THE GREAT BOOKS FOUNDATION

SHORT STORY OMNIBUS

Canisius University
Library
Buffalo, New York

SELECTED AND EDITED BY

Daniel Born

Judith McCue

Donald H. Whitfield

CONTRIBUTORS

Carolyn Groenewold

Fred Hang

Patrick Hurley

Abigail Mitchell

Daniel Raeburn

Gary Schoepfel

Donald C. Smith

Kathy Swain

Mary Williams

THE GREAT BOOKS FOUNDATION

SHORT STORY OMNIBUS

THE GREAT BOOKS FOUNDATION

A nonprofit educational organization

With generous support from Harrison Middleton University,
a Great Books distance-learning college

Published and distributed by

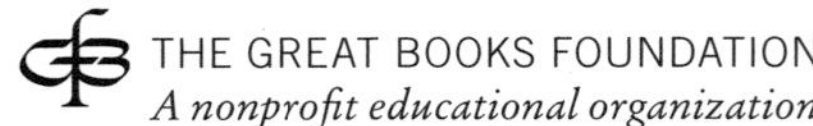

35 E. Wacker Drive, Suite 400
Chicago, IL 60601
www.greatbooks.org

With generous support from
Harrison Middleton University,
a Great Books distance-learning college
www.chumsci.edu

Shared Inquiry™ is a trademark of the Great Books Foundation. The contents of this publication include proprietary trademarks and copyrighted materials, and may be used or quoted only with permission and appropriate credit to the Foundation.

Copyright © 2009 by the Great Books Foundation
Chicago, Illinois
All rights reserved
ISBN 978-1-880323-73-1

First printing
9 8 7 6 5 4 3 2 1

Library of Congress Cataloging-in-Publication Data
The Great Books Foundation short story omnibus / selected and edited by Daniel Born, Judith McCue, Donald H. Whitfield.
p. cm.
ISBN 978-1-880323-73-1
1. Short stories—Translations into English. 2. Short stories, English. 3. Short stories, American. I. Born, Daniel. II. McCue, Judith. III. Whitfield, Donald. IV. Great Books Foundation (U.S.) V. Title: Short story omnibus.
PN6120.2.G716 2009
808.83'1—dc22

2008038875

Cover illustration: Lisa Haney
Book design: Think Design Group LLC

About the Great Books Foundation

The Great Books Foundation was established in 1947 by two University of Chicago educators, Robert Maynard Hutchins and Mortimer Adler. An independent, nonprofit educational organization whose mission is to help people learn how to think and share ideas, the Foundation promotes the reading and discussion of classic and contemporary texts across the disciplines, and publishes books and anthologies for readers of all ages. It also conducts professional development courses in Shared Inquiry,™ a text-based Socratic method of learning that helps participants read actively, pose evocative questions, and listen and respond to others effectively in dialogue.

Footnotes by the author are not bracketed; footnotes by the Great Books Foundation, an editor, or a translator are [bracketed]. Spelling and punctuation have been modernized and slightly altered for clarity.

Contents

SUDDEN FICTION

NOVELLAS

GRAPHIC STORIES

Introduction

Storytelling is a universal human tradition, and to acquire language means to become immersed in a world of stories. For the species Homo sapiens these facts of life are so common that we sometimes forget to pay conscious attention to them.

Furthermore, we cannot learn without stories. They are both inevitable and indispensable. The fancy term for story, "narrative," can be traced to its Latin root *narrare,* "to make known." Linguists talk about the grammar, or deep structure, of a language, to make sense of how words are arranged and used to create meaning. Yet when we attempt to understand how this system of meaning functions, we are caught up in the telling of yet another story. We use stories to communicate information—that is true—but just as important, we come to understand ourselves through them. We are ineluctably caught in their web. We make stories, and stories make us.

One can argue that without language there would be no stories, but more important, without stories language would have no purpose. To convey knowledge, whether in oral or written form, depends on the ability to create a story. Data, even when generated by numerical equations, must at some point be converted into narrative before it is recognized as knowledge—knowledge always comes packaged in some kind of story. Literary critic Susan Lohafer has spent much of her career investigating the way short fiction works. In her essay "A Cognitive Approach to Storyness," she writes about realizing some years ago "how very partial was my claim on the notion of 'story.' It belonged also to journalists, historians, cultural anthropologists, and . . . to discourse analysts, social psychologists, psycholinguists, and cognitive scientists." Stories convey make-believe entertainment, but they are also the method of imparting truth claims and hypotheses about the world.

If human beings have been telling stories for millennia, the "short story" as a recognized form of written entertainment has to be acknowledged as a relatively recent arrival. Although many critics point to ancient antecedents, including folktales, biblical stories, and even jokes and riddles, it was not until 1842 that Edgar Allan Poe, while writing about Nathaniel Hawthorne's *Twice-Told Tales*, made a key observation. "The short prose narrative," he noted, is one that can be read within "a half hour to one or two hours," or, as he puts it more succinctly, "at one sitting." Lohafer observes the genius of this definition: "What could be more practical than to measure one's span of attention by the seat of one's pants?"

What's more, Poe's rule that the short story be short is the only generalization about this literary form that readers and critics have been able to agree on. Poe made other claims about the short story, such as the importance of "unity of effect," and much like a fight promoter, he enthused that the story affords "unquestionably the fairest field for the exercise of the loftiest talent." But to this day, attempts to produce a comprehensive catalog of the short story's features have failed. As Valerie Shaw observes in *The Short Story: A Critical Introduction*, "No sooner is a definition of the short story formulated than exceptions begin to multiply, insisting on their value as literature and properly upsetting the tidiness of a homogenizing approach."

If Poe was insistent on the unity of effect or atmosphere—so obvious a factor in the success of his gothic horror stories—other critics have expressed different biases. Many nineteenth-century commentators believed a well-made plot to be central. For certain modernist writers, it was the exploration of a single subjective moment of experience, or epiphany, that sufficed to germinate a short story. Nowadays, one hears frequently in both the literature class and creative writing workshop about the importance of character-driven narrative. But such single-minded efforts toward generalization are blown away when we consider the stunning variety of stories that have evolved since Poe made his manifesto. As Ian Reid points out in *The Short Story*, because of the looseness of the form, writers have experimented endlessly. Some have even gone so far as to challenge altogether such traditional elements as plot, character, setting, and consistent narrative voice. Furthermore, the short story genre has developed a repertoire of subject matter that includes romance, science fiction, horror, crime, and erotica—all of these variants also flourishing in the novel, in longer form.

This collection of short stories is not intended to put on display these particular subgenres (though subsequent volumes in our Omnibus series will take up several of these in turn). Rather, this anthology gathers together some of the best short stories ever written, stories exemplary in the demands they make on a reader. They can be profitably read and discussed by literature students in classrooms or book groups, as well as by aspiring authors in creative writing workshops.

What do we mean by great literature? It is, simply, literature that generations of readers can't stop talking about. Great stories are the ones we return to again and again because they are not easily exhausted. We can keep mining them without worrying that the ore will run out. They are the ones likely to generate lively discussion, differing interpretations, and sometimes even spirited disagreement within a community of readers. They challenge our capacity to interpret them. They arouse us to think and feel with heightened intensity.

The four-part structure of this collection—"Short Stories," "Sudden Fiction," "Novellas," and "Graphic Stories"—serves a distinct purpose. These categories all comply with Poe's requirement that a short story be read in one sitting. Yet the selections here also demonstrate the kinds of freedom and experimentation that are practiced within the limits of the form. The short story has evolved, and continues to evolve, with an ever more diverse range of possibilities.

The first section of this book provides a glimpse of just how rich the tradition can be. It ranges across the past 150 years and includes stories in a realist mode, in which the imagined world is made plausible through the implementation of prose narrative conventions such as character, setting, and plot. It also includes narratives that stretch the boundaries of verisimilitude, in some cases dispensing with this aim altogether. In other cases, the story becomes a vehicle for philosophical exposition or inquiry. The subject may not be a character or characters in the usual sense, but the story itself, a kind of exploration that is sometimes called "metafiction."

This collection's second section consists of stories in the mode of "sudden fiction." Sudden fiction is what it sounds like. Sometimes called "flash fiction," "microfiction," or "the short short," it ends almost as soon as it has begun, packing a great deal into a compressed time zone. It is condensed, distilled storytelling at its most refined. It might just as easily be read on the fly as in an easy chair. Writing about its unique qualities in his introduction to *Short Shorts*, critic Irving Howe has observed that the short short is "almost like a lyric poem; it explodes in a burst of revelation or illumination; it confines itself to a single, overpowering incident; it bears symbolic weight." And as he also suggests, there are certain things that this kind of abbreviated story doesn't do. Exhaustive character development or complex plotting are not what it is about. Rather, in Howe's words, "Everything depends on intensity, one sweeping blow of perception. In the short short the writer gets no second chance."

At the other end of the duration scale is the novella, featured in the third section of this book. Longer than most short stories, and shorter than most novels, the novella is a hybrid form. Scholar Mary Doyle Springer, author of *Forms of the Modern Novella*, suggests its word count at between fifteen thousand and fifty thousand words; if we use the two-hour ceiling for reading time and consider that fast readers usually devour forty to fifty pages in an hour, then the upper-reach limit for the novella is around a hundred pages. The novella, because of its relatively relaxed length, provides writers with opportunities to do what novelists often do: develop an imaginative world in which the reader can luxuriate; present more characters, and in more depth; and, sometimes, play with shifting points of view or perspective.

The fourth and final category includes three graphic stories, or as they are popularly known, comics. That term, however, with its connotations of the newspaper "funnies" or superhero comic books, hardly does justice to the quality of writing, artwork, and thematic subject matter found in the best graphic stories, which have emerged in the past few decades as a form demanding attention from thoughtful readers.

Many readers who believe in the idea of great books consider graphic stories beneath their notice, as one more example of adolescent pop culture ephemera unlikely to stand the test of time. To these readers we offer a cautionary note: self-consciously literary readers in the early nineteenth century considered the novel an inferior kind of popular entertainment, and as recently as the mid-twentieth century, English literary critic F. R. Leavis looked down on Charles Dickens as more of a cheap entertainer than a serious literary artist. Leavis would later change his opinion.

At this time, graphic stories, or at least the best of them, seem closer to memoir or autobiography or even journalism than to fiction, yet there is no question that they constitute a new form of short story. For one thing, graphic stories put special demands on readers. We who are accustomed to processing only written text are suddenly confronted with the experience of simultaneous words and images—and how we interpret the pictures matters as much as our take on the words. Neither the analogy of text with illustrations, nor the experience of watching a foreign film with subtitles, quite captures the cognitive experience of reading a graphic story. We expect that this kind of complicated reading will force us, in the years to come, to develop new kinds of questions to ask about the graphic "text" as well as new vocabularies for describing the unique aesthetic qualities of a form that blends textual and visual art.

Each story in this anthology is followed by a few questions. These are meant to stir discussion among groups of readers, and to begin the process of interpreting what are in some cases very challenging stories. These are not offered as exhaustive by any means, nor are they put forward here as writing prompts. And at the back of this book we include a description of Shared Inquiry, a Socratic, text-based method of learning that offers a way to open up a text to every engaged reader through discussion. It is a method that has been successfully used in hundreds of book groups and thousands of classrooms for more than six decades.

SHORT STORIES

HONORÉ DE BALZAC (1799–1850) is one of the most important innovators of the modern, realist novel, in which detailed descriptions of setting and incident contribute to psychologically discerning portraits of men and women. Born in provincial France, Balzac made his home in Paris. In the early 1830s, he conceived the idea of a vast literary project depicting all aspects of human society, which he titled *The Human Comedy.* He eventually added dozens of novels, short stories, and plays to this collection, many of them concerned with conflicts arising from class and financial ambition. Among Balzac's major works are the novels *Eugénie Grandet* (1833), *Père Goriot* (1835), and *Lost Illusions*, 3 vols. (1837–1843). Balzac was an important influence on the writings of Henry James and Marcel Proust.

A Passion in the Desert

"The sight was fearful!" she exclaimed, as we left the menagerie of Monsieur Martin.

She had been watching that daring speculator as he went through his wonderful performance in the den of the hyena.

"How is it possible," she continued, "to tame those animals so as to be certain that he can trust them?"

"You think it a problem," I answered, interrupting her, "and yet it is a natural fact."

"Oh!" she cried, an incredulous smile flickering on her lip.

"Do you think that beasts are devoid of passions?" I asked. "Let me assure you that we teach them all the vices and virtues of our own state of civilization."

She looked at me in amazement.

"The first time I saw Monsieur Martin," I added, "I exclaimed, as you do, with surprise. I happened to be sitting beside an old soldier whose right leg was amputated, and whose appearance had attracted my notice as I entered the building. His face, stamped with the scars of battle, wore the undaunted look of a veteran of the wars of Napoleon. Moreover, the old hero had a frank and joyous manner that attracts me wherever I meet it. He was, doubtless, one of those old campaigners whom nothing can surprise, who find something to laugh at in the last contortions of a comrade, and will bury a friend or rifle his body gayly; challenging bullets with indifference; making short shrift for themselves or others; and fraternizing, as a usual thing, with the devil. After looking very attentively at the proprietor of the menagerie as he entered the den, my companion curled his lip with that expression of satirical contempt that well-informed men sometimes put on to mark the difference between themselves and dupes. As I uttered my exclamation of surprise at the coolness and courage of Monsieur Martin, the old soldier smiled, shook his head, and said with a knowing glance, 'An old story!'

" 'How do you mean, an old story?' I asked. 'If you could explain the secret of this mysterious power, I should be greatly obliged to you.'

"After a while, during which we became better acquainted, we went to dine at the first restaurant we could find after leaving the menagerie. A bottle of champagne with our dessert brightened the recollections of the old man and made them singularly vivid. He related to me a circumstance in his early history that proved that he had ample cause to pronounce Monsieur Martin's performance 'an old story.' "

When we reached her house, she was so persuasive and captivating, and made me so many pretty promises, that I consented to write down for her benefit the story told me by the old hero. On the following day I sent her this episode of an historical epic, which might be entitled, "The French in Egypt."

At the time of General Desaix's expedition to Upper Egypt a Provençal soldier, who had fallen into the hands of the Maugrabins, was marched by those tireless Arabs across the desert that lies beyond the cataracts of the Nile. To put sufficient distance between themselves and the French army and thus insure their safety, the Maugrabins made a forced march, and did not halt until after nightfall. They then camped about a well shaded with palm trees, near which they had previously buried a stock of provisions. Not dreaming that the thought of escape could enter their captive's mind, they merely bound his wrists, and lay down to sleep themselves, after eating a few dates and giving their horses a feed of barley. When the bold Provençal saw his enemies too soundly asleep to watch him, he used his teeth to pick up a scimitar, with which, steadying the blade by means of his knees, he contrived to cut through the cord that bound his hands, and thus recovered his liberty. He at once seized a carbine and a poniard, took the precaution to lay in a supply of dates, a small bag of barley, some powder and ball, buckled on the scimitar, mounted one of the horses, and spurred him in the direction where he supposed the French army to be. Impatient to meet the outposts, he pressed the horse, which was already wearied, so severely that the poor animal fell dead with his flanks torn, leaving the Frenchman alone in the midst of the desert.

After marching for a long time through the sand with the dogged courage of an escaping galley slave, the soldier was forced to halt as the darkness drew on; for his utter weariness compelled him to rest, though the exquisite sky of an Eastern night might well have tempted him to continue the journey. Happily he had reached a slight elevation, at the top of which a few palm trees shot upward, whose leafage, seen from a long distance against the sky, had helped to sustain his hopes. His fatigue was so great that he threw himself down on a block of granite, cut by nature into the shape of a camp bed, and slept heavily, without taking the least precaution to protect himself while asleep. He accepted the loss of his life as inevitable, and his last waking thought was one of regret for having left the Maugrabins, whose nomad life began to charm him now that he was far away from them and from every other hope of succor.

He was wakened by the sun, whose pitiless beams falling vertically upon the granite rock produced an intolerable heat. The Provençal had ignorantly flung himself down in a contrary direction to the shadows thrown by the verdant and majestic fronds of the palm trees. He gazed at these solitary monarchs and shuddered. They recalled to his mind the graceful shafts crowned with long weaving leaves that distinguish the Saracenic columns of the cathedral of Arles. The thought overcame him, and when, after counting the trees, he threw his eyes upon the scene around him, an agony of despair convulsed his soul. He saw a limitless ocean. The somber sands of the desert stretched out till lost to sight in all directions; they glittered with dark luster like a steel blade shining in the sun. He could not tell if it were an ocean or a chain of lakes that lay mirrored before him. A hot vapor swept in waves above the surface of this heaving continent. The sky had the Oriental glow of translucent purity that disappoints because it leaves nothing for the imagination to desire. The heavens and the earth were both on fire. Silence added its awful and desolate majesty. Infinitude, immensity pressed down upon the soul on every side; not a cloud in the sky, not a breath in the air, not a rift on the breast of the sand, which was ruffled only with little ridges scarcely rising above its surface. Far as the eye could reach the horizon fell away into space, marked by a slender line, slim as the edge of a saber—like as in summer seas a thread of light parts this earth from the heaven it meets.

The Provençal clasped the trunk of a palm tree as if it were the body of a friend. Sheltered from the sun by its straight and slender shadow, he wept; and presently sitting down he remained motionless, contemplating with awful dread the implacable nature stretched out before him. He cried aloud, as if to tempt the solitude to answer him. His voice, lost in the hollows of the hillock, sounded afar with a thin resonance that returned no echo; the echo came from the soldier's heart. He was twenty-two years old, and he loaded his carbine.

"Time enough!" he muttered, as he put the liberating weapon on the sand beneath him.

Gazing by turns at the burnished blackness of the sand and the blue expanse of the sky, the soldier dreamed of France. He smelt in fancy the gutters of Paris; he remembered the towns through which he had passed, the faces of his comrades, and the most trifling incidents of his life. His southern imagination saw the pebbles of his own Provence in the undulating play of the heated air, as it seemed to roughen the far-reaching surface of the desert. Dreading the dangers of this cruel mirage, he went down the little hill on the side opposite to that by which he had gone up the night before. His joy was great when he discovered a natural grotto, formed by the immense blocks of granite that made a foundation for the rising ground. The remnants of a mat showed that the place had once been inhabited, and close to the entrance were a few palm trees loaded with fruit. The instinct that binds men to life woke in his heart. He now hoped to live until some Maugrabin should pass that way; possibly he might even hear the roar of cannon, for Bonaparte was at that time overrunning Egypt. Encouraged by these thoughts, the Frenchman shook down a cluster of the ripe fruit under the weight of which the palms were bending; and as he tasted this unhoped-for manna, he thanked the former inhabitant of the grotto for the cultivation of the trees, which the rich and luscious flesh of the fruit amply attested. Like a true Provençal, he passed from the gloom of despair to a joy that was half insane. He ran back to the top of the hill, and busied himself for the rest of the day in cutting down one of the sterile trees that had been his shelter the night before.

Some vague recollection made him think of the wild beasts of the desert, and foreseeing that they would come to drink at a spring that bubbled through the sand at the foot of the rock, he resolved to protect his hermitage by felling a tree across the entrance. Notwithstanding his eagerness, and the strength that the fear of being attacked while asleep gave to his muscles, he was unable to cut the palm tree in pieces during the day; but he succeeded in bringing it down. Toward evening the king of the desert fell; and the noise of his fall, echoing far, was like a moan from the breast of Solitude. The soldier shuddered, as though he had heard a voice predicting evil. But, like an heir who does not long mourn a parent, he stripped from the beautiful tree the arching green fronds—its poetical adornment—and made a bed of them in his refuge. Then, tired with his work and by the heat of the day, he fell asleep beneath the red vault of the grotto.

In the middle of the night his sleep was broken by a strange noise. He sat up; the deep silence that reigned everywhere enabled him to hear the alternating rhythm of a respiration whose savage vigor could not belong to a human being. A terrible fear, increased by the darkness, by the silence, by the rush of his waking fancies, numbed his heart. He felt the contraction of his hair, which rose on end as his eyes, dilating to their full strength, beheld through the darkness two faint amber lights. At first he thought them an optical delusion; but by degrees the clearness of the night enabled him to distinguish objects in the grotto, and he saw, within two feet of him, an enormous animal lying at rest.

Was it a lion? Was it a tiger? Was it a crocodile? The Provençal had not enough education to know in what subspecies he ought to class the intruder; but his terror was all the greater because his ignorance made it vague. He endured the cruel trial of listening, of striving to catch the peculiarities of this breathing without losing one of its inflections, and without daring to make the slightest movement. A strong odor, like that exhaled by foxes, only far more pungent and penetrating, filled the grotto. When the soldier had tasted it, so to speak, by the nose, his fear became terror; he could no longer doubt the nature of the terrible companion whose royal lair he had taken for a bivouac. Before long, the reflection of the moon, as it sank to the horizon, lighted up the den and gleamed upon the shining, spotted skin of a panther.

The lion of Egypt lay asleep, curled up like a dog, the peaceable possessor of a kennel at the gate of a mansion; its eyes, which had opened for a moment, were now closed; its head was turned toward the Frenchman. A hundred conflicting thoughts rushed through the mind of the panther's prisoner. Should he kill it with a shot from his musket? But ere the thought was formed, he saw there was no room to take aim; the muzzle would have gone beyond the animal. Suppose he were to wake it? The fear kept him motionless. As he heard the beating of his heart through the dead silence, he cursed the strong pulsations of his vigorous blood, lest they should disturb the sleep that gave him time to think and plan for safety. Twice he put his hand on his scimitar, with the idea of striking off the head of his enemy; but the difficulty of cutting through the close-haired skin made him renounce the bold attempt. Suppose he missed his aim? It would, he knew, be certain death. He preferred the chances of a struggle, and resolved to await the dawn. It was not long in coming. As daylight broke, the Frenchman was able to examine the animal. Its muzzle was stained with blood. "It has eaten a good meal," thought he, not caring whether the feast were human flesh or not; "it will not be hungry when it wakes."

It was a female. The fur on the belly and on the thighs was of sparkling whiteness. Several little spots like velvet made pretty bracelets round her paws. The muscular tail was also white, but it terminated with black rings. The fur of the back, yellow as dead gold and very soft and glossy, bore the characteristic spots, shaded like a full-blown rose, that distinguish the panther from all other species of *felis.* This terrible hostess lay tranquilly snoring, in an attitude as easy and graceful as that of a cat on the cushions of an ottoman. Her bloody paws, sinewy and well-armed, were stretched beyond her head, which lay upon them; and from her muzzle projected a few straight hairs called whiskers, which shimmered in the early light like silver wires. If he had seen her lying thus imprisoned in a cage, the Provençal would have admired the creature's grace, and the strong contrasts of vivid color that gave to her robe an imperial splendor; but as it was, his sight was jaundiced by sinister forebodings. The presence of the panther, though she was still asleep, had the same effect upon his mind as the magnetic eyes of a snake produce, we are told, upon the nightingale. The soldier's courage oozed away in presence of this silent peril, though he was a man who gathered nerve before the mouths of cannon belching grapeshot. And yet, ere long, a bold thought entered his mind, and checked the cold sweat that was rolling from his brow. Roused to action, as some men are when, driven face to face with death, they defy it and offer themselves to their doom, he saw a tragedy before him, and he resolved to play his part with honor to the last.

"Yesterday," he said, "the Arabs might have killed me."

Regarding himself as dead, he waited bravely, but with anxious curiosity, for the waking of his enemy. When the sun rose, the panther suddenly opened her eyes; then she stretched her paws violently, as if to unlimber them from the cramp of their position. Presently she yawned and showed the frightful armament of her teeth, and her cloven tongue, rough as a grater.

"She is like a dainty woman," thought the Frenchman, watching her as she rolled and turned on her side with an easy and coquettish movement. She licked the blood from her paws, and rubbed her head with a reiterated movement full of grace.

"Well done! Dress yourself prettily, my little woman," said the Frenchman, who recovered his gaiety as soon as he had recovered his courage. "We are going to bid each other good morning;" and he felt for the short poniard that he had taken from the Maugrabins.

At this instant the panther turned her head toward the Frenchman and looked at him fixedly, without moving. The rigidity of her metallic eyes and their insupportable clearness made the Provençal shudder. The beast moved toward him; he looked at her caressingly, with a soothing glance by which he hoped to magnetize her. He let her come quite close to him before he stirred; then, with a touch as gentle and loving as he might have used to a pretty woman, he slid his hand along her spine from the head to the flanks, scratching with his nails the flexible vertebrae that divide the yellow back of a panther. The creature drew up her tail voluptuously, her eyes softened, and when for the third time the Frenchman bestowed this self-interested caress, she gave vent to a purr like that with which a cat expresses pleasure; but it issued from a throat so deep and powerful that the sound echoed through the grotto like the last chords of an organ rolling along the roof of a church. The Provençal, perceiving the value of his caresses, redoubled them, until they had completely soothed and lulled the imperious courtesan.

When he felt that he had subdued the ferocity of his capricious companion, whose hunger had so fortunately been appeased the night before, he rose to leave the grotto. The panther let him go; but as soon as he reached the top of the little hill she bounded after him with the lightness of a bird hopping from branch to branch, and rubbed against his legs, arching her back with the gesture of a domestic cat. Then looking at her guest with an eye that was growing less inflexible, she uttered the savage cry that naturalists liken to the noise of a saw.

"My lady is exacting," cried the Frenchman, smiling. He began to play with her ears and stroke her belly, and at last he scratched her head firmly with his nails. Encouraged by success, he tickled her skull with the point of his dagger, looking for the right spot where to stab her; but the hardness of the bone made him pause, dreading failure.

The sultana of the desert acknowledged the talents of her slave by lifting her head and swaying her neck to his caresses, betraying satisfaction by the tranquillity of her relaxed attitude. The Frenchman suddenly perceived that he could assassinate the fierce princess at a blow, if he struck her in the throat; and he had raised the weapon, when the panther, surfeited perhaps with his caresses, threw herself gracefully at his feet, glancing up at him with a look in which, despite her natural ferocity, a flicker of kindness could be seen. The poor Provençal, frustrated for the moment, ate his dates as he leaned against a palm tree, casting from time to time an interrogating eye across the desert in the hope of discerning rescue from afar, and then lowering it upon his terrible companion, to watch the chances of her uncertain clemency. Each time that he threw away a date stone the panther eyed the spot where it fell with an expression of keen distrust; and she examined the Frenchman with what might be called commercial prudence. The examination, however, seemed favorable, for when the man had finished his meager meal she licked his shoes and wiped off the dust, which was caked into the folds of the leather, with her rough and powerful tongue.

"How will it be when she is hungry?" thought the Provençal. In spite of the shudder that this reflection cost him, his attention was attracted by the symmetrical proportions of the animal, and he began to measure them with his eye. She was three feet in height to the shoulder, and four feet long, not including the tail. That powerful weapon, which was round as a club, measured three feet. The head, as large as that of a lioness, was remarkable for an expression of crafty intelligence; the cold cruelty of a tiger was its ruling trait, and yet it bore a vague resemblance to the face of an artful woman. As the soldier watched her, the countenance of this solitary queen shone with savage gaiety like that of Nero in his cups: she had slaked her thirst for blood, and now wished for play. The Frenchman tried to come and go, and accustom her to his movements. The panther left him free, as if contented to follow him with her eyes, seeming, however, less like a faithful dog watching his master's movements with affection, than a huge Angora cat uneasy and suspicious of them. A few steps brought him to the spring, where he saw the carcass of his horse, which the panther had evidently carried there. Only two thirds was eaten. The sight reassured the Frenchman; for it explained the absence of his terrible companion and the forbearance that she had shown to him while asleep.

This first good luck encouraged the reckless soldier as he thought of the future. The wild idea of making a home with the panther until some chance of escape occurred entered his mind, and he resolved to try every means of taming her and of turning her goodwill to account. With these thoughts he returned to her side, and noticed joyfully that she moved her tail with an almost imperceptible motion. He sat down beside her fearlessly, and they began to play with each other. He held her paws and her muzzle, twisted her ears, threw her over on her back, and stroked her soft, warm flanks. She allowed him to do so; and when he began to smooth the fur of her paws, she carefully drew in her murderous claws, which were sharp and curved like a Damascus blade. The Frenchman kept one hand on his dagger, again watching his opportunity to plunge it into the belly of the too-confiding beast; but the fear that she might strangle him in her last convulsions once more stayed his hand. Moreover, he felt in his heart a foreboding of remorse that warned him not to destroy a hitherto inoffensive creature. He even fancied that he had found a friend in the limitless desert. His mind turned back, involuntarily, to his first mistress, whom he had named in derision "Mignonne," because her jealousy was so furious that throughout the whole period of their intercourse he lived in dread of the knife with which she threatened him. This recollection of his youth suggested the idea of teaching the young panther, whose soft agility and grace he now admired with less terror, to answer to the caressing name. Toward evening he had grown so familiar with his perilous position that he was half in love with its dangers, and his companion was so far tamed that she had caught the habit of turning to him when he called, in falsetto tones, "Mignonne!"

As the sun went down Mignonne uttered at intervals a prolonged, deep, melancholy cry.

"She is well brought up," thought the gay soldier. "She says her prayers." But the jest only came into his mind as he watched the peaceful attitude of his comrade.

"Come, my pretty blond, I will let you go to bed first," he said, relying on the activity of his legs to get away as soon as she fell asleep, and trusting to find some other resting place for the night. He waited anxiously for the right moment, and when it came he started vigorously in the direction of the Nile. But he had scarcely marched for half an hour through the sand before he heard the panther bounding after him, giving at intervals the sawlike cry that was more terrible to hear than the thud of her bounds.

"Well, well!" he cried, "she must have fallen in love with me! Perhaps she has never met anyone else. It is flattering to be her first love."

So thinking, he fell into one of the treacherous quicksands that deceive the inexperienced traveler in the desert, and from which there is seldom any escape. He felt he was sinking, and he uttered a cry of despair. The panther seized him by the collar with her teeth, and sprang vigorously backward, drawing him, like magic, from the sucking sand.

"Ah, Mignonne!" cried the soldier, kissing her with enthusiasm, "we belong to each other now—for life, for death! But play me no tricks," he added, as he turned back the way he came.

From that moment the desert was, as it were, peopled for him. It held a being to whom he could talk, and whose ferocity was now lulled into gentleness, although he could scarcely explain to himself the reasons for this extraordinary friendship. His anxiety to keep awake and on his guard succumbed to excessive weariness both of body and mind, and throwing himself down on the floor of the grotto he slept soundly. At his waking Mignonne was gone. He mounted the little hill to scan the horizon, and perceived her in the far distance returning with the long bounds peculiar to these animals, who are prevented from running by the extreme flexibility of their spinal column.

Mignonne came home with bloody jaws, and received the tribute of caresses that her slave hastened to pay, all the while manifesting her pleasure by reiterated purring.

Her eyes, now soft and gentle, rested kindly on the Provençal, who spoke to her lovingly as he would to a domestic animal.

"Ah! Mademoiselle—for you are an honest girl, are you not? You like to be petted, don't you? Are you not ashamed of yourself? You have been eating a Maugrabin. Well, well! they are animals like the rest of you. But you are not to crunch up a Frenchman; remember that! If you do, I will not love you."

She played like a young dog with her master, and let him roll her over and pat and stroke her, and sometimes she would coax him to play by laying a paw upon his knee with a pretty soliciting gesture.

Several days passed rapidly. This strange companionship revealed to the Provençal the sublime beauties of the desert. The alternations of hope and fear, the sufficiency of food, the presence of a creature who occupied his thoughts,—all this kept his mind alert, yet free: it was a life full of strange contrasts. Solitude revealed to him her secrets, and wrapped him with her charm. In the rising and the setting of the sun he saw splendors unknown to the world of men. He quivered as he listened to the soft whirring of the wings of a bird—a rare visitant!—or watched the blending of the fleeting clouds—those changeful and many-tinted voyagers. In the waking hours of the night he studied the play of the moon upon the sandy ocean, where the strong simoom had rippled the surface into waves and ever-varying undulations. He lived in the Eastern day; he worshipped its marvelous glory. He rejoiced in the grandeur of the storms when they rolled across the vast plain, and tossed the sand upward till it looked like a dry red fog or a solid death-dealing vapor; and as the night came on he welcomed it with ecstasy, grateful for the blessed coolness of the light of the stars. His ears listened to the music of the skies. Solitude taught him the treasures of meditation. He spent hours in recalling trifles, and in comparing his past life with the weird present.

He grew fondly attached to his panther; for he was a man who needed an affection. Whether it was that his own will, magnetically strong, had modified the nature of his savage princess, or that the wars then raging in the desert had provided her with an ample supply of food, it is certain that she showed no sign of attacking him, and became so tame that he soon felt no fear of her. He spent much of his time in sleeping; though with his mind awake, like a spider in its web, lest he should miss some deliverance that might chance to cross the sandy sphere marked out by the horizon. He had made his shirt into a banner and tied it to the top of a palm tree that he had stripped of its leafage. Taking counsel of necessity, he kept the flag extended by fastening the corners with twigs and wedges; for the fitful wind might have failed to wave it at the moment when the longed-for succor came in sight.

Nevertheless, there were long hours of gloom when hope forsook him; and then he played with his panther. He learned to know the different inflections of her voice and the meanings of her expressive glance; he studied the variegation of the spots that shaded the dead gold of her robe. Mignonne no longer growled when he caught the tuft of her dangerous tail and counted the black and white rings that glittered in the sunlight like a cluster of precious stones. He delighted in the soft lines of her lithe body, the whiteness of her belly, the grace of her charming head: but above all he loved to watch her as she gamboled at play. The agility and youthfulness of her movements were a constantly fresh surprise to him. He admired the suppleness of the flexible body as she bounded, crept, and glided, or clung to the trunk of palm trees, or rolled over and over, crouching sometimes to the ground, and gathering herself together as she made ready for her vigorous spring. Yet, however vigorous the bound, however slippery the granite block on which she landed, she would stop short, motionless, at the one word "Mignonne."

One day, under a dazzling sun, a large bird hovered in the sky. The Provençal left his panther to watch the new guest. After a moment's pause the neglected sultana uttered a low growl.

"The devil take me! I believe she is jealous!" exclaimed the soldier, observing the rigid look that once more appeared in her metallic eyes. "The soul of Sophronie has got into her body!"

The eagle disappeared in ether, and the Frenchman, recalled by the panther's displeasure, admired afresh her rounded flanks and the perfect grace of her attitude. She was as pretty as a woman. The blond brightness of her robe shaded, with delicate gradations, to the dead-white tones of her furry thighs; the vivid sunshine brought out the brilliancy of this living gold and its variegated brown spots with indescribable luster. The panther and the Provençal gazed at each other with human comprehension. She trembled with delight—the coquettish creature!—as she felt the nails of her friend scratching the strong bones of her skull. Her eyes glittered like flashes of lightning, and then she closed them tightly.

"She has a soul!" cried the soldier, watching the tranquil repose of this sovereign of the desert, golden as the sands, white as their pulsing light, solitary and burning as they.

"Well," she said, "I have read your defense of the beasts. But tell me what was the end of this friendship between two beings so formed to understand each other."

"Ah, exactly," I replied. "It ended as all great passions end—by a misunderstanding. Both sides imagine treachery, pride prevents an explanation, and the rupture comes about through obstinacy."

"Yes," she said, "and sometimes a word, a look, an exclamation suffices. But tell me the end of the story."

"That is difficult," I answered. "But I will give it to you in the words of the old veteran, as he finished the bottle of champagne and exclaimed: 'I don't know how I could have hurt her, but she suddenly turned upon me as if in fury, and seized my thigh with her sharp teeth; and yet (as I afterward remembered) not cruelly. I thought she meant to devour me, and I plunged my dagger into her throat. She rolled over with a cry that froze my soul; she looked at me in her death struggle, but without anger. I would have given all the world—my cross, which I had not then gained, all, everything—to have brought her back to life. It was as if I had murdered a friend, a human being. When the soldiers who saw my flag came to my rescue they found me weeping. 'Monsieur,' he resumed, after a moment's silence, 'I went through the wars in Germany, Spain, Russia, France; I have marched my carcass well-nigh over all the world; but I have seen nothing comparable to the desert. Ah, it is grand! glorious!'

" 'What were your feelings there?' I asked.

" 'They cannot be told, young man. Besides, I do not always regret my panther and my palm tree oasis: I must be very sad for that. But I will tell you this: In the desert there is all—and yet nothing.'

" 'Stay!—explain that.'

" 'Well, then,' he said, with a gesture of impatience, 'God is there, and man is not.' "

---

1. What does the old soldier mean when he explains his comment that "in the desert there is all—and yet nothing," by saying, "God is there, and man is not"?

2. Why does the Provençal soldier give the panther the name of his first mistress, Mignonne?

3. Why does the soldier kill the panther even though the panther and the soldier had gazed at each other with "human comprehension"?

EDGAR ALLAN POE (1809–1849), known today as a poet and author of horror and mystery stories, first achieved public recognition as an editor of American literary journals and magazines. During the last ten years of his brief and troubled life, Poe published his most famous poem, "The Raven," as well as his major stories, including "The Fall of the House of Usher," "The Murders in the Rue Morgue," and "The Tell-Tale Heart." Poe's horror stories emphasize the conflicted workings of the human mind as much as terrifying incidents, while his detective stories, a genre he is often credited with inventing, portray clearheaded objectivity and ratiocination confronting the unknown. Poe was the first writer to offer a theory of the short story genre.

The Black Cat

For the most wild, yet most homely narrative which I am about to pen, I neither expect nor solicit belief. Mad indeed would I be to expect it, in a case where my very senses reject their own evidence. Yet mad am I not, and very surely do I not dream. But tomorrow I die, and today I would unburden my soul. My immediate purpose is to place before the world, plainly, succinctly, and without comment, a series of mere household events. In their consequences, these events have terrified, have tortured, have destroyed me. Yet I will not attempt to expound them. To me they have presented little but horror; to many they will seem less terrible than *baroques*. Hereafter, perhaps, some intellect may be found which will reduce my phantasm to the commonplace—some intellect more calm, more logical, and far less excitable than my own, which will perceive, in the circumstances I detail with awe, nothing more than an ordinary succession of very natural causes and effects.

From my infancy I was noted for the docility and humanity of my disposition. My tenderness of heart was even so conspicuous as to make me the jest of my companions. I was especially fond of animals, and was indulged by my parents with a great variety of pets. With these I spent most of my time, and never was so happy as when feeding and caressing them. This peculiarity of character grew with my growth, and in my manhood I derived from it one of my principal sources of pleasure. To those who have cherished an affection for a faithful and sagacious dog I need hardly be at the trouble of explaining the nature or the intensity of the gratification thus derivable. There is something in the unselfish and self-sacrificing love of a brute which goes directly to the heart of him who has had frequent occasion to test the paltry friendship and gossamer fidelity of mere man.

I married early, and was happy to find in my wife a disposition not uncongenial with my own. Observing my partiality for domestic pets, she lost no opportunity of procuring those of the most agreeable kind. We had birds, goldfish, a fine dog, rabbits, a small monkey, and a cat.

This latter was a remarkably large and beautiful animal, entirely black, and sagacious to an astonishing degree. In speaking of his intelligence, my wife, who at heart was not a little tinctured with superstition, made frequent allusion to the ancient popular notion, which regarded all black cats as witches in disguise. Not that she was ever serious upon this point, and I mention the matter at all for no better reason than that it happens, just now, to be remembered.

Pluto—this was the cat's name—was my favorite pet and playmate. I alone fed him, and he attended me wherever I went about the house. It was even with difficulty that I could prevent him from following me through the streets.

Our friendship lasted in this manner for several years, during which my general temperament and character, through the instrumentality of the fiend intemperance, had (I blush to confess it) experienced a radical alteration for the worse. I grew, day by day, more moody, more irritable, more regardless of the feelings of others. I suffered myself to use intemperate language to my wife. At length I even offered her personal violence. My pets, of course, were made to feel the change in my disposition. I not only neglected, but ill-used, them. For Pluto, however, I still retained sufficient regard to restrain me from maltreating him, as I made no scruple of maltreating the rabbits, the monkey, or even the dog, when, by accident, or through affection, they came in my way. But my disease grew upon me—for what disease is like alcohol!—and at length even Pluto, who was now becoming old and consequently somewhat peevish—even Pluto began to experience the effects of my ill temper.

One night, returning home much intoxicated from one of my haunts about town, I fancied that the cat avoided my presence. I seized him, when, in his fright at my violence, he inflicted a slight wound upon my hand with his teeth. The fury of a demon instantly possessed me. I knew myself no longer. My original soul seemed, at once, to take its flight from my body; and a more than fiendish malevolence, gin nurtured, thrilled every fibre of my frame. I took from my waistcoat pocket a penknife, opened it, grasped the poor beast by the throat, and deliberately cut one of its eyes from the socket! I blush, I burn, I shudder, while I pen the damnable atrocity.

When reason returned with the morning—when I had slept off the fumes of the night's debauch—I experienced a sentiment half of horror, half of remorse, for the crime of which I had been guilty; but it was, at best, a feeble and equivocal feeling, and the soul remained untouched. I again plunged into excess and soon drowned in wine all memory of the deed.

In the meantime the cat slowly recovered. The socket of the lost eye presented, it is true, a frightful appearance, but he no longer appeared to suffer any pain. He went about the house as usual, but, as might be expected, fled in extreme terror at my approach. I had so much of my old heart left as to be at first grieved by this evident dislike on the part of a creature which had once so loved me. But this feeling soon gave place to irritation. And then came as if to my final and irrevocable overthrow, the spirit of perverseness. Of this spirit philosophy takes no account. Yet I am not more sure that my soul lives than I am that perverseness is one of the primitive impulses of the human heart—one of the indivisible primary faculties, or sentiments, which give direction to the character of man. Who has not, a hundred times, found himself committing a vile or a stupid action, for no other reason than because he knows he should not? Have we not a perpetual inclination, in the teeth of our best judgment, to violate that which is law, merely because we understand it to be such? This spirit of perverseness, I say, came to my final overthrow. It was this unfathomable longing of the soul to vex itself, to offer violence to its own nature, to do wrong for the wrong's sake only, that urged me to continue and finally to consummate the injury I had inflicted upon the unoffending brute. One morning, in cold blood, I slipped a noose about its neck and hung it to the limb of a tree; hung it with the tears streaming from my eyes, and with the bitterest remorse at my heart; hung it because I knew that it had loved me, and because I felt it had given me no reason of offence; hung it because I knew that in so doing I was committing a sin, a deadly sin that would so jeopardize my immortal soul as to place it, if such a thing were possible, even beyond the reach of the infinite mercy of the most merciful and most terrible God.

On the night of the day on which this most cruel deed was done, I was aroused from sleep by the cry of fire. The curtains of my bed were in flames. The whole house was blazing. It was with great difficulty that my wife, a servant, and myself made our escape from the conflagration. The destruction was complete. My entire worldly wealth was swallowed up, and I resigned myself thenceforward to despair.

I am above the weakness of seeking to establish a sequence of cause and effect between the disaster and the atrocity. But I am detailing a chain of facts, and wish not to leave even a possible link imperfect. On the day succeeding the fire I visited the ruins. The walls, with one exception, had fallen in. This exception was found in a compartment wall, not very thick, which stood about the middle of the house, and against which had rested the head of my bed. The plastering had here, in great measure, resisted the action of the fire, a fact which I attributed to its having been recently spread. About this wall a dense crowd were collected, and many persons seemed to be examining a particular portion of it with very minute and eager attention. The words "strange!" "singular!" and other similar expressions excited my curiosity. I approached and saw, as if graven in bas-relief upon the white surface, the figure of a gigantic cat. The impression was given with an accuracy truly marvellous. There was a rope about the animal's neck.

When I first beheld this apparition, for I could scarcely regard it as less, my wonder and my terror were extreme. But at length reflection came to my aid. The cat, I remembered, had been hung in a garden adjacent to the house. Upon the alarm of fire, this garden had been immediately filled by the crowd—by some one of whom the animal must have been cut from the tree and thrown, through an open window, into my chamber. This had probably been done with the view of arousing me from sleep. The falling of other walls had compressed the victim of my cruelty into the substance of the freshly spread plaster; the lime of which, with the flames, and the ammonia from the carcass, had then accomplished the portraiture as I saw it.

Although I thus readily accounted to my reason, if not altogether to my conscience, for the startling fact just detailed, it did not the less fail to make a deep impression upon my fancy. For months I could not rid myself of the phantasm of the cat; and, during this period there came back into my spirit a half sentiment that seemed, but was not, remorse. I went so far as to regret the loss of the animal, and to look about me, among the vile haunts which I now habitually frequented, for another pet of the same species and of somewhat similar appearance, with which to supply its place.

One night as I sat, half stupefied, in a den of more than infamy, my attention was suddenly drawn to some black object reposing upon the head of one of the immense hogsheads of gin or of rum which constituted the chief furniture of the apartment. I had been looking steadily at the top of this hogshead for some minutes, and what now caused me surprise was the fact that I had not sooner perceived the object thereupon. I approached it and touched it with my hand. It was a black cat, a very large one, fully as large as Pluto, and closely resembling him in every respect but one. Pluto had not a white hair upon any portion of his body; but this cat had a large, although indefinite splotch of white, covering nearly the whole region of the breast.

Upon my touching him he immediately arose, purred loudly, rubbed against my hand, and appeared delighted with my notice. This, then, was the very creature of which I was in search. I at once offered to purchase it of the landlord; but this person made no claim to it, knew nothing of it, had never seen it before.

I continued my caresses, and when I prepared to go home the animal evinced a disposition to accompany me. I permitted it to do so, occasionally stooping and patting it as I proceeded. When it reached the house it domesticated itself at once, and became immediately a great favorite with my wife.

For my own part, I soon found a dislike to it arising within me. This was just the reverse of what I had anticipated; but, I know not how or why it was, its evident fondness for myself rather disgusted and annoyed me. By slow degrees these feelings of disgust and annoyance rose into the bitterness of hatred. I avoided the creature; a certain sense of shame, and the remembrance of my former deed of cruelty, preventing me from physically abusing it. I did not, for some weeks, strike or otherwise violently ill-use it; but gradually—very gradually—I came to look upon it with unutterable loathing, and to flee silently from its odious presence as from the breath of a pestilence.

What added, no doubt, to my hatred of the beast was the discovery, on the morning after I brought it home, that, like Pluto, it also had been deprived of one of its eyes. This circumstance, however, only endeared it to my wife, who, as I have already said, possessed, in a high degree, that humanity of feeling which had once been my distinguishing trait, and the source of many of my simplest and purest pleasures.

With my aversion to this cat, however, its partiality for myself seemed to increase. It followed my footsteps with a pertinacity which it would be difficult to make the reader comprehend. Whenever I sat, it would crouch beneath my chair or spring upon my knees, covering me with its loathsome caresses. If I arose to walk it would get between my feet and thus nearly throw me down, or, fastening its long and sharp claws in my dress, clamber, in this manner, to my breast. At such times, although I longed to destroy it with a blow, I was yet withheld from so doing, partly by a memory of my former crime, but chiefly—let me confess it at once—by absolute dread of the beast.

This dread was not exactly a dread of physical evil, and yet I should be at a loss how otherwise to define it. I am almost ashamed to own—yes, even in this felon's cell, I am almost ashamed to own—that the terror and horror with which the animal inspired me had been heightened by one of the merest chimeras it would be possible to conceive. My wife had called my attention, more than once, to the character of the mark of white hair, of which I have spoken, and which constituted the sole visible difference between the strange beast and the one I had destroyed. The reader will remember that this mark, although large, had been originally very indefinite; but, by slow degrees—degrees nearly imperceptible, and which for a long time my reason struggled to reject as fanciful—it had at length assumed a rigorous distinctness of outline. It was now the representation of an object that I shudder to name; and for this, above all, I loathed and dreaded, and would have rid myself of the monster had I dared; it was now, I say, the image of a hideous, of a ghastly thing—of the gallows!—oh, mournful and terrible engine of horror and of crime, of agony and of death!

And now was I indeed wretched beyond the wretchedness of mere humanity. And a brute beast, whose fellow I had contemptuously destroyed—a brute beast to work out for me—for me, a man fashioned in the image of the High God, so much of insufferable woe! Alas! neither by day nor by night knew I the blessing of rest anymore! During the former the creature left me no moment alone, and in the latter I started hourly from dreams of unutterable fear to find the hot breath of the thing upon my face, and its vast weight, an incarnate nightmare that I had no power to shake off, incumbent eternally upon my heart!

Beneath the pressure of torments such as these, the feeble remnant of the good within me succumbed. Evil thoughts became my sole intimates—the darkest and most evil of thoughts. The moodiness of my usual temper increased to hatred of all things and of all mankind; while from the sudden, frequent, and ungovernable outbursts of a fury to which I now blindly abandoned myself, my uncomplaining wife, alas! was the most usual and the most patient of sufferers.

One day she accompanied me upon some household errand into the cellar of the old building which our poverty compelled us to inhabit. The cat followed me down the steep stairs, and, nearly throwing me headlong, exasperated me to madness. Uplifting an axe, and forgetting in my wrath the childish dread which had hitherto stayed my hand, I aimed a blow at the animal, which, of course, would have proved instantly fatal had it descended as I wished. But this blow was arrested by the hand of my wife. Goaded by the interference into a rage more than demoniacal, I withdrew my arm from her grasp and buried the axe in her brain. She fell dead upon the spot without a groan.

This hideous murder accomplished, I set myself forthwith, and with entire deliberation, to the task of concealing the body. I knew that I could not remove it from the house, either by day or by night, without the risk of being observed by the neighbors. Many projects entered my mind. At one period I thought of cutting the corpse into minute fragments and destroying them by fire. At another, I resolved to dig a grave for it in the floor of the cellar. Again, I deliberated about casting it in the well in the yard; about packing it in a box, as if merchandise, with the usual arrangements, and so getting a porter to take it from the house. Finally I hit upon what I considered a far better expedient than either of these. I determined to wall it up in the cellar, as the monks of the Middle Ages are recorded to have walled up their victims.

For a purpose such as this the cellar was well adapted. Its walls were loosely constructed, and had lately been plastered throughout with a rough plaster, which the dampness of the atmosphere had prevented from hardening. Moreover, in one of the walls was a projection, caused by a false chimney, or fireplace, that had been filled up and made to resemble the rest of the cellar. I made no doubt that I could readily displace the bricks at this point, insert the corpse, and wall the whole up as before, so that no eye could detect anything suspicious.

And in this calculation I was not deceived. By means of a crowbar I easily dislodged the bricks, and, having carefully deposited the body against the inner wall, I propped it in that position, while with little trouble I relaid the whole structure as it originally stood. Having procured mortar, sand, and hair, with every possible precaution I prepared a plaster which could not be distinguished from the old, and with this I very carefully went over the new brickwork. When I had finished, I felt satisfied that all was right. The wall did not present the slightest appearance of having been disturbed. The rubbish on the floor was picked up with the minutest care. I looked around triumphantly and said to myself: "Here at least, then, my labor has not been in vain."

My next step was to look for the beast which had been the cause of so much wretchedness; for I had at length firmly resolved to put it to death. Had I been able to meet with it at the moment, there could have been no doubt of its fate; but it appeared that the crafty animal had been alarmed at the violence of my previous anger, and forbore to present itself in my present mood. It is impossible to describe, or to imagine, the deep, the blissful sense of relief which the absence of the detested creature occasioned in my bosom. It did not make its appearance during the night; and thus for one night, at least, since its introduction into the house, I soundly and tranquilly slept; aye, slept even with the burden of murder upon my soul.

The second and the third day passed, and still my tormentor came not. Once again I breathed as a freeman. The monster, in terror, had fled the premises for ever; I should behold it no more! My happiness was supreme! The guilt of my dark deed disturbed me but little. Some few inquiries had been made, but these had been readily answered. Even a search had been instituted, but, of course, nothing was to be discovered. I looked upon my future felicity as secured.

Upon the fourth day of the assassination, a party of the police came, very unexpectedly, into the house, and proceeded again to make rigorous investigation of the premises. Secure, however, in the inscrutability of my place of concealment, I felt no embarrassment whatever. The officers bade me accompany them in their search. They left no nook or corner unexplored. At length, for the third or fourth time, they descended into the cellar. I quivered not in a muscle. My heart beat calmly as that of one who slumbers in innocence. I walked the cellar from end to end. I folded my arms upon my bosom and roamed easily to and fro. The police were thoroughly satisfied and prepared to depart. The glee at my heart was too strong to be restrained. I burned to say if but one word, by way of triumph, and to render doubly sure their assurance of my guiltlessness.

"Gentlemen," I said at last, as the party ascended the steps, "I delight to have allayed your suspicions. I wish you all health and a little more courtesy. By the bye, gentlemen, this—this is a very well-constructed house." (In the rabid desire to say something easily, I scarcely knew what I uttered at all.) "I may say an excellently well-constructed house. These walls—are you going, gentlemen?—these walls are solidly put together"; and here, through the mere frenzy of bravado, I rapped heavily with a cane which I held in my hand upon that very portion of the brickwork behind which stood the corpse of the wife of my bosom.

But may God shield and deliver me from the fangs of the arch-fiend! No sooner had the reverberation of my blows sunk into silence than I was answered by a voice from within the tomb!—by a cry, at first muffled and broken, like the sobbing of a child, and then quickly swelling into one long, loud, and continuous scream, utterly anomalous and inhuman—a howl, a wailing shriek, half of horror and half of triumph, such as might have arisen only out of hell, conjointly from the throats of the damned in their agony and of the demons that exult in the damnation.

Of my own thoughts it is folly to speak. Swooning, I staggered to the opposite wall. For one instant the party on the stairs remained motionless, through extremity of terror and awe. In the next a dozen stout arms were toiling at the wall. It fell bodily. The corpse, already greatly decayed and clotted with gore, stood erect before the eyes of the spectators. Upon its head, with red extended mouth and solitary eye of fire, sat the hideous beast whose craft had seduced me into murder, and whose informing voice had consigned me to the hangman. I had walled the monster up within the tomb.

---

1. Why does the narrator insist that he is detailing a chain of facts, not seeking to explain them?

2. Why does the narrator give his knowledge of committing a deadly sin as one of the reasons for hanging Pluto?

3. Why does the second black cat's evident fondness for the narrator cause him disgust and annoyance?

4. After having satisfied the police, why does the narrator want to "render doubly sure their assurance"?

HENRY JAMES (1843–1916), brother of psychologist and philosopher William James, was born in America but lived many years as an expatriate in England, cultivating the cosmopolitan perspective reflected in his writings. Many of his novels and stories, including *Daisy Miller* (1878), *The Portrait of a Lady* (1881), and *The Ambassadors* (1903), portray the cross-cultural confrontation of the New World and the Old World. His fictional works employ a complex style that includes such techniques as stream of consciousness; they are penetrating psychological studies of individuals that also explore larger philosophical and social issues. James was also a skillful writer of supernatural stories, the most famous of which is *The Turn of the Screw* (1898). His literary criticism and essays, particularly "The Art of Fiction," are as highly regarded as his fiction.

The Real Thing

1

When the porter's wife (she used to answer the house bell) announced "A gentleman—with a lady, sir," I had, as I often had in those days, for the wish was father to the thought, an immediate vision of sitters. Sitters my visitors in this case proved to be; but not in the sense I should have preferred. However, there was nothing at first to indicate that they might not have come for a portrait. The gentleman, a man of fifty, very high and very straight, with a moustache slightly grizzled and a dark grey walking coat admirably fitted, both of which I noted professionally—I don't mean as a barber or yet as a tailor—would have struck me as a celebrity if celebrities often were striking. It was a truth of which I had for some time been conscious that a figure with a good deal of frontage was, as one might say, almost never a public institution. A glance at the lady helped to remind me of this paradoxical law:

she also looked too distinguished to be a "personality." Moreover one would scarcely come across two variations together.

Neither of the pair spoke immediately—they only prolonged the preliminary gaze which suggested that each wished to give the other a chance. They were visibly shy; they stood there letting me take them in—which, as I afterwards perceived, was the most practical thing they could have done. In this way their embarrassment served their cause. I had seen people painfully reluctant to mention that they desired anything so gross as to be represented on canvas; but the scruples of my new friends appeared almost insurmountable. Yet the gentleman might have said "I should like a portrait of my wife," and the lady might have said "I should like a portrait of my husband." Perhaps they were not husband and wife—this naturally would make the matter more delicate. Perhaps they wished to be done together—in which case they ought to have brought a third person to break the news.

"We come from Mr. Rivet," the lady said at last, with a dim smile which had the effect of a moist sponge passed over a "sunk" piece of painting, as well as of a vague allusion to vanished beauty. She was as tall and straight, in her degree, as her companion, and with ten years less to carry. She looked as sad as a woman could look whose face was not charged with expression; that is her tinted oval mask showed friction as an exposed surface shows it. The hand of time had played over her freely, but only to simplify. She was slim and stiff, and so well dressed, in dark blue cloth, with lappets and pockets and buttons, that it was clear she employed the same tailor as her husband. The couple had an indefinable air of prosperous thrift—they evidently got a good deal of luxury for their money. If I was to be one of their luxuries it would behove me to consider my terms.

"Ah, Claude Rivet recommended me?" I inquired; and I added that it was very kind of him, though I could reflect that, as he only painted landscape, this was not a sacrifice.

The lady looked very hard at the gentleman, and the gentleman looked round the room. Then staring at the floor a moment and stroking his moustache, he rested his pleasant eyes on me with the remark: "He said you were the right one."

"I try to be, when people want to sit."

"Yes, we should like to," said the lady anxiously.

"Do you mean together?"

My visitors exchanged a glance. "If you could do anything with *me*, I suppose it would be double," the gentleman stammered.

"Oh yes, there's naturally a higher charge for two figures than for one."

"We should like to make it pay," the husband confessed.

"That's very good of you," I returned, appreciating so unwonted a sympathy—for I supposed he meant pay the artist.

A sense of strangeness seemed to dawn on the lady. "We mean for the illustrations—Mr. Rivet said you might put one in."

"Put one in—an illustration?" I was equally confused.

"Sketch her off, you know," said the gentleman, colouring.

It was only then that I understood the service Claude Rivet had rendered me; he had told them that I worked in black and white, for magazines, for storybooks, for sketches of contemporary life, and consequently had frequent employment for models. These things were true, but it was not less true (I may confess it now—whether because the aspiration was to lead to everything or to nothing I leave the reader to guess), that I couldn't get the honours, to say nothing of the emoluments, of a great painter of portraits out of my head. My "illustrations" were my potboilers; I looked to a different branch of art (far and away the most interesting it had always seemed to me), to perpetuate my fame. There was no shame in looking to it also to make my fortune; but that fortune was by so much further from being made from the moment my visitors wished to be "done" for nothing. I was disappointed; for in the pictorial sense I had immediately *seen* them. I had seized their type—I had already settled what I would do with it. Something that wouldn't absolutely have pleased them, I afterwards reflected.

"Ah, you're—you're—a—?" I began, as soon as I had mastered my surprise. I couldn't bring out the dingy word *models*; it seemed to fit the case so little.

"We haven't had much practice," said the lady.

"We've got to *do* something, and we've thought that an artist in your line might perhaps make something of us," her husband threw off. He further mentioned that they didn't know many artists and that they had gone first, on the off chance (he painted views of course, but sometimes put in figures—perhaps I remembered), to Mr. Rivet, whom they had met a few years before at a place in Norfolk where he was sketching.

"We used to sketch a little ourselves," the lady hinted.

"It's very awkward, but we absolutely *must* do something," her husband went on.

"Of course we're not so *very* young," she admitted, with a wan smile.

With the remark that I might as well know something more about them, the husband had handed me a card extracted from a neat new pocketbook (their appurtenances were all of the freshest) and inscribed with the words "Major Monarch." Impressive as these words were they didn't carry my knowledge much further; but my visitor presently added: "I've left the army, and we've had the misfortune to lose our money. In fact our means are dreadfully small."

"It's an awful bore," said Mrs. Monarch.

They evidently wished to be discreet—to take care not to swagger because they were gentlefolks. I perceived they would have been willing to recognise this as something of a drawback, at the same time that I guessed at an underlying sense—their consolation in adversity—that they *had* their points. They certainly had; but these advantages struck me as preponderantly social; such for instance as would help to make a drawing room look well. However, a drawing room was always, or ought to be, a picture.

In consequence of his wife's allusion to their age Major Monarch observed: "Naturally, it's more for the figure that we thought of going in. We can still hold ourselves up." On the instant I saw that the figure was indeed their strong point. His "naturally" didn't sound vain, but it lighted up the question. "*She* has got the best," he continued, nodding at his wife, with a pleasant after-dinner absence of circumlocution. I could only reply, as if we were in fact sitting over our wine, that this didn't prevent his own from being very good; which led him in turn to rejoin: "We thought that if you ever had to do people like us, we might be something like it. *She*, particularly—for a lady in a book, you know."

I was so amused by them that, to get more of it, I did my best to take their point of view; and though it was an embarrassment to find myself appraising physically, as if they were animals on hire or useful blacks, a pair whom I should have expected to meet only in one of the relations in which criticism is tacit, I looked at Mrs. Monarch judicially enough to be able to exclaim, after a moment, with conviction: "Oh yes, a lady in a book!" She was singularly like a bad illustration.

"We'll stand up, if you like," said the Major; and he raised himself before me with a really grand air.

I could take his measure at a glance—he was six feet two and a perfect gentleman. It would have paid any club in process of formation and in want of a stamp to engage him at a salary to stand in the principal window. What struck me immediately was that in coming to me they had rather missed their vocation; they could surely have been turned to better account for advertising purposes. I couldn't of course see the thing in detail, but I could see them make someone's fortune—I don't mean their own. There was something in them for a waistcoat maker, an hotelkeeper or a soap vendor. I could imagine "We always use it" pinned on their bosoms with the greatest effect; I had a vision of the promptitude with which they would launch a table d'hôte.

Mrs. Monarch sat still, not from pride but from shyness, and presently her husband said to her: "Get up my dear and show how smart you are." She obeyed, but she had no need to get up to show it. She walked to the end of the studio, and then she came back blushing, with her fluttered eyes on her husband. I was reminded of an incident I had accidentally had a glimpse of in Paris—being with a friend there, a dramatist about to produce a play—when an actress came to him to ask to be intrusted with a part. She went through her paces before him, walked up and down as Mrs. Monarch was doing. Mrs. Monarch did it quite as well, but I asbstained from applauding. It was very odd to see such people apply for such poor pay. She looked as if she had ten thousand a year. Her husband had used the word that described her: she was, in the London current jargon, essentially and typically "smart." Her figure was, in the same order of ideas, conspicuously and irreproachably "good." For a woman of her age her waist was surprisingly small; her elbow moreover had the orthodox crook. She held her head at the conventional angle; but why did she come to *me*? She ought to have tried on jackets at a big shop. I feared my visitors were not only destitute, but "artistic"—which would be a great complication. When she sat down again I thanked her, observing that what a draughtsman most valued in his model was the faculty of keeping quiet.

"Oh, *she* can keep quiet," said Major Monarch. Then he added, jocosely: "I've always kept her quiet."

"I'm not a nasty fidget, am I?" Mrs. Monarch appealed to her husband.

He addressed his answer to me. "Perhaps it isn't out of place to mention—because we ought to be quite businesslike, oughtn't we?—that when I married her she was known as the Beautiful Statue."

"Oh dear!" said Mrs. Monarch, ruefully.

"Of course I should want a certain amount of expression," I rejoined.

"Of *course*!" they both exclaimed.

"And then I suppose you know that you'll get awfully tired."

"Oh, we *never* get tired!" they eagerly cried.

"Have you had any kind of practice?"

They hesitated—they looked at each other. "We've been photographed, *immensely*," said Mrs. Monarch.

"She means the fellows have asked us," added the Major.

"I see—because you're so good-looking."

"I don't know what they thought, but they were always after us."

"We always got our photographs for nothing," smiled Mrs. Monarch.

"We might have brought some, my dear," her husband remarked.

"I'm not sure we have any left. We've given quantities away," she explained to me.

"With our autographs and that sort of thing," said the Major.

"Are they to be got in the shops?" I inquired, as a harmless pleasantry.

"Oh, yes; *hers*—they used to be."

"Not now," said Mrs. Monarch, with her eyes on the floor.

2

I could fancy the "sort of thing" they put on the presentation copies of their photographs, and I was sure they wrote a beautiful hand. It was odd how quickly I was sure of everything that concerned them. If they were now so poor as to have to earn shillings and pence, they never had had much of a margin. Their good looks had been their capital, and they had good-humouredly made the most of the career that this resource marked out for them. It was in their faces, the blankness, the deep intellectual repose of the twenty years of country-house visiting which had given them pleasant intonations. I could see the sunny drawing rooms, sprinkled with periodicals she didn't read, in which Mrs. Monarch had continuously sat; I could see the wet shrubberies in which she had walked, equipped to admiration for either exercise. I could see the rich covers the Major had helped to shoot and the wonderful garments in which, late at night, he repaired to the smoking room to talk about them. I could imagine their leggings and waterproofs, their knowing tweeds and rugs, their rolls of sticks and cases of tackle and neat umbrellas; and I could evoke the exact appearance of their servants and the compact variety of their luggage on the platforms of country stations.

They gave small tips, but they were liked; they didn't do anything themselves, but they were welcome. They looked so well everywhere; they gratified the general relish for stature, complexion and "form." They knew it without fatuity or vulgarity, and they respected themselves in consequence. They were not superficial; they were thorough and kept themselves up—it had been their line. People with such a taste for activity had to have some line. I could feel how, even in a dull house, they could have been counted upon for cheerfulness. At present something had happened—it didn't matter what, their little income had grown less, it had grown least—and they had to do something for pocket money. Their friends liked them, but didn't like to support them. There was something about them that represented credit—their clothes, their manners, their type; but if credit is a large empty pocket in which an occasional chink reverberates, the chink at least must be audible. What they wanted of me was to help to make it so. Fortunately they had no children—I soon divined that. They would also perhaps wish our relations to be kept secret: this was why it was "for the figure"—the reproduction of the face would betray them.

I liked them—they were so simple; and I had no objection to them if they would suit. But, somehow, with all their perfections I didn't easily believe in them. After all they were amateurs, and the ruling passion of my life was the detestation of the amateur. Combined with this was another perversity—an innate preference for the represented subject over the real one: the defect of the real one was so apt to be a lack of representation. I liked things that appeared; then one was sure. Whether they *were* or not was a subordinate and almost always a profitless question. There were other considerations, the first of which was that I already had two or three people in use, notably a young person with big feet, in alpaca, from Kilburn, who for a couple of years had come to me regularly for my illustrations and with whom I was still—perhaps ignobly—satisfied. I frankly explained to my visitors how the case stood; but they had taken more precautions than I supposed. They had reasoned out their opportunity, for Claude Rivet had told them of the projected *édition de luxe* of one of the writers of our day—the rarest of the novelists—who, long neglected by the multitudinous vulgar and dearly prized by the attentive (need I mention Philip Vincent?) had had the happy fortune of seeing, late in life, the dawn and then the full light of a higher criticism—an estimate in which, on the part of the public, there was something really of expiation. The edition in question, planned by a publisher of taste, was practically an act of high reparation; the woodcuts with which it was to be enriched were the homage of English art to one of the most independent representatives of English letters. Major and Mrs. Monarch confessed to me that they had hoped I might be able to work *them* into my share of the enterprise. They knew I was to do the first of the books, "Rutland Ramsay," but I had to make clear to them that my participation in the rest of the affair—this first book was to be a test—was to depend on the satisfaction I should give. If this should be limited my employers would drop me without a scruple. It was therefore a crisis for me, and naturally I was making special preparations, looking about for new people, if they should be necessary, and securing the best types. I admitted however that I should like to settle down to two or three good models who would do for everything.

"Should we have often to—a—put on special clothes?" Mrs. Monarch timidly demanded.

"Dear, yes—that's half the business."

"And should we be expected to supply our own costumes?"

"Oh, no; I've got a lot of things. A painter's models put on—or put off—anything he likes."

"And do you mean—a—the same?"

"The same?"

Mrs. Monarch looked at her husband again.

"Oh, she was just wondering," he explained, "if the costumes are in *general* use." I had to confess that they were, and I mentioned further that some of them (I had a lot of genuine, greasy last-century things), had served their time, a hundred years ago, on living, world-stained men and women. "We'll put on anything that *fits*," said the Major.

"Oh, I arrange that—they fit in the pictures."

"I'm afraid I should do better for the modern books. I would come as you like," said Mrs. Monarch.

"She has got a lot of clothes at home: they might do for contemporary life," her husband continued.

"Oh, I can fancy scenes in which you'd be quite natural." And indeed I could see the slipshod rearrangements of stale properties—the stories I tried to produce pictures for without the exasperation of reading them—whose sandy tracts the good lady might help to people. But I had to return to the fact that for this sort of work—the daily mechanical grind—I was already equipped; the people I was working with were fully adequate.

"We only thought we might be more like *some* characters," said Mrs. Monarch mildly, getting up.

Her husband also rose; he stood looking at me with a dim wistfulness that was touching in so fine a man. "Wouldn't it be rather a pull sometimes to have—a—to have—?" He hung fire; he wanted me to help him by phrasing what he meant. But I couldn't—I didn't know. So he brought it out, awkwardly: "The *real* thing; a gentleman, you know, or a lady." I was quite ready to give a general assent—I admitted that there was a great deal in that. This encouraged Major Monarch to say, following up his appeal with an unacted gulp: "It's awfully hard—we've tried everything." The gulp was communicative; it proved too much for his wife. Before I knew it Mrs. Monarch had dropped again upon a divan and burst into tears. Her husband sat down beside her, holding one of her hands; whereupon she quickly dried her eyes with the other, while I felt embarrassed as she looked up at me. "There isn't a confounded job I haven't applied for—waited for—prayed for. You can fancy we'd be pretty bad first. Secretaryships and that sort of thing? You might as well ask for a peerage. I'd be *anything*—I'm strong; a messenger or a coal heaver. I'd put on a gold-laced cap and open carriage doors in front of the haberdasher's; I'd hang about a station, to carry portmanteaus; I'd be a postman. But they won't *look* at you; there are thousands, as good as yourself, already on the ground. *Gentlemen*, poor beggars, who have drunk their wine, who have kept their hunters!"

I was as reassuring as I knew how to be, and my visitors were presently on their feet again while, for the experiment, we agreed on an hour. We were discussing it when the door opened and Miss Churm came in with a wet umbrella. Miss Churm had to take the omnibus to Maida Vale and then walk half a mile. She looked a trifle blowsy and slightly splashed. I scarcely ever saw her come in without thinking afresh how odd it was that, being so little in herself, she should yet be so much in others. She was a meagre little Miss Churm, but she was an ample heroine of romance. She was only a freckled cockney, but she could represent everything, from a fine lady to a shepherdess; she had the faculty, as she might have had a fine voice or long hair. She couldn't spell, and she loved beer, but she had two or three "points," and practice, and a knack, and mother wit, and a kind of whimsical sensibility, and a love of the theatre, and seven sisters, and not an ounce of respect, especially for the *h*. The first thing my visitors saw was that her umbrella was wet, and in their spotless perfection they visibly winced at it. The rain had come on since their arrival.

"I'm all in a soak; there *was* a mess of people in the 'bus. I wish you lived near a stytion," said Miss Churm. I requested her to get ready as quickly as possible, and she passed into the room in which she always changed her dress. But before going out she asked me what she was to get into this time.

"It's the Russian princess, don't you know?" I answered; "the one with the 'golden eyes,' in black velvet, for the long thing in the *Cheapside*."

"Golden eyes? I *say*!" cried Miss Churm, while my companions watched her with intensity as she withdrew. She always arranged herself, when she was late, before I could turn round; and I kept my visitors a little, on purpose, so that they might get an idea, from seeing her, what would be expected of themselves. I mentioned that she was quite my notion of an excellent model—she was really very clever.

"Do you think she looks like a Russian princess?" Major Monarch asked, with lurking alarm.

"When I make her, yes."

"Oh, if you have to *make* her—!" he reasoned, acutely.

"That's the most you can ask. There are so many that are not makeable."

"Well now, *here's* a lady"—and with a persuasive smile he passed his arm into his wife's—"who's already made!"

"Oh, I'm not a Russian princess," Mrs. Monarch protested, a little coldly. I could see that she had known some and didn't like them. There, immediately, was a complication of a kind that I never had to fear with Miss Churm.

This young lady came back in black velvet—the gown was rather rusty and very low on her lean shoulders—and with a Japanese fan in her red hands. I reminded her that in the scene I was doing she had to look over someone's head. "I forget whose it is; but it doesn't matter. Just look over a head."

"I'd rather look over a stove," said Miss Churm; and she took her station near the fire. She fell into position, settled herself into a tall attitude, gave a certain backward inclination to her head and a certain forward droop to her fan, and looked, at least to my prejudiced sense, distinguished and charming, foreign and dangerous. We left her looking so, while I went downstairs with Major and Mrs. Monarch.

"I think I could come about as near it as that," said Mrs. Monarch.

"Oh, you think she's shabby, but you must allow for the alchemy of art."

However, they went off with an evident increase of comfort, founded on their demonstrable advantage in being the real thing. I could fancy them shuddering over Miss Churm. She was very droll about them when I went back, for I told her what they wanted.

"Well, if *she* can sit I'll tyke to bookkeeping," said my model.

"She's very ladylike," I replied, as an innocent form of aggravation.

"So much the worse for *you*. That means she can't turn round."

"She'll do for the fashionable novels."

"Oh yes, she'll *do* for them!" my model humorously declared. "Ain't they bad enough without her?" I had often sociably denounced them to Miss Churm.

3

It was for the elucidation of a mystery in one of these works that I first tried Mrs. Monarch. Her husband came with her, to be useful if necessary—it was sufficiently clear that as a general thing he would prefer to come with her. At first I wondered if this were for "propriety's" sake—if he were going to be jealous and meddling. The idea was too tiresome, and if it had been confirmed it would speedily have brought our acquaintance to a close. But I soon saw there was nothing in it and that if he accompanied Mrs. Monarch it was (in addition to the chance of being wanted), simply because he had nothing else to do. When she was away from him his occupation was gone—she never *had* been away from him. I judged, rightly, that in their awkward situation their close union was their main comfort and that this union had no weak spot. It was a real marriage, an encouragement to the hesitating, a nut for pessimists to crack. Their address was humble (I remember afterwards thinking it had been the only thing about them that was really professional), and I could fancy the lamentable lodgings in which the Major would have been left alone. He could bear them with his wife—he couldn't bear them without her.

He had too much tact to try and make himself agreeable when he couldn't be useful; so he simply sat and waited, when I was too absorbed in my work to talk. But I liked to make him talk—it made my work, when it didn't interrupt it, less sordid, less special. To listen to him was to combine the excitement of going out with the economy of staying at home. There was only one hindrance: that I seemed not to know any of the people he and his wife had known. I think he wondered extremely, during the term of our intercourse, whom the deuce I *did* know. He hadn't a stray sixpence of an idea to fumble for; so we didn't spin it very fine—we confined ourselves to questions of leather and even of liquor (saddlers and breeches makers and how to get good claret cheap), and matters like "good trains" and the habits of small game. His lore on these last subjects was astonishing, he managed to interweave the stationmaster with the ornithologist. When he couldn't talk about greater things he could talk cheerfully about smaller, and since I couldn't accompany him into reminiscences of the fashionable world he could lower the conversation without a visible effort to my level.

So earnest a desire to please was touching in a man who could so easily have knocked one down. He looked after the fire and had an opinion on the draught of the stove, without my asking him, and I could see that he thought many of my arrangements not half clever enough. I remember telling him that if I were only rich I would offer him a salary to come and teach me how to live. Sometimes he gave a random sigh, of which the essence was: "Give me even such a bare old barrack as *this*, and I'd do something with it!" When I wanted to use him he came alone; which was an illustration of the superior courage of women. His wife could bear her solitary second floor, and she was in general more discreet; showing by various small reserves that she was alive to the propriety of keeping our relations markedly professional—not letting them slide into sociability. She wished it to remain clear that she and the Major were employed, not cultivated, and if she approved of me as a superior, who could be kept in his place, she never thought me quite good enough for an equal.

She sat with great intensity, giving the whole of her mind to it, and was capable of remaining for an hour almost as motionless as if she were before a photographer's lens. I could see she had been photographed often, but somehow the very habit that made her good for that purpose unfitted her for mine. At first I was extremely pleased with her ladylike air, and it was a satisfaction, on coming to follow her lines, to see how good they were and how far they could lead the pencil. But after a few times I began to find her too insurmountably stiff; do what I would with it my drawing looked like a photograph or a copy of a photograph. Her figure had no variety of expression—she herself had no sense of variety. You may say that this was my business, was only a question of placing her. I placed her in every conceivable position, but she managed to obliterate their differences. She was always a lady certainly, and into the bargain was always the same lady. She was the real thing, but always the same thing. There were moments when I was oppressed by the serenity of her confidence that she *was* the real thing. All her dealings with me and all her husband's were an implication that this was lucky for *me*. Meanwhile I found myself trying to invent types that approached her own, instead of making her own transform itself—in the clever way that was not impossible, for instance, to poor Miss Churm. Arrange as I would and take the precautions I would, she always, in my pictures, came out too tall—landing me in the dilemma of having represented a fascinating woman as seven feet high, which, out of respect perhaps to my own very much scantier inches, was far from my idea of such a personage.

The case was worse with the Major—nothing I could do would keep *him* down, so that he became useful only for the representation of brawny giants. I adored variety and range, I cherished human accidents, the illustrative note; I wanted to characterise closely, and the thing in the world I most hated was the danger of being ridden by a type. I had quarrelled with some of my friends about it—I had parted company with them for maintaining that one *had* to be, and that if the type was beautiful (witness Raphael and Leonardo), the servitude was only a gain. I was neither Leonardo nor Raphael; I might only be a presumptuous young modern searcher, but I held that everything was to be sacrificed sooner than character. When they averred that the haunting type in question could easily *be* character, I retorted, perhaps superficially: "Whose?" It couldn't be everybody's—it might end in being nobody's.

After I had drawn Mrs. Monarch a dozen times I perceived more clearly than before that the value of such a model as Miss Churm resided precisely in the fact that she had no positive stamp, combined of course with the other fact that what she did have was a curious and inexplicable talent for imitation. Her usual appearance was like a curtain which she could draw up at request for a capital performance. This performance was simply suggestive; but it was a word to the wise—it was vivid and pretty. Sometimes, even, I thought it, though she was plain herself, too insipidly pretty; I made it a reproach to her that the figures drawn from her were monotonously (*bêtement*,[1] as we used to say) graceful. Nothing made her more angry: it was so much her pride to feel that she could sit for characters that had nothing in common with each other. She would accuse me at such moments of taking away her "reputytion."

It suffered a certain shrinkage, this queer quantity, from the repeated visits of my new friends. Miss Churm was greatly in demand,

1. [Stupidity.]

never in want of employment, so I had no scruple in putting her off occasionally, to try them more at my ease. It was certainly amusing at first to do the real thing—it was amusing to do Major Monarch's trousers. They *were* the real thing, even if he did come out colossal. It was amusing to do his wife's back hair (it was so mathematically neat,) and the particular "smart" tension of her tight stays. She lent herself especially to positions in which the face was somewhat averted or blurred; she abounded in ladylike back views and *profils perdus.*[2] When she stood erect she took naturally one of the attitudes in which court painters represent queens and princesses; so that I found myself wondering whether, to draw out this accomplishment, I couldn't get the editor of the *Cheapside* to publish a really royal romance, "A Tale of Buckingham Palace." Sometimes, however, the real thing and the make-believe came into contact; by which I mean that Miss Churm, keeping an appointment or coming to make one on days when I had much work in hand, encountered her invidious rivals. The encounter was not on their part, for they noticed her no more than if she had been the housemaid; not from intentional loftiness, but simply because, as yet, professionally, they didn't know how to fraternise, as I could guess that they would have liked—or at least that the Major would. They couldn't talk about the omnibus—they always walked; and they didn't know what else to try—she wasn't interested in good trains or cheap claret. Besides, they must have felt—in the air—that she was amused at them, secretly derisive of their ever knowing how. She was not a person to conceal her scepticism if she had had a chance to show it. On the other hand Mrs. Monarch didn't think her tidy; for why else did she take pains to say to me (it was going out of the way, for Mrs. Monarch), that she didn't like dirty women?

One day when my young lady happened to be present with my other sitters (she even dropped in, when it was convenient, for a chat), I asked her to be so good as to lend a hand in getting tea—a service with which she was familiar and which was one of a class that, living as I did in a small way, with slender domestic resources, I often appealed to my models to render. They liked to lay hands on my property, to break

2. [Obscured profiles.]

the sitting, and sometimes the china—I made them feel Bohemian. The next time I saw Miss Churm after this incident she surprised me greatly by making a scene about it—she accused me of having wished to humiliate her. She had not resented the outrage at the time, but had seemed obliging and amused, enjoying the comedy of asking Mrs. Monarch, who sat vague and silent, whether she would have cream and sugar, and putting an exaggerated simper into the question. She had tried intonations—as if she too wished to pass for the real thing; till I was afraid my other visitors would take offence.

Oh, *they* were determined not to do this; and their touching patience was the measure of their great need. They would sit by the hour, uncomplaining, till I was ready to use them; they would come back on the chance of being wanted and would walk away cheerfully if they were not. I used to go to the door with them to see in what magnificent order they retreated. I tried to find other employment for them—I introduced them to several artists. But they didn't "take," for reasons I could appreciate, and I became conscious, rather anxiously, that after such disappointments they fell back upon me with a heavier weight. They did me the honour to think that it was I who was most *their* form. They were not picturesque enough for the painters, and in those days there were not so many serious workers in black and white. Besides, they had an eye to the great job I had mentioned to them—they had secretly set their hearts on supplying the right essence for my pictorial vindication of our fine novelist. They knew that for this undertaking I should want no costume effects, none of the frippery of past ages—that it was a case in which everything would be contemporary and satirical and, presumably, genteel. If I could work them into it their future would be assured, for the labour would of course be long and the occupation steady.

One day Mrs. Monarch came without her husband—she explained his absence by his having had to go to the City. While she sat there in her usual anxious stiffness there came, at the door, a knock which I immediately recognised as the subdued appeal of a model out of work. It was followed by the entrance of a young man whom I easily perceived to be a foreigner and who proved in fact an Italian acquainted with no English word but my name, which he uttered in a way that made it seem to include all others. I had not then visited his country, nor was

I proficient in his tongue; but as he was not so meanly constituted—what Italian is?—as to depend only on that member for expression he conveyed to me, in familiar but graceful mimicry, that he was in search of exactly the employment in which the lady before me was engaged. I was not struck with him at first, and while I continued to draw I emitted rough sounds of discouragement and dismissal. He stood his ground, however, not importunately, but with a dumb, doglike fidelity in his eyes which amounted to innocent impudence—the manner of a devoted servant (he might have been in the house for years), unjustly suspected. Suddenly I saw that this very attitude and expression made a picture, whereupon I told him to sit down and wait till I should be free. There was another picture in the way he obeyed me, and I observed as I worked that there were others still in the way he looked wonderingly, with his head thrown back, about the high studio. He might have been crossing himself in St. Peter's. Before I finished I said to myself: "The fellow's a bankrupt orange monger, but he's a treasure."

When Mrs. Monarch withdrew he passed across the room like a flash to open the door for her, standing there with the rapt, pure gaze of the young Dante spellbound by the young Beatrice. As I never insisted, in such situations, on the blankness of the British domestic, I reflected that he had the making of a servant (and I needed one, but couldn't pay him to be only that), as well as of a model; in short I made up my mind to adopt my bright adventurer if he would agree to officiate in the double capacity. He jumped at my offer, and in the event my rashness (for I had known nothing about him), was not brought home to me. He proved a sympathetic though a desultory ministrant, and had in a wonderful degree the *sentiment de la pose*. It was uncultivated, instinctive; a part of the happy instinct which had guided him to my door and helped him to spell out my name on the card nailed to it. He had had no other introduction to me than a guess, from the shape of my high north window, seen outside, that my place was a studio and that as a studio it would contain an artist. He had wandered to England in search of fortune, like other itinerants, and had embarked, with a partner and a small green handcart, on the sale of penny ices. The ices had melted away and the partner had dissolved in their train. My young man wore tight yellow trousers with reddish stripes and his name was Oronte. He was sallow but fair, and when I put him into some old clothes of my own he looked like an Englishman. He was as good as Miss Churm, who could look, when required, like an Italian.

4

I thought Mrs. Monarch's face slightly convulsed when, on her coming back with her husband, she found Oronte installed. It was strange to have to recognise in a scrap of a lazzarone a competitor to her magnificent Major. It was she who scented danger first, for the Major was anecdotically unconscious. But Oronte gave us tea, with a hundred eager confusions (he had never seen such a queer process), and I think she thought better of me for having at last an "establishment." They saw a couple of drawings that I had made of the establishment, and Mrs. Monarch hinted that it never would have struck her that he had sat for them. "Now the drawings you make from *us*, they look exactly like us," she reminded me, smiling in triumph; and I recognised that this was indeed just their defect. When I drew the Monarchs I couldn't, somehow, get away from them—get into the character I wanted to represent; and I had not the least desire my model should be discoverable in my picture. Miss Churm never was, and Mrs. Monarch thought I hid her, very properly, because she was vulgar; whereas if she was lost it was only as the dead who go to heaven are lost—in the gain of an angel the more.

By this time I had got a certain start with "Rutland Ramsay," the first novel in the great projected series; that is I had produced a dozen drawings, several with the help of the Major and his wife, and I had sent them in for approval. My understanding with the publishers, as I have already hinted, had been that I was to be left to do my work, in this particular case, as I liked, with the whole book committed to me; but my connection with the rest of the series was only contingent. There were moments when, frankly, it *was* a comfort to have the real thing under one's hand; for there were characters in "Rutland Ramsay" that were very much like it. There were people presumably as straight as the Major and women of as good a fashion as Mrs. Monarch. There was a great deal of country-house life—treated, it is true, in a fine, fanciful, ironical, generalised way—and there was a considerable implication of knickerbockers and kilts. There were certain things I had to settle at the outset; such things for instance as the exact appearance of the hero, the particular bloom of the heroine. The author of course gave me a lead, but there was a margin for interpretation. I took the Monarchs into my confidence, I told them frankly what I was about, I mentioned my embarrassments and alternatives. "Oh, take *him*!" Mrs. Monarch murmured sweetly, looking at her husband; and "What could you want better than my wife?" the Major inquired, with the comfortable candour that now prevailed between us.

I was not obliged to answer these remarks—I was only obliged to place my sitters. I was not easy in mind, and I postponed, a little timidly perhaps, the solution of the question. The book was a large canvas, the other figures were numerous, and I worked off at first some of the episodes in which the hero and the heroine were not concerned. When once I had set *them* up I should have to stick to them—I couldn't make my young man seven feet high in one place and five feet nine in another. I inclined on the whole to the latter measurement, though the Major more than once reminded me that *he* looked about as young as anyone. It was indeed quite possible to arrange him, for the figure, so that it would have been difficult to detect his age. After the spontaneous Oronte had been with me a month, and after I had given him to understand several different times that his native exuberance would presently constitute an insurmountable barrier to our further intercourse, I waked to a sense of his heroic capacity. He was only five feet seven, but the remaining inches were latent. I tried him almost secretly at first, for I was really rather afraid of the judgment my other models would pass on such a choice. If they regarded Miss Churm as little better than a snare, what would they think of the representation by a person so little the real thing as an Italian street vendor of a protagonist formed by a public school?

If I went a little in fear of them it was not because they bullied me, because they had got an oppressive foothold, but because in their really pathetic decorum and mysteriously permanent newness they counted on me so intensely. I was therefore very glad when Jack Hawley came home: he was always of such good counsel. He painted badly himself, but there was no one like him for putting his finger on the place. He had been absent from England for a year; he had been somewhere—I don't remember where—to get a fresh eye. I was in a good deal of dread of any such organ, but we were old friends; he had been away for months and a sense of emptiness was creeping into my life. I hadn't dodged a missile for a year.

He came back with a fresh eye, but with the same old black velvet blouse, and the first evening he spent in my studio we smoked cigarettes till the small hours. He had done no work himself, he had only got the eye; so the field was clear for the production of my little things. He wanted to see what I had done for the *Cheapside*, but he was disappointed in the exhibition. That at least seemed the meaning of two or three comprehensive groans which, as he lounged on my big divan, on a folded leg, looking at my latest drawings, issued from his lips with the smoke of the cigarette.

"What's the matter with you?" I asked.

"What's the matter with *you*?"

"Nothing save that I'm mystified."

"You are indeed. You're quite off the hinge. What's the meaning of this new fad?" And he tossed me, with visible irreverence, a drawing in which I happened to have depicted both my majestic models. I asked if he didn't think it good, and he replied that it struck him as execrable, given the sort of thing I had always represented myself to him as wishing to arrive at; but I let that pass, I was so anxious to see exactly what he meant. The two figures in the picture looked colossal, but I supposed this was *not* what he meant, inasmuch as, for aught he knew to the contrary, I might have been trying for that. I maintained that I was working exactly in the same way as when he last had done me the honour to commend me. "Well, there's a big hole somewhere," he answered; "wait a bit and I'll discover it." I depended upon him to do so: where else was the fresh eye? But he produced at last nothing more luminous than "I don't know—I don't like your types." This was lame, for a critic who had never consented to discuss with me anything but the question of execution, the direction of strokes and the mystery of values.

"In the drawings you've been looking at I think my types are very handsome."

"Oh, they won't do!"

"I've had a couple of new models."

"I see you have. *They* won't do."

"Are you very sure of that?"

"Absolutely—they're stupid."

"You mean *I* am—for I ought to get round that."

"You *can't*—with such people. Who are they?"

I told him, as far as was necessary, and he declared, heartlessly: "*Ce sont des gens qu'il faut mettre à la porte.*"[3]

"You've never seen them; they're awfully good," I compassionately objected.

"Not seen them? Why, all this recent work of yours drops to pieces with them. It's all I want to see of them."

"No one else has said anything against it—the *Cheapside* people are pleased."

"Everyone else is an ass, and the *Cheapside* people the biggest asses of all. Come, don't pretend, at this time of day, to have pretty illusions about the public, especially about publishers and editors. It's not for *such* animals you work—it's for those who know, *coloro che sanno*,[4] so keep straight for *me* if you can't keep straight for yourself. There's a certain sort of thing you tried for from the first—and a very good thing it is. But this twaddle isn't *in* it." When I talked with Hawley later about "Rutland Ramsay" and its possible successors he declared that I must get back into my boat again or I would go to the bottom. His voice in short was the voice of warning.

I noted the warning, but I didn't turn my friends out of doors. They bored me a good deal; but the very fact that they bored me admonished me not to sacrifice them—if there was anything to be done with them—simply to irritation. As I look back at this phase they seem to me to have pervaded my life not a little. I have a vision of them as most of the time in my studio, seated, against the wall, on an old velvet bench to be out of the way, and looking like a pair of patient courtiers in a royal antechamber. I am convinced that during the coldest weeks of the winter they held their ground because it saved them fire. Their newness

3. [They are people one must show to the door.]

4. [Those in the know, the cognoscenti.]

was losing its gloss, and it was impossible not to feel that they were objects of charity. Whenever Miss Churm arrived they went away, and after I was fairly launched in "Rutland Ramsay" Miss Churm arrived pretty often. They managed to express to me tacitly that they supposed I wanted her for the lowlife of the book, and I let them suppose it, since they had attempted to study the work—it was lying about the studio—without discovering that it dealt only with the highest circles. They had dipped into the most brilliant of our novelists without deciphering many passages. I still took an hour from them, now and again, in spite of Jack Hawley's warning: it would be time enough to dismiss them, if dismissal should be necessary, when the rigour of the season was over. Hawley had made their acquaintance—he had met them at my fireside—and thought them a ridiculous pair. Learning that he was a painter they tried to approach him, to show him too that they were the real thing; but he looked at them, across the big room, as if they were miles away: they were a compendium of everything that he most objected to in the social system of his country. Such people as that, all convention and patent leather, with ejaculations that stopped conversation, had no business in a studio. A studio was a place to learn to see, and how could you see through a pair of featherbeds?

The main inconvenience I suffered at their hands was that, at first, I was shy of letting them discover how my artful little servant had begun to sit to me for "Rutland Ramsay." They knew that I had been odd enough (they were prepared by this time to allow oddity to artists), to pick a foreign vagabond out of the streets, when I might have had a person with whiskers and credentials; but it was some time before they learned how high I rated his accomplishments. They found him in an attitude more than once, but they never doubted I was doing him as an organ grinder. There were several things they never guessed, and one of them was that for a striking scene in the novel, in which a footman briefly figured, it occurred to me to make use of Major Monarch as the menial. I kept putting this off, I didn't like to ask him to don the livery—besides the difficulty of finding a livery to fit him. At last, one day late in the winter, when I was at work on the despised Oronte (he caught one's idea in an instant), and was in the glow of feeling that I was going very straight, they came in, the Major and his wife, with their society laugh about nothing (there was less and less to laugh at), like country callers—they always reminded me of that—who have walked across the park after church and are presently persuaded to stay to luncheon. Luncheon was over, but they could stay to tea—I knew they wanted it. The fit was on me, however, and I couldn't let my ardour cool and my work wait, with the fading daylight, while my model prepared it. So I asked Mrs. Monarch if she would mind laying it out—a request which, for an instant, brought all the blood to her face. Her eyes were on her husband's for a second, and some mute telegraphy passed between them. Their folly was over the next instant; his cheerful shrewdness put an end to it. So far from pitying their wounded pride, I must add, I was moved to give it as complete a lesson as I could. They bustled about together and got out the cups and saucers and made the kettle boil. I know they felt as if they were waiting on my servant, and when the tea was prepared I said: "He'll have a cup, please—he's tired." Mrs. Monarch brought him one where he stood, and he took it from her as if he had been a gentleman at a party, squeezing a crush-hat with an elbow.

Then it came over me that she had made a great effort for me—made it with a kind of nobleness—and that I owed her a compensation. Each time I saw her after this I wondered what the compensation could be. I couldn't go on doing the wrong thing to oblige them. Oh, it *was* the wrong thing, the stamp of the work for which they sat—Hawley was not the only person to say it now. I sent in a large number of the drawings I had made for "Rutland Ramsay," and I received a warning that was more to the point than Hawley's. The artistic adviser of the house for which I was working was of opinion that many of my illustrations were not what had been looked for. Most of these illustrations were the subjects in which the Monarchs had figured. Without going into the question of what *had* been looked for, I saw at this rate I shouldn't get the other books to do. I hurled myself in despair upon Miss Churm, I put her through all her paces. I not only adopted Oronte publicly as my hero, but one morning when the Major looked in to see if I didn't require him to finish a figure for the *Cheapside*, for which he had begun to sit the week before, I told him that I had changed my mind—I would do the drawing from my man. At this my visitor turned pale and stood looking at me. "Is *he* your idea of an English gentleman?" he asked.

I was disappointed, I was nervous, I wanted to get on with my work; so I replied with irritation: "Oh, my dear Major—I can't be ruined for *you*!"

He stood another moment; then, without a word, he quitted the studio. I drew a long breath when he was gone, for I said to myself that I shouldn't see him again. I had not told him definitely that I was in danger of having my work rejected, but I was vexed at his not having felt the catastrophe in the air, read with me the moral of our fruitless collaboration, the lesson that, in the deceptive atmosphere of art, even the highest respectability may fail of being plastic.

I didn't owe my friends money, but I did see them again. They reappeared together, three days later, and under the circumstances there was something tragic in the fact. It was a proof to me that they could find nothing else in life to do. They had threshed the matter out in a dismal conference—they had digested the bad news that they were not in for the series. If they were not useful to me even for the *Cheapside* their function seemed difficult to determine, and I could only judge at first that they had come, forgivingly, decorously, to take a last leave. This made me rejoice in secret that I had little leisure for a scene; for I had placed both my other models in position together and I was pegging away at a drawing from which I hoped to derive glory. It had been suggested by the passage in which Rutland Ramsay, drawing up a chair to Artemisia's piano stool, says extraordinary things to her while she ostensibly fingers out a difficult piece of music. I had done Miss Churm at the piano before—it was an attitude in which she knew how to take on an absolutely poetic grace. I wished the two figures to "compose" together, intensely, and my little Italian had entered perfectly into my 'conception. The pair were vividly before me, the piano had been pulled out; it was a charming picture of blended youth and murmured love, which I had only to catch and keep. My visitors stood and looked at it, and I was friendly to them over my shoulder.

They made no response, but I was used to silent company and went on with my work, only a little disconcerted (even though exhilarated by the sense that *this* was at least the ideal thing), at not having got rid of them after all. Presently I heard Mrs. Monarch's sweet voice beside, or rather above me: "I wish her hair was a little better done." I looked up and she was staring with a strange fixedness at Miss Churm, whose back was turned to her. "Do you mind my just touching it?" she went on—a question which made me spring up for an instant, as with the instinctive fear that she might do the young lady a harm. But she quieted me with a glance I shall never forget—I confess I should like to have been able to paint *that*—and went for a moment to my model. She spoke to her softly, laying a hand upon her shoulder and bending over her; and as the girl, understanding, gratefully assented, she disposed her rough curls, with a few quick passes, in such a way as to make Miss Churm's head twice as charming. It was one of the most heroic personal services I have ever seen rendered. Then Mrs. Monarch turned away with a low sigh and, looking about her as if for something to do, stooped to the floor with a noble humility and picked up a dirty rag that had dropped out of my paint box.

The Major meanwhile had also been looking for something to do and, wandering to the other end of the studio, saw before him my breakfast things, neglected, unremoved. "I say, can't I be useful *here*?" he called out to me with an irrepressible quaver. I assented with a laugh that I fear was awkward and for the next ten minutes, while I worked, I heard the light clatter of china and the tinkle of spoons and glass. Mrs. Monarch assisted her husband—they washed up my crockery, they put it away. They wandered off into my little scullery, and I afterwards found that they had cleaned my knives and that my slender stock of plate had an unprecedented surface. When it came over me, the latent eloquence of what they were doing, I confess that my drawing was blurred for a moment—the picture swam. They had accepted their failure, but they couldn't accept their fate. They had bowed their heads in bewilderment to the perverse and cruel law in virtue of which the real thing could be so much less precious than the unreal; but they didn't want to starve. If my servants were my models, my models might be my servants. They would reverse the parts—the others would sit for the ladies and gentleman, and *they* would do the work. They would still be in the studio—it was an intense dumb appeal to me not to turn them out. "Take us on," they wanted to say—"we'll do *anything*."

When all this hung before me the afflatus vanished—my pencil dropped from my hand. My sitting was spoiled and I got rid of my sitters, who were also evidently rather mystified and awestruck. Then, alone with the Major and his wife, I had a most uncomfortable moment. He put their prayer into a single sentence: "I say, you know—just let *us* do for you, can't you?" I couldn't—it was dreadful to see them emptying my slops; but I pretended I could, to oblige them, for about a week. Then I gave them a sum of money to go away; and I never saw them again. I obtained the remaining books, but my friend Hawley repeats that Major and Mrs. Monarch did me a permanent harm, got me into a second-rate trick. If it be true I am content to have paid the price—for the memory.

---

1. How is the narrator's life and work affected by his aversion to painting "types" and his opinion that "everything was to be sacrificed sooner than character"?
2. What does Hawley mean when he says that the Monarchs are "stupid"?
3. What is the significance of the servants becoming models and the models becoming servants?

ANTON CHEKHOV (1860–1904) became a physician in 1884, but by that time he was already well known for his writings. He wrote hundreds of short stories, and his writing style influenced many of the twentieth century's greatest authors. His plays are world-renowned and frequently performed. Chekhov's earliest works, written to support his family, are comic and satirical, qualities that subtly persist in his later and darker works, which keenly portray the entire range of Russian society. During his last twelve years, often in failing health, Chekhov wrote many of his best-known stories, including "Ward Number Six" and "A Lady with a Dog," as well as the plays *The Seagull* (1896), *Uncle Vanya* (1897), *Three Sisters* (1901), and *The Cherry Orchard* (1904).

A Lady with a Dog

1

There was said to be a new arrival on the esplanade: a lady with a dog.

After spending a fortnight at Yalta, Dmitry Gurov had quite settled in and was now beginning to take an interest in new faces. As he sat outside Vernet's café he saw a fair-haired young woman, not tall, walking on the promenade—wearing a beret, with a white Pomeranian dog trotting after her.

Then he encountered her several times a day in the municipal park and square. She walked alone, always with that beret, always with the white Pomeranian. Who she was no one knew, everyone just called her "the dog lady."

"If she has no husband or friends here she might be worth picking up," calculated Gurov.

He was still in his thirties, but had a twelve-year-old daughter and two schoolboy sons. His marriage had been arranged early—during his second college year—and now his wife seemed half as old again as he. She was a tall, dark-browed woman: outspoken, earnest, stolid and—she maintained—an "intellectual." She was a great reader, she favored spelling reform, she called her husband "Demetrius" instead of plain "Dmitry," while he privately thought her narrow-minded, inelegant, and slow on the uptake. He was afraid of her, and disliked being at home. He had begun deceiving her long ago, and his infidelities were frequent—which is probably why he nearly always spoke so disparagingly of women, calling them an "inferior species" when the subject cropped up.

He was, he felt, sufficiently schooled by bitter experience to call them any name he liked, yet he still couldn't live two days on end without his "inferior species." Men's company bored him, making him ill at ease, tongue-tied, and apathetic, whereas with women he felt free. He knew what to talk about, how to behave—he even found it easy to be with them without talking at all. In his appearance and character, in his whole nature, there was an alluring, elusive element that charmed and fascinated women. He knew it, and he was himself strongly attracted in return.

As experience multiple and—in the full sense of the word—bitter had long since taught him, every intimacy that so pleasantly diversifies one's life, that seems so easy, so delightfully adventurous at the outset . . . such an intimacy does, when reasonable people are involved (not least Muscovites—so hesitant and slow off the mark), develop willy-nilly into some vast, extraordinarily complex problem until the whole business finally becomes quite an ordeal. Somehow, though, on every new encounter with an attractive woman all this experience went for nothing—he wanted a bit of excitement and it all seemed so easy and amusing.

Well, he was eating in an open-air restaurant late one afternoon when the lady in the beret sauntered along and took the next table. Her expression, walk, clothes, hairstyle . . . all told him that she was socially presentable, married, in Yalta for the first time, alone—and bored.

Much nonsense is talked about the looseness of morals in these parts, and he despised such stories, knowing that they were largely fabricated by people who would have been glad to misbehave themselves, given the aptitude! But when the young woman sat down at the next table, three paces away, he recalled those tales of trips into the mountains and easy conquests. The seductive thought of a swift, fleeting *affaire*—the romance with the stranger whose very name you don't know—suddenly possessed him. He made a friendly gesture to the dog. It came up. He wagged his finger. The dog growled and Gurov shook his finger again.

The lady glanced at him, lowered her eyes at once.

"He doesn't bite." She blushed.

"May I give him a bone?"

She nodded.

"Have you been in Yalta long, madam?" he asked courteously.

"Five days."

"Oh, I've nearly survived my first fortnight."

There was a short pause.

"Time goes quickly, but it *is* so boring," she said, not looking at him.

"That's what they all say, what a bore this place is. Your average tripper from Belyov, Zhizdra, or somewhere . . . he doesn't know what boredom means till he comes here. Then it's 'Oh, what a bore! Oh, what dust!' You might think he'd just blown in from sunny Spain!"

She laughed. Then both continued their meal in silence, as strangers. After dinner, though, they left together and embarked on the bantering chat of people who feel free and easy, who don't mind where they go or what they talk about. As they strolled they discussed the strange light on the sea: the water was of a soft, warm, mauve hue, crossed by a stripe of golden moonlight. How sultry it was after the day's heat, they said. Gurov described himself as a Muscovite who had studied literature but worked in a bank. He had once trained as an opera singer but had given that up and owned two houses in Moscow.

From her he learnt that she had grown up in St. Petersburg, but had married in the provincial town where she had now been living for two years, that she was staying in Yalta for another month, that her husband (who also wanted a holiday) might come and fetch her. She was quite unable to explain her husband's job—was it with the County Council or the Rural District?—and even she saw the funny side of this. Gurov also learnt that she was called Anne.

In his hotel room afterward he thought about her. He was very likely to meet her tomorrow, bound to. As he went to bed he remembered that she had not long left boarding school, that she had been a schoolgirl like his own daughter—remembered, too, how much shyness and stiffness she still showed when laughing and talking to a stranger. This must be her first time ever alone in such a place, with men following her around, watching her, talking to her: all with a certain privy aim that she could not fail to divine. He remembered her slender, frail neck, her lovely gray eyes.

"You can't help feeling sorry for her, though," he thought. And dozed off.

2

A week had passed since their first meeting. It was a Sunday or some other holiday. Indoors was stifling, and outside flurries of dust swept the streets, whipping off hats. It was a thirsty day, and Gurov kept calling in at the cafe to fetch Anne a soft drink or an ice cream. There was no escaping the heat.

In the evening things were a little easier, and they went on the pier to watch a steamer come in. There were a lot of people hanging around on the landing stage: they were here to meet someone, and held bunches of flowers. Two features of the Yalta smart set were now thrown into sharp relief. The older women dressed like young ones. There were lots of generals.

As the sea was rough the steamer arrived late, after sunset, and maneuvered for some time before putting in at the jetty. Anne watched boat and passengers through her lorgnette as if seeking someone she knew. Whenever she turned to Gurov her eyes shone. She spoke a lot, asking quick-fire questions and immediately forgetting what they were. Then she lost her lorgnette: dropped it in the crowd.

The gaily dressed gathering dispersed, no more faces could be seen, and the wind dropped completely while Gurov and Anne stood as if waiting for someone else to disembark. Anne had stopped talking, and sniffed her flowers without looking at Gurov.

"The weather's better now that it's evening," said he. "So where shall we go? How about driving somewhere?"

She did not answer.

Then he stared at her hard, embraced her suddenly, and kissed her lips. The scent of her flowers, their dampness, enveloped him, and he immediately glanced around fearfully: had they been observed?

"Let's go to your room," he said softly.

They set off quickly together.

Her room was stuffy and smelt of the scent that she had bought in the Japanese shop.

"What encounters one does have in life," thought Gurov as he looked at her now.

He still retained memories of the easygoing, lighthearted women in his past: women happy in their love and grateful to him for that happiness, however brief. He also recalled those who, like his wife, made love insincerely, with idle chatter, affectations, and hysteria, their expressions conveying that this was neither love nor passion but something more significant. He thought of two or three very beautiful frigid women whose faces would suddenly flash a rapacious, stubborn look of lust to seize, to snatch more from life than it can give . . . women no longer young, these: fractious, unreasonable, overbearing and obtuse. When Gurov had cooled toward them their beauty had aroused his hatred, and the lace on their underclothes had looked like a lizard's scales.

In this case, though, all was hesitancy, the awkwardness of inexperienced youth. There was the impression of her being taken aback, too, as by a sudden knock on the door. Anne, this "lady with a dog," had her own special view—a very serious one—of what had happened. She thought of it as her "downfall," it seemed, which was all very strange and inappropriate. Her features had sunk and faded, her long hair drooped sadly down each side of her face. She had struck a pensive, despondent pose, like the Woman Taken in Adultery in an old-fashioned picture.

"This is all wrong," she said. "Now you'll completely despise me."

There was a watermelon on the table. Gurov cut a slice and slowly ate. Half an hour, at least, passed in silence.

He found Anne touching. She had that air of naive innocence of a thoroughly nice unworldly woman. A solitary candle, burning on the table, barely lit her face, but it was obvious that she was ill at ease.

"Why should I lose respect for you?" asked Gurov. "You don't know what you're saying."

"God forgive me," she said, her eyes brimming with tears. "This is terrible."

"You seem very much on the defensive, Anne."

"How *can* I defend what I've done? I'm a bad, wicked woman; I despise myself and I'm not trying to make excuses. It's not my husband, it is *myself* I've deceived. I don't just mean what happened here; I've been deceiving myself for a long time. My husband may be a good, honorable nun, but he *is* such a worm. What he does at that job of his I don't know—all I know is, he's a worm. I was twenty when I married him—I longed to know more of life. Then I wanted something better. There must *be* a different life, mustn't there? Or so I told myself. I wanted a little—well, rather *more* than a little—excitement. I was avid for experience. You won't understand me, I'm sure, but I could control myself no longer. I swear, something had happened to me, there was no holding me. So I told my husband I was ill and I came here. And I've been going round here in a daze as if I was off my head. But now I'm just another vulgar, worthless woman whom everyone is free to despise."

Gurov was bored with all this. He was irritated by the naive air, the unexpected, uncalled-for remorse. But for the tears in her eyes he might have thought her to be joking or play-acting.

"I don't understand," said he softly. "What is it you want?"

She hid her face on his breast and clung to him.

"Please, please believe me," she implored. "I long for a decent, moral life. Sin disgusts me, I don't know what I'm doing myself. The common people say the 'Evil One' tempted them, and now I can say the same: I was tempted by the Evil One."

"There there, that's enough," he muttered.

He looked into her staring, frightened eyes, kissed her, spoke softly and gently. She gradually relaxed and cheered up again. Both laughed.

Then they went out. The promenade was deserted, the town with its cypresses looked quite dead, but the sea still roared, breaking on the beach. A single launch with a sleepily glinting lamp tossed on the waves.

They found a cab and drove to Oreanda.

"I've only just discovered your surname, downstairs in your hotel," Gurov told her. "'Von Diederitz,' it says on the board. Is your husband German?"

"No, his grandfather was, I think, but he's Russian."

They sat on a bench near the church at Oreanda, gazing silently down at the sea. Yalta was barely visible through the dawn mist, white clouds hung motionless on the mountain peaks. Not a leaf stirred on the trees, cicadas chirped. Borne up from below, the sea's monotonous, muffled boom spoke of peace, of the everlasting sleep awaiting us. Before Yalta or Oreanda yet existed that surf had been thundering down there, it was roaring away now, and it will continue its dull booming with the same unconcern when we are no more. This persistence, this utter aloofness from all our lives and deaths . . . do they perhaps hold the secret pledge of our eternal salvation, of life's perpetual motion on earth, of its uninterrupted progress? As he sat there, lulled and entranced by the magic panorama—sea, mountains, clouds, broad sky—beside a young woman who looked so beautiful in the dawn, Gurov reflected that everything on earth is beautiful, really, when you consider it—everything except what we think and do ourselves when we forget the lofty goals of being and our human dignity.

Someone—a watchman, no doubt—came up, looked at them, went away. Even this incident seemed mysterious—beautiful, too. In the dawn they saw a steamer arrive from Feodosiya, its lights already extinguished.

"There's dew on the grass," Anne said, after a pause.

"Yes, time to go home."

They went back to town.

After this they met on the promenade each noon, lunched, dined, strolled, enthused about the sea together. She complained of sleeping badly, of palpitations. Disturbed by jealousy, and by the fear that he did not respect her enough, she kept repeating the same old questions. And often in the square or gardens, when there was nobody near them, he would suddenly draw her to him and kiss her ardently. This utter idleness, these kisses in broad daylight, these glances over the shoulder, this fear of being seen, the heat, the sea's smell, the repeated glimpses of idle, elegant, sleek persons . . . it all seemed to revitalize him. He told Anne how pretty she was, how provocative. He was impetuous, he was passionate, he never left her side, while she was forever brooding and begging him to admit that he did not respect her, that he loved her not at all, that he could see in her no more than a very ordinary woman. Late almost every evening they would drive out of town: to Oreanda or the waterfall. These trips were invariably a great success, leaving an impression of majesty and beauty.

They had been expecting the husband to arrive, but he sent a letter to say that he had eye trouble, and begged his wife to come home soon. Anne bestirred herself.

"It's just as well I *am* leaving," she told Gurov. "This is fate."

She left by carriage and he drove with her. This part of her journey took all day. When she took her seat in the express train, which was due to leave in five minutes, she asked to look at him once more.

"One last look—that's right."

She did not cry, but was so sad that she seemed ill. Her face quivered.

"I'll think of you, I'll remember you," she said. "God bless and keep you. Don't think ill of me. We're parting forever. We must, because we should never have met at all. God bless you."

The train departed swiftly, its lights soon vanishing and its noise dying away within a minute, as though everything had conspired to make a quick end of that sweet trance, that madness. Alone on the platform, gazing into the dark distance, Gurov heard the chirp of grasshoppers and the hum of telegraph wires, feeling as if he had just awoken. Well, there went another adventure or episode in his life, he reflected. It too had ended, now only the memory was left.

He was troubled, sad, somewhat penitent. This young woman whom he would never see again . . . she hadn't been happy with him, now, had she? He had treated her kindly and affectionately. And yet his attitude to her, his tone, his caresses had betrayed a faint irony: the rather crude condescension of your conquering male—of a man nearly twice her age into the bargain. She had kept calling him kind, exceptional, noble—so she hadn't seen him as he really was, obviously, and he must have been deceiving her without meaning to.

Here at the station there was already a whiff of autumn in the air, and the evening was cool.

"It's time I went north too," thought Gurov, leaving the platform. "High time."

3

Back home in Moscow it was already like winter. The stoves were alight. It was dark when his children breakfasted and got ready for school in the mornings, so their nanny lit the light for a short time. The frosts had begun. It is always such a joy to see the white ground and white roofs when the snow first falls, on that first day of sleigh riding. The air is so fresh and good to breathe, and you remember the years of your youth. White with frost, the old limes and birches have a kindly look, they are dearer to your heart than any cypresses or palm trees, and near them you no longer hanker after mountains and sea.

A Moscow man himself, Gurov had come home on a fine frosty day. He put on his fur coat and warm gloves and strolled down the Petrovka, he heard church bells pealing on Saturday evening . . . and his recent trip, all the places he had visited, lost all charm for him. He gradually plunged into Moscow life. He was zealously reading his three newspapers a day, now—while claiming to read no Moscow newspapers on principle! He felt the lure of restaurants, clubs, dinner parties, anniversary celebrations; he was flattered to be visited by famous lawyers and actors, flattered to play cards with a professor at the Doctors' Club. He could tackle a large helping of "Moscow hot pot" straight from the pan.

In a month or two's time the memory of Anne would become blurred, thought he—he would just dream of her, of her adorable smile, occasionally as he used to dream of those other ones. But more than a month passed, real winter set in, and yet everything was still as clear in his mind as if they had parted only yesterday. His memories flared up ever more brightly. When, in the quiet of evening, his children's voices reached his study as they did their homework, when he heard a sentimental song or a barrel organ in a restaurant, when a blizzard howled in his chimney . . . it would all suddenly come back to him: that business on the pier, the early morning with the mist on the mountains, the Feodosiya steamer, the kisses. He would pace the room for hours, remembering and smiling until these recollections merged into fantasies: until, in his imagination, past fused with future. Though he did not dream of Anne, she pursued him everywhere like his shadow, watching him. If he closed his eyes he could see her vividly—younger, gentler, more beautiful than she really was. He even saw himself as a better man than he had been back in Yalta. She gazed at him from the bookcase in the evenings, from the hearth, from a corner of the room. He heard her breathing, heard the delightful rustle of her dress. In the street he followed women with his eyes, seeking one like her.

He was plagued, now, by the urge to share his memories. But he could not talk about his love at home, and outside his home there was no one to tell—he couldn't very well discuss it with his tenants or at the bank! What was there to say, anyway? Had he really been in love? Had there really been anything beautiful or idyllic, anything edifying—anything merely interesting, even—in his relations with Anne? He was reduced to vague remarks about love and women, and no one guessed what he had in mind. His wife just twitched those dark eyebrows and told him that "the role of lady-killer doesn't suit you at all, Demetrius."

As he was leaving the Doctors' club one night with his partner, a civil servant, he could not help saying that he had "met such an enchanting woman in Yalta—did you but know!"

The civil servant climbed into his sledge and drove off, but suddenly turned round and shouted Gurov's name.

"What is it?"

"You were quite right just now, the sturgeon *was* a bit off."

For some reason these words, humdrum though they were, suddenly infuriated Gurov, striking him as indelicate and gross. What barbarous manners, what faces, what meaningless nights, what dull, featureless days! Frantic card playing, guzzling, drunkenness, endless chatter always on one and the same topic. Futile activities, repetitious talk, talk, talk . . . they engross most of your time, your best efforts, and you end up with a sort of botched, pedestrian life: a form of imbecility from which there's no way out, no escape. You might as well be in jail or in a madhouse!

Gurov lay awake all night, fuming—then had a headache all next day. He slept badly on the following nights, too, sitting up in bed thinking, or pacing the room. He was fed up with his children, fed up with his bank, there was nowhere he wanted to go, nothing he wanted to talk about.

Toward Christmas he prepared for a journey. He told his wife that he was going to St. Petersburg on a certain young man's business—but he actually went to the town where Anne lived. Why? He didn't really know himself. He wanted to see her, speak to her—make an assignation if he could.

He reached the town one morning and put up at a hotel, in the "best" room with wall-to-wall carpeting in coarse field-gray material. On the table stood an inkstand, gray with dust and shaped as a horseman holding his hat up in one hand and minus a head. The porter told him what he needed to know: von Diederitz lived in Old Pottery Street in his own house near the hotel. He did things in style, kept his own horses, was known to everyone in town. The porter pronounced the name as "Drearydits." Gurov sauntered off to old Pottery Street, found the house. Immediately facing it was a long, gray fence crowned with nails: "a fence to run away from," thought Gurov, looking from windows to fence and back.

Local government offices were closed today, so the husband was probably at home, Gurov reckoned. In any case it would be tactless to go into the house and create a disturbance. If he sent a note, though, it might fall into the husband's hands and ruin everything. Better trust to chance. He paced the street near the fence, awaiting this chance. He saw a beggar go through the gate, saw him set upon by dogs. An hour later he heard the faint, muffled sound of a piano—that must be Anne playing. Suddenly the front door opened, and out came an old woman with the familiar white Pomeranian running after her. Gurov wanted to call the dog, but his heart suddenly raced and he was too excited to remember its name.

He paced about, loathing that gray fence more and more. In his irritation, he fancied that Anne had forgotten him and might be amusing herself with another man—what else could be expected of a young woman compelled to contemplate this confounded fence morning, noon, and night? He went back to his room, sat on the sofa for hours not knowing what to do, then lunched and dozed for hours.

"It's all so stupid and distressing," he thought, waking up and seeing the dark windows—it was already evening. "Now I've had a good sleep for some reason, but what shall I do tonight?"

He sat on the bed—it was covered with a cheap, gray hospital blanket.

"So much for your ladies with dogs!" said he in petulant self-mockery. "So much for your holiday romances—now you're stuck in this dump."

In the station that morning his eye had been caught by a poster in bold lettering advertising the opening of *The Geisha*. Recalling this, he drove to the theater, reflecting that she very probably attended first nights.

The theater was full. As usual in provincial theaters a mist hung above the chandelier, while the gallery was restive and rowdy. In the first row before the performance began stood the local gallants, hands clasped behind their backs. In the governor's box, in front, sat that worthy's daughter complete with feather boa, while the governor himself lurked modestly behind a *portière*, only his hands showing. The curtain shook, the orchestra tuned up protractedly. As the audience came in and took its seats, Gurov peered frantically around.

In came Anne. She sat down in the third row, and when Gurov glimpsed her his heart seemed to miss a beat. He saw clearly, now, that she was nearer, dearer, more important to him than anyone in the whole world. Lost in the provincial crowd, this very ordinary little woman carrying her vulgar lorgnette now absorbed his whole being. She was his grief, his joy—the only happiness he wanted, now. To the strains of that abominable orchestra with its atrocious, tasteless fiddling he thought how lovely she was . . . thought and brooded.

A young man with short dundrearies, very tall, round-shouldered, had come in with Anne and sat down beside her. He kept bobbing his head as if making obeisance with every step he took. It must be the husband whom, in that bitter outburst back in Yalta, she had dubbed a "worm." His lanky figure, his sidewhiskers, his small bald patch . . . there actually *was* something menial and flunkylike about them. He gave an ingratiating smile, the emblem of some learned society glinting in his buttonhole like a hotel servant's number.

The husband went for a smoke in the first interval, while she remained seated. Gurov—his seat was also in the stalls—approached her. His voice trembling, forcing a smile, he wished her good evening.

She glanced at him, she blenched. Then she looked again—aghast, not believing her eyes, crushing fan and lorgnette together in her hands in an obvious effort to prevent herself from fainting. Neither spoke. She sat, he remained standing—alarmed by her discomfiture, not venturing to sit down beside her. Fiddles and flute started tuning up, and he suddenly panicked: from all the boxes eyes seemed to be staring at them. Then she stood up and quickly made for the exit, while he followed, both walking at random along corridors, up and down stairways, glimpsing men in the uniforms of the courts, the schools, and the administration of crown lands, all wearing their decorations. There were glimpses of ladies and fur coats on pegs. A draft enveloped them with the smell of cigarette ends.

"Oh God—why all these people, this orchestra?" wondered Gurov, his heart pounding.

Suddenly he recalled the evening when he had seen Anne off at the station, when he had told himself that it was all over and that they would never meet again. How far they were now, though, from any ending!

On a narrow, gloomy staircase labeled ENTRANCE TO CIRCLE she stopped.

"How you did scare me," she panted, still pale and dazed. "I nearly died, you scared me so. Why, why, why are you here?"

"Try and understand, Anne," he said in a rapid undertone. "Understand, I implore you—"

She looked at him—fearfully, pleadingly, lovingly. She stared, trying to fix his features in her memory.

"I'm so miserable," she went on, not hearing him. "I've thought only of you all this time, my thoughts of you have kept me alive. Oh, I did so want to forget you—why, why, why are you here?"

On a landing higher up two schoolboys were smoking and looking down, but Gurov did not care. He pulled Anne to him, kissed her face, cheek, hands.

"Whatever are you doing?" she asked—horrified, pushing him from her. "We must be out of our minds. You must go away today—leave this very instant, I implore you, I beg you in the name of all that is holy. Someone's coming."

Someone indeed was coming upstairs.

"You *must* leave," Anne went on in a whisper. "Do you hear me, Gurov? I'll visit you in Moscow. I've never been happy, I'm unhappy now, and I shall never, never, never be happy. So don't add to my sufferings. I'll come to Moscow, I swear it, but we must part now. We must say goodbye, my good, kind darling."

She pressed his hand and went quickly downstairs, looking back at him, and he could see from her eyes that she really was unhappy. Gurov waited a little, cocked an ear and, when all was quiet, found the peg with his coat and left the theater.

4

Anne took to visiting him in Moscow. Once every two or three months she would leave her hometown, telling her husband that she was going to consult a professor about a female complaint. The husband neither believed nor disbelieved her. In Moscow she would put up at the Slav Fair Hotel, and at once send a red-capped messenger to Gurov. Gurov would visit her hotel, and no one in Moscow knew anything about it.

It thus chanced that he was on his way to see her one winter morning—her messenger had called on the previous evening, but had not found him at home. He was walking with his daughter, wanting to take her to her school, which was on his way. There was a heavy downpour of sleet.

"It's three degrees above zero, yet look at the sleet," said Gurov to his daughter. "But it's only the ground that is warm, you see—the temperature in the upper strata of the atmosphere is quite different."

"Why doesn't it thunder in winter, Daddy?"

He explained this too, reflecting as he spoke that he was on his way to an assignation. Not a soul knew about it—or ever would know, probably. He was living two lives. One of them was open to view by—and known to—the people concerned. It was full of stereotyped truths and stereotyped untruths, it was identical with the life of his friends and acquaintances. The other life proceeded in secret. Through some strange and possibly arbitrary chain of coincidences everything vital, interesting, and crucial to him, everything that called his sincerity and integrity into play, everything that made up the core of his life . . . all that took place in complete secrecy, whereas everything false about him, the façade behind which he hid to conceal the truth—his work at the bank, say, his arguments at the club, that "inferior species" stuff, attending anniversary celebrations with his wife—all that was in the open. He judged others by himself, disbelieving the evidence of his eyes, and attributing to everyone a real, fascinating life lived under the cloak of secrecy as in the darkness of the night. Each individual existence is based on mystery, which is perhaps why civilized man makes such a neurotic fuss about having his privacy respected.

After taking his daughter to school, Gurov made for the Slav Fair. He removed his coat downstairs, went up, tapped on the door. Anne was wearing his favorite gray dress, she was tired by the journey—and by the wait, after expecting him since the previous evening. She was pale, she looked at him without smiling, and no sooner was he in the room than she flung herself against his chest. Their kiss was as protracted and lingering as if they had not met for two years.

"Well, how are things with you?" he asked. "What's the news?"

"Wait, I'll tell you in a moment—I can't now."

Unable to speak for crying, she turned away and pressed a handkerchief to her eyes.

"Let her cry, I'll sit down for a bit," thought he, and sat in the armchair.

Then he rang and ordered tea. Then he drank it while she still stood with her back to him, facing the window.

She wept as one distressed and woefully aware of the melancholy turn that their lives had taken. They met only in secret, they hid from other people like thieves. Their lives were in ruins, were they not?

"Now, do stop it," he said.

He could see that this was no fleeting affair—there was no telling when it would end. Anne was growing more and more attached to him. She adored him, and there was no question of telling her that all this must finish one day. Besides, she would never believe him.

He went up to her, laid his hands on her shoulders, meaning to soothe her with a little banter—and then caught sight of himself in the mirror.

His hair was turning gray. He wondered why he had aged so much in the last few years and lost his looks. The shoulders on which his hands rested were warm and trembling. He pitied this life—still so warm and beautiful, but probably just about to fade and wither like his own. Why did she love him so? Women had never seen him as he really was. What they loved in him was not his real self but a figment of their own imaginations—someone whom they had dreamed of meeting all their lives. Then, when they realized their mistake, they had loved him all the same. Yet none of them had been happy with him. Time had passed, he had met new ones, been intimate with them, parted from them. Not once had he been in love, though. He had known everything conceivable—except love, that is.

Only now that his head was gray had he well and truly fallen in love: for the first time in his life.

Anne and he loved each other very, very dearly, like man and wife or bosom friends. They felt themselves predestined for each other. That he should have a wife, and she a husband . . . it seemed to make no sense. They were like two migratory birds, a male and a female, caught and put in separate cages. They had forgiven each other the shameful episodes of their past, they forgave each other for the present too, and they felt that their love had transformed them both.

Once, in moments of depression, he had tried to console himself with any argument that came into his head—but now he had no use for arguments. His deepest sympathies were stirred, he only wanted to be sincere and tender.

"Stop, darling," he said. "You've had your cry—that's enough. Now let's talk, let's think of something."

Then they consulted at length about avoiding the need for concealment and deception, for living in different towns, for meeting only at rare intervals. How could they break these intolerable bonds? How, how, how?

He clutched his head and asked the question again and again.

Soon, it seemed, the solution would be found and a wonderful new life would begin. But both could see that they still had a long, long way to travel—and that the most complicated and difficult part was only just beginning.

---

1. Why was it “strange and inappropriate” for Anne to think of her relationship with Gurov as her “downfall”?
2. If, as Anne believes, their lives are already “in ruins,” then why is “the most complicated and difficult part” just beginning?
3. Why does Gurov fall in love for the first time in his life with Anne?
4. Why are Anne and Gurov unable to break their “intolerable” bonds?

CHARLOTTE PERKINS GILMAN (1860–1935) is primarily known today for her short story "The Yellow Wallpaper" (first published in 1892), reflecting her stifling experience of marriage and domestic life, and *Herland* (1915), a feminist novel about a society in which women and men are equals. However, during her lifetime she was also noted for a series of books advocating deep social change in the family roles of men and women, including *Women and Economics* (1898) and *The Home: Its Work and Influence* (1903). Among Gilman's early influences was her relative, Harriet Beecher Stowe, author of *Uncle Tom's Cabin.* Besides writing, Gilman worked as a teacher and commercial artist and also became a popular speaker on the lecture circuit, promoting women's rights.

The Yellow Wallpaper

It is very seldom that mere ordinary people like John and myself secure ancestral halls for the summer.

A colonial mansion, a hereditary estate, I would say a haunted house, and reach the height of romantic felicity—but that would be asking too much of fate!

Still I will proudly declare that there is something queer about it.

Else, why should it be let so cheaply? And why have stood so long untenanted?

John laughs at me, of course, but one expects that in marriage.

John is practical in the extreme. He has no patience with faith, an intense horror of superstition, and he scoffs openly at any talk of things not to be felt and seen and put down in figures.

John is a physician, and *perhaps*—(I would not say it to a living soul, of course, but this is dead paper and a great relief to my mind—) *perhaps* that is one reason I do not get well faster.

You see, he does not believe I am sick!

And what can one do?

If a physician of high standing, and one's own husband, assures friends and relatives that there is really nothing the matter with one but temporary nervous depression—a slight hysterical tendency—what is one to do?

My brother is also a physician, and also of high standing, and he says the same thing.

So I take phosphates or phosphites—whichever it is, and tonics, and journeys, and air, and exercise, and am absolutely forbidden to "work" until I am well again.

Personally, I disagree with their ideas.

Personally, I believe that congenial work, with excitement and change, would do me good.

But what is one to do?

I did write for a while in spite of them; but it *does* exhaust me a good deal—having to be so sly about it, or else meet with heavy opposition.

I sometimes fancy that in my condition if I had less opposition and more society and stimulus—but John says the very worst thing I can do is to think about my condition, and I confess it always makes me feel bad.

So I will let it alone and talk about the house.

The most beautiful place! It is quite alone, standing well back from the road, quite three miles from the village. It makes me think of English places that you read about, for there are hedges and walls and gates that lock, and lots of separate little houses for the gardeners and people.

There is a *delicious* garden! I never saw such a garden—large and shady, full of box-bordered paths, and lined with long grape-covered arbors with seats under them.

There were greenhouses, too, but they are all broken now.

There was some legal trouble, I believe, something about the heirs and coheirs; anyhow, the place has been empty for years.

That spoils my ghostliness, I am afraid, but I don't care—there is something strange about the house—I can feel it.

I even said so to John one moonlight evening, but he said what I felt was a *draught*, and shut the window.

I get unreasonably angry with John sometimes. I'm sure I never used to be so sensitive. I think it is due to this nervous condition.

But John says if I feel so, I shall neglect proper self-control; so I take pains to control myself—before him, at least, and that makes me very tired.

I don't like our room a bit. I wanted one downstairs that opened on the piazza and had roses all over the window, and such pretty old-fashioned chintz hangings! but John would not hear of it.

He said there was only one window and not room for two beds, and no near room for him if he took another.

He is very careful and loving, and hardly lets me stir without special direction.

I have a schedule prescription for each hour in the day; he takes all care from me, and so I feel basely ungrateful not to value it more.

He said we came here solely on my account, that I was to have perfect rest and all the air I could get. "Your exercise depends on your strength, my dear," said he, "and your food somewhat on your appetite; but air you can absorb all the time." So we took the nursery at the top of the house.

It is a big, airy room, the whole floor nearly, with windows that look all ways, and air and sunshine galore. It was nursery first and then playroom and gymnasium, I should judge; for the windows are barred for little children, and there are rings and things in the walls.

The paint and paper look as if a boys' school had used it. It is stripped off—the paper—in great patches all around the head of my bed, about as far as I can reach, and in a great place on the other side of the room low down. I never saw a worse paper in my life.

One of those sprawling flamboyant patterns committing every artistic sin.

It is dull enough to confuse the eye in following, pronounced enough to constantly irritate and provoke study, and when you follow the lame uncertain curves for a little distance they suddenly commit suicide—plunge off at outrageous angles, destroy themselves in unheard of contradictions.

The color is repellant, almost revolting; a smouldering unclean yellow, strangely faded by the slow-turning sunlight.

It is a dull yet lurid orange in some places, a sickly sulphur tint in others.

No wonder the children hated it! I should hate it myself if I had to live in this room long.

There comes John, and I must put this away—he hates to have me write a word.

We have been here two weeks, and I haven't felt like writing before, since that first day.

I am sitting by the window now, up in this atrocious nursery, and there is nothing to hinder my writing as much as I please, save lack of strength.

John is away all day, and even some nights when his cases are serious.

I am glad my case is not serious!

But these nervous troubles are dreadfully depressing.

John does not know how much I really suffer. He knows there is no *reason* to suffer, and that satisfies him.

Of course it is only nervousness. It does weigh on me so not to do my duty in any way!

I meant to be such a help to John, such a real rest and comfort, and here I am a comparative burden already!

Nobody would believe what an effort it is to do what little I am able—to dress and entertain, and order things.

It is fortunate Mary is so good with the baby. Such a dear baby!

And yet I *cannot* be with him, it makes me so nervous.

I suppose John never was nervous in his life. He laughs at me so about this wallpaper!

At first he meant to repaper the room, but afterwards he said that I was letting it get the better of me, and that nothing was worse for a nervous patient than to give way to such fancies.

He said that after the wallpaper was changed it would be the heavy bedstead, and then the barred windows, and then that gate at the head of the stairs, and so on.

"You know the place is doing you good,"‘ he said, "and really, dear, I don't care to renovate the house just for a three months' rental."

"Then do let us go downstairs," I said, "there are such pretty rooms there."

Then he took me in his arms and called me a blessed little goose, and said he would go down cellar, if I wished, and have it whitewashed into the bargain.

But he is right enough about the beds and windows and things.

It is an airy and comfortable room as anyone need wish, and, of course, I would not be so silly as to make him uncomfortable just for a whim.

I'm really getting quite fond of the big room, all but that horrid paper.

Out of one window I can see the garden, those mysterious deep-shaded arbors, the riotous old-fashioned flowers, and bushes and gnarly trees.

Out of another I get a lovely view of the bay and a little private wharf belonging to the estate. There is a beautiful shaded lane that runs down there from the house. I always fancy I see people walking in these numerous paths and arbors, but John has cautioned me not to give way to fancy in the least. He says that with my imaginative power and habit of story making, a nervous weakness like mine is sure to lead to all manner of excited fancies, and that I ought to use my will and good sense to check the tendency. So I try.

I think sometimes that if I were only well enough to write a little it would relieve the press of ideas and rest me.

But I find I get pretty tired when I try.

It is so discouraging not to have any advice and companionship about my work. When I get really well, John says we will ask Cousin Henry and Julia down for a long visit; but he says he would as soon put fireworks in my pillowcase as to let me have those stimulating people about now.

I wish I could get well faster.

But I must not think about that. This paper looks to me as if it *knew* what a vicious influence it had!

There is a recurrent spot where the pattern lolls like a broken neck and two bulbous eyes stare at you upside down.

I get positively angry with the impertinence of it and the everlastingness. Up and down and sideways they crawl, and those absurd, unblinking eyes are everywhere. There is one place where two breadths didn't match, and the eyes go all up and down the line, one a little higher than the other.

I never saw so much expression in an inanimate thing before, and we all know how much expression they have! I used to lie awake as a child and get more entertainment and terror out of blank walls and plain furniture than most children could find in a toy store.

I remember what a kindly wink the knobs of our big, old bureau used to have, and there was one chair that always seemed like a strong friend.

I used to feel that if any of the other things looked too fierce I could always hop into that chair and be safe.

The furniture in this room is no worse than inharmonious, however, for we had to bring it all from downstairs. I suppose when this was used as a playroom they had to take the nursery things out, and no wonder! I never saw such ravages as the children have made here.

The wallpaper, as I said before, is torn off in spots, and it sticketh closer than a brother—they must have had perseverance as well as hatred.

Then the floor is scratched and gouged and splintered, the plaster itself is dug out here and there, and this great heavy bed which is all we found in the room, looks as if it had been through the wars.

But I don't mind it a bit—only the paper.

There comes John's sister. Such a dear girl as she is, and so careful of me! I must not let her find me writing.

She is a perfect and enthusiastic housekeeper, and hopes for no better profession. I verily believe she thinks it is the writing which made me sick!

But I can write when she is out, and see her a long way off from these windows.

There is one that commands the road, a lovely shaded winding road, and one that just looks off over the country. A lovely country, too, full of great elms and velvet meadows.

This wallpaper has a kind of subpattern in a different shade, a particularly irritating one, for you can only see it in certain lights, and not clearly then.

But in the places where it isn't faded and where the sun is just so—I can see a strange, provoking, formless sort of figure, that seems to skulk about behind that silly and conspicuous front design.

There's sister on the stairs!

Well, the Fourth of July is over! The people are all gone and I am tired out. John thought it might do me good to see a little company, so we just had mother and Nellie and the children down for a week.

Of course I didn't do a thing. Jennie sees to everything now.

But it tired me all the same.

John says if I don't pick up faster he shall send me to Weir Mitchell in the fall.

But I don't want to go there at all. I had a friend who was in his hands once, and she says he is just like John and my brother, only more so!

Besides, it is such an undertaking to go so far.

I don't feel as if it was worthwhile to turn my hand over for anything, and I'm getting dreadfully fretful and querulous.

I cry at nothing, and cry most of the time.

Of course I don't when John is here, or anybody else, but when I am alone.

And I am alone a good deal just now. John is kept in town very often by serious cases, and Jennie is good and lets me alone when I want her to.

So I walk a little in the garden or down that lovely lane, sit on the porch under the roses, and lie down up here a good deal.

I'm getting really fond of the room in spite of the wallpaper. Perhaps *because* of the wallpaper.

It dwells in my mind so!

I lie here on this great immovable bed—it is nailed down, I believe—and follow that pattern about by the hour. It is as good as gymnastics, I assure you. I start, we'll say, at the bottom, down in the corner over there where it has not been touched, and I determine for the thousandth time that I *will* follow that pointless pattern to some sort of a conclusion.

I know a little of the principle of design, and I know this thing was not arranged on any laws of radiation, or alternation, or repetition, or symmetry, or anything else that I ever heard of.

It is repeated, of course, by the breadths, but not otherwise.

Looked at in one way each breadth stands alone, the bloated curves and flourishes—a kind of "debased Romanesque" with delirium tremens—go waddling up and down in isolated columns of fatuity.

But, on the other hand, they connect diagonally, and the sprawling outlines run off in great slanting waves of optic horror, like a lot of wallowing seaweeds in full chase.

The whole thing goes horizontally, too, at least it seems so, and I exhaust myself in trying to distinguish the order of its going in that direction.

They have used a horizontal breadth for a frieze, and that adds wonderfully to the confusion.

There is one end of the room where it is almost intact, and there, when the crosslights fade and the low sun shines directly upon it, I can almost fancy radiation after all—the interminable grotesque seem to form around a common centre and rush off in headlong plunges of equal distraction.

It makes me tired to follow it. I will take a nap I guess.

I don't know why I should write this.

I don't want to.

I don't feel able.

And I know John would think it absurd. But I *must* say what I feel and think in some way—it is such a relief!

But the effort is getting to be greater than the relief.

Half the time now I am awfully lazy, and lie down ever so much.

John says I mustn't lose my strength, and has me take cod-liver oil and lots of tonics and things, to say nothing of ale and wine and rare meat.

Dear John! He loves me very dearly, and hates to have me sick. I tried to have a real earnest reasonable talk with him the other day, and tell him how I wish he would let me go and make a visit to Cousin Henry and Julia.

But he said I wasn't able to go, nor able to stand it after I got there; and I did not make out a very good case for myself, for I was crying before I had finished.

It is getting to be a great effort for me to think straight. Just this nervous weakness I suppose.

And dear John gathered me up in his arms, and just carried me upstairs and laid me on the bed, and sat by me and read to me till it tired my head.

He said I was his darling and his comfort and all he had, and that I must take care of myself for his sake, and keep well.

He says no one but myself can help me out of it, that I must use my will and self-control and not let any silly fancies run away with me.

There's one comfort, the baby is well and happy, and does not have to occupy this nursery with the horrid wallpaper.

If we had not used it, that blessed child would have! What a fortunate escape! Why, I wouldn't have a child of mine, an impressionable little thing, live in such a room for worlds.

I never thought of it before, but it is lucky that John kept me here after all, I can stand it so much easier than a baby, you see.

Of course I never mention it to them anymore—I am too wise—but I keep watch of it all the same.

There are things in that paper that nobody knows but me, or ever will.

Behind that outside pattern the dim shapes get clearer every day.

It is always the same shape, only very numerous.

And it is like a woman stooping down and creeping about behind that pattern. I don't like it a bit. I wonder—I begin to think—I wish John would take me away from here!

It is so hard to talk with John about my case, because he is so wise, and because he loves me so.

But I tried it last night.

It was moonlight. The moon shines in all around just as the sun does.

I hate to see it sometimes, it creeps so slowly, and always comes in by one window or another.

John was asleep and I hated to waken him, so I kept still and watched the moonlight on that undulating wallpaper till I felt creepy.

The faint figure behind seemed to shake the pattern, just as if she wanted to get out.

I got up softly and went to feel and see if the paper *did* move, and when I came back John was awake.

"What is it, little girl?" he said. "Don't go walking about like that—you'll get cold."

I thought it was a good time to talk, so I told him that I really was not gaining here, and that I wished he would take me away.

"Why, darling!" said he, "our lease will be up in three weeks, and I can't see how to leave before.

"The repairs are not done at home, and I cannot possibly leave town just now. Of course if you were in any danger, I could and would, but you really are better, dear, whether you can see it or not. I am a doctor, dear, and I know. You are gaining flesh and color, your appetite is better, I feel really much easier about you."

"I don't weigh a bit more," said I, "nor as much; and my appetite may be better in the evening when you are here, but it is worse in the morning when you are away!"

"Bless her little heart!" said he with a big hug, "she shall be as sick as she pleases! But now let's improve the shining hours by going to sleep, and talk about it in the morning!"

"And you won't go away?" I asked gloomily.

"Why, how can I, dear? It is only three weeks more and then we will take a nice little trip of a few days while Jennie is getting the house ready. Really dear you are better!"

"Better in body perhaps—" I began, and stopped short, for he sat up straight and looked at me with such a stern, reproachful look that I could not say another word.

"My darling," said he, "I beg of you, for my sake and for our child's sake, as well as for your own, that you will never for one instant let that idea enter your mind! There is nothing so dangerous, so fascinating, to a temperament like yours. It is a false and foolish fancy. Can you not trust me as a physician when I tell you so?"

So of course I said no more on that score, and we went to sleep before long. He thought I was asleep first, but I wasn't, and lay there for hours trying to decide whether that front pattern and the back pattern really did move together or separately.

. . .

On a pattern like this, by daylight, there is a lack of sequence, a defiance of law, that is a constant irritant to a normal mind.

The color is hideous enough, and unreliable enough, and infuriating enough, but the pattern is torturing.

You think you have mastered it, but just as you get well underway in following, it turns a back somersault and there you are. It slaps you in the face, knocks you down, and tramples upon you. It is like a bad dream.

The outside pattern is a florid arabesque, reminding one of a fungus. If you can imagine a toadstool in joints, an interminable string of toadstools, budding and sprouting in endless convolutions—why, that is something like it.

That is, sometimes!

There is one marked peculiarity about this paper, a thing nobody seems to notice but myself, and that is that it changes as the light changes.

When the sun shoots in through the east window—I always watch for that first long, straight ray—it changes so quickly that I never can quite believe it.

That is why I watch it always.

By moonlight—the moon shines in all night when there is a moon—I wouldn't know it was the same paper.

At night in any kind of light, in twilight, candlelight, lamplight, and worst of all by moonlight, it becomes bars! The outside pattern I mean, and the woman behind it is as plain as can be.

I didn't realize for a long time what the thing was that showed behind, that dim subpattern, but now I am quite sure it is a woman.

By daylight she is subdued, quiet. I fancy it is the pattern that keeps her so still. It is so puzzling. It keeps me quiet by the hour.

I lie down ever so much now. John says it is good for me, and to sleep all I can.

Indeed he started the habit by making me lie down for an hour after each meal.

It is a very bad habit I am convinced, for you see I don't sleep.

And that cultivates deceit, for I don't tell them I'm awake—O no!

The fact is I am getting a little afraid of John.

He seems very queer sometimes, and even Jennie has an inexplicable look.

It strikes me occasionally, just as a scientific hypothesis—that perhaps it is the paper!

I have watched John when he did not know I was looking, and come into the room suddenly on the most innocent excuses, and I've caught him several times *looking at the paper*! And Jennie too. I caught Jennie with her hand on it once.

She didn't know I was in the room, and when I asked her in a quiet, a very quiet voice, with the most restrained manner possible, what she was doing with the paper—she turned around as if she had been caught stealing, and looked quite angry—asked me why I should frighten her so!

Then she said that the paper stained everything it touched, that she had found yellow smooches on all my clothes and John's, and she wished we would be more careful!

Did not that sound innocent? But I know she was studying that pattern, and I am determined that nobody shall find it out but myself!

Life is very much more exciting now than it used to be. You see I have something more to expect, to look forward to, to watch. I really do eat better, and am more quiet than I was.

John is so pleased to see me improve! He laughed a little the other day, and said I seemed to be flourishing in spite of my wallpaper.

I turned it off with a laugh. I had no intention of telling him it was *because* of the wallpaper—he would make fun of me. He might even want to take me away.

I don't want to leave now until I have found it out. There is a week more, and I think that will be enough.

I'm feeling ever so much better! I don't sleep much at night, for it is so interesting to watch developments; but I sleep a good deal in the daytime.

In the daytime it is tiresome and perplexing.

There are always new shoots on the fungus, and new shades of yellow all over it. I cannot keep count of them, though I have tried conscientiously.

It is the strangest yellow, that wallpaper! It makes me think of all the yellow things I ever saw—not beautiful ones like buttercups, but old foul, bad yellow things.

But there is something else about that paper—the smell! I noticed it the moment we came into the room, but with so much air and sun it was not bad. Now we have had a week of fog and rain, and whether the windows are open or not, the smell is here.

It creeps all over the house.

I find it hovering in the dining room, skulking in the parlor, hiding in the hall, lying in wait for me on the stairs.

It gets into my hair.

Even when I go to ride, if I turn my head suddenly and surprise it—there is that smell!

Such a peculiar odor, too! I have spent hours in trying to analyze it, to find what it smelled like.

It is not bad—at first, and very gentle, but quite the subtlest, most enduring odor I ever met.

In this damp weather it is awful, I wake up in the night and find it hanging over me.

It used to disturb me at first. I thought seriously of burning the house—to reach the smell.

But now I am used to it. The only thing I can think of that it is like is the *color* of the paper! A yellow smell.

There is a very funny mark on this wall, low down, near the mopboard. A streak that runs round the room. It goes behind every piece of furniture, except the bed, a long, straight, even *smooch*, as if it had been rubbed over and over.

I wonder how it was done and who did it, and what they did it for. Round and round and round—round and round and round—it makes me dizzy!

I really have discovered something at last.

Through watching so much at night, when it changes so, I have finally found out.

The front pattern *does* move—and no wonder! The woman behind shakes it!

Sometimes I think there are a great many women behind, and sometimes only one, and she crawls around fast, and her crawling shakes it all over.

Then in the very bright spots she keeps still, and in the very shady spots she just takes hold of the bars and shakes them hard.

And she is all the time trying to climb through. But nobody could climb through that pattern—it strangles so; I think that is why it has so many heads.

They get through, and then the pattern strangles them off and turns them upside down, and makes their eyes white! If those heads were covered or taken off it would not be half so bad.

I think that woman gets out in the daytime!

And I'll tell you why—privately—I've seen her!

I can see her out of every one of my windows!

It is the same woman, I know, for she is always creeping, and most women do not creep by daylight.

I see her in that long shaded lane, creeping up and down. I see her in those dark grape arbors, creeping all around the garden.

I see her on that long road under the trees, creeping along, and when a carriage comes she hides under the blackberry vines.

I don't blame her a bit. It must be very humiliating to be caught creeping by daylight!

I always lock the door when I creep by daylight. I can't do it at night, for I know John would suspect something at once.

And John is so queer now, that I don't want to irritate him. I wish he would take another room! Besides, I don't want anybody to get that woman out at night but myself.

I often wonder if I could see her out of all the windows at once.

But, turn as fast as I can, I can only see out of one at one time.

And though I always see her, she *may* be able to creep faster than I can turn!

I have watched her sometimes away off in the open country, creeping as fast as a cloud shadow in a high wind.

. . .

If only that top pattern could be gotten off from the under one! I mean to try it, little by little.

I have found out another funny thing, but I shan't tell it this time! It does not do to trust people too much.

There are only two more days to get this paper off, and I believe John is beginning to notice. I don't like the look in his eyes.

And I heard him ask Jennie a lot of professional questions about me. She had a very good report to give.

She said I slept a good deal in the daytime.

John knows I don't sleep very well at night, for all I'm so quiet!

He asked me all sorts of questions, too, and pretended to be very loving and kind.

As if I couldn't see through him!

Still, I don't wonder he acts so, sleeping under this paper for three months.

It only interests me, but I feel sure John and Jennie are secretly affected by it.

Hurrah! This is the last day, but it is enough. John to stay in town overnight, and won't be out until this evening.

Jennie wanted to sleep with me—the sly thing! but I told her I should undoubtedly rest better for a night all alone.

That was clever, for really I wasn't alone a bit! As soon as it was moonlight and that poor thing began to crawl and shake the pattern, I got up and ran to help her.

I pulled and she shook, I shook and she pulled, and before morning we had peeled off yards of that paper.

A strip about as high as my head and half around the room.

And then when the sun came and that awful pattern began to laugh at me, I declared I would finish it today!

We go away tomorrow, and they are moving all my furniture down again to leave things as they were before.

Jennie looked at the wall in amazement, but I told her merrily that I did it out of pure spite at the vicious thing.

She laughed and said she wouldn't mind doing it herself, but I must not get tired.

How she betrayed herself that time!

But I am here, and no person touches this paper but me—not *alive*!

She tried to get me out of the room—it was too patent! But I said it was so quiet and empty and clean now that I believed I would lie down again and sleep all I could; and not to wake me even for dinner—I would call when I woke.

So now she is gone, and the servants are gone, and the things are gone, and there is nothing left but that great bedstead nailed down, with the canvas mattress we found on it.

We shall sleep downstairs tonight, and take the boat home tomorrow.

I quite enjoy the room, now it is bare again.

How those children did tear about here!

This bedstead is fairly gnawed!

But I must get to work.

I have locked the door and thrown the key down into the front path.

I don't want to go out, and I don't want to have anybody come in, till John comes.

I want to astonish him.

I've got a rope up here that even Jennie did not find. If that woman does get out, and tries to get away, I can tie her!

But I forgot I could not reach far without anything to stand on!

This bed will *not* move!

I tried to lift and push it until I was lame, and then I got so angry I bit off a little piece of one corner—but it hurt my teeth.

Then I peeled off all the paper I could reach standing on the floor. It sticks horribly and the pattern just enjoys it! All those strangled heads and bulbous eyes and waddling fungus growths just shriek with derision!

I am getting angry enough to do something desperate. To jump out of the window would be admirable exercise, but the bars are too strong even to try.

Besides I wouldn't do it. Of course not. I know well enough that a step like that is improper and might be misconstrued.

I don't like to *look* out of the windows even—there are so many of those creeping women, and they creep so fast.

I wonder if they all come out of that wallpaper as I did?

But I am securely fastened now by my well-hidden rope—you don't get *me* out in the road there!

I suppose I shall have to get back behind the pattern when it comes night, and that is hard!

It is so pleasant to be out in this great room and creep around as I please!

I don't want to go outside. I won't, even if Jennie asks me to.

For outside you have to creep on the ground, and everything is green instead of yellow.

But here I can creep smoothly on the floor, and my shoulder just fits in that long smooch around the wall, so I cannot lose my way.

Why there's John at the door!

It is no use, young man, you can't open it!

How he does call and pound!

Now he's crying for an axe.

It would be a shame to break down that beautiful door!

"John dear!" said I in the gentlest voice, "the key is down by the front steps, under a plantain leaf!"

That silenced him for a few moments.

Then he said—very quietly indeed, "Open the door, my darling!"

"I can't," said I. "The key is down by the front door under a plantain leaf!"

And then I said it again, several times, very gently and slowly, and said it so often that he had to go and see, and he got it of course, and came in. He stopped short by the door.

"What is the matter?" he cried. "For God's sake, what are you doing?"

I kept on creeping just the same, but I looked at him over my shoulder.

"I've got out at last," said I, "in spite of you and Jane. And I've pulled off most of the paper, so you can't put me back!"

Now why should that man have fainted? But he did, and right across my path by the wall, so that I had to creep over him every time!

---

1. Why does the narrator feel so much better after she sees the woman behind the wallpaper?
2. Why does the narrator come to believe that she is the woman behind the wallpaper?
3. If its pattern is "torturing" to the narrator, then why does she claim, later on, to feel better "*because* of the wallpaper"?
4. Is the narrator correct when she says that John does not believe she is sick, or does John merely fail to understand the nature of her illness?

KATHERINE MANSFIELD (1888–1923) was born in New Zealand but as a young woman moved to London to pursue a career as a writer. Her first collection of short stories, *In a German Pension* (1911), portrays disillusioned women and failed sexual relationships, reflecting her own experience and prefiguring many of the themes of her later work. While continuing to refine her storytelling art, Mansfield wrote literary reviews for various magazines edited by the critic John Middleton Murry, whom she married in 1918. Her collections *Bliss and Other Stories* (1920) and *The Garden Party and Other Stories* (1922) were critically praised for their innovative use of modernist techniques such as stream-of-consciousness narration, and greatly influenced the development of the modern short story, in particular the work of Virginia Woolf.

Her First Ball

Exactly when the ball began Leila would have found it hard to say. Perhaps her first real partner was the cab. It did not matter that she shared the cab with the Sheridan girls and their brother. She sat back in her own little corner of it, and the bolster on which her hand rested felt like the sleeve of an unknown young man's dress suit; and away they bowled, past waltzing lampposts and houses and fences and trees.

"Have you really never been to a ball before, Leila? But, my child, how too weird—" cried the Sheridan girls.

"Our nearest neighbour was fifteen miles," said Leila softly, gently opening and shutting her fan.

Oh, dear, how hard it was to be indifferent like the others! She tried not to smile too much; she tried not to care. But every single thing was so new and exciting . . . Meg's tuberoses, Jose's long loop of amber, Laura's little dark head, pushing above her white fur like a flower through snow. She would remember forever. It even gave her a pang to see her cousin Laurie throw away the wisps of tissue paper he pulled from the fastenings of his new gloves. She would like to have kept those wisps as a keepsake, as a remembrance. Laurie leaned forward and put his hand on Laura's knee.

"Look here, darling," he said. "The third and the ninth as usual. Twig?"

Oh, how marvellous to have a brother! In her excitement Leila felt that if there had been time, if it hadn't been impossible, she couldn't have helped crying because she was an only child, and no brother had ever said "Twig?" to her; no sister would ever say, as Meg said to Jose that moment, "I've never known your hair go up more successfully than it has tonight!"

But, of course, there was no time. They were at the drill hall already; there were cabs in front of them and cabs behind. The road was bright on either side with moving fanlike lights, and on the pavement gay couples seemed to float through the air; little satin shoes chased each other like birds.

"Hold on to me, Leila; you'll get lost," said Laura.

"Come on, girls, let's make a dash for it," said Laurie.

Leila put two fingers on Laura's pink velvet cloak, and they were somehow lifted past the big golden lantern, carried along the passage, and pushed into the little room marked "Ladies." Here the crowd was so great there was hardly space to take off their things; the noise was deafening. Two benches on either side were stacked high with wraps. Two old women in white aprons ran up and down tossing fresh armfuls. And everybody was pressing forward trying to get at the little dressing table and mirror at the far end.

A great quivering jet of gas lighted the ladies' room. It couldn't wait; it was dancing already. When the door opened again and there came a burst of tuning from the drill hall, it leaped almost to the ceiling.

Dark girls, fair girls were patting their hair, tying ribbons again, tucking handkerchiefs down the fronts of their bodices, smoothing marble-white gloves. And because they were all laughing it seemed to Leila that they were all lovely.

"Aren't there any invisible hairpins?" cried a voice. "How most extraordinary! I can't see a single invisible hairpin."

"Powder my back, there's a darling," cried someone else.

"But I must have a needle and cotton. I've torn simply miles and miles of the frill," wailed a third.

Then, "Pass them along, pass them along!" The straw basket of programmes was tossed from arm to arm. Darling little pink and silver programmes, with pink pencils and fluffy tassels. Leila's fingers shook as she took one out of the basket. She wanted to ask someone, "Am I meant to have one too?" but she had just time to read: "Waltz 3. '*Two, Two in a Canoe.*' Polka 4. '*Making the Feathers Fly,*' " when Meg cried, "Ready, Leila?" and they pressed their way through the crush in the passage towards the big double doors of the drill hall.

Dancing had not begun yet, but the band had stopped tuning, and the noise was so great it seemed that when it did begin to play it would never be heard. Leila, pressing close to Meg, looking over Meg's shoulder, felt that even the little quivering coloured flags strung across the ceiling were talking. She quite forgot to be shy; she forgot how in the middle of dressing she had sat down on the bed with one shoe off and one shoe on and begged her mother to ring up her cousins and say she couldn't go after all. And the rush of longing she had had to be sitting on the veranda of their forsaken up-country home, listening to the baby owls crying "More pork" in the moonlight, was changed to a rush of joy so sweet that it was hard to bear alone. She clutched her fan, and, gazing at the gleaming, golden floor, the azaleas, the lanterns, the stage at one end with its red carpet and gilt chairs and the band in a corner, she thought breathlessly, "How heavenly; how simply heavenly!"

All the girls stood grouped together at one side of the doors, the men at the other, and the chaperones in dark dresses, smiling rather foolishly, walked with little careful steps over the polished floor towards the stage.

"This is my little country cousin Leila. Be nice to her. Find her partners; she's under my wing," said Meg, going up to one girl after another.

Strange faces smiled at Leila—sweetly, vaguely. Strange voices answered, "Of course, my dear." But Leila felt the girls didn't really see her. They were looking towards the men. Why didn't the men begin? What were they waiting for? There they stood, smoothing their gloves, patting their glossy hair, and smiling among themselves. Then, quite suddenly, as if they had only just made up their minds that that was what they had to do, the men came gliding over the parquet. There was a joyful flutter among the girls. A tall, fair man flew up to Meg, seized her programme, scribbled something; Meg passed him on to Leila. "May I have the pleasure?" He ducked and smiled. There came a dark man wearing an eyeglass, then cousin Laurie with a friend, and Laura with a little freckled fellow whose tie was crooked. Then quite an old man—fat, with a big bald patch on his head—took her programme and murmured, "Let me see, let me see!" And he was a long time comparing his programme, which looked black with names, with hers. It seemed to give him so much trouble that Leila was ashamed. "Oh, please don't bother," she said eagerly. But instead of replying the fat man wrote something, glanced at her again. "Do I remember this bright little face?" he said softly. "Is it known to me of yore?" At that moment the band began playing; the fat man disappeared. He was tossed away on a great wave of music that came flying over the gleaming floor, breaking the groups up into couples, scattering them, sending them spinning. . . .

Leila had learned to dance at boarding school. Every Saturday afternoon the boarders were hurried off to a little corrugated iron mission hall where Miss Eccles (of London) held her "select" classes. But the difference between that dusty-smelling hall—with calico texts on the walls, the poor terrified little woman in a brown velvet toque with rabbit's ears thumping the cold piano, Miss Eccles poking the girls' feet with her long white wand—and this was so tremendous that Leila was sure if her partner didn't come and she had to listen to that marvellous music and to watch the others sliding, gliding over the golden floor, she would die at least, or faint, or lift her arms and fly out of one of those dark windows that showed the stars.

"Ours, I think—" Someone bowed, smiled, and offered her his arm; she hadn't to die after all. Someone's hand pressed her waist, and she floated away like a flower that is tossed into a pool.

"Quite a good floor, isn't it?" drawled a faint voice close to her ear.

"I think it's most beautifully slippery," said Leila.

"Pardon!" The faint voice sounded surprised. Leila said it again. And there was a tiny pause before the voice echoed, "Oh, quite!" and she was swung round again.

He steered so beautifully. That was the great difference between dancing with girls and men, Leila decided. Girls banged into each other, and stamped on each other's feet; the girl who was gentleman always clutched you so.

The azaleas were separate flowers no longer; they were pink and white flags streaming by.

"Were you at the Bells' last week?" the voice came again. It sounded tired. Leila wondered whether she ought to ask him if he would like to stop.

"No, this is my first dance," said she.

Her partner gave a little gasping laugh. "Oh, I say," he protested.

"Yes, it is really the first dance I've ever been to." Leila was most fervent. It was such a relief to be able to tell somebody. "You see, I've lived in the country all my life up until now. . . ."

At that moment the music stopped, and they went to sit on two chairs against the wall. Leila tucked her pink satin feet under and fanned herself, while she blissfully watched the other couples passing and disappearing through the swing doors.

"Enjoying yourself, Leila?" asked Jose, nodding her golden head.

Laura passed and gave her the faintest little wink; it made Leila wonder for a moment whether she was quite grown up after all. Certainly her partner did not say very much. He coughed, tucked his handkerchief away, pulled down his waistcoat, took a minute thread off his sleeve. But it didn't matter. Almost immediately the band started, and her second partner seemed to spring from the ceiling.

"Floor's not bad," said the new voice. Did one always begin with the floor? And then, "Were you at the Neaves' on Tuesday?" And again Leila explained. Perhaps it was a little strange that her partners were not more interested. For it was thrilling. Her first ball! She was only at the beginning of everything. It seemed to her that she had never known what the night was like before. Up till now it had been dark, silent, beautiful very often—oh, yes—but mournful somehow. Solemn. And now it would never be like that again—it had opened dazzling bright.

"Care for an ice?" said her partner. And they went through the swing doors, down the passage, to the supper room. Her cheeks burned, she was fearfully thirsty. How sweet the ices looked on little glass plates, and how cold the frosted spoon was, iced too! And when they came back to the hall there was the fat man waiting for her by the door. It gave her quite a shock again to see how old he was; he ought to have been on the stage with the fathers and mothers. And when Leila compared him with her other partners he looked shabby. His waistcoat was creased, there was a button off his glove, his coat looked as if it was dusty with French chalk.

"Come along, little lady," said the fat man. He scarcely troubled to clasp her, and they moved away so gently, it was more like walking than dancing. But he said not a word about the floor. "Your first dance, isn't it?" he murmured.

"How *did* you know?"

"Ah," said the fat man, "that's what it is to be old!" He wheezed faintly as he steered her past an awkward couple. "You see, I've been doing this kind of thing for the last thirty years."

"Thirty years?" cried Leila. Twelve years before she was born!

"It hardly bears thinking about, does it?" said the fat man gloomily. Leila looked at his bald head, and she felt quite sorry for him.

"I think it's marvellous to be still going on," she said kindly.

"Kind little lady," said the fat man, and he pressed her a little closer, and hummed a bar of the waltz. "Of course," he said, "you can't hope to last anything like as long as that. No-o," said the fat man, "long before that you'll be sitting up there on the stage, looking on, in your nice black velvet. And these pretty arms will have turned into little short fat ones, and you'll beat time with such a different kind of fan—a black bony one." The fat man seemed to shudder. "And you'll smile away like the poor old dears up there, and point to your daughter, and tell the elderly lady next to you how some dreadful man tried to kiss her at the club ball. And your heart will ache, ache"—the fat man squeezed her closer still, as if he really was sorry for that poor heart—"because no one wants to kiss you now. And you'll say how unpleasant these polished floors are to walk on, how dangerous they are. Eh, Mademoiselle Twinkletoes?" said the fat man softly.

Leila gave a light little laugh, but she did not feel like laughing. Was it—could it all be true? It sounded terribly true. Was this first ball only the beginning of her last ball after all? At that the music seemed to change; it sounded sad, sad; it rose upon a great sigh. Oh, how quickly things changed! Why didn't happiness last forever? Forever wasn't a bit too long.

"I want to stop," she said in a breathless voice. The fat man led her to the door.

"No," she said, "I won't go outside. I won't sit down. I'll just stand here, thank you." She leaned against the wall, tapping with her foot, pulling up her gloves and trying to smile. But deep inside her a little girl threw her pinafore over her head and sobbed. Why had he spoiled it all?

"I say, you know," said the fat man, "you mustn't take me seriously, little lady."

"As if I should!" said Leila, tossing her small dark head and sucking her underlip. . . .

Again the couples paraded. The swing doors opened and shut. Now new music was given out by the bandmaster. But Leila didn't want to dance anymore. She wanted to be home, or sitting on the veranda listening to those baby owls. When she looked through the dark windows at the stars, they had long beams like wings. . . .

But presently a soft, melting, ravishing tune began, and a young man with curly hair bowed before her. She would have to dance, out of politeness, until she could find Meg. Very stiffly she walked into the middle; very haughtily she put her hand on his sleeve. But in one minute, in one turn, her feet glided, glided. The lights, the azaleas, the dresses, the pink faces, the velvet chairs, all became one beautiful flying wheel. And when her next partner bumped her into the fat man and he said, "Par*don*," she smiled at him more radiantly than ever. She didn't even recognize him again.

---

1. Why does the fat man tell Leila that she "can't hope to last anything like as long" as thirty years?
2. If the fat man knows it is Leila's first ball, why does he try to spoil it for her?
3. Why doesn't Leila recognize the fat man when she bumps into him a little later on the dance floor?

ERNEST HEMINGWAY (1899–1961) established himself as the most influential prose writer of his generation by the age of thirty. His first two major novels, *The Sun Also Rises* (1926) and *A Farewell to Arms* (1929), display the lean style that would become his trademark. Heavily relying on the rhythms of the simple sentence, he delivered stories of individuals dealing with extremes of violence and pain who show, at their best, the "grace under pressure" that Hemingway affirmed as his personal credo. Perhaps for this reason he was drawn to such subjects as war, revolution, and bullfighting—any arena where death was insistently present. Hemingway became internationally renowned and won the Nobel Prize in Literature in 1954, but his last years were marked by alcoholism and depression, ending with his suicide in Ketchum, Idaho.

Indian Camp

At the lakeshore there was another rowboat drawn up. The two Indians stood waiting.

Nick and his father got in the stern of the boat and the Indians shoved it off and one of them got in to row. Uncle George sat in the stern of the camp rowboat. The young Indian shoved the camp boat off and got in to row Uncle George.

The two boats started off in the dark. Nick heard the oarlocks of the other boat quite a way ahead of them in the mist. The Indians rowed with quick choppy strokes. Nick lay back with his father's arm around him. It was cold on the water. The Indian who was rowing them was working very hard, but the other boat moved further ahead in the mist all the time.

"Where are we going, Dad?" Nick asked.

"Over to the Indian camp. There is an Indian lady very sick."

"Oh," said Nick.

Across the bay they found the other boat beached. Uncle George was smoking a cigar in the dark. The young Indian pulled the boat way up on the beach. Uncle George gave both the Indians cigars.

They walked up from the beach through a meadow that was soaking wet with dew, following the young Indian who carried a lantern. Then they went into the woods and followed a trail that led to the logging road that ran back into the hills. It was much lighter on the logging road as the timber was cut away on both sides. The young Indian stopped and blew out his lantern and they all walked on along the road.

They came around a bend and a dog came out barking. Ahead were the lights of the shanties where the Indian bark-peelers lived. More dogs rushed out at them. The two Indians sent them back to the shanties. In the shanty nearest the road there was a light in the window. An old woman stood in the doorway holding a lamp.

Inside on a wooden bunk lay a young Indian woman. She had been trying to have her baby for two days. All the old women in the camp had been helping her. The men had moved off up the road to sit in the dark and smoke out of range of the noise she made. She screamed just as Nick and the two Indians followed his father and Uncle George into the shanty. She lay in the lower bunk, very big under a quilt. Her head was turned to one side. In the upper bunk was her husband. He had cut his foot very badly with an ax three days before. He was smoking a pipe. The room smelled very bad.

Nick's father ordered some water to be put on the stove, and while it was heating he spoke to Nick.

"This lady is going to have a baby, Nick," he said.

"I know," said Nick.

"You don't know," said his father. "Listen to me. What she is going through is called being in labor. The baby wants to be born and she wants it to be born. All her muscles are trying to get the baby born. That is what is happening when she screams."

"I see," Nick said.

Just then the woman cried out.

"Oh, Daddy, can't you give her something to make her stop screaming?" asked Nick.

"No. I haven't any anesthetic," his father said. "But her screams are not important. I don't hear them because they are not important."

The husband in the upper bunk rolled over against the wall.

The woman in the kitchen motioned to the doctor that the water was hot. Nick's father went into the kitchen and poured about half of the water out of the big kettle into a basin. Into the water left in the kettle he put several things he unwrapped from a handkerchief.

"Those must boil" he said, and began to scrub his hands in the basin of hot water with a cake of soap he had brought from the camp. Nick watched his father's hands scrubbing each other with the soap. While his father washed his hands very carefully and thoroughly, he talked.

"You see, Nick, babies are supposed to be born head first but sometimes they're not. When they're not they make a lot of trouble for everybody. Maybe I'll have to operate on this lady. We'll know in a little while."

When he was satisfied with his hands he went in and went to work.

"Pull back that quilt, will you, George?" he said. "I'd rather not touch it."

Later when he started to operate Uncle George and three Indian men held the woman still. She bit Uncle George on the arm and Uncle George said, "Damn squaw bitch!" and the young Indian who had rowed Uncle George over laughed at him. Nick held the basin for his father. It all took a long time. His father picked the baby up and slapped it to make it breathe and handed it to the old woman.

"See, it's a boy, Nick," he said. "How do you like being an interne?"

Nick said, "All right." He was looking away so as not to see what his father was doing.

"There. That gets it," said his father and put something into the basin.

Nick didn't look at it.

"Now," his father said, "there's some stitches to put in. You can watch this or not, Nick, just as you like. I'm going to sew up the incision I made."

Nick did not watch. His curiosity had been gone for a long time.

His father finished and stood up. Uncle George and the three Indian men stood up. Nick put the basin out in the kitchen.

Uncle George looked at his arm. The young Indian smiled reminiscently.

"I'll put some peroxide on that, George," the doctor said. He bent over the Indian woman. She was quiet now and her eyes were closed. She looked very pale. She did not know what had become of the baby or anything.

"I'll be back in the morning," the doctor said, standing up. "The nurse should be here from St. Ignace by noon and she'll bring everything we need."

He was feeling exalted and talkative as football players are in the dressing room after a game.

"That's one for the medical journal, George," he said. "Doing a caesarian with a jackknife and sewing it up with nine-foot, tapered gut leaders."

Uncle George was standing against the wall, looking at his arm.

"Oh, you're a great man, all right," he said.

"Ought to have a look at the proud father. They're usually the worst sufferers in these little affairs," the doctor said. "I must say he took it all pretty quietly."

He pulled back the blanket from the Indian's head. His hand came away wet. He mounted on the edge of the lower bunk with the lamp in one hand and looked in. The Indian lay with his face toward the wall. His throat had been cut from ear to ear. The blood had flowed down into a pool where his body sagged the bunk. His head rested on his left arm. The open razor lay, edge up, in the blankets.

"Take Nick out of the shanty, George," the doctor said.

There was no need of that. Nick, standing in the door of the kitchen, had a good view of the upper bunk when his father, the lamp in one hand, tipped the Indian's head back.

It was just beginning to be daylight when they walked along the logging road back toward the lake.

"I'm terribly sorry I brought you along, Nickie," said his father, all his postoperative exhilaration gone. "It was an awful mess to put you through."

"Do ladies always have such a hard time having babies?" Nick asked.

"No, that was very, very exceptional."

"Why did he kill himself, Daddy?"

"I don't know, Nick. He couldn't stand things, I guess."

"Do many men kill themselves, Daddy?"

"Not very many, Nick."

"Do many women?"

"Hardly ever."

"Don't they ever?"

"Oh, yes. They do sometimes."

"Daddy?"

"Yes."

"Where did Uncle George go?"

"He'll turn up all right."

"Is dying hard, Daddy?"

"No, I think it's pretty easy, Nick. It all depends."

They were seated in the boat, Nick in the stern, his father rowing. The sun was coming up over the hills. A bass jumped, making a circle in the water. Nick trailed his hand in the water. It felt warm in the sharp chill of the morning.

In the early morning on the lake sitting in the stern of the boat with his father rowing, he felt quite sure that he would never die.

---

1. Why does Nick's father say that he does not hear the woman's screams "because they are not important"?

2. Is Uncle George sincere when he calls Nick's father "a great man"?

3. Why does the woman's husband kill himself while his wife is giving birth?

4. Why does Nick's father tell him that dying is "pretty easy"? Why is Nick quite sure he'll never die?

V. S. PRITCHETT (1900–1997) was born in Ipswich, England, and received some formal education at Alleyn's School in London. Largely self-taught, he became a freelance journalist for the *Christian Science Monitor*, traveling extensively in Ireland, Spain, Morocco, and the United States. With a keen eye for detail and deliberate effort to avoid academic jargon, he wrote for the common reader. His successful career spanned more than seventy years, during which he wrote novels and short stories, literary criticism and biographies, including *The Living Novel* (1946) and an award-winning autobiography, *A Cab at the Door* (1968). He also edited the periodical the *New Statesman* for several years, was knighted for his service to literature, and won a number of awards including the Royal Society of Literature Award.

The Diver

In a side street on the Right Bank of the Seine where the river divides at the Île de la Cité, there is a yellow and red brick building shared by a firm of leather merchants. When I was twenty I worked there. The hours were long, the pay was low, and the place smelled of cigarettes and boots. I hated it. I had come to Paris to be a writer but my money had run out, and in this office I had to stick. How often I looked across the river, envying the free lives of the artists and writers on the other bank. Being English, I was the joke of the office. The sight of my fat pink innocent face and fair hair made everyone laugh; my accent was bad, for I could not pronounce a full *o*; worst of all, like a fool, I not only admitted I hadn't got a mistress, but boasted about it. To the office boys this news was extravagant. It doubled them up. It was a favourite trick of theirs, and even of the salesman, a man called Claudel with whom I had to work, to call me to the street door at lunchtime and then, if any girl or woman passed, they would give me a punch and shout:

"How much to sleep with this one? Twenty? Forty? A hundred?" I put on a grin, but, to tell the truth, a sheet of glass seemed to come down between me and any female I saw.

About one woman the lads did not play this game. She was a woman between thirty and forty I suppose, Mme. Chamson, who kept the menders and cleaners down the street. You could hear her heels as she came, half-running, to see Claudel, with jackets and trousers of his on her arm. He had some arrangement with her for getting his suits cleaned and repaired on the cheap. In return—well, there was a lot of talk. She had sinfully tinted hair built up high over arching, exclaiming eyebrows, hard as varnish and when she got near our door there was always a joke coming out of the side of her mouth. She would bounce into the office in her tight navy blue skirt, call the boys and Claudel together, shake hands with them all, and tell them some tale which always ended, with a dirty glance around, in whispering. Then she stood back and shouted with laughter. I was never in this secret circle and if I happened to grin, she gave me a severe and offended look and marched out scowling. One day, when one of her tales was over, she called back from the door:

"Standing all day in that gallery with all those naked women, he comes home done for, finished."

The office boys squeezed each other with pleasure. She was talking about her husband who was an attendant at the Louvre, a small moist-looking fellow whom we sometimes saw with her, a man fond of fishing, whose breath smelled of white wine. Because of her arrangement with Claudel, and her stories, she was a very respected woman.

I did not like Mme. Chamson; she looked to me like some predatory bird; but I could not take my eyes off her pushing bosom and her crooked mouth. I was afraid of her tongue. She caught on quickly to the fact that I was the office joke, but when they told her on top of this I wanted to be a writer, any curiosity she had about me was finished. "I could tell him a tale," she said. For her I didn't exist. She didn't even bother to shake hands with me.

Streets and avenues in Paris are named after writers; there are statues to poets, novelists and dramatists, making gestures to the birds, nursemaids and children in the gardens. How was it these men had become famous? How had they begun? For myself, it was impossible to begin. I walked about packed with stories, but when I sat in cafés or in my room with a pen in my hand and a bare sheet of paper before me, I could not touch it. I seemed to swell in the head, the chest, the arms and legs, as if I was trying to heave an enormous load onto the page and could not move. The portentous moment had not yet come. And there was another reason. The longer I worked in the leather trade and talked to the office boys, the typists there and Claudel, the more I acquired a double personality; when I left the office and walked to the Metro, I practised French to myself. In this bizarre language the stories inside me flared up, I was acting and speaking them as I walked, often in the subjunctive: but when I sat before my paper, the English language closed its sullen mouth.

And what were these stories? Impossible to say. I would set off in the morning and see the grey, ill-painted buildings of the older quarters leaning together like people, their shutters thrown back, so that the open windows looked like black and empty eyes. In the mornings the bedding was thrown over the sills to air and hung out, wagging like tongues about what goes on in the night between men and women. The houses looked sunken-shouldered, exhausted, by what they told; and crowning the city was the church of Sacré Coeur, very white, standing like some dry Byzantine bird, to my mind, hollow-eyed and without conscience, presiding over the habits of the flesh and—to judge by what I read in newspapers—its crimes also; its murders, rapes, its shootings for jealousy and robbery. As my French improved the secrets of Paris grew worse. It amazed me that the crowds I saw on the street had survived the night and many indeed looked as sleepless as the houses.

After I had been a little more than a year in Paris, fourteen months in fact, a drama broke the monotonous life of our office. A consignment of dressed skins had been sent to us from Rouen. It had been sent by barge—not the usual method in our business. The barge was an old one and was carrying a mixed cargo and, within a few hundred yards from our warehouse, it was rammed and sunk one misty morning, by a Dutch boat taking the wrong channel. The manager, the whole office, especially Claudel, who saw his commission go to the bottom, were outraged. Fortunately the barge had gone down slowly near the bank, close to us; the water was not too deep. A crane was brought down on another barge to the water's edge and soon, in an exciting week, a diver was let down to salvage what he could. Claudel and I had to go to the quay and, if a bale of our stuff came up, we had to get it to the warehouse and see what the damage was.

Anything to get out of the office. For me the diver was the hero of the week. He stood in his round helmet and suit on a wide tray of wood hanging from four chains and then, the motor spat, the chains rattled and down he went with great dignity under the water. While the diver was under the water, Claudel would be reckoning his commission over again—would it be calculated only on the sale price or on what was saved? "Five bales so far," he would mutter fanatically. "One and a half per cent." His teeth and his eyes were agitated with changing figures. I, in imagination, was groping in the gloom of the river bed with the hero. Then we'd step forward; the diver was coming up. Claudel would hold my arm as the man appeared with a tray of sodden bales and the brown water streaming off them. He would step off the plank onto the barge where the crane was installed and look like a swollen frog. A workman unscrewed his helmet, the vizor was raised and then we saw the young diver's rosy, cheerful face. A workman lit a cigarette and gave it to him and out of the helmet came a long surprising jet of smoke. There was always a crowd watching from the quay wall and when he did this, they all smiled and many laughed. "See that?" they would say. "He is having a puff," and the diver grinned and waved to the crowd.

Our job was to grab the bale. Claudel would check the numbers of the bales on his list. Then we saw them wheeled to our warehouse, dripping all the way, and there I had to hang up the skins on poles. It was like hanging up drowned animals—even, I thought, human beings.

On the Friday afternoon of that week, when everyone was tired and even the crowd looking down from the street wall had thinned to next to nothing, Claudel and I were still down on the quay waiting for the final load. The diver had come up. We were seeing him for the last time before the weekend. I was waiting to watch what I had not yet seen: how he got out of his suit. I walked down nearer at the quay's edge to get a good view. Claudel shouted to me to get on with the job and as he shouted I heard a whizzing noise above my head and then felt a large, heavy slopping lump hit me on the shoulders. I turned round and the next thing I was flying in the air, arms outspread with wonder. Paris turned upside down. A second later, I crashed into cold darkness, water was running up my legs swallowing me. I had fallen into the river.

The wall of the quay was not high. In a couple of strokes I came up spitting mud and caught an iron ring on the quay wall. Two men pulled my hands. Everyone was laughing as I climbed out.

I stood there drenched and mud-smeared, with straw in my hair, pouring water into a puddle that came from me, getting larger and larger.

"Didn't you hear me shout?" said Claudel.

Laughing and arguing, two or three men led me to the shelter of the wall where I began to wring out my jacket and shirt and squeeze the water out of my trousers. It was a warm day and I stood in the sun and saw my trousers steam and heard my shoes squelch.

"Give him a hot rum," someone said. Claudel was torn between looking after our few bales left on the quay and taking me across the street to a bar. But, checking the numbers and muttering a few more figures to himself, he decided to enjoy the drama and go with me. He called out that we'd be back in a minute.

We got to the bar and Claudel saw to it that my arrival was a sensation. Always nagging at me in the office, he was now proud of me.

"He fell into the river. He nearly drowned. I warned him. I shouted. Didn't I?"

The one or two customers admired me. The barman brought me the rum. I could not get my hand into my pocket because it was wet.

"You pay me tomorrow," said Claudel, putting a coin on the counter.

"Drink it quickly," said the barman.

I was laughing and explaining now.

"One moment he was on dry land, the next he was flying in the air, then plonk in the water. Three elements," said Claudel.

"Only fire is missing," said the barman.

They argued about how many elements there were. A whole history of swimming feats, drowning stories, bodies bound, murders in the Seine, sprang up. Someone said the morgue used to be full of corpses. And then an argument started, as it sometimes did in this part of Paris, about the exact date at which the morgue was moved from the island. I joined in but my teeth had begun to chatter.

"Another rum," the barman said.

And then I felt a hand fingering my jacket and my trousers. It was the hand of Mme. Chamson. She had been down at the quay once or twice during the week to have a word with Claudel. She had seen what had happened.

"He ought to go home and change into dry things at once," she said in a firm voice. "You ought to take him home."

"I can't do that. We've left five bales on the quay," said Claudel.

"He can't go back," said Mme. Chamson. "He's shivering."

I sneezed.

"You'll catch pneumonia," she said. And to Claudel: "You ought to have kept an eye on him. He might have drowned."

She was very stern with him.

"Where do you live?" she said to me.

I told her.

"It will take you an hour," she said.

Everyone was silent before the decisive voice of Mme. Chamson.

"Come with me to the shop," she ordered and pulled me brusquely by the arm. She led me out of the bar and said, as we walked away, my boots squeaking and squelching:

"That man thinks of nothing but money. Who'd pay for your funeral? Not he!"

Twice, as she got me, her prisoner, past the shops, she called out to people at their doors:

"They nearly let him drown."

Three girls used to sit mending in the window of her shop and behind them was usually a man pressing clothes. But it was half past six now and the shop was closed. Everyone had gone. I was relieved. This place had disturbed me. When I first went to work for our firm Claudel had told me he could fix me up with one of the mending girls; if we shared a room it would halve our expenses and she could cook and look after my clothes. That was what started the office joke about my not having a mistress. When we got to the shop Mme. Chamson led me down a passage inside which was muggy with the smell of dozens of dresses and suits hanging there, into a dim parlour beyond. It looked out on to the smeared grey wall of a courtyard.

"Stay here," said Mme. Chamson planting me by a sofa. "Don't sit on it in those wet things. Take them off."

I took off my jacket.

"No. Don't wring it. Give it to me. I'll get a towel."

I started drying my hair.

"All of them," she said.

Mme. Chamson looked shorter in her room, her hair looked duller, her eyebrows less dramatic. I had never really seen her closely. She had become a plain, domestic woman; her mouth had straightened. There was not a joke in her. Her bosom swelled with management. The rumour that she was Claudel's mistress was obviously an office tale.

"I'll see what I can find for you. You can't wear these."

I waited for her to leave the room and then I took off my shirt and dried my chest, picking off the bits of straw from the river that had stuck to my skin. She came back.

"Off with your trousers, I said. Give them to me. What size are they?"

My head went into the towel. I pretended not to hear. I could not bring myself to undress before Mme. Chamson. But while I hesitated she bent down and her sharp fingernails were at my belt.

"I'll do it," I said anxiously.

Our hands touched and our fingers mixed as I unhitched my belt. Impatiently she began on my buttons, but I pushed her hands away.

She stood back, blank-faced and peremptory in her stare. It was the blankness of her face, her indifference to me, her ordinary womanliness, the touch of her practical fingers that left me without defence. She was not the ribald, coquettish, dangerous woman who came wagging her hips to our office, not one of my Paris fantasies of sex and danger. She was simply a woman. The realisation of this was disastrous to me. An unbelievable change was throbbing in my body. It was uncontrollable. My eyes angrily, helplessly, asked her to go away. She stood there implacably. I half-turned, bending to conceal my enormity as I lowered my trousers, but as I lowered them inch by inch so the throbbing manifestation increased. I got my foot out of one leg but my shoe caught in the other. On one leg I tried to dance my other trouser leg off. The towel slipped and I glanced at her in red-faced angry appeal. My trouble was only too clear. I was stiff with terror. I was almost in tears.

The change in Mme. Chamson was quick. From busy indifference, she went to anger.

"Young man," she said. "Cover yourself. How dare you. What indecency. How dare you insult me!"

"I'm sorry. I couldn't help . . ." I said.

Mme. Chamson's bosom became a bellows puffing outrage.

"What manners," she said. "I am not one of your tarts. I am a respectable woman. This is what I get for helping you. What would your parents say? If my husband were here!"

She had got my trousers in her hand. The shoe that had betrayed me fell now out of the leg to the floor.

She bent down coolly and picked it up.

"In any case," she said and now I saw for the first time this afternoon the strange twist of her mouth return to her, as she nodded at my now concealing towel—"that is nothing to boast about."

My blush had gone. I was nearly fainting. I felt the curious, brainless stupidity that goes with the state nature had put me in. A miracle saved me. I sneezed and then sneezed again; the second time with force.

"What did I tell you!" said Mme. Chamson, passing now to angry self-congratulation. She flounced out to the passage that led to the shop and coming back with a pair of trousers she threw them at me and, red in the face, said:

"Try those. If they don't fit I don't know what you'll do. I'll get a shirt," and she went past me to the door of the room beyond saying:

"You can thank your lucky stars my husband has gone fishing."

I heard her muttering as she opened drawers. She did not return. There was silence.

In the airless little salon, looking out (as if it were a cell in which I was caught) on the stained smudgy grey wall of the courtyard, the silence lengthened. It began to seem that Mme. Chamson had shut herself away in her disgust and was going to have no more to do with me. I saw a chance of getting out but she had taken away my wet clothes. I pulled on the pair of trousers she had thrown; they were too long but I could tuck them in. I should look an even bigger fool if I went out in the street dressed only in these. What was Mme. Chamson doing? Was she torturing me? Fortunately my impromptu disorder had passed. I stood listening. I studied the mantelpiece where I saw what I supposed was a photograph of Mme. Chamson as a girl in the veil of her first communion. Presently I heard her voice:

"Young man," she called harshly, "do you expect me to wait on you. Come and fetch your things."

Putting on a polite and apologetic look, I went to the inner door which led into a short passage only a yard long. She was not there.

"In here," she said curtly.

I pushed the next door open. This room was dim also and the first thing I saw was the end of a bed and in the corner a chair with a dark skirt on it and a stocking hanging from the arm, and on the floor a pair of shoes, one of them on its side. Then, suddenly, I saw at the end of the bed a pair of bare feet. I looked at the toes; how had they got there? And then I saw: without a stitch of clothing on her, Mme. Chamson—but could this naked body be she?—was lying on the bed, her chin propped on her hand, her lips parted as they always were when she came in on the point of laughing to the office, but now with no sound coming from them; her eyes, generally wide open, were now half-closed, watching me with the stillness of some large white cat. I looked away and then I saw two other large brown eyes gazing at me, two other faces: her breasts. It was the first time in my life I had ever seen a naked woman, and it astonished me to see the rise of a haunch, the slope of her belly and the black hair like a moustache beneath it. Mme. Chamson's face was always strongly made up with some almost orange colour, and it astonished me to see how white her body was from the neck down, but not the white of statues, but some sallow colour of white and shadow, marked at the waist by the tightness of the clothes she had taken off. I had thought of her as old, but she was not; her body was young and idle.

The sight of her transfixed me. It did not stir me. I simply stood there gaping. My heart seemed to have stopped. I wanted to rush from the room, but I could not. She was so very near. My horror must have been on my face but she seemed not to notice that, but simply stared at me. There was a small movement of her lips and I dreaded that she was going to laugh; but she did not; slowly she closed her lips and said at last between her teeth in a voice low and mocking:

"Is this the first time you have seen a woman?"

And after she said this, a sad look came into her face.

I could not answer.

She lay on her back and put out her hand and smiled fully.

"Well?" she said. And she moved her hips.

"I," I began, but I could not go on. All the fantasies of my walks about Paris, as I practised French, rushed into my head. This was the secret of all those open windows of Paris, of the vulturelike head of Sacré Coeur looking down on it. In a room like this, with a wardrobe in the corner and with clothes thrown on a chair, was enacted—what? Everything—but, above all, to my panicking mind, the crimes I read about in the newspapers. I was desperate as her hand went out.

"You have never seen a woman before?" she said again.

I moved a little and out of reach of her hand I said, fiercely:

"Yes, I have." I was amazed at myself.

"Ah!" she said and when I did not answer, she laughed: "Where was that? Who was she?"

It was her laughter, so dreaded by me, that released something in me. I said something terrible. The talk of the morgue at the bar jumped into my head.

I said coldly: "She was dead. In London."

"Oh my God," said Mme. Chamson sitting up and pulling at the coverlet, but it was caught and she could only cover her feet.

It was her turn to be frightened. Across my brain newspaper headlines were tapping out.

"She was murdered," I said. I hesitated. I was playing for time. Then it came out.

"She was strangled."

"Oh no!" she said and she pulled the coverlet violently up with both hands, until she had got some of it to her breast.

"I saw her," I said. "On her bed."

"You *saw* her? *How* did you see her?" she said. "Where was this?"

Suddenly the story sprang out of me, it unrolled as I spoke.

"It was in London," I said. "In our street. The woman was a neighbour of ours, we knew her well. She used to pass our window every morning on her way up from the bank."

"She was robbed!" said Mme. Chamson. Her mouth buckled with horror.

I saw I had caught her.

"Yes," I said. "She kept a shop."

"Oh my God, my God," said Mme. Chamson looking at the door behind me, then anxiously round the room.

"It was a sweets shop," I said, "where we bought our papers too."

"Killed in her shop," groaned Mme. Chamson. "Where was her husband?"

"No," I said, "in her bedroom at the back. Her husband was out at work all day and this man must have been watching for him to go. Well, we knew he did. He was the laundry man. He used to go in there twice a week. She'd been carrying on with him. She was lying there with her head on one side and a scarf twisted round her neck."

Mme. Chamson dropped the coverlet and hid her face in her hands; then she lowered them and said suspiciously:

"But how did *you* see her like this?"

"Well," I said, "it happened like this. My little sister had been whining after breakfast and wouldn't eat anything and Mother said, 'That kid will drive me out of my mind. Go up to Mrs Blake's'—that was her name—'and get her a bar of chocolate, milk chocolate, no nuts, she only spits them out.' And Mother said, 'You may as well tell her we don't want any papers after Friday because we're going to Brighton. Wait, I haven't finished yet—here take this money and pay the bill. Don't forget that, you forgot last year and the papers were littering up my hall. We owe for a month.'"

Mme. Chamson nodded at this detail. She had forgotten she was naked. She was the shopkeeper and she glanced again at the door as if listening for some customer to come in.

"I went up to the shop and there was no one there when I got in . . ."

"A woman alone!" said Mme. Chamson.

"So I called, 'Mrs Blake,' but there was no answer. I went to the inner door and called up a small flight of stairs, 'Mrs Blake'—Mother had been on at me as I said, about paying the bill. So I went up."

"You went up?" said Mme. Chamson, shocked.

"I'd often been up there with Mother, once when she was ill. We knew the family. Well—there she was. As I said, lying on the bed, naked, strangled, dead."

Mme. Chamson gazed at me. She looked me slowly up and down from my hair, then studied my face and then down my body to my feet. I had come barefooted into the room. And then she looked at my bare arms, until she came to my hands. She gazed at these as if she had never seen hands before. I rubbed them on my trousers, for she confused me.

"Is this true?" she accused me.

"Yes," I said, "I opened the door and there . . ."

"How old were you?"

I hadn't thought of that but I quickly decided.

"Twelve," I said.

Mme. Chamson gave a deep sigh. She had been sitting taut, holding her breath. It was a sigh in which I could detect just a twinge of disappointment. I felt my story had lost its hold.

"I ran home," I said quickly, "and said to my mother, 'Someone has killed Mrs Blake.' Mother did not believe me. She couldn't realise it. I had to tell her again and again. 'Go and see for yourself,' I said."

"Naturally," said Mme. Chamson. "You were only a child."

"We rang the police," I said.

At the word *police* Mme. Chamson groaned peacefully.

"There is a woman at the laundry," she said, "who was in the hospital with eight stitches in her head. She had been struck with an iron. But that was her husband. The police did nothing. But what does my husband do? He stands in the Louvre all day. Then he goes fishing, like this evening. Anyone," she said vehemently to me, "could break in here."

She was looking through me into some imagined scene and it was a long time before she came out of it. Then she saw her own bare shoulder and pouting she said, slowly:

"Is it true you were only twelve?"

"Yes."

She studied me for a long time.

"You poor boy," she said. "Your poor mother."

And she put her hand to my arm and let her hand slide down it gently to my wrist; then she put out her other hand to my other arm and took that hand too, as the coverlet slipped a little from her. She looked at my hands and lowered her head. Then she looked up slyly at me.

"You didn't do it, did you?" she said.

"No," I said indignantly, pulling back my hands, but she held on to them. My story vanished from my head.

"It is a bad memory," she said. She looked to me, once more, as she had looked when I had first come with her into her salon soaking wet—a soft, ordinary, decent woman. My blood began to throb.

"You must forget about it," she said. And then, after a long pause, she pulled me to her. I was done for, lying on the bed.

"Ah," she laughed, pulling at my trousers. "The diver's come up again. Forget. Forget."

And then there was no more laughter. Once in the height of our struggle I caught sight of her eyes; the pupils had disappeared and there were only the blind whites and she cried out: "Kill me. Kill me," from her twisted mouth.

Afterwards we lay talking. She asked if it was true I was going to be a writer and when I said, "Yes," she said:

"You want talent for that. Stay where you are. It's a good firm. Claudel has been there for twelve years. And now, get up. My little husband will be back."

She got off the bed. Quickly she gave me a complete suit belonging to one of her customers, a grey one, the jacket rather tight.

"It suits you," she said. "Get a grey one next time."

I was looking at myself in a mirror when her husband came in, carrying his fishing rod and basket. He did not seem surprised. She picked up my sodden clothes and rushed angrily at him:

"Look at these. Soaked. That fool Claudel let this boy fall into the river. He brought him here."

Her husband simply stared.

"And where have you been? Leaving me alone like this," she carried on. "Anyone could break in. This boy saw a woman strangled in her bed in London. She had a shop. Isn't that it? A man came in and murdered her. What d'you say to that?"

Her husband stepped back and looked with appeal at me.

"Did you catch anything?" she said to him, still accusing.

"No," said her husband.

"Well, not like me," she said, mocking me. "I caught this one."

"Will you have a drop of something?" said her husband.

"No, he won't," said Mme. Chamson. "He'd better go straight home to bed."

So we shook hands. M. Chamson let me out through the shop door while Mme. Chamson called down the passage to me, "Bring the suit back tomorrow. It belongs to a customer."

Everything was changed for me after this. At the office I was a hero.

"Is it true that you saw a murder?" the office boys said.

And when Mme. Chamson came along and I gave her back the suit, she said: "Ah, here he is—my fish."

And then boldly: "When are you coming to collect your things?"

And then she went over to whisper to Claudel and ran out.

"You know what she said just now," said Claudel to me, looking very shrewd: "She said 'I am afraid of that young Englishman. Have you seen his hands?' "

---

1. What does the diver in the story represent for the narrator? What does he have to do with the narrator's ability to find his voice as a writer?

2. Why does the narrator become defenseless when he views Mme. Chamson not as a "ribald, coquettish, dangerous woman . . . [one of his] Paris fantasies of sex and danger," but as "simply a woman"?

3. Why does the narrator make up the story about seeing a dead woman in London? Why does Mme. Chamson say, "Kill me" while she and the narrator are making love?

4. Why, after returning home from his fishing trip, does Mme. Chamson's husband look "with appeal" at the narrator?

ISAAC BASHEVIS SINGER (1904–1991) was born into a family of Hasidic rabbis in Poland. Anticipating the invasion of Poland by Germany, Singer immigrated to the United States in 1934, where he worked for the *Jewish Daily Forward*, a Yiddish language newspaper. He published his first novel, *Satan in Goray*, in 1935. Singer would typically first write in Yiddish and then oversee the translation of his works into English. His rich body of work includes more than twelve collections of short stories and numerous novels, such as *The Family Moskat* (1950), *The Magician of Lublin* (1960), and *Enemies, a Love Story* (1972). Many of Singer's stories portray the eastern European small-town Jewish culture that largely vanished during World War II. He was awarded the Nobel Prize in Literature in 1978.

Gimpel the Fool

1

I am Gimpel the Fool. I don't think myself a fool. On the contrary. But that's what folks call me. They gave me the name while I was still in school. I had seven names in all: imbecile, donkey, flax-head, dope, glump, ninny, and fool. The last name stuck. What did my foolishness consist of? I was easy to take in. They said, "Gimpel, you know the rabbi's wife has been brought to childbed?" So I skipped school. Well, it turned out to be a lie. How was I supposed to know? She hadn't had a big belly. But I never looked at her belly. Was that really so foolish? The gang laughed and heehawed, stomped and danced and chanted a good-night prayer. And instead of the raisins they give when a woman's lying in, they stuffed my hand full of goat turds. I was no weakling. If I slapped someone he'd see all the way to Cracow. But I'm really not a slugger by nature. I think to myself, Let it pass. So they take advantage of me.

I was coming home from school and heard a dog barking. I'm not afraid of dogs, but of course I never want to start up with them. One of them may be mad, and if he bites there's not a Tartar in the world who can help you. So I made tracks. Then I looked around and saw the whole marketplace wild with laughter. It was no dog at all but Wolf-Leib the Thief. How was I supposed to know it was he? It sounded like a howling bitch.

When the pranksters and leg-pullers found that I was easy to fool, every one of them tried his luck with me. "Gimpel, the czar is coming to Frampol; Gimpel, the moon fell down in Turbeen; Gimpel, little Hodel Furpiece found a treasure behind the bathhouse." And I like a golem believed everyone. In the first place, everything is possible, as it is written in the Wisdom of the Fathers, I've forgotten just how. Second, I had to believe when the whole town came down on me! If I ever dared to say, "Ah, you're kidding!" there was trouble. People got angry. "What do you mean! You want to call everyone a liar?" What was I to do? I believed them, and I hope at least that did them some good.

I was an orphan. My grandfather who brought me up was already bent toward the grave. So they turned me over to a baker, and what a time they gave me there! Every woman or girl who came to bake a pan of cookies or dry a batch of noodles had to fool me at least once. "Gimpel, there's a fair in heaven; Gimpel, the rabbi gave birth to a calf in the seventh month; Gimpel, a cow flew over the roof and laid brass eggs." A student from the yeshiva came once to buy a roll, and he said, "You, Gimpel, while you stand here scraping with your baker's shovel the Messiah has come. The dead have arisen." "What do you mean?" I said. "I heard no one blowing the ram's horn!" He said, "Are you deaf?" And all began to cry, "We heard it, we heard!" Then in came Reitze the Candle-dipper and called out in her hoarse voice, "Gimpel, your father and mother have stood up from the grave. They're looking for you."

To tell the truth, I knew very well that nothing of the sort had happened, but all the same, as folks were talking, I threw on my wool vest and went out. Maybe something had happened. What did I stand to lose by looking? Well, what a cat music went up! And then I took a vow to believe nothing more. But that was no go either. They confused me so that I didn't know the big end from the small.

I went to the rabbi to get some advice. He said, "It is written, better to be a fool all your days than for one hour to be evil. You are not a fool. They are the fools. For he who causes his neighbor to feel shame loses paradise himself." Nevertheless the rabbi's daughter took me in. As I left the rabbinical court she said, "Have you kissed the wall yet?" I said, "No, what for?" She answered, "It's a law. You've got to do it after every visit." Well, there didn't seem to be any harm in it. And she burst out laughing. It was a fine trick. She put one over on me, all right.

I wanted to go off to another town, but then everyone got busy matchmaking, and they were after me so they nearly tore my coattails off. They talked at me and talked until I got water on the ear. She was no chaste maiden, but they told me she was virgin pure. She had a limp, and they said it was deliberate, from coyness. She had a bastard, and they told me the child was her little brother. I cried, "You're wasting your time. I'll never marry that whore." But they said indignantly, "What a way to talk! Aren't you ashamed of yourself? We can take you to the rabbi and have you fined for giving her a bad name." I saw then that I wouldn't escape them so easily and I thought, They're set on making me their butt. But when you're married the husband's the master, and if that's all right with her it's agreeable to me too. Besides, you can't pass through life unscathed, nor expect to.

I went to her clay house, which was built on the sand, and the whole gang, hollering and chorusing, came after me. They acted like bear baiters. When we came to the well they stopped all the same. They were afraid to start anything with Elka. Her mouth would open as if it were on a hinge, and she had a fierce tongue. I entered the house. Lines were strung from wall to wall and clothes were drying. Barefoot she stood by the tub, doing the wash. She was dressed in a worn hand-me-down gown of plush. She had her hair put up in braids and pinned across her head. It took my breath away, almost, the reek of it all.

Evidently she knew who I was. She took a look at me and said, "Look who's here! He's come, the drip. Grab a seat."

I told her all; I denied nothing. "Tell me the truth," I said, "are you really a virgin, and is that mischievous Yechiel actually your little brother? Don't be deceitful with me, for I'm an orphan."

"I'm an orphan myself," she answered, "and whoever tries to twist you up, may the end of his nose take a twist. But don't let them think they can take advantage of me. I want a dowry of fifty guilders, and let them take up a collection besides. Otherwise they can kiss my you-know-what." She was very plainspoken. I said, "It's the bride and not the groom who gives a dowry." Then she said, "Don't bargain with me. Either a flat 'yes' or a flat 'no'—go back where you came from."

I thought, No bread will ever be baked from *this* dough. But ours is not a poor town. They consented to everything and proceeded with the wedding. It so happened that there was a dysentery epidemic at the time. The ceremony was held at the cemetery gates, near the little corpse-washing hut. The fellows got drunk. While the marriage contract was being drawn up I heard the most pious high rabbi ask, "Is the bride a widow or a divorced woman?" And the sexton's wife answered for her, "Both a widow and divorced." It was a black moment for me. But what was I to do, run away from under the marriage canopy?

There was singing and dancing. An old granny danced opposite me, hugging a braided white challah. The master of revels made a "God 'a mercy" in memory of the bride's parents. The schoolboys threw burrs, as on Tishah b'Av fast day. There were a lot of gifts after the sermon: a noodle board, a kneading trough, a bucket, brooms, ladles, household articles galore. Then I took a look and saw two strapping young men carrying a crib. "What do we need this for?" I asked. So they said, "Don't rack your brains about it. It's all right, it'll come in handy." I realized I was going to be rooked. Take it another way though, what did I stand to lose? I reflected, I'll see what comes of it. A whole town can't go altogether crazy.

2

At night I came where my wife lay, but she wouldn't let me in. "Say, look here, is this what they married us for?" I said. And she said, "My monthly has come." "But yesterday they took you to the ritual bath, and that's afterward, isn't it supposed to be?" "Today isn't yesterday," said she, "and yesterday's not today. You can beat it if you don't like it." In short, I waited.

Not four months later she was in childbed. The townsfolk hid their laughter with their knuckles. But what could I do? She suffered intolerable pains and clawed at the walls. "Gimpel," she cried, "I'm going. Forgive me!" The house filled with women. They were boiling pans of water. The screams rose to the welkin.

The thing to do was to go to the house of prayer to repeat Psalms, and that was what I did.

The townsfolk liked that, all right. I stood in a corner saying Psalms and prayers, and they shook their heads at me. "Pray, pray!" they told me. "Prayer never made any woman pregnant." One of the congregation put a straw to my mouth and said, "Hay for the cows." There was something to that too, by God!

She gave birth to a boy. Friday at the synagogue the sexton stood up before the Ark, pounded on the reading table, and announced, "The wealthy Reb Gimpel invites the congregation to a feast in honor of the birth of a son." The whole House of Prayer rang with laughter. My face was flaming. But there was nothing I could do. After all, I *was* the one responsible for the circumcision honors and rituals.

Half the town came running. You couldn't wedge another soul in. Women brought peppered chickpeas, and there was a keg of beer from the tavern. I ate and drank as much as anyone, and they all congratulated me. Then there was a circumcision, and I named the boy after my father, may he rest in peace. When all were gone and I was left with my wife alone, she thrust her head through the bed curtain and called me to her.

"Gimpel," said she, "why are you silent? Has your ship gone and sunk?"

"What shall I say?" I answered. "A fine thing you've done to me! If my mother had known of it she'd have died a second time."

She said, "Are you crazy, or what?"

"How can you make such a fool," I said, "of one who should be the lord and master?"

"What's the matter with you?" she said. "What have you taken it into your head to imagine?"

I saw that I must speak bluntly and openly. "Do you think this is the way to use an orphan?" I said. "You have borne a bastard."

She answered, "Drive this foolishness out of your head. The child is yours."

"How can he be mine?" I argued. "He was born seventeen weeks after the wedding."

She told me then that he was premature. I said, "Isn't he a little too premature?" She said she had had a grandmother who carried just as short a time and she resembled this grandmother of hers as one drop of water does another. She swore to it with such oaths that you would have believed a peasant at the fair if he had used them. To tell the plain truth, I didn't believe her; but when I talked it over next day with the schoolmaster he told me that the very same thing had happened to Adam and Eve. Two they went up to bed, and four they descended.

"There isn't a woman in the world who is not the granddaughter of Eve," he said.

That was how it was—they argued me dumb. But then, who really knows how such things are?

I began to forget my sorrow. I loved the child madly, and he loved me too. As soon as he saw me he'd wave his little hands and want me to pick him up, and when he was colicky I was the only one who could pacify him. I bought him a little bone teething ring and a little gilded cap. He was forever catching the evil eye from someone, and then I had to run to get one of those abracadabras for him that would get him out of it. I worked like an ox. You know how expenses go up when there's an infant in the house. I don't want to lie about it; I didn't dislike Elka either, for that matter. She swore at me and cursed, and I couldn't get enough of her. What strength she had! One of her looks could rob you of the power of speech. And her orations! Pitch and sulfur, that's what they were full of, and yet somehow also full of charm. I adored her every word. She gave me bloody wounds though.

In the evening I brought her a white loaf as well as a dark one, and also poppy seed rolls I baked myself. I thieved because of her and swiped everything I could lay hands on, macaroons, raisins, almonds, cakes. I hope I may be forgiven for stealing from the Saturday pots the women left to warm in the baker's oven. I would take out scraps of meat, a chunk of pudding, a chicken leg or head, a piece of tripe, whatever I could nip quickly. She ate and became fat and handsome.

I had to sleep away from home all during the week, at the bakery. On Friday nights when I got home she always made an excuse of some sort. Either she had heartburn, or a stitch in the side, or hiccups, or headaches. You know what women's excuses are. I had a bitter time of it. It was rough. To add to it, this little brother of hers, the bastard, was growing bigger. He'd put lumps on me, and when I wanted to hit back she'd open her mouth and curse so powerfully I saw a green haze floating before my eyes. Ten times a day she threatened to divorce me. Another man in my place would have taken French leave and disappeared. But I'm the type that bears it and says nothing. What's one to do? Shoulders are from God, and burdens too.

One night there was a calamity in the bakery; the oven burst, and we almost had a fire. There was nothing to do but go home, so I went home. Let me, I thought, also taste the joy of sleeping in bed in midweek. I didn't want to wake the sleeping mite and tiptoed into the house. Coming in, it seemed to me that I heard not the snoring of one but, as it were, a double snore, one a thin enough snore and the other like the snoring of a slaughtered ox. Oh, I didn't like that! I didn't like it at all. I went up to the bed, and things suddenly turned black. Next to Elka lay a man's form. Another in my place would have made an uproar, and enough noise to rouse the whole town, but the thought occurred to me that I might wake the child. A little thing like that—why frighten a little swallow like that, I thought. All right then, I went back to the bakery and stretched out on a sack of flour, and till morning I never shut an eye. I shivered as if I had had malaria. "Enough of being a donkey," I said to myself. "Gimpel isn't going to be a sucker all his life. There's a limit even to the foolishness of a fool like Gimpel."

In the morning I went to the rabbi to get advice, and it made a great commotion in the town. They sent the beadle for Elka right away. She came, carrying the child. And what do you think she did? She denied it, denied everything, bone and stone! "He's out of his head," she said. "I know nothing of dreams or divinations." They yelled at her, warned her, hammered on the table, but she stuck to her guns: it was a false accusation, she said.

The butchers and the horse traders took her part. One of the lads from the slaughterhouse came by and said to me, "We've got our eye on you, you're a marked man." Meanwhile the child started to bear down and soiled itself. In the rabbinical court there was an Ark of the Covenant, and they couldn't allow that, so they sent Elka away.

I said to the rabbi, "What shall I do?"

"You must divorce her at once," said he.

"And what if she refuses?" I asked.

He said, "You must serve the divorce, that's all you'll have to do."

I said, "Well, all right, Rabbi. Let me think about it."

"There's nothing to think about," said he. "You mustn't remain under the same roof with her."

"And if I want to see the child?" I asked.

"Let her go, the harlot," said he, "and her brood of bastards with her."

The verdict he gave was that I mustn't even cross her threshold—never again, as long as I should live.

During the day it didn't bother me so much. I thought, It was bound to happen, the abscess had to burst. But at night when I stretched out upon the sacks I felt it all very bitterly. A longing took me, for her and for the child. I wanted to be angry, but that's my misfortune exactly, I don't have it in me to be really angry. In the first place—this was how my thoughts went—there's bound to be a slip sometimes. You can't live without errors. Probably that lad who was with her led her on and gave her presents and what not, and women are often long on hair and short on sense, and so he got around her. And then since she denies it so, maybe I was only seeing things? Hallucinations do happen. You see a figure or a manikin or something, but when you come up closer it's nothing, there's not a thing there. And if that's so, I'm doing her an injustice. And when I got so far in my thoughts I started to weep. I sobbed so that I wet the flour where I lay. In the morning I went to the rabbi and told him that I had made a mistake. The rabbi wrote on with his quill, and he said that if that were so he would have to reconsider the whole case. Until he had finished I wasn't to go near my wife, but I might send her bread and money by messenger.

3

Nine months passed before all the rabbis could come to an agreement. Letters went back and forth. I hadn't realized that there could be so much erudition about a matter like this.

Meantime Elka gave birth to still another child, a girl this time. On the Sabbath I went to the synagogue and invoked a blessing on her.

They called me up to the Torah, and I named the child for my mother-in-law, may she rest in peace. The louts and loudmouths of the town who came into the bakery gave me a going-over. All Frampol refreshed its spirits because of my trouble and grief. However, I resolved that I would always believe what I was told. What's the good of *not* believing? Today it's your wife you don't believe; tomorrow it's God himself you won't take stock in.

By an apprentice who was her neighbor I sent her daily a corn or a wheat loaf, or a piece of pastry, rolls or bagels, or, when I got the chance, a slab of pudding, a slice of honeycake, or wedding strudel—whatever came my way. The apprentice was a goodhearted lad, and more than once he added something on his own. He had formerly annoyed me a lot, plucking my nose and digging me in the ribs, but when he started to be a visitor to my house he became kind and friendly. "Hey, you, Gimpel," he said to me, "you have a very decent little wife and two fine kids. You don't deserve them."

"But the things people say about her," I said.

"Well, they have long tongues," he said, "and nothing to do with them but babble. Ignore it as you ignore the cold of last winter."

One day the rabbi sent for me and said, "Are you certain, Gimpel, that you were wrong about your wife?"

I said, "I'm certain."

"Why, but look here! You yourself saw it."

"It must have been a shadow," I said.

"The shadow of what?"

"Just of one of the beams, I think."

"You can go home then. You owe thanks to the Yanover rabbi. He found an obscure reference in Maimonides that favored you."

I seized the rabbi's hand and kissed it.

I wanted to run home immediately. It's no small thing to be separated for so long a time from wife and child. Then I reflected, I'd better go back to work now, and go home in the evening. I said nothing to anyone, although as far as my heart was concerned it was like one of the holy days. The women teased and twitted me as they did every day, but my thought was, Go on, with your loose talk. The truth is out, like the oil upon the water. Maimonides says it's right, and therefore it is right!

At night, when I had covered the dough to let it rise, I took my share of bread and a little sack of flour and started homeward. The moon was full and the stars were glistening, something to terrify the soul. I hurried onward, and before me darted a long shadow. It was winter, and a fresh snow had fallen. I had a mind to sing, but it was growing late and I didn't want to wake the householders. Then I felt like whistling, but remembered that you don't whistle at night because it brings the demons out. So I was silent and walked as fast as I could.

Dogs in the Christian yards barked at me when I passed, but I thought, Bark your teeth out! What are you but mere dogs? Whereas I am a man, the husband of a fine wife, the father of promising children.

As I approached the house my heart started to pound as though it were the heart of a criminal. I felt no fear, but my heart went thump! thump! Well, no drawing back. I quietly lifted the latch and went in. Elka was asleep. I looked at the infant's cradle. The shutter was closed, but the moon forced its way through the cracks. I saw the newborn child's face and loved it as soon as I saw it—immediately—each tiny bone.

Then I came nearer to the bed. And what did I see but the apprentice lying there beside Elka. The moon went out all at once. It was utterly black, and I trembled. My teeth chattered. The bread fell from my hands and my wife waked and said, "Who is that, ah?"

I muttered, "It's me."

"Gimpel?" she asked. "How come you're here? I thought it was forbidden."

"The rabbi said," I answered and shook as with a fever.

"Listen to me, Gimpel," she said, "go out to the shed and see if the goat's all right. It seems she's been sick." I have forgotten to say that we had a goat. When I heard she was unwell I went into the yard. The nanny goat was a good little creature. I had a nearly human feeling for her.

With hesitant steps I went up to the shed and opened the door. The goat stood there on her four feet. I felt her everywhere, drew her by the horns, examined her udders, and found nothing wrong. She had probably eaten too much bark. "Good night, little goat," I said. "Keep well." And the little beast answered with a "Maa" as though to thank me for the good will.

I went back. The apprentice had vanished.

"Where," I asked, "is the lad?"

"What lad?" my wife answered.

"What do you mean?" I said. "The apprentice. You were sleeping with him."

"The things I have dreamed this night and the night before," she said, "may they come true and lay you low, body and soul! An evil spirit has taken root in you and dazzles your sight." She screamed out, "You hateful creature! You moon calf! You spook! You uncouth man! Get out, or I'll scream all Frampol out of bed!"

Before I could move, her brother sprang out from behind the oven and struck me a blow on the back of the head. I thought he had broken my neck. I felt that something about me was deeply wrong, and I said, "Don't make a scandal. All that's needed now is that people should accuse me of raising spooks and dybbuks." For that was what she had meant. "No one will touch bread of my baking."

In short, I somehow calmed her.

"Well," she said, "that's enough. Lie down, and be shattered by wheels."

Next morning I called the apprentice aside. "Listen here, brother!" I said. And so on and so forth. "What do you say?" He stared at me as though I had dropped from the roof or something.

"I swear," he said, "you'd better go to an herb doctor or some healer. I'm afraid you have a screw loose, but I'll hush it up for you." And that's how the thing stood.

To make a long story short, I lived twenty years with my wife. She bore me six children, four daughters and two sons. All kinds of things happened, but I neither saw nor heard. I believed, and that's all. The rabbi recently said to me, "Belief in itself is beneficial. It is written that a good man lives by his faith."

Suddenly my wife took sick. It began with a trifle, a little growth upon the breast. But she evidently was not destined to live long; she had no years. I spent a fortune on her. I have forgotten to say that by this time I had a bakery of my own and in Frampol was considered to be something of a rich man. Daily the healer came, and every witch doctor in the neighborhood was brought. They decided to use leeches, and after that to try cupping. They even called a doctor from Lublin, but it was too late. Before she died she called me to her bed and said, "Forgive me, Gimpel."

I said, "What is there to forgive? You have been a good and faithful wife."

"Woe, Gimpel!" she said. "It was ugly how I deceived you all these years. I want to go clean to my Maker, and so I have to tell you that the children are not yours."

If I had been clouted on the head with a piece of wood it couldn't have bewildered me more.

"Whose are they?" I asked.

"I don't know," she said, "there were a lot . . . but they're not yours." And as she spoke she tossed her head to the side, her eyes turned glassy, and it was all up with Elka. On her whitened lips there remained a smile.

I imagined that, dead as she was, she was saying, "I deceived Gimpel. That was the meaning of my brief life."

4

One night, when the period of mourning was done, as I lay dreaming on the flour sacks, there came the Spirit of Evil himself and said to me, "Gimpel, why do you sleep?"

I said, "What should I be doing? Eating kreplach?"

"The whole world deceives you," he said, "and you ought to deceive the world in your turn."

"How can I deceive all the world?" I asked him.

He answered, "You might accumulate a bucket of urine every day and at night pour it into the dough. Let the sages of Frampol eat filth."

"What about judgment in the world to come?" I said.

"There is no world to come," he said. "They've sold you a bill of goods and talked you into believing you carried a cat in your belly. What nonsense!"

"Well then," I said, "and is there a God?"

He answered, "There is no God either."

"What," I said, "*is* there, then?"

"A thick mire."

He stood before my eyes with a goatish beard and horns, long toothed, and with a tail. Hearing such words, I wanted to snatch him by the tail, but I tumbled from the flour sacks and nearly broke a rib. Then it happened that I had to answer the call of nature, and, passing, I saw the risen dough, which seemed to say to me, "Do it!" In brief, I let myself be persuaded.

At dawn the apprentice came. We kneaded the bread, scattered caraway seeds on it, and set it to bake. Then the apprentice went away, and I was left sitting in the little trench by the oven, on a pile of rags. Well, Gimpel, I thought, you've revenged yourself on them for all the shame they've put on you. Outside the frost glittered, but it was warm beside the oven. The flames heated my face. I bent my head and fell into a doze.

I saw in a dream, at once, Elka in her shroud. She called to me, "What have you done, Gimpel?"

I said to her, "It's all your fault," and started to cry.

"You fool!" she said. "You fool! Because I was false is everything false too? I never deceived anyone but myself. I'm paying for it all, Gimpel. They spare you nothing here."

I looked at her face. It was black. I was startled and waked, and remained sitting dumb. I sensed that everything hung in the balance. A false step now and I'd lose eternal life. But God gave me his help. I seized the long shovel and took out the loaves, carried them into the yard, and started to dig a hole in the frozen earth.

My apprentice came back as I was doing it. "What are you doing, boss?" he said, and grew pale as a corpse.

"I know what I'm doing," I said, and I buried it all before his very eyes.

Then I went home, took my hoard from its hiding place, and divided it among the children. "I saw your mother tonight," I said. "She's turning black, poor thing."

They were so astounded they couldn't speak a word.

"Be well," I said, "and forget that such a one as Gimpel ever existed." I put on my short coat, a pair of boots, took the bag that held my prayer shawl in one hand, my stick in the other, and kissed the mezuzah. When people saw me in the street they were greatly surprised.

"Where are you going?" they said.

I answered, "Into the world." And so I departed from Frampol.

I wandered over the land, and good people did not neglect me. After many years I became old and white; I heard a great deal, many lies and falsehoods, but the longer I lived the more I understood that there were really no lies. Whatever doesn't really happen is dreamed at night. It happens to one if it doesn't happen to another, tomorrow if not today, or a century hence if not next year. What difference can it make? Often I heard tales of which I said, "Now this is a thing that cannot happen." But before a year had elapsed I heard that it actually had come to pass somewhere.

Going from place to place, eating at strange tables, it often happens that I spin yarns—improbable things that could never have happened—about devils, magicians, windmills, and the like. The children run after me, calling, "Grandfather, tell us a story." Sometimes they ask for particular stories, and I try to please them. A fat young boy once said to me, "Grandfather, it's the same story you told us before." The little rogue, he was right.

So it is with dreams too. It is many years since I left Frampol, but as soon as I shut my eyes I am there again. And whom do you think I see? Elka. She is standing by the washtub, as at our first encounter, but her face is shining and her eyes are as radiant as the eyes of a saint, and she speaks outlandish words to me, strange things. When I wake I have forgotten it all. But while the dream lasts I am comforted. She answers all my queries, and what comes out is that all is right. I weep and implore, "Let me be with you." And she consoles me and tells me to be patient. The time is nearer than it is far. Sometimes she strokes and kisses me and weeps upon my face. When I awaken I feel her lips and taste the salt of her tears.

No doubt the world is entirely an imaginary world, but it is only once removed from the true world. At the door of the hovel where I lie, there stands the plank on which the dead are taken away. The gravedigger Jew has his spade ready. The grave waits and the worms are hungry; the shrouds are prepared—I carry them in my beggar's sack. Another schnorrer is waiting to inherit my bed of straw. When the time comes I will go joyfully. Whatever may be there, it will be real, without complication, without ridicule, without deception. God be praised: there even Gimpel cannot be deceived.

---

1. What "good" does Gimpel hope to accomplish by believing those who fooled him? What explains his statement that, "I believed them, and I hope at least that did them some good."?
2. What does Gimpel mean when he says toward the end of his life that "the longer I lived the more I understood that there were really no lies"?
3. Is Singer asking readers to believe that acceptance of what life brings, no matter how absurd, is actually wisdom?

JEAN-PAUL SARTRE (1905–1980) was one of France's leading twentieth-century philosophers and literary writers. His work strongly advocates existentialist philosophy, emphasizing the freedom of human beings to assert their dignity and create their own values in an indifferent universe. A native of Paris, Sartre was active in the French Resistance during the German occupation in World War II. After the war, he became deeply engaged in Marxist movements, holding that literature and philosophy should serve political ends. In 1964, Sartre declined to accept the Nobel Prize in Literature. Though never married, he maintained a lifelong partnership with the writer Simone de Beauvoir. Among Sartre's major works are *L'être et le néant* (1943; *Being and Nothingness*, 1956), the novels *La nausée* (1938; *Nausea*, 1949) and *La mort dans l'âme* (1945; *Troubled Sleep*, 1950), the play *Huis clos* (1945; *No Exit*, 1946), and the memoir *Les mots* (1963; *Words*, 1964).

The Wall

They pushed us into a big white room and I began to blink because the light hurt my eyes. Then I saw a table and four men behind the table, civilians, looking over the papers. They had bunched another group of prisoners in the back and we had to cross the whole room to join them. There were several I knew and some others who must have been foreigners. The two in front of me were blond with round skulls; they looked alike. I suppose they were French. The smaller one kept hitching up his pants; nerves.

It lasted about three hours; I was dizzy and my head was empty; but the room was well heated and I found that pleasant enough: for the past twenty-four hours we hadn't stopped shivering. The guards brought the prisoners up to the table, one after the other. The four men asked each one his name and occupation. Most of the time they didn't go any further—or they would simply ask a question here and there:

"Did you have anything to do with the sabotage of munitions?" Or "Where were you the morning of the ninth and what were you doing?" They didn't listen to the answers or at least didn't seem to. They were quiet for a moment and then looking straight in front of them began to write. They asked Tom if it were true he was in the International Brigade; Tom couldn't tell them otherwise because of the papers they found in his coat. They didn't ask Juan anything but they wrote for a long time after he told them his name.

"My brother José is the anarchist," Juan said, "you know he isn't here any more. I don't belong to any party, I never had anything to do with politics."

They didn't answer. Juan went on, "I haven't done anything. I don't want to pay for somebody else."

His lips trembled. A guard shut him up and took him away. It was my turn.

"Your name is Pablo Ibbieta?"

"Yes."

The man looked at the papers and asked me, 'Where's Ramon Gris?"

"I don't know."

"You hid him in your house from the sixth to the nineteenth."

"No."

They wrote for a minute and then the guards took me out. In the corridor Tom and Juan were waiting between two guards. We started walking. Tom asked one of the guards, "So?"

"So what?" the guard said.

"Was that the cross-examination or the sentence?"

"Sentence," the guard said.

"What are they going to do with us?"

The guard answered dryly, "Sentence will be read in your cell."

As a matter of fact, our cell was one of the hospital cellars. It was terrifically cold there because of the drafts. We shivered all night and it wasn't much better during the day. I had spent the previous five days in a cell in a monastery, a sort of hole in the wall that must have dated from the middle ages: since there were a lot of prisoners and not much room, they locked us up anywhere. I didn't miss my cell; I hadn't suffered too much from the cold but I was alone; after a long time it gets irritating. In the cellar I had company. Juan hardly ever spoke: he was afraid and he was too young to have anything to say. But Tom was a good talker and he knew Spanish well.

There was a bench in the cellar and four mats. When they took us back we sat and waited in silence. After a long moment, Tom said, "We're screwed."

"I think so too," I said, "but I don't think they'll do anything to the kid."

"They don't have a thing against him," said Tom. "He's the brother of a militiaman and that's all."

I looked at Juan: he didn't seem to hear. Tom went on, "You know what they do in Saragossa? They lay the men down on the road and run over them with trucks. A Moroccan deserter told us that. They said it was to save ammunition."

"It doesn't save gas," I said.

I was annoyed at Tom: he shouldn't have said that.

"Then there's officers walking along the road," he went on, "supervising it all. They stick their hands in their pockets and smoke cigarettes. You think they finish off the guys? Hell no. They let them scream. Sometimes for an hour. The Moroccan said he damned near puked the first time."

"I don't believe they'll do that here," I said. "Unless they're really short on ammunition."

Day was coming in through four air holes and a round opening they had made in the ceiling on the left, and you could see the sky through it. Through this hole, usually closed by a trap, they unloaded coal into the cellar. Just below the hole there was a big pile of coal dust; it had been used to heat the hospital but since the beginning of the war the patients were evacuated and the coal stayed there, unused; sometimes it even got rained on because they had forgotten to close the trap.

Tom began to shiver. "Good Jesus Christ, I'm cold," he said. "Here it goes again."

He got up and began to do exercises. At each movement his shirt opened on his chest, white and hairy. He lay on his back, raised his legs in the air and bicycled. I saw his great rump trembling. Tom was husky but he had too much fat. I thought how rifle bullets or the sharp points of bayonets would soon be sunk into this mass of tender flesh as in a lump of butter. It wouldn't have made me feel like that if he'd been thin.

I wasn't exactly cold, but I couldn't feel my arms and shoulders any more. Sometimes I had the impression I was missing something and began to look around for my coat and then suddenly remembered they hadn't given me a coat. It was rather uncomfortable. They took our clothes and gave them to their soldiers leaving us only our shirts—and those canvas pants that hospital patients wear in the middle of summer. After a while Tom got up and sat next to me, breathing heavily.

"Warmer?"

"Good Christ, no. But I'm out of wind."

Around eight o'clock in the evening a major came in with two *falangistas*. He had a sheet of paper in his hand. He asked the guard, "What are the names of those three?"

"Steinbock, Ibbieta, and Mirbal," the guard said.

The major put on his eyeglasses and scanned the list, "Steinbock . . . Steinbock . . . oh yes . . . you are sentenced to death. You will be shot tomorrow morning." He went on looking. "The other two as well."

"That's not possible," Juan said. "Not me."

The major looked at him amazed. "What's your name?"

"Juan Mirbal," he said.

'Well, your name is there," said the major. "You're sentenced."

"I didn't do anything," Juan said.

The major shrugged his shoulders and turned to Tom and me.

"You're Basque?"

"Nobody is Basque."

He looked annoyed. "They told me there were three Basques. I'm not going to waste my time running after them. Then naturally you don't want a priest?"

We didn't even answer.

He said, "A Belgian doctor is coming shortly. He is authorized to spend the night with you." He made a military salute and left.

"What did I tell you," Tom said. "We get it."

"Yes," I said, "it's a rotten deal for the kid."

I said that to be decent but I didn't like the kid. His face was too thin and fear and suffering had disfigured it, twisting all his features. Three days before he was a smart sort of kid, not too bad; but now he looked like an old fairy and I thought how he'd never be young again, even if they were to let him go. It wouldn't have been too hard to have a little pity for him but pity disgusts me, or rather it horrifies me. He hadn't said anything more but he had turned gray; his face and hands were both gray. He sat down again and looked at the ground with round eyes. Tom was goodhearted, he wanted to take his arm, but the kid tore himself away violently and made a face.

"Let him alone," I said in a low voice, "you can see he's going to blubber."

Tom obeyed regretfully; he would have liked to comfort the kid, it would have passed his time and he wouldn't have been tempted to think about himself. But it annoyed me: I'd never thought about death because I never had any reason to, but now the reason was here and there was nothing to do but think about it.

Tom began to talk. "So you think you've knocked guys off, do you?" he asked me. I didn't answer. He began explaining to me that he had knocked off six since the beginning of August; he didn't realize the situation and I could tell he didn't *want* to realize it. I hadn't quite realized it myself, I wondered if it hurt much, I thought of bullets, I imagined their burning hail through my body. All that was beside the real question; but I was calm: we had all night to understand. After a while Tom stopped talking and I watched him out of the corner of my eye; I saw he too had turned gray and he looked rotten; I told myself "Now it starts." It was almost dark, a dim glow filtered through the air holes and the pile of coal and made a big stain beneath the spot of sky; I could already see a star through the hole in the ceiling: the night would be pure and icy.

The door opened and two guards came in, followed by a blond man in a tan uniform. He saluted us. "I am the doctor," he said. "I have authorization to help you in these trying hours."

He had an agreeable and distinguished voice. I said, "What do you want here?"

"I am at your disposal. I shall do all I can to make your last moments less difficult."

"What did you come here for? There are others, the hospital's full of them."

"I was sent here," he answered with a vague look. "Ah! Would you like to smoke?" he added hurriedly, "I have cigarettes and even cigars."

He offered us English cigarettes and *puros*, but we refused. I looked him in the eyes and he seemed irritated. I said to him, "You aren't here on an errand of mercy. Besides, I know you. I saw you with the fascists in the barracks yard the day I was arrested."

I was going to continue, but something surprising suddenly happened to me; the presence of this doctor no longer interested me. Generally when I'm on somebody I don't let go. But the desire to talk left me completely; I shrugged and turned my eyes away. A little later I raised my head; he was watching me curiously. The guards were sitting on a mat. Pedro, the tall thin one, was twiddling his thumbs, the other shook his head from time to time to keep from falling asleep.

"Do you want a light?" Pedro suddenly asked the doctor. The other nodded yes: I think he was about as smart as a log, but he surely wasn't bad. Looking in his cold blue eyes it seemed to me that his only sin was lack of imagination. Pedro went out and came back with an oil lamp which he set on the corner of the bench. It gave a bad light but it was better than nothing: they had left us in the dark the night before. For a long time I watched the circle of light the lamp made on the ceiling. I was fascinated. Then suddenly I woke up, the circle of light disappeared and I felt myself crushed under an enormous weight. It was not the thought of death, or fear; it was nameless. My cheeks burned and my head ached.

I shook myself and looked at my two friends. Tom had hidden his face in his hands. I could only see the fat white nape of his neck. Little Juan was the worst, his mouth was open and his nostrils trembled. The doctor went to him and put his hand on his shoulder to comfort him: but his eyes stayed cold. Then I saw the Belgian's hand drop stealthily along Juan's arm, down to the wrist. Juan paid no attention. The Belgian took his wrist between three fingers, distractedly, the same time drawing back a little and turning his back to me. But I leaned backward and saw him take a watch from his pocket and look at it for a moment, never letting go of the wrist. After a minute he let the hand fall inert and went and leaned his back against the wall, then, as if he suddenly remembered something very important which had to be jotted down on the spot, he took a notebook from his pocket and wrote a few lines. "Bastard," I thought angrily, "let him come and take my pulse. I'll shove my fist in his rotten face."

He didn't come but I felt him watching me. I raised my head and returned his look. Impersonally, he said to me, "Doesn't it seem cold to you here?" He looked cold, he was blue.

"I'm not cold," I told him.

He never took his hard eyes off me. Suddenly I understood and my hands went to my face: I was drenched in sweat. In this cellar, in the midst of winter, in the midst of drafts, I was sweating. I ran my hands through my hair, gummed together with perspiration; at the same time I saw my shirt was damp and sticking to my skin: I had been dripping for an hour and hadn't felt it. But that swine of a Belgian hadn't missed a thing; he had seen the drops rolling down my cheeks and thought: this is the manifestation of an almost pathological state of terror; and he had felt normal and proud of being alive because he was cold. I wanted to stand up and smash his face but no sooner had I made the slightest gesture than my rage and shame were wiped out; I fell back on the bench with indifference.

I satisfied myself by rubbing my neck with my handkerchief because now I felt the sweat dropping from my hair onto my neck and it was unpleasant. I soon gave up rubbing, it was useless; my handkerchief was already soaked and I was still sweating. My buttocks were sweating too and my damp trousers were glued to the bench.

Suddenly Juan spoke. "You're a doctor?"

"Yes," the Belgian said.

"Does it hurt . . . very long?"

"Huh? When . . . ? Oh, no," the Belgian said paternally. "Not at all. It's over quickly." He acted as though he were calming a cash customer.

"But I . . . they told me . . . sometimes they have to fire twice."

"Sometimes," the Belgian said, nodding. "It may happen that the first volley reaches no vital organs."

"Then they have to reload their rifles and aim all over again?" He thought for a moment and then added hoarsely, "That takes time!"

He had a terrible fear of suffering, it was all he thought about: it was his age. I never thought much about it and it wasn't fear of suffering that made me sweat.

I got up and walked to the pile of coal dust. Tom jumped up and threw me a hateful look: I had annoyed him because my shoes squeaked.

I wondered if my face looked as frightened as his: I saw he was sweating too. The sky was superb, no light filtered into the dark corner and I had only to raise my head to see the Big Dipper. But it wasn't like it had been: the night before I could see a great piece of sky from my monastery cell and each hour of the day brought me a different memory. Morning, when the sky was a hard, light blue, I thought of beaches on the Atlantic; at noon I saw the sun and I remembered a bar in Seville where I drank manzanilla and ate olives and anchovies; afternoons I was in the shade and I thought of the deep shadow which spreads over half a bullring leaving the other half shimmering in sunlight; it was really hard to see the whole world reflected in the sky like that. But now I could watch the sky as much as I pleased, it no longer evoked anything in me. I liked that better. I came back and sat near Tom. A long moment passed.

Tom began speaking in a low voice. He had to talk, without that he wouldn't have been able to recognize himself in his own mind. I thought he was talking to me but he wasn't looking at me. He was undoubtedly afraid to see me as I was, gray and sweating: we were alike and worse than mirrors of each other. He watched the Belgian, the living.

"Do you understand?" he said. "I don't understand."

I began to speak in a low voice too. I watched the Belgian. "Why? What's the matter?"

"Something is going to happen to us that I can't understand."

There was a strange smell about Tom. It seemed to me I was more sensitive than usual to odors. I grinned. "You'll understand in a while."

"It isn't clear," he said obstinately. "I want to be brave but first I have to know. . . . Listen, they're going to take us into the courtyard. Good. They're going to stand up in front of us. How many?"

"I don't know. Five or eight. Not more."

"All right. There'll be eight. Someone'll holler 'aim!' and I'll see eight rifles looking at me. I'll think how I'd like to get inside the wall, I'll push against it with my back . . . with every ounce of strength I have, but the wall will stay, like in a nightmare. I can imagine all that. If you only knew how well I can imagine it."

"All right, all right!" I said, "I can imagine it too."

"It must hurt like hell. You know, they aim at the eyes and mouth to disfigure you," he added mechanically. "I can feel the wounds already; I've had pains in my head and in my neck for the past hour. Not real pains. Worse. This is what I'm going to feel tomorrow morning. And then what?"

I well understood what he meant but I didn't want to act as if I did. I had pains too, pains in my body like a crowd of tiny scars. I couldn't get used to it. But I was like him, I attached no importance to it. "After," I said, "you'll be pushing up daisies."

He began to talk to himself: he never stopped watching the Belgian. The Belgian didn't seem to be listening. I knew what he had come to do; he wasn't interested in what we thought; he came to watch our bodies, bodies dying in agony while yet alive.

"It's like a nightmare," Tom was saying. "You want to think something, you always have the impression that it's all right, that you're going to understand and then it slips, it escapes you and fades away. I tell myself there will be nothing afterwards. But I don't understand what it means. Sometimes I almost can . . . and then it fades away and I start thinking about the pains again, bullets, explosions. I'm a materialist, I swear it to you; I'm not going crazy. But something's the matter. I see my corpse; that's not hard but *I'm* the one who sees it, with *my* eyes. I've got to think . . . think that I won't see anything anymore and the world will go on for the others. We aren't made to think that, Pablo. Believe me: I've already stayed up a whole night waiting for something. But this isn't the same: this will creep up behind us, Pablo, and we won't be able to prepare for it."

"Shut up," I said. "Do you want me to call a priest?"

He didn't answer. I had already noticed he had the tendency to act like a prophet and call me Pablo, speaking in a toneless voice. I didn't like that: but it seems all the Irish are that way. I had the vague impression he smelled of urine. Fundamentally, I hadn't much sympathy for Tom and I didn't see why, under the pretext of dying together, I should have any more. It would have been different with some others. With Ramon Gris, for example. But I felt alone between Tom and Juan. I liked that better, anyhow: with Ramon I might have been more deeply moved. But I was terribly hard just then and I wanted to stay hard.

He kept on chewing his words, with something like distraction. He certainly talked to keep himself from thinking. He smelled of urine like an old prostate case. Naturally, I agreed with him, I could have said everything he said: it isn't *natural* to die. And since I was going to die, nothing seemed natural to me, not this pile of coal dust, or the bench, or Pedro's ugly face. Only it didn't please me to think the same things as Tom. And I knew that, all through the night, every five minutes, we would keep on thinking things at the same time. I looked at him sideways and for the first time he seemed strange to me: he wore death on his face. My pride was wounded: for the past twenty-four hours I had lived next to Tom, I had listened to him, I had spoken to him and I knew we had nothing in common. And now we looked as much alike as twin brothers, simply because we were going to die together. Tom took my hand without looking at me.

"Pablo, I wonder . . . I wonder if it's really true that everything ends."

I took my hand away and said, "Look between your feet, you pig."

There was a big puddle between his feet and drops fell from his pantsleg.

"What is it?" he asked, frightened.

"You're pissing in your pants," I told him.

"It isn't true," he said furiously. "I'm not pissing. I don't feel anything."

The Belgian approached us. He asked with false solicitude, "Do you feel ill?"

Tom did not answer. The Belgian looked at the puddle and said nothing.

"I don't know what it is," Tom said ferociously. "But I'm not afraid. I swear I'm not afraid."

The Belgian did not answer. Tom got up and went to piss in a corner. He came back buttoning his fly, and sat down without a word. The Belgian was taking notes.

All three of us watched him because he was alive. He had the motions of a living human being, the cares of a living human being; he shivered in the cellar the way the living are supposed to shiver; he had an obedient, well-fed body. The rest of us hardly felt ours—not in the same way anyhow. I wanted to feel my pants between my legs but I didn't dare; I watched the Belgian, balancing on his legs, master of his muscles, someone who could think about tomorrow. There we were, three bloodless shadows; we watched him and we sucked his life like vampires.

Finally he went over to little Juan. Did he want to feel his neck for some professional motive or was he obeying an impulse of charity? If he was acting by charity it was the only time during the whole night.

He caressed Juan's head and neck. The kid let himself be handled, his eyes never leaving him, then suddenly, he seized the hand and looked at it strangely. He held the Belgian's hand between his own two hands and there was nothing pleasant about them, two gray pincers gripping this fat and reddish hand. I suspected what was going to happen and Tom must have suspected it too: but the Belgian didn't see a thing, he smiled paternally. After a moment the kid brought the fat red hand to his mouth and tried to bite it. The Belgian pulled away quickly and stumbled back against the wall. For a second he looked at us with horror, he must have suddenly understood that we were not men like him. I began to laugh and one of the guards jumped up. The other was asleep, his wide-open eyes were blank.

I felt relaxed and overexcited at the same time. I didn't want to think anymore about what would happen at dawn, at death. It made no sense. I only found words or emptiness. But as soon as I tried to think of anything else I saw rifle barrels pointing at me. Perhaps I lived through my execution twenty times; once I even thought it was for good: I must have slept a minute. They were dragging me to the wall and I was struggling; I was asking for mercy. I woke up with a start and looked at the Belgian: I was afraid I might have cried out in my sleep. But he was stroking his moustache, he hadn't noticed anything. If I had wanted to, I think I could have slept a while; I had been awake for forty-eight hours. I was at the end of my rope. But I didn't want to lose two hours of life: they would come to wake me up at dawn, I would follow them, stupefied with sleep and I would have croaked without so much as an "Oof!"; I didn't want that, I didn't want to die like an animal, I wanted to understand. Then I was afraid of having nightmares. I got up, walked back and forth, and, to change my ideas, I began to think about my past life. A crowd of memories came back to me pell-mell. There were good and bad ones—or at least I called them that *before*. There were faces and incidents. I saw the face of a little novillero who was gored in Valencia during the *feria*, the face of one of my uncles, the face of Ramon Gris. I remembered my whole life: how I was out of work for three months in 1926, how I almost starved to death. I remembered a night I spent on a beach in Granada: I hadn't eaten for three days. I was angry, I didn't want to die. That made me smile. How madly I ran after happiness, after women, after liberty. Why? I wanted to free Spain, I admired Pi y Margall, I joined the anarchist movement, I spoke in public meetings: I took everything as seriously as if I were immortal.

At that moment I felt that I had my whole life in front of me and I thought, "It's a damned lie." It was worth nothing because it was finished. I wondered how I'd been able to walk, to laugh with the girls: I wouldn't have moved so much as my little finger if I had only imagined I would die like this. My life was in front of me, shut, closed, like a bag and yet everything inside of it was unfinished. For an instant I tried to judge it. I wanted to tell myself, this is a beautiful life. But I couldn't pass judgment on it; it was only a sketch; I had spent my time counterfeiting eternity, I had understood nothing. I missed nothing: there were so many things I could have missed, the taste of manzanilla or the baths I took in summer in a little creek near Cadiz; but death had disenchanted everything.

The Belgian suddenly had a bright idea. "My friends," he told us, "I will undertake—if the military administration will allow it—to send a message for you, a souvenir to those who love you. . . ."

Tom mumbled, "I don't have anybody."

I said nothing. Tom waited an instant then looked at me with curiosity. "You don't have anything to say to Concha?"

"No."

I hated this tender complicity: it was my own fault, I had talked about Concha the night before, I should have controlled myself. I was with her for a year. Last night I would have given an arm to see her again for five minutes. That was why I talked about her, it was stronger than I was. Now I had no more desire to see her, I had nothing more to say to her. I would not even have wanted to hold her in my arms: my body filled me with horror because it was gray and sweating—and

I wasn't sure that her body didn't fill me with horror. Concha would cry when she found out I was dead, she would have no taste for life for months afterward. But I was still the one who was going to die. I thought of her soft, beautiful eyes. When she looked at me something passed from her to me. But I knew it was over: if she looked at me *now* the look would stay in her eyes, it wouldn't reach me. I was alone.

Tom was alone too but not in the same way. Sitting cross-legged, he had begun to stare at the bench with a sort of smile, he looked amazed. He put out his hand and touched the wood cautiously as if he were afraid of breaking something, then drew back his hand quickly and shuddered. If I had been Tom I wouldn't have amused myself by touching the bench; this was some more Irish nonsense, but I too found that objects had a funny look: they were more obliterated, less dense than usual. It was enough for me to look at the bench, the lamp, the pile of coal dust, to feel that I was going to die. Naturally I couldn't think clearly about my death but I saw it everywhere, on things, in the way things fell back and kept their distance, discreetly, as people who speak quietly at the bedside of a dying man. It was *his* death which Tom had just touched on the bench.

In the state I was in, if someone had come and told me I could go home quietly, that they would leave me my life whole, it would have left me cold: several hours or several years of waiting is all the same when you have lost the illusion of being eternal. I clung to nothing, in a way I was calm. But it was a horrible calm—because of my body; my body, I saw with its eyes, I heard with its ears, but it was no longer me; it sweated and trembled by itself and I didn't recognize it anymore. I had to touch it and look at it to find out what was happening, as if it were the body of someone else. At times I could still feel it, I felt sinkings, and fallings, as when you're in a plane taking a nose dive, or I felt my heart beating. But that didn't reassure me. Everything that came from my body was all cockeyed. Most of the time it was quiet and I felt no more than a sort of weight, a filthy presence against me; I had the impression of being tied to an enormous vermin. Once I felt my pants and I felt they were damp; I didn't know whether it was sweat or urine, but I went to piss on the coal pile as a precaution.

The Belgian took out his watch, looked at it. He said, "It is three thirty."

Bastard! He must have done it on purpose. Tom jumped; he hadn't noticed time was running out; night surrounded us like a shapeless, somber mass, I couldn't even remember that it had begun.

Little Juan began to cry. He wrung his hands, pleaded, "I don't want to die. I don't want to die."

He ran across the whole cellar waving his arms in the air then fell sobbing on one of the mats. Tom watched him with mournful eyes, without the slightest desire to console him. Because it wasn't worth the trouble: the kid made more noise than we did, but he was less touched: he was like a sick man who defends himself against illness by fever. It's much more serious when there isn't any fever.

He wept: I could clearly see he was pitying himself; he wasn't thinking about death. For one second, one single second, I wanted to weep myself, to weep with pity for myself. But the opposite happened: I glanced at the kid, I saw his thin sobbing shoulders and felt inhuman: I could pity neither the others nor myself. I said to myself, "I want to die cleanly."

Tom had gotten up, he placed himself just under the round opening and began to watch for daylight. I was determined to die cleanly and I only thought of that. But ever since the doctor told us the time, I felt time flying, flowing away drop by drop.

It was still dark when I heard Tom's voice: "Do you hear them?"

Men were marching in the courtyard.

"Yes."

"What the hell are they doing? They can't shoot in the dark."

After a while we heard no more. I said to Tom, "It's day."

Pedro got up, yawning, and came to blow out the lamp. He said to his buddy, "Cold as hell."

The cellar was all gray. We heard shots in the distance.

"It's starting," I told Tom. "They must do it in the court in the rear."

Tom asked the doctor for a cigarette. I didn't want one; I didn't want cigarettes or alcohol. From that moment on they didn't stop firing.

"Do you realize what's happening?" Tom said.

He wanted to add something but kept quiet, watching the door. The door opened and a lieutenant came in with four soldiers. Tom dropped his cigarette.

"Steinbock?"

Tom didn't answer. Pedro pointed him out.

"Juan Mirbal?"

"On the mat."

"Get up," the lieutenant said.

Juan did not move. Two soldiers took him under the arms and set him on his feet. But he fell as soon as they released him.

The soldiers hesitated.

"He's not the first sick one," said the lieutenant. "You two carry him; they'll fix it up down there."

He turned to Tom. "Let's go."

Tom went out between two soldiers. Two others followed, carrying the kid by the armpits. He hadn't fainted; his eyes were wide open and tears ran down his cheeks. When I wanted to go out the lieutenant stopped me.

"You Ibbieta?"

"Yes."

"You wait here; they'll come for you later."

They left. The Belgian and the two jailers left too, I was alone. I did not understand what was happening to me but I would have liked it better if they had gotten it over with right away. I heard shots at almost regular intervals; I shook with each one of them. I wanted to scream and tear out my hair. But I gritted my teeth and pushed my hands in my pockets because I wanted to stay clean.

After an hour they came to get me and led me to the first floor, to a small room that smelt of cigars and where the heat was stifling. There were two officers sitting smoking in the armchairs, papers on their knees.

"You're Ibbieta?"

"Yes."

"Where is Ramon Gris?"

"I don't know."

The one questioning me was short and fat. His eyes were hard behind his glasses. He said to me, "Come here."

I went to him. He got up and took my arms, staring at me with a look that should have pushed me into the earth. At the same time he pinched my biceps with all his might. It wasn't to hurt me, it was only a game: he wanted to dominate me. He also thought he had to blow his stinking breath square in my face. We stayed for a moment like that, and I almost felt like laughing. It takes a lot to intimidate a man who is going to die; it didn't work. He pushed me back violently and sat down again. He said, "It's his life against yours. You can have yours if you tell us where he is."

These men dolled up with their riding crops and boots were still going to die. A little later than I, but not too much. They busied themselves looking for names in their crumpled papers, they ran after other men to imprison or suppress them; they had opinions on the future of Spain and on other subjects. Their little activities seemed shocking and burlesqued to me; I couldn't put myself in their place, I thought they were insane. The little man was still looking at me, whipping his boots with the riding crop. All his gestures were calculated to give him the look of a live and ferocious beast.

"So? You understand?"

"I don't know where Gris is," I answered. "I thought he was in Madrid."

The other officer raised his pale hand indolently. This indolence was also calculated. I saw through all their little schemes and I was stupefied to find there were men who amused themselves that way.

"You have a quarter of an hour to think it over," he said slowly. "Take him to the laundry, bring him back in fifteen minutes. If he still refuses he will be executed on the spot."

They knew what they were doing: I had passed the night in waiting; then they had made me wait an hour in the cellar while they shot Tom and Juan and now they were locking me up in the laundry; they must have prepared their game the night before. They told themselves that nerves eventually wear out and they hoped to get me that way.

They were badly mistaken. In the laundry I sat on a stool because I felt very weak and I began to think. But not about their proposition. Of course I knew where Gris was; he was hiding with his cousins, four kilometers from the city. I also knew that I would not reveal his hiding place unless they tortured me (but they didn't seem to be thinking about that). All that was perfectly regulated, definite, and in no way interested me. Only I would have liked to understand the reasons for my conduct. I would rather die than give up Gris. Why? I didn't like

Ramon Gris anymore. My friendship for him had died a little while before dawn at the same time as my love for Concha, at the same time as my desire to live. Undoubtedly I thought highly of him: he was tough. But it was not for this reason that I consented to die in his place; his life had no more value than mine; no life had value. They were going to slap a man up against a wall and shoot at him till he died, whether it was I or Gris or somebody else made no difference. I knew he was more useful than I to the cause of Spain but I thought to hell with Spain and anarchy; nothing was important. Yet I was there, I could save my skin and give up Gris and I refused to do it. I found that somehow comic; it was obstinacy. I thought, "I must be stubborn!" And a droll sort of gaiety spread over me.

They came for me and brought me back to the two officers. A rat ran out from under my feet and that amused me. I turned to one of the falangistas and said, "Did you see the rat?"

He didn't answer. He was very sober, he took himself seriously. I wanted to laugh but I held myself back because I was afraid that once I got started I wouldn't be able to stop. The falangista had a moustache. I said to him again, "You ought to shave off your moustache, idiot." I thought it funny that he would let the hairs of his living being invade his face. He kicked me without great conviction and I kept quiet.

"Well," said the fat officer, "have you thought about it?"

I looked at them with curiosity, as insects of a very rare species. I told them, "I know where he is. He is hidden in the cemetery. In a vault or in the gravediggers' shack."

It was a farce. I wanted to see them stand up, buckle their belts and give orders busily.

They jumped to their feet. "Let's go. Molés, go get fifteen men from Lieutenant Lopez. You," the fat man said, "I'll let you off if you're telling the truth, but it'll cost you plenty if you're making monkeys out of us."

They left in a great clatter and I waited peacefully under the guard of falangistas. From time to time I smiled, thinking about the spectacle they would make. I felt stunned and malicious. I imagined them lifting up tombstones, opening the doors of the vaults one by one. I represented this situation to myself as if I had been someone else: this prisoner obstinately playing the hero, these grim falangistas with their moustaches and their men in uniform running among the graves; it was irresistibly funny. After half an hour the little fat man came back alone. I thought he had come to give the orders to execute me. The others must have stayed in the cemetery.

The officer looked at me. He didn't look at all sheepish. "Take him into the big courtyard with the others," he said. "After the military operations a regular court will decide what happens to him."

"Then they're not . . . not going to shoot me . . . ?"

"Not now, anyway. What happens afterwards is none of my business."

I still didn't understand. I asked, "But why . . . ?"

He shrugged his shoulders without answering and the soldiers took me away. In the big courtyard there were about a hundred prisoners, women, children and a few old men. I began walking around the central grassplot, I was stupefied. At noon they let us eat in the mess hall. Two or three people questioned me. I must have known them, but I didn't answer: I didn't even know where I was.

Around evening they pushed about ten new prisoners into the court. I recognized Garcia, the baker. He said, "What damned luck you have! I didn't think I'd see you alive."

"They sentenced me to death," I said, "and then they changed their minds. I don't know why."

"They arrested me at two o'clock," Garcia said.

"Why?" Garcia had nothing to do with .politics.

"I don't know," he said. "They arrest everybody who doesn't think the way they do. He lowered his voice. "They got Gris."

I began to tremble. "When?"

"This morning. He messed it up. He left his cousin's on Tuesday because they had an argument. There were plenty of people to hide him but he didn't want to owe anything to anybody. He said, 'I'd go and hide in Ibbieta's place, but they got him, so I'll go hide in the cemetery."

"In the cemetery?"

"Yes. What a fool. Of course they went by there this morning, that was sure to happen. They found him in the gravediggers' shack. He shot at them and they got him."

"In the cemetery!"

Everything began to spin and I found myself sitting on the ground: I laughed so hard I cried.

1. Why does Pablo Ibbieta dislike his fellow prisoner Juan?
2. Why does Ibbieta decide not to give up the actual whereabouts of Gris, even though he doesn't care anymore about Gris as a person or the anarchist political cause?
3. Does Ibbieta betray Gris?
4. Is Ibietta's resolve broken by his captors? If so, at what point?

JOHN CHEEVER (1912–1982) was born in Quincy, Massachusetts. He sold his first short story to the *New Republic* at the age of seventeen. During his career he published most of his fiction in the *New Yorker,* and his collection *The Stories of John Cheever* (1978) earned the Pulitzer Prize for fiction. He also wrote five novels, including *The Wapshot Chronicle* (1957), which won the National Book Award. In his stories, Cheever explores the human tendencies toward both self-loathing and self-deception, all the while imbuing his characters—generally successful, suburban, white commuters—with the desire for aesthetic and spiritual wholeness. Nearly destroyed by alcoholism, Cheever stopped drinking in 1975. Toward the end of his life, he summed up what his writing was about: "Literature is the only continuous and coherent account of our struggle to be illustrious, a monument of aspiration, a vast pilgrimage."

The Country Husband

To begin at the beginning, the airplane from Minneapolis in which Francis Weed was traveling east ran into heavy weather. The sky had been a hazy blue, with the clouds below the plane lying so close together that nothing could be seen of the earth. Then mist began to form outside the windows, and they flew into a white cloud of such density that it reflected the exhaust fires. The color of the cloud darkened to gray, and the plane began to rock. Francis had been in heavy weather before, but he had never been shaken up so much. The man in the seat beside him pulled a flask out of his pocket and took a drink. Francis smiled at his neighbor, but the man looked away; he wasn't sharing his painkiller with anyone. The plane began to drop and flounder wildly. A child was crying. The air in the cabin was overheated and stale, and Francis's left foot went to sleep. He read a little from a paper book that he had bought at the airport, but the violence of the storm divided his attention. It was black outside the ports. The exhaust fires blazed and shed sparks in the dark, and, inside, the shaded lights, the stuffiness, and the window curtains gave the cabin an atmosphere of intense and misplaced domesticity. Then the lights flickered and went out. "You know what I've always wanted to do?" the man beside Francis said suddenly. "I've always wanted to buy a farm in New Hampshire and raise beef cattle." The stewardess announced that they were going to make an emergency landing. All but the children saw in their minds the spreading wings of the Angel of Death. The pilot could be heard singing faintly, "I've got sixpence, jolly, jolly sixpence. I've got sixpence to last me all my life . . ." There was no other sound.

The loud groaning of the hydraulic valves swallowed up the pilot's song, and there was a shrieking high in the air, like automobile brakes, and the plane hit flat on its belly in a cornfield and shook them so violently that an old man up forward howled, "Me kidneys! Me kidneys!" The stewardess flung open the door, and someone opened an emergency door at the back, letting in the sweet noise of their continuing mortality—the idle splash and smell of a heavy rain. Anxious for their lives, they filed out of the doors and scattered over the cornfield in all directions, praying that the thread would hold. It did. Nothing happened. When it was clear that the plane would not burn or explode, the crew and the stewardess gathered the passengers together and led them to the shelter of a barn. They were not far from Philadelphia, and in a little while a string of taxis took them into the city. "It's just like the Marne," someone said, but there was surprisingly little relaxation of that suspiciousness with which many Americans regard their fellow travelers.

In Philadelphia, Francis Weed got a train to New York. At the end of that journey, he crossed the city and caught just as it was about to pull out the commuting train that he took five nights a week to his home in Shady Hill.

He sat with Trace Bearden. "You know, I was in that plane that just crashed outside Philadelphia," he said. "We came down in a field . . ." He had traveled faster than the newspapers or the rain, and the weather in New York was sunny and mild. It was a day in late September, as fragrant and shapely as an apple. Trace listened to the story, but how could he get excited? Francis had no powers that would let him re-create a brush with death—particularly in the atmosphere of a commuting train, journeying through a sunny countryside where already, in the slum gardens, there were signs of harvest. Trace picked up his newspaper, and Francis was left alone with his thoughts. He said good night to Trace on the platform at Shady Hill and drove in his secondhand Volkswagen up to the Blenhollow neighborhood, where he lived.

The Weeds' Dutch colonial house was larger than it appeared to be from the driveway. The living room was spacious and divided like Gaul into three parts. Around an ell to the left as one entered from the vestibule was the long table, laid for six, with candles and a bowl of fruit in the center. The sounds and smells that came from the open kitchen door were appetizing, for Julia Weed was a good cook. The largest part of the living room centered on a fireplace. On the right were some bookshelves and a piano. The room was polished and tranquil, and from the windows that opened to the west there was some late-summer sunlight, brilliant and as clear as water. Nothing here was neglected; nothing had not been burnished. It was not the kind of household where, after prying open a stuck cigarette box, you would find an old shirt button and a tarnished nickel. The hearth was swept, the roses on the piano were reflected in the polish of the broad top, and there was an album of Schubert waltzes on the rack. Louisa Weed, a pretty girl of nine, was looking out the western windows. Her younger brother Henry was standing beside her. Her still younger brother, Toby, was studying the figures of some tonsured monks drinking beer on the polished brass of the woodbox. Francis, taking off his hat and putting down his paper, was not consciously pleased with the scene; he was not that reflective. It was his element, his creation, and he returned to it with that sense of lightness and strength with which any creature returns to his home. "Hi, everybody," he said. "The plane from Minneapolis . . ."

Nine times out of ten, Francis would be greeted with affection, but tonight the children are absorbed in their own antagonisms. Francis had not finished his sentence about the plane crash before Henry plants a kick in Louisa's behind. Louisa swings around, saying, "*Damn* you!" Francis makes the mistake of scolding Louisa for bad language before he punishes Henry. Now Louisa turns on her father and accuses him of favoritism. Henry is always right; she is persecuted and lonely; her lot is hopeless. Francis turns to his son, but the boy has justification for the kick—she hit him first; she hit him on the ear, which is dangerous. Louisa agrees with this passionately. She hit him on the ear, and she *meant* to hit him on the ear, because he messed up her china collection. Henry says that this is a lie. Little Toby turns away from the woodbox to throw in some evidence for Louisa. Henry claps his hand over little Toby's mouth. Francis separates the two boys but accidentally pushes Toby into the woodbox. Toby begins to cry. Louisa is already crying. Just then, Julia Weed comes into that part of the room where the table is laid. She is a pretty, intelligent woman, and the white in her hair is premature. She does not seem to notice the fracas. "Hello, darling," she says serenely to Francis. "Wash your hands, everyone. Dinner is ready." She strikes a match and lights the six candles in this vale of tears.

This simple announcement, like the war cries of the Scottish chieftains, only refreshes the ferocity of the combatants. Louisa gives Henry a blow on the shoulder. Henry, although he seldom cries, has pitched nine innings and is tired. He bursts into tears. Little Toby discovers a splinter in his hand and begins to howl. Francis says loudly that he has been in a plane crash and that he is tired. Julia appears again from the kitchen and, still ignoring the chaos, asks Francis to go upstairs and tell Helen that everything is ready. Francis is happy to go; it is like getting back to headquarters company. He is planning to tell his oldest daughter about the airplane crash, but Helen is lying on her bed reading a *True Romance* magazine, and the first thing Francis does is to take the magazine from her hand and remind Helen that he has forbidden her to buy it. She did not buy it, Helen replies. It was given to her by her best friend, Bessie Black. Everybody reads *True Romance.* Bessie Black's father reads *True Romance.* There isn't a girl in Helen's class who doesn't read *True Romance.* Francis expresses his detestation of the magazine and then tells her that dinner is ready—although from the sounds downstairs it doesn't seem so. Helen follows him down the stairs. Julia has seated herself in the candlelight and spread a napkin over her lap. Neither Louisa nor Henry has come to the table. Little Toby is still howling, lying face down on the floor. Francis speaks to him gently: "Daddy was in a plane crash this afternoon, Toby. Don't you want to hear about it?" Toby goes on crying. "If you don't come to the table now, Toby," Francis says, "I'll have to send you to bed without any supper." The little boy rises, gives him a cutting look, flies up the stairs to his bedroom, and slams the door. "Oh dear," Julia says, and starts to go after him. Francis says that she will spoil him. Julia says that Toby is ten pounds underweight and has to be encouraged to eat. Winter is coming, and he will spend the cold months in bed unless he has his dinner. Julia goes upstairs. Francis sits down at the table with Helen. Helen is suffering from the dismal feeling of having read too intently on a fine day, and she gives her father and the room a jaded look. She doesn't understand about the plane crash, because there wasn't a drop of rain in Shady Hill.

Julia returns with Toby, and they all sit down and are served. "Do I have to look at that big, fat slob?" Henry says, of Louisa. Everybody but Toby enters into this skirmish, and it rages up and down the table for five minutes. Toward the end, Henry puts his napkin over his head and, trying to eat that way, spills spinach all over his shirt. Francis asks Julia if the children couldn't have their dinner earlier. Julia's guns are loaded for this. She can't cook two dinners and lay two tables. She paints with lightning strokes that panorama of drudgery in which her youth, her beauty, and her wit have been lost. Francis says that he must be understood; he was nearly killed in an airplane crash, and he doesn't like to come home every night to a battlefield. Now Julia is deeply concerned. Her voice trembles. He doesn't come home every night to a battlefield. The accusation is stupid and mean. Everything was tranquil until he arrived. She stops speaking, puts down her knife and fork, and looks into her plate as if it is a gulf. She begins to cry. "Poor Mummy!" Toby says, and when Julia gets up from the table, drying her tears with a napkin, Toby goes to her side. "Poor Mummy," he says. "Poor Mummy!" And they climb the stairs together. The other children drift away from the battlefield, and Francis goes into the back garden for a cigarette and some air.

It was a pleasant garden, with walks and flower beds and places to sit. The sunset had nearly burned out, but there was still plenty of light. Put into a thoughtful mood by the crash and the battle, Francis listened to the evening sounds of Shady Hill. "Varmints! Rascals!" old Mr. Nixon shouted to the squirrels in his bird-feeding station. "Avaunt and quit my sight!" A door slammed. Someone was cutting grass. Then Donald Goslin, who lived at the corner, began to play the *Moonlight Sonata*. He did this nearly every night. He threw the tempo out the window and played it *rubato* from beginning to end, like an outpouring of tearful petulance, lonesomeness, and self-pity—of everything it was Beethoven's greatness not to know. The music rang up and down the street beneath the trees like an appeal for love, for tenderness, aimed at some lovely housemaid—some fresh-faced, homesick girl from Galway, looking at old snapshots in her third-floor room. "Here, Jupiter, here, Jupiter," Francis called to the Mercers' retriever. Jupiter crashed through the tomato vines with the remains of a felt hat in his mouth.

Jupiter was an anomaly. His retrieving instincts and his high spirits were out of place in Shady Hill. He was as black as coal, with a long, alert, intelligent, rakehell face. His eyes gleamed with mischief, and he held his head high. It was the fierce, heavily collared dog's head that appears in heraldry, in tapestry, and that used to appear on umbrella handles and walking sticks. Jupiter went where he pleased, ransacking wastebaskets, clotheslines, garbage pails, and shoe bags. He broke up garden parties and tennis matches, and got mixed up in the processional at Christ Church on Sunday, barking at the men in red dresses. He crashed through old Mr. Nixon's rose garden two or three times a day, cutting a wide swath through the Condesa de Sastagos, and as soon as Donald Goslin lighted his barbecue fire on Thursday nights, Jupiter would get the scent. Nothing the Goslins did could drive him away. Sticks and stones and rude commands only moved him to the edge of the terrace, where he remained, with his gallant and heraldic muzzle, waiting for Donald Goslin to turn his back and reach for the salt. Then he would spring onto the terrace, lift the steak lightly off the fire, and run away with the Goslins' dinner. Jupiter's days were numbered. The Wrightsons' German gardener or the Farquarsons' cook would soon poison him. Even old Mr. Nixon might put some arsenic in the garbage that Jupiter loved. "Here, Jupiter, Jupiter!" Francis called, but the dog pranced off, shaking the hat in his white teeth. Looking at the windows of his house, Francis saw that Julia had come down and was blowing out the candles.

Julia and Francis Weed went out a great deal. Julia was well liked and gregarious, and her love of parties sprang from a most natural dread of chaos and loneliness. She went through her morning mail with real anxiety, looking for invitations, and she usually found some, but she was insatiable, and if she had gone out seven nights a week, it would not have cured her of a reflective look—the look of someone who hears distant music—for she would always suppose that there was a more brilliant party somewhere else. Francis limited her to two weeknight parties, putting a flexible interpretation on Friday, and rode through the weekend like a dory in a gale. The day after the airplane crash, the Weeds were to have dinner with the Farquarsons.

Francis got home late from town, and Julia got the sitter while he dressed, and then hurried him out of the house. The party was small and pleasant, and Francis settled down to enjoy himself. A new maid passed the drinks. Her hair was dark, and her face was round and pale and seemed familiar to Francis. He had not developed his memory as a sentimental faculty. Wood smoke, lilac, and other such perfumes did not stir him, and his memory was something like his appendix—a vestigial repository. It was not his limitation at all to be unable to escape the past; it was perhaps his limitation that he had escaped it so successfully. He might have seen the maid at other parties, he might have seen her taking a walk on Sunday afternoons, but in either case he would not be searching his memory now. Her face was, in a wonderful way, a moon face—Norman or Irish—but it was not beautiful enough to account for his feeling that he had seen her before, in circumstances that he ought to be able to remember. He asked Nellie Farquarson who she was. Nellie said that the maid had come through an agency, and that her home was Trenon, in Normandy—a small place with a church and a restaurant that Nellie had once visited. While Nellie talked on about her travels abroad, Francis realized where he had seen the woman before. It had been at the end of the war. He had left a replacement depot with some other men and taken a three-day pass in Trenon. On their second day, they had walked out to a crossroads to see the public chastisement of a young woman who had lived with the German commandant during the Occupation.

It was a cool morning in the fall. The sky was overcast, and poured down onto the dirt crossroads a very discouraging light. They were on high land and could see how like one another the shapes of the clouds and the hills were as they stretched off toward the sea. The prisoner arrived sitting on a three-legged stool in a farm cart. She stood by the cart while the mayor read the accusation and the sentence. Her head was bent and her face was set in that empty half smile behind which the whipped soul is suspended. When the mayor was finished, she undid her hair and let it fall across her back. A little man with a gray mustache cut off her hair with shears and dropped it on the ground. Then, with a bowl of soapy water and a straight razor, he shaved her skull clean. A woman approached and began to undo the fastenings of her clothes, but the prisoner pushed her aside and undressed herself. When she pulled her chemise over her head and threw it on the ground, she was naked. The women jeered; the men were still. There was no change in the falseness or the plaintiveness of the prisoner's smile. The cold wind made her white skin rough and hardened the nipples of her breasts. The jeering ended gradually, put down by the recognition of their common humanity. One woman spat on her, but some inviolable grandeur in her nakedness lasted through the ordeal. When the crowd was quiet, she turned—she had begun to cry—and, with nothing on but a pair of worn black shoes and stockings, walked down the dirt road alone away from the village. The round white face had aged a little, but there was no question but that the maid who passed his cocktails and later served Francis his dinner was the woman who had been punished at the crossroads.

The war seemed now so distant and that world where the cost of partisanship had been death or torture so long ago. Francis had lost track of the men who had been with him in Vesey. He could not count on Julia's discretion. He could not tell anyone. And if he had told the story now, at the dinner table, it would have been a social as well as a human error. The people in the Farquarsons' living room seemed united in their tacit claim that there had been no past, no war—that there was no danger or trouble in the world. In the recorded history of human arrangements, this extraordinary meeting would have fallen into place, but the atmosphere of Shady Hill made the memory unseemly and impolite. The prisoner withdrew after passing the coffee, but the encounter left Francis feeling languid; it had opened his memory and his senses, and left them dilated. Julia went into the house. Francis stayed in the car to take the sitter home.

Expecting to see Mrs. Henlein, the old lady who usually stayed with the children, he was surprised when a young girl opened the door and came out onto the lighted stoop. She stayed in the light to count her textbooks. She was frowning and beautiful. Now, the world is full of beautiful young girls, but Francis saw here the difference between beauty and perfection. All those endearing flaws, moles, birthmarks, and healed wounds were missing, and he experienced in his consciousness that moment when music breaks glass, and felt a pang of recognition as strange, deep, and wonderful as anything in his life. It hung from her frown, from an impalpable darkness in her face—a look that impressed him as a direct appeal for love. When she had counted her books, she came down the steps and opened the car door. In the light, he saw that her checks were wet. She got in and shut the door.

"You're new," Francis said.

"Yes. Mrs. Henlein is sick. I'm Anne Murchison."

"Did the children give you any trouble?"

"Oh, no, no." She turned and smiled at him unhappily in the dim dashboard light. Her light hair caught on the collar of her jacket, and she shook her head to set it loose.

"You've been crying."

"Yes."

"I hope it was nothing that happened in our house."

"No, no, it was nothing that happened in your house." Her voice was bleak. "It's no secret. Everybody in the village knows. Daddy's an alcoholic, and he just called me from some saloon and gave me a piece of his mind. He thinks I'm immoral. He called just before Mrs. Weed came back."

"I'm sorry."

"Oh, *Lord*!" She gasped and began to cry. She turned toward Francis, and he took her in his arms and let her cry on his shoulder. She shook in his embrace, and this movement accentuated his sense of the fineness of her flesh and bone. The layers of their clothing felt thin, and when her shuddering began to diminish, it was so much like a paroxysm of love that Francis lost his head and pulled her roughly against him. She drew away. "I live on Belleview Avenue," she said. "You go down Lansing Street to the railroad bridge."

"All right." He started the car.

"You turn left at that traffic light. . . . Now you turn right here and go straight on toward the tracks."

The road Francis took brought him out of his own neighborhood, across the tracks, and toward the river, to a street where the near-poor lived, in houses whose peaked gables and trimmings of wooden lace conveyed the purest feelings of pride and romance, although the houses themselves could not have offered much privacy or comfort, they were all so small. The street was dark, and, stirred by the grace and beauty of the troubled girl, he seemed, in turning into it, to have come into the deepest part of some submerged memory. In the distance, he saw a porch light burning. It was the only one, and she said that the house with the light was where she lived. When he stopped the car, he could see beyond the porch light into a dimly lighted hallway with an old-fashioned clothes tree. "Well, here we are," he said, conscious that a young man would have said something different.

She did not move her hands from the books, where they were folded, and she turned and faced him. There were tears of lust in his eyes. Determinedly—not sadly—he opened the door on his side and walked around to open hers. He took her free hand, letting his fingers in between hers, climbed at her side the two concrete steps, and went up a narrow walk through a front garden where dahlias, marigolds, and roses—things that had withstood the light frosts—still bloomed, and made a bittersweet smell in the night air. At the steps, she freed her hand and then turned and kissed him swiftly. Then she crossed the porch and shut the door. The porch light went out, then the light in the hall. A second later, a light went on upstairs at the side of the house, shining into a tree that was still covered with leaves. It took her only a few minutes to undress and get into bed, and then the house was dark.

Julia was asleep when Francis got home. He opened a second window and got into bed to shut his eyes on that night, but as soon as they were shut—as soon as he had dropped off to sleep—the girl entered his mind, moving with perfect freedom through its shut doors and filling chamber after chamber with her light, her perfume, and the music of her voice. He was crossing the Atlantic with her on the old *Mauretania* and, later, living with her in Paris. When he woke from his dream, he got up and smoked a cigarette at the open window. Getting back into bed, he cast around in his mind for something he desired to do that would injure no one, and he thought of skiing. Up through the dimness in his mind rose the image of a mountain deep in snow. It was late in the day. Wherever his eyes looked, he saw broad and heartening things. Over his shoulder, there was a snow-filled valley, rising into wooded hills where the trees dimmed the whiteness like a sparse coat of hair. The cold deadened all sound but the loud, iron clanking of the lift machinery. The light on the trails was blue, and it was harder than it had been a minute or two earlier to pick the turns, harder to judge—now that the snow was all deep blue—the crust, the ice, the bare spots, and the deep piles of dry powder. Down the mountain he swung, matching his speed against the contours of a slope that had been formed in the first ice age, seeking with ardor some simplicity of feeling and circumstance. Night fell then, and he drank a martini with some old friend in a dirty country bar.

In the morning, Francis's snow-covered mountain was gone, and he was left with his vivid memories of Paris and the *Mauretania*. He had been bitten gravely. He washed his body, shaved his jaws, drank his coffee, and missed the seven-thirty-one. The train pulled out just as he brought his car to the station, and the longing he felt for the coaches as they drew stubbornly away from him reminded him of the humors of love. He waited for the eight-two, on what was now an empty platform. It was a clear morning; the morning seemed thrown like a gleaming bridge of light over his mixed affairs. His spirits were feverish and high. The image of the girl seemed to put him into a relationship to the world that was mysterious and enthralling. Cars were beginning to fill up the parking lot, and he noticed that those that had driven down from the high land above Shady Hill were white with hoarfrost. This first clear sign of autumn thrilled him. An express train—a night train from Buffalo or Albany—came down the tracks between the platforms, and he saw that the roofs of the foremost cars were covered with a skin of ice. Struck by the miraculous physicalness of everything, he smiled at the passengers in the dining car, who could be seen eating eggs and wiping their mouths with napkins as they traveled. The sleeping-car compartments, with their soiled bed linen, trailed through the fresh morning like a string of rooming-house windows. Then he saw an extraordinary thing; at one of the bedroom windows sat an unclothed woman of exceptional beauty, combing her golden hair. She passed like an apparition through Shady Hill, combing and combing her hair, and

Francis followed her with his eyes until she was out of sight. Then old Mrs. Wrightson joined him on the platform and began to talk.

"Well, I guess you must be surprised to see me here the third morning in a row," she said, "but because of my window curtains I'm becoming a regular commuter. The curtains I bought on Monday I returned on Tuesday, and the curtains I bought Tuesday I'm returning today. On Monday, I got exactly what I wanted—it's a wool tapestry with roses and birds—but when I got them home, I found they were the wrong length. Well, I exchanged them yesterday, and when I got them home, I found they were still the wrong length. Now I'm praying to high heaven that the decorator will have them in the right length, because you know my house, you *know* my living room windows, and you can imagine what a problem they present. I don't know what to do with them."

"I know what to do with them," Francis said.

"What?"

"Paint them black on the inside, and shut up."

There was a gasp from Mrs. Wrightson, and Francis looked down at her to be sure that she knew he meant to be rude. She turned and walked away from him, so damaged in spirit that she limped. A wonderful feeling enveloped him, as if light were being shaken about him, and he thought again of Venus combing and combing her hair as she drifted through the Bronx. The realization of how many years had passed since he had enjoyed being deliberately impolite sobered him. Among his friends and neighbors, there were brilliant and gifted people—he saw that—but many of them, also, were bores and fools, and he had made the mistake of listening to them all with equal attention. He had confused a lack of discrimination with Christian love, and the confusion seemed general and destructive. He was grateful to the girl for this bracing sensation of independence. Birds were singing—cardinals and the last of the robins. The sky shone like enamel. Even the smell of ink from his morning paper honed his appetite for life, and the world that was spread out around him was plainly a paradise.

If Francis had believed in some hierarchy of love—in spirits armed with hunting bows, in the capriciousness of Venus and Eros—or even in magical potions, philters, and stews, in scapulae and quarters of the moon, it might have explained his susceptibility and his feverish high spirits. The autumnal loves of middle age are well publicized, and he guessed that he was face to face with one of these, but there was not a trace of autumn in what he felt. He wanted to sport in the green woods, scratch where he itched, and drink from the same cup.

His secretary, Miss Rainey, was late that morning—she went to a psychiatrist three mornings a week—and when she came in, Francis wondered what advice a psychiatrist would have for him. But the girl promised to bring back into his life something like the sound of music. The realization that this music might lead him straight to a trial for statutory rape at the county courthouse collapsed his happiness. The photograph of his four children laughing into the camera on the beach at Gay Head reproached him. On the letterhead of his firm there was a drawing of the Laocoön, and the figure of the priest and his sons in the coils of the snake appeared to him to have the deepest meaning.

He had lunch with Pinky Trabert. At a conversational level, the mores of his friends were robust and elastic, but he knew that the moral card house would come down on them all—on Julia and the children as well—if he got caught taking advantage of a babysitter. Looking back over the recent history of Shady Hill for some precedent, he found there was none. There was no turpitude; there had not been a divorce since he lived there; there had not even been a breath of scandal. Things seemed arranged with more propriety even than in the Kingdom of Heaven. After leaving Pinky, Francis went to a jeweler's and bought the girl a bracelet. How happy this clandestine purchase made him, how stuffy and comical the jeweler's clerks seemed, how sweet the women who passed at his back smelled! On Fifth Avenue, passing Atlas with his shoulders bent under the weight of the world, Francis thought of the strenuousness of containing his physicalness within the patterns he had chosen.

He did not know when he would see the girl next. He had the bracelet in his inside pocket when he got home. Opening the door of his house, he found her in the hall. Her back was to him, and she turned when she heard the door close. Her smile was open and loving. Her perfection stunned him like a fine day—a day after a thunderstorm. He seized her and covered her lips with his, and she struggled but she did not have to struggle for long, because just then little Gertrude Flannery appeared from somewhere and said, "Oh, Mr. Weed . . ."

Gertrude was a stray. She had been born with a taste for exploration, and she did not have it in her to center her life with her affectionate parents. People who did not know the Flannerys concluded from Gertrude's behavior that she was the child of a bitterly divided family, where drunken quarrels were the rule. This was not true. The fact that little Gertrude's clothing was ragged and thin was her own triumph over her mother's struggle to dress her warmly and neatly. Garrulous, skinny, and unwashed, she drifted from house to house around the Blenhollow neighborhood, forming and breaking alliances based on an attachment to babies, animals, children her own age, adolescents, and sometimes adults. Opening your front door in the morning, you would find Gertrude sitting on your stoop. Going into the bathroom to shave, you would find Gertrude using the toilet. Looking into your son's crib, you would find it empty, and, looking further, you would find that Gertrude had pushed him in his baby carriage into the next village. She was helpful, pervasive, honest, hungry, and loyal. She never went home of her own choice. When the time to go arrived, she was indifferent to all its signs. "Go home, Gertrude," people could be heard saying in one house or another, night after night. "Go home, Gertrude. It's time for you to go home now, Gertrude." "You had better go home and get your supper, Gertrude." "I told you to go home twenty minutes ago, Gertrude." "Your mother will be worrying about you, Gertrude." "Go home, Gertrude, go home."

There are times when the lines around the human eye seem like shelves of eroded stone and when the staring eye itself strikes us with such a wilderness of animal feeling that we are at a loss. The look Francis gave the little girl was ugly and queer, and it frightened her. He reached into his pockets—his hands were shaking—and took out a quarter. "Go home, Gertrude, go home, and don't tell anyone, Gertrude. Don't—" He choked and ran into the living room as Julia called down to him from upstairs to hurry and dress.

The thought that he would drive Anne Murchison home later that night ran like a golden thread through the events of the party that Francis and Julia went to, and he laughed uproariously at dull jokes, dried a tear when Mabel Mercer told him about the death of her kitten, and stretched, yawned, sighed, and grunted like any other man with a rendezvous at the back of his mind. The bracelet was in his pocket. As he sat talking, the smell of grass was in his nose, and he was wondering where he would park the car. Nobody lived in the old Parker mansion, and the driveway was used as a lovers' lane. Townsend Street was a dead end, and he could park there, beyond the last house. The old lane that used to connect Elm Street to the riverbanks was overgrown, but he had walked there with his children, and he could drive his car deep enough into the brushwoods to be concealed.

The Weeds were the last to leave the party, and their host and hostess spoke of their own married happiness while they all four stood in the hallway saying good night. "She's my girl," their host said, squeezing his wife. "She's my blue sky. After sixteen years, I still bite her shoulders. She makes me feel like Hannibal crossing the Alps."

The Weeds drove home in silence. Francis brought the car up the driveway and sat still, with the motor running. "You can put the car in the garage," Julia said as she got out. "I told the Murchison girl she could leave at eleven. Someone drove her home." She shut the door, and Francis sat in the dark. He would be spared nothing then, it seemed, that a fool was not spared: ravening lewdness, jealousy, this hurt to his feelings that put tears in his eyes, even scorn—for he could see clearly the image he now presented, his arms spread over the steering wheel and his head buried in them for love.

Francis had been a dedicated Boy Scout when he was young, and, remembering the precepts of his youth, he left his office early the next afternoon and played some round-robin squash, but, with his body toned up by exercise and a shower, he realized that he might better have stayed at his desk. It was a frosty night when he got home. The air smelled sharply of change. When he stepped into the house, he sensed an unusual stir. The children were in their best clothes, and when Julia came down, she was wearing a lavender dress and her diamond sunburst. She explained the stir: Mr. Hubber was coming at seven to take their photograph for the Christmas card. She had put out Francis's blue suit and a tie with some color in it, because the picture was going to be in color this year. Julia was lighthearted at the thought of being photographed for Christmas. It was the kind of ceremony she enjoyed.

Francis went upstairs to change his clothes. He was tired from the day's work and tired with longing, and sitting on the edge of the bed had the effect of deepening his weariness. He thought of Anne Murchison, and the physical need to express himself, instead of being restrained by the pink lamps of Julia's dressing table, engulfed him. He went to Julia's desk, took a piece of writing paper, and began to write on it. "Dear Anne, I love you, I love you, I love you . . ." No one would see the letter, and he used no restraint. He used phrases like "heavenly bliss," and "love nest." He salivated, sighed, and trembled. When Julia called him to come down, the abyss between his fantasy and the practical world opened so wide that he felt it affected the muscles of his heart.

Julia and the children were on the stoop, and the photographer and his assistant had set up a double battery of floodlights to show the family and the architectural beauty of the entrance to their house. People who had come home on a late train slowed their cars to see the Weeds being photographed for their Christmas card. A few waved and called to the family. It took half an hour of smiling and wetting their lips before Mr. Hubber was satisfied. The heat of the lights made an unfresh smell in the frosty air, and when they were turned off, they lingered on the retina of Francis's eyes.

Later that night, while Francis and Julia were drinking their coffee in the living room, the doorbell rang. Julia answered the door and let in Clayton Thomas. He had come to pay for some theatre tickets that she had given his mother some time ago, and that Helen Thomas had scrupulously insisted on paying for, though Julia had asked her not to. Julia invited him in to have a cup of coffee. "I won't have any coffee," Clayton said, "but I will come in for a minute." He followed her into the living room, said good evening to Francis, and sat awkwardly in a chair.

Clayton's father had been killed in the war, and the young man's fatherlessness surrounded him like an element. This may have been conspicuous in Shady Hill because the Thomases were the only family that lacked a piece; all the other marriages were intact and productive. Clayton was in his second or third year of college, and he and his mother lived alone in a large house, which she hoped to sell. Clayton had once made some trouble. Years ago, he had stolen some money and run away; he had got to California before they caught up with him. He was tall and homely, wore horn-rimmed glasses, and spoke in a deep voice.

"When do you go back to college, Clayton?" Francis asked.

"I'm not going back," Clayton said. "Mother doesn't have the money, and there's no sense in all this pretense. I'm going to get a job, and if we sell the house, we'll take an apartment in New York."

"Won't you miss Shady Hill?" Julia asked.

"No," Clayton said. "I don't like it."

"Why not?" Francis asked.

"Well, there's a lot here I don't approve of," Clayton said gravely. "Things like the club dances. Last Saturday night, I looked in toward the end and saw Mr. Granner trying to put Mrs. Minot into the trophy case. They were both drunk. I disapprove of so much drinking."

"It was Saturday night," Francis said.

"And all the dovecotes are phony," Clayton said. "And the way people clutter up their lives. I've thought about it a lot, and what seems to me to be really wrong with Shady Hill is that it doesn't have any future. So much energy is spent in perpetuating the place—in keeping out undesirables, and so forth—that the only idea of the future anyone has is just more and more commuting trains and more parties. I don't think that's healthy. I think people ought to be able to dream big dreams about the future. I think people ought to be able to dream great dreams."

"It's too bad you couldn't continue with college," Julia said.

"I wanted to go to divinity school," Clayton said.

"What's your church?" Francis asked.

"Unitarian, Theosophist, Transcendentalist, Humanist," Clayton said.

"Wasn't Emerson a transcendentalist?" Julia asked.

"I mean the English transcendentalists," Clayton said. "All the American transcendentalists were goops."

"What kind of job do you expect to get?" Francis asked.

"Well, I'd like to work for a publisher," Clayton said, "but everyone tells me there's nothing doing. But it's the kind of thing I'm interested in. I'm writing a long verse play about good and evil. Uncle Charlie might get me into a bank, and that would be good for me. I need the discipline. I have a long way to go in forming my character. I have some terrible habits. I talk too much. I think I ought to take vows of silence. I ought to try not to speak for a week, and discipline myself. I've thought of making a retreat at one of the Episcopalian monasteries, but I don't like Trinitarianism."

"Do you have any girlfriends?" Francis asked.

"I'm engaged to be married," Clayton said. "Of course, I'm not old enough or rich enough to have my engagement observed or respected or anything, but I bought a simulated emerald for Anne Murchison with the money I made cutting lawns this summer. We're going to be married as soon as she finishes school."

Francis recoiled at the mention of the girl's name. Then a dingy light seemed to emanate from his spirit, showing everything—Julia, the boy, the chairs—in their true colorlessness. It was like a bitter turn of the weather.

"We're going to have a large family," Clayton said. "Her father's a terrible rummy, and I've had my hard times, and we want to have lots of children. Oh, she's wonderful, Mr. and Mrs. Weed, and we have so much in common. We like all the same things. We sent out the same Christmas card last year without planning it, and we both have an allergy to tomatoes, and our eyebrows grow together in the middle. Well, good night."

Julia went to the door with him. When she returned, Francis said that Clayton was lazy, irresponsible, affected, and smelly. Julia said that Francis seemed to be getting intolerant; the Thomas boy was young and should be given a chance. Julia had noticed other cases where Francis had been short-tempered. "Mrs. Wrightson has asked everyone in Shady Hill to her anniversary party but us," she said.

"I'm sorry, Julia."

"Do you know why they didn't ask us?"

"Why?"

"Because you insulted Mrs. Wrightson."

"Then you know about it?"

"June Masterson told me. She was standing behind you."

Julia walked in front of the sofa with a small step that expressed, Francis knew, a feeling of anger.

"I did insult Mrs. Wrightson, Julia, and I meant to. I've never liked her parties, and I'm glad she's dropped us."

"What about Helen?"

"How does Helen come into this?"

"Mrs. Wrightson's the one who decides who goes to the assemblies."

"You mean she can keep Helen from going to the dances?"

"Yes."

"I hadn't thought of that."

"Oh. I knew you hadn't thought of it," Julia cried, thrusting hilt-deep into this chink of his armor. "And it makes me furious to see this kind of stupid thoughtlessness wreck everyone's happiness."

"I don't think I've wrecked anyone's happiness."

"Mrs. Wrightson runs Shady Hill and has run it for the last forty years. I don't know what makes you think that in a community like this you can indulge every impulse you have to be insulting, vulgar, and offensive."

"I have very good manners," Francis said, trying to give the evening a turn toward the light.

"Damn you, Francis Weed!" Julia cried, and the spit of her words struck him in the face. "I've worked hard for the social position we enjoy in this place, and I won't stand by and see you wreck it. You must have understood when you settled here that you couldn't expect to live like a bear in a cave."

"I've got to express my likes and dislikes."

"You can conceal your dislikes. You don't have to meet everything head on, like a child. Unless you're anxious to be a social leper. It's no accident that we get asked out a great deal! It's no accident that Helen has so many friends. How would you like to spend your Saturday nights at the movies? How would you like to spend your Sundays raking up dead leaves? How would you like it if your daughter spent the assembly nights sitting at her window, listening to the music from the club? How would you like it—" He did something then that was, after all, not so unaccountable, since her words seemed to raise up between them a wall so deadening that he gagged. He struck her full in the face. She staggered and then, a moment later, seemed composed. She went up the stairs to their room. She didn't slam the door. When Francis followed, a few minutes later, he found her packing a suitcase.

"Julia, I'm very sorry."

"It doesn't matter," she said. She was crying.

"Where do you think you're going?"

"I don't know. I just looked at a timetable. There's an eleven-sixteen into New York. I'll take that."

"You can't go, Julia."

"I can't stay. I know that."

"I'm sorry about Mrs. Wrightson, Julia, and I'm—"

"It doesn't matter about Mrs. Wrightson. That isn't the trouble."

"What is the trouble?"

"You don't love me."

"I do love you, Julia."

"No, you don't."

"Julia, I do love you, and I would like to be as we were—sweet and bawdy and dark—but now there are so many people."

"You hate me."

"I don't hate you, Julia."

"You have no idea of how much you hate me. I think it's subconscious. You don't realize the cruel things you've done."

"What cruel things, Julia?"

"The cruel acts your subconscious drives you to in order to express your hatred of me."

"What, Julia?"

"I've never complained."

"Tell me."

"Your clothes."

"What do you mean?"

"I mean the way you leave your dirty clothes around in order to express your subconscious hatred of me."

"I don't understand."

"I mean your dirty socks and your dirty pajamas and your dirty underwear and your dirty shirts!" She rose from kneeling by the suitcase and faced him, her eyes blazing and her voice ringing with emotion. "I'm talking about the fact that you've never learned to hang up anything. You just leave your clothes all over the floor where they drop, in order to humiliate me. You do it on purpose!" She fell on the bed, sobbing.

"Julia, darling!" he said, but when she felt his hand on her shoulder she got up.

"Leave me alone," she said. "I have to go." She brushed past him to the closet and came back with a dress. "I'm not taking any of the things you've given me," she said. "I'm leaving my pearls and the fur jacket."

"Oh, Julia!" Her figure, so helpless in its self-deceptions, bent over the suitcase made him nearly sick with pity. She did not understand how desolate her life would be without him. She didn't understand the hours that working women have to keep. She didn't understand that most of her friendships existed within the framework of their marriage, and that without this she would find herself alone. She didn't understand about travel, about hotels, about money. "Julia, I can't let you go! What you don't understand, Julia, is that you've come to be dependent on me."

She tossed her head back and covered her face with her hands. "Did you say that *I* was dependent on *you*?" she asked. "Is that what you said? And who is it that tells you what time to get up in the morning and when to go to bed at night? Who is it that prepares your meals and picks up your dirty clothes and invites your friends to dinner? If it weren't for me, your neckties would be greasy and your clothing would be full of moth holes. You were alone when I met you, Francis Weed, and you'll be alone when I leave. When Mother asked you for a list to send out invitations to our wedding, how many names did you have to give her? Fourteen!"

"Cleveland wasn't my home, Julia."

"And how many of your friends came to the church? Two!"

"Cleveland wasn't my home, Julia."

"Since I'm not taking the fur jacket," she said quietly, "you'd better put it back into storage. There's an insurance policy on the pearls that comes due in January. The name of the laundry and the maid's telephone number—all those things are in my desk. I hope you won't drink too much, Francis. I hope that nothing bad will happen to you. If you do get into serious trouble you can call me."

"Oh, my darling, I can't let you go!" Francis said. "I can't let you go, Julia!" He took her in his arms.

"I guess I'd better stay and take care of you for a little while longer," she said.

Riding to work in the morning, Francis saw the girl walk down the aisle of the coach. He was surprised; he hadn't realized that the school she went to was in the city, but she was carrying books, she seemed to be going to school. His surprise delayed his reaction, but then he got up clumsily and stepped into the aisle. Several people had come between them, but he could see her ahead of him, waiting for someone to open the car door, and then, as the train swerved, putting out her hand to support herself as she crossed the platform into the next car. He followed her through that car and halfway through another before calling her name—"Anne! Anne!"—but she didn't turn. He followed her into still another car, and she sat down in an aisle seat. Coming up to her, all his feelings warm and bent in her direction, he put his hand on the back of her seat—even this touch warmed him—and leaning down to speak to her, he saw that it was not Anne. It was an older woman wearing glasses. He went on deliberately into another car, his face red with embarrassment and the much deeper feeling of having his good sense challenged; for if he couldn't tell one person from another, what evidence was there that his life with Julia and the children had as much reality as his dreams of iniquity in Paris or the litter, the grass smell, and the cave-shaped trees in Lovers' Lane.

Late that afternoon, Julia called to remind Francis that they were going out for dinner. A few minutes later, Trace Bearden called. "Look, fellar," Trace said. "I'm calling for Mrs. Thomas. You know? Clayton, that boy of hers, doesn't seem able to get a job, and I wondered if you could help. If you'd call Charlie Bell—I know he's indebted to you—and say a good word for the kid, I think Charlie would—"

"Trace, I hate to say this," Francis said, "but I don't feel that I can do anything for that boy. The kid's worthless. I know it's a harsh thing to say, but it's a fact. Any kindness done for him would backfire in everybody's face. He's just a worthless kid, Trace, and there's nothing to be done about it. Even if we got him a job, he wouldn't be able to keep it for a week. I know that to be a fact. It's an awful thing, Trace, and I know it is, but instead of recommending that kid, I'd feel obligated to warn people against him—people who knew his father and would naturally want to step in and do something. I'd feel obliged to warn them. He's a thief . . ."

The moment this conversation was finished, Miss Rainey came in and stood by his desk. "I'm not going to be able to work for you any more, Mr. Weed," she said. "I can stay until the seventeenth if you need me, but I've been offered a whirlwind of a job, and I'd like to leave as soon as possible."

She went out, leaving him to face alone the wickedness of what he had done to the Thomas boy. His children in their photograph laughed and laughed, glazed with all the bright colors of summer, and he remembered that they had met a bagpiper on the beach that day and he had paid the piper a dollar to play them a battle song of the Black Watch. The girl would be at the house when he got home. He would spend another evening among his kind neighbors, picking and choosing dead-end streets, cart tracks, and the driveways of abandoned houses. There was nothing to mitigate his feeling—nothing that laughter or a game of softball with the children would change—and, thinking back over the plane crash, the Farquarsons' new maid, and Anne Murchison's difficulties with her drunken father, he wondered how he could have avoided arriving at just where he was. He was in trouble. He had been lost once in his life, coming back from a trout stream in the north woods, and he had now the same bleak realization that no amount of cheerfulness or hopefulness or valor or perseverance could help him find, in the gathering dark, the path that he'd lost. He smelled the forest. The feeling of bleakness was intolerable, and he saw clearly that he had reached the point where he would have to make a choice.

He could go to a psychiatrist, like Miss Rainey; he could go to church and confess his lusts; he could go to a Danish massage parlor in the West Seventies that had been recommended by a salesman; he could rape the girl or trust that he would somehow be prevented from doing this; or he could get drunk. It was his life, his boat, and, like every other man, he was made to be the father of thousands, and what harm could there be in a tryst that would make them both feel more kindly toward the world? This was the wrong train of thought, and he came back to the first, the psychiatrist. He had the telephone number of Miss Rainey's doctor, and he called and asked for an immediate appointment. He was insistent with the doctor's secretary—it was his manner in business—and when she said that the doctor's schedule was full for the next few weeks, Francis demanded an appointment that day and was told to come at five.

The psychiatrist's office was in a building that was used mostly by doctors and dentists, and the hallways were filled with the candy smell of mouthwash and memories of pain. Francis's character had been formed upon a series of private resolves—resolves about cleanliness, about going off the high diving board or repeating any other feat that challenged his courage, about punctuality, honesty, and virtue. To abdicate the perfect loneliness in which he had made his most vital decisions shattered his concept of character and left him now in a condition that felt like shock. He was stupefied. The scene for his *miserere mei Deus* was, like the waiting room of so many doctor's offices, a crude token gesture toward the sweets of domestic bliss: a place arranged with antiques, coffee tables, potted plants, and etchings of snow-covered bridges and geese in flight, although there were no children, no marriage bed, no stove, even, in this travesty of a house, where no one had ever spent the night and where the curtained windows looked straight onto a dark air shaft. Francis gave his name and address to a secretary and then saw, at the side of the room, a policeman moving toward him. "Hold it, hold it," the policeman said. "Don't move. Keep your hands where they are."

"I think it's all right, Officer," the secretary began. "I think it will be—"

"Let's make sure," the policeman said, and he began to slap Francis's clothes, looking for what—pistols, knives, an icepick? Finding nothing, he went off and the secretary began a nervous apology: "When you called on the telephone, Mr. Weed, you seemed very excited, and one of the doctor's patients has been threatening his life, and we have to be careful. If you want to go in now?" Francis pushed open a door connected to an electrical chime, and in the doctor's lair sat down heavily, blew his nose into a handkerchief, searched in his pockets for cigarettes, for matches, for something, and said hoarsely, with tears in his eyes, "I'm in love, Dr. Herzog."

. . .

It is a week or ten days later in Shady Hill. The seven-fourteen has come and gone, and here and there dinner is finished and the dishes are in the dishwashing machine. The village hangs, morally and economically, from a thread; but it hangs by its thread in the evening light. Donald Goslin has begun to worry the *Moonlight Sonata* again. *Marcato ma sempre pianissimo!* He seems to be wringing out a wet bath towel, but the housemaid does not heed him. She is writing a letter to Arthur Godfrey. In the cellar of his house, Francis Weed is building a coffee table. Dr. Herzog recommends woodwork as a therapy, and Francis finds some true consolation in the simple arithmetic involved and in the holy smell of new wood. Francis is happy. Upstairs, little Toby is crying, because he is tired. He puts off his cowboy hat, gloves, and fringed jacket, unbuckles the belt studded with gold and rubies, the silver bullets and holsters, slips off his suspenders, his checked shirt, and Levi's, and sits on the edge of his bed to pull off his high boots. Leaving this equipment in a heap, he goes to the closet and takes his space suit off a nail. It is a struggle for him to get into the long tights, but he succeeds. He loops the magic cape over his shoulders and, climbing onto the footboard of his bed, he spreads his arms and flies the short distance to the floor, landing with a thump that is audible to everyone in the house but himself.

"Go home, Gertrude, go home," Mrs. Masterson says. "I told you to go home an hour ago, Gertrude. It's way past your suppertime, and your mother will be worried. Go home!" A door on the Babcocks' terrace flies open, and out comes Mrs. Babcock without any clothes on, pursued by a naked husband. (Their children are away at boarding school, and their terrace is screened by a hedge.) Over the terrace they go and in at the kitchen door, as passionate and handsome a nymph and satyr as you will find on any wall in Venice. Cutting the last of the roses in her garden, Julia hears old Mr. Nixon shouting at the squirrels in his bird-feeding station. "Rapscallions! Varmints! Avaunt and quit my sight!" A miserable cat wanders into the garden, sunk in spiritual and physical discomfort. Tied to its head is a small straw hat—a doll's hat—and it is securely buttoned into a doll's dress, from the skirts of which protrudes its long, hairy tail. As it walks, it shakes its feet, as if it had fallen into water.

"Here, pussy, pussy, pussy!" Julia calls.

"Here, pussy, here, poor pussy!" But the cat gives her a skeptical look and stumbles away in its skirts. The last to come is Jupiter. He prances through the tomato vines, holding in his generous mouth the remains of an evening slipper. Then it is dark; it is a night where kings in golden suits ride elephants over the mountains.

---

1. Why does Francis think that telling the story of the French maid would constitute "a social as well as a human error"?
2. Francis is rude to Mrs. Wrightson, makes a pass at the babysitter, and refuses to help Clayton Thomas get a job. Why does Francis do these things?
3. Does the reality of Shady Hill confirm the claim that things there "seemed arranged with more propriety even than in the Kingdom of Heaven"?
4. What is the meaning of the last line of this story: "Then it is dark; it is a night where kings in golden suits ride elephants over the mountains"?

LAWRENCE SARGENT HALL (1915–1993) was born in Haverhill, Massachusetts, and after graduating from Yale University he served in the U.S. Naval Reserve, including a stint of active sea duty during World War II. From 1946 until his retirement in 1967, he was a professor of English at Bowdoin College. Hall's nautical interests included operating an old-time Maine coast boatyard and navigating the length of the Mississippi River on an ocean-going dory. He wrote several books of literary criticism and contributed to such periodicals as the *Hudson Review* and the *North American Review.* "The Ledge" received a first place O. Henry Award in 1960.

The Ledge

On Christmas morning before sunup the fisherman embraced his warm wife and left his close bed. She did not want him to go. It was Christmas morning. He was a big, raw man, with too much strength, whose delight in winter was to hunt the sea ducks that flew in to feed by the outer ledges, bare at low tide.

As his bare feet touched the cold floor and the frosty air struck his nude flesh, he might have changed his mind in the dark of this special day. It was a home day, which made it seem natural to think of the outer ledges merely as some place he had shot ducks in the past. But he had promised his son, thirteen, and his nephew, fifteen, who came from inland. That was why he had given them his present of an automatic shotgun each the night before, on Christmas Eve. Rough man though he was known to be, and no spoiler of boys, he kept his promises when he understood what they meant. And to the boys, as to him, home meant where you came for rest after you had had your Christmas fill of action and excitement.

His legs astride, his arms raised, the fisherman stretched as high as he could in the dim privacy of his bedroom. Above the snug murmur of his wife's protest he heard the wind in the pines and knew it was easterly as the boys had hoped and he had surmised the night before. Conditions would be ideal, and when they were, anybody ought to take advantage of them. The birds would be flying. The boys would get a man's sport their first time outside on the ledges.

His son at thirteen, small but steady and experienced, was fierce to grow up in hunting, to graduate from sheltered waters and the blinds along the shores of the inner bay. His nephew at fifteen, an overgrown farm boy, had a farm boy's love of the sea, though he could not swim a stroke and was often sick in choppy weather. That was the reason his father, the fisherman's brother, was a farmer and chose to sleep in on the holiday morning at his brother's house. Many of the ones the farmer had grown up with were regularly seasick and could not swim, but they were unafraid of the water. They could not have dreamed of being anything but fishermen. The fisherman himself could swim like a seal and was never sick, and he would sooner die than be anything else.

He dressed in the cold and dark, and woke the boys gruffly. They tumbled out of bed, their instincts instantly awake while their thoughts still fumbled slumbrously. The fisherman's wife in the adjacent bedroom heard them apparently trying to find their clothes, mumbling sleepily and happily to each other, while her husband went down to the hot kitchen to fry eggs—sunny-side up, she knew, because that was how they all liked them.

Always in winter she hated to have them go outside, the weather was so treacherous and there were so few others out in case of trouble. To the fisherman these were no more than woman's fears, to be taken for granted and laughed off. When they were first married they fought miserably every fall because she was after him constantly to put his boat up until spring. The fishing was all outside in winter, and though prices were high the storms made the rate of attrition high on gear. Nevertheless he did well. So she could do nothing with him.

People thought him a hard man, and gave him the reputation of being all out for himself because he was inclined to brag and be disdainful. If it was true, and his own brother was one of those who strongly felt it was, they lived better than others, and his brother had small right to criticize. There had been times when in her loneliness she had yearned to leave him for another man. But it would have been dangerous. So over the years she had learned to shut her mind to his hard-driving, and take what comfort she might from his unsympathetic competence. Only once or twice, perhaps, had she gone so far as to dwell guiltily on what it would be like to be a widow.

The thought that her boy, possibly because he was small, would not be insensitive like his father, and the rattle of dishes and smell of frying bacon downstairs in the kitchen shut off from the rest of the chilly house, restored the cozy feeling she had had before she was alone in bed. She heard them after a while go out and shut the back door.

Under her window she heard the snow grind dryly beneath their boots, and her husband's sharp, exasperated commands to the boys. She shivered slightly in the envelope of her own warmth. She listened to the noise of her son and nephew talking elatedly. Twice she caught the glimmer of their lights on the white ceiling above the window as they went down the path to the shore. There would be frost on the skiff and freezing suds at the water's edge. She herself used to go gunning when she was younger; now, it seemed to her, anyone going out like that on Christmas morning had to be incurably male. They would none of them think about her until they returned and piled the birds they had shot on top of the sink for her to dress.

Ripping into the quiet predawn cold she heard the hot snarl of the outboard taking them out to the boat. It died as abruptly as it had burst into life. Two or three or four or five minutes later the big engine broke into a warm reassuring roar. He had the best of equipment, and he kept it in the best of condition. She closed her eyes. It would not be too long before the others would be up for Christmas. The summer drone of the exhaust deepened. Then gradually it faded in the wind until it was lost at sea, or she slept.

The engine had started immediately in spite of the temperature. This put the fisherman in a good mood. He was proud of his boat. Together he and the two boys heaved the skiff and outboard onto the stern and secured it athwartships. His son went forward along the deck, iridescent in the ray of the light the nephew shone through the windshield, and cast the mooring pennant loose into darkness. The fisherman swung to starboard, glanced at his compass, and headed seaward down the obscure bay.

There would be just enough visibility by the time they reached the headland to navigate the crooked channel between the islands. It was the only nasty stretch of water. The fisherman had done it often in fog or at night—he always swore he could go anywhere in the bay blindfolded—but there was no sense in taking chances if you didn't have to. From the mouth of the channel he could lay a straight course for Brown Cow Island, anchor the boat out of sight behind it, and from the skiff set their tollers off Devil's Hump three hundred yards to seaward. By then the tide would be clearing the ledge and they could land and be ready to shoot around half tide.

It was early, it was Christmas, and it was farther out than most hunters cared to go in this season of the closing year, so that he felt sure no one would be taking possession ahead of them. He had shot thousands of ducks there in his day. The Hump was by far the best hunting. Only thing was you had to plan for the right conditions because you didn't have too much time. About four hours was all, and you had to get it before three in the afternoon when the birds left and went out to sea ahead of nightfall.

They had it figured exactly right for today. The ledge would not be going under until after the gunning was over, and they would be home for supper in good season. With a little luck the boys would have a skiff-load of birds to show for their first time outside. Well beyond the legal limit, which was no matter. You took what you could get in this life, or the next man made out and you didn't.

The fisherman had never failed to make out gunning from Devil's Hump. And this trip, he had a hunch, would be above ordinary. The easterly wind would come up just stiff enough, the tide was right, and it was going to storm by tomorrow morning so the birds would be moving. Things were perfect.

The old fierceness was in his bones. Keeping a weather eye to the murk out front and a hand on the wheel, he reached over and cuffed both boys playfully as they stood together close to the heat of the exhaust pipe running up through the center of the house. They poked back at him and shouted above the drumming engine, making bets as they always did on who would shoot the most birds. This trip they had the thrill of new guns, the best money could buy, and a man's hunting ground. The black retriever wagged at them and barked. He was too old and arthritic to be allowed in December water, but he was jaunty anyway at being brought along.

Groping in his pocket for his pipe the fisherman suddenly had his high spirits rocked by the discovery that he had left his tobacco at home. He swore. Anticipation of a day out with nothing to smoke made him incredulous. He searched his clothes, and then he searched them again, unable to believe the tobacco was not somewhere. When the boys inquired what was wrong he spoke angrily to them, blaming them for being in some devious way at fault. They were instantly crestfallen and willing to put back after the tobacco, though they could appreciate what it meant only through his irritation. But he bitterly refused. That would throw everything out of phase. He was a man who did things the way he set out to do.

He clamped his pipe between his teeth, and twice more during the next few minutes he ransacked his clothes in disbelief. He was no stoic. For one relaxed moment he considered putting about and gunning somewhere nearer home. Instead he held his course and sucked the empty pipe, consoling himself with the reflection that at least he had whiskey enough if it got too uncomfortable on the ledge. Peremptorily he made the boys check to make certain the bottle was really in the knapsack with the lunches where he thought he had taken care to put it. When they reassured him he despised his fate a little less.

The fisherman's judgment was as usual accurate. By the time they were abreast of the headland there was sufficient light so that he could wind his way among the reefs without slackening speed. At last he turned his bows toward open ocean, and as the winter dawn filtered upward through long layers of smoky cloud on the eastern rim his spirits rose again with it.

He opened the throttle, steadied on his course, and settled down to the two-hour run. The wind was stronger but seemed less cold coming from the sea. The boys had withdrawn from the fisherman and were talking together while they watched the sky through the windows. The boat churned solidly through a light chop, flinging spray off her flaring bows. Astern the headland thinned rapidly till it lay like a blackened sill on the gray water. No other boats were abroad.

The boys fondled their new guns, sighted along the barrels, worked the mechanisms, compared notes, boasted, and gave each other contradictory advice. The fisherman got their attention once and pointed at the horizon. They peered through the windows and saw what looked like a black scum floating on top of gently agitated water. It wheeled and tilted, rippled, curled, then rose, strung itself out and became a huge raft of ducks escaping over the sea. A good sign.

The boys rushed out and leaned over the washboards in the wind and spray to see the flock curl below the horizon. Then they went and hovered around the hot engine, bewailing their lot. If only they had been already set out and waiting. Maybe these ducks would be crazy enough to return later and be slaughtered. Ducks were known to be foolish.

In due course and right on schedule they anchored at midmorning in the lee of Brown Cow Island. They put the skiff overboard and loaded it with guns, knapsacks, and tollers. The boys showed their eagerness by being clumsy. The fisherman showed his in bad temper and abuse which they silently accepted in the absorbed tolerance of being boys. No doubt they laid it to lack of tobacco.

By outboard they rounded the island and pointed due east in the direction of a ridge of foam which could be seen whitening the surface three hundred yards away. They set the decoys in a broad, straddling V opening wide into the ocean. The fisherman warned them not to get their hands wet, and when they did he made them carry on with red and painful fingers, in order to teach them. Once the last toller was bobbing among his fellows, brisk and alluring, they got their numbed fingers inside their oilskins and hugged their warm crotches. In the meantime the fisherman had turned the skiff toward the patch of foam where as if by magic, like a black glossy rib of earth, the ledge had broken through the belly of the sea.

Carefully they inhabited their slipper nub of the North American continent, while the unresting Atlantic swelled and swirled as it had for eons round the indomitable edges. They hauled the skiff after them, established themselves as comfortably as they could in a shallow sump on top, lay on their sides a foot or so above the water, and waited, guns in hand.

In time the fisherman took a thermos bottle from the knapsack and they drank steaming coffee, and waited for the nodding decoys to lure in the first flight to the rock. Eventually the boys got hungry and restless. The fisherman let them open the picnic lunch and eat one sandwich apiece, which they both shared with the dog. Having no tobacco the fisherman himself would not eat.

Actually the day was relatively mild, and they were warm enough at present in their woolen clothes and socks underneath oilskins and hip boots. After a while, however, the boys began to feel cramped. Their nerves were agonized by inactivity. The nephew complained and was severely told by the fisherman—who pointed to the dog, crouched unmoving except for his white-rimmed eyes—that part of doing a man's hunting was learning how to wait. But he was beginning to have misgivings of his own. This could be one of those days where all the right conditions masked an incalculable flaw.

If the fisherman had been alone, as he often was, stopping off when the necessary coincidence of tide and time occurred on his way home from hauling trawls, and had plenty of tobacco, he would not have fidgeted. The boys' being nervous made him nervous. He growled at them again. When it came it was likely to come all at once, and then in a few moments be over. He warned them not to slack off, never to slack off, to be always ready. Under his rebuke they kept their tortured peace, though they could not help shifting and twisting until he lost what patience he had left and bullied them into lying still. A duck could see an eyelid twitch. If the dog could go without moving so could they.

"Here it comes!" the fisherman said tersely at last.

The boys quivered with quick relief. The flock came in downwind, quartering slightly, myriad, black, and swift.

"Beautiful—" breathed the fisherman's son.

"All right," said the fisherman, intense and precise. "Aim at singles in the thickest part of the flock. Wait for me to fire and then don't stop shooting till your gun's empty." He rolled up onto his left elbow and spread his legs to brace himself. The flock bore down, arrowy and vibrant, then a hundred yards beyond the decoys it veered off.

"They're going away!" the boys cried, sighting in.

"Not yet!" snapped the fisherman. "They're coming round."

The flock changed shape, folded over itself, and drove into the wind in a tight arc. "Thousands—" the boys hissed through their teeth. All at once a whistling storm of black and white broke over the decoys.

"Now!" the fisherman shouted. "Perfect!" And he opened fire at the flock just as it hung suspended in momentary chaos above the tollers. The three pulled at their triggers and the birds splashed into the water, until the last report went off unheard, the last smoking shell flew unheeded over their shoulders, and the last of the routed flock scattered diminishing, diminishing, diminishing in every direction.

Exultantly the boys dropped their guns, jumped up and scrambled for the skiff.

"I'll handle that skiff!" the fisherman shouted at them. They stopped. Gripping the painter and balancing himself he eased the skiff into the water stern first and held the bow hard against the side of the rock shelf the skiff had rested on. "You stay here," he said to his nephew. "No sense in all three of us going in the boat.'

The boy on the reef gazed at the gray water rising and falling hypnotically along the glistening edge. It had dropped about a foot since their arrival. "I want to go with you," he said in a sullen tone, his eyes on the streaming eddies.

"You want to do what I tell you if you want to gun with me," answered the fisherman harshly. The boy couldn't swim, and he wasn't going to have him climbing in and out of the skiff any more than necessary. Besides he was too big.

The fisherman took his son in the skiff and cruised round and round among the decoys picking up dead birds. Meanwhile the other boy stared unmoving after them from the highest part of the ledge. Before they had quite finished gathering the dead birds, the fisherman cut the outboard and dropped to his knees in the skiff. "Down!" he yelled. "Get down!" About a dozen birds came tolling in. "Shoot—shoot!" his son hollered from the bottom of the boat to the boy on the ledge.

The dog, who had been running back and forth whining, sank to his belly, his muzzle on his forepaws. But the boy on the ledge never stirred. The ducks took late alarm at the skiff, swerved aside and into the air, passing with a whirr no more than fifty feet over the head of the boy, who remained on the ledge like a statue, without his gun, watching the two crouching in the boat.

The fisherman's son climbed onto the ledge and held the painter. The bottom of the skiff was covered with feathery black and white bodies with feet upturned and necks lolling. He was jubilant. "We got twenty-seven!" he told his cousin. "How's that? Nine apiece. Boy—" he added, "what a cool Christmas!"

The fisherman pulled the skiff onto its shelf and all three went and lay down again in anticipation of the next flight. The son, reloading, patted his shotgun affectionately. "I'm going to get me ten next time," he said. Then he asked his cousin, "Whatsamatter—didn't you see the strays?"

"Yeah," the boy said.

"How come you didn't shoot at 'em?"

"Didn't feel like it," replied the boy, still with a trace of sullenness.

"You stupid or something?" The fisherman's son was astounded. "What a highlander!" But the fisherman, though he said nothing, knew that the older boy had had an attack of ledge fever.

"Cripes!" his son kept at it. "I'd at least of tried."

"Shut up," the fisherman finally told him, "and leave him be."

At slack water three more flocks came in, one right after the other, and when it was over, the skiff was half full of clean, dead birds. During the subsequent lull they broke out the lunch and ate it all and finished the hot coffee. For a while the fisherman sucked away on his cold pipe. Then he had himself a swig of whiskey.

The boys passed the time contentedly jabbering about who shot the most—there were ninety-two all told—which of their friends they would show the biggest ones to, how many each could eat at a meal provided they didn't have to eat any vegetables. Now and then they heard sporadic distant gunfire on the mainland, at its nearest point about two miles to the north. Once far off they saw a fishing boat making in the direction of home.

At length the fisherman got a hand inside his oilskins and produced his watch.

"Do we have to go now?" asked his son.

"Not just yet," he replied. "Pretty soon." Everything had been perfect. As good as he had ever had it. Because he was getting tired of the boys' chatter he got up, heavily in his hip boots, and stretched. The tide had turned and was coming in, the sky was more ashen, and the wind had freshened enough so that whitecaps were beginning to blossom. It would be a good hour before they had to leave the ledge and pick up the tollers. However, he guessed they would leave a little early. On account of the rising wind he doubted there would be much more shooting. He stepped carefully along the back of the ledge, to work his kinks out. It was also getting a little colder.

The whiskey had begun to warm him, but he was unprepared for the sudden blaze that flashed upward inside him from belly to head. He was standing looking at the shelf where the skiff was. Only the foolish skiff was not there!

For the second time that day the fisherman felt the deep vacuity of disbelief. He gaped, seeing nothing but the flat shelf of rock. He whirled, started toward the boys, slipped, recovered himself, fetched a complete circle, and stared at the unimaginably empty shelf. Its emptiness made him feel as if everything he had done that day so far, his life so far, he had dreamed. What could have happened? The tide was still nearly a foot below. There had been no sea to speak of. The skiff could hardly have slid off by itself. For the life of him, consciously careful as he inveterately was, he could not now remember hauling it up the last time. Perhaps in the heat of hunting he had left it to the boy. Perhaps he could not remember which was the last time.

"Christ—" he exclaimed loudly, without realizing it because he was so entranced by the invisible event.

"What's wrong, Dad?" asked his son, getting to his feet.

The fisherman went blind with uncontainable rage. "Get back down there where you belong!" he screamed. He scarcely noticed the boy sink back in amazement. In a frenzy he ran along the ledge thinking the skiff might have been drawn up at another place, though he knew better. There was no other place.

He stumbled, half falling, back to the boys who were gawking at him in consternation, as though he had gone insane. "God damn it!" he yelled savagely, grabbing both of them and yanking them to their knees. "Get on your feet!"

"What's wrong?" his son repeated in a stifled voice.

"Never mind what's wrong," he snarled. "Look for the skiff—it's adrift!" When they peered around he gripped their shoulders, brutally facing them about. "Downwind—" He slammed his fist against his thigh. "Jesus!" he cried, struck to madness at their stupidity.

At last he sighted the skiff himself, magically bobbing along the grim sea like a toller, a quarter of a mile to leeward on a direct course for home. The impulse to strip himself naked was succeeded instantly by a queer calm. He simply sat down on the ledge and forgot everything except the marvelous mystery.

As his awareness partially returned he glanced toward the boys. They were still observing the skiff speechlessly. Then he was gazing into the clear young eyes of his son.

"Dad," asked the boy steadily, "what do we do now?"

That brought the fisherman upright. "The first thing we have to do," he heard himself saying with infinite tenderness as if he were making love, "is think."

"Could you swim it?" asked his son.

He shook his head and smiled at them. They smiled quickly back, too quickly. "A hundred yards, maybe, in this water. I wish I could," he added. It was the most intimate and pitiful thing he had ever said. He walked in circles round them, trying to break the stall his mind was left in.

He gauged the level of the water. To the eye it was quite stationary, six inches from the shelf at this second. The fisherman did not have to mark it on the side of the rock against the passing of time to prove to his reason that it was rising, always rising. Already it was over the brink of reason, beyond the margins of thought—a senseless measurement. No sense to it.

All his life the fisherman had tried to lick the element of time, by getting up earlier and going to bed later, owning a faster boat, planning more than the day would hold, and tackling just one other job before the deadline fell. If, as on rare occasions he had the grand illusion, he ever really had beaten the game, he would need to call on all his reserves of practice and cunning now.

He sized up the scant but unforgivable three hundred yards to Brown Cow Island. Another hundred yards behind it his boat rode at anchor, where, had he been aboard, he could have cut in a Fathometer to plumb the profound and occult seas, or a ship-to-shore radio on which in an interminably short time he would have heard his wife's voice talking to him over the air about homecoming.

"Couldn't we wave something so somebody would see us?" his nephew suggested.

The fisherman spun round. "Load your guns!" he ordered. They loaded as if the air had suddenly gone frantic with birds. "I'll fire once and count to five. Then you fire. Count to five. That way they won't just think it's only somebody gunning ducks. We'll keep doing that."

"We've only got just two and a half boxes left," said his son.

The fisherman nodded, understanding that from beginning to end their situation was purely mathematical, like the ticking of the alarm clock in his silent bedroom. Then he fired. The dog, who had been keeping watch over the decoys, leaped forward and yelped in confusion. They all counted off, fired the first five rounds by threes, and reloaded. The fisherman scanned first the horizon, then the contracting borders of the ledge, which was the sole place the water appeared to be climbing. Soon it would be over the shelf.

They counted off and fired the second five rounds. "We'll hold off awhile on the last one," the fisherman told the boys. He sat down and pondered what a trivial thing was a skiff. This one he and the boy had knocked together in a day. Was a gun, manufactured for killing.

His son tallied up the remaining shells, grouping them symmetrically in threes on the rock when the wet box fell apart. "Two short," he announced. They reloaded and laid the guns on their knees.

Behind thickening clouds they could not see the sun going down. The water, coming up, was growing blacker. The fisherman thought he might have told his wife they would be home before dark since it was Christmas Day. He realized he had forgotten about its being any particular day. The tide would not be high until two hours after sunset. When they did not get in by nightfall, and could not be raised by radio, she might send somebody to hunt for them right away. He rejected this arithmetic immediately, with a sickening shock, recollecting it was a two-and-a-half-hour run at best. Then it occurred to him that she might send somebody on the mainland who was nearer. She would think he had engine trouble.

He rose and searched the shoreline, barely visible. Then his glance dropped to the toy shoreline at the edges of the reef. The shrinking ledge, so sinister from a boat, grew dearer minute by minute as though the whole wide world he gazed on from horizon to horizon balanced on its contracting rim. He checked the water level and found the shelf awash.

Some of what went through his mind the fisherman told to the boys. They accepted it without comment. If he caught their eyes they looked away to spare him or because they were not yet old enough to face what they saw. Mostly they watched the rising water. The fisherman was unable to initiate a word of encouragement. He wanted one of them to ask him whether somebody would reach them ahead of the tide. He would have found it possible to say yes. But they did not inquire.

The fisherman was not sure how much, at their age, they were able to imagine. Both of them had seen from the docks drowned bodies put ashore out of boats. Sometimes they grasped things, and sometimes not. He supposed they might be longing for the comfort of their mothers, and was astonished, as much as he was capable of any astonishment except the supreme one, to discover himself wishing he had not left his wife's dark, close, naked bed that morning.

"Is it time to shoot now?" asked his nephew.

"Pretty soon," he said, as if he were putting off making good on a promise. "Not yet."

His own boy cried softly for a brief moment, like a man, his face averted in an effort neither to give or show pain.

"Before school starts," the fisherman said, wonderfully detached, "we'll go to town and I'll buy you boys anything you want."

With great difficulty, in a dull tone as though he did not in the least desire it, his son said after a pause, "I'd like one of those new thirty-horse outboards."

"All right," said the fisherman. And to his nephew, "How about you?"

The nephew shook his head desolately. "I don't want anything," he said.

After another pause the fisherman's son said, "Yes he does, Dad. He wants one too."

"All right—" the fisherman said again, and said no more.

The dog whined in uncertainty and licked the boys' faces where they sat together. Each threw an arm over his back and hugged him. Three strays flew in and sat companionably down among the stiff-necked decoys. The dog crouched, obedient to his training. The boys observed them listlessly. Presently, sensing something untoward, the ducks took off, splashing the wave tops with feet and wingtips, into the dusky waste.

The sea began to make up in the mounting wind, and the wind bore a new and deathly chill. The fisherman, scouring the somber, dwindling shadow of the mainland for a sign, hoped it would not snow. But it did. First a few flakes, then a flurry, then storming past horizontally. The fisherman took one long, bewildered look at Brown Cow Island three hundred yards dead to leeward, and got to his feet.

Then it shut in, as if what was happening on the ledge was too private even for the last wan light of the expiring day.

"Last round," the fisherman said austerely.

The boys rose and shouldered their tacit guns. The fisherman fired into the flying snow. He counted methodically to five. His son fired and counted. His nephew. All three fired and counted. Four rounds.

"You've got one left, Dad," his son said.

The fisherman hesitated another second, then he fired the final shell. Its pathetic report, like the spat of a popgun, whipped away on the wind and was instantly blanketed in falling snow.

Night fell all in a moment to meet the ascending sea. They were now barely able to make one another out through driving snowflakes, dim as ghosts in their yellow oilskins. The fisherman heard a sea break and glanced down where his feet were. They seemed to be wound in a snowy sheet. Gently he took the boys by the shoulders and pushed them in front of him, feeling with his feet along the shallow sump to the place where it triangulated into a sharp crevice at the highest point of the ledge. "Face ahead," he told them. "Put the guns down."

"I'd like to hold mine, Dad," begged his son.

"Put it down," said the fisherman. "The tide won't hurt it. Now brace your feet against both sides and stay there."

They felt the dog, who was pitch black, running up and down in perplexity between their straddled legs. "Dad," said his son, "what about the pooch?"

If he had called the dog by name it would have been too personal. The fisherman would have wept. As it was he had all he could do to keep from laughing. He bent his knees, and when he touched the dog hoisted him under one arm. The dog's belly was soaking wet.

So they waited, marooned in their consciousness, surrounded by a monstrous tidal space which was slowly, slowly closing them out. In this space the periwinkle beneath the fisherman's boots was king. While hovering airborne in his mind he had an inward glimpse of his house as curiously separate, like a June mirage.

Snow, rocks, seas, wind the fisherman had lived by all his life. Now he thought he had never comprehended what they were, and he hated them. Though they had not changed. He was deadly chilled. He set out to ask the boys if they were cold. There was no sense. He thought of the whiskey, and sidled backward, still holding the awkward dog, till he located the bottle under water with his toe. He picked it up squeamishly as though afraid of getting his sleeve wet, worked his way forward and bent over his son. "Drink it," he said, holding the bottle against the boy's ribs. The boy tipped his head back, drank, coughed hotly, then vomited.

"I can't," he told his father wretchedly.

"Try—try—" the fisherman pleaded, as if it meant the difference between life and death.

The boy obediently drank, and again he vomited hotly. He shook his head against his father's chest and passed the bottle forward to his cousin, who drank and vomited also. Passing the bottle back, the boys dropped it in the frigid water between them.

When the waves reached his knees the fisherman set the warm dog loose and said to his son, "Turn around and get up on my shoulders." The boy obeyed. The fisherman opened his oilskin jacket and twisted his hands behind him through his suspenders, clamping the boy's booted ankles with his elbows.

"What about the dog?" the boy asked.

"He'll make his own way all right," the fisherman said. "He can take the cold water." His knees were trembling. Every instinct shrieked for gymnastics. He ground his teeth and braced like a colossus against the sides of the submerged crevice.

The dog, having lived faithfully as though one of them for eleven years, swam a few minutes in and out around the fisherman's legs, not knowing what was happening, and left them without a whimper. He would swim and swim at random by himself, round and round in the blinding night, and when he had swum routinely through the paralyzing water all he could, he would simply, in one incomprehensible moment, drown. Almost the fisherman, waiting out infinity, envied him his pattern.

Freezing seas swept by, flooding inexorably up and up as the earth sank away imperceptibly beneath them. The boy called out once to his cousin. There was no answer. The fisherman, marvelling on a terror without voice, was dumbly glad when the boy did not call again. His own boots were long full of water. With no sensation left in his straddling legs he dared not move them. So long as the seas came sidewise against his hips, and then sidewise against his shoulders, he might balance—no telling how long. The upper half of him was what felt frozen. His legs, disengaged from his nerves and his will, he came to regard quite scientifically. They were the absurd, precarious axis around which reeled and surged universal tumult. The waves would come on and on; he could not visualize how many tossing reinforcements lurked in the night beyond—inexhaustible numbers, and he wept in supernatural fury at each because it was higher, till he transcended hate and took them, swaying like a convert, one by one as they lunged against him and away aimlessly into their own undisputed, wild realm.

From his hips upward the fisherman stretched to his utmost as a man does whose spirit reaches out of dead sleep. The boy's head, none too high, must be at least seven feet above the ledge. Though growing larger every minute, it was a small light life. The fisherman meant to hold it there, if need be, through a thousand tides.

By and by the boy, slumped on the head of his father, asked, "Is it over your boots, Dad?"

"Not yet," the fisherman said. Then through his teeth he added, "If I fall—kick your boots off—swim for it—downwind—to the island. . . ."

"You . . . ?" the boy finally asked.

The fisherman nodded against the boy's belly. "—Won't see each other," he said.

The boy did for the fisherman the greatest thing that can be done. He may have been too young for perfect terror, but he was old enough to know there were things beyond the power of any man. All he could do he did, by trusting his father to do all he could, and asking nothing more.

The fisherman, rocked to his soul by a sea, held his eyes shut upon the interminable night.

"Is it time now?" the boy said.

The fisherman could hardly speak. "Not yet," he said. "Not just yet. . . ."

As the land mass pivoted toward sunlight the day after Christmas, a tiny fleet of small craft converged off shore like iron filings to a magnet. At daybreak they found the skiff floating unscathed off the headland, half full of ducks and snow. The shooting *had* been good, as someone hearing on the nearby mainland the previous afternoon had supposed. Two hours afterward they found the unharmed boat adrift five miles at sea. At high noon they found the fisherman at ebb tide, his right foot jammed cruelly into a glacial crevice of the ledge beside three shotguns, his hands tangled behind him in his suspenders, and under his right elbow a rubber boot with a sock and a live starfish in it. After dragging unlit depths all day for the boys, they towed the fisherman home in his boat at sundown, and in the frost of evening, mute with discovering purgatory, laid him on his wharf for his wife to see.

She, somehow, standing on the dock as in her frequent dream, gazing at the fisherman pure as crystal on the icy boards, a small rubber boot still frozen under one clenched arm, saw him exaggerated beyond remorse or grief, absolved of his mortality.

---

1. Why does the fisherman begin to have misgivings about the hunt, thinking that this could be "one of those days where all the right conditions masked an incalculable flaw"?

2. Why is the fisherman astonished "to discover himself wishing he had not left his wife's dark, close, naked bed that morning"?

3. Why does the fisherman, "waiting out infinity," almost envy the dog?

4. What does the narrator mean when he says that the boy "did for the fisherman the greatest thing that can be done"?

SAUL BELLOW (1915–2005) was one of the leading Jewish American writers in the second half of the twentieth century. He received three National Book Awards, the Pulitzer Prize, and in 1976, the Nobel Prize in Literature. Beginning with his first novel, *Dangling Man* (1944), Bellow created a series of protagonists who, despite being buffeted by social and economic forces beyond their control, retain their psychological buoyancy and humor. His unique style is one that moves rapidly between registers of high-minded philosophical speculation and warm, earthy, and sometimes hilariously vulgar expressions of the human flesh. Some of Bellow's most notable works include *The Adventures of Augie March* (1953), *Herzog* (1964), and *Mr. Sammler's Planet* (1970).

Looking for Mr. Green

Whatsoever thy hand findeth to do,
do it with thy might. . . .

Hard work? No, it wasn't really so hard. He wasn't used to walking and stair climbing, but the physical difficulty of his new job was not what George Grebe felt most. He was delivering relief checks in the Negro district, and although he was a native Chicagoan this was not a part of the city he knew much about—it needed a depression to introduce him to it. No, it wasn't literally hard work, not as reckoned in foot-pounds, but yet he was beginning to feel the strain of it, to grow aware of its peculiar difficulty. He could find the streets and numbers, but the clients were not where they were supposed to be, and he felt like a hunter inexperienced in the camouflage of his game. It was an unfavorable day, too—fall, and cold, dark weather, windy. But, anyway, instead of shells in his deep trench-coat pocket he had the cardboard of checks, punctured for the spindles of the file, the holes reminding him of the holes in player-piano paper. And he didn't look much like a hunter, either; his was a city figure entirely, belted up in this Irish conspirator's coat. He was slender without being tall, stiff in the back, his legs looking shabby in a pair of old tweed pants gone through and fringy at the cuffs. With this stiffness, he kept his head forward, so that his face was red from the sharpness of the weather; and it was an indoors sort of face with gray eyes that persisted in some kind of thought and yet seemed to avoid definiteness of conclusion. He wore sideburns that surprised you somewhat by the tough curl of the blond hair and the effect of assertion in their length. He was not so mild as he looked, nor so youthful; and nevertheless there was no effort on his part to seem what he was not. He was an educated man; he was a bachelor; he was in some ways simple; without lushing, he liked a drink; his luck had not been good. Nothing was deliberately hidden.

He felt that his luck was better than usual today. When he had reported for work that morning he had expected to be shut up in the relief office at a clerk's job, for he had been hired downtown as a clerk, and he was glad to have, instead, the freedom of the streets and welcomed, at least at first, the vigor of the cold and even the blowing of the hard wind. But on the other hand he was not getting on with the distribution of the checks. It was true that it was a city job; nobody expected you to push too hard at a city job. His supervisor, that young Mr. Raynor, had practically told him that. Still, he wanted to do well at it. For one thing, when he knew how quickly he could deliver a batch of checks, he would know also how much time he could expect to clip for himself. And then, too, the clients would be waiting for their money. That was not the most important consideration, though it certainly mattered to him. No, but he wanted to do well, simply for doing-well's sake, to acquit himself decently of a job because he so rarely had a job to do that required just this sort of energy. Of this peculiar energy he now had a superabundance; once it had started to flow, it flowed all too heavily. And, for the time being anyway, he was balked. He could not find Mr. Green.

So he stood in his big-skirted trench coat with a large envelope in his hand and papers showing from his pocket, wondering why people should be so hard to locate who were too feeble or sick to come to the station to collect their own checks. But Raynor had told him that tracking them down was not easy at first and had offered him some advice on how to proceed. "If you can see the postman, he's your first man to ask, and your best bet. If you can't connect with him, try the stores and tradespeople around. Then the janitor and the neighbors. But you'll find the closer you come to your man the less people will tell you. They don't want to tell you anything."

"Because I'm a stranger."

"Because you're white. We ought to have a Negro doing this, but we don't at the moment, and of course you've got to eat, too, and this is public employment. Jobs have to be made. Oh, that holds for me too. Mind you, I'm not letting myself out. I've got three years of seniority on you, that's all. And a law degree. Otherwise, you might be back of the desk and I might be going out into the field this cold day. The same dough pays us both and for the same, exact, identical reason. What's my law degree got to do with it? But you have to pass out these checks, Mr. Grebe, and it'll help if you're stubborn, so I hope you are."

"Yes, I'm fairly stubborn."

Raynor sketched hard with an eraser in the old dirt of his desk, left-handed, and said, "Sure, what else can you answer to such a question. Anyhow, the trouble you're going to have is that they don't like to give information about anybody. They think you're a plainclothes dick or an installment collector, or summons server or something like that. Till you've been seen around the neighborhood for a few months and people know you're only from the relief."

It was dark, ground-freezing, pre-Thanksgiving weather; the wind played hob with the smoke, rushing it down, and Grebe missed his gloves, which he had left in Raynor's office. And no one would admit knowing Green. It was past three o'clock and the postman had made his last delivery. The nearest grocer, himself a Negro, had never heard the name Tulliver Green, or said he hadn't. Grebe was inclined to think that it was true, that he had in the end convinced the man that he wanted only to deliver a check. But he wasn't sure. He needed experience in interpreting looks and signs and, even more, the will not to be put off or denied and even the force to bully if need be. If the grocer did know, he had got rid of him easily. But since most of his trade was with reliefers, why should he prevent the delivery of a check? Maybe Green, or Mrs. Green, if there was a Mrs. Green, patronized another grocer. And was there a Mrs. Green? It was one of Grebe's great handicaps that he hadn't looked at any of the case records. Raynor should have let him read files for a few hours. But he apparently saw no need for that, probably considering the job unimportant. Why prepare systematically to deliver a few checks?

But now it was time to look for the janitor. Grebe took in the building in the wind and gloom of the late November day—trampled, frost-hardened lots on one side; on the other, an automobile junkyard and then the infinite work of Elevated frames, weak looking, gaping with rubbish fires; two sets of leaning brick porches three stories high and a flight of cement stairs to the cellar. Descending, he entered the underground passage, where he tried the doors until one opened and he found himself in the furnace room. There someone rose toward him and approached, scraping on the coal grit and bending under the canvas-jacketed pipes.

"Are you the janitor?"

"What do you want?"

"I'm looking for a man who's supposed to be living here. Green."

"What Green?"

"Oh, you maybe have more than one Green?" said Grebe with new, pleasant hope. "This is Tulliver Green."

"I don't think I c'n help you, mister. I don't know any."

"A crippled man."

The janitor stood bent before him. Could it be that he was crippled? Oh, God! what if he was. Grebe's gray eyes sought with excited difficulty to see. But no, he was only very short and stooped. A head awakened from meditation, a strong-haired beard, low, wide shoulders. A staleness of sweat and coal rose from his black shirt and the burlap sack he wore as an apron.

"Crippled how?"

Grebe thought and then answered with the light voice of unmixed candor, "I don't know. I've never seen him." This was damaging, but his only other choice was to make a lying guess, and he was not up to it. "I'm delivering checks for the relief to shut-in cases. If he weren't crippled he'd come to collect himself. That's why I said crippled. Bedridden, chair ridden—is there anybody like that?"

This sort of frankness was one of Grebe's oldest talents, going back to childhood. But it gained him nothing here.

"No suh. I've got four buildin's same as this that I take care of. I don' know all the tenants, leave alone the tenants' tenants. The rooms turn over so fast, people movin' in and out every day. I can't tell you."

The janitor opened his grimy lips, but Grebe did not hear him in the piping of the valves and the consuming pull of air to flame in the body of the furnace. He knew, however, what he had said.

"Well, all the same, thanks. Sorry I bothered you. I'll prowl around upstairs again and see if I can turn up someone who knows him."

Once more in the cold air and early darkness he made the short circle from the cellarway to the entrance crowded between the brickwork pillars and began to climb to the third floor. Pieces of plaster ground under his feet; strips of brass tape from which the carpeting had been torn away marked old boundaries at the sides. In the passage, the cold reached him worse than in the street; it touched him to the bone. The hall toilets ran like springs. He thought grimly as he heard the wind burning around the building with a sound like that of the furnace, that this was a great piece of constructed shelter. Then he struck a match in the gloom and searched for names and numbers among the writings and scribbles on the walls. He saw WHOODY-DOODY GO TO JESUS, and zigzags, caricatures, sexual scrawls, and curses. So the sealed rooms of pyramids were also decorated, and the caves of human dawn.

The information on his card was, TULLIVER GREEN—APT 3D. There were no names, however, and no numbers. His shoulders drawn up, tears of cold in his eyes, breathing vapor, he went the length of the corridor and told himself that if he had been lucky enough to have the temperament for it he would bang on one of the doors and bawl out "Tulliver Green!" until he got results. But it wasn't in him to make an uproar and he continued to burn matches, passing the light over the walls. At the rear, in a corner off the hall, he discovered a door he had not seen before and he thought it best to investigate. It sounded empty when he knocked, but a young Negress answered, hardly more than a girl. She opened only a bit, to guard the warmth of the room.

"Yes suh?"

"I'm from the district relief station on Prairie Avenue. I'm looking for a man named Tulliver Green to give him his check. Do you know him?"

No, she didn't; but he thought she had not understood anything of what he had said. She had a dream-bound, dream-blind face, very soft and black, shut off. She wore a man's jacket and pulled the ends together at her throat. Her hair was parted in three directions, at the sides and transversely, standing up at the front in a dull puff.

"Is there somebody around here who might know?"

"I jus' taken this room las' week."

He observed that she shivered, but even her shiver was somnambulistic and there was no sharp consciousness of cold in the big smooth eyes of her handsome face.

"All right, miss, thank you. Thanks," he said, and went to try another place.

Here he was admitted. He was grateful, for the room was warm. It was full of people, and they were silent as he entered—ten people, or a dozen, perhaps more, sitting on benches like a parliament. There was no light, properly speaking, but a tempered darkness that the window gave, and everyone seemed to him enormous, the men padded out in heavy work clothes and winter coats, and the women huge, too, in their sweaters, hats, and old furs. And, besides, bed and bedding, a black cooking range, a piano piled towering to the ceiling with papers, a dining room table of the old style of prosperous Chicago. Among these people Grebe, with his cold-heightened fresh color and his smaller stature, entered like a schoolboy. Even though he was met with smiles and goodwill, he knew, before a single word was spoken, that all the currents ran against him and that he would make no headway. Nevertheless he began. "Does anybody here know how I can deliver a check to Mr. Tulliver Green?"

"Green?" It was the man that had let him in who answered. He was in short sleeves, in a checkered shirt, and had a queer, high head, profusely overgrown and long as a shako; the veins entered it strongly from his forehead. "I never heard mention of him. Is this where he live?"

"This is the address they gave me at the station. He's a sick man, and he'll need his check. Can't anybody tell me where to find him?"

He stood his ground and waited for a reply, his crimson wool scarf wound about his neck and drooping outside his trench coat, pockets weighted with the block of checks and official forms. They must have realized that he was not a college boy employed afternoons by a bill collector, trying foxily to pass for a relief clerk, recognized that he was an older man who knew himself what need was, who had had more than an average seasoning in hardship. It was evident enough if you looked at the marks under his eyes and at the sides of his mouth.

"Anybody know this sick man?"

"No suh." On all sides he saw heads shaken and smiles of denial. No one knew. And maybe it was true, he considered, standing silent in the earthen, musky human gloom of the place as the rumble continued. But he could never really be sure.

"What's the matter with this man?" said shako-head.

"I've never seen him. All I can tell you is that he can't come in person for his money. It's my first day in this district."

"Maybe they given you the wrong number?"

"I don't believe so. But where else can I ask about him?" He felt that this persistence amused them deeply, and in a way he shared their amusement that he should stand up so tenaciously to them. Though smaller, though slight, he was his own man, he retracted nothing about himself, and he looked back at them, gray-eyed, with amusement and also with a sort of courage. On the bench some man spoke in his throat, the words impossible to catch, and a woman answered with a wild, shrieking laugh, which was quickly cut off.

"Well, so nobody will tell me?"

"Ain't nobody who knows."

"At least, if he lives here, he pays rent to someone. Who manages the building?"

"Greatham Company. That's on Thirty-ninth Street."

Grebe wrote it in his pad. But, in the street again, a sheet of wind-driven paper clinging to his leg while he deliberated what direction to take next, it seemed a feeble lead to follow. Probably this Green didn't rent a flat, but a room. Sometimes there were as many as twenty people in an apartment; the real-estate agent would know only the lessee. And not even the agent could tell you who the renters were. In some places the beds were even used in shifts, watchmen or jitney drivers or short-order cooks in night joints turning out after a day's sleep and surrendering their beds to a sister, a nephew, or perhaps a stranger, just off the bus. There were large numbers of newcomers in this terrific, blight-bitten portion of the city between Cottage Grove and Ashland, wandering from house to house and room to room. When you saw them, how could you know them? They didn't carry bundles on their backs or look picturesque. You only saw a man, a Negro, walking in the street or riding in the car, like everyone else, with his thumb closed on a transfer. And therefore how were you supposed to tell? Grebe thought the Greatham agent would only laugh at his question.

But how much it would have simplified the job to be able to say that Green was old, or blind, or consumptive. An hour in the files, taking a few notes, and he needn't have been at such a disadvantage. When Raynor gave him the block of checks Grebe asked, "How much should I know about these people?" Then Raynor had looked as though Grebe were preparing to accuse him of trying to make the job more important than it was. Grebe smiled, because by then they were on fine terms, but nevertheless he had been getting ready to say something like that when the confusion began in the station over Staika and her children.

Grebe had waited a long time for this job. It came to him through the pull of an old schoolmate in the Corporation Counsel's office, never a close friend, but suddenly sympathetic and interested—pleased to show, moreover, how well he had done, how strongly he was coming on even in these miserable times. Well, he was coming through strongly, along with the Democratic administration itself. Grebe had gone to see him in City Hall, and they had had a counter lunch or beers at least once a month for a year, and finally it had been possible to swing the job. He didn't mind being assigned the lowest clerical grade, nor even being a messenger, though Raynor thought he did.

This Raynor was an original sort of guy and Grebe had taken to him immediately. As was proper on the first day, Grebe had come early, but he waited long, for Raynor was late. At last he darted into his cubicle of an office as though he had just jumped from one of those hurtling huge red Indian Avenue cars. His thin, rough face was wind stung and he was grinning and saying something breathlessly to himself. In his hat, a small fedora, and his coat, the velvet collar a neat fit about his neck, and his silk muffler that set off the nervous twist of his chin, he swayed and turned himself in his swivel chair, feet leaving the ground, so that he pranced a little as he sat. Meanwhile he took Grebe's measure out of his eyes, eyes of an unusual vertical length and slightly sardonic. So the two men sat for a while, saying nothing, while the supervisor raised his hat from his miscombed hair and put it in his lap. His cold-darkened hands were not clean. A steel beam passed through the little makeshift room, from which machine belts once had hung. The building was an old factory.

"I'm younger than you; I hope you won't find it hard taking orders from me," said Raynor. "But I don't make them up, either. You're how old, about?"

"Thirty-five."

"And you thought you'd be inside doing paperwork. But it so happens I have to send you out."

"I don't mind."

"And it's mostly a Negro load we have in this district."

"So I thought it would be."

"Fine. You'll get along. *C'est un bon boulot*. Do you know French?"

"Some."

"I thought you'd be a university man."

"Have you been in France?" said Grebe.

"No, that's the French of the Berlitz School. I've been at it for more than a year, just as I'm sure people have been, all over the world, office boys in China and braves in Tanganyika. In fact, I damn well know it. Such is the attractive power of civilization. It's overrated, but what do you want? *Que voulez-vous?* I get *Le Rire* and all the spicy papers, just like in Tanganyika. It must be mystifying, out there. But my reason is that I'm aiming at the diplomatic service. I have a cousin who's a courier, and the way he describes it is awfully attractive. He rides in the *wagon-lits* and reads books. While we—What did you do before?"

"I sold."

"Where?"

"Canned meat at Stop and Shop. In the basement."

"And before that?"

"Window shades, at Goldblatt's."

"Steady work?"

"No, Thursdays and Saturdays. I also sold shoes."

"You've been a shoe-dog too. Well. And prior to that? Here it is in your folder." He opened the record. "Saint Olaf's College, instructor in classical languages. Fellow, University of Chicago, 1926–27. I've had Latin, too. Let's trade quotations—'*Dum spiro spero.*'"

"'*De dextram misero.*'"

"'*Alea jacta est.*'"

"'*Excelsior.*'"

Raynor shouted with laughter, and other workers came to look at him over the partition. Grebe also laughed, feeling pleased and easy. The luxury of fun on a nervous morning.

When they were done and no one was watching or listening, Raynor said rather seriously, "What made you study Latin in the first place? Was it for the priesthood?"

"No."

"Just for the hell of it? For the culture? Oh, the things people think they can pull!" He made his cry hilarious and tragic. "I ran my pants off so I could study for the bar, and I've passed the bar, so I get twelve dollars a week more than you as a bonus for having seen life straight and whole. I'll tell you, as a man of culture, that even though nothing looks to be real, and everything stands for something else, and that thing for another thing, and that thing for a still further one—there ain't any comparison between twenty-five and thirty-seven dollars a week, regardless of the last reality. Don't you think that was clear to your Greeks? They were a thoughtful people, but they didn't part with their slaves."

This was a great deal more than Grebe had looked for in his first interview with his supervisor. He was too shy to show all the astonishment he felt. He laughed a little, aroused, and brushed at the sunbeam that covered his head with its dust. "Do you think my mistake was so terrible?"

"Damn right it was terrible, and you know it now that you've had the whip of hard times laid on your back. You should have been preparing yourself for trouble. Your people must have been well-off to send you to the university. Stop me, if I'm stepping on your toes. Did your mother pamper you? Did your father give in to you? Were you brought up tenderly, with permission to go and find out what were the last things that everything else stands for while everybody else labored in the fallen world of appearances?"

"Well, no, it wasn't exactly like that." Grebe smiled. *The fallen world of appearances!* no less. But now it was his turn to deliver a surprise. "We weren't rich. My father was the last genuine English butler in Chicago—"

"Are you kidding?"

"Why should I be?"

"In a livery?"

"In livery. Up on the Gold Coast."

"And he wanted you to be educated like a gentleman?"

"He did not. He sent me to the Armour Institute to study chemical engineering. But when he died I changed schools."

He stopped himself, and considered how quickly Raynor had reached him. In no time he had your valise on the table and all your stuff unpacked. And afterward, in the streets, he was still reviewing how far he might have gone, and how much he might have been led to tell if they had not been interrupted by Mrs. Staika's great noise.

But just then a young woman, one of Raynor's workers, ran into the cubicle exclaiming, "Haven't you heard all the fuss?"

"We haven't heard anything."

"It's Staika, giving out with all her might. The reporters are coming. She said she phoned the papers, and you know she did."

"But what is she up to?" said Raynor.

"She brought her wash and she's ironing it here, with our current, because the relief won't pay her electric bill. She has her ironing board set up by the admitting desk, and her kids are with her, all six. They never are in school more than once a week. She's always dragging them around with her because of her reputation."

"I don't want to miss any of this," said Raynor, jumping up. Grebe, as he followed with the secretary, said, "Who is this Staika?"

"They call her the 'Blood Mother of Federal Street.' She's a professional donor at the hospitals. I think they pay ten dollars a pint. Of course it's no joke, but she makes a very big thing out of it and she and the kids are in the papers all the time."

A small crowd, staff and clients divided by a plywood barrier, stood in the narrow space of the entrance, and Staika was shouting in a gruff, mannish voice, plunging the iron on the board and slamming it on the metal rest.

"My father and mother came in a steerage, and I was born in our house, Robey by Huron. I'm no dirty immigrant. I'm a U.S. citizen.

My husband is a gassed veteran from France with lungs weaker'n paper, that hardly can he go to the toilet by himself. These six children of mine, I have to buy the shoes for their feet with my own blood. Even a lousy little white Communion necktie, that's a couple of drops of blood; a little piece of mosquito veil for my Vadja so she won't be ashamed in church for the other girls, they take my blood for it by Goldblatt. That's how I keep goin'. A fine thing if I had to depend on the relief. And there's plenty of people on the rolls—fakes! There's nothin' *they* can't get, that can go and wrap bacon at Swift and Armour anytime. They're lookin' for them by the Yards. They never have to be out of work. Only they rather lay in their lousy beds and eat the public's money." She was not afraid, in a predominantly Negro station, to shout this way about Negroes.

Grebe and Raynor worked themselves forward to get a closer view of the woman. She was flaming with anger and with pleasure at herself, broad and huge, a golden-headed woman who wore a cotton cap laced with pink ribbon. She was barelegged and had on black gym shoes, her Hoover apron was open and her great breasts, not much restrained by a man's undershirt, hampered her arms as she worked at the kid's dress on the ironing board. And the children, silent and white, with a kind of locked obstinacy, in sheepskins and lumber jackets, stood behind her. She had captured the station, and the pleasure this gave her was enormous. Yet her grievances were true grievances. She was telling the truth. But she behaved like a liar. The look of her small eyes was hidden, and while she raged she also seemed to be spinning and planning.

"They send me out college caseworkers in silk pants to talk me out of what I got comin'. Are they better'n me? Who told them? Fire them. Let 'em go and get married, and then you won't have to cut electric from people's budget."

The chief supervisor, Mr. Ewing, couldn't silence her and he stood with folded arms at the head of his staff, bald, bald-headed, saying to his subordinates like the ex–school principal he was, "Pretty soon she'll be tired and go."

"No she won't," said Raynor to Grebe. "She'll get what she wants. She knows more about the relief even than Ewing. She's been on the rolls for years, and she always gets what she wants because she puts on a noisy show. Ewing knows it. He'll give in soon. He's only saving face. If he gets bad publicity, the commissioner'll have him on the carpet, downtown. She's got him submerged; she'll submerge everybody in time, and that includes nations and governments."

Grebe replied with his characteristic smile, disagreeing completely. Who would take Staika's orders, and what changes could her yelling ever bring about?

No, what Grebe saw in her, the power that made people listen, was that her cry expressed the war of flesh and blood, perhaps turned a little crazy and certainly ugly, on this place and this condition. And at first, when he went out, the spirit of Staika somehow presided over the whole district for him, and it took color from her; he saw her color, in the spotty curb fires, and the fires under the El, the straight alley of flamey gloom. Later, too, when he went into a tavern for a shot of rye, the sweat of beer, association with West Side Polish streets, made him think of her again.

He wiped the corners of his mouth with his muffler, his handkerchief being inconvenient to reach for, and went out again to get on with the delivery of his checks. The air bit cold and hard and a few flakes of snow formed near him. A train struck by and left a quiver in the frames and a bristling icy hiss over the rails.

Crossing the street, he descended a flight of board steps into a basement grocery, setting off a little bell. It was a dark, long store and it caught you with its stinks of smoked meat, soap, dried peaches, and fish. There was a fire wrinkling and flapping in the little stove, and the proprietor was waiting, an Italian with a long, hollow face and stubborn bristles. He kept his hands warm under his apron.

No, he didn't know Green. You knew people but not names. The same man might not have the same name twice. The police didn't know, either, and mostly didn't care. When somebody was shot or knifed they took the body away and didn't look for the murderer. In the first place, nobody would tell them anything. So they made up a name for the coroner and called it quits. And in the second place, they didn't give a goddamn anyhow. But they couldn't get to the bottom of a thing even if they wanted to. Nobody would get to know even a tenth of what went on among these people. They stabbed and stole, they did every crime and abomination you ever heard of, men and men, women and women, parents and children, worse than the animals. They carried on their own way, and the horrors passed off like a smoke. There was never anything like it in the history of the whole world.

It was a long speech, deepening with every word in its fantasy and passion and becoming increasingly senseless and terrible: a swarm amassed by suggestion and invention, a huge, hugging, despairing knot, a human wheel of heads, legs, bellies, arms, rolling through his shop.

Grebe felt that he must interrupt him. He said sharply, "What are you talking about! All I asked was whether you knew this man."

"That isn't even the half of it. I been here six years. You probably don't want to believe this. But suppose it's true?"

"All the same," said Grebe, "there must be a way to find a person."

The Italian's close-spaced eyes had been queerly concentrated, as were his muscles, while he leaned across the counter trying to convince Grebe. Now he gave up the effort and sat down on his stool. "Oh—I suppose. Once in a while. But I been telling you, even the cops don't get anywhere."

"They're always after somebody. It's not the same thing."

"Well, keep trying if you want. I can't help you."

But he didn't keep trying. He had no more time to spend on Green. He slipped Green's check to the back of the block. The next name on the list was FIELD, WINSTON.

He found the backyard bungalow without the least trouble; it shared a lot with another house, a few feet of yard between. Grebe knew these two-shack arrangements. They had been built in vast numbers in the days before the swamps were filled and the streets raised, and they were all the same—a boardwalk along the fence, well under street level, three or four ball-headed posts for clotheslines, greening wood, dead shingles, and a long, long flight of stairs to the rear door.

A twelve-year-old boy let him into the kitchen, and there the old man was, sitting by the table in a wheelchair.

"Oh, it's d' Government man," he said to the boy when Grebe drew out his checks. "Go bring me my box of papers." He cleared a space on the table.

"Oh, you don't have to go to all that trouble," said Grebe. But Field laid out his papers: Social Security card, relief certification, letters from the state hospital Manteno, and a naval discharge dated San Diego, 1920.

"That's plenty," Grebe said. "Just sign."

"You got to know who I am," the old man said. "You're from the Government. It's not your check, it's a Government check and you got no business to hand it over till everything is proved."

He loved the ceremony of it, and Grebe made no more objections. Field emptied his box and finished out the circle of cards and letters.

"There's everything I done and been. Just the death certificate and they can close book on me." He said this with a certain happy pride and magnificence. Still he did not sign; he merely held the little pen upright on the golden-green corduroy of his thigh. Grebe did not hurry him. He felt the old man's hunger for conversation.

"I got to get better coal," he said. "I send my little gran'son to the yard with my order and they fill his wagon with screening. The stove ain't made for it. It fall through the grate. The order says Franklin County egg-size coal."

"I'll report it and see what can be done."

"Nothing can be done, I expect. You know and I know. There ain't no little ways to make things better, and the only big thing is money. That's the only sunbeams, money. Nothing is black where it shines, and the only place you see black is where it ain't shining. What we colored have to have is our own rich. There ain't no other way."

Grebe sat, his reddened forehead bridged levelly by his close-cut hair and his cheeks lowered in the wings of his collar—the caked fire shone hard within the isinglass-and-iron frames but the room was not comfortable—sat and listened while the old man unfolded his scheme. This was to create one Negro millionaire a month by subscription. One clever, goodhearted young fellow elected every month would sign a contract to use the money to start a business employing Negroes. This would be advertised by chain letters and word of mouth, and every Negro wage earner would contribute a dollar a month. Within five years there would be sixty millionaires.

"That'll fetch respect," he said with a throat-stopped sound that came out like a foreign syllable. "You got to take and organize all the money that gets thrown away on the policy wheel and horse race. As long as they can take it away from you, they got no respect for you.

Money, that's d' sum of humankind!" Field was a Negro of mixed blood, perhaps Cherokee, or Natchez; his skin was reddish. And he sounded, speaking about a golden sun in this dark room, and looked—shaggy and slab-headed—with the mingled blood of his face and broad lips, and with the little pen still upright in his hand, like one of the underground kings of mythology, old judge Minos himself.

And now he accepted the check and signed. Not to soil the slip, he held it down with his knuckles. The table budged and creaked, the center of the gloomy, heathen midden of the kitchen covered with bread, meat, and cans, and the scramble of papers.

"Don't you think my scheme'd work?"

"It's worth thinking about. Something ought to be done, I agree."

"It'll work if people will do it. That's all. That's the only thing, anytime. When they understand it in the same way, all of them."

"That's true," said Grebe, rising. His glance met the old man's.

"I know you got to go," he said. "Well, God bless you, boy, you ain't been sly with me. I can tell it in a minute."

He went back through the buried yard. Someone nursed a candle in a shed, where a man unloaded kindling wood from a sprawl-wheeled baby buggy and two voices carried on a high conversation. As he came up the sheltered passage he heard the hard boost of the wind in the branches and against the house fronts, and then, reaching the sidewalk, he saw the needle-eye red of cable towers in the open icy height hundreds of feet above the river and the factories—those keen points. From here, his view was obstructed all the way to the South Branch and its timber banks, and the cranes beside the water. Rebuilt after the Great Fire, this part of the city was, not fifty years later, in ruins again, factories boarded up, buildings deserted or fallen, gaps of prairie between. But it wasn't desolation that this made you feel, but rather a faltering of organization that set free a huge energy, an escaped, unattached, unregulated power from the giant raw place. Not only must people feel it but, it seemed to Grebe, they were compelled to match it. In their very bodies. He no less than others, he realized. Say that his parents had been servants in their time, whereas he was supposed not to be one. He thought that they had never done any service like this, which no one visible asked for, and probably flesh and blood could not even perform. Nor could anyone show why it should be performed;

or see where the performance would lead. That did not mean that he wanted to be released from it, he realized with a grimly pensive face. On the contrary. He had something to do. To be compelled to feel this energy and yet have no task to do—that was horrible; that was suffering; he knew what that was. It was now quitting time. Six o'clock. He could go home if he liked, to his room, that is, to wash in hot water, to pour a drink, lie down on his quilt, read the paper, eat some liver paste on crackers before going out to dinner. But to think of this actually made him feel a little sick, as though he had swallowed hard air. He had six checks left, and he was determined to deliver at least one of these: Mr. Green's check.

So he started again. He had four or five dark blocks to go, past open lots, condemned houses, old foundations, closed schools, black churches, mounds, and he reflected that there must be many people alive who had once seen the neighborhood rebuilt and new. Now there was a second layer of ruins; centuries of history accomplished through human massing. Numbers had given the place forced growth; enormous numbers had also broken it down. Objects once so new, so concrete that it could never have occurred to anyone they stood for other things, had crumbled. Therefore, reflected Grebe, the secret of them was out. It was that they stood for themselves by agreement, and were natural and not unnatural by agreement, and when the things themselves collapsed the agreement became visible. What was it, otherwise, that kept cities from looking peculiar? Rome, that was almost permanent, did not give rise to thoughts like these. And was it abidingly real? But in Chicago, where the cycles were so fast the familiar died out, and again rose changed, and died again in thirty years, you saw the common agreement or covenant, and you were forced to think about appearances and realities. (He remembered Raynor and he smiled. Raynor was a clever boy.) Once you had grasped this, a great many things became intelligible. For instance, why Mr. Field should conceive such a scheme. Of course, if people were to agree to create a millionaire, a real millionaire would come into existence. And if you wanted to know how Mr. Field was inspired to think of this, why, he had within sight of his kitchen window the chart, the very bones of a successful scheme—the El with its blue and green confetti of signals. People consented to pay dimes and ride the crash-box cars, and so it was a success. Yet how absurd it looked; how little reality there was to start with. And yet Yerkes, the great financier who built it, had known that he could get people to agree to do it. Viewed as itself, what a scheme of a scheme it seemed, how close to an appearance. Then why wonder at Mr. Field's idea? He had grasped a principle. And then Grebe remembered, too, that Mr. Yerkes had established the Yerkes Observatory and endowed it with millions. Now how did the notion come to him in his New York museum of a palace or his Aegean-bound yacht to give money to astronomers? Was he awed by the success of his bizarre enterprise and therefore ready to spend money to find out where in the universe being and seeming were identical? Yes, he wanted to know what abides; and whether flesh is Bible grass; and he offered money to be burned in the fire of suns. Okay, then, Grebe thought further, these things exist because people consent to exist with them—we have got so far—and also there is a reality which doesn't depend on consent but within which consent is a game. But what about need, the need that keeps so many vast thousands in position? You tell me that, you *private* little gentleman and *decent* soul—he used these words against himself scornfully. Why is the consent given to misery? And why so painfully ugly? Because there is *something* that is dismal and permanently ugly? Here he sighed and gave it up, and thought it was enough for the present moment that he had a real check in his pocket for a Mr. Green who must be real beyond question. If only his neighbors didn't think they had to conceal him.

This time he stopped at the second floor. He struck a match and found a door. Presently a man answered his knock and Grebe had the check ready and showed it even before he began. "Does Tulliver Green live here? I'm from the relief."

The man narrowed the opening and spoke to someone at his back.

"Does he live here?"

"Uh-uh. No."

"Or anywhere in this building? He's a sick man and he can't come for his dough." He exhibited the check in the light, which was smoky—the air smelled of charred lard—and the man held off the brim of his cap to study it.

"Uh-uh. Never seen the name."

"There's nobody around here that uses crutches?"

He seemed to think, but it was Grebe's impression that he was simply waiting for a decent interval to pass.

"No, suh. Nobody I ever see."

"I've been looking for this man all afternoon"—Grebe spoke out with sudden force—"and I'm going to have to carry this check back to the station. It seems strange not to be able to find a person to *give* him something when you're looking for him for a good reason. I suppose if I had bad news for him I'd find him quick enough."

There was a responsive motion in the other man's face. "That's right, I reckon."

"It almost doesn't do any good to have a name if you can't be found by it. It doesn't stand for anything. He might as well not have any," he went on, smiling. It was as much of a concession as he could make to his desire to laugh.

"Well, now, there's a little old knot-back man I see once in a while. He might be the one you lookin' for. Downstairs."

"Where? Right side or left? Which door?"

"I don't know which. Thin-face little knot-back with a stick."

But no one answered at any of the doors on the first floor. He went to the end of the corridor, searching by matchlight, and found only a stairless exit to the yard, a drop of about six feet. But there was a bungalow near the alley, an old house like Mr. Field's. To jump was unsafe. He ran from the front door, through the underground passage and into the yard. The place was occupied. There was a light through the curtains, upstairs. The name on the ticket under the broken, scoop-shaped mailbox was Green! He exultantly rang the bell and pressed against the locked door. Then the lock clicked faintly and a long staircase opened before him. Someone was slowly coming down—a woman. He had the impression in the weak light that she was shaping her hair as she came, making herself presentable, for he saw her arms raised. But it was for support that they were raised; she was feeling her way downward, down the wall, stumbling. Next he wondered about the pressure of her feet on the treads; she did not seem to be wearing shoes. And it was a freezing stairway. His ring had got her out of bed, perhaps, and she had forgotten to put them on. And then he saw that she was not only shoeless but naked; she was entirely naked, climbing down while she talked to herself, a heavy woman, naked and drunk. She blundered into him. The contact of her breasts, though they touched only his coat, made him go back against the door with a blind shock. See what he had tracked down, in his hunting game!

The woman was saying to herself, furious with insult, "So I cain't fuck, huh? I'll show that son of a bitch kin I, cain't I."

What should he do now? Grebe asked himself. Why, he should go. He should turn away and go. He couldn't talk to this woman. He couldn't keep her standing naked in the cold. But when he tried he found himself unable to turn away.

He said, "Is this where Mr. Green lives?"

But she was still talking to herself and did not hear him.

"Is this Mr. Green's house?"

At last she turned her furious drunken glance on him. "What do you want?"

Again her eyes wandered from him; there was a dot of blood in their enraged brilliance. He wondered why she didn't feel the cold.

"I'm from the relief."

"Awright, what?"

"I've got a check for Tulliver Green."

This time she heard him and put out her hand.

"No, no, for *Mr.* Green. He's got to sign," he said. How was he going to get Green's signature tonight!

"I'll take it. He cain't."

He desperately shook his head, thinking of Mr. Field's precautions about identification. "I can't let you have it. It's for him. Are you Mrs. Green?"

"Maybe I is, and maybe I ain't. Who want to know?"

"Is he upstairs?"

"Awright. Take it up yourself, you goddamn fool."

Sure, he was a goddamn fool. Of course he could not go up because Green would probably be drunk and naked, too. And perhaps he would appear on the landing soon. He looked eagerly upward. Under the light was a high narrow brown wall. Empty! It remained empty!

"Hell with you, then!" he heard her cry. To deliver a check for coal and clothes, he was keeping her in the cold. She did not feel it, but his face was burning with frost and self-ridicule. He backed away from her.

"I'll come tomorrow, tell him."

"Ah, hell with you. Don't never come. What you doin' here in the nighttime? Don' come back." She yelled so that he saw the breadth of her tongue. She stood astride in the long cold box of the hall and held on to the banister and the wall. The bungalow itself was shaped something like a box, a clumsy, high box pointing into the freezing air with its sharp, wintry lights.

"If you are Mrs. Green, I'll give you the check," he said, changing his mind.

"Give here, then." She took it, took the pen offered with it in her left hand, and tried to sign the receipt on the wall. He looked around, almost as though to see whether his madness was being observed, and came near to believing that someone was standing on a mountain of used tires in the auto-junking shop next door.

"But are you Mrs. Green?" he now thought to ask. But she was already climbing the stairs with the check, and it was too late, if he had made an error, if he was now in trouble, to undo the thing. But he wasn't going to worry about it. Though she might not be Mrs. Green, he was convinced that Mr. Green was upstairs. Whoever she was, the woman stood for Green, whom he was not to see this time. Well, you silly bastard, he said to himself, so you think you found him. So what? Maybe you really did find him—what of it? But it was important that there was a real Mr. Green whom they could not keep him from reaching because he seemed to come as an emissary from hostile appearances. And though the self-ridicule was slow to diminish, and his face still blazed with it, he had, nevertheless, a feeling of elation, too. "For after all," he said, "he *could* be found!"

---

1. What does the scene with Staika and her children add to the story? What does the narrator mean when he says that Staika "was telling the truth. But she behaved like a liar"?

2. Why does Grebe find that he is unable to turn away from the naked woman as she approaches him at the end of the story?

3. Why does the story leave the reader uncertain as to whether Grebe has actually found Mr. Green?
4. What does Grebe discover about appearance and reality during his search for Mr. Green?

JAMES BALDWIN (1924–1987) was born into a poor family in New York City. At the age of fourteen he underwent a dramatic conversion to Christianity and began preaching as a children's minister, an experience he later chronicled in *Go Tell It on the Mountain* (1953). Still in his teens and growing disillusioned with his faith, Baldwin determined to be a writer, and after a short stint working for a defense contractor in New Jersey, he moved to Greenwich Village, where he met Richard Wright and started to write a novel. In 1948 he moved to Paris, spending his next eight years there writing plays and essays that portray the black experience in a predominantly white society. Baldwin was a powerful public speaker and spokesman for the civil rights movement, and he gained much critical attention for his essays collected in *Notes of a Native Son* (1955) and *Nobody Knows My Name: More Notes of a Native Son* (1961).

Sonny's Blues

I read about it in the paper, in the subway, on my way to work. I read it, and I couldn't believe it, and I read it again. Then perhaps I just stared at it, at the newsprint spelling out his name, spelling out the story. I stared at it in the swinging lights of the subway car, and in the faces and bodies of the people, and in my own face, trapped in the darkness which roared outside.

It was not to be believed and I kept telling myself that, as I walked from the subway station to the high school. And at the same time I couldn't doubt it. I was scared, scared for Sonny. He became real to me again. A great block of ice got settled in my belly and kept melting there slowly all day long, while I taught my classes algebra. It was a special kind of ice. It kept melting, sending trickles of ice water all up and down my veins, but it never got less. Sometimes it hardened and seemed to expand until I felt my guts were going to come spilling out or that I was going to choke or scream. This would always be at a moment when I was remembering some specific thing Sonny had once said or done.

When he was about as old as the boys in my classes his face had been bright and open, there was a lot of copper in it; and he'd had wonderfully direct brown eyes, and great gentleness and privacy. I wondered what he looked like now. He had been picked up, the evening before, in a raid on an apartment downtown, for peddling and using heroin.

I couldn't believe it: but what I mean by that is that I couldn't find any room for it anywhere inside me. I had kept it outside me for a long time. I hadn't wanted to know. I had had suspicions, but I didn't name them, I kept putting them away. I told myself that Sonny was wild, but he wasn't crazy. And he'd always been a good boy, he hadn't ever turned hard or evil or disrespectful, the way kids can, so quick, so quick, especially in Harlem. I didn't want to believe that I'd ever see my brother going down, coming to nothing, all that light in his face gone out, in the condition I'd already seen so many others. Yet it had happened and here I was, talking about algebra to a lot of boys who might, every one of them for all I knew, be popping off needles every time they went to the head. Maybe it did more for them than algebra could.

I was sure that the first time Sonny had ever had horse, he couldn't have been much older than these boys were now. These boys, now, were living as we'd been living then, they were growing up with a rush and their heads bumped abruptly against the low ceiling of their actual possibilities. They were filled with rage. All they really knew were two darknesses, the darkness of their lives, which was now closing in on them, and the darkness of the movies, which had blinded them to that other darkness, and in which they now, vindictively, dreamed, at once more together than they were at any other time, and more alone.

When the last bell rang, the last class ended, I let out my breath. It seemed I'd been holding it for all that time. My clothes were wet—I may have looked as though I'd been sitting in a steam bath, all dressed up, all afternoon. I sat alone in the classroom a long time. I listened to the boys outside, downstairs, shouting and cursing and laughing. Their laughter struck me for perhaps the first time. It was not the joyous laughter which—God knows why—one associates with children. It was mocking and insular, its intent to denigrate. It was disenchanted, and in this, also, lay the authority of their curses. Perhaps I was listening to them because I was thinking about my brother and in them I heard my brother. And myself.

One boy was whistling a tune, at once very complicated and very simple, it seemed to be pouring out of him as though he were a bird, and it sounded very cool and moving through all that harsh, bright air, only just holding its own through all those other sounds.

I stood up and walked over to the window and looked down into the courtyard. It was the beginning of the spring and the sap was rising in the boys. A teacher passed through them every now and again, quickly, as though he or she couldn't wait to get out of that courtyard, to get those boys out of their sight and off their minds. I started collecting my stuff. I thought I'd better get home and talk to Isabel.

The courtyard was almost deserted by the time I got downstairs. I saw this boy standing in the shadow of a doorway, looking just like Sonny. I almost called his name. Then I saw that it wasn't Sonny, but somebody we used to know, a boy from around our block. He'd been Sonny's friend. He'd never been mine, having been too young for me, and, anyway, I'd never liked him. And now, even though he was a grown-up man, he still hung around that block, still spent hours on the street corners, was always high and raggy. I used to run into him from time to time and he'd often work around to asking me for a quarter or fifty cents. He always had some real good excuse, too, and I always gave it to him, I don't know why.

But now, abruptly, I hated him. I couldn't stand the way he looked at me, partly like a dog, partly like a cunning child. I wanted to ask him what the hell he was doing in the school courtyard.

He sort of shuffled over to me, and he said, "I see you got the papers. So you already know about it."

"You mean about Sonny? Yes, I already know about it. How come they didn't get you?"

He grinned. It made him repulsive and it also brought to mind what he'd looked like as a kid. "I wasn't there. I stay away from them people."

"Good for you." I offered him a cigarette and I watched him through the smoke. "You come all the way down here just to tell me about Sonny?"

“That’s right.” He was sort of shaking his head and his eyes looked strange, as though they were about to cross. The bright sun deadened his damp dark brown skin and it made his eyes look yellow and showed up the dirt in his kinked hair. He smelled funky. I moved a little away from him and I said, “Well, thanks. But I already know about it and I got to get home.”

“I’ll walk you a little ways,” he said. We started walking. There were a couple of kids still loitering in the courtyard and one of them said goodnight to me and looked strangely at the boy beside me.

“What’re you going to do?” he asked me, “I mean, about Sonny?”

“Look. I haven’t seen Sonny for over a year, I’m not sure I’m going to do anything. Anyway, what the hell *can* I do?”

“That’s right,” he said quickly, “ain’t nothing you can do. Can’t much help old Sonny no more, I guess.”

It was what I was thinking and so it seemed to me he had no right to say it.

“I’m surprised at Sonny, though,” he went on—he had a funny way of talking, he looked straight ahead as though he were talking to himself—“I thought Sonny was a smart boy, I thought he was too smart to get hung.”

“I guess he thought so too,” I said sharply, “and that’s how he got hung. And how about you? You’re pretty goddamn smart, I bet.”

Then he looked directly at me, just for a minute. “I ain’t smart,” he said. “If I was smart, I’d have reached for a pistol a long time ago.”

“Look. Don’t tell *me* your sad story, if it was up to me, I’d give you one.” Then I felt guilty—guilty, probably, for never having supposed that the poor bastard *had* a story of his own, much less a sad one, and I asked, quickly, “What’s going to happen to him now?”

He didn’t answer this. He was off by himself some place. “Funny thing,” he said, and from his tone we might have been discussing the quickest way to get to Brooklyn, “when I saw the papers this morning, the first thing I asked myself was if I had anything to do with it. I felt sort of responsible.”

I began to listen more carefully. The subway station was on the corner, just before us, and I stopped. He stopped, too. We were in front of a bar and he ducked slightly, peering in, but whoever he was looking for didn’t seem to be there. The jukebox was blasting away with something black and bouncy and I half watched the barmaid as she danced her way from the jukebox to her place behind the bar. And I watched her face as she laughingly responded to something someone said to her, still keeping time to the music. When she smiled one saw the little girl, one sensed the doomed, still-struggling woman beneath the battered face of the semiwhore.

"I never *give* Sonny nothing," the boy said finally, "but a long time ago I come to school high and Sonny asked me how it felt." He paused, I couldn't bear to watch him, I watched the barmaid, and I listened to the music which seemed to be causing the pavement to shake. "I told him it felt great." The music stopped, the barmaid paused and watched the jukebox until the music began again. "It did."

All this was carrying me some place I didn't want to go. I certainly didn't want to know how it felt. It filled everything, the people, the houses, the music, the dark, quicksilver barmaid, with menace; and this menace was their reality.

"What's going to happen to him now?" I asked again.

"They'll send him away some place and they'll try to cure him." He shook his head. "Maybe he'll even think he's kicked the habit. Then they'll let him loose"—he gestured, throwing his cigarette into the gutter. "That's all."

"What do you mean, that's *all*?"

But I knew what he meant.

"I *mean*, that's *all*." He turned his head and looked at me, pulling down the corners of his mouth. "Don't you know what I mean?" he asked, softly.

"How the hell *would* I know what you mean?" I almost whispered it, I don't know why.

"That's right," he said to the air, "how would *he* know what I mean?" He turned toward me again, patient and calm, and yet I somehow felt him shaking, shaking as though he were going to fall apart. I felt that ice in my guts again, the dread I'd felt all afternoon; and again I watched the barmaid, moving about the bar, washing glasses, and singing. "Listen. They'll let him out and then it'll just start all over again. That's what I mean."

"You mean—they'll let him out. And then he'll just start working his way back in again. You mean he'll never kick the habit. Is that what you mean?"

"That's right," he said, cheerfully. "*You* see what I mean."

"Tell me," I said at last, "why does he want to die? He must want to die, he's killing himself, why does he want to die?"

He looked at me in surprise. He licked his lips. "He don't want to die. He wants to live. Don't nobody want to die, ever."

Then I wanted to ask him—too many things. He could not have answered, or if he had, I could not have borne the answers. I started walking. "Well, I guess it's none of my business."

"It's going to be rough on old Sonny," he said. We reached the subway station. "This is your station?" he asked. I nodded. I took one step down. "Damn!" he said, suddenly. I looked up at him. He grinned again. "Damn it if I didn't leave all my money home. You ain't got a dollar on you, have you? Just for a couple of days, is all."

All at once something inside gave and threatened to come pouring out of me. I didn't hate him anymore. I felt that in another moment I'd start crying like a child.

"Sure," I said. "Don't sweat." I looked in my wallet and didn't have a dollar, I only had a five. "Here," I said. "That hold you?"

He didn't look at it—he didn't want to look at it. A terrible closed look came over his face, as though he were keeping the number on the bill a secret from him and me. "Thanks," he said, and now he was dying to see me go. "Don't worry about Sonny. Maybe I'll write him or something."

"Sure," I said. "You do that. So long."

"Be seeing you," he said. I went on down the steps.

And I didn't write Sonny or send him anything for a long time. When I finally did, it was just after my little girl died, he wrote me back a letter which made me feel like a bastard.

Here's what he said:

> Dear brother,
>
> You don't know how much I needed to hear from you. I wanted to write you many a time but I dug how much I must have hurt you and so I didn't write. But now I feel like a man who's been trying to climb up out of some deep, real deep and funky hole and just saw the sun up there, outside. I got to get outside.

I can't tell you much about how I got here. I mean I don't know how to tell you. I guess I was afraid of something or I was trying to escape from something and you know I have never been very strong in the head (smile). I'm glad Mama and Daddy are dead and can't see what's happened to their son and I swear if I'd known what I was doing I would never have hurt you so, you and a lot of other fine people who were nice to me and who believed in me.

I don't want you to think it had anything to do with me being a musician. It's more than that. Or maybe less than that. I can't get anything straight in my head down here and I try not to think about what's going to happen to me when I get outside again. Sometime I think I'm going to flip and *never* get outside and sometime I think I'll come straight back. I tell you one thing, though, I'd rather blow my brains out than go through this again. But that's what they all say, so they tell me. If I tell you when I'm coming to New York and if you could meet me, I sure would appreciate it. Give my love to Isabel and the kids and I was sure sorry to hear about little Gracie. I wish I could be like Mama and say the Lord's will be done, but I don't know it seems to me that trouble is the one thing that never does get stopped and I don't know what good it does to blame it on the Lord. But maybe it does some good if you believe it.

Your brother,
Sonny

Then I kept in constant touch with him and I sent him whatever I could and I went to meet him when he came back to New York. When I saw him many things I thought I had forgotten came flooding back to me. This was because I had begun, finally, to wonder about Sonny, about the life that Sonny lived inside. This life, whatever it was, had made him older and thinner and it had deepened the distant stillness in which he had always moved. He looked very unlike my baby brother. Yet, when he smiled, when we shook hands, the baby brother I'd never known looked out from the depths of his private life, like an animal waiting to be coaxed into the light.

"How you been keeping?" he asked me.

"All right. And you?"

"Just fine." He was smiling all over his face. "It's good to see you again."

"It's good to see you."

The seven years' difference in our ages lay between us like a chasm: I wondered if these years would ever operate between us as a bridge. I was remembering, and it made it hard to catch my breath, that I had been there when he was born; and I had heard the first words he had ever spoken. When he started to walk, he walked from our mother straight to me. I caught him just before he fell when he took the first steps he ever took in this world.

"How's Isabel?"

"Just fine. She's dying to see you."

"And the boys?"

"They're fine, too. They're anxious to see their uncle."

"Oh, come on. You know they don't remember me."

"Are you kidding? Of course they remember you."

He grinned again. We got into a taxi. We had a lot to say to each other, far too much to know how to begin.

As the taxi began to move, I asked, "You still want to go to India?"

He laughed. "You still remember that. Hell, no. This place is Indian enough for me."

"It used to belong to them," I said.

And he laughed again. "They damn sure knew what they were doing when they got rid of it."

Years ago, when he was around fourteen, he'd been all hipped on the idea of going to India. He read books about people sitting on rocks, naked, in all kinds of weather, but mostly bad, naturally, and walking barefoot through hot coals and arriving at wisdom. I used to say that it sounded to me as though they were getting away from wisdom as fast as they could. I think he sort of looked down on me for that.

"Do you mind," he asked, "if we have the driver drive alongside the park? On the west side—I haven't seen the city in so long."

"Of course not," I said. I was afraid that I might sound as though I were humoring him, but I hoped he wouldn't take it that way.

So we drove along, between the green of the park and the stony, lifeless elegance of hotels and apartment buildings, toward the vivid, killing streets of our childhood. These streets hadn't changed, though housing projects jutted up out of them now like rocks in the middle of a boiling sea. Most of the houses in which we had grown up had vanished, as had the stores from which we had stolen, the basements in which we had first tried sex, the rooftops from which we had hurled tin cans and bricks. But houses exactly like the houses of our past yet dominated the landscape, boys exactly like the boys we once had been found themselves smothering in these houses, came down into the streets for light and air and found themselves encircled by disaster. Some escaped the trap, most didn't. Those who got out always left something of themselves behind, as some animals amputate a leg and leave it in the trap. It might be said, perhaps, that I had escaped, after all, I was a school teacher; or that Sonny had, he hadn't lived in Harlem for years. Yet, as the cab moved uptown through streets which seemed, with a rush, to darken with dark people, and as I covertly studied Sonny's face, it came to me that what we both were seeking through our separate cab windows was that part of ourselves which had been left behind. It's always at the hour of trouble and confrontation that the missing member aches.

We hit 110th Street and started rolling up Lenox Avenue. And I'd known this avenue all my life, but it seemed to me again, as it had seemed on the day I'd first heard about Sonny's trouble, filled with a hidden menace which was its very breath of life.

"We almost there," said Sonny.

"Almost." We were both too nervous to say anything more.

We live in a housing project. It hasn't been up long. A few days after it was up it seemed uninhabitably new, now, of course, it's already rundown. It looks like a parody of the good, clean, faceless life—God knows the people who live in it do their best to make it a parody. The beat-looking grass lying around isn't enough to make their lives green, the hedges will never hold out the streets, and they know it. The big windows fool no one, they aren't big enough to make space out of no space. They don't bother with the windows, they watch the TV screen instead. The playground is most popular with the children who don't play at jacks, or skip rope, or roller skate, or swing, and they can be found in it after dark. We moved in partly because it's not too far from where I teach, and partly for the kids; but it's really just like the houses in which Sonny and I grew up. The same things happen, they'll have the same things to remember. The moment Sonny and I started into the house I had the feeling that I was simply bringing him back into the danger he had almost died trying to escape.

Sonny has never been talkative. So I don't know why I was sure he'd be dying to talk to me when supper was over the first night. Everything went fine, the oldest boy remembered him, and the youngest boy liked him, and Sonny had remembered to bring something for each of them; and Isabel, who is really much nicer than I am, more open and giving, had gone to a lot of trouble about dinner and was genuinely glad to see him. And she's always been able to tease Sonny in a way that I haven't. It was nice to see her face so vivid again and to hear her laugh and watch her make Sonny laugh. She wasn't, or, anyway, she didn't seem to be, at all uneasy or embarrassed. She chatted as though there were no subject which had to be avoided and she got Sonny past his first, faint stiffness. And thank God she was there, for I was filled with that icy dread again. Everything I did seemed awkward to me, and everything I said sounded freighted with hidden meaning. I was trying to remember everything I'd heard about dope addiction and I couldn't help watching Sonny for signs. I wasn't doing it out of malice. I was trying to find out something about my brother. I was dying to hear him tell me he was safe.

"Safe!" my father grunted, whenever Mama suggested trying to move to a neighborhood which might be safer for children. "Safe, hell! Ain't no place safe for kids, nor nobody."

He always went on like this, but he wasn't, ever, really as bad as he sounded, not even on weekends, when he got drunk. As a matter of fact, he was always on the lookout for "something a little better," but he died before he found it. He died suddenly, during a drunken weekend in the middle of the war, when Sonny was fifteen. He and Sonny hadn't ever got on too well. And this was partly because Sonny was the apple of his father's eye. It was because he loved Sonny so much and was frightened for him, that he was always fighting with him. It doesn't do any good to fight with Sonny. Sonny just moves back, inside himself, where he can't be reached. But the principal reason that they never hit it off is that they were so much alike. Daddy was big and rough and loud-talking, just the opposite of Sonny, but they both had—that same privacy.

Mama tried to tell me something about this, just after Daddy died. I was home on leave from the army.

This was the last time I ever saw my mother alive. Just the same, this picture gets all mixed up in my mind with pictures I had of her when she was younger. The way I always see her is the way she used to be on a Sunday afternoon, say, when the old folks were talking after the big Sunday dinner. I always see her wearing pale blue. She'd be sitting on the sofa. And my father would be sitting in the easy chair, not far from her. And the living room would be full of church folks and relatives. There they sit, in chairs all around the living room, and the night is creeping up outside, but nobody knows it yet. You can see the darkness growing against the windowpanes and you hear the street noises every now and again, or maybe the jangling beat of a tambourine from one of the churches close by, but it's real quiet in the room. For a moment nobody's talking, but every face looks darkening, like the sky outside. And my mother rocks a little from the waist, and my father's eyes are closed. Everyone is looking at something a child can't see. For a minute they've forgotten the children. Maybe a kid is lying on the rug, half asleep. Maybe somebody's got a kid in his lap and is absent-mindedly stroking the kid's head. Maybe there's a kid, quiet and big eyed, curled up in a big chair in the corner. The silence, the darkness coming, and the darkness in the faces frightens the child obscurely. He hopes that the hand which strokes his forehead will never stop—will never die. He hopes that there will never come a time when the old folks won't be sitting around the living room, talking about where they've come from, and what they've seen, and what's happened to them and their kinfolk.

But something deep and watchful in the child knows that this is bound to end, is already ending. In a moment someone will get up and turn on the light. Then the old folks will remember the children and they won't talk anymore that day. And when light fills the room, the child is filled with darkness. He knows that every time this happens he's moved just a little closer to that darkness outside. The darkness outside is what the old folks have been talking about. It's what they've come from. It's what they endure. The child knows that they won't talk anymore because if he knows too much about what's happened to *them*, he'll know too much too soon, about what's going to happen to *him*.

The last time I talked to my mother, I remember I was restless. I wanted to get out and see Isabel. We weren't married then and we had a lot to straighten out between us.

There Mama sat, in black, by the window. She was humming an old church song, *Lord, you brought me from a long ways off.* Sonny was out somewhere. Mama kept watching the streets.

"I don't know," she said, "if I'll ever see you again, after you go off from here. But I hope you'll remember the things I tried to teach you."

"Don't talk like that," I said, and smiled. "You'll be here a long time yet."

She smiled, too, but she said nothing. She was quiet for a long time. And I said, "Mama, don't you worry about nothing. I'll be writing all the time, and you be getting the checks. . . ."

"I want to talk to you about your brother," she said, suddenly. "If anything happens to me he ain't going to have nobody to look out for him."

"Mama," I said, "ain't nothing going to happen to you *or* Sonny. Sonny's all right. He's a good boy and he's got good sense."

"It ain't a question of his being a good boy," Mama said, "nor of his having good sense. It ain't only the bad ones, nor yet the dumb ones that gets sucked under." She stopped, looking at me. "Your daddy once had a brother," she said, and she smiled in a way that made me feel she was in pain. "You didn't never know that, did you?"

"No," I said, "I never knew that," and I watched her face.

"Oh, yes," she said, "your daddy had a brother." She looked out of the window again. "I know you never saw your daddy cry. But *I* did—many a time, through all these years."

I asked her, "What happened to his brother? How come nobody's ever talked about him?"

This was the first time I ever saw my mother look old.

"His brother got killed," she said, "when he was just a little younger than you are now. I knew him. He was a fine boy. He was maybe a little full of the devil, but he didn't mean nobody no harm."

Then she stopped and the room was silent, exactly as it had sometimes been on those Sunday afternoons. Mama kept looking out into the streets.

"He used to have a job in the mill," she said, "and, like all young folks, he just liked to perform on Saturday nights. Saturday nights, him and your father would drift around to different places, go to dances and things like that, or just sit around with people they knew, and your father's brother would sing, he had a fine voice, and play along with himself on his guitar. Well, this particular Saturday night, him and your father was coming home from some place, and they were both a little drunk and there was a moon that night, it was bright like day. Your father's brother was feeling kind of good, and he was whistling to himself, and he had his guitar slung over his shoulder. They was coming down a hill and beneath them was a road that turned off from the highway. Well, your father's brother, being always kind of frisky, decided to run down this hill, and he did, with that guitar banging and clanging behind him, and he ran across the road, and he was making water behind a tree. And your father was sort of amused at him and he was still coming down the hill, kind of slow. Then he heard a car motor and that same minute his brother stepped from behind the tree, into the road, in the moonlight. And he started to cross the road. And your father started to run down the hill, he says he don't know why. This car was full of white men. They was all drunk, and when they seen your father's brother they let out a great whoop and holler and they aimed the car straight at him. They was having fun, they just wanted to scare him, the way they do sometimes, you know. But they was drunk. And I guess the boy, being drunk, too, and scared, kind of lost his head. By the time he jumped it was too late. Your father says he heard his brother scream when the car rolled over him, and he heard the wood of that guitar when it give, and he heard them strings go flying, and he heard them white men shouting, and the car kept on a-going and it ain't stopped till this day. And, time your father got down the hill, his brother weren't nothing but blood and pulp."

Tears were gleaming on my mother's face. There wasn't anything I could say.

"He never mentioned it," she said, "because I never let him mention it before you children. Your daddy was like a crazy man that night and for many a night thereafter. He says he never in his life seen anything as dark as that road after the lights of that car had gone away. Weren't nothing, weren't nobody on that road, just your daddy and his brother and that busted guitar. Oh, yes. Your daddy never did really get right again. Till the day he died he weren't sure but that every white man he saw was the man that killed his brother."

She stopped and took out her handkerchief and dried her eyes and looked at me.

"I ain't telling you all this," she said, "to make you scared or bitter or to make you hate nobody. I'm telling you this because you got a brother. And the world ain't changed."

I guess I didn't want to believe this. I guess she saw this in my face. She turned away from me, toward the window again, searching those streets.

"But I praise my Redeemer," she said at last, "that he called your daddy home before me. I ain't saying it to throw no flowers at myself, but, I declare, it keeps me from feeling too cast down to know I helped your father get safely through this world. Your father always acted like he was the roughest, strongest man on earth. And everybody took him to be like that. But if he hadn't had *me* there—to see his tears!"

She was crying again. Still, I couldn't move. I said, "Lord, Lord, Mama, I didn't know it was like that."

"Oh, honey," she said, "there's a lot that you don't know. But you are going to find it out." She stood up from the window and came over to me. "You got to hold on to your brother," she said, "and don't let him fall, no matter what it looks like is happening to him and no matter how evil you gets with him. You going to be evil with him many a time. But don't you forget what I told you, you hear?"

"I won't forget," I said. "Don't you worry, I won't forget. I won't let nothing happen to Sonny."

My mother smiled as though she were amused at something she saw in my face. Then, "You may not be able to stop nothing from happening. But you got to let him know you's *there*."

Two days later I was married, and then I was gone. And I had a lot of things on my mind and I pretty well forgot my promise to Mama until I got shipped home on a special furlough for her funeral.

And, after the funeral, with just Sonny and me alone in the empty kitchen, I tried to find out something about him.

"What do you want to do?" I asked him.

"I'm going to be a musician," he said.

For he had graduated, in the time I had been away, from dancing to the jukebox to finding out who was playing what, and what they were doing with it, and he had bought himself a set of drums.

"You mean, you want to be a drummer?" I somehow had the feeling that being a drummer might be all right for other people but not for my brother Sonny.

"I don't think," he said, looking at me very gravely, "that I'll ever be a good drummer. But I think I can play a piano."

I frowned. I'd never played the role of the older brother quite so seriously before, had scarcely ever, in fact, *asked* Sonny a damn thing. I sensed myself in the presence of something I didn't really know how to handle, didn't understand. So I made my frown a little deeper as I asked: "What kind of musician do you want to be?"

He grinned. "How many kinds do you think there are?"

"Be *serious*," I said.

He laughed, throwing his head back, and then looked at me. "I *am* serious."

"Well, then, for Christ's sake, stop kidding around and answer a serious question. I mean, do you want to be a concert pianist, you want to play classical music and all that, or—or what?" Long before I finished he was laughing again. "For Christ's *sake*, Sonny!"

He sobered, but with difficulty. "I'm sorry. But you sound so—*scared*!" and he was off again.

"Well, you may think it's funny now, baby, but it's not going to be so funny when you have to make your living at it, let me tell you *that*." I was furious because I knew he was laughing at me and I didn't know why.

"No," he said, very sober now, and afraid, perhaps, that he'd hurt me, "I don't want to be a classical pianist. That isn't what interests me. I mean"—he paused, looking hard at me, as though his eyes would help me to understand, and then gestured helplessly, as though perhaps his hand would help—"I mean, I'll have a lot of studying to do, and I'll have to study *everything*, but, I mean, I want to play *with*—jazz musicians." He stopped. "I want to play jazz," he said.

Well, the word had never before sounded as heavy, as real, as it sounded that afternoon in Sonny's mouth. I just looked at him and

I was probably frowning a real frown by this time. I simply couldn't see why on earth he'd want to spend his time hanging around nightclubs, clowning around on bandstands, while people pushed each other around a dance floor. It seemed—beneath him, somehow. I had never thought about it before, had never been forced to, but I suppose I had always put jazz musicians in a class with what Daddy called "good-time people."

"Are you *serious*?"

"Hell, *yes*, I'm serious."

He looked more helpless than ever, and annoyed, and deeply hurt.

I suggested, helpfully: "You mean—like Louis Armstrong?"

His face closed as though I'd struck him. "No. I'm not talking about none of that old-time, down-home crap."

"Well, look, Sonny, I'm sorry, don't get mad. I just don't altogether get it, that's all. Name somebody—you know, a jazz musician you admire."

"Bird."

"Who?"

"Bird! Charlie Parker! Don't they teach you nothing in the goddamn army?"

I lit a cigarette. I was surprised and then a little amused to discover that I was trembling. "I've been out of touch," I said. "You'll have to be patient with me. Now. Who's this Parker character?"

"He's just one of the greatest jazz musicians alive," said Sonny, sullenly, his hands in his pockets, his back to me. "Maybe *the* greatest," he added, bitterly, "that's probably why *you* never heard of him."

"All right," I said, "I'm ignorant. I'm sorry. I'll go out and buy all the cat's records right away, all right?"

"It don't," said Sonny, with dignity, "make any difference to me. I don't care what you listen to. Don't do me no favors."

I was beginning to realize that I'd never seen him so upset before. With another part of my mind I was thinking that this would probably turn out to be one of those things kids go through and that I shouldn't make it seem important by pushing it too hard. Still, I didn't think it would do any harm to ask: "Doesn't all this take a lot of time? Can you make a living at it?"

He turned back to me and half leaned, half sat, on the kitchen table. "Everything takes time," he said, "and—well, yes, sure, I can make a living at it. But what I don't seem to be able to make you understand is that it's the only thing I want to do."

"Well, Sonny," I said, gently, "you know people can't always do exactly what they *want* to do—"

"*No*, I don't know that," said Sonny, surprising me. "I think people *ought* to do what they want to do, what else are they alive for?"

"You getting to be a big boy," I said desperately, "it's time you started thinking about your future."

"I'm thinking about my future," said Sonny, grimly. "I think about it all the time."

I gave up. I decided, if he didn't change his mind, that we could always talk about it later. "In the meantime," I said, "you got to finish school." We had already decided that he'd have to move in with Isabel and her folks. I knew this wasn't the ideal arrangement because Isabel's folks are inclined to be dicty and they hadn't especially wanted Isabel to marry me. But I didn't know what else to do. "And we have to get you fixed up at Isabel's."

There was a long silence. He moved from the kitchen table to the window. "That's a terrible idea. You know it yourself."

"Do you have a *better* idea?"

He just walked up and down the kitchen for a minute. He was as tall as I was. He had started to shave. I suddenly had the feeling that I didn't know him at all.

He stopped at the kitchen table and picked up my cigarettes. Looking at me with a kind of mocking, amused defiance, he put one between his lips. "You mind?"

"You smoking already?"

He lit the cigarette and nodded, watching me through the smoke. "I just wanted to see if I'd have the courage to smoke in front of you." He grinned and blew a great cloud of smoke to the ceiling. "It was easy." He looked at my face. "Come on, now. I bet you was smoking at my age, tell the truth."

I didn't say anything but the truth was on my face, and he laughed. But now there was something very strained in his laugh. "Sure. And I bet that ain't all you was doing."

He was frightening me a little. "Cut the crap," I said. "We already decided that you was going to go and live at Isabel's. Now what's got into you all of a sudden?"

"*You* decided it," he pointed out. "*I* didn't decide nothing." He stopped in front of me, leaning against the stove, arms loosely folded. "Look, brother. I don't want to stay in Harlem no more, I really don't." He was very earnest. He looked at me, then over toward the kitchen window. There was something in his eyes I'd never seen before, some thoughtfulness, some worry all his own. He rubbed the muscle of one arm. "It's time I was getting out of here."

"Where do you want to *go*, Sonny?"

"I want to join the army. Or the navy, I don't care. If I say I'm old enough, they'll believe me."

Then I got mad. It was because I was so scared. "You must be crazy. You goddamn fool, what the hell do you want to go and join the *army* for?"

"I just told you. To get out of Harlem."

"Sonny, you haven't even finished *school*. And if you really want to be a musician, how do you expect to study if you're in the *army*?"

He looked at me, trapped, and in anguish. "There's ways. I might be able to work out some kind of deal. Anyway, I'll have the GI Bill when I come out."

"*If* you come out." We stared at each other. "Sonny, please. Be reasonable. I know the setup is far from perfect. But we got to do the best we can."

"I ain't learning nothing in school," he said. "Even when I go." He turned away from me and opened the window and threw his cigarette out into the narrow alley. I watched his back. "At least, I ain't learning nothing you'd want me to learn." He slammed the window so hard I thought the glass would fly out, and turned back to me. "And I'm sick of the stink of these garbage cans!"

"Sonny," I said, "I know how you feel. But if you don't finish school now, you're going to be sorry later that you didn't." I grabbed him by the shoulders. "And you only got another year. It ain't so bad. And I'll come back and I swear I'll help you do *whatever* you want to do. Just try to put up with it till I come back. Will you please do that? For me?"

He didn't answer and he wouldn't look at me.

"Sonny. You hear me?"

He pulled away. "I hear you. But you never hear anything *I* say."

I didn't know what to say to that. He looked out of the window and then back at me. "OK," he said, and sighed. "I'll try."

Then I said, trying to cheer him up a little, "They got a piano at Isabel's. You can practice on it."

And as a matter of fact, it did cheer him up for a minute. "That's right," he said to himself. "I forgot that." His face relaxed a little. But the worry, the thoughtfulness, played on it still, the way shadows play on a face which is staring into the fire.

But I thought I'd never hear the end of that piano. At first, Isabel would write me, saying how nice it was that Sonny was so serious about his music and how, as soon as he came in from school, or wherever he had been when he was supposed to be at school, he went straight to that piano and stayed there until suppertime. And, after supper, he went back to that piano and stayed there until everybody went to bed. He was at the piano all day Saturday and all day Sunday. Then he bought a record player and started playing records. He'd play one record over and over again, all day long sometimes, and he'd improvise along with it on the piano. Or he'd play one section of the record, one chord, one change, one progression, then he'd do it on the piano. Then back to the record. Then back to the piano.

Well, I really don't know how they stood it. Isabel finally confessed that it wasn't like living with a person at all, it was like living with sound. And the sound didn't make any sense to her, didn't make any sense to any of them—naturally. They began, in a way, to be afflicted by this presence that was living in their home. It was as though Sonny were some sort of god, or monster. He moved in an atmosphere which wasn't like theirs at all. They fed him and he ate, he washed himself, he walked in and out of their door; he certainly wasn't nasty or unpleasant or rude, Sonny isn't any of those things; but it was as though he were all wrapped up in some cloud, some fire, some vision all his own; and there wasn't any way to reach him.

At the same time, he wasn't really a man yet, he was still a child, and they had to watch out for him in all kinds of ways. They certainly couldn't throw him out. Neither did they dare to make a great scene about that piano because even they dimly sensed, as I sensed, from so many thousands of miles away, that Sonny was at that piano playing for his life.

But he hadn't been going to school. One day a letter came from the school board and Isabel's mother got it—there had, apparently, been other letters but Sonny had torn them up. This day, when Sonny came in, Isabel's mother showed him the letter and asked where he'd been spending his time. And she finally got it out of him that he'd been down in Greenwich Village, with musicians and other characters, in a white girl's apartment. And this scared her and she started to scream at him and what came up, once she began—though she denies it to this day—was what sacrifices they were making to give Sonny a decent home and how little he appreciated it.

Sonny didn't play the piano that day. By evening, Isabel's mother had calmed down but then there was the old man to deal with, and Isabel herself. Isabel says she did her best to be calm but she broke down and started crying. She says she just watched Sonny's face. She could tell, by watching him, what was happening with him. And what was happening was that they penetrated his cloud, they had reached him. Even if their fingers had been a thousand times more gentle than human fingers ever are, he could hardly help feeling that they had stripped him naked and were spitting on that nakedness. For he also had to see that his presence, that music, which was life or death to him, had been torture for them and that they had endured it, not at all for his sake, but only for mine. And Sonny couldn't take that. He can take it a little better today than he could then but he's still not very good at it and, frankly, I don't know anybody who is.

The silence of the next few days must have been louder than the sound of all the music ever played since time began. One morning, before she went to work, Isabel was in his room for something and she suddenly realized that all of his records were gone. And she knew for certain that he was gone. And he was. He went as far as the navy would carry him. He finally sent me a postcard from some place in Greece and that was the first I knew that Sonny was still alive. I didn't see him anymore until we were both back in New York and the war had long been over.

He was a man by then, of course, but I wasn't willing to see it. He came by the house from time to time, but we fought almost every time we met. I didn't like the way he carried himself, loose and dreamlike all the time, and I didn't like his friends, and his music seemed to be merely an excuse for the life he led. It sounded just that weird and disordered.

Then we had a fight, a pretty awful fight, and I didn't see him for months. By and by I looked him up, where he was living, in a furnished room in the Village, and I tried to make it up. But there were lots of people in the room and Sonny just lay on his bed, and he wouldn't come downstairs with me, and he treated these other people as though they were his family and I weren't. So I got mad and then he got mad, and then I told him that he might just as well be dead as live the way he was living. Then he stood up and he told me not to worry about him anymore in life, that he *was* dead as far as I was concerned. Then he pushed me to the door and the other people looked on as though nothing were happening, and he slammed the door behind me. I stood in the hallway, staring at the door. I heard somebody laugh in the room and then the tears came to my eyes. I started down the steps, whistling to keep from crying, I kept whistling to myself, *You going to need me, baby, one of these cold, rainy days.*

I read about Sonny's trouble in the spring. Little Grace died in the fall. She was a beautiful little girl. But she only lived a little over two years. She died of polio and she suffered. She had a slight fever for a couple of days, but it didn't seem like anything and we just kept her in bed. And we would certainly have called the doctor, but the fever dropped, she seemed to be all right. So we thought it had just been a cold. Then, one day, she was up, playing, Isabel was in the kitchen fixing lunch for the two boys when they'd come in from school, and she heard Grace fall down in the living room. When you have a lot of children you don't always start running when one of them falls, unless they start screaming or something. And, this time, Grace was quiet. Yet, Isabel says that when she heard that *thump* and then that silence, something happened in her to make her afraid. And she ran to the living room and there was little Grace on the floor, all twisted up, and the reason she hadn't screamed was that she couldn't get her breath. And when she did scream, it was the worst sound, Isabel says, that she'd ever heard in all her life, and she still hears it sometimes in her dreams. Isabel will sometimes wake me up with a low, moaning, strangled sound and I have to be quick to awaken her and hold her to me and where Isabel is weeping against me seems a mortal wound.

I think I may have written Sonny the very day that little Grace was buried. I was sitting in the living room in the dark, by myself, and I suddenly thought of Sonny. My trouble made his real.

One Saturday afternoon, when Sonny had been living with us, or, anyway, been in our house, for nearly two weeks, I found myself wandering aimlessly about the living room, drinking from a can of beer, and trying to work up the courage to search Sonny's room. He was out, he was usually out whenever I was home, and Isabel had taken the children to see their grandparents. Suddenly I was standing still in front of the living room window, watching Seventh Avenue. The idea of searching Sonny's room made me still. I scarcely dared to admit to myself what I'd be searching for. I didn't know what I'd do if I found it. Or if I didn't.

On the sidewalk across from me, near the entrance to a barbecue joint, some people were holding an old-fashioned revival meeting. The barbecue cook, wearing a dirty white apron, his conked hair reddish and metallic in the pale sun, and a cigarette between his lips, stood in the doorway, watching them. Kids and older people paused in their errands and stood there, along with some older men and a couple of very tough-looking women who watched everything that happened on the avenue, as though they owned it, or were maybe owned by it. Well, they were watching this, too. The revival was being carried on by three sisters in black, and a brother. All they had were their voices and their Bibles and a tambourine. The brother was testifying and while he testified two of the sisters stood together, seeming to say, amen, and the third sister walked around with the tambourine outstretched and a couple of people dropped coins into it. Then the brother's testimony ended and the sister who had been taking up the collection dumped the coins into her palm and transferred them to the pocket of her long black robe. Then she raised both hands, striking the tambourine against the air, and then against one hand, and she started to sing. And the two other sisters and the brothers joined in.

It was strange, suddenly, to watch, though I had been seeing these street meetings all my life. So, of course, had everybody else down there. Yet, they paused and watched and listened and I stood still at the window. "*Tis the old ship of Zion*," they sang, and the sister with the tambourine kept a steady, jangling beat, "*it has rescued many a thousand!*" Not a soul under the sound of their voices was hearing this song for the first time, not one of them had been rescued. Nor had they seen much in the way of rescue work being done around them. Neither did they especially believe in the holiness of the three sisters and the brother, they knew too much about them, knew where they lived, and how. The woman with the tambourine, whose voice dominated the air, whose face was bright with joy, was divided by very little from the woman who stood watching her, a cigarette between her heavy, chapped lips, her hair a cuckoo's nest, her face scarred and swollen from many beatings, and her black eyes glittering like coal. Perhaps they both knew this, which was why, when, as rarely, they addressed each other, they addressed each other as Sister. As the singing filled the air the watching, listening faces underwent a change, the eyes focusing on something within; the music seemed to soothe a poison out of them; and time seemed, nearly, to fall away from the sullen, belligerent, battered faces, as though they were fleeing back to their first condition, while dreaming of their last. The barbecue cook half shook his head and smiled, and dropped his cigarette and disappeared into his joint. A man fumbled in his pockets for change and stood holding it in his hand impatiently, as though he had just remembered a pressing appointment further up the avenue. He looked furious. Then I saw Sonny, standing on the edge of the crowd. He was carrying a wide, flat notebook with a green cover, and it made him look, from where I was standing, almost like a schoolboy. The coppery sun brought out the copper in his skin, he was very faintly smiling, standing very still. Then the singing stopped, the tambourine turned into a collection plate again. The furious man dropped in his coins and vanished, so did a couple of the women, and Sonny dropped some change in the plate, looking directly at the woman with a little smile. He started across the avenue, toward the house. He has a slow, loping walk, something like the way Harlem hipsters walk, only he's imposed on this his own half beat. I had never really noticed it before.

I stayed at the window, both relieved and apprehensive. As Sonny disappeared from my sight, they began singing again. And they were still singing when his key turned in the lock.

"Hey," he said.

"Hey, yourself. You want some beer?"

"No. Well, maybe." But he came up to the window and stood beside me, looking out. "What a warm voice," he said.

They were singing "*If I could only hear my mother pray again!*"

"Yes," I said, "and she can sure beat that tambourine."

"But what a terrible song," he said, and laughed. He dropped his notebook on the sofa and disappeared into the kitchen. "Where's Isabel and the kids?"

"I think they went to see their grandparents. You hungry?"

"No." He came back into the living room with his can of beer. "You want to come some place with me tonight?"

I sensed, I don't know how, that I couldn't possibly say no. "Sure. Where?"

He sat down on the sofa and picked up his notebook and started leafing through it. "I'm going to sit in with some fellows in a joint in the Village."

"You mean, you're going to play, tonight?"

"That's right." He took a swallow of his beer and moved back to the window. He gave me a sidelong look. "If you can stand it."

"I'll try," I said.

He smiled to himself and we both watched as the meeting across the way broke up. The three sisters and the brother, heads bowed, were singing "*God be with you till we meet again.*" The faces around them were very quiet. Then the song ended. The small crowd dispersed. We watched the three women and the lone man walk slowly up the avenue.

"When she was singing before," said Sonny, abruptly, "her voice reminded me for a minute of what heroin feels like sometimes—when it's in your veins. It makes you feel sort of warm and cool at the same time. And distant. And—and sure." He sipped his beer, very deliberately not looking at me. I watched his face. "It makes you feel—in control. Sometimes you've got to have that feeling."

"Do you?" I sat down slowly in the easy chair.

"Sometimes." He went to the sofa and picked up his notebook again. "Some people do."

"In order," I asked, "to play?" And my voice was very ugly, full of contempt and anger.

"Well"—he looked at me with great, troubled eyes, as though, in fact, he hoped his eyes would tell me things he could never otherwise say—"they *think* so. And *if* they think so—!"

"And what do *you* think?" I asked.

He sat on the sofa and put his can of beer on the floor. "I don't know," he said, and I couldn't be sure if he were answering my question or pursuing his thoughts. His face didn't tell me. "It's not so much to *play*. It's to *stand* it, to be able to make it at all. On any level." He frowned and smiled: "In order to keep from shaking to pieces."

"But these friends of yours," I said, "they seem to shake themselves to pieces pretty goddamn fast."

"Maybe." He played with the notebook. And something told me that I should curb my tongue, that Sonny was doing his best to talk, that I should listen. "But of course you only know the ones that've gone to pieces. Some don't—or at least they haven't *yet* and that's just about all *any* of us can say." He paused. "And then there are some who just live, really, in hell, and they know it and they see what's happening and they go right on. I don't know." He sighed, dropped the notebook, folded his arms. "Some guys, you can tell from the way they play, they on something *all* the time. And you can see that, well, it makes something real for them. But of course," he picked up his beer from the floor and sipped it and put the can down again, "they *want* to, too, you've got to see that. Even some of them that say they don't—*some*, not all."

"And what about you?" I asked—I couldn't help it. "What about you? Do *you* want to?"

He stood up and walked to the window and remained silent for a long time. Then he sighed. "Me," he said. Then: "While I was downstairs before, on my way here, listening to that woman sing, it struck me all of a sudden how much suffering she must have had to go through—to sing like that. It's *repulsive* to think you have to suffer that much."

I said: "But there's no way not to suffer—is there, Sonny?"

"I believe not," he said and smiled, "but that's never stopped anyone from trying." He looked at me. "Has it?" I realized, with this mocking look, that there stood between us, forever, beyond the power of time or forgiveness, the fact that I had held silence—so long!—when he had needed human speech to help him. He turned back to the window. "No, there's no way not to suffer. But you try all kinds of ways to keep from drowning in it, to keep on top of it, and to make it seem—well, like *you*. Like you did something, all right, and now you're suffering for it. You know?" I said nothing. "Well you know," he said, impatiently, "why *do* people suffer? Maybe it's better to do something to give it a reason, *any* reason."

"But we just agreed," I said, "that there's no way not to suffer. Isn't it better, then, just to—take it?"

"But nobody just takes it," Sonny cried, "that's what I'm telling you! *Everybody* tries not to. You're just hung up on the *way* some people try—it's not *your* way!"

The hair on my face began to itch, my face felt wet. "That's not true," I said, "that's not true. I don't give a damn what other people do, I don't even care how they suffer. I just care how *you* suffer." And he looked at me. "Please believe me," I said, "I don't want to see you—die—trying not to suffer."

"I won't," he said, flatly, "die trying not to suffer. At least, not any faster than anybody else."

"But there's no need," I said, trying to laugh, "is there? in killing yourself."

I wanted to say more, but I couldn't. I wanted to talk about willpower and how life could be—well, beautiful. I wanted to say that it was all within; but was it? or, rather, wasn't that exactly the trouble? And I wanted to promise that I would never fail him again. But it would all have sounded—empty words and lies.

So I made the promise to myself and prayed that I would keep it.

"It's terrible sometimes, inside," he said, "that's what's the trouble. You walk these streets, black and funky and cold, and there's not really a living ass to talk to, and there's nothing shaking, and there's no way of getting it out—that storm inside. You can't talk it and you can't make love with it, and when you finally try to get with it and play it, you realize *nobody's* listening. So *you've* got to listen. You got to find a way to listen."

And then he walked away from the window and sat on the sofa again, as though all the wind had suddenly been knocked out of him. "Sometimes you'll do *anything* to play, even cut your mother's throat." He laughed and looked at me. "Or your brother's." Then he sobered. "Or your own." Then: "Don't worry. I'm all right now and I think I'll *be* all right. But I can't forget—where I've been. I don't mean just the physical place I've been, I mean where I've *been*. And *what* I've been."

"What have you been, Sonny?" I asked.

He smiled—but sat sideways on the sofa, his elbow resting on the back, his fingers playing with his mouth and chin, not looking at me. "I've been something I didn't recognize, didn't know I could be. Didn't know anybody could be." He stopped, looking inward, looking helplessly young, looking old. "I'm not talking about it now because I feel *guilty* or anything like that—maybe it would be better if I did, I don't know. Anyway, I can't really talk about it. Not to you, not to anybody," and now he turned and faced me. "Sometimes, you know, and it was actually when I was most *out* of the world, I felt that I was in it, that I was *with* it, really, and I could play or I didn't really have to *play*, it just came out of me, it was there. And I don't know how I played, thinking about it now, but I know I did awful things, those times, sometimes, to people. Or it wasn't that I *did* anything to them—it was that they weren't real." He picked up the beer can; it was empty; he rolled it between his palms: "And other times—well, I needed a fix, I needed to find a place to lean, I needed to clear a space to *listen*—and I couldn't find it, and I—went crazy, I did terrible things to *me*, I was terrible *for* me." He began pressing the beer can between his hands, I watched the metal begin to give. It glittered, as he played with it, like a knife, and I was afraid he would cut himself, but I said nothing. "Oh well. I can never tell you. I was all by myself at the bottom of something, stinking and sweating and crying and shaking, and I smelled it, you know? *my* stink, and I thought I'd die if I couldn't get away from it and yet, all the same, I knew that everything I was doing was just locking me in with it. And I didn't know," he paused, still flattening the beer can, "I didn't know, I still *don't* know, something kept telling me that maybe it was good to smell your own stink, but I didn't think that *that* was what I'd been trying to do—and—who can stand it?" and he abruptly dropped the ruined beer can, looking at me with a small, still smile, and then rose, walking to the window as though it were the lodestone rock. I watched his face, he watched the avenue. "I couldn't tell you when Mama died—but the reason I wanted to leave Harlem so bad was to get away from drugs. And then, when I ran away, that's what I was running from—really. When I came back, nothing had changed, *I* hadn't changed, I was just—older." And he stopped, drumming with his fingers on the windowpane. The sun had vanished, soon darkness would fall. I watched his face. "It can come again," he said, almost as though speaking to himself. Then he turned to me. "It can come again," he repeated. "I just want you to know that."

"All right," I said, at last. "So it can come again. All right."

He smiled, but the smile was sorrowful. "I had to try to tell you," he said.

"Yes," I said. "I understand that."

"You're my brother," he said, looking straight at me, and not smiling at all.

"Yes," I repeated, "yes. I understand that."

He turned back to the window, looking out. "All that hatred down there," he said, "all that hatred and misery and love. It's a wonder it doesn't blow the avenue apart."

We went to the only nightclub on a short, dark street, downtown. We squeezed through the narrow, chattering, jam-packed bar to the entrance of the big room, where the bandstand was. And we stood there for a moment, for the lights were very dim in this room and we couldn't see. Then, "Hello, boy," said a voice and an enormous black man, much older than Sonny or myself, erupted out of all that atmospheric lighting and put an arm around Sonny's shoulder. "I been sitting right here," he said, "waiting for you."

He had a big voice, too, and heads in the darkness turned toward us.

Sonny grinned and pulled a little away, and said, "Creole, this is my brother. I told you about him."

Creole shook my hand. "I'm glad to meet you, son," he said, and it was clear that he was glad to meet me *there*, for Sonny's sake. And he smiled, "You got a real musician in *your* family," and he took his arm from Sonny's shoulder and slapped him, lightly, affectionately, with the back of his hand.

"Well. Now I've heard it all," said a voice behind us. This was another musician, and a friend of Sonny's, a coal-black, cheerful-looking man, built close to the ground. He immediately began confiding to me, at the top of his lungs, the most terrible things about Sonny, his teeth gleaming like a lighthouse and his laugh coming up out of him like the beginning of an earthquake. And it turned out that everyone at the bar knew Sonny, or almost everyone; some were musicians, working there, or nearby, or not working, some were simply hangers-on, and some were there to hear Sonny play. I was introduced to all of them and they were all very polite to me. Yet, it was clear that, for them, I was only Sonny's brother. Here, I was in Sonny's world. Or, rather: his kingdom. Here, it was not even a question that his veins bore royal blood.

They were going to play soon and Creole installed me, by myself, at a table in a dark corner. Then I watched them, Creole, and the little black man, and Sonny, and the others, while they horsed around, standing just below the bandstand. The light from the bandstand spilled just a little short of them and, watching them laughing and gesturing and moving about, I had the feeling that they, nevertheless, were being most careful not to step into that circle of light too suddenly: that if they moved into the light too suddenly, without thinking, they would perish in flame. Then, while I watched, one of them, the small, black man, moved into the light and crossed the bandstand and started fooling around with his drums. Then—being funny and being, also, extremely ceremonious—Creole took Sonny by the arm and led him to the piano. A woman's voice called Sonny's name and a few hands started clapping. And Sonny, also being funny and being ceremonious, and so touched, I think, that he could have cried, but neither hiding it nor showing it, riding it like a man, grinned, and put both hands to his heart and bowed from the waist.

Creole then went to the bass fiddle and a lean, very bright-skinned brown man jumped up on the bandstand and picked up his horn. So there they were, and the atmosphere on the bandstand and in the room began to change and tighten. Someone stepped up to the microphone and announced them. Then there were all kinds of murmurs. Some people at the bar shushed others. The waitress ran around, frantically getting in the last orders, guys and chicks got closer to each other, and the lights on the bandstand, on the quartet, turned to a kind of indigo. Then they all looked different there. Creole looked about him for the last time, as though he were making certain that all his chickens were in the coop, and then he—jumped and struck the fiddle. And there they were.

All I know about music is that not many people ever really hear it. And even then, on the rare occasions when something opens within, and the music enters, what we mainly hear, or hear corroborated, are personal, private, vanishing evocations. But the man who creates the music is hearing something else, is dealing with the roar rising from the void and imposing order on it as it hits the air. What is evoked in him, then, is of another order, more terrible because it has no words, and triumphant, too, for that same reason. And his triumph, when he triumphs, is ours. I just watched Sonny's face. His face was troubled, he was working hard, but he wasn't with it. And I had the feeling that, in a way, everyone on the bandstand was waiting for him, both waiting for him and pushing him along. But as I began to watch Creole, I realized that it was Creole who held them all back. He had them on a short rein. Up there, keeping the beat with his whole body, wailing on the fiddle, with his eyes half closed, he was listening to everything, but he was listening to Sonny. He was having a dialogue with Sonny. He wanted Sonny to leave the shoreline and strike out for the deep water. He was Sonny's witness that deep water and drowning were not the same thing—he had been there, and he knew. And he wanted Sonny to know. He was waiting for Sonny to do the things on the keys which would let Creole know that Sonny was in the water.

And, while Creole listened, Sonny moved, deep within, exactly like someone in torment. I had never before thought of how awful the relationship must be between the musician and his instrument. He has to fill it, this instrument, with the breath of life, his own. He has to make it do what he wants it to do. And a piano is just a piano. It's made out of so much wood and wires and little hammers and big ones, and ivory. While there's only so much you can do with it, the only way to find this out is to try; to try and make it do everything.

And Sonny hadn't been near a piano for over a year. And he wasn't on much better terms with his life, not the life that stretched before him now. He and the piano stammered, started one way, got scared, stopped; started another way, panicked, marked time, started again; then seemed to have found a direction, panicked again, got stuck. And the face I saw on Sonny I'd never seen before. Everything had been burned out of it, and, at the same time, things usually hidden were being burned in, by the fire and fury of the battle which was occurring in him up there.

Yet, watching Creole's face as they neared the end of the first set, I had the feeling that something had happened, something I hadn't heard. Then they finished, there was scattered applause, and then, without an instant's warning, Creole started into something else, it was almost sardonic, it was "Am I Blue". And, as though he commanded, Sonny began to play. Something began to happen. And Creole let out the reins. The dry, low, black man said something awful on the drums, Creole answered, and the drums talked back. Then the horn insisted, sweet and high, slightly detached perhaps, and Creole listened, commenting now and then, dry, and driving, beautiful and calm and old. Then they all came together again, and Sonny was part of the family again. I could tell this from his face. He seemed to have found, right there beneath his fingers, a damn brand-new piano. It seemed that he couldn't get over it. Then, for awhile, just being happy with Sonny, they seemed to be agreeing with him that brand-new pianos certainly were a gas.

Then Creole stepped forward to remind them that what they were playing was the blues. He hit something in all of them, he hit something in me, myself, and the music tightened and deepened, apprehension began to beat the air. Creole began to tell us what the blues were all about. They were not about anything very new. He and his boys up there were keeping it new, at the risk of ruin, destruction, madness, and death, in order to find new ways to make us listen. For, while the tale of how we suffer, and how we are delighted, and how we may triumph is never new, it always must be heard. There isn't any other tale to tell, it's the only light we've got in all this darkness.

And this tale, according to that face, that body, those strong hands on those strings, has another aspect in every country, and a new depth in every generation. Listen, Creole seemed to be saying, listen. Now these are Sonny's blues. He made the little black man on the drums know it, and the bright, brown man on the horn. Creole wasn't trying any longer to get Sonny in the water. He was wishing him Godspeed. Then he stepped back, very slowly, filling the air with the immense suggestion that Sonny speak for himself.

Then they all gathered around Sonny and Sonny played. Every now and again one of them seemed to say, amen. Sonny's fingers filled the air with life, his life. But that life contained so many others. And Sonny went all the way back, he really began with the spare, flat statement of the opening phrase of the song. Then he began to make it his. It was very beautiful because it wasn't hurried and it was no longer a lament. I seemed to hear with what burning he had made it his, with what burning we had yet to make it ours, how we could cease lamenting. Freedom lurked around us and I understood, at last, that he could help us to be free if we would listen, that he would never be free until we did. Yet, there was no battle in his face now. I heard what he had gone through, and would continue to go through until he came to rest in earth. He had made it his: that long line, of which we knew only Mama and Daddy. And he was giving it back, as everything must be given back, so that, passing through death, it can live forever. I saw my mother's face again, and felt, for the first time, how the stones of the road she had walked on must have bruised her feet. I saw the moonlit road where my father's brother died. And it brought something else back to me, and carried me past it. I saw my little girl again and felt Isabel's tears again, and I felt my own tears begin to rise. And I was yet aware that this was only a moment, that the world waited outside, as hungry as a tiger, and that trouble stretched above us, longer than the sky.

Then it was over. Creole and Sonny let out their breath, both soaking wet, and grinning. There was a lot of applause and some of it was real. In the dark, the girl came by and I asked her to take drinks to the bandstand. There was a long pause, while they talked up there in the indigo light and after awhile I saw the girl put a Scotch and milk on top of the piano for Sonny. He didn't seem to notice it, but just before they started playing again, he sipped from it and looked toward me, and nodded. Then he put it back on top of the piano. For me, then, as they began to play again, it glowed and shook above my brother's head like the very cup of trembling.

---

1. When Sonny's friend asks the narrator for a dollar, why does the narrator say, "I didn't hate him anymore"?
2. Does the narrator agree with Sonny that people are alive in order to do what they want to do?
3. Does the narrator come to an understanding of Sonny's blues? If so, what is that understanding?
4. How can the narrator best exercise his responsibility toward Sonny?

DONALD HALL (1928–) was born in New Haven, Connecticut. He was educated at Phillips Exeter Academy and received bachelor's degrees in literature at both Harvard and Oxford universities. At Oxford he won the prestigious Newdigate Prize for his poetry—a feat seldom achieved by an American poet. In 1957 he began his teaching career at the University of Michigan, prolifically publishing volumes of prose, poetry, and children's literature. Upon the death of his grandmother in 1975, he bought Eagle Pond Farm, which she had owned, and moved there with his second wife, the poet Jane Kenyon, to devote himself full-time to writing. His work reflects his passion for the land and his connection to it. He has won numerous literary prizes; *The One Day: A Poem in Three Parts* (1988) received the National Book Critics Circle Award and the Los Angeles Times Book Prize in poetry.

Argument and Persuasion

1

A husband and wife named Raoul and Marie lived in a house beside a river next to a forest. One afternoon Raoul told Marie that he had to travel to Paris overnight on business. As soon as he left, Marie paid the Ferryman one franc to row her across the river to the house of her lover Pierre. Marie and Pierre made love all night. Just before dawn, Marie dressed to go home, to be sure that she arrived before Raoul returned. When she reached the Ferryman, she discovered that she had neglected to bring a second franc for her return journey. She asked the Ferryman to trust her; she would pay him back. He refused: A rule is a rule, he said.

If she walked north by the river she could cross it on a bridge, but between the bridge and her house a Murderer lived in the forest and killed anybody who entered. So Marie returned to Pierre's house to wake him and borrow a franc. She found the door locked; she banged on it; she shouted as loud as she could; she threw pebbles against Pierre's bedroom windows. Pierre awoke hearing her but he was tired and did not want to get out of bed. "Women!" he thought. "Once you give in, they take advantage of you. . . ." Pierre went back to sleep.

Marie returned to the Ferryman: She would give him *ten* francs by midmorning. He refused to break the rules of his job; they told him cash only; he did what they told him. . . . Marie returned to Pierre, with the same lack of result, as the sun started to rise.

Desperate, she ran north along the riverbank, crossed the bridge, and entered the Murderer's forest.

2

At 9:00 a.m. on a cool April morning, seventeen young women sat in plastic classroom chairs, each with a paddle-shaped writing surface. When Dr. Silva finished telling the story, he paused until the girls stopped their note taking and looked up at him. He smiled as he had smiled in a hundred other composition classes when he had told about Raoul and Marie. He continued: "This is not a trick story. There is no *correct* answer, but for forty minutes, please argue an answer to the question: Which of the characters in this story is morally most responsible for Marie's death?"

He wrote the question on the board and turned back to the class. "This impromptu gives you the opportunity to shape an argument. Be logical. In the next five minutes you may ask questions. There will be no further questions after five minutes are up. Do your thinking now." Myra Bobnick was already writing. "Do not start writing your impromptu before you have thought it out." Myra raced into her second page as if there were a contest for the most pages. Helen DeVane looked puzzled as ever and put her hand up. "I will list and spell all names on the blackboard," Dr. Silva said; he wrote:

Raoul
Marie
Ferryman

Pierre
Murderer

When he finished he nodded in Helen's direction.

"Did like this really happen?"

He could never tell what Helen's question would be, but he knew it would be dull witted. He also knew that she didn't really want an answer; she wanted only to postpone the moment of writing. When he answered Helen, he feared that he sounded so patient that he revealed his annoyance. "It doesn't matter, Helen. Certainly; why not? But it's just a story, something to write about." She nodded her head but the puzzlement never left her face.

Young women crossed their blue-jeaned legs and addressed the lined pads before them. This class was the first of three on Wednesday. All would do the same impromptu and if some of the later classes heard the story ahead of time, he knew it would make no difference. The girls chewed their fingernails or their Bics, either thinking or trying to look as if they were thinking. Magda had a question. "The ferry guy, did he work for himself, I mean with his own boat?"

"In the story," said Dr. Silva, "he implies that somebody else makes the rules."

There were no more questions. Now he could daydream for half an hour. He enjoyed this moment of English Composition 101, when fifteen or twenty pens scratched in front of him and he could look out the window at the grosbeaks coming to the feeder he had put there. Young female heads bent over paper like so many birds poking for sunflower seed. He checked his class list. There would have been eighteen but Jeanette was still in the infirmary. A year ago they had been graduating seniors in their suburban high schools; now they were freshmen at Connecticut Hills, a two-year college once called a finishing school, where he knew himself fortunate to have a job. He did not write books; for the good jobs you had to write books. Most of his work was three or four sections of English Composition—teaching the art of English prose to girls who could not, most of them, read anything more complicated than the labels of their cashmere sweaters. One term a year he relaxed into a section of the Sophomore Introduction to Great Books, a soft reward for all his labor over comma splices: *The Odyssey*, a touch of Thucydides, *Othello.*

Mary Ellen Budd was walking up to the desk. He shook his head; no questions after five minutes. Mary Ellen looked hopeless, sat down, and wrote nothing for the next ten minutes. He understood: She was demonstrating Dr. Silva's injustice; he also understood that she would get over it.

He could not remember who had told him the story of Raoul and Marie. It was early in graduate school, those happy-go-lucky first three years of marriage and provisional adulthood, in-between time that was also the best time, he often acknowledged, though not out loud; Anne did enough acknowledging out loud, when she had had something to drink. Back then in Ann Arbor someone at a party had told the story; it was supposed to be an anecdote Camus liked to tell, asking: "Who's most to blame?" Arthur Silva had said from the start that he knew the answer even if there wasn't supposed to be one: the Murderer. It made him feel morally clear-sighted to give this answer and defend it.

He looked at the pretty heads bent down before him: children of privilege, growing up rich in America—no brains . . . And when they had brains, which happened at Connecticut Hills more often than you might expect, the brains were well trained to believe that they were stupid; or to know by an un-stated rule that if they wished to remain daughters who were loved, cherished, and protected, they had better *act* stupid.

Bethany had finished her page and a half and checked it over: obedient girl—and now stupid by half. It was Dr. Silva's task, as he saw it, to teach girls like Bethany Adams—not to write sentences, not to employ the major rhetorical patterns, not to write A themes—but: *I am not dumb.* This was his mission at Connecticut Hills, and when he succeeded it was gratifying. He sighed, reminding himself that it was opposite to the lesson that he had learned. After five years in the PhD program at the University of Michigan, with the MA behind him and generals twice failed, he had been summoned by the Graduate Faculty Committee and requested to withdraw from the PhD program. Of course they would help him get a job, they assured him, for he was a competent teacher of composition. They apologized that their judgment had failed when they admitted him to the program, but they could not therefore compound the error by permitting him to continue. After he pleaded his case, the textual scholar Waldo Slaughter silenced him with one sentence: "You are not PhD material." The words remained permanently attached to him, as if they were printed on his forehead in diploma script. He remembered how old Braithewaite kept nodding his head, as if with encouragement, at every devastating generalization.

Oh, to take those words home to Anne, with Joanie only two years old!—Anne who had quit the MA program in French to take a job when they married, then quit her job to have Joanie. As it happened, the promised support consisted of a one-year job at an academy outside Detroit. After which, with a certain amount of backdoor help from the guiltier senior professors, Arthur Silva had been accepted into the doctoral program of the education department of an old normal school turned state university, and in two years he wore the desired letters after his name.

"Time's up!" he said. "You have an extra minute for checking." Five hours later—two more classes, brown bag lunch, office hours—he bicycled home with fifty-seven impromptus about a murder in a forest in generalized France.

3

When Raoul returned from Paris at noon he was exhausted and hungry. It annoyed him that Marie was nowhere about. It was unlike her, although she sometimes took a *fin* in the morning with one of her gabby oldwife friends. There was of course her ridiculous *affaire du coeur* with Pierre, about which Raoul pretended convenient ignorance. They had, after all, been married a dozen years. And after all, what was he doing in Paris? He sighed in delicious recollection of a seamstress.

Raoul was too tired to make the rounds of the cafés. He swallowed some stale bread with sweet butter and a slab of cold pink lamb. He read three pages in *L'Encyclopédie* and slept until seven o'clock in the evening. He woke and called Marie's name, intent on complaining about her absence. When she did not answer he was suddenly frightened. Where in hell was Marie?

4

Thursday was Dr. Silva's day without classes; therefore he let Wednesday be theme day, and spent all Thursday at the breakfast table, blitzing through a stack of papers with his red pencil and his *Harbrace College Handbook*—a dreadful text, but he knew the symbols for correction so well that they appeared as characters in his dreams. When you had sixty themes on the same subject—Dr. Silva had worked at schools where he taught composition to a hundred students a term—the first twenty went quickly. You began with one or two of the best, to set a measure. You knew who the best would be. After one class meeting, you knew which students would have As at the end of the term. This knowledge depressed him—what was the purpose of his teaching?—but he used this knowledge. You set the rest against the models, almost like grading on a curve. With a free theme it was harder but he rarely gave free themes anymore. The students complained that they had no ideas; freedom was the last thing they wanted: They wanted to know what he wanted so that they could do what he wanted so that they could receive the Cs that they wanted.

Anne brought him a pot of coffee in a thermal jug before she went to work in the travel agency. Familiar sarcasms dropped sleepily from the corner of her mouth. Now that Joanie had finished college and worked in San Francisco, they could survive without her job, and usually her jobs didn't last very long. Usually she was fired for being unpleasant to customers. What people called sarcasm he knew for disappointment. He knew who had let her down, and that was why, as he told himself, he never answered her bitterness with bitterness. Every now and then she was fired for drinking, and if she were home all day—Dr. Silva's teaching schedule was long, with conferences, office hours, and the writing lab on Mondays and Fridays—what would she do with her time but drink? She was holding onto her present job, although her complaints accelerated. One day she would leave work early; one day he would bicycle home to find her sitting with a bottle.

On this Thursday he was more than halfway through by the time Anne came home for lunch. But the remaining themes always took half again as long, and sometimes he put the last papers off until the next morning, working from six to eight before the nine o'clock class that began his long Friday.

"What's the score?" Anne said as she came in.

"About like last year," he said. He looked at the sheet where he kept tab, four upright marks slanted through to make five. "Marie 20, Pierre 5, Raoul 4, Ferryman 1."

5

Pierre woke in his house across the river about the time Raoul returned from Paris. The cook who doubled as serving maid brought him brioches and café au lait while he read *Le Monde.*

For a long time he felt slightly ill at ease, as if there were something he had forgotten to do. Twice he checked his calendar, but there was nothing on until teatime. He adjusted his foulard in the mirror and drank more coffee. Then he remembered: That slut Marie had knocked at his door all night! He filled with indignation for the sake of his friend Raoul. Perhaps it was time to give Marie her walking papers, amusing as she had seemed at the beginning. Pierre curled his lip. Pierre sharpened the points of his black mustache.

He allowed himself to think of potential replacements. Perhaps it was time to allow Marguerite the pleasures of his bed. She seemed ready a month ago, and surely Alphonse would be complaisant if not downright grateful. On the other hand there was Sylvie, a touch young perhaps at fifteen, but therefore perhaps amusing. At any rate, he felt certain, there would soon be an opening. These ruminations relieved him of his annoyance and cheered him up. He allowed *la petite bonne,* who was a great-grandmother at forty-seven, to leave when she had cleaned up after lunch, although Rose-Rose was not due until four o'clock.

6

After lunch Arthur Silva worked until 3:45, when he had to interrupt his day at home. He stood, stretched, unlocked his bike and pumped toward the campus for a special conference with Jeanette, who had been ill for two weeks and required make-up assignments. He enjoyed the break in his day of correcting impromptus, but as he pedaled he could not clear them from his mind. Marie kept getting most of the votes: She should have done this, she should have done that; she was at fault because she forgot to bring her return fare for the Ferryman, because of her taste in rotten Pierre, because she knew that the Murderer was in the forest—and always, implicit if unmentioned, because she was an unfaithful wife.

Tomorrow he would arch his eyebrows and ask Myra Bobnick if she really felt that infidelity was a capital offense? In his ten o'clock, he would ask Ginger Hagstrom about the idea behind her conclusion: "Marie was begging for it." He was not sure that he would raise Mary Ellen Budd's argument in class. It had surprised him a little, for Mary Ellen was only quietly attractive—not heavily made-up, not tightly jeaned—and Mary Ellen had poured scorn upon Marie for her stupidity in not lying her way out of her predicament. Marie was morally responsible for her own death, according to Mary Ellen, because she was so dumb—because after daylight she could have borrowed a franc from practically anybody on Pierre's side of the river, and if Raoul was already back by the time the Ferryman rowed her across, she could just tell him that she had felt like taking a walk after a restless night. Professor Silva sighed for Mary Ellen and for her husbands and lovers; then he sighed for himself and everybody else.

No more lies, thank goodness. Most of the lies happened while Joanie was still little, when he and Anne lurched more than once toward the cliffs of divorce. There had been a long period of calm before Anne's last fling, four years ago at St. Hilda's. And even earlier, he reminded himself, there had been stretches of good time when they had been loyal and kind to each other. He remembered with gratitude the first year of his graduate work at State, when they had joined the Presbyterian Church so that Joanie could go to Sunday school, and to their surprise followed their minister in his clear love of Jesus, whose figure clarified momentarily for both of them and allowed them notions of compassion and grace. But every good memory slid into something bad. That idyll ended when Anne discovered the letters a student of nursing had written Arthur. He could not for the life of him remember how he had allowed himself to ruin their calm by drifting into a casual affair. He remembered only feeling powerless, fated, carried like a chip on the stream.

Deliberately he turned his mind back to the present. Maybe he could write a paper for *College English* about this assignment. He had often thought about it; he had made some notes. He used this impromptu every term when he introduced the subject of Argumentation. It revealed unstated hypotheses, unacknowledged and unexamined; it revealed Logical Fallacies.

Every year a few students named Raoul on the grounds of priority. First, he was a bad husband or Marie would not have been unfaithful; second, since leaving her alone was the earliest fault, it was the most grievous. Few students, in all the years, voted for the Ferryman—because he was only following orders, because his motive seemed less passionate. When they did vote for him, it was on the same grounds: Because his motive seemed least important, mercy would have cost him least; therefore his refusal to transport Marie was capricious, which made him morally most responsible. Dr. Silva rather liked this argument, because he remembered (part of the story told in Ann Arbor) that in France the Ferryman always won the vote: Gallic disgust over the small bureaucrat, *le petit fonctionnaire*. The Ferryman had won Anne's vote, years back in Ann Arbor; she thought it was because she had spent her Junior Year Abroad in France.

Students who found Pierre guiltiest usually showed the most illogic—and they were the sweetest students, unsophisticated believers in romantic love. He could imagine how cynical Mary Ellen Budd would be about such arguments: We could use her, during the class meeting, to argue with the illogic of romantic outrage. The question of greater culpability—he would explain after Mary Ellen had made the point unclearly—is not the same as the question of foulness of character. Similarly, of course, he could find another student to rebut Mary Ellen's equation of Marie's moral culpability with Marie's disinclination to lie.

He smiled with fondness as he remembered how Joanie, who was only sixteen when he told her the story, had turned furious at Pierre. It was in the living room of the dormitory apartment at St. Hilda's, while Anne was still sober and faithful and Joanie a devoted daughter, when things for a while went well. He had never known Joanie so outraged, as he gently questioned her premises. But it had turned sour. Anne's sarcasm sent Joanie in a rage to her room, as a few years later it sent her across the continent to San Francisco.

Dr. Silva pushed uphill toward the bicycle rack. Every pleasant memory started a rabbit that, when it found its hole, found sour defeat. He tried remembering how lucky he was, in his job at Connecticut Hills, but it made him remember how St. Hilda's was good for two years only; then it became a job he left on his own initiative, because Anne carried on with the famously philandering bursar and humiliated Arthur, showing affection to her lover even in public, even at a Christmas party with students. That January in his classroom he had found a map rolled down in front of his blackboard and when he zipped it up had read: DR. SILVA IS A WIMP.

But nobody voted for the Murderer. He locked his bike, walking to his office. Once half a dozen years ago, at St. Hilda's as a matter of fact, a freshman intellectual turned up in his class. Clearly the system had failed. When she advanced her theory that the person who committed the crime was the most responsible for the crime, the class unanimously proclaimed that she was crazy. If you were a murderer, murder was part of the job description, wasn't it?

7

The Ferryman rode his bicycle home at 8:00 a.m. after his twelve-hour stint. The daytime help had showed up on time for once. His wife bustled at the stove, flour whitening her arms up to her elbows—fat, ugly, and agreeable.

"How'd it go?" she said. "Much work?"

He hung his beret on a peg and slouched to the table yawning. "Seventeen trips. Seventeen francs. What's for dinner?"

"Oeufs à la Russe, truite au beurre, Châteaubriand (bleu, d'accord), pommes frites, Bruxelles, salade verte, and napoleon. Somebody go just one way?"

With his mouth full of egg and mayonnaise, he took a moment to answer. "That slut with the brown curls who screws around with that fruit on the other side of the river when her husband visits his whore in Paris. Can you beat it? She didn't bring money for the ride back!"

His wife turned the steak in the skillet, stirred the sprouts, and drained the potatoes. "What did she do, try the forest?"

"Hey, how do I know? No skin off my ass. *Tant pis. Merde alors.* People get what's coming to them. When they call your number, your number's up. The bullet's got your name on it, you're dead. The moving finger writes. Rules are rules. I was only following orders."

She served the salad. "You always were a bunghole, honey," she said.

8

Although he was two minutes early, Jeanette was waiting in her baggy jeans and sweatshirt outside his office, looking pale and anxious as she always did.

"Sorry if I'm late," said Dr. Silva. He made a mental note that his feeder was empty outside his classroom next door; he would bring sunflower seed in the morning. When Jeanette sat down and took out her notebook he asked if she felt able to undertake her make-up work. She nodded, poised with pen and notebook. Dr. Silva read from his class schedule, first the reading assignments, then last week's theme—a three-hundred word essay using a rhetorical pattern and keyed to a reading assignment. Could she finish this theme in the next ten days? Jeanette nodded.

Then he told her that beginning tomorrow the class hour would be devoted to Argumentation. He asked her if she could spend forty minutes, tonight, writing something like an impromptu—he smiled as he said he trusted her not to spend more than forty minutes—and bring it to class tomorrow. If she could do the latest thing first, he explained, she would be ready to keep up with the class work—and she could catch up on the old work as she was able. He was conscious again that he was an easy and generous teacher, as he intended to be.

Jeanette thought she could manage, and Dr. Silva for the nth time in his life told the story of Raoul and Marie. Coming to the part where Marie was refused a second time by the Ferryman, and a second time by Pierre, he hurried because Jeanette turned pale until she looked the color of a rainy day. Before he could finish she vomited over his desk.

With a secretary's help, and with the help of another student waiting outside another office, Dr. Silva walked Jeanette to the college infirmary although she whimpered that she did not want to return.

When she was put to bed and sedated he paused by the desk of the head nurse, Mrs. Williams. He asked what Jeanette's illness had been. Mrs. Williams was surprised that he did not know, although they tried to keep such things quiet. After a pause for discretion's sake, she told him: Jeanette had visited a boy's college on a blind date, got drunk, and fraternity boys gang-raped her. She was doing quite well, the nurse told him; the school psychologist was reassuring, although this relapse would trouble him. . . .

Something like this happened *every year*, Mrs. Williams said, at the same place more often than not. Those fraternities should be abolished! But for all the warnings every autumn—deans and house-mothers and seniors—something like this happened almost *every year*. Mrs. Williams shook her head. Tears filled her eyes. Tears filled Dr. Silva's eyes also; shame started in him. Mrs. Williams pulled herself together and acknowledged that the girls, even those most brutalized, by and large *survived*. She could mention, but she wouldn't, one or two prominent alumnae who had endured something like Jeanette's humiliation. . . .

Dr. Silva knew that his face was a bright red as he returned to his office and with paper towels from the washroom cleaned up vomit. He left the window open six inches and bicycled home. Maybe this would be a good night for going to the movies, he thought. He remembered that there was a western at the shopping mall. He and Anne liked westerns, with their clear, simplified morality. Anne had picked up a taste for them during her year in France, where the Parisian critics were making much of them. But he found her already ironical with her second whiskey, smoking Camel after Camel between yellowed fingers, her grayed hair straggling and her face smudged. Dr. Silva recognized marks of boredom and self-loathing. He poured himself a drink and threw it away. He could not speak to Anne, not now when she had been drinking. His mind kept giving him one excuse: How could he have known? The excuse did not help; when he looked at the papers left to be corrected he felt revulsion. "I guess I'll do them in the morning," he said as if to Anne.

"What else is new?" she said.

All night he was restless with guilty and defensive thoughts. He would no sooner fall asleep than Anne would snore and wake him. He turned her gently onto her side and lay still, awake and miserable. At six o'clock he made a pot of coffee and settled down to correct the last dozen themes mechanically. He wrote in the margins, "Is this a capital offense?" with the same mild irony that he had used yesterday and twenty years earlier.

When Anne woke up at seven thirty he had finished the papers and made more coffee. His mind wandered while *Good Morning, America* talked about famine in Ethiopia, a plane crash in Russia, Princess Di's pregnancy, an Iranian boat capsizing, the execution of a crazed killer in Florida, a high pressure zone over the East, and Wayne Gretzky's hat trick. He bicycled to his nine o'clock class trembling and uncertain, as if he were meeting his first class twenty-five years ago.

9

When the nighttime Ferryman came back to work at 8:00 p.m., fresh from breakfast, Raoul and Pierre waited for him. Raoul asked questions and the Ferryman answered them defiantly, making the point that rules are rules and he was only following orders. At this last remark Pierre spat in the dust at his feet, then twirled the ends of his mustache. The two men stared at each other. Doubtless Pierre had been less than forthright in recounting his own behavior the previous night, and therefore showed contempt for the Ferryman's petty rigidity. Raoul remained cool as he watched the confrontation.

Then he interrupted, "OK," he said. "She must have gone into the forest. What are we going to do?"

"*Merde alors*," said the Ferryman. "I'm on duty."

Pierre supplied a solution. "Let's all go to sleep," he said. "She's probably just hanging around somewhere. With a friend. Have you tried the saloon? If she isn't back by tomorrow, maybe we ought to call the sheriff."

Raoul turned suddenly bitter. "And then some liberal judge will put the Murderer in an insane asylum. I say we raise a posse."

Pierre said he'd drink to that, and the Ferryman jumped up and yodeled. "Well, I'll be hornswoggled," he declared, slapping his ten-gallon hat against his thigh. "Heh, heh, heh," he croaked, banging his friend Pierre on the back. "I reckon we just got ourselves invited to A NECKTIE PARTY!"

10

Dr. Silva waited until the seventeen young female bodies, sleepy in their sweaters at nine o'clock, gathered before him. It was Jeanette's class and to his relief she was not there. He realized as he waited for quiet that all the young women in his classes had known about Jeanette's assault from the day it happened. When he had told the story day before yesterday, what could they have thought?

They watched him take the elastic off the papers and quieted down, looking up at him expectantly.

"It was Marie, wasn't it?" said Helen DeVane, followed by a small cheer from most of the class.

"Now I told you that there was no correct answer," he said, "but, yes, you agreed as a class that Marie's moral responsibility was the greatest." He read from his tally sheet for the 9:00 a.m. class: "Marie 14, Raoul 2, Pierre 1."

Girls applauded. It was the game side of this assignment that made it effective. Today it disturbed him and he spoke almost as if he were cross: "But the point is your arguments. Remember, we are studying Argumentation. I am sure that you all spent last night rereading Chapter Eight of *Writing Well,* 'Argument and Persuasion.' Magda, tell us why Marie was the most responsible?"

Magda put down an unlit cigarette. "Because she cheated on her husband is why. I mean, if she hadn't cheated it would never have happened?"

Bethany Adams was pumping her arm. He nodded in her direction. "But if her husband hadn't gone off and left her it wouldn't have happened in the first place, or if the Ferryboat guy had trusted her.

I say Raoul because he *started* it by going away, because he was the *first*."

Deriding voices defended Raoul from the charge, and said the Ferryman had the *least* to do with it . . . He heard a voice proclaiming Pierre. "Pearl?" he said.

"Yeah," she said, "Pierre did it, I mean he's the worst, you know? I mean there they are, you know, doing it all night and he won't even open the door for her when she's screaming and crying? What a rat."

At this point the class erupted with laughter and argument. It always happened so—and this year he did not want it to happen. He let them shout for a moment, out of control, as the Marie-majority poured scorn on the rest. After a moment he waved his hands for silence. In desperation he tried playing the old tape: "Helen," he said, "you said Marie was guilty for her own death because she had committed adultery. Does anyone find anything to criticize in Helen's logic?" No one spoke.

"You all know what logic is; you all read the chapter." More silence. "Helen, do you think that adultery should be punished?"

Helen lit a cigarette and looked as if she felt picked on.

Dr. Silva continued: "Do you think adultery should be punished by death?" Looking out the window he realized: He had forgotten to bring sunflower seed.

After a sullen moment Barbie Hawkes put up her hand. Dr. Silva nodded, feeling his stomach tremble. "But, I know," she said, "but she really was asking for it, you've got to admit, right?" Dr. Silva's nausea rose as he watched the girls in front of him nod their heads in sage agreement. "She was a dope," somebody said, and through the noise of general agreement he heard Mary Ellen laughing as she described the ways in which Marie could have lied her way out. Somebody's voice, louder than the rest, summed it all up: "She got what was coming to her." Dr. Silva stared at the floor, no longer listening. After a moment the class quieted, as if they felt that they had assumed an authority that wasn't theirs. Silence forced Dr. Silva to speak.

"I wonder," he said, "if any of you gave thought to the notion that the guiltiest person might be the Murderer."

When in earlier years he had made this suggestion, his class usually erupted into a hubbub of derision that he gradually tamed by argument. This time, when he spoke, he caused no hubbub. Someone said "awww," but the sentiment drifted away unconfirmed. As he looked from face to face, the girls lowered their eyes. They were embarrassed, and at first he did not know why. Then Bethany Adams took pity. "I thought about him," she said, "but then I decided: If he's just a Murderer, if that's all he is, then he must be crazy, and if you're crazy how can you be guilty?"

Dr. Silva spoke gently, reaching back to old words because he didn't know how to speak new ones. "You're making an assumption," he said. "The story doesn't say the Murderer is crazy. The story says someone murders people who come through the woods. Haven't we convicted and executed people who did that? Multiple murderers? Haven't we called them guilty? If murdering is crazy, then, by your logic, are all murderers innocent?"

There might be a number of answers to that one, he knew; of course, as he often said to Anne after he had stated a conviction, he didn't mean that he was *right*. . . . He felt his face grow red; he felt his heart pound; he did not want to speak the old words. "You made another assumption," he said. "You said that you 'thought about him.' Do you see why that's an assumption?"

Bethany shook her head. Dr. Silva went on, "How do you know that the Murderer is a man?"

Bethany's face showed a quick glint of intelligence. At the same time, Dr. Silva became aware of a sound from the rest of the room like air escaping from a tire, a collective sigh that expressed mild boredom and mild disgust. He looked at the faces—Mary Ellen, Magda, Pearl, Barbie, Helen, Joan, Tracy, Stacy, Myra, Susan, Kimberly, Hulda, Bethany . . . Pretty faces, most of them, parentally cherished faces of young American women. Mostly they looked at him, he realized, with contempt—or if it was not so strong as contempt it was condescension: *Dr. Silva is a Wimp.* They knew what men do and what women do to outwit or evade what men do. They were sorry for him or contemptuous of him because he did not know.

Suddenly he heard himself plead: "*Please* don't accept this! You don't have to accept this! You think it's all right that Marie got murdered. You think it's *natural.* Why do you think you have to put up with this? Why don't you . . . ?"

He stopped short of mentioning Jeanette, and he did not know what to say next. He did not know what they should do.

11

As soon as Marie entered the forest she heard footsteps behind her. When she entered the clearing she turned about quickly to face him. He showed no hesitation but emerged from the underbrush to face her in the grassy opening gradually lightening with dawn. He was dressed like a clerk from the Second Empire, or like the emperor himself, with a derby set squarely on his head, a small mustache, and a pince-nez that made his eyes look narrow. He wore clean gray gloves and carried an umbrella.

Marie: I take it that you are the Murderer.

Murderer: I take it that you are my next victim, since you have voluntarily entered the forest that is my domain.

Marie: If you wish it I shall be your next victim. I do, however, question your use of the word "voluntarily," or the idea implicit in the word.

Murderer: You are well-spoken.

Marie: I enter the forest not voluntarily but under compulsion because of the action, inaction, and potential action of three men. You are the fourth man.

Murderer: In your opinion, is the compulsion singular or plural? I speak of course in metaphor. Are we four men, one man, or all men?

Marie: Speaking historically, you are one man. But one or many, your violence is not requisite. It is within the power of your will to commit not murder but mercy.

Murderer: For what reason would I spare your life when I have spared no one else's?

Marie: By sparing my life you proclaim your freedom. Are you an automaton, able only to perform according to rote?

Murderer: And if I spared you, how would it affect my reputation? It would be taken as a sign of weakness. Your fear recognizes my power, which neighborhood anxiety confirms.

Marie: On the contrary, mercy would prove your power and your strength. What power resides in the predictable?

Murderer: A deal of power resides in the predictable—unless and until power shows itself mutable, capricious, whimsical. . . . Invariable obligation, not to say routine, sustains my omnipotence.

Marie: And in your inflexibility you make danger for yourself. If you showed mercy on occasion, your neighbors could allow themselves hope in connection with your power and your forest.

Murderer: A moderate acquaintance with human history makes evident: *Power's use is ineluctable.* Allow me to ask: From what does my power derive?

Marie: From physical strength.

Murderer: From what do your concepts of pity and compassion derive?

Marie: From my physical weakness, or from slave morality, if you will; you are indebted to the insane philosopher Nietzsche. Jesus had a number of things to say about weakness and strength.

Murderer: Jesus, I need hardly inform you, bred no progeny. Remarkable indeed for moral suggestions and personal behavior, he did not disturb the characteristics of the double helix. Although we may differ on the etiology of ethics, you will agree that ideas are acquired characteristics that do not alter the gene pool.

Marie: The dove descended.

Murderer: And quickened one womb. In order to rid the woods of murderers, the Holy Ghost—possibly in the form of gene-altering radiation—must descend with regularity, must perhaps quicken every womb for three generations. I kill you for the reason that you understand, that you even accept: I am stronger than you are.

Marie: It is my part to tell you: When you kill me because you are stronger than I am, the politics of this murder is only incidentally sexual or I should say physiological—an incidence, naturally enough, that I find poignant—for you authorize your own murder, on the same principle of strength, as soon as a younger or more muscular or more determined Murderer enters the woods. Or a lynch mob, which is your body multiplied by other bodies both weak and strong.

Murderer: Well understood. Are we ready, can-be, for to begin?

Marie: "Let my cry come into Thee."

12

Dr. Silva canceled his classes and bicycled back to the apartment. He lay on the bed with his head whirling, nauseated when he closed his eyes, desperately tired when he kept them open. After a while he heard Anne come home for lunch, fix a tuna fish sandwich, watch part of a game show, and return to work. With the shades still drawn in the bedroom he lay on his back looking at the ceiling without making a sound until she was gone. Then he rose and paced, bedroom through living room to kitchen and back again. On one of his passes he chewed a sprig of celery; later he ate a handful of bologna and heated bitter coffee.

By the time Anne returned at five thirty he had made a decision. On Monday, he said, he would submit his resignation to the dean of Connecticut Hills. Over the weekend he would update his curriculum vitae and draft a letter seeking employment. By the end of next week he would have written every community college in California, maybe four-year schools as well—but California's community colleges were famous. Wherever they wound up, he said while Anne nodded, they would be closer to Joanie.

Anne drank Dubonnet slowly while Arthur daydreamed aloud, growing more enthusiastic as his plans turned more concrete. When he paused Anne was agreeable: They should see the country before they got too old; maybe after a few years in California they could take early retirement; maybe they should think again about a trailer in Arizona; maybe she should return to school; maybe she should go into social work, as she had often thought.

By the time they went to bed that evening, Dr. Silva had almost forgotten his shame. Then he remembered: He would have to find a new way to introduce Argument and Persuasion. He had the notion again, which he usually dismissed quickly: Maybe it was time to leave teaching. But what could he do instead? He smiled sleepily thinking: I could be rich. When he was a child he had wanted a car as long as a Pullman. He dove toward sleep remembering a Pierce Arrow that parked on Thursdays when he was a small boy in front of his father's grocery. The chauffeur teased him gently while the old lady went inside to feel the vegetables. His mother told him that he could not be a chauffeur because he was not black. When he said that then he wanted to be a widow, because he knew that Archibald's boss was a widow, his mother repeated his remark all week to everyone who came into the store.

---

1. Why is Dr. Silva overcome by shame when he learns about Jeannette's gang rape?
2. Why does Dr. Silva return to school the next day "trembling and uncertain, as if he were meeting his first class twenty-five years ago"?
3. What does the conversation between Marie and the Murderer contribute to the larger story?
4. Why does Dr. Silva decide that he "would have to find a new way to introduce Argument and Persuasion"?

URSULA K. LE GUIN (1929–) was born in Berkeley, California. As the daughter of Alfred L. Kroeber, a leading twentieth-century anthropologist, Le Guin gained exposure to the study of Native American cultures, particularly their mythologies, and this stimulated her interest in writing about complex, imaginary societies. Sometimes labeled a science fiction writer, Le Guin has elevated this genre to a high level through her subtle portrayal of issues of gender, power, and social values. She has written prolifically in many genres, including short stories, novellas, poetry, and children's literature, and she has won numerous awards. Her novels include *The Left Hand of Darkness* (1969) and *The Dispossessed* (1974), both of which won Hugo and Nebula awards.

The Professor's Houses

The professor had two houses, one inside the other. He lived with his wife and child in the outer house, which was comfortable, clean, disorderly, not quite big enough for all his books, her papers, their daughter's bright deciduous treasures. The roof leaked after heavy rains early in the fall before the wood swelled, but a bucket in the attic sufficed. No rain fell upon the inner house, where the professor lived without his wife and child; or so he said jokingly sometimes: "Here's where I live. My house." His daughter often added, without resentment, for the visitor's information, "It started out to be for me, but it's really his." And she might reach in to bring forth an inch-high table lamp with fluted shade, or a blue dish the size of her little fingernail, marked "Kitty" and half full of eternal milk; but she was sure to replace these, after they had been admired, pretty near exactly where they had been. The little house was very orderly, and just big enough for all it contained, though to some tastes the bric-a-brac in the parlor might seem excessive. The daughter's preference was for the store-bought gimmicks and appliances, the toasters and carpet sweepers of Lilliput, but she knew that most adult visitors would admire the perfection of the furnishings her father himself had so delicately and finely made and finished. He was inclined to be a little shy of showing off his own work, so she would point out the more ravishing elegances: the glass-fronted sideboard, the hardwood parquetry and the dadoes, the widow's walk. No visitor, child or adult, could withstand the fascination of the Venetian blinds, the infinitesimal slats that slanted and slid in perfect order on their cords of double-weight sewing thread. "Do you know how to make a Venetian blind?" the professor would inquire, setting up the visitor for his daughter, who would forestall or answer the hesitant negative with a joyful, "Put his eyes out!" Her father, who was entertained by involutions, and like all teachers willing to repeat a good thing, would then remark that after working for two weeks on those blinds, he had established that a Venetian blind can also make an American blind.

"I did that awful rug in the nursery," the professor's wife, Julia, might say, evidencing her participation in the inner house, her approbation, her incompetence. "It's not up to Ian's standard, but he accepted the intent." The crocheted rug was, in fact, coarse-looking and curly-edged; the needlepoint rugs in the other rooms, miniature Orientals and a gaudy floral in the master bedroom, lay flat and flawless.

The inner house stood on a low table in an open alcove, called "the bookshelf end," of the long living room of the outer house. Friends of the family checked the progress of its construction, furnishing, and fitting-out as they came to dinner or for a drink from time to time, from year to year. Occasional visitors assumed that it belonged to the daughter and was kept downstairs on display because it was a really fine doll's house, a regular work of art, and miniatures were coming into or recently had been in vogue. To certain rather difficult guests, including the dean of his college, the professor, without affirming or denying his part as architect, cabinetmaker, roofer, glazier, electrician, and *tapissier*, might quote Claude Lévi-Strauss. "It's in *La pensée sauvage*, I think," he would say. "His idea is that the reduced model—the miniature—allows a knowledge of the whole to precede the knowledge of the parts. A reversal of the usual process of knowing. Essentially, all the arts proceed that way, reducing a material dimension in favor of an intellectual dimension." He found that persons entirely incapable of, and averse to, the kind of concrete thought that was his chief pleasure in working on the house went rigid as bird dogs at the name of the father of structuralism, and sometimes continued to gaze at the doll's house for some minutes with the tense and earnest gaze of a pointer at a sitting duck. The professor's wife had to entertain a good many strangers when she became state coordinator of the conservation organization for which she worked, but her guests, with urgent business on their mind, admired the doll's house perfunctorily if they noticed it at all.

As the daughter, Victoria, passed through the Vickie period and, at thirteen, entered upon the Tori period, her friends no longer had to be restrained or distracted from fiddling with the fittings of the little house, wearing out the fragile mechanisms, sometimes handling the furniture carelessly in their story-games with its occupants. For there was, or had been, a family living in it. Victoria at eight had requested and received for Christmas a rather expensive European mama, papa, brother, sister, and baby, all cleverly articulated so that they could sit in the armchairs, and reach up to the copper-bottom saucepans hung above the stove, and hit or clasp one another in moments of passion. Family dramas of great intensity were enacted from time to time in the then incompletely furnished house. The brother's left leg came off at the hip and was never properly mended. Papa Bendsky received a marking-pen mustache and eyebrows that gave him an evil squint, like the half-breed Lascar in an Edwardian thriller. The baby got lost. Victoria no longer played with the survivors; and the professor gratefully put them into the drawer of the table on which the house stood. He had always hated them, invaders, especially the papa, so thin, so flexible, with his nasty little Austrian-looking green jacket and his beady Lascar eyes.

Victoria had recently bought with her earnings from babysitting a gift to the house and her father: a china cat to drink the eternal milk from the blue bowl marked "Kitty." The professor did not put the cat in the drawer. He believed it to be worthy of the house, as the Bendsky family had never been. It was a finely modelled little figure, glazed orange and tabby on white. Curled on the hearthrug at twilight in the ruddy glow of the flames (red cellophane and a penlight bulb), it looked very comfortable indeed. But since it lay curled up, it could never go into the kitchen to drink from the blue bowl; and this was evidently a trouble or burden to the professor's unconscious mind, for he had not exactly a dream about it, one night while he was going to sleep after working late on a complex and difficult piece of writing, a response he was to give to a paper to be presented later in the year at the A.A.A.S.; not a dream, but a kind of half-waking experience. He was looking into or was in the kitchen of the inner house. That was not unusual, for when fitting the cabinets and wall panelling and building in the sink, he had become deeply familiar with the proportions and aspects of the kitchen from every angle, and had frequently and deliberately visualized it from the perspective of a six-inch person standing by the stove or at the pantry door. But in this case he had no sense of volition; he was merely there; and while standing there, near the big wood-burning stove, he saw the cat come in, look up at him, and settle itself down to drink the milk. The experience included the auditory: he heard the neat and amusing sound a cat makes lapping.

Next day he remembered this little vision clearly. His mind ran upon it, now and then. Walking across campus after a lecture, he thought with some intensity that it would be very pleasant to have an animal in the house, a live animal. Not a cat, of course. Something very small. But his precise visual imagination at once presented him with a gerbil the size of the sofa, a monstrous hamster in the master bedroom, like the dreadful Mrs. Bhoolaboy in *Staying On*, billowing in the bed, immense, and he laughed inwardly, and winced away from the spectacle.

Once, indeed, when he had been installing the pull-chain toilet—the house and its furnishings were generally Victorian; that was the original eponymous joke—he had glanced up to see that a moth had got into the attic, but only after a moment of shock did he recognize it as a moth, the marvellous, soft-winged, unearthly owl beating there beneath the rafters. Flies, however, which often visited the house, brought only thoughts of horror movies about professors who tampered with what man was not meant to know and ended up buzzing at the window pane, crying vainly, "Don't! No!" as the housewife's inexorable swatter fell. And serve them right. Would a ladybug do for a tortoise? The size was right, the colors wrong. The Victorians did not hesitate to paint live tortoise's shells. But tortoises do not raise their shells and fly away home. There was no pet suitable for the house.

Lately he had not been working much on the house; weeks and months went by before he got the tiny Landseer framed, and then it was a plain gilt frame fitted up on a Sunday afternoon, not the scrollwork masterpiece he had originally planned. Sketches for a glassed-in sun porch were never, as his dean would have put it, implemented. The personal and professional stresses in his department at the university, which had first driven him to this small escape hatch, were considerably eased under the new chairman; he and Julia had worked out their problems well enough to go on with; and anyway, the house and all its furnishings were done, in place, complete. Every armchair its antimacassars. Now that the Bendskys were gone, nothing got lost or broken, nothing even got moved. And no rain fell. The outer house was in real need of reroofing; it had required three attic buckets this October, and even so there had been some damage to the study ceiling. But the cedar shingles on the inner house were still blond, virginal. They knew little of sunlight, and nothing of the rain.

I could, the professor thought, pour water on the roof, to weather the shingles a bit. It ought to be sprinkled on, somehow, so it would be more like rain. He saw himself stand with Julia's green plastic half-gallon watering can at the low table in the book-lined alcove of the living room; he saw water falling on the little shingles, pooling on the table, dripping to the ancient but serviceable domestic Oriental rug. He saw a mad professor watering a toy house. Will it grow, Doctor? Will it grow?

That night he dreamed that the inner house, his house, was outside. It stood in a garden patch on a rickety support of some kind. The ground around it had been partly dug up as if for planting. The sky was low and dingy, though it was not raining yet. Some slats had come away from the back of the house, and he was worried about the glue. "I'm worried about the glue," he said to the gardener or whoever it was that was there with a short-handled shovel, but the person did not understand. The house should not be outside, but it was outside, and it was too late to do anything about it.

He woke in great distress from this dream and could not find rest from it until his mind came upon the notion of, as it were, obeying the dream: actually moving the inner house outdoors, into the garden, which would then become the garden of both houses. An inner garden within the outer garden could be designed. Julia's advice would be needed for that. Miniature roses for hawthorn trees, surely. Scotch moss for the lawn? What could you use for hedges? She might know. A fountain? . . . He drifted back to sleep contentedly planning the garden of the house. And for months, even years, after that he amused or consoled himself from time to time, on troubled nights or in boring meetings, by reviving the plans for the miniature garden. But really it was not a practicable idea, given the rainy weather of his part of the world.

He and Julia got their house reroofed eventually, and brought the buckets down from the attic. The inner house was moved upstairs into Victoria's room when she went off to college. Looking into that room towards dusk of a November evening, the professor saw the peaked roofs and widow's walk sharp against the window light. They were still dry. Dust falls here, not rain, he thought. It isn't fair. He opened the front of the house and turned on the fireplace. The little cat lay curled up on the rug before the ruddy glow, the illusion of warmth, the illusion of shelter. And the dry milk in the half-full bowl marked "Kitty" by the kitchen door. And the child gone.

---

1. Why is the professor's inner house so "orderly" and perfectly furnished and the outer house "comfortable, clean, disorderly," with a leaky roof?
2. Why is it "a trouble or burden to the professor's unconscious mind" that the china cat can never drink from the blue bowl?
3. When looking at the inner house in Victoria's room, why does the professor think, "Dust falls here, not rain . . . It isn't fair"?

JOHN BARTH (1930–) was born in Dorchester County, Maryland. After attending Juilliard School of Music and playing drums in various jazz groups, he studied journalism at Johns Hopkins University, receiving an MA in 1952. He went on to teach English and creative writing at various universities including Pennsylvania State University, the State University of New York, and Johns Hopkins. Barth's short stories and novels, including *The Sot-Weed Factor* (1960); *Chimera* (1972), for which he won the National Book Award for Fiction; and *Where Three Roads Meet: Novellas* (2005), are characterized by their philosophical depth and satirical humor. "Lost in the Funhouse," the title story of a collection that Barth published in 1968, explores the limits of realist conventions in the short story form itself.

Lost in the Funhouse

For whom is the funhouse fun? Perhaps for lovers. For Ambrose it is *a place of fear and confusion.* He has come to the seashore with his family for the holiday, *the occasion of their visit is Independence Day, the most important secular holiday of the United States of America.* A single straight underline is the manuscript mark for italic type, *which in turn* is the printed equivalent to oral emphasis of words and phrases as well as the customary type for titles of complete works, not to mention. Italics are also employed, in fiction stories especially, for "outside," intrusive, or artificial voices, such as radio announcements, the texts of telegrams and newspaper articles, et cetera. They should be used *sparingly.* If passages originally in roman type are italicized by someone repeating them, it's customary to acknowledge the fact. *Italics mine.*

Ambrose was "at that awkward age." His voice came out high pitched as a child's if he let himself get carried away; to be on the safe side, therefore, he moved and spoke with *deliberate calm* and *adult gravity.* Talking soberly of unimportant or irrelevant matters and listening consciously to the sound of your own voice are useful habits for maintaining control in this difficult interval. *En route* to Ocean City he sat in the back seat of the family car with his brother Peter, age fifteen, and Magda G——, age fourteen, a pretty girl and exquisite young lady, who lived not far from them on B—— Street in the town of D——, Maryland. Initials, blanks, or both were often substituted for proper names in nineteenth-century fiction to enhance the illusion of reality. It is as if the author felt it necessary to delete the names for reasons of tact or legal liability. Interestingly, as with other aspects of realism, it is an *illusion* that is being enhanced, by purely artificial means. Is it likely, does it violate the principle of verisimilitude, that a thirteen-year-old boy could make such a sophisticated observation? A girl of fourteen is *the psychological coeval* of a boy of fifteen or sixteen; a thirteen-year-old boy, therefore, even one precocious in some other respects, might be three years *her emotional junior.*

Thrice a year—on Memorial, Independence, and Labor Days—the family visits Ocean City for the afternoon and evening. When Ambrose and Peter's father was their age, the excursion was made by train, as mentioned in the novel *The 42nd Parallel*, by John Dos Passos. Many families from the same neighborhood used to travel together, with dependent relatives and often with Negro servants; schoolfuls of children swarmed through the railway cars; everyone shared everyone else's Maryland fried chicken, Virginia ham, deviled eggs, potato salad, beaten biscuits, iced tea. Nowadays (that is, in 19——, the year of our story) the journey is made by automobile—more comfortably and quickly though without the extra fun though without the *camaraderie* of a general excursion. It's all part of the deterioration of American life, their father declares; Uncle Karl supposes that when the boys take *their* families to Ocean City for the holidays they'll fly in autogiros. Their mother, sitting in the middle of the front seat like Magda in the second, only with her arms on the seatback behind the men's shoulders, wouldn't want the good old days back again, the steaming trains and stuffy long dresses; on the other hand she can do without autogiros, too, if she has to become a grandmother to fly in them.

Description of physical appearance and mannerisms is one of several standard methods of characterization used by writers of fiction. It is also important to "keep the senses operating"; when a detail from one of the five senses, say visual, is "crossed" with a detail from another, say auditory, the reader's imagination is oriented to the scene, perhaps unconsciously. This procedure may be compared to the way surveyors and navigators determine their positions by two or more compass bearings, a process known as triangulation. The brown hair on Ambrose's mother's forearms gleamed in the sun like. Though right-handed, she took her left arm from the seatback to press the dashboard cigar lighter for Uncle Karl. When the glass bead in its handle glowed red, the lighter was ready for use. The smell of Uncle Karl's cigar smoke reminded one of. The fragrance of the ocean came strong to the picnic ground where they always stopped for lunch, two miles inland from Ocean City. Having to pause for a full hour almost within sound of the breakers was difficult for Peter and Ambrose when they were younger; even at their present age it was not easy to keep their anticipation, *stimulated by the briny spume*, from turning into short temper. The Irish author James Joyce, in his unusual novel entitled *Ulysses*, now available in this country, uses the adjectives *snot-green* and *scrotum-tightening* to describe the sea. Visual, auditory, tactile, olfactory, gustatory. Peter and Ambrose's father, while steering their black 1936 LaSalle sedan with one hand, could with the other remove the first cigarette from a white pack of Lucky Strikes and, more remarkably, light it with a match forefingered from its book and thumbed against the flint paper without being detached. The matchbook cover merely advertised U.S. war bonds and stamps. A fine metaphor, simile, or other figure of speech, in addition to its obvious "first-order" relevance to the thing it describes, will be seen upon reflection to have a second order of significance: it may be drawn from the *milieu* of the action, for example, or be particularly appropriate to the sensibility of the narrator, even hinting to the reader things of which the narrator is unaware; or it may cast further and subtler lights upon the thing it describes, sometimes ironically qualifying the more evident sense of the comparison.

To say that Ambrose's and Peter's mother was *pretty* is to accomplish nothing; the reader may acknowledge the proposition, but his imagination is not engaged. Besides, Magda was also pretty, yet in an altogether different way. Although she lived on B—— Street she had very good manners and did better than average in school. Her figure was very well developed for her age. Her right hand lay casually on the plush upholstery of the seat, very near Ambrose's left leg, on which his own hand rested. The space between their legs, between her right and his left leg, was out of the line of sight of anyone sitting on the other side of Magda, as well as anyone glancing into the rearview mirror. Uncle Karl's face resembled Peter's—rather, vice versa. Both had dark hair and eyes, short husky statures, deep voices. Magda's left hand was probably in a similar position on her left side. The boy's father is difficult to describe; no particular feature of his appearance or manner stood out. He wore glasses and was principal of a T—— County grade school. Uncle Karl was a masonry contractor.

Although Peter must have known as well as Ambrose that the latter, because of his position in the car, would be the first to see the electrical towers of the power plant at V——, the halfway point of their trip, he leaned forward and slightly toward the center of the car and pretended to be looking for them through the flat pinewoods and tuckahoe creeks along the highway. For as long as the boys could remember, "looking for the Towers" had been a feature of the first half of their excursions to Ocean City, "looking for the standpipe" of the second. Though the game was childish, their mother preserved the tradition of rewarding the first to see the Towers with a candy bar or piece of fruit. She insisted now that Magda play the game; the prize, she said, was "something hard to get nowadays." Ambrose decided not to join in; he sat far back in his seat. Magda, like Peter, leaned forward. Two sets of straps were discernible through the shoulders of her sundress; the inside right one, a brassiere strap, was fastened or shortened with a small safety pin. The right armpit of her dress, presumably the left as well, was damp with perspiration. The simple strategy for being first to espy the Towers, which Ambrose had understood by the age of four, was to sit on the right-hand side of the car. Whoever sat there, however, had also to put up with the worst of the sun, and so Ambrose, without mentioning the matter, chose sometimes the one and sometimes the other. Not impossibly Peter had never caught on to the trick, or thought that his brother hadn't simply because Ambrose on occasion preferred shade to a Baby Ruth or tangerine.

The shade-sun situation didn't apply to the front seat, owing to the windshield; if anything the driver got more sun, since the person on the passenger side not only was shaded below by the door and dashboard but might swing down his sun visor all the way too.

"Is that them?" Magda asked. Ambrose's mother teased the boys for letting Magda win, insinuating that "somebody [had] a girlfriend." Peter and Ambrose's father reached a long thin arm across their mother to butt his cigarette in the dashboard ashtray, under the lighter. The prize this time for seeing the Towers first was a banana. Their mother bestowed it after chiding their father for wasting a half-smoked cigarette when everything was so scarce. Magda, to take the prize, moved her hand from so near Ambrose's that he could have touched it as though accidentally. She offered to share the prize, things like that were so hard to find; but everyone insisted it was hers alone. Ambrose's mother sang an iambic trimeter couple from a popular song, femininely rhymed:

> *"What's good is in the Army;*
> *What's left will never harm me."*

Uncle Karl tapped his cigar ash out the ventilator window; some particles were sucked by the slipstream back into the car through the rear window on the passenger side. Magda demonstrated her ability to hold a banana in one hand and peel it with her teeth. She still sat forward; Ambrose pushed his glasses back onto the bridge of his nose with his left hand, which he then negligently let fall to the seat cushion immediately behind her. He even permitted the single hair, gold, on the second joint of his thumb to brush the fabric of her skirt. Should she have sat back at that instant, his hand would have been caught under her.

Plush upholstery prickles uncomfortably through gabardine slacks in the July sun. The function of the *beginning* of a story is to introduce the principal characters, establish their initial relationships, set the scene for the main action, expose the background of the situation if necessary, plant motifs and foreshadowings where appropriate, and initiate the first complication or whatever of the "rising action." Actually, if one imagines a story called "The Funhouse," or "Lost in the Funhouse," the details of the drive to Ocean City don't seem especially relevant. The *beginning* should recount the events between Ambrose's first sight of the funhouse early in the afternoon and his entering it with Magda and Peter in the evening. The *middle* would narrate all relevant events from the time he goes in to the time he loses his way; middles have the double and contradictory function of delaying the climax while at the same time preparing the reader for it and fetching him to it. Then the *ending* would tell what Ambrose does while he's lost, how he finally finds his way out, and what everybody makes of the experience. So far there's been no real dialogue, very little sensory detail, and nothing in the way of a *theme*. And a long time has gone by already without anything happening; it makes a person wonder. We haven't even reached Ocean City yet: we will never get out of the funhouse.

The more closely an author identifies with the narrator, literally or metaphorically, the less advisable it is, as a rule, to use the first-person narrative viewpoint. Once three years previously the young people *aforementioned* played Niggers and Masters in the backyard; when it was Ambrose's turn to be Master and theirs to be Niggers Peter had to go serve his evening papers; Ambrose was afraid to punish Magda alone, but she led him to the whitewashed Torture Chamber between the woodshed and the privy in the Slaves Quarters; there she knelt sweating among bamboo rakes and dusty Mason jars, pleadingly embraced his knees, and while bees droned in the lattice as if on an ordinary summer afternoon, purchased clemency at a surprising price set by herself. Doubtless she remembered nothing of this event; Ambrose on the other hand seemed unable to forget the least detail of his life. He even recalled how, standing beside himself with awed impersonality in the reeky heat, he'd stared the while at an empty cigar box in which Uncle Karl kept stone-cutting chisels: beneath the words *El Producto*, a laureled, loose-toga'd lady regarded the sea from a marble bench; beside her, forgotten or not yet turned to, was a five-stringed lyre. Her chin reposed on the back of her right hand; her left depended negligently from the bench arm. The lower half of scene and lady was peeled away; the words EXAMINED BY —— were inked there into the wood. Nowadays cigar boxes are made of pasteboard. Ambrose wondered what Magda would have done, Ambrose wondered what Magda would do when she sat back on his hand as he resolved she should. Be angry. Make a teasing joke of it. Give no sign at all. For a long time she leaned forward, playing Cow Poker with Peter against Uncle Karl and Mother and watching for the first sign of Ocean City. At nearly the same instant, picnic ground and Ocean City standpipe hove into view; an Amoco filling station on their side of the road cost Mother and Uncle Karl fifty cows and the game; Magda bounced back, clapping her right hand on Mother's right arm; Ambrose moved clear "in the nick of time."

At this rate our hero, at this rate our protagonist will remain in the funhouse forever. Narrative ordinarily consists of alternating dramatization and summarization. One symptom of nervous tension, paradoxically, is repeated and violent yawning; neither Peter nor Magda nor Uncle Karl nor Mother reacted in this manner. Although they were no longer small children, Peter and Ambrose were each given a dollar to spend on boardwalk amusements in addition to what money of their own they'd brought along. Magda too, though she protested she had ample spending money. The boys' mother made a little scene out of distributing the bills; she pretended that her sons and Magda were small children and cautioned them not to spend the sum too quickly or in one place. Magda promised with a merry laugh and, having both hands free, took the bill with her left. Peter laughed also and pledged in a falsetto to be a good boy. His imitation of a child was not clever. The boys' father was tall and thin, balding, fair complexioned. Assertions of that sort are not effective; the reader may acknowledge the proposition, but. We should be much farther along than we are; something has gone wrong; not much of this preliminary rambling seems relevant. Yet everyone begins in the same place; how is it that most go along without difficulty but a few lose their way?

"Stay out from under the boardwalk," Uncle Karl growled from the side of his mouth. The boys' mother pushed his shoulder *in mock annoyance*. They were all standing before Fat May the Laughing Lady who advertised the funhouse. Larger than life, Fat May mechanically shook, rocked on her heels, slapped her thighs while recorded laughter—uproarious, female—came amplified from a hidden loudspeaker. It chuckled, wheezed, wept; tried in vain to catch its breath; tittered, groaned, exploded raucous and anew. You couldn't hear it without laughing yourself, no matter how you felt. Father came back from talking to a Coast Guardsman on duty and reported that the surf was spoiled with crude oil from tankers recently torpedoed offshore. Lumps of it, difficult to remove, made tarry tidelines on the beach and stuck on swimmers. Many bathed in the surf nevertheless and came out speckled; others paid to use a municipal pool and only sunbathed on the beach. We would do the latter. We would do the latter. We would do the latter.

Under the boardwalk, matchbook covers, grainy other things. What is the story's theme? Ambrose is ill. He perspires in the dark passages; candied apples-on-a-stick, delicious looking, disappointing to eat. Funhouses need men's and ladies' room at intervals. Others perhaps have also vomited in corners and corridors; may even have had bowel movements liable to be stepped in in the dark. The word *fuck* suggests suction and/or and/or flatulence. Mother and Father; grandmothers and grandfathers on both sides; great-grandmothers and great-grandfathers on four sides, et cetera. Count a generation as thirty years: in approximately the year when Lord Baltimore was granted charter to the province of Maryland by Charles I, five hundred twelve women—English, Welsh, Bavarian, Swiss—of every class and character, received into themselves the penises the intromittent organs of five hundred twelve men, ditto, in every circumstance and posture, to conceive the five hundred twelve ancestors of the two hundred fifty-six ancestors of the et cetera et cetera et cetera et cetera et cetera et cetera et cetera et cetera of the author, of the narrator, of this story, *Lost in the Funhouse*. In alleyways, ditches, canopy beds, pinewoods, bridal suites, ship's cabins, coach-and-fours, coaches-and-four, sultry toolsheds; on the cold sand under boardwalks, littered with *El Producto* cigar butts, treasured with Lucky Strike cigarette stubs, Coca-Cola caps, gritty turds, cardboard lollipop sticks, matchbook covers warning that A Slip of the Lip Can Sink a Ship. The shluppish whisper, continuous as seawash round the globe, tidelike falls and rises with the circuit of dawn and dusk.

Magda's teeth. She *was* left-handed. Perspiration. They've gone all the way, through, Magda and Peter, they've been waiting for hours with Mother and Uncle Karl while Father searches for his lost son; they draw french-fried potatoes from a paper cup and shake their heads. They've named the children they'll one day have and bring to Ocean City on holidays. Can spermatozoa properly be thought of as male animalcules when there are no female spermatozoa? They grope through hot, dark windings, past Love's Tunnel's fearsome obstacles. Some perhaps lose their way.

Peter suggested then and there that they do the funhouse; he had been through it before, so had Magda, Ambrose hadn't and suggested, his voice cracking on account of Fat May's laughter, that they swim first. All were chuckling, couldn't help it; Ambrose's father, Ambrose's and Peter's father came up grinning like a lunatic with two boxes of syrup-coated popcorn, one for Mother, one for Magda; the men were to help themselves. Ambrose walked on Magda's right; being by nature left-handed, she carried the box in her left hand. Up front the situation was reversed.

"What are you limping for?" Magda inquired of Ambrose. He supposed in a husky tone that his foot had gone to sleep in the car. Her teeth flashed. "Pins and needles?" It was the honeysuckle on the lattice of the former privy that drew the bees. Imagine being stung there. How long is this going to take?

The adults decided to forgo the pool; but Uncle Karl insisted they change into swimsuits and do the beach. "He wants to watch the pretty girls," Peter teased, and ducked behind Magda from Uncle Karl's pretended wrath. "You've got all the pretty girls you need right here," Magda declared, and Mother said: "Now that's the gospel truth." Magda scolded Peter, who reached over her shoulder to sneak some popcorn. "Your brother and father aren't getting any." Uncle Karl wondered if they were going to have fireworks that night, what with the shortages. It wasn't the shortages, Mr. M—— replied; Ocean City had fireworks from prewar. But it was too risky on account of the enemy submarines, some people thought.

"Don't seem like Fourth of July without fireworks," said Uncle Karl. The inverted tag in dialogue writing is still considered permissible with proper names or epithets, but sounds old-fashioned with personal pronouns. "We'll have 'em again soon enough," predicted the boys' father. Their mother declared she could do without fireworks: they reminded her too much of the real thing. Their father said all the more reason to shoot off a few now and again. Uncle Karl asked *rhetorically* who needed reminding, just look at people's hair and skin.

"The oil, yes," said Mrs. M——.

Ambrose had a pain in his stomach and so didn't swim but enjoyed watching the others. He and his father burned red easily. Magda's figure was exceedingly well developed for her age. She too declined to swim, and got mad, and became angry when Peter attempted to drag her into the pool. She always swam, he insisted; what did she mean not swim? Why did a person come to Ocean City?

"Maybe I want to lay here with Ambrose," Magda teased.

Nobody likes a pedant.

"Aha," said Mother. Peter grabbed Magda by one ankle and ordered Ambrose to grab the other. She squealed and rolled over on the beach blanket. Ambrose pretended to help hold her back. Her tan was darker than even Mother's and Peter's. "Help out, Uncle Karl!" Peter cried. Uncle Karl went to seize the other ankle. Inside the top of her swimsuit, however, you could see the line where the sunburn ended and, when she hunched her shoulders and squealed again, one nipple's auburn edge. Mother made them behave themselves. "*You* should certainly know," she said to Uncle Karl. Archly. "That when a lady says she doesn't feel like swimming, a gentleman doesn't ask questions." Uncle Karl said excuse *him*; Mother winked at Magda; Ambrose blushed; stupid Peter kept saying "Phooey on *feel like*!" and tugging at Magda's ankle; then even he got the point, and cannonballed with a holler into the pool.

"I swear," Magda said, in mock *in feigned* exasperation.

The diving would make a suitable literary symbol. To go off the high board you had to wait in a line along the poolside and up the ladder. Fellows tickled girls and goosed one another and shouted to the ones at the top to hurry up, or razzed them for bellyfloppers. Once on the springboard some took a great while posing or clowning or deciding on a dive or getting up their nerve; others ran right off. Especially among the younger fellows the idea was to strike the funniest pose or do the craziest stunt as you fell, a thing that got harder to do as you kept on and kept on. But whether you hollered *Geronimo!* or *Sieg heil!*, held your nose or "rode a bicycle," pretended to be shot or did a perfect jacknife or changed your mind halfway down and ended up with nothing, it was over in two seconds, after all that wait. Spring, pose, splash. Spring, neato-o, splash. Spring, aw fooey, splash.

The grown-ups had gone on; Ambrose wanted to converse with Magda; she was remarkably well developed for her age; it was said that that came from rubbing with a turkish towel, and there were other theories. Ambrose could think of nothing to say except how good a diver Peter was, who was showing off for her benefit. You could pretty well tell by looking at their bathing suits and arm muscles how far along the different fellows were. Ambrose was glad he hadn't gone in swimming, the cold water shrank you up so. Magda pretended to be uninterested in the diving; she probably weighed as much as he did. If you knew your way around in the funhouse like your own bedroom, you could wait until a girl came along and then slip away without ever getting caught, even if her boyfriend was right with her. She'd think *he* did it! It would be better to be the boyfriend, and act outraged, and tear the funhouse apart.

Not act; *be*.

"He's a master diver," Ambrose said. In feigned admiration. "You really have to slave away at it to get that good." What would it matter anyhow if he asked her right out whether she remembered, even teased her with it as Peter would have?

There's no point in going farther; this isn't getting anybody anywhere; they haven't even come to the funhouse yet. Ambrose is off the track, in some new or old part of the place that's not supposed to be used; he strayed into it by some one-in-a-million chance, like the time the roller-coaster car left the tracks in the nineteen-teens against all the laws of physics and sailed over the boardwalk in the dark. And they can't locate him because they don't know where to look. Even the designer and operator have forgotten this other part, that winds around on itself like a whelk shell. That winds around the right part like the snakes on Mercury's caduceus. Some people, perhaps, don't "hit their stride" until their twenties, when the growing-up business is over and women appreciate other things besides wisecracks and teasing and strutting. Peter didn't have one-tenth the imagination *he* had, not one-tenth. Peter did this naming-their-children thing as a joke, making up names like Aloysius and Murgatroyd, but Ambrose knew *exactly* how it would feel to be married and have children of your own, and be a loving husband and father, and go comfortably to work in the mornings and to bed with your wife at night, and wake up with her there. With a breeze coming through the sash and birds and mockingbirds singing in the Chinese cigar trees. His eyes watered, there aren't enough ways to say that. He would be quite famous in his line of work. Whether Magda was his wife or not, one evening when he was wise lined and gray at the temples he'd smile gravely, at a fashionable dinner party, and remind her of his youthful passion. The times they went with his family to Ocean City; the *erotic fantasies* he used to have about her. How long ago it seemed, and childish! Yet tender, too, *n'est-ce pas*? Would she have imagined that the world-famous whatever remembered how many strings were on the lyre on the bench beside the girl on the label of the cigar box he'd stared at in the toolshed at age ten while she, age eleven. Even then he had felt *wise beyond his years*; he'd stroked her hair and said in his deepest voice and correctest English, as to a dear child: "I shall never forget this moment."

But though he had breathed heavily, groaned as if ecstatic, what he'd really felt throughout was an odd detachment, as though someone else were Master. Strive as he might to be transported, he heard his mind take notes upon the scene: *This is what they call* passion. *I am experiencing it.* Many of the digger machines were out of order in the penny arcades and could not be repaired or replaced for the duration. Moreover the prizes, made now in USA, were less interesting than formerly, pasteboard items for the most part, and some of the machines wouldn't work on white pennies. The gypsy fortune-teller machine might have provided a foreshadowing of the climax of this story if Ambrose had operated it. It was even dilapidateder than most: the silver coating was worn off the brown metal handles, the glass windows around the dummy were cracked and taped, her kerchiefs and silks long-faded. If a man lived by himself, he could take a department-store mannequin with flexible joints and modify her in certain ways. *However*: by the time he was that old he'd have a real woman. There was a machine that stamped your name around a white-metal coin with a star in the middle: *A*——. His son would be the second, and when the lad reached thirteen or so he would put a strong arm around his shoulder and tell him calmly: "It is perfectly normal. We have all been through it. It will not last forever." Nobody knew how to be what they were right. He'd smoke a pipe, teach his son how to fish and softcrab, assure him he needn't worry about himself. Magda would certainly give, Magda would certainly yield a great deal of milk, although guilty of occasional solecisms. It don't taste so bad. Suppose the lights came on now!

The day wore on. You think you're yourself, but there are other persons in you. Ambrose gets hard when Ambrose doesn't want to, *and obversely.* Ambrose watches them disagree; Ambrose watches him watch. In the funhouse mirror-room you can't see yourself go on forever, because no matter how you stand, your head gets in the way. Even if you had a glass periscope, the image of your eye would cover up the thing you really wanted to see. The police will come; there'll be a story in the papers. That must be where it happened. Unless he can find a surprise exit, an unofficial back door or escape hatch opening on an alley, say, and then stroll up to the family in front of the funhouse and ask where everybody's been; *he's* been out of the place for ages. That's just where it happened, in that last lighted room: Peter and Magda found the right exit; he found one that you weren't supposed to find and strayed off into the works somewhere. In a perfect funhouse you'd be able to go only one way, like the divers off the highboard; getting lost would be impossible; the doors and halls would work like minnow traps or the valves in veins.

On account of German U-boats, Ocean City was "browned out": streetlights were shaded on the seaward side; shop windows and boardwalk amusement places were kept dim, not to silhouette tankers and Liberty ships for torpedoing. In a short story about Ocean City, Maryland, during World War II, the author could make use of the image of sailors on leave in the penny arcades and shooting galleries, sighting through the crosshairs of toy machine guns at swastika'd subs, while out in the black Atlantic a U-boat skipper squints through his periscope at real ships outlined by the glow of penny arcades. After dinner the family strolled back to the amusement end of the boardwalk. The boys' father had burnt red as always and was masked with Noxzema, a minstrel in reverse. The grown-ups stood at the end of the boardwalk where the hurricane of '33 had cut an inlet from the ocean to Assawoman Bay.

"Pronounced with a long *o*," Uncle Karl reminded Magda with a wink. His shirt sleeves were rolled up; Mother punched his brown biceps with the arrowed heart on it and said his mind was naughty. Fat May's laugh came suddenly from the funhouse, as if she'd just got the joke; the family laughed too at the coincidence. Ambrose went under the boardwalk to search for out-of-town matchbook covers with the aid of his pocket flashlight; he looked out from the edge of the North American continent and wondered how far their laughter carried over the water. Spies in rubber rafts; survivors in lifeboats. If the joke had been beyond his understanding, he could have said: "*The laughter was over his head.*" And let the reader see the serious wordplay on second reading.

He turned the flashlight on and then off at once even before the woman whooped. He sprang away, heart athud, dropping the light. What had the man grunted? Perspiration drenched and chilled him by the time he scrambled up to the family. "See anything?" his father asked. His voice wouldn't come; he shrugged and violently brushed sand from his pants legs.

"Let's ride the old flying horses!" Magda cried. I'll never be an author. It's been forever already, everybody's gone home, Ocean City's deserted, the ghost crabs are tickling across the beach and down the littered cold streets. And the empty halls of clapboard hotels and abandoned funhouses. A tidal wave; an enemy air raid; a monster crab swelling like an island from the sea. *The inhabitants fled in terror.* Magda clung to his trouser leg; he alone knew the maze's secret. "He gave his life that we might live," said Uncle Karl with a scowl of pain, as he. The fellow's hands had been tattooed; the woman's legs, the woman's fat white legs had. *An astonishing coincidence.* He yearned to tell Peter. He wanted to throw up for excitement. They hadn't even chased him. He wished he were dead.

One possible ending would be to have Ambrose come across another lost person in the dark. They'd match their wits together against the funhouse, struggle like Ulysses past obstacle after obstacle, help and encourage each other. Or a girl. By the time they found the exit they'd be closest friends, sweethearts if it were a girl; they'd know each other's inmost souls, be bound together *by the cement of shared adventure*; then they'd emerge into the light and it would turn out that his friend was a Negro. A blind girl. President Roosevelt's son. Ambrose's former archenemy.

Shortly after the mirror room he'd groped along a musty corridor, his heart already misgiving him at the absence of phosphorescent arrows and other signs. He'd found a crack of light—not a door, it turned out, but a seam between the plyboard wall panels—and squinting up to it, espied a small old man, *in appearance not unlike* the photographs at home of Ambrose's late grandfather, nodding upon a stool beneath a bare, speckled bulb. A crude panel of toggle and knife switches hung beside the open fuse box near his head; elsewhere in the little room were wooden levers and ropes belayed to boat cleats. At the time, Ambrose wasn't lost enough to rap or call; later he couldn't find that crack. Now it seemed to him that he'd possibly dozed off for a few minutes somewhere along the way; certainly he was exhausted from the afternoon's sunshine and the evening's problems; he couldn't be sure he hadn't dreamed part or all of the sight. Had an old black wall fan droned like bees and shimmied two flypaper streamers? Had the funhouse operator—gentle, somewhat sad and tired-appearing, in expression not unlike the photographs at home of Ambrose's late Uncle Konrad—murmured in his sleep? Is there really such a person as Ambrose, or is he a figment of the author's imagination? Was it Assawoman Bay or Sinepuxent? Are there other errors of fact in this fiction? Was there another sound besides the little slap slap of thigh on ham, like water sucking at the chine boards of a skiff?

When you're lost, the smartest thing to do is stay put till you're found, hollering if necessary. But to holler guarantees humiliation as well as rescue; keeping silent permits some saving of face—you can act surprised at the fuss when your rescuers find you and swear you weren't lost, if they do. What's more you might find your own way yet, *however belatedly.*

"Don't tell me your foot's still asleep!" Magda exclaimed as the three young people walked from the inlet to the area set aside for Ferris wheels, carrousels, and other carnival rides, they having decided in favor of the vast and ancient merry-go-round instead of the funhouse. What a sentence, everything was wrong from the outset. People don't know what to make of him, he doesn't know what to make of himself, he's only thirteen, *athletically and socially inept*, not astonishingly bright, but there are antennae; he has . . . some sort of receivers in his head; things speak to him, he understands more than he should, the world winks at him through its objects, grabs grinning at his coat. Everybody else is in on some secret he doesn't know; they've forgotten to tell him. Through simple *procrastination* his mother put off his baptism until this year. Everyone else had it done as a baby; he'd assumed the same of himself, as had his mother, so she claimed, until it was time for him to join Grace Methodist–Protestant and the oversight came out. He was mortified, but pitched sleepless through his private catechizing, intimidated by the ancient mysteries, a thirteen-year-old would never say that, resolved to experience conversion like St. Augustine. When the water touched his brow and Adam's sin left him, he contrived by a strain like defecation to bring tears into his eyes—but felt nothing. There was some simple, radical difference about him; he hoped it was genius, feared it was madness, devoted himself to amiability and inconspicuousness. Alone on the seawall near his house he was seized by the terrifying transports he'd thought to find in toolshed, in Communion cup. The grass was alive! The town, the river, himself, were not imaginary; time roared in his ears like wind; the world was *going on*! This part ought to be dramatized. The Irish author James Joyce once wrote. Ambrose M—— is going to scream.

There is no *texture of rendered sensory detail*, for one thing. The faded distorting mirrors beside Fat May; the impossibility of choosing a mount when one had but a single ride on the great carrousel; *the vertigo attendant on his recognition* that Ocean City was worn out, the place of fathers and grandfathers, straw-boatered men and parasoled ladies survived by their amusements. Money spent, the three paused at Peter's insistence beside Fat May to watch the girls get their skirts blown up. The object was to tease Magda, who said: "I swear, Peter M——, you've got a one-track mind! Amby and me aren't *interested* in such things." In the tumbling barrel, too, just inside the Devil's mouth entrance to the funhouse, the girls were upended and their boyfriends and others could see up their dresses if they cared to. Which was the whole point, Ambrose realized. Of the entire funhouse! If you looked around, you noticed that almost all the people on the boardwalk were paired off into couples except the small children; in a way, that was the whole point of Ocean City! If you had X-ray eyes and could see everything going on at that instant under the boardwalk and in all the hotel rooms and cars and alleyways, you'd realize that all that normally *showed*, like restaurants and dance halls and clothing and test-your-strength machines, was merely preparation and intermission. Fat May screamed.

Because he watched the goings-on from the corner of his eye, it was Ambrose who spied the half-dollar on the boardwalk near the tumbling barrel. Losers weepers. The first time he'd heard some people moving through a corridor not far away, just after he'd lost sight of the crack of light, he'd decided not to call to them, for fear they'd guess he was scared and poke fun; it sounded like roughnecks; he'd hoped they'd come by and he could follow in the dark without their knowing. Another time he'd heard just one person, unless he imagined it, bumping along as if on the other side of the plywood; perhaps Peter coming back for him, or Father, or Magda lost too. Or the owner and operator of the funhouse. He'd called out once, as though merrily, "Anybody know where the heck we are?" But the query was too stiff, his voice cracked, when the sounds stopped he was terrified: maybe it was a queer who waited for fellows to get lost, or a long-haired filthy monster that lived in some cranny of the funhouse. He stood rigid for hours it seemed like, scarcely respiring. His future was shockingly clear, in outline. He tried holding his breath to the point of unconsciousness. There ought to be a button you could push to end your life absolutely without pain; disappear in a flick, like turning out a light. He would push it instantly! He despised Uncle Karl. But he despised his father too, for not being what he was supposed to be. Perhaps his father hated *his* father, and so on, and his son would hate him, and so on. Instantly!

Naturally he didn't have nerve enough to ask Magda to go through the funhouse with him. With incredible nerve and to everyone's surprise he invited Magda, quietly and politely, to go through the funhouse with him. "I warn you, I've never been through it before," he added, *laughing easily*; "but I reckon we can manage somehow. The important thing to remember, after all, is that it's meant to be a *fun*house; that is, a place of amusement. If people really got lost or injured or too badly frightened in it, the owner'd go out of business. There'd even be lawsuits. No character in a work of fiction can make a speech this long without interruption or acknowledgment from the other characters."

Mother teased Uncle Karl: "Three's a crowd, I always heard." But actually Ambrose was relieved that Peter now had a quarter too. Nothing was what it looked like. Every instant, under the surface of the Atlantic Ocean, millions of living animals devoured one another. Pilots were falling in flames over Europe; women were being forcibly raped in the South Pacific. His father should have taken him aside and said: "There is a simple secret to getting through the funhouse, as simple as being first to see the Towers. Here it is. Peter does not know it; neither does your Uncle Karl. You and I are different. Not surprisingly, you've often wished you weren't. Don't think I haven't noticed how unhappy your childhood has been! But you'll understand, when I tell you, why it had to be kept secret until now. And you won't regret not being like your brother and your uncle. *On the contrary!*" If you knew all the stories behind all the people on the boardwalk, you'd see that *nothing* was what it looked like. Husbands and wives often hated each other; parents didn't necessarily love their children; et cetera. A child took things for granted because he had nothing to compare his life to and everybody acted as if things were as they should be. Therefore each saw himself as the hero of the story, when the truth might turn out to be that he's the villain, or the coward. And there wasn't one thing you could do about it!

Hunchbacks, fat ladies, fools—that no one chose what he was was unbearable. In the movies he'd meet a beautiful young girl in the funhouse; they'd have hairsbreadth escapes from real dangers; he'd do and say the right thing; she also; in the end they'd be lovers; their dialogue lines would match up; he'd be perfectly at ease; she'd not only like him well enough, she'd think he was *marvelous*; she'd lie awake thinking about *him,* instead of vice versa—the way *his* face looked in different lights and how he stood and exactly what he'd said—and yet that would be only one small episode in his wonderful life, among many many others. Not a *turning point* at all. What had happened in the toolshed was nothing. He hated, he loathed his parents! One reason for not writing a lost-in-the-funhouse story is that either everybody's felt what Ambrose feels, in which case it goes without saying, or else no normal person feels such things, in which case Ambrose is a freak. "Is anything more tiresome, in fiction, than the problems of sensitive adolescents?" And it's all too long and rambling, as if the author. For all a person knows the first time through, the end could be just around any corner; perhaps, *not impossibly* it's been within reach any number of times. On the other hand he may be scarcely past the start, with everything yet to get through, an intolerable idea.

Fill in: His father's raised eyebrows when he announced his decision to do the funhouse with Magda. Ambrose understands now, but didn't then, that his father was wondering whether he knew what the funhouse was *for*—especially since he didn't object, as he should have, when Peter decided to come along too. The ticket woman, witch-like, mortifying him when inadvertently he gave her his name-coin instead of the half-dollar, then unkindly calling Magda's attention to the birthmark on his temple: "Watch out for him, girlie, he's a marked man!" She wasn't even cruel, he understood, only vulgar and insensitive. Somewhere in the world there was a young woman with such splendid understanding that she'd see him entire, like a poem or story, and find his words so valuable after all that when he confessed his apprehensions she would explain why they were in fact the very things that made him precious to her . . . and to Western civilization! There was no such girl, the simple truth being. Violent yawns as they approached the mouth. Whispered advice from an old-timer on a bench near the barrel: "Go crabwise and ye'll get an eyeful without upsetting!" Composure vanished at the first pitch: Peter hollered joyously, Magda tumbled, shrieked, clutched her skirt; Ambrose scrambled crabwise, tightlipped with terror, was soon out, watched his dropped name-coin slide among the couples. Shamefaced he saw that to get through expeditiously was not the point; Peter feigned assistance in order to trip Magda up, shouted "I see Christmas!" when her legs went flying. The old man, his latest betrayer, cacked approval. A dim hall then of black-thread cobwebs and recorded gibber: he took Magda's elbow to steady her against revolving discs set in the slanted floor to throw your feet out from under, and explained to her in a calm, deep voice his theory that each phase of the funhouse was triggered either automatically, by a series of photoelectric devices, or else manually by operators stationed at peepholes. But he lost his voice thrice as the discs unbalanced him; Magda was anyhow squealing; but at one point she clutched him about the waist to keep from falling, and her right cheek pressed for a moment against his belt buckle. Heroically he drew her up, it was his chance to clutch her close as if for support and say: "I love you." He even put an arm lightly about the small of her back before a sailor and girl pitched into them from behind, sorely treading his left big toe and knocking Magda asprawl with them. The sailor's girl was a string-haired hussy with a loud laugh and light blue drawers; Ambrose realized that he wouldn't have said "I love you" anyhow, and was smitten with self-contempt. How much better it would be to be that common sailor! A wiry little Seaman 3rd, the fellow squeezed a girl to each side and stumbled hilarious into the mirror room, closer to Magda in thirty seconds than Ambrose had got in thirteen years. She giggled at something the fellow said to Peter; she drew her hair from her eyes with a movement so womanly it struck Ambrose's heart; Peter's smacking her backside then seemed particularly coarse. But Magda made a pleased indignant face and cried, "All right for *you*, mister!" and pursued Peter into the maze without a backward glance. The sailor followed after, leisurely, drawing his girl against his hip; Ambrose understood not only that they were all so relieved to be rid of his burdensome company that they didn't even notice his absence, but that he himself shared their relief. Stepping from the treacherous passage at last into the mirror maze, he saw once again, more clearly than ever, how readily he deceived himself into supposing he was a person. He even foresaw, wincing at his dreadful self-knowledge, that he would repeat the deception, at ever-rarer intervals, all his wretched life, so fearful were the alternatives. Fame, madness, suicide; perhaps all three. It's not believable that so young a boy could articulate that reflection, and in fiction the merely true must always yield to the plausible. Moreover, the symbolism is in places heavy-footed. Yet Ambrose M—— understood, as few adults do, that the famous loneliness of the great was no popular myth but a general truth—furthermore, that it was as much cause as effect.

All the preceding except the last few sentences is exposition that should've been done earlier or interspersed with the present action instead of lumped together. No reader would put up with so much with such *prolixity*. It's interesting that Ambrose's father, though presumably an intelligent man (as indicated by his role as grade school principal), neither encouraged nor discouraged his sons at all in any way—as if he either didn't care about them or cared all right but didn't know how to act. If this fact should contribute to one of them's becoming a celebrated but wretchedly unhappy scientist, was it a good thing or not? He too might someday face the question; it would be useful to know whether it had tortured his father for years, for example, or never once crossed his mind.

In the maze two important things happened. First, our hero found a name-coin someone else had lost or discarded: AMBROSE, suggestive of the famous lightship and of his late grandfather's favorite dessert, which his mother used to prepare on special occasions out of coconut, oranges, grapes, and what else. Second, as he wondered at the endless replication of his image in the mirrors, second, as he *lost himself in the reflection* that the necessity for an observer makes perfect observation impossible, better make him eighteen at least, yet that would render other things unlikely, he heard Peter and Magda chuckling somewhere together in the maze. "Here!" "No, here!" they shouted to each other; Peter said, "Where's Amby?" Magda murmured. "Amb?" Peter called. In a pleased, friendly voice. He didn't reply. The truth was, his brother was a *happy-go-lucky youngster* who'd've been better off with a regular brother of his own, but who seldom complained of his lot and was generally cordial. Ambrose's throat ached; there aren't enough different ways to say that. He stood quietly while the two young people giggled and thumped through the glittering maze, hurrah'd their discovery of its exit, cried out in joyful alarm at what next beset them. Then he set his mouth and followed after, as he supposed, took a wrong turn, strayed into the pass *wherein he lingers yet*.

The action of conventional dramatic narrative may be represented by a diagram called Freitag's triangle:

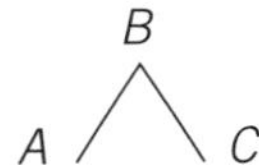

or more accurately by a variant of that diagram:

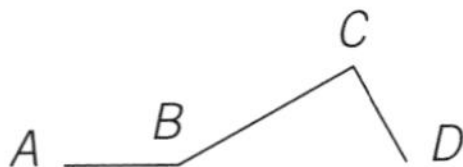

in which *AB* represents the exposition, *B* the introduction of conflict, *BC* the "rising action," complication, or development of the conflict, *C* the climax, or turn of the action, *CD* the dénouement, or resolution of the conflict. While there is no reason to regard this pattern as an absolute necessity, like many other conventions it became conventional because great numbers of people over many years learned by trial and error that it was effective; one ought not to forsake it, therefore, unless one wishes to forsake as well the effect of drama or has clear cause to feel that deliberate violation of the "normal" pattern can better can better effect that effect. This can't go on much longer; it can go on forever. He died telling stories to himself in the dark; years later, when that vast unsuspected area of the funhouse came to light, the first expedition found his skeleton in one of its labyrinthine corridors and mistook it for part of the entertainment. He died of starvation telling himself stories in the dark; but unbeknownst unbeknownst to him, an assistant operator of the funhouse, happening to overhear him, crouched just behind the plyboard partition and wrote down his every word. The operator's daughter, an exquisite young woman with a figure unusually well developed for her age, crouched just behind the partition and transcribed his every word. Though she had never laid eyes on him, she recognized that here was one of Western culture's truly great imaginations, the eloquence of whose suffering would be an inspiration to unnumbered. And her heart was torn between her love for the misfortunate young man (yes, she loved him, though she had never laid though she knew him only—but how well!—through his words, and the deep, calm voice in which he spoke them) between her love et cetera and her womanly intuition that only in suffering and isolation could he give voice et cetera. Lone dark dying. Quietly she kissed the rough plyboard, and a tear fell upon the page. Where she had written in shorthand *Where she had written in shorthand* Where she had written in shorthand *Where she* et cetera. A long time ago we should have passed the apex of Freitag's triangle and made brief work of the *dénouement*; the plot doesn't rise by meaningful steps but winds upon itself, digresses, retreats, hesitates, sighs, collapses, expires. The climax of the story must be its protagonist's discovery of a way to get through the funhouse. But he has found none, may have ceased to search.

What relevance does the war have to the story? Should there be fireworks outside or not?

Ambrose wandered, languished, dozed. Now and then he fell into his habit of rehearsing to himself the unadventurous story of his life, narrated from the third-person point of view, from his earliest memory parenthesis of maple leaves stirring in the summer breath of tidewater Maryland end of parenthesis to the present moment. Its principal events, on this telling, would appear to have been *A*, *B*, *C*, and *D*.

He imagined himself years hence, successful, married, at ease in the world, the trials of his adolescence far behind him. He has come to the seashore with his family for the holiday: how Ocean City has changed! But at one seldom at one ill-frequented end of the boardwalk a few derelict amusements survive from times gone by: the great carrousel from the turn of the century, with its monstrous griffins and mechanical concert band; the roller coaster rumored since 1916 to have been condemned; the mechanical shooting gallery in which only the image of our enemies changed. His own son laughs with Fat May and wants to know what a funhouse is; Ambrose hugs the sturdy lad close and smiles around his pipestem at his wife.

The family's going home. Mother sits between Father and Uncle Karl, who teases him good-naturedly who chuckles over the fact that the comrade with whom he'd fought his way shoulder to shoulder through the funhouse had turned out to be a blind Negro girl—to their mutual discomfort, as they'd opened their souls. But such are the walls of custom, which even. Whose arm is where? How must it feel. He dreams of a funhouse vaster by far than any yet constructed; but by then they may be out of fashion, like steamboats and excursion trains. Already quaint and seedy: the draperied ladies on the frieze of the carrousel are his father's father's mooncheeked dreams; if he thinks of it more he will vomit his apple-on-a-stick.

He wonders: will he become a regular person? Something has gone wrong; his vaccination didn't take; at the Boy Scout initiation campfire he only pretended to be deeply moved, as he pretends to this hour that it is not so bad after all in the funhouse, and that he has a little limp. How long will it last? He envisions a truly astonishing funhouse, incredibly complex yet utterly controlled from a great central switchboard like the console of a pipe organ. Nobody had enough imagination. He could design such a place himself, wiring and all, and he's only thirteen years old. He would be its operator: panel lights would show what was up in every cranny of its cunning of its multifarious vastness; a switch-flick would ease this fellow's way, complicate that's, to balance things out; if anyone seemed lost or frightened, all the operator had to do was.

He wishes he had never entered the funhouse. But he has. Then he wishes he were dead. But he's not. Therefore he will construct funhouses for others and be their secret operator—though he would rather be among the lovers for whom funhouses are designed.

---

1. What does his experience in the funhouse teach Ambrose?
2. What is the funhouse, or what does being lost in it represent?
3. Why does Barth make the main point of view that of a thirteen-year-old boy who, in one ending, dies telling himself stories in the dark, and in another ending, imagines constructing funhouses for others?
4. Does this story reveal how most of the effects of the funhouse are manufactured?

JOHN UPDIKE (1932–2009) was born in Reading, Pennsylvania, and spent much of his childhood living on a farm in nearby Shillington. While studying English at Harvard University, he wrote and drew cartoons for the *Harvard Lampoon*, and in 1955 he joined the staff of the *New Yorker* magazine. Despite his claims that what he wanted to be was a cartoonist, Updike became an accomplished and prolific writer in four genres—the novel, short story, poem, and essay—chronicling issues such as the spiritual uncertainty and domestic unrest faced by ordinary Americans living in middle-class suburbia. He won numerous literary prizes, and his most acclaimed novels include the quartet written about the character Harry "Rabbit" Angstrom—*Rabbit is Rich* (1981) and *Rabbit at Rest* (1990) each won the Pulitzer Prize.

Tomorrow and Tomorrow and So Forth

Whirling, talking, 11D began to enter Room 109. From the quality of their excitement, Mark Prosser guessed it would rain. He had been teaching high school for three years, yet his students still impressed him; they were such sensitive animals. They reacted so infallibly to merely barometric pressure.

In the doorway, Brute Young paused while little Barry Snyder giggled at his elbow. Barry's stagy laugh rose and fell, dipping down toward some vile secret that had to be tasted and retasted, then soaring artificially to proclaim that he, little Barry, shared such a secret with the school's fullback. Being Brute's stooge was precious to Barry. The fullback paid no attention to him; he twisted his neck to stare at something not yet coming through the door. He yielded reluctantly to the procession pressing him forward.

Right under Prosser's eyes, like a murder suddenly appearing in an annalistic frieze of kings and queens, someone stabbed a girl in the back with a pencil; she ignored the assault saucily. Another hand yanked out Geoffrey Langer's shirttail. Geoffrey, a bright student, was uncertain whether to laugh it off or defend himself with anger, and made a weak, half-turning gesture of compromise, wearing an expression of distant arrogance that Prosser recognized as having been his own in moments of schoolyard fear. All along the line, in the glitter of key chains and the acute angles of turned-back shirt cuffs, an electricity was expressed which simple weather couldn't generate.

Mark wondered if today Gloria Andrews would wear that sweater, an ember-pink angora, with very short sleeves. The virtual sleevelessness was the disturbing factor: the exposure of those two serene arms to the air, white as thighs against the delicate wool.

His guess was correct. A vivid pink patch flashed through the jiggle of arms and shoulders as the final knot of youngsters entered the room.

"Take your seats," Mr. Prosser said. "Come on. Let's go."

Most obeyed, but Peter Forry, who had been at the center of the group around Gloria, still lingered in the doorway with her, finishing some story, apparently determined to make her laugh or gasp. When she did gasp, he tossed his head with satisfaction. His apricot-colored hair bounced. Red-haired boys are all alike, Mark thought, with their white eyelashes and wise-guy faces, their mouths always twisted with an unearned self-confidence. Bluffers, the bunch of them.

When Gloria, moving in a considered, stately way, had taken her seat, and Peter had swerved into his, Mr. Prosser said, "Peter Forry."

"Yes?" Peter rose, scrabbling through his book for the assigned pages.

"Kindly tell the class the exact meaning of the words 'Tomorrow, and tomorrow, and tomorrow, / Creeps in this petty pace from day to day.' "

Peter glanced down at the high school edition of *Macbeth* lying open on his desk. One of the duller girls tittered expectantly from the back of the room. Peter was popular with the girls; girls that age had minds like moths.

"Peter. With your book shut. We have all memorized this passage for today. Remember?" The girl in the back of the room squealed in delight. Gloria laid her own book face-open on her desk, where Peter could see it.

Peter shut his book with a bang and stared into Gloria's. "Why," he said at last, "I think it means pretty much what it says."

"Which is?"

"Why, that tomorrow is something we often think about. It creeps into our conversation all the time. We couldn't make any plans without thinking about tomorrow."

"I see. Then you would say that Macbeth is here referring to the, the datebook aspect of life?"

Geoffrey Langer laughed, no doubt to please Mr. Prosser. For a moment, Mark *was* pleased. But he shouldn't play for laughs at a student's expense. His paraphrase had made Peter's reading of the lines seem more ridiculous than it was. He began to retract. "I admit—"

But Peter was going on; redheads never know when to quit. "Macbeth means that if we quit worrying about tomorrow, and just lived for today, we could appreciate all the wonderful things that are going on under our noses."

Mark considered this a moment before he spoke. He would not be sarcastic. "Uh, without denying that there is truth in what you say, Peter, do you think it likely that Macbeth, in his situation, would be expressing such"—he couldn't help himself—"such sunny sentiments?"

Geoffrey laughed again. Peter's neck reddened; he studied the floor. Gloria glared at Mr. Prosser, the anger in her face clearly meant for him to see.

Mark hurried to undo his mistake. "Don't misunderstand me, please," he told Peter. "I don't have all the answers myself. But it seems to me the whole speech, down to 'Signifying nothing,' is saying that life is—well, a *fraud*. Nothing wonderful about it."

"Did Shakespeare really think that?" Geoffrey Langer asked, a nervous quickness pitching his voice high.

Mark read into Geoffrey's question his own adolescent premonitions of the terrible truth. The attempt he must make was plain. He turned his attention from Peter and looked through the window toward the steadying sky. The clouds were lowering, getting darker. "There is," Mr. Prosser slowly began, "much darkness in Shakespeare's work, and no play is darker than *Macbeth.* The atmosphere is poisonous, oppressive. One critic has said that in this play humanity suffocates." This was too fancy.

"In the middle of his career, Shakespeare wrote plays about men like Hamlet and Othello and Macbeth—men who aren't allowed by their society, or bad luck, or some minor flaw in themselves, to become the great men they might have been. Even Shakespeare's comedies of this period deal with a world gone sour. It is as if he had seen through the bright, bold surface of his earlier comedies and histories and had looked upon something terrible. It frightened him, just as some day it may frighten some of you." In his determination to find the right words, he had been staring at Gloria, without meaning to. Embarrassed, she nodded, and, realizing what had been happening, he nodded back.

He tried to make his remarks more diffident. "But then I think Shakespeare sensed a redeeming truth. His last plays are serene and symbolical, as if he had pierced through the ugly facts and reached a realm where the facts are again beautiful. In this way, Shakespeare's total work is a more complete image of life than that of any other writer, except perhaps for Dante, an Italian poet who wrote three centuries earlier." He had been taken far from the *Macbeth* soliloquy. Other teachers had been happy to tell him how the kids made a game of getting him talking. He looked toward Geoffrey. The boy was doodling on his table, indifferent. Mr. Prosser concluded, "The last play Shakespeare wrote is an extraordinary poem called *The Tempest.* Some of you may want to read it for your next book reports—the ones due May tenth. It's a short play."

The class had been taking a holiday. Barry Snyder was snicking BBs off the blackboard and glancing over at Brute Young to see if he noticed. "Once more, Barry," Mr. Prosser said, "and out you go." Barry blushed, and grinned to cover the blush, his eyeballs sliding toward Brute. The dull girl in the rear of the room was putting on lipstick. "Put that away, Alice," Mr. Prosser commanded. She giggled and obeyed. Sejak, the Polish boy who worked nights, was asleep at his desk, his cheek white with pressure against the varnished wood, his mouth sagging sidewise. Mr. Prosser had an impulse to let him sleep. But the impulse might not be true kindness, just the self-congratulatory, kindly pose in which he sometimes discovered himself. Besides, one breach of discipline encouraged others. He moved down the aisle and gently shook Sejak awake. Then he turned his attention to the mumble growing at the front of the room.

Peter Forry was whispering to Gloria, trying to make her laugh. The girl's face, though, was cool and solemn, as if a thought had been provoked in her head. Perhaps at least *she* had been listening to what Mr. Prosser had been saying. With a bracing sense of chivalrous intercession, Mark said, "Peter. I gather from this noise that you have something to add to your theories."

Peter responded courteously. "No, sir. I honestly don't understand the speech. Please, sir, what *does* it mean?"

This candid admission and odd request stunned the class. Every white, round face, eager, for once, to learn, turned toward Mark. He said, "I don't know. I was hoping *you* would tell *me.*"

In college, when a professor made such a remark, it was with grand effect. The professor's humility, the necessity for creative interplay between teacher and student were dramatically impressed upon the group. But to 11D, ignorance in an instructor was as wrong as a hole in the roof. It was as if he had held thirty strings pulling thirty faces taut toward him and then had slashed the strings. Heads waggled, eyes dropped, voices buzzed. Some of the discipline problems, like Peter Forry, smirked signals to one another.

"Quiet!" Mr. Prosser shouted. "All of you. Poetry isn't arithmetic. There's no single right answer. I don't want to force my own impression on you, even if I *have* had much more experience with literature." He made this last clause very loud and distinct, and some of the weaker students seemed reassured. "I know none of *you* want that," he told them.

Whether or not they believed him, they subsided, somewhat. Mark judged he could safely assume his human-among-humans attitude again. He perched on the edge of the desk and leaned forward beseechingly. "Now, honestly. Don't any of you have some personal feeling about the lines that you would like to share with the class and me?"

One hand, with a flowered handkerchief balled in it, unsteadily rose. "Go ahead, Teresa," Mr. Prosser said encouragingly. She was a timid, clumsy girl whose mother was a Seventh-day Adventist.

"It makes me think of cloud shadows," Teresa said.

Geoffrey Langer laughed. "Don't be rude, Geoff," Mr. Prosser said sideways, softly, before throwing his voice forward: "Thank you, Teresa. I think that's an interesting and valid impression. Cloud movement has something in it of the slow, monotonous rhythm one feels in the line 'Tomorrow, and tomorrow, and tomorrow.' It's a very gray line, isn't it, class?" No one agreed or disagreed.

Beyond the windows actual clouds were moving rapidly, and erratic sections of sunlight slid around the room. Gloria's arm, crooked gracefully above her head, turned gold. "Gloria?" Mr. Prosser asked.

She looked up from something on her desk with a face of sullen radiance. "I think what Teresa said was very good," she said, glaring in the direction of Geoffrey Langer. Geoffrey snickered defiantly. "And I have a question. What does 'petty pace' mean?"

"It means the trivial day-to-day sort of life that, say, a bookkeeper or a bank clerk leads. Or a schoolteacher," he added, smiling.

She did not smile back. Thought wrinkles irritated her shining brow. "But Macbeth has been fighting wars, and killing kings, and being a king himself, and all," she pointed out.

"Yes, but it's just these acts Macbeth is condemning as 'nothing.' Can you see that?"

Gloria shook her head. "Another thing I worry about—isn't it silly for Macbeth to be talking to himself right in the middle of this war, with his wife just dead, and all?"

"I don't think so, Gloria. No matter how fast events happen, thought is faster."

His answer was weak; everyone knew it, even if Gloria hadn't mused, supposedly to herself, but in a voice the entire class could hear, "It seems so *stupid.*"

Mark winced, pierced by the awful clarity with which his students saw him. Through their eyes, how queer he looked, with his soft hands, and his horn-rimmed glasses, and his hair never slicked down, all wrapped up in "literature," where, when things get rough, the king mumbles a poem nobody understands. The delight Mr. Prosser took in such crazy junk made not only his good sense but his masculinity a matter of doubt. It was gentle of them not to laugh him out of the room. He looked down and rubbed his fingertips together, trying to erase the chalk dust. The class noise sifted into unnatural quiet. "It's getting late," he said finally. "Let's start the recitations of the memorized passage. Bernard Amilson, you begin."

Bernard had trouble enunciating, and his rendition began, " 'T'mau 'n' t'mau 'n' t'mau.' " Mr. Prosser admired the extent to which the class tried to repress its amusement, and wrote "A" in his marking book opposite Bernard's name. He always gave Bernard A on recitations, despite the school nurse, who claimed there was nothing organically wrong with the boy's mouth.

It was the custom, cruel but traditional, to deliver recitations from the front of the room. Alice, when her turn came, was reduced to a helpless state by the first funny face Peter Forry made at her. Mark let her hang up there a good minute while her face ripened to cherry redness, and at last relented: "Very well, Alice—you may try again later."

Many of the youngsters knew the passage gratifyingly well, though there was a tendency to leave out the line "To the last syllable of recorded time" and to turn "struts and frets" into "frets and struts" or simply "struts and struts." Even Sejak, who couldn't have looked at the passage before he came to class, got through it as far as "And then is heard no more."

Geoffrey Langer showed off, as he always did, by interrupting his own recitation with bright questions. " 'Tomorrow, and tomorrow, and tomorrow,' " he said, " 'creeps in'—shouldn't that be '*creep* in,' Mr. Prosser?"

"It is 'creep*s*.' The trio is in effect singular. Go on." Mr. Prosser was tired of coddling Langer. If you let them, these smart students will run away with the class. "Without the footnotes."

" 'Creep*sss* in this petty pace from day to day, / To the last syllable of recorded time; / And all our yesterdays have lighted fools / The way to dusty death. Out, out—' "

"No, no!" Mr. Prosser jumped out of his chair. "This is poetry. Don't mushmouth it! Pause a little after 'fools.' " Geoffrey looked genuinely startled this time, and Mark himself did not quite understand his annoyance and, mentally turning to see what was behind him, seemed to glimpse in the humid undergrowth the two stern eyes of the indignant look Gloria had thrown Geoffrey. He glimpsed himself in the absurd position of acting as Gloria's champion in her inscrutable private war with this intelligent boy. He signed apologetically. "Poetry is made up of *lines*," he began, turning to the class. Gloria was passing a note to Peter Forry.

The rudeness of it! To pass notes during a scolding that she herself had caused! Mark caged in his hand the girl's wrist—how small and frail it was!—and ripped the note from her fingers. He read it to himself, letting the class see he was reading it, though he despised such methods of discipline. The note went:

> Pete—I think you're *wrong* about Mr. Prosser. I think he's wonderful and I get a lot out of his class. He's heavenly with poetry. I think I love him. I really do *love* him. So there.

Mr. Prosser folded the note once and slipped it into his side coat pocket. "See me after class, Gloria," he said. Then, to Geoffrey, "Let's try it again. Begin at the beginning. Let the *words* talk, Geoffrey."

While the boy was reciting the passage, the buzzer sounded the end of the period. It was the last class of the day. The room quickly emptied, except for Gloria. The noise of lockers slamming open and books being thrown against metal and shouts drifted in:

"Who has a car?"

"Lend me a cig, pig."

"We can't have practice in this slop."

Mark hadn't noticed exactly when the rain started, but it was coming down hard now. He moved around the room with the window pole, closing windows and pulling down shades. Spray bounced in on his hands. He began to talk to Gloria in a crisp voice that, like his device of shutting the windows, was intended to protect them both from embarrassment.

"About note passing." She sat motionless at her desk in the front of the room, her short, brushed-up hair like a cool torch. From the way she sat, her naked arms folded at her breasts and her shoulders hunched, he felt she was chilly. "It is not only rude to scribble when a teacher is talking, it is stupid to put one's words down on paper, where they look much more foolish than they might have sounded if spoken."

He leaned the window pole in its corner and walked toward his desk.

"And about love. 'Love' is one of those words that illustrate what happens to an old, overworked language. These days, with movie stars and crooners and preachers and psychiatrists all pronouncing the word, it's come to mean nothing but a vague fondness for something. In this sense, I love the rain, this blackboard, these desks, you. It means nothing, you see, whereas once the word signified a quite explicit thing—a desire to share all you own and are with someone else. It is time we coined a new word to mean that, and when you think up the word *you* want to use, I suggest that you be economical with it. Treat it as something you can spend only once—if not for your own sake, for the good of the language." He walked over to his own desk and dropped two pencils on it, as if to say, "That's all."

"I'm sorry," Gloria said.

Rather surprised, Mr. Prosser said, "Don't be."

"But you don't understand."

"Of course I don't. I probably never did. At your age, I was like Geoffrey Langer."

"I bet you weren't." The girl was almost crying; he was sure of that.

"Come on, Gloria. Run along. Forget it." She slowly cradled her books between her bare arm and her sweater, and left the room with that melancholy teenage shuffle, so that her body above her hips seemed to float over the desks.

What was it, Mark asked himself, these young people were after? What did they want? *Glide,* he decided, the quality of *glide.* To slip along, always in rhythm, always cool, the little wheels humming under you, going nowhere special. If heaven existed, that's the way it would be there. "He's heavenly with poetry." They loved the word. Heaven was in half their songs.

"Christ, he's humming." Strunk, the phys-ed teacher, had come into the room without Prosser's noticing. Gloria had left the door ajar.

"Ah," Mark said, "a fallen angel, full of grit."

"What the hell makes you so happy?"

"I'm not happy, I'm just serene. Now the day is over, et cetera."

"Say." Strunk came up an aisle with a disagreeably effeminate waddle, pregnant with gossip. "Did you hear about Murchison?"

"No." Mark mimicked Strunk's whisper.

"He got the pants kidded off him today."

"Oh dear."

Strunk started to laugh, as he often did before beginning a story. "You know what a goddamn ladies' man he thinks he is?"

"You bet," Mark said, although Strunk said that about every male member of the faculty.

"You have Gloria Andrews, don't you?"

"You bet."

"Well, this morning Murky intercepts a note she was writing, and the note says what a damn neat guy she thinks Murchison is and how she *loves* him!" Strunk waited for Mark to say something, and then, when he didn't, continued, "You could see he was tickled pink. But—get this—it turns out at lunch that the same damn thing happened to Freyburg in history yesterday!" Strunk laughed and, still getting no response, gave Mark a little push—a schoolyard push. "The girl's too dumb to have thought it up herself. We all think it was Peter Forry's idea."

"Probably was," Mark agreed. Strunk followed him out to his locker, describing Murchison's expression when Freyburg (in all innocence, mind you) told what had happened to him.

Mark turned the combination of his locker: 18, 24, 3. "Would you excuse me, Dave?" he said. "My wife may be out front waiting. She picks me up when it rains."

Strunk was too thick to catch Mark's anger. "Help yourself," he said. "I got to get over to the gym. Can't take the little darlings outside in the rain; their mommies'll write notes to Teacher." He clattered down the hall and wheeled at the far end, shouting, "Now, don't tell You-know-who! The ladies' man!"

Mr. Prosser took his coat from the locker and shrugged it on. He placed his hat upon his head. He fitted his rubbers over his shoes, pinching his fingers painfully, and lifted his umbrella off the hook. He thought of opening it right there in the vacant hall, as a kind of joke on himself, and decided not to. The girl had been almost crying; he was sure of that.

---

1. Why is Mr. Prosser unable to help his class arrive at a satisfactory interpretation of the passage from *Macbeth*?
2. Why does Mr. Prosser tell Gloria that when he was her age, he was like Geoffrey Langer?
3. What explains Mr. Prosser's belief, even after Mr. Strunk's revelations, that Gloria was "almost crying"?
4. How do Mr. Strunk's revelations change our view of Mr. Prosser? Of Gloria?

RAYMOND CARVER (1938–1988) grew up in Yakima, Washington, where his father was a sawmill worker and his mother worked in retail and waited tables. Carver moved to California when he was twenty and enrolled at Chico State College, where he began to take creative writing classes. Upon graduating from Humboldt State, he attended the Iowa Writers' Workshop. In the years that followed, Carver struggled with alcoholism, bounced between various jobs, and continued to write. His breakthrough collection of stories, *Will You Please Be Quiet, Please?* (1976), was nominated for a National Book Award. Carver achieved sobriety shortly thereafter, and his collection *What We Talk About When We Talk About Love* (1981) established him as a major influence among short story writers. *Where I'm Calling From: New & Selected Stories*, came out the year that Carver died of lung cancer. He has been compared to Hemingway and Cheever.

Cathedral

This blind man, an old friend of my wife's, he was on his way to spend the night. His wife had died. So he was visiting the dead wife's relatives in Connecticut. He called my wife from his in-laws'. Arrangements were made. He would come by train, a five-hour trip, and my wife would meet him at the station. She hadn't seen him since she worked for him one summer in Seattle ten years ago. But she and the blind man had kept in touch. They made tapes and mailed them back and forth. I wasn't enthusiastic about his visit. He was no one I knew. And his being blind bothered me. My idea of blindness came from the movies. In the movies, the blind moved slowly and never laughed. Sometimes they were led by Seeing Eye dogs. A blind man in my house was not something I looked forward to.

That summer in Seattle she had needed a job. She didn't have any money. The man she was going to marry at the end of the summer was in officers' training school. He didn't have any money, either. But she was in love with the guy, and he was in love with her, etc. She'd seen something in the paper: HELP WANTED—*Reading to Blind Man*, and a telephone number. She phoned and went over, was hired on the spot. She'd worked with this blind man all summer. She read stuff to him, case studies, reports, that sort of thing. She helped him organize his little office in the county social-service department. They'd become good friends, my wife and the blind man. How do I know these things? She told me. And she told me something else. On her last day in the office, the blind man asked if he could touch her face. She agreed to this. She told me he touched his fingers to every part of her face, her nose—even her neck! She never forgot it. She even tried to write a poem about it. She was always trying to write a poem. She wrote a poem or two every year, usually after something really important had happened to her.

When we first started going out together, she showed me the poem. In the poem, she recalled his fingers and the way they had moved around over her face. In the poem, she talked about what she had felt at the time, about what went through her mind when the blind man touched her nose and lips. I can remember I didn't think much of the poem. Of course, I didn't tell her that. Maybe I just don't understand poetry. I admit it's not the first thing I reach for when I pick up something to read.

Anyway, this man who'd first enjoyed her favors, the officer-to-be, he'd been her childhood sweetheart. So okay. I'm saying that at the end of the summer she let the blind man run his hands over her face, said good-bye to him, married her childhood etc., who was now a commissioned officer, and she moved away from Seattle. But they'd kept in touch, she and the blind man. She made the first contact after a year or so. She called him up one night from an Air Force base in Alabama. She wanted to talk. They talked. He asked her to send him a tape and tell him about her life. She did this. She sent the tape. On the tape, she told the blind man about her husband and about their life together in the military. She told the blind man she loved her husband but she didn't like it where they lived and she didn't like it that he was a part of the military-industrial thing. She told the blind man she'd written a poem and he was in it. She told him that she was writing a poem about what it was like to be an Air Force officer's wife. The poem wasn't finished yet. She was still writing it. The blind man made a tape. He sent her the tape. She made a tape. This went on for years. My wife's officer was posted to one base and then another. She sent tapes from Moody AFB, McGuire, McConnell, and finally Travis, near Sacramento, where one night she got to feeling lonely and cut off from people she kept losing in that moving-around life. She got to feeling she couldn't go it another step. She went in and swallowed all the pills and capsules in the medicine chest and washed them down with a bottle of gin. Then she got into a hot bath and passed out.

But instead of dying, she got sick. She threw up. Her officer—why should he have a name? he was the childhood sweetheart, and what more does he want?—came home from somewhere, found her, and called the ambulance. In time, she put it all on a tape and sent the tape to the blind man. Over the years, she put all kinds of stuff on tapes and sent the tapes off lickety-split. Next to writing a poem every year, I think it was her chief means of recreation. On one tape, she told the blind man she'd decided to live away from her officer for a time. On another tape, she told him about her divorce. She and I began going out, and of course she told her blind man about it. She told him everything, or so it seemed to me. Once she asked me if I'd like to hear the latest tape from the blind man. This was a year ago. I was on the tape, she said. So I said okay, I'd listen to it. I got us drinks and we settled down in the living room. We made ready to listen. First she inserted the tape into the player and adjusted a couple of dials. Then she pushed a lever. The tape squeaked and someone began to talk in this loud voice. She lowered the volume. After a few minutes of harmless chitchat, I heard my own name in the mouth of this stranger, this blind man I didn't even know! And then this: "From all you've said about him, I can only conclude—" But we were interrupted, a knock at the door, something, and we didn't ever get back to the tape. Maybe it was just as well. I'd heard all I wanted to.

Now this same blind man was coming to sleep in my house.

"Maybe I could take him bowling," I said to my wife. She was at the draining board doing scalloped potatoes. She put down the knife she was using and turned around.

"If you love me," she said, "you can do this for me. If you don't love me, okay. But if you had a friend, any friend, and the friend came to visit, I'd make him feel comfortable." She wiped her hands with the dish towel.

"I don't have any blind friends," I said.

"You don't have *any* friends," she said. "Period. Besides," she said, "goddamn it, his wife's just died! Don't you understand that? The man's lost his wife!"

I didn't answer. She'd told me a little about the blind man's wife. Her name was Beulah. Beulah! That's a name for a colored woman.

"Was his wife a Negro?" I asked.

"Are you crazy?" my wife said. "Have you just flipped or something?" She picked up a potato. I saw it hit the floor, then roll under the stove. "What's wrong with you?" she said. "Are you drunk?"

"I'm just asking," I said.

Right then my wife filled me in with more detail than I cared to know. I made a drink and sat at the kitchen table to listen. Pieces of the story began to fall into place.

Beulah had gone to work for the blind man the summer after my wife had stopped working for him. Pretty soon Beulah and the blind man had themselves a church wedding. It was a little wedding—who'd want to go to such a wedding in the first place?—just the two of them, plus the minister and the minister's wife. But it was a church wedding just the same. It was what Beulah had wanted, he'd said. But even then Beulah must have been carrying the cancer in her glands. After they had been inseparable for eight years—my wife's word, *inseparable*—Beulah's health went into a rapid decline. She died in a Seattle hospital room, the blind man sitting beside the bed and holding on to her hand. They'd married, lived and worked together, slept together—had sex, sure—and then the blind man had to bury her. All this without his having ever seen what the goddamned woman looked like. It was beyond my understanding. Hearing this, I felt sorry for the blind man for a little bit. And then I found myself thinking what a pitiful life this woman must have led. Imagine a woman who could never see herself as she was seen in the eyes of her loved one. A woman who could go on day after day and never receive the smallest compliment from her beloved. A woman whose husband could never read the expression on her face, be it misery or something better. Someone who could wear makeup or not—what difference to him? She could, if she wanted, wear green eye shadow around one eye, a straight pin in her nostril, yellow slacks, and purple shoes, no matter. And then to slip off into death, the blind man's hand on her hand, his blind eyes streaming tears—I'm imagining now—her last thought maybe this: that he never even knew what she looked like, and she on an express to the grave. Robert was left with a small insurance policy and half of a twenty-peso Mexican coin. The other half of the coin went into the box with her. Pathetic.

So when the time rolled around, my wife went to the depot to pick him up. With nothing to do but wait—sure, I blamed him for that—I was having a drink and watching the TV when I heard the car pull into the drive. I got up from the sofa with my drink and went to the window to have a look.

I saw my wife laughing as she parked the car. I saw her get out of the car and shut the door. She was still wearing a smile. Just amazing. She went around to the other side of the car to where the blind man was already starting to get out. This blind man, feature this, he was wearing a full beard! A beard on a blind man! Too much, I say. The blind man reached into the backseat and dragged out a suitcase. My wife took his arm, shut the car door, and, talking all the way, moved him down the drive and then up the steps to the front porch. I turned off the TV. I finished my drink, rinsed the glass, dried my hands. Then I went to the door.

My wife said, "I want you to meet Robert. Robert, this is my husband. I've told you all about him." She was beaming. She had this blind man by his coat sleeve.

The blind man let go of his suitcase and up came his hand.

I took it. He squeezed hard, held my hand, and then he let it go.

"I feel like we've already met," he boomed.

"Likewise," I said. I didn't know what else to say. Then I said, "Welcome. I've heard a lot about you." We began to move then, a little group, from the porch into the living room, my wife guiding him by the arm. The blind man was carrying his suitcase in his other hand. My wife said things like, "To your left here, Robert. That's right. Now watch it, there's a chair. That's it. Sit down right here. This is the sofa. We just bought this sofa two weeks ago."

I started to say something about the old sofa. I'd liked that old sofa. But I didn't say anything. Then I wanted to say something else, small talk, about the scenic ride along the Hudson. How going *to* New York, you should sit on the right-hand side of the train, and coming *from* New York, the left-hand side.

"Did you have a good train ride?" I said. "Which side of the train did you sit on, by the way?"

"What a question, which side!" my wife said. "What's it matter which side?" she said.

"I just asked," I said.

"Right side," the blind man said. "I hadn't been on a train in nearly forty years. Not since I was a kid. With my folks. That's been a long time. I'd nearly forgotten the sensation. I have winter in my beard now," he said. "So I've been told, anyway. Do I look distinguished, my dear?" the blind man said to my wife.

"You look distinguished, Robert," she said. "Robert," she said. "Robert, it's just so good to see you."

My wife finally took her eyes off the blind man and looked at me. I had the feeling she didn't like what she saw. I shrugged.

I've never met, or personally known, anyone who was blind. This blind man was late forties, a heavy-set, balding man with stooped shoulders, as if he carried a great weight there. He wore brown slacks, brown shoes, a light-brown shirt, a tie, a sports coat. Spiffy. He also had this full beard. But he didn't use a cane and he didn't wear dark glasses. I'd always thought dark glasses were a must for the blind. Fact was, I wished he had a pair. At first glance, his eyes looked like anyone else's eyes. But if you looked close, there was something different about them. Too much white in the iris, for one thing, and the pupils seemed to move around in the sockets without his knowing it or being able to stop it. Creepy. As I stared at his face, I saw the left pupil turn in toward his nose while the other made an effort to keep in one place. But it was only an effort, for that eye was on the roam without his knowing it or wanting it to be.

I said, "Let me get you a drink. What's your pleasure? We have a little of everything. It's one of our pastimes."

"Bub, I'm a Scotch man myself," he said fast enough in this big voice.

"Right," I said. Bub! "Sure you are. I knew it."

He let his fingers touch his suitcase, which was sitting alongside the sofa. He was taking his bearings. I didn't blame him for that.

"I'll move that up to your room," my wife said.

"No, that's fine," the blind man said loudly. "It can go up when I go up."

"A little water with the Scotch?" I said.

"Very little," he said.

"I knew it," I said.

He said, "Just a tad. The Irish actor, Barry Fitzgerald? I'm like that fellow. When I drink water, Fitzgerald said, I drink water. When I drink whiskey, I drink whiskey." My wife laughed. The blind man brought his hand up under his beard. He lifted his beard slowly and let it drop.

I did the drinks, three big glasses of Scotch with a splash of water in each. Then we made ourselves comfortable and talked about Robert's travels. First the long flight from the West Coast to Connecticut, we covered that. Then from Connecticut up here by train. We had another drink concerning that leg of the trip.

I remembered having read somewhere that the blind didn't smoke because, as speculation had it, they couldn't see the smoke they exhaled. I thought I knew that much and that much only about blind people. But this blind man smoked his cigarette down to the nubbin and then lit another one. This blind man filled his ashtray and my wife emptied it.

When we sat down at the table for dinner, we had another drink. My wife heaped Robert's plate with cube steak, scalloped potatoes, green beans. I buttered him up two slices of bread. I said, "Here's bread and butter for you." I swallowed some of my drink. "Now let us pray," I said, and the blind man lowered his head. My wife looked at me, her mouth agape. "Pray the phone won't ring and the food doesn't get cold," I said.

We dug in. We ate everything there was to eat on the table. We ate like there was no tomorrow. We didn't talk. We ate. We scarfed. We grazed that table. We were into serious eating. The blind man had right away located his foods, he knew just where everything was on his plate. I watched with admiration as he used his knife and fork on the meat. He'd cut two pieces of meat, fork the meat into his mouth, and then go all out for the scalloped potatoes, the beans next, and then he'd tear off a hunk of buttered bread and eat that. He'd follow this up with a big drink of milk. It didn't seem to bother him to use his fingers once in a while, either.

We finished everything, including half a strawberry pie. For a few moments, we sat as if stunned. Sweat beaded on our faces. Finally, we got up from the table and left the dirty plates. We didn't look back. We took ourselves into the living room and sank into our places again. Robert and my wife sat on the sofa. I took the big chair. We had us two or three more drinks while they talked about the major things that had come to pass for them in the past ten years. For the most part, I just listened. Now and then I joined in. I didn't want him to think I'd left the room, and I didn't want her to think I was feeling left out. They talked of things that had happened to them—to them!—these past ten years. I waited in vain to hear my name on my wife's sweet lips: "And then my dear husband came into my life"—something like that. But I heard nothing of the sort. More talk of Robert. Robert had done a little of everything, it seemed, a regular blind jack-of-all-trades. But most recently he and his wife had had an Amway distributorship, from which, I gathered, they'd earned their living, such as it was. The blind man was also a ham radio operator. He talked in his loud voice about conversations he'd had with fellow operators in Guam, in the Philippines, in Alaska, and even in Tahiti. He said he'd have a lot of friends there if he ever wanted to go visit those places. From time to time, he'd turn his blind face toward me, put his hand under his beard, ask me something. How long had I been in my present position? (Three years.) Did I like my work? (I didn't.) Was I going to stay with it? (What were the options?) Finally, when I thought he was beginning to run down, I got up and turned on the TV.

My wife looked at me with irritation. She was heading toward a boil. Then she looked at the blind man and said, "Robert, do you have a TV?"

The blind man said, "My dear, I have two TVs. I have a color set and a black-and-white thing, an old relic. It's funny, but if I turn the TV on, and I'm always turning it on, I turn on the color set. It's funny, don't you think?"

I didn't know what to say to that. I had absolutely nothing to say to that. No opinion. So I watched the news program and tried to listen to what the announcer was saying.

"This is a color TV," the blind man said. "Don't ask me how, but I can tell."

"We traded up a while ago," I said.

The blind man had another taste of his drink. He lifted his beard, sniffed it, and let it fall. He leaned forward on the sofa. He positioned his ashtray on the coffee table, then put the lighter to his cigarette. He leaned back on the sofa and crossed his legs at the ankles.

My wife covered her mouth, and then she yawned. She stretched. She said, "I think I'll go upstairs and put on my robe. I think I'll change into something else. Robert, you make yourself comfortable," she said.

"I'm comfortable," the blind man said.

"I want you to feel comfortable in this house," she said.

"I am comfortable," the blind man said.

After she'd left the room, he and I listened to the weather report and then to the sports roundup. By that time, she'd been gone so long I didn't know if she was going to come back. I thought she might have gone to bed. I wished she'd come back downstairs. I didn't want to be left alone with a blind man. I asked him if he wanted another drink, and he said sure. Then I asked if he wanted to smoke some dope with me. I said I'd just rolled a number. I hadn't, but I planned to do so in about two shakes.

"I'll try some with you," he said.

"Damn right," I said. "That's the stuff."

I got our drinks and sat down on the sofa with him. Then I rolled us two fat numbers. I lit one and passed it. I brought it to his fingers. He took it and inhaled.

"Hold it as long as you can," I said. I could tell he didn't know the first thing.

My wife came back downstairs wearing her pink robe and her pink slippers.

"What do I smell?" she said.

"We thought we'd have us some cannabis," I said.

My wife gave me a savage look. Then she looked at the blind man and said, "Robert, I didn't know you smoked."

He said, "I do now, my dear. There's a first time for everything. But I don't feel anything yet."

"This stuff is pretty mellow," I said. "This stuff is mild. It's dope you can reason with," I said. "It doesn't mess you up."

"Not much it doesn't, bub," he said, and laughed.

My wife sat on the sofa between the blind man and me. I passed her the number. She took it and toked and then passed it back to me. "Which way is this going?" she said. Then she said, "I shouldn't be smoking this. I can hardly keep my eyes open as it is. That dinner did me in. I shouldn't have eaten so much."

"It was the strawberry pie," the blind man said. "That's what did it," he said, and he laughed his big laugh. Then he shook his head.

"There's more strawberry pie," I said.

"Do you want some more, Robert?" my wife said.

"Maybe in a little while," he said.

We gave our attention to the TV. My wife yawned again. She said, "Your bed is made up when you feel like going to bed, Robert. I know you must have had a long day. When you're ready to go to bed, say so." She pulled his arm. "Robert?"

He came to and said, "I've had a real nice time. This beats tapes, doesn't it?"

I said, "Coming at you," and I put the number between his fingers. He inhaled, held the smoke, and then let it go. It was like he'd been doing it since he was nine years old.

"Thanks, bub," he said. "But I think this is all for me. I think I'm beginning to feel it," he said. He held the burning roach out for my wife.

"Same here," she said. "Ditto. Me, too." She took the roach and passed it to me. "I may just sit here for a while between you two guys with my eyes closed. But don't let me bother you, okay? Either one of you. If it bothers you, say so. Otherwise, I may just sit here with my eyes closed until you're ready to go to bed," she said. "Your bed's made up, Robert, when you're ready. It's right next to our room at the top of the stairs. We'll show you up when you're ready. You wake me up now, you guys, if I fall asleep." She said that and then she closed her eyes and went to sleep.

The news program ended. I got up and changed the channel. I sat back down on the sofa. I wished my wife hadn't pooped out. Her head lay across the back of the sofa, her mouth open. She'd turned so that her robe had slipped away from her legs, exposing a juicy thigh. I reached to draw her robe back over her, and it was then that I glanced at the blind man. What the hell! I flipped the robe open again.

"You say when you want some strawberry pie," I said.

"I will," he said.

I said, "Are you tired? Do you want me to take you up to your bed? Are you ready to hit the hay?"

"Not yet," he said. "No, I'll stay up with you, bub. If that's all right. I'll stay up until you're ready to turn in. We haven't had a chance to talk. Know what I mean? I feel like me and her monopolized the evening." He lifted his beard and he let it fall. He picked up his cigarettes and his lighter.

"That's all right," I said. Then I said, "I'm glad for the company."

And I guess I was. Every night I smoked dope and stayed up as long as I could before I fell asleep. My wife and I hardly ever went to bed at the same time. When I did go to sleep, I had these dreams. Sometimes I'd wake up from one of them, my heart going crazy.

Something about the church and the Middle Ages was on the TV. Not your run-of-the-mill TV fare. I wanted to watch something else. I turned to the other channels. But there was nothing on them, either. So I turned back to the first channel and apologized.

"Bub, it's all right," the blind man said. "It's fine with me. Whatever you want to watch is okay. I'm always learning something. Learning never ends. It won't hurt me to learn something tonight. I got ears," he said.

We didn't say anything for a time. He was leaning forward with his head turned at me, his right ear aimed in the direction of the set. Very disconcerting. Now and then his eyelids drooped and then they snapped open again. Now and then he put his fingers into his beard and tugged, like he was thinking about something he was hearing on the television.

On the screen, a group of men wearing cowls was being set upon and tormented by men dressed in skeleton costumes and men dressed as devils. The men dressed as devils wore devil masks, horns, and long tails. This pageant was part of a procession. The Englishman who was narrating the thing said it took place in Spain once a year. I tried to explain to the blind man what was happening.

"Skeletons," he said. "I know about skeletons," he said, and he nodded.

The TV showed this one cathedral. Then there was a long, slow look at another one. Finally, the picture switched to the famous one in Paris, with its flying buttresses and its spires reaching up to the clouds. The camera pulled away to show the whole of the cathedral rising above the skyline.

There were times when the Englishman who was telling the thing would shut up, would simply let the camera move around over the cathedrals. Or else the camera would tour the countryside, men in fields walking behind oxen. I waited as long as I could. Then I felt I had to say something. I said, "They're showing the outside of this cathedral now. Gargoyles. Little statues carved to look like monsters. Now I guess they're in Italy. Yeah, they're in Italy. There's paintings on the walls of this one church."

"Are those fresco paintings, bub?" he asked, and he sipped from his drink.

I reached for my glass. But it was empty. I tried to remember what I could remember. "You're asking me are those frescoes?" I said. "That's a good question. I don't know."

The camera moved to a cathedral outside Lisbon. The differences in the Portuguese cathedral compared with the French and Italian were not that great. But they were there. Mostly the interior stuff. Then something occurred to me, and I said, "Something has occurred to me. Do you have any idea what a cathedral is? What they look like, that is? Do you follow me? If somebody says cathedral to you, do you have any notion what they're talking about? Do you know the difference between that and a Baptist church, say?"

He let the smoke dribble from his mouth. "I know they took hundreds of workers fifty or a hundred years to build," he said. "I just heard the man say that, of course. I know generations of the same families worked on a cathedral. I heard him say that, too. The men who began their life's work on them, they never lived to see the completion of their work. In that wise, bub, they're no different from the rest of us, right?" He laughed. Then his eyelids drooped again. His head nodded. He seemed to be snoozing. Maybe he was imagining himself in Portugal. The TV was showing another cathedral now. This one was in Germany. The Englishman's voice droned on. "Cathedrals," the blind man said. He sat up and rolled his head back and forth. "If you want the truth, bub, that's about all I know. What I just said. What I heard him say. But maybe you could describe one to me? I wish you'd do it. I'd like that. If you want to know, I really don't have a good idea."

I stared hard at the shot of the cathedral on the TV. How could I even begin to describe it? But say my life depended on it. Say my life was being threatened by an insane guy who said I had to do it or else.

I stared some more at the cathedral before the picture flipped off into the countryside. There was no use. I turned to the blind man and said, "To begin with, they're very tall." I was looking around the room for clues. "They reach way up. Up and up. Toward the sky. They're so big, some of them, they have to have these supports. To help hold them up, so to speak. These supports are called buttresses. They remind me of viaducts, for some reason. But maybe you don't know viaducts, either? Sometimes the cathedrals have devils and such carved into the front. Sometimes lords and ladies. Don't ask me why this is," I said.

He was nodding. The whole upper part of his body seemed to be moving back and forth.

"I'm not doing so good, am I?" I said.

He stopped nodding and leaned forward on the edge of the sofa. As he listened to me, he was running his fingers through his beard. I wasn't getting through to him, I could see that. But he waited for me to go on just the same. He nodded, like he was trying to encourage me. I tried to think what else to say. "They're really big," I said. "They're massive. They're built of stone. Marble, too, sometimes. In those olden days, when they built cathedrals, men wanted to be close to God. In those olden days, God was an important part of everyone's life. You could tell this from their cathedral-building. I'm sorry," I said, "but it looks like that's the best I can do for you. I'm just no good at it."

"That's all right, bub," the blind man said. "Hey, listen. I hope you don't mind my asking you. Can I ask you something? Let me ask you a simple question, yes or no. I'm just curious and there's no offense. You're my host. But let me ask if you are in any way religious? You don't mind my asking?"

I shook my head. He couldn't see that, though. A wink is the same as a nod to a blind man. "I guess I don't believe in it. In anything. Sometimes it's hard. You know what I'm saying?"

"Sure, I do," he said.

"Right," I said.

The Englishman was still holding forth. My wife sighed in her sleep. She drew a long breath and went on with her sleeping.

"You'll have to forgive me," I said. "But I can't tell you what a cathedral looks like. It just isn't in me to do it. I can't do any more than I've done."

The blind man sat very still, his head down, as he listened to me.

I said, "The truth is, cathedrals don't mean anything special to me. Nothing. Cathedrals. They're something to look at on late-night TV. That's all they are."

It was then that the blind man cleared his throat. He brought something up. He took a handkerchief from his back pocket. Then he said, "I get it, bub. It's okay. It happens. Don't worry about it," he said. "Hey, listen to me. Will you do me a favor? I got an idea. Why don't you find us some heavy paper? And a pen. We'll do something. We'll draw one together. Get us a pen and some heavy paper. Go on, bub, get the stuff," he said.

So I went upstairs. My legs felt like they didn't have any strength in them. They felt like they did after I'd done some running. In my wife's room, I looked around. I found some ballpoints in a little basket on her table. And then I tried to think where to look for the kind of paper he was talking about.

Downstairs, in the kitchen, I found a shopping bag with onion skins in the bottom of the bag. I emptied the bag and shook it. I brought it into the living room and sat down with it near his legs. I moved some things, smoothed the wrinkles from the bag, spread it out on the coffee table.

The blind man got down from the sofa and sat next to me on the carpet.

He ran his fingers over the paper. He went up and down the sides of the paper. The edges, even the edges. He fingered the corners.

"All right," he said. "All right, let's do her."

He found my hand, the hand with the pen. He closed his hand over my hand. "Go ahead, bub, draw," he said. "Draw. You'll see. I'll follow along with you. It'll be okay. Just begin now like I'm telling you. You'll see. Draw," the blind man said.

So I began. First I drew a box that looked like a house. It could have been the house I lived in. Then I put a roof on it. At either end of the roof, I drew spires. Crazy.

"Swell," he said. "Terrific. You're doing fine," he said. "Never thought anything like this could happen in your lifetime, did you, bub? Well, it's a strange life, we all know that. Go on now. Keep it up."

I put in windows with arches. I drew flying buttresses. I hung great doors. I couldn't stop. The TV station went off the air. I put down the pen and closed and opened my fingers. The blind man felt around over the paper. He moved the tips of his fingers over the paper, all over what I had drawn, and he nodded.

"Doing fine," the blind man said.

I took up the pen again, and he found my hand. I kept at it. I'm no artist. But I kept drawing just the same.

My wife opened up her eyes and gazed at us. She sat up on the sofa, her robe hanging open. She said, "What are you doing? Tell me, I want to know."

I didn't answer her.

The blind man said, "We're drawing a cathedral. Me and him are working on it. Press hard," he said to me. "That's right. That's good," he said. "Sure. You got it, bub. I can tell. You didn't think you could. But you can, can't you? You're cooking with gas now. You know what I'm saying? We're going to really have us something here in a minute. How's the old arm?" he said. "Put some people in there now. What's a cathedral without people?"

My wife said, "What's going on? Robert, what are you doing? What's going on?"

"It's all right," he said to her. "Close your eyes now," the blind man said to me.

I did it. I closed them just like he said.

"Are they closed?" he said. "Don't fudge."

"They're closed," I said.

"Keep them that way," he said. He said, "Don't stop now. Draw."

So we kept on with it. His fingers rode my fingers as my hand went over the paper. It was like nothing else in my life up to now.

Then he said, "I think that's it. I think you got it," he said. "Take a look. What do you think?"

But I had my eyes closed. I thought I'd keep them that way for a little longer. I thought it was something I ought to do.

"Well?" he said. "Are you looking?"

My eyes were still closed. I was in my house. I knew that. But I didn't feel like I was inside anything.

"It's really something," I said.

---

1. What explains the narrator's initial distrust of the blind man?

2. Why does it bother the narrator to imagine a woman "who could never see herself as she was seen in the eyes of her loved one"?

3. Why do the narrator and the blind man end up drawing a cathedral together?

4. Why does the narrator think he ought to keep his eyes closed longer when Robert tells him to look at the drawing?

MARGARET ATWOOD (1939–) is one of Canada's most prominent authors and has written in a wide range of genres, including poetry, novels, short stories, children's literature, and literary essays. Born in Ottawa, she has lived for many years in Toronto and has received numerous awards for her work. Her books are not only highly regarded by critics around the world, but are also widely popular with general readers. Many of Atwood's stories and novels center on complex women characters and deal with social and political issues from a feminist perspective. Her novels include *The Edible Woman* (1969), *The Handmaid's Tale* (1985), *The Robber Bride* (1993), and *The Blind Assassin* (2000), for which she won the Booker Prize.

The Man from Mars

A long time ago Christine was walking through the park. She was still wearing her tennis dress; she hadn't had time to shower and change, and her hair was held back with an elastic band. Her chunky reddish face, exposed with no softening fringe, looked like a Russian peasant's, but without the elastic band the hair got in her eyes. The afternoon was too hot for April; the indoor courts had been steaming, her skin felt poached.

The sun had brought the old men out from wherever they spent the winter: she had read a story recently about one who lived for three years in a manhole. They sat weedishly on the benches or lay on the grass with their heads on squares of used newspaper. As she passed, their wrinkled toadstool faces drifted towards her, drawn by the movement of her body, then floated away again, uninterested.

The squirrels were out, too, foraging; two or three of them moved towards her in darts and pauses, eyes fixed on her expectantly, mouths with the ratlike receding chins open to show the yellowed front teeth. Christine walked faster, she had nothing to give them. People shouldn't feed them, she thought; it makes them anxious and they get mangy.

Halfway across the park she stopped to take off her cardigan. As she bent over to pick up her tennis racquet again someone touched her on her freshly bared arm. Christine seldom screamed; she straightened up suddenly, gripping the handle of her racquet. It was not one of the old men, however; it was a dark-haired boy of twelve or so.

"Excuse me," he said, "I search for Economics Building. Is it there?" He motioned towards the west.

Christine looked at him more closely. She had been mistaken: he was not young, just short. He came a little above her shoulder, but then, she was above the average height; "statuesque," her mother called it when she was straining. He was also what was referred to in their family as "a person from another culture": oriental without a doubt, though perhaps not Chinese. Christine judged he must be a foreign student and gave him her official welcoming smile. In high school she had been president of the United Nations Club; that year her school had been picked to represent the Egyptian delegation at the Mock Assembly. It had been an unpopular assignment—nobody wanted to be the Arabs—but she had seen it through. She had made rather a good speech about the Palestinian refugees.

"Yes," she said, "that's it over there. The one with the flat roof. See it?"

The man had been smiling nervously at her the whole time. He was wearing glasses with transparent plastic rims, through which his eyes bulged up at her as though through a goldfish bowl. He had not followed where she was pointing. Instead he thrust towards her a small pad of green paper and a ballpoint pen.

"You make map," he said.

Christine set down her tennis racquet and drew a careful map. "We are here," she said, pronouncing distinctly. "You go this way. The building is here." She indicated the route with a dotted line and an *X*. The man leaned close to her, watching the progress of the map attentively; he smelled of cooked cauliflower and an unfamiliar brand of hair grease. When she had finished Christine handed the paper and pen back to him with a terminal smile.

"Wait," the man said. He tore the piece of paper with the map off the pad, folded it carefully and put it in his jacket pocket; the jacket sleeves came down over his wrists and had threads at the edges. He began to write something; she noticed with a slight feeling of revulsion that his nails and the ends of his fingers were so badly bitten they seemed almost deformed. Several of his fingers were blue from the leaky ballpoint.

"Here is my name," he said, holding the pad out to her.

Christine read an odd assemblage of *G*s, *Y*s, and *N*s, neatly printed in block letters. "Thank you," she said.

"You now write *your* name," he said, extending the pen.

Christine hesitated. If this had been a person from her own culture she would have thought he was trying to pick her up. But then, people from her own culture never tried to pick her up; she was too big. The only one who had made the attempt was the Moroccan waiter at the beer parlour where they sometimes went after meetings, and he had been direct. He had just intercepted her on the way to the Ladies' Room and asked and she said no; that had been that. This man was not a waiter though, but a student; she didn't want to offend him. In his culture, whatever it was, this exchange of names on pieces of paper was probably a formal politeness, like saying thank you. She took the pen from him.

"That is a very pleasant name," he said. He folded the paper and placed it in his jacket pocket with the map.

Christine felt she had done her duty. "Well, goodbye," she said. "It was nice to have met you." She bent for her tennis racquet but he had already stooped and retrieved it and was holding it with both hands in front of him, like a captured banner.

"I carry this for you."

"Oh no, please. Don't bother, I am in a hurry," she said, articulating clearly. Deprived of her tennis racquet she felt weaponless. He started to saunter along the path; he was not nervous at all now, he seemed completely at ease.

"*Vous parlez français?*" he asked conversationally.

"*Oui, un petit peu,*" she said. "Not very well." How am I going to get my racquet away from him without being rude? she was wondering.

"*Maís vous avez un bel accent.*" His eyes goggled at her through the glasses: was he being flirtatious? She was well aware that her accent was wretched.

"Look," she said, for the first time letting her impatience show, "I really have to go. Give me my racquet, please."

He quickened his pace but gave no sign of returning the racquet. "Where you are going?"

"Home," she said. "My house."

"I go with you now," he said hopefully.

"*No*," she said: she would have to be firm with him. She made a lunge and got a grip on her racquet; after a brief tug of war it came free.

"Goodbye," she said, turning away from his puzzled face and setting off at what she hoped was a discouraging jog trot. It was like walking away from a growling dog: you shouldn't let on you were frightened. Why should she be frightened anyway? He was only half her size and she had the tennis racquet, there was nothing he could do to her.

Although she did not look back she could tell he was still following. Let there be a streetcar, she thought, and there was one, but it was far down the line, stuck behind a red light. He appeared at her side, breathing audibly, a moment after she reached the stop. She gazed ahead, rigid.

"You are my friend," he said tentatively.

Christine relented: he hadn't been trying to pick her up after all, he was a stranger, he just wanted to meet some of the local people; in his place she would have wanted the same thing.

"Yes," she said, doling him out a smile.

"That is good," he said. "My country is very far."

Christine couldn't think of an apt reply. "That's interesting," she said. "*Très interessant*." The streetcar was coming at last; she opened her purse and got out a ticket.

"I go with you now," he said. His hand clamped on her arm above the elbow.

"You . . . stay . . . *here*," Christine said, resisting the impulse to shout but pausing between each word as though for a deaf person. She detached his hand—his hold was quite feeble and could not compete with her tennis biceps—and leapt off the curb and up the streetcar steps, hearing with relief the doors grind shut behind her. Inside the car and a block away she permitted herself a glance out a side window. He was standing where she had left him; he seemed to be writing something on his little pad of paper.

When she reached home she had only time for a snack, and even then she was almost late for the Debating Society. The topic was, "Resolved: That War Is Obsolete." Her team took the affirmative and won.

Christine came out of her last examination feeling depressed. It was not the exam that depressed her but the fact that it was the last one: it meant the end of the school year. She dropped into the coffee shop as usual, then went home early because there didn't seem to be anything else to do.

"Is that you, dear?" her mother called from the living room. She must have heard the front door close. Christine went in and flopped on the sofa, disturbing the neat pattern of cushions.

"How was your exam, dear?" her mother asked.

"Fine," said Christine flatly. It had been fine; she had passed. She was not a brilliant student, she knew that, but she was conscientious. Her professors always wrote things like "A serious attempt" and "Well thought out but perhaps lacking in élan" on her term papers; they gave her Bs, the occasional B+. She was taking Political Science and Economics, and hoped for a job with the Government after she graduated; with her father's connections she had a good chance.

"That's nice."

Christine felt, resentfully, that her mother had only a hazy idea of what an exam was. She was arranging gladioli in a vase; she had rubber gloves on to protect her hands as she always did when engaged in what she called "housework." As far as Christine could tell her housework consisted of arranging flowers in vases: daffodils and tulips and hyacinths through gladioli, irises, and roses, all the way to asters and mums. Sometimes she cooked, elegantly and with chafing dishes, but she thought of it as a hobby. The girl did everything else. Christine thought it faintly sinful to have a girl. The only ones available now were either foreign or pregnant; their expressions usually suggested they were being taken advantage of somehow. But her mother asked what they would do otherwise; they'd either have to go into a Home or stay in their own countries, and Christine had to agree this was probably true. It was hard, anyway, to argue with her mother. She was so delicate, so preserved-looking, a harsh breath would scratch the finish.

"An interesting young man phoned today," her mother said. She had finished the gladioli and was taking off her rubber gloves. "He asked to speak with you and when I said you weren't in we had quite a little chat. You didn't tell me about him, dear." She put on the glasses which she wore on a decorative chain around her neck, a signal that she was in her modern, intelligent mood rather than her old-fashioned whimsical one.

"Did he leave his name?" Christine asked. She knew a lot of young men but they didn't often call her; they conducted their business with her in the coffee shop or after meetings.

"He's a person from another culture. He said he would call back later."

Christine had to think a moment. She was vaguely acquainted with several people from other cultures, Britain mostly; they belonged to the Debating Society.

"He's studying Philosophy in Montreal," her mother prompted. "He sounded French."

Christine began to remember the man in the park. "I don't think he's French, exactly," she said.

Her mother had taken off her glasses again and was poking absent-mindedly at a bent gladiolus. "Well, he sounded French." She meditated, flowery sceptre in hand. "I think it would be nice if you had him to tea."

Christine's mother did her best. She had two other daughters, both of whom took after her. They were beautiful; one was well married already and the other would clearly have no trouble. Her friends consoled her about Christine by saying, "She's not fat, she's just big-bones, it's the father's side," and "Christine is so healthy." Her other daughters had never gotten involved in activities when they were at school, but since Christine could not possibly ever be beautiful even if she took off weight, it was just as well she was so athletic and political, it was a good thing she had interests. Christine's mother tried to encourage her interests whenever possible. Christine could tell when she was making an extra effort, there was a reproachful edge to her voice.

She knew her mother expected enthusiasm but she could not supply it. "I don't know, I'll have to see," she said dubiously.

"You look tired, darling," said her mother. "Perhaps you'd like a glass of milk."

Christine was in the bathtub when the phone rang. She was not prone to fantasy but when she was in the bathtub she often pretended she was a dolphin, a game left over from one of the girls who used to bathe her when she was small. Her mother was being bell-voiced and gracious in the hall; then there was a tap at the door.

"It's that nice young French student, Christine," her mother said.

"Tell him I'm in the bathtub," Christine said, louder than necessary. "He isn't French."

She could hear her mother frowning. "That wouldn't be very polite, Christine. I don't think he'd understand."

"Oh, all right," Christine said. She heaved herself out of the bathtub, swathed her pink bulk in a towel and splattered to the phone.

"Hello," she said gruffly. At a distance he was not pathetic, he was a nuisance. She could not imagine how he had tracked her down: most likely he went through the phone book, calling all the numbers with her last name until he hit on the right one.

"It is your friend."

"I know," she said. "How are you?"

"I am very fine." There was a long pause, during which Christine had a vicious urge to say, "Well goodbye then," and hang up; but she was aware of her mother poised figurine-like in her bedroom doorway. Then he said, "I hope you also are very fine."

"Yes," said Christine. She wasn't going to participate.

"I come to tea," he said.

This took Christine by surprise. "You do?"

"Your pleasant mother ask me. I come Thursday, four o'clock."

"Oh," Christine said, ungraciously.

"See you then," he said, with the conscious pride of one who has mastered a difficult idiom.

Christine set down the phone and went along the hall. Her mother was in her study, sitting innocently at her writing desk.

"Did you ask him to tea on Thursday?"

"Not exactly, dear," her mother said. "I did mention he might come round to tea *some*time, though."

"Well, he's coming Thursday. Four o'clock."

"What's wrong with that?" her mother said serenely. "I think it's a very nice gesture for us to make. I do think you might try to be a little more cooperative." She was pleased with herself.

"Since you invited him," said Christine, "you can bloody well stick around and help me entertain him. I don't want to be left making nice gestures all by myself."

"Christine, *dear*," her mother said, above being shocked. "You ought to put on your dressing gown, you'll catch a chill."

After sulking for an hour Christine tried to think of the tea as a cross between an examination and an executive meeting: not enjoyable, certainly, but to be got through as tactfully as possible. And it *was* a nice gesture. When the cakes her mother had ordered arrived from The Patisserie on Thursday morning she began to feel slightly festive; she even resolved to put on a dress, a good one, instead of a skirt and blouse. After all, she had nothing against him, except the memory of the way he had grabbed her tennis racquet and then her arm. She suppressed a quick impossible vision of herself pursued around the living room, fending him off with thrown sofa cushions and vases of gladioli; nevertheless she told the girl they would have tea in the garden. It would be a treat for him, and there was more space outdoors.

She had suspected her mother would dodge the tea, would contrive to be going out just as he was arriving: that way she could size him up and then leave them alone together. She had done things like that to Christine before; the excuse this time was the Symphony Committee. Sure enough, her mother carefully mislaid her gloves and located them with a faked murmur of joy when the doorbell rang. Christine relished for weeks afterwards the image of her mother's dropped jaw and flawless recovery when he was introduced: he wasn't quite the foreign potentate her optimistic, veil-fragile mind had concocted.

He was prepared for celebration. He had slicked on so much hair cream that his head seemed to be covered with a tight black patent leather cap, and he had cut the threads off his jacket sleeves. His orange tie was overpoweringly splendid. Christine noticed, however, as he shook her mother's suddenly braced white glove that the ballpoint ink on his fingers was indelible. His face had broken out, possibly in anticipation of the delights in store for him; he had a tiny camera slung over his shoulder and was smoking an exotic-smelling cigarette.

Christine led him through the cool flowery softly padded living room and out by the French doors into the garden. "You sit here," she said. "I will have the girl bring tea."

This girl was from the West Indies: Christine's parents had been enraptured with her when they were down at Christmas and had brought her back with them. Since that time she had become pregnant, but Christine's mother had not dismissed her. She said she was slightly disappointed but what could you expect, and she didn't see any real difference between a girl who was pregnant before you hired her and one who got that way afterwards. She prided herself on her tolerance; also there was a scarcity of girls. Strangely enough, the girl became progressively less easy to get along with. Either she did not share Christine's mother's view of her own generosity, or she felt she had gotten away with something and was therefore free to indulge in contempt. At first Christine had tried to treat her as an equal. "Don't call me 'Miss Christine,'" she had said with an imitation of light, comradely laughter. "What you want me to call you then?" the girl had said, scowling. They had begun to have brief, surly arguments in the kitchen, which Christine decided were like the arguments between one servant and another: her mother's attitude towards each of them was similar, they were not altogether satisfactory but they would have to do.

The cakes, glossy with icing, were set out on a plate and the teapot was standing ready; on the counter the electric kettle boiled. Christine headed for it, but the girl, till then sitting with her elbows on the kitchen table and watching her expressionlessly, made a dash and intercepted her. Christine waited until she had poured the water into the pot. Then, "I'll carry it out, Elvira," she said. She had just decided she didn't want the girl to see her visitor's orange tie; already, she knew, her position in the girl's eyes had suffered because no one had yet attempted to get *her* pregnant.

"What you think they pay me for, Miss Christine?" the girl said insolently. She swung towards the garden with the tray; Christine trailed her, feeling lumpish and awkward. The girl was at least as big as she was but in a different way.

"Thank you, Elvira," Christine said when the tray was in place. The girl departed without a word, casting a disdainful backward glance at the frayed jacket sleeves, the stained fingers. Christine was now determined to be especially kind to him.

"You are very rich," he said.

"No," Christine protested, shaking her head, "we're not." She had never thought of her family as rich; it was one of her father's sayings that nobody made any money with the Government.

"Yes," he repeated, "you are very rich." He sat back in his lawn chair, gazing about him as though dazed.

Christine set his cup of tea in front of him. She wasn't in the habit of paying much attention to the house or the garden; they were nothing special, far from being the largest on the street; other people took care of them. But now she looked where he was looking, seeing it all as though from a different height: the long expanses, the border flowers blazing in the early-summer sunlight, the flagged patio and walks, the high walls and the silence.

He came back to her face, sighing a little. "My English is not good," he said, "but I improve."

"You do," Christine said, nodding encouragement.

He took sips of his tea, quickly and tenderly, as though afraid of injuring the cup. "I like to stay here."

Christine passed him the cakes. He took only one, making a slight face as he ate it; but he had several more cups of tea while she finished the cakes. She managed to find out from him that he had come over on a church fellowship—she could not decode the denomination—and was studying Philosophy or Theology, or possibly both. She was feeling well-disposed towards him: he had behaved himself, he had caused her no inconvenience.

The teapot was at last empty. He sat up straight in his chair, as though alerted by a soundless gong. "You look this way, please," he said. Christine saw that he had placed his miniature camera on the stone sundial her mother had shipped back from England two years before. He wanted to take her picture. She was flattered, and settled herself to pose, smiling evenly.

He took off his glasses and laid them beside his plate. For a moment she saw his myopic, unprotected eyes turned towards her, with something tremulous and confiding in them she wanted to close herself off from knowing about. Then he went over and did something to the camera, his back to her. The next instant he was crouched beside her, his arm around her waist as far as it could reach, his other hand covering her own hands which she had folded in her lap, his cheek jammed up against hers. She was too startled to move. The camera clicked.

He stood up at once and replaced his glasses, which glittered now with a sad triumph. "Thank you, miss," he said to her. "I go now." He slung the camera back over his shoulder, keeping his hand on it as though to hold the lid on and prevent escape. "I send to my family; they will like."

He was out the gate and gone before Christine had recovered; then she laughed. She had been afraid he would attack her, she could admit it now, and he had; but not in the usual way. He had raped, *rapeo, rapere, rapui, to seize and carry off*, not herself but her celluloid image, and incidentally that of the silver tea service, which glinted mockingly at her as the girl bore it away, carrying it regally, the insignia, the official jewels.

Christine spent the summer as she had for the past three years: she was the sailing instructress at an expensive all-girls camp near Algonquin Park. She had been a camper there, everything was familiar to her; she sailed almost better than she played tennis.

The second week she got a letter from him, postmarked Montreal and forwarded from her home address. It was printed in block letters on a piece of the green paper, two or three sentences. It began, "I hope you are well," then described the weather in monosyllables and ended, "I am fine." It was signed, "Your friend." Each week she got another of these letters, more or less identical. In one of them a colour print was enclosed: himself, slightly cross-eyed and grinning hilariously, even more spindly than she remembered him against her billowing draperies, flowers exploding around them like firecrackers, one of his hands an equivocal blur in her lap, the other out of sight; on her own face, astonishment and outrage, as though he was sticking her in the behind with his hidden thumb.

She answered the first letter, but after that the seniors were in training for the races. At the end of the summer, packing to go home, she threw all the letters away.

. . .

When she had been back for several weeks she received another of the green letters. This time there was a return address printed at the top which Christine noted with foreboding was in her own city. Every day she waited for the phone to ring; she was so certain his first attempt at contact would be a disembodied voice that when he came upon her abruptly in midcampus she was unprepared.

"How are you?"

His smile was the same, but everything else about him had deteriorated. He was, if possible, thinner; his jacket sleeves had sprouted a lush new crop of threads, as though to conceal hands now so badly bitten they appeared to have been gnawed by rodents. His hair fell over his eyes, uncut, ungreased; his eyes in the hollowed face, a delicate triangle of skin stretched on bone, jumped behind his glasses like hooded fish. He had the end of a cigarette in the corner of his mouth, and as they walked he lit a new one from it.

"I'm fine," Christine said. She was thinking, I'm not going to get involved again, enough is enough, I've done my bit for internationalism. "How are you?"

"I live here now," he said. "Maybe I study Economics."

"That's nice." He didn't sound as though he was enrolled anywhere.

"I come to see you."

Christine didn't know whether he meant he had left Montreal in order to be near her or just wanted to visit her at her house as he had done in the spring; either way she refused to be implicated. They were outside the Political Science Building. "I have a class here," she said. "Goodbye." She was being callous, she realized that, but a quick chop was more merciful in the long run, that was what her beautiful sisters used to say.

Afterwards she decided it had been stupid of her to let him find out where her class was. Though a timetable was posted in each of the colleges: all he had to do was look her up and record her every probable movement in block letters on his green notepad. After that day he never left her alone.

Initially he waited outside the lecture rooms for her to come out. She said hello to him curtly at first and kept on going, but this didn't work; he followed her at a distance, smiling his changeless smile. Then she stopped speaking altogether and pretended to ignore him, but it made no difference, he followed her anyway. The fact that she was in some way afraid of him—or was it just embarrassment?—seemed only to encourage him. Her friends started to notice, asking her who he was and why he was tagging along behind her; she could hardly answer because she hardly knew.

As the weekdays passed and he showed no signs of letting up, she began to jog trot between classes, finally to run. He was tireless, and had an amazing wind for one who smoked so heavily: he would speed along behind her, keeping the distance between them the same, as though he were a pull toy attached to her by a string. She was aware of the ridiculous spectacle they must make, galloping across campus, something out of a cartoon short, a lumbering elephant stampeded by a smiling, emaciated mouse, both of them locked in the classic pattern of comic pursuit and flight; but she found that to race made her less nervous than to walk sedately, the skin on the back of her neck crawling with the feel of his eyes on it. At least she could use her muscles. She worked out routines, escapes: she would dash in the front door of the Ladies' Room in the coffee shop and out the back door, and he would lose the trail, until he discovered the other entrance. She would try to shake him by detours through baffling archways and corridors, but he seemed as familiar with the architectural mazes as she was herself. As a last refuge she could head for the women's dormitory and watch from safety as he was skidded to a halt by the receptionist's austere voice: men were not allowed past the entrance.

Lunch became difficult. She would be sitting, usually with other members of the Debating Society, just digging nicely into a sandwich, when he would appear suddenly as though he'd come up through an unseen manhole. She then had the choice of barging out through the crowded cafeteria, sandwich half eaten, or finishing her lunch with him standing behind her chair, everyone at the table acutely aware of him, the conversation stilting and dwindling. Her friends learned to spot him from a distance; they posted lookouts. "Here he comes," they would whisper, helping her collect her belongings for the sprint they knew would follow.

Several times she got tired of running and turned to confront him. "What do you want?" she would ask, glowering belligerently down at him, almost clenching her fists; she felt like shaking him, hitting him.

"I wish to talk with you."

"Well, here I am," she would say. "What do you want to talk about?"

But he would say nothing; he would stand in front of her, shifting his feet, smiling perhaps apologetically (though she could never pinpoint the exact tone of that smile, chewed lips stretched apart over the nicotine-yellowed teeth, rising at the corners, flesh held stiffly in place for an invisible photographer), his eyes jerking from one part of her face to another as though he saw her in fragments.

Annoying and tedious though it was, his pursuit of her had an odd result: mysterious in itself, it rendered her equally mysterious. No one had ever found Christine mysterious before. To her parents she was a beefy heavyweight, a plodder, lacking in flair, ordinary as bread. To her sisters she was the plain one, treated with an indulgence they did not give to each other: they did not fear her as a rival. To her male friends she was the one who could be relied on. She was helpful and a hard worker, always good for a game of tennis with the athletes among them. They invited her along to drink beer with them so they could get into the cleaner, more desirable Ladies and Escorts side of the beer parlour, taking it for granted she would buy her share of the rounds. In moments of stress they confided to her their problems with women. There was nothing devious about her and nothing interesting.

Christine had always agreed with these estimates of herself. In childhood she had identified with the false bride or the ugly sister; whenever a story had begun, "Once there was a maiden as beautiful as she was good," she had known it wasn't her. That was just how it was, but it wasn't so bad. Her parents never expected her to be a brilliant social success and weren't overly disappointed when she wasn't. She was spared the manoeuvering and anxiety she witnessed among others her age, and she even had a kind of special position among men: she was an exception, she fitted none of the categories they commonly used when talking about girls; she wasn't a cockteaser, a cold fish, an easy lay, or a snarky bitch; she was an honorary person. She had grown to share their contempt for most women.

Now, however, there was something about her that could not be explained. A man was chasing her, a peculiar sort of man, granted, but still a man, and he was without doubt attracted to her, he couldn't leave her alone. Other men examined her more closely than they ever had, appraising her, trying to find out what it was those twitching bespectacled eyes saw in her. They started to ask her out, though they returned from these excursions with their curiosity unsatisfied, the secret of her charm still intact. Her opaque dumpling face, her solid bearshaped body became for them parts of a riddle no one could solve. Christine sensed this. In the bathtub she no longer imagined she was a dolphin; instead she imagined she was an elusive water nixie, or sometimes, in moments of audacity, Marilyn Monroe. The daily chase was becoming a habit; she even looked forward to it. In addition to its other benefits she was losing weight.

All these weeks he had never phoned her or turned up at the house. He must have decided however that his tactics were not having the desired result, or perhaps he sensed she was becoming bored. The phone began to ring in the early morning or late at night when he could be sure she would be there. Sometimes he would simply breathe (she could recognize, or thought she could, the quality of his breathing), in which case she would hang up. Occasionally he would say again that he wanted to talk to her, but even when she gave him lots of time nothing else would follow. Then he extended his range: she would see him on her streetcar, smiling at her silently from a seat never closer than three away; she could feel him tracking her down her own street, though when she would break her resolve to pay no attention and would glance back he would be invisible or in the act of hiding behind a tree or hedge.

Among crowds of people and in daylight she had not really been afraid of him; she was stronger than he was and he had made no recent attempt to touch her. But the days were growing shorter and colder, it was almost November. Often she was arriving home in twilight or a darkness broken only by the feeble orange streetlamps. She brooded over the possibility of razors, knives, guns; by acquiring a weapon he could quickly turn the odds against her. She avoided wearing scarves, remembering the newspaper stories about girls who had been strangled by them. Putting on her nylons in the morning gave her a funny feeling. Her body seemed to have diminished, to have become smaller than his.

Was he deranged, was he a sex maniac? He seemed so harmless, yet it was that kind who often went berserk in the end. She pictured those ragged fingers at her throat, tearing at her clothes, though she could not think of herself as screaming. Parked cars, the shrubberies near her house, the driveways on either side of it, changed as she passed them from unnoticed background to sinister shadowed foreground, every detail distinct and harsh: they were places a man might crouch, leap out from. Yet every time she saw him in the clear light of morning or afternoon (for he still continued his old methods of pursuit), his aging jacket and jittery eyes convinced her that it was she herself who was the tormentor, the persecutor. She was in some sense responsible; from the folds and crevices of the body she had treated for so long as a reliable machine was emanating, against her will, some potent invisible odour, like a dog's in heat or a female moth's, that made him unable to stop following her.

Her mother, who had been too preoccupied with the unavoidable fall entertaining to pay much attention to the number of phone calls Christine was getting or to the hired girl's complaints of a man who hung up without speaking, announced that she was flying down to New York for the weekend; her father decided to go too. Christine panicked: she saw herself in the bathtub with her throat slit, the blood drooling out of her neck and running in a little spiral down the drain (for by this time she believed he could walk through walls, could be everywhere at once). The girl would do nothing to help; she might even stand in the bathroom door with her arms folded, watching. Christine arranged to spend the weekend at her married sister's.

When she arrived back Sunday evening she found the girl close to hysterics. She said that on Saturday she had gone to pull the curtains across the French doors at dusk and had found a strangely contorted face, a man's face, pressed against the glass, staring in at her from the garden. She claimed she had fainted and had almost had her baby a month too early right there on the living room carpet. Then she had called the police. He was gone by the time they got there but she had recognized him from the afternoon of the tea; she had informed them he was a friend of Christine's.

They called Monday evening to investigate, two of them. They were very polite, they knew who Christine's father was. Her father greeted them heartily; her mother hovered in the background, fidgeting with her porcelain hands, letting them see how frail and worried she was. She didn't like having them in the living room but they were necessary.

Christine had to admit he'd been following her around. She was relieved he'd been discovered, relieved also that she hadn't been the one to tell, though if he'd been a citizen of the country she would have called the police a long time ago. She insisted he was not dangerous, he had never hurt her.

"That kind don't hurt you," one of the policemen said. "They just kill you. You're lucky you aren't dead."

"Nut cases," the other one said.

Her mother volunteered that the thing about people from another culture was that you could never tell whether they were insane or not because their ways were so different. The policemen agreed with her, deferential but also condescending, as though she was a royal half-wit who had to be humoured.

"You know where he lives?" the first policeman asked.

Christine had long ago torn up the letter with his address on it; she shook her head.

"We'll have to pick him up tomorrow then," he said. "Think you can keep him talking outside your class if he's waiting for you?"

After questioning her they held a murmured conversation with her father in the front hall. The girl, clearing away the coffee cups, said if they didn't lock him up she was leaving, she wasn't going to be scared half out of her skin like that again.

Next day when Christine came out of her Modern History lecture he was there, right on schedule. He seemed puzzled when she did not begin to run. She approached him, her heart thumping with treachery and the prospect of freedom. Her body was back to its usual size; she felt herself a giantess, self-controlled, invulnerable.

"How are you?" she asked, smiling brightly.

He looked at her with distrust.

"How have you been?" she ventured again. His own perennial smile faded; he took a step back from her.

"This the one?" said the policeman, popping out from behind a notice board like a Keystone cop and laying a competent hand on the worn jacket shoulder. The other policeman lounged in the background; force would not be required.

"Don't *do* anything to him," she pleaded as they took him away. They nodded and grinned, respectful, scornful. He seemed to know perfectly well who they were and what they wanted.

The first policeman phoned that evening to make his report. Her father talked with him, jovial and managing. She herself was now out of the picture; she had been protected, her function was over.

"What did they *do* to him?" she asked anxiously as he came back into the living room. She was not sure what went on in police stations.

"They didn't do anything to him," he said, amused by her concern. "They could have booked him for Watching and Besetting, they wanted to know if I'd like to press charges. But it's not worth a court case: he's got a visa that says he's only allowed in the country as long as he studies in Montreal, so I told them to just ship him down there. If he turns up here again they'll deport him. They went around to his rooming house, his rent's two weeks overdue; the landlady said she was on the point of kicking him out. He seems happy enough to be getting his back rent paid and a free train ticket to Montreal." He paused. "They couldn't get anything out of him though."

"*Out* of him?" Christine asked.

"They tried to find out why he was doing it; following you, I mean." Her father's eyes swept her as though it was a riddle to him also. "They said when they asked him about that he just clammed up. Pretended he didn't understand English. He understood well enough, but he wasn't answering."

Christine thought this would be the end, but somehow between his arrest and the departure of the train he managed to elude his escort long enough for one more phone call.

"I see you again," he said. He didn't wait for her to hang up.

Now that he was no longer an embarrassing present reality, he could be talked about, he could become an amusing story. In fact, he was the only amusing story Christine had to tell, and telling it preserved both for herself and for others the aura of her strange allure. Her friends and the men who continued to ask her out speculated about his motives.

One suggested he had wanted to marry her so he could remain in the country; another said that oriental men were fond of well-built women: "It's your Rubens quality."

Christine thought about him a lot. She had not been attracted to him, rather the reverse, but as an idea only he was a romantic figure, the one man who had found her irresistible; though she often wondered, inspecting her unchanged pink face and hefty body in her full-length mirror, just what it was about her that had done it. She avoided whenever it was proposed the theory of his insanity: it was only that there was more than one way of being sane.

But a new acquaintance, hearing the story for the first time, had a different explanation. "So he got you, too," he said, laughing. "That has to be the same guy who was hanging around our day camp a year ago this summer. He followed all the girls like that, a short guy, Japanese or something, glasses, smiling all the time."

"Maybe it was another one," Christine said.

"There couldn't be two of them, everything fits. This was a pretty weird guy."

"What . . . *kind* of girls did he follow?" Christine asked.

"Oh, just anyone who happened to be around. But if they paid any attention to him at first, if they were nice to him or anything, he was unshakeable. He was a bit of a pest, but harmless."

Christine ceased to tell her amusing story. She had been one among many, then. She went back to playing tennis, she had been neglecting her game.

A few months later the policeman who had been in charge of the case telephoned her again.

"Like you to know, miss, that fellow you were having the trouble with was sent back to his own country. Deported."

"What for?" Christine asked. "Did he try to come back here?" Maybe she had been special after all, maybe he had dared everything for her.

"Nothing like it," the policeman said. "He was up to the same tricks in Montreal but he really picked the wrong woman this time—a Mother Superior of a convent. They don't stand for things like that in Quebec—had him out of here before he knew what happened. I guess he'll be better off in his own place."

"How old was she?" Christine asked, after a silence.

"Oh, around sixty, I guess."

"Thank you very much for letting me know," Christine said in her best official manner. "It's such a relief." She wondered if the policeman had called to make fun of her.

She was almost crying when she put down the phone. What *had* he wanted from her then? A Mother Superior. Did she really look sixty, did she look like a mother? What did convents mean? Comfort, charity? Refuge? Was it that something had happened to him, some intolerable strain just from being in this country; her tennis dress and exposed legs too much for him, flesh and money seemingly available everywhere but withheld from him wherever he turned, the nun the symbol of some final distortion, the robe and veil reminiscent to his near-sighted eyes of the women of his homeland, the ones he was able to understand? But he was back in his own country, remote from her as another planet; she would never know.

He hadn't forgotten her though. In the spring she got a postcard with a foreign stamp and the familiar block-letter writing. On the front was a picture of a temple. He was fine, he hoped she was fine also, he was her friend. A month later another print of the picture he had taken in the garden arrived, in a sealed manila envelope otherwise empty.

Christine's aura of mystery soon faded; anyway, she herself no longer believed in it. Life became again what she had always expected. She graduated with mediocre grades and went into the Department of Health and Welfare; she did a good job, and was seldom discriminated against for being a woman because nobody thought of her as one. She could afford a pleasant-sized apartment, though she did not put much energy into decorating it. She played less and less tennis; what had been muscle with a light coating of fat turned gradually into fat with a thin substratum of muscle. She began to get headaches.

As the years were used up and the war began to fill the newspapers and magazines, she realized which Eastern country he had actually been from. She had known the name but it hadn't registered at the time, it was such a minor place; she could never keep them separate in her mind.

But though she tried, she couldn't remember the name of the city, and the postcard was long gone—had he been from the North or the South, was he near the battle zone or safely far from it? Obsessively she bought magazines and pored over the available photographs, dead villagers, soldiers on the march, colour blowups of frightened or angry faces, spies being executed; she studied maps, she watched the late-night newscasts, the distant country and terrain becoming almost more familiar to her than her own. Once or twice she thought she could recognize him but it was no use, they all looked like him.

Finally she had to stop looking at the pictures. It bothered her too much, it was bad for her; she was beginning to have nightmares in which he was coming through the French doors of her mother's house in his shabby jacket, carrying a packsack and a rifle and a huge bouquet of richly coloured flowers. He was smiling in the same way but with blood streaked over his face, partly blotting out the features. She gave her television set away and took to reading nineteenth-century novels instead; Trollope and Galsworthy were her favourites. When, despite herself, she would think about him, she would tell herself that he had been crafty and agile-minded enough to survive, more or less, in her country, so surely he would be able to do it in his own, where he knew the language. She could not see him in the army, on either side; he wasn't the type, and to her knowledge he had not believed in any particular ideology. He would be something nondescript, something in the background, like herself; perhaps he had become an interpreter.

---

1. How does Christine's understanding of "culture" influence her perceptions?
2. Why does Christine begin to look forward to "the daily chase," even though she has images of the man attacking her?
3. What does it mean that Christine "had been protected, her function was over"?
4. Why does Christine think the man might have become an interpreter?

THOM JONES (1945–) was born in Aurora, Illinois, the son of a professional heavyweight boxer. He joined the Marines, and in 1963, shortly before deployment to Vietnam, he received a medical discharge due to epileptic fits that began after a boxing match. He earned a BA from the University of Washington in 1970 and an MFA from the Iowa Writers' Workshop in 1973. He struggled with alcoholism and worked for a time as a janitor at the school where his wife was the librarian, but then decided to dedicate himself to writing. His short story "The Pugilist at Rest" won the O. Henry Award in 1993; his story collection by that title was nominated for the National Book Award. He has written two other collections of short stories: *Cold Snap: Stories* (1995) and *Sonny Liston Was a Friend of Mine* (1999).

The Pugilist at Rest

Hey Baby got caught writing a letter to his girl when he was supposed to be taking notes on the specs of the M-14 rifle. We were sitting in a stifling hot Quonset hut during the first weeks of boot camp, August 1966, at the Marine Corps Recruit Depot in San Diego. Sergeant Wright snatched the letter out of Hey Baby's hand, and later that night in the squad bay he read the letter to the Marine recruits of Platoon 263, his voice laden with sarcasm. "*Hey, Baby*!" he began, and then as he went into the body of the letter he worked himself into a state of outrage and disgust. It was a letter to *Rosie Rottencrotch*, he said at the end, and what really mattered, what was really at issue and what was of utter importance was not *Rosie Rottencrotch* and her steaming-hot panties but rather the muzzle velocity of the M-14 rifle.

Hey Baby paid for the letter by doing a hundred squat thrusts on the concrete floor of the squad bay, but the main prize he won that night was that he became forever known as Hey Baby to the recruits of Platoon 263—in addition to being a shitbird, a faggot, a turd, a maggot, and other such standard appellations. To top it all off, shortly after the incident, Hey Baby got a Dear John from his girl back in Chicago, of whom Sergeant Wright, myself, and seventy-eight other Marine recruits had come to know just a little.

Hey Baby was not in the Marine Corps for very long. The reason for this was that he started in on my buddy, Jorgeson. Jorgeson was my main man, and Hey Baby started calling him Jorgepussy and began harassing him and pushing him around. He was down on Jorgeson because whenever we were taught some sort of combat maneuver or tactic, Jorgeson would say, under his breath, "You could get *killed* if you try that." Or, "Your ass is *had*, if you do that." You got the feeling that Jorgeson didn't think loving the American flag and defending democratic ideals in Southeast Asia were all that important. He told me that what he really wanted to do was have an artist's loft in the SoHo district of New York City, wear a beret, eat liver-sausage sandwiches made with stale baguettes, drink Tokay wine, smoke dope, paint pictures, and listen to the wailing, sorrowful songs of that French singer Edith Piaf, otherwise known as "The Little Sparrow."

After the first half hour of boot camp most of the other recruits wanted to get out, too, but they nourished dreams of surfboards, Corvettes, and blond babes. Jorgeson wanted to be a beatnik and hang out with Jack Kerouac and Neal Cassady, slam down burning shots of amber whiskey, and hear Charles Mingus play real cool jazz on the bass fiddle. He wanted to practice Zen Buddhism, throw the I Ching, eat couscous, and study astrology charts. All of this was foreign territory to me. I had grown up in Aurora, Illinois, and had never heard of such things. Jorgeson had a sharp tongue and was so supercilious in his remarks that I didn't know quite how seriously I should take this talk, but I enjoyed his humor and I did believe he had the sensibilities of an artist. It was not some vague yearning. I believed very much that he could become a painter of pictures. At that point he wasn't putting his heart and soul into becoming a Marine. He wasn't a true believer like me.

Some weeks after Hey Baby began hassling Jorgeson, Sergeant Wright gave us his best speech: "You men are going off to war, and it's not a pretty thing," etc. & etc., "and if Luke the Gook knocks down one of your buddies, a fellow Marine, you are going to risk your life and go in and get that Marine and you are going to bring him out. Not because I said so. No! You are going after that Marine because *you* are a Marine, a member of the most elite fighting force in the world, and that man out there who's gone down is a Marine, and he's your *buddy*. He is your brother! Once you are a Marine, you are *always* a Marine and you will never let another Marine down." Etc. & etc. "You can take a Marine out of the Corps but you can't take the Corps out of a Marine." Etc. & etc. At the time it seemed to me a very good speech, and it stirred me deeply. Sergeant Wright was no candy ass. He was one squared-away dude, and he could call cadence. Man, it puts a lump in my throat when I remember how that man could sing cadence. Apart from Jorgeson, I think all of the recruits in Platoon 263 were proud of Sergeant Wright. He was the real thing, the genuine article. He was a crackerjack Marine.

In the course of training, lots of the recruits dropped out of the original platoon. Some couldn't pass the physical-fitness tests and had to go to a special camp for pussies. This was a particularly shameful shortcoming, the most humiliating apart from bed-wetting. Other recruits would get pneumonia, strep throat, infected foot blisters, or whatever, and lose time that way. Some didn't qualify at the rifle range. One would break a leg. Another would have a nervous breakdown (and this was also deplorable). People dropped out right and left. When the recruit corrected whatever deficiency he had, or when he got better, he would be picked up by another platoon that was in the stage of basic training that he had been in when his training was interrupted. Platoon 263 picked up dozens of recruits in this fashion. If everything went well, however, you got through with the whole business in twelve weeks. That's not a long time, but it seemed like a long time. You did not see a female in all that time. You did not see a newspaper or a television set. You did not eat a candy bar. Another thing was the fact that you had someone on top of you, watching every move you made. When it was time to "shit, shower, and shave," you were given just ten minutes, and had to confront lines and so on to complete the entire affair. Head calls were so infrequent that I spent a lot of time that might otherwise have been neutral or painless in the eye-watering anxiety that I was going to piss my pants. We *ran* to chow, where we were faced with enormous steam vents that spewed out a sickening smell of rancid, super-heated grease. Still, we entered the mess hall with ravenous appetites, ate a huge tray of food in just a few minutes, and then *ran* back to our company area in formation, choking back the burning bile of a meal too big to be eaten so fast. God forbid that you would lose control and vomit.

If all had gone well in the preceding hours, Sergeant Wright would permit us to smoke one cigarette after each meal. Jorgeson had shown me the wisdom of switching from Camels to Pall Malls—they were much longer, packed a pretty good jolt, and when we snapped open our brushed chrome Zippos, torched up, and inhaled the first few drags, we shared the overmastering pleasure that tobacco can bring if you use it seldom and judiciously. These were always the best moments of the day—brief respites from the tyrannical repression of recruit training. As we got close to the end of it all Jorgeson liked to play a little game. He used to say to me (with fragrant blue smoke curling out of his nostrils), "If someone said, 'I'll give you ten thousand dollars to do all of this again,' what would you say?" "No way, Jack!" He would keep on upping it until he had John Beresford Tipton, the guy from *The Millionaire*, offering me a check for a million bucks. "Not for any money," I'd say.

While they were all smoldering under various pressures, the recruits were also getting pretty "salty"—they were beginning to believe. They were beginning to think of themselves as Marines. If you could make it through this, the reasoning went, you wouldn't crack in combat. So I remember that I had tears in my eyes when Sergeant Wright gave us the spiel about how a Marine would charge a machine-gun nest to save his buddies, dive on a hand grenade, do whatever it takes—and yet I was ashamed when Jorgeson caught me wiping them away. All of the recruits were teary except Jorgeson. He had these very clear cobalt-blue eyes. They were so remarkable that they caused you to notice Jorgeson in a crowd. There was unusual beauty in these eyes, and there was an extraordinary power in them. Apart from having a pleasant enough face, Jorgeson was small and unassuming except for these eyes. Anyhow, when he caught me getting sentimental he gave me this look that penetrated to the core of my being. It was the icy look of absolute contempt, and it caused me to doubt myself. I said, "Man! Can't you get into it? For Christ's sake!"

"I'm not like you," he said. "But I am into it, more than you could ever know. I never told you this before, but I am Kal-El, born on the planet Krypton and rocketed to Earth as an infant, moments before my world exploded. Disguised as a mild-mannered Marine, I have resolved to use my powers for the good of mankind. Whenever danger appears on the scene, truth and justice will be served as I slip into the green U.S.M.C. utility uniform and become Earth's greatest hero."

I got highly pissed and didn't talk to him for a couple of days after this. Then, about two weeks before boot camp was over, when we were running out to the parade field for drill with our rifles at port arms, all assholes and elbows, I saw Hey Baby give Jorgeson a nasty shove with his M-14. Hey Baby was a large and fairly tough young man who liked to displace his aggressive impulses on Jorgeson, but he wasn't as big or as tough as I.

Jorgeson nearly fell down as the other recruits scrambled out to the parade field, and Hey Baby gave a short, malicious laugh. I ran past Jorgeson and caught up to Hey Baby; he picked me up in his peripheral vision, but by then it was too late. I set my body so that I could put everything into it, and with one deft stroke I hammered him in the temple with the sharp edge of the steel butt plate of my M-14. It was not exactly a premeditated crime, although I had been laying to get him. My idea before this had simply been to lay my hands on him, but now I had blood in my eye. I was a skilled boxer, and I knew the temple was a vulnerable spot; the human skull is otherwise hard and durable, except at its base. There was a sickening crunch, and Hey Baby dropped into the ice plants along the side of the company street.

The entire platoon was out on the parade field when the house mouse screamed at the assistant D.I., who rushed back to the scene of the crime to find Hey Baby crumpled in a fetal position in the ice plants with blood all over the place. There was blood from the scalp wound as well as a froth of blood emitting from his nostrils and his mouth. Blood was leaking from his right ear. Did I see skull fragments and brain tissue? It seemed that I did. To tell you the truth, I wouldn't have cared in the least if I had killed him, but like most criminals I was very much afraid of getting caught. It suddenly occurred to me that I could be headed for the brig for a long time. My heart was pounding out of my chest. Yet the larger part of me didn't care. Jorgeson was my buddy, and I wasn't going to stand still and let someone fuck him over.

The platoon waited at parade rest while Sergeant Wright came out of the duty hut and took command of the situation. An ambulance was called, and it came almost immediately. A number of corpsmen squatted down alongside the fallen man for what seemed an eternity. Eventually they took Hey Baby off with a fractured skull. It would be the last we ever saw of him. Three evenings later, in the squad bay, the assistant D.I. told us rather ominously that Hey Baby had recovered consciousness. That's all he said. What did *that* mean? I was worried, because Hey Baby had seen me make my move, but, as it turned out, when he came to he had forgotten the incident and all events of the preceding two weeks. Retrograde amnesia. Lucky for me. I also knew that at least three other recruits had seen what I did, but none of them reported me. Every member of the platoon was called in and grilled by a team of hard-ass captains and a light colonel from the Criminal Investigation Detachment. It took a certain amount of balls to lie to them, yet none of my fellow jarheads reported me. I was well liked and Hey Baby was not. Indeed, many felt that he got exactly what was coming to him.

The other day—Memorial Day, as it happened—I was cleaning some stuff out of the attic when I came upon my old dress-blue uniform. It's a beautiful uniform, easily the most handsome worn by any of the U.S. armed forces. The rich color recalled Jorgeson's eyes for me—not that the color matched, but in the sense that the color of each was so startling. The tunic does not have lapels, of course, but a high collar with red piping and the traditional golden eagle, globe, and anchor insignia on either side of the neck clasp. The tunic buttons are not brassy—although they are in fact made of brass—but are a delicate gold in color, like Florentine gold. On the sleeves of the tunic my staff sergeant's chevrons are gold on red. High on the left breast is a rainbow display of fruit salad representing my various combat citations. Just below these are my marksmanship badges; I shot Expert in rifle as well as pistol.

I opened a sandalwood box and took my various medals out of the large plastic bag I had packed them in to prevent them from tarnishing.

The Navy Cross and the two Silver Stars are the best; they are such pretty things they dazzle you. I found a couple of Thai sticks in the sandalwood box as well. I took a whiff of the box and smelled the smells of Saigon—the whores, the dope, the saffron, cloves, jasmine, and patchouli oil. I put the Thai sticks back, recalling the three-day hangover that particular batch of dope had given me more than twenty-three years before. Again I looked at my dress-blue tunic. My most distinctive badge, the crowning glory, and the one of which I am most proud, is the set of Airborne wings. I remember how it was, walking around Oceanside, California—the Airborne wings and the high-and-tight haircut were recognized by all the Marines; they meant you were the crème de la crème, you were a recon Marine.

Recon was all Jorgeson's idea. We had lost touch with each other after boot camp. I was sent to com school in San Diego, where I had to sit in a hot Class A wool uniform all day and learn the Morse code. I deliberately flunked out, and when I was given the perfunctory option for a second shot, I told the colonel, "Hell no, sir. I want to go 003—infantry. I want to be a ground pounder. I didn't join the service to sit at a desk all day."

I was on a bus to Camp Pendleton three days later, and when I got there I ran into Jorgeson. I had been thinking of him a lot. He was a clerk in headquarters company. Much to my astonishment, he was fifteen pounds heavier, and had grown two inches, and he told me he was hitting the weight pile every night after running seven miles up and down the foothills of Pendleton in combat boots, carrying a rifle and a full field pack. After the usual what's-been-happening? b.s., he got down to business and said, "They need people in Force Recon, what do you think? Headquarters is one boring motherfucker."

I said, "Recon? Paratrooper? You got to be shittin' me! When did you get so gung-ho, man?"

He said, "Hey, you were the one who *bought* the program. Don't fade on me now, goddamm it! Look, we pass the physical fitness test and then they send us to jump school at Benning. If we pass that, we're in. And we'll pass. Those doggies ain't got jack. Semper fi, motherfucker! Let's do it."

There was no more talk of Neal Cassady, Edith Piaf, or the artist's loft in SoHo. I said, "If Sergeant Wright could only see you now!"

. . .

We were just three days in country when we got dropped in somewhere up north near the DMZ. It was a routine reconnaissance patrol. It was not supposed to be any kind of big deal at all—just acclimation. The morning after our drop we approached a clear field. I recall that it gave me a funny feeling, but I was too new to fully trust my instincts. *Everything* was spooky; I was fresh meat, F.N.G.—a Fucking New Guy.

Before moving into the field, our team leader sent Hanes—a lance corporal, a short-timer, with only twelve days left before his rotation was over—across the field as a point man. This was a bad omen and everyone knew it. Hanes had two Purple Hearts. He followed the order with no hesitation and crossed the field without drawing fire. The team leader signaled for us to fan out and told me to circumvent the field and hump through the jungle to investigate a small mound of loose red dirt that I had missed completely but that he had picked up with his trained eye. I remember I kept saying, "Where?" He pointed to a heap of earth about thirty yards along the tree line and about ten feet back in the bushes. Most likely it was an anthill, but you never knew—it could have been an NVA tunnel. "Over there," he hissed. "Goddamn it, do I have to draw pictures for you?"

I moved smartly in the direction of the mound while the rest of the team reconverged to discuss something. As I approached the mound I saw that it was in fact an anthill, and I looked back at the team and saw they were already halfway across the field, moving very fast.

Suddenly there were several loud hollow pops and the cry "Incoming!" Seconds later the first of a half-dozen mortar rounds landed in the loose earth surrounding the anthill. For a millisecond, everything went black. I was blown back and lifted up on a cushion of warm air. At first it was like the thrill of a carnival ride, but it was quickly followed by that stunned, jangly, electric feeling you get when you hit your crazy bone. Like that, but not confined to a small area like the elbow. I felt it shoot through my spine and into all four limbs. A thick plaster of sand and red clay plugged up my nostrils and ears. Grit was blown in between my teeth. If I hadn't been wearing a pair of Ray-Ban aviator shades, I would certainly have been blinded permanently—as it was, my eyes were loaded with grit. (I later discovered that fine red earth was somehow blown in behind the crystal of my pressure-tested Rolex Submariner, underneath my fingernails and toenails, and deep into the pores of my skin.) When I was able to, I pulled out a canteen filled with lemon-lime Kool-Aid and tried to flood my eyes clean. This helped a little, but my eyes still felt like they were on fire. I rinsed them again and blinked furiously.

I rolled over on my stomach in the prone position and leveled my field-issue M-16. A company of screaming NVA soldiers ran into the field, firing as they came—I saw their green tracer rounds blanket the position where the team had quickly congregated to lay out a perimeter, but none of our own red tracers were going out. Several of the Marines had been killed outright by the mortar rounds. Jorgeson was all right, and I saw him cast a nervous glance in my direction. Then he turned to the enemy and began to fire his M-16. I clicked my rifle on to automatic and pulled the trigger, but the gun was loaded with dirt and it wouldn't fire.

Apart from Jorgeson, the only other American putting out any fire was Second Lieutenant Milton, also a fairly new guy, a "cherry," who was down on one knee firing his .45, an exercise in almost complete futility. I assumed that Milton's 16 had jammed, like mine, and watched as AK-47 rounds, having penetrated his flak jacket and then his chest, ripped through the back of his field pack and buzzed into the jungle beyond like a deadly swarm of bees. A few seconds later, I heard the swoosh of an RPG rocket, a dud round that dinged the lieutenant's left shoulder before it flew off in the bush behind him. It took off his whole arm, and for an instant I could see the white bone and ligaments of his shoulder, and then red flesh of muscle tissue, looking very much like fresh prime beef, well marbled and encased in a thin layer of yellowish white adipose tissue that quickly became saturated with dark-red blood. What a lot of blood there was. Still, Milton continued to fire his .45. When he emptied his clip, I watched him remove a fresh one from his web gear and attempt to load the pistol with one hand. He seemed to fumble with the fresh clip for a long time, until at last he dropped it, along with his .45. The lieutenant's head slowly sagged forward, but he stayed up on one knee with his remaining arm extended out to the enemy, palm upward in the soulful, heart-rending gesture of Al Jolson doing a rendition of "Mammy."

A hail of green tracer rounds buzzed past Jorgeson, but he coolly returned fire in short, controlled bursts. The light, tinny pops from his M-16 did not sound very reassuring, but I saw several NVA go down. AK-47 fire kicked up red dust all around Jorgeson's feet. He was basically out in the open, and if ever a man was totally alone it was Jorgeson. He was dead meat and he had to know it. It was very strange that he wasn't hit immediately.

Jorgeson zigged his way over to the body of a large black Marine who carried an M-60 machine gun. Most of the recon Marines carried grease guns or Swedish Ks; an M-60 was too heavy for traveling light and fast, but this Marine had been big and he had been paranoid. I had known him least of anyone in the squad. In three days he had said nothing to me, I suppose because I was F.N.G., and had spooked him. Indeed, now he was dead. That august seeker of truth, Schopenhauer, was correct: *We are like lambs in a field, disporting themselves under the eye of the butcher, who chooses out first one and then another for his prey. So it is that in our good days we are all unconscious of the evil Fate may have presently in store for us—sickness, poverty, mutilation, loss of sight or reason.*

It was difficult to judge how quickly time was moving. Although my senses had been stunned by the concussion of the mortar rounds, they were, however paradoxical this may seem, more acute than ever before. I watched Jorgeson pick up the machine gun and begin to spread an impressive field of fire back at the enemy. *Thuk thuk thuk, thuk thuk thuk, thuk thuk thuk!* I saw several more bodies fall, and began to think that things might turn out all right after all. The NVA dropped for cover, and many of them turned back and headed for the tree line. Jorgeson fired off a couple of bandoliers, and after he stopped to load another, he turned back and looked at me with those blue eyes and a smile like "How am I doing?" Then I heard the steel-cork pop of an M-79 launcher and saw a rocket grenade explode through Jorgeson's upper abdomen, causing him to do something like a back flip. His M-60 machine gun flew straight up into the air. The barrel was glowing red like a hot poker, and continued to fire in a "cook off" until the entire bandolier had run through.

In the meantime I had pulled a cleaning rod out of my pack and worked it through the barrel of my M-16. When I next tried to shoot, the Tonka-toy son of a bitch remained jammed, and at last I frantically broke it down to find the source of the problem. I had a dirty bolt. Fucking dirt everywhere. With numbed fingers I removed the firing pin and worked it over with a toothbrush, dropping it in the red dirt, picking it up, cleaning it, and dropping it again. My fingers felt like Novocain, and while I could see far away, I was unable to see up close. I poured some more Kool-Aid over my eyes. It was impossible for me to get my weapon clean. Lucky for me, ultimately.

Suddenly NVA soldiers were running through the field shoving bayonets into the bodies of the downed Marines. It was not until an NVA trooper kicked Lieutenant Milton out of his tripod position that he finally fell to the ground. Then the soldiers started going through the dead Marines' gear. I was still frantically struggling with my weapon when it began to dawn on me that the enemy had forgotten me in the excitement of the firefight. I wondered what had happened to Hanes and if he had gotten clear. I doubted it, and hopped on my survival radio to call in an air strike when finally a canny NVA trooper did remember me and headed in my direction most ricky tick.

With a tight grip on the spoon, I pulled the pin on a fragmentation grenade and then unsheathed my K-bar. About this time Jorgeson let off a horrendous shriek—a gut shot is worse than anything. Or did Jorgeson scream to save my life? The NVA moving in my direction turned back to him, studied him for a moment, and then thrust a bayonet into his heart. As badly as my own eyes hurt, I was able to see Jorgeson's eyes—a final flash of glorious azure before they faded into the unfocused and glazed gray of death. I repinned the grenade, got up on my knees, and scrambled away until finally I was on my feet with a useless and incomplete handful of M-16 parts, and I was running as fast and as hard as I have ever run in my life. A pair of Phantom F-4s came in very low with delayed-action high-explosive rounds and napalm. I could feel the almost unbearable heat waves of the latter, volley after volley. I can still feel it and smell it to this day.

Concerning Lance Corporal Hanes: they found him later, fried to a crisp by the napalm, but it was nonetheless ascertained that he had been mutilated while alive. He was like the rest of us—eighteen, nineteen, twenty years old. What did we know of life? Before Vietnam, Hanes didn't think he would ever die. I mean, yes, he knew that in theory he would die, but he *felt* like he was going to live forever. I know that I felt that way. Hanes was down to twelve days and a wake-up. When other Marines saw a short-timer get greased, it devastated their morale. However, when I saw them zip up the body bag on Hanes I became incensed. Why hadn't Milton sent him back to the rear to burn shit or something when he got so short? Twelve days to go and then mutilated. Fucking Milton! Fucking second lieutenant!

Theogenes was the greatest of gladiators. He was a boxer who served under the patronage of a cruel nobleman, a prince who took great delight in bloody spectacles. Although this was several hundred years before the times of those most enlightened of men Socrates, Plato, and Aristotle, and well after the Minoans of Crete, it still remains a high point in the history of Western civilization and culture. It was the approximate time of Homer, the greatest poet who ever lived. Then, as now, violence, suffering, and the cheapness of life were the rule.

The sort of boxing Theogenes practiced was not like modern-day boxing with those kindergarten Queensberry rules. The two contestants were not permitted the freedom of a ring. Instead, they were strapped to flat stones, facing each other nose to nose. When the signal was given, they would begin hammering each other with fists encased in heavy leather thongs. It was a fight to the death. Fourteen hundred and twenty-five times Theogenes was strapped to the stone and fourteen hundred and twenty-five times he emerged a victor.

Perhaps it is Theogenes who is depicted in the famous Roman statue (based on the earlier Greek original) of *The Pugilist at Rest*. I keep a grainy black-and-white photograph of it in my room. The statue depicts a muscular athlete approaching his middle age. He has a thick beard and a full head of curly hair. In addition to the telltale broken nose and cauliflower ears of a boxer, the pugilist has the slanted, drooping brows that bespeak torn nerves. Also, the forehead is piled with scar tissue. As may be expected, the pugilist has the musculature of a fighter. His neck and trapezius muscles are well developed. His shoulders are enormous; his chest is thick and flat, without the bulging pectorals of the bodybuilder. His back, oblique, and abdominal muscles are highly pronounced, and he has that greatest asset of the modern boxer—sturdy legs. The arms are large, particularly the forearms, which are reinforced with the leather wrappings of the cestus. It is the body of a small heavyweight—lithe rather than bulky, but by no means lacking in power: a Jack Johnson or a Dempsey, say. If you see the authentic statue at the Terme Museum, in Rome, you will see that the seated boxer is really not much more than a light-heavyweight. People were small in those days. The important thing was that he was perfectly proportioned.

The pugilist is sitting on a rock with his forearms balanced on his thighs. That he is seated and not pacing implies that he has been through all this many times before. It appears that he is conserving his strength. His head is turned as if he were looking over his shoulder—as if someone had just whispered something to him. It is in this that the "art" of the sculpture is conveyed to the viewer. Could it be that someone has just summoned him to the arena? There is a slight look of befuddlement on his face, but there is no trace of fear. There is an air about him that suggests that he is eager to proceed and does not wish to cause anyone any trouble or to create a delay, even though his life will soon be on the line. Besides the deformities on his noble face, there is also the suggestion of weariness and philosophical resignation. *All the world's a stage, and all the men and women merely players.* Exactly! He knew this more than two thousand years before Shakespeare penned the line. How did he come to be at this place in space and time? Would he rather be safely removed to the countryside—an obscure, stinking peasant shoving a plow behind a mule? Would that be better? Or does he revel in his role? Perhaps he once did, but surely not now. Is this the great Theogenes or merely a journeyman fighter, a former slave or criminal bought by one of the many contractors who for months trained the condemned for their brief moment in the arena? I wonder if Marcus Aurelius loved the *Pugilist* as I do, and came to study it and to meditate before it.

I cut and ran from that field in Southeast Asia. I've read that Davy Crockett, hero of the American frontier, was cowering under a bed when Santa Anna and his soldiers stormed into the Alamo. What is the truth? Jack Dempsey used to get so scared before his fights that he sometimes wet his pants. But look what he did to Willard and to Luis Firpo, the Wild Bull of the Pampas! It was something close to homicide. What is courage? What is cowardice? The magnificent Roberto Duran gave us "*No más*," but who had a greater fighting heart than Duran?

I got over that first scare and saw that I was something quite other than that which I had known myself to be. Hey Baby proved only my warm-up act. There was a reservoir of malice, poison, and vicious sadism in my soul, and it poured forth freely in the jungles and rice paddies of Vietnam. I pulled three tours. I wanted some payback for Jorgeson. I grieved for Lance Corporal Hanes. I grieved for myself and what I had lost. I committed unspeakable crimes and got medals for it.

It was only fair that I got a head injury myself. I never got a scratch in Vietnam, but I got tagged in a boxing smoker at Pendleton. Fought a bad-ass light heavyweight from artillery. Nobody would fight this guy. He could box. He had all the moves. But mainly he was a puncher—it was said that he could punch with either hand. It was said that his hand speed was superb. I had finished off at least a half rack of Hamm's before I went in with him and started getting hit with head shots I didn't even see coming. They were right. His hand speed *was* superb.

I was twenty-seven years old, smoked two packs a day, was a borderline alcoholic. I shouldn't have fought him—I knew that—but he had been making noise. A very long time before, I had been the middleweight champion of the First Marine Division. I had been a so-called war hero. I had been a recon Marine. But now I was a garrison Marine and in no kind of shape.

He put me down almost immediately, and when I got up I was terribly afraid. I was tight and I could not breathe. It felt like he was hitting me in the face with a ball-peen hammer. It felt like he was busting light bulbs in my face. Rather than one opponent, I saw three. I was convinced his gloves were loaded, and a wave of self-pity ran through me.

I began to move. He made a mistake by expending a lot of energy trying to put me away quickly. I had no intention of going down again, and I knew I wouldn't. My buddies were watching, and I had to give them a good show. While I was afraid, I was also exhilarated; I had not felt this alive since Vietnam. I began to score with my left jab, and because of this I was able to withstand his bull charges and divert them. I thought he would throw his bolt, but in the beginning he was tireless. I must have hit him with four hundred left jabs. It got so that I could score at will, with either hand, but he would counter, trap me on the ropes, and pound. He was the better puncher and was truly hurting me, but I was scoring, and as the fight went on the momentum shifted and I took over. I staggered him again and again. The Marines at ringside were screaming for me to put him away, but however much I tried, I could not. Although I could barely stand by the end, I was sorry that the fight was over. Who had won? The referee raised my arm in victory, but I think it was pretty much a draw. Judging a prizefight is a very subjective thing.

About an hour after the bout, when the adrenaline had subsided, I realized I had a terrible headache. It kept getting worse, and I rushed out of the NCO Club, where I had gone with my buddies to get loaded.

I stumbled outside, struggling to breathe, and I headed away from the company area toward Sheepshit Hill, one of the many low brown foothills in the vicinity. Like a dog who wants to die alone, so it was with me. Everything got swirly, and I dropped in the bushes.

I was unconscious for nearly an hour, and for the next two weeks I walked around like I was drunk, with double vision. I had constant headaches and seemed to have grown old overnight. My health was gone.

I became a very timid individual. I became introspective. I wondered what had made me act the way I had acted. Why had I killed my fellow men in war, without any feeling, remorse, or regret? And when the war was over, why did I continue to drink and swagger around and get into fistfights? Why did I like to dish out pain, and why did I take positive delight in the suffering of others? Was I insane? Was it too much testosterone? Women don't do things like that. The rapacious will to power lost its hold on me. Suddenly I began to feel sympathetic to the cares and sufferings of all living creatures. You lose your health and you start thinking this way.

Has man become any better since the times of Theogenes? The world is replete with badness. I'm not talking about that old routine where you drag out the Spanish Inquisition, the Holocaust, Joseph Stalin, the Khmer Rouge, etc. It happens in our own backyard. Twentieth-century America is one of the most materially prosperous nations in history. But take a walk through an American prison, a nursing home, the slums where the homeless live in cardboard boxes, a cancer ward. Go to a Vietnam vets' meeting, or an A.A. meeting, or an Overeaters Anonymous meeting. *How hollow and unreal a thing is life, how deceitful are its pleasures, what horrible aspects it possesses.* Is the world not rather like a hell, as Schopenhauer, that clearheaded seer—who has helped me transform my suffering into an object of understanding—was so quick to point out? They called him a pessimist and dismissed him with a word, but it is peace and self-renewal that I have found in his pages.

About a year after my fight with the guy from artillery I started having seizures. I suffered from a form of left-temporal-lobe seizure which is sometimes called Dostoyevsky's epilepsy. It's so rare as to be almost unknown. Freud, himself a neurologist, speculated that Dostoyevsky was a hysterical epileptic, and that his fits were unrelated to brain damage—psychogenic in origin. Dostoyevsky did not have his first attack until the age of twenty-five, when he was imprisoned in Siberia and received fifty lashes after complaining about the food. Freud figured that after Dostoyevsky's mock execution, the four years' imprisonment in Siberia, the tormented childhood, the murder of his tyrannical father, etc. & etc.—he had all the earmarks of hysteria, of grave psychological trauma. And Dostoyevsky had displayed the trademark features of the psychomotor epileptic long before his first attack. These days physicians insist there is no such thing as the "epileptic personality." I think they say this because they do not want to add to the burden of the epileptic's suffering with an extra stigma. Privately they do believe in these traits. Dostoyevsky was nervous and depressed, a tormented hypochondriac, a compulsive writer obsessed with religious and philosophic themes. He was hyperloquacious, raving, etc. & etc. His gambling addiction is well known. By most accounts he was a sick soul.

The peculiar and most distinctive thing about his epilepsy was that in the split second before his fit—in the aura, which is in fact officially a part of the attack—Dostoyevsky experienced a sense of felicity, of ecstatic well-being unlike anything an ordinary mortal could hope to imagine. It was the experience of satori. Not the nickel-and-dime satori of Abraham Maslow, but the Supreme. He said that he wouldn't trade ten years of life for this feeling, and I, who have had it, too, would have to agree. I can't explain it, I don't understand it—it becomes slippery and elusive when it gets any distance on you—but I have felt this down to the core of my being. Yes, God exists! But then it slides away and I lose it. I become a doubter. Even Dostoyevsky, the fervent Christian, makes an almost airtight case against the possibility of the existence of God in the Grand Inquisitor digression in *The Brothers Karamazov*. It is probably the greatest passage in all of world literature, and it tilts you to the court of the atheist. This is what happens when you approach Him with the intellect.

It is thought that St. Paul had a temporal-lobe fit on the road to Damascus. Paul warns us in First Corinthians that God will confound the intellectuals. It is known that Muhammad composed the Koran after attacks of epilepsy. Black Elk experienced fits before his grand "buffalo" vision. Joan of Arc is thought to have been a left-temporal-lobe epileptic. Each of these in a terrible flash of brain lightning was able to pierce the murky veil of illusion which is spread over all things. Just so did the scales fall from my eyes. It is called the "sacred disease."

But what a price. I rarely leave the house anymore. To avoid falling injuries, I always wear my old boxer's headgear, and I always carry my mouthpiece. Rather more often than the aura where "every common bush is afire with God," I have the typical epileptic aura, which is that of terror and impending doom. If I can keep my head and think of it, and if there is time, I slip the mouthpiece in and thus avoid biting my tongue. I bit it in half once, and when they sewed it back together it swelled enormously, like a huge red and black sausage. I was unable to close my mouth for more than two weeks.

The fits are coming more and more. I'm loaded on Depakene, phenobarbital, Tegretol, Dilantin—the whole shitload. A nurse from the V.A. bought a pair of Staffordshire terriers for me and trained them to watch me as I sleep, in case I have a fit and smother face-down in my bedding. What delightful companions these dogs are! One of them, Gloria, is especially intrepid and clever. Inevitably, when I come to I find that the dogs have dragged me into the kitchen, away from blankets and pillows, rugs, and objects that might suffocate me; and that they have turned me on my back. There's Gloria, barking in my face. Isn't this incredible?

My sister brought a neurosurgeon over to my place around Christmas—not some V.A. butcher but a guy from the university hospital. He was a slick dude in a nine-hundred-dollar suit. He came down on me hard, like a used-car salesman. He wants to cauterize a small spot in a nerve bundle in my brain. "It's not a lobotomy, it's a *cingulotomy*," he said.

Reckless, desperate, last-ditch psychosurgery is still pretty much unthinkable in the conservative medical establishment. That's why he made a personal visit to my place. A house call. Drumming up some action to make himself a name. "See that bottle of Thorazine?" he said. "You can throw that poison away," he said. "All that amitriptyline. That's garbage, you can toss that, too." He said, "Tell me something. How can you take all of that shit and still walk?" He said, "You take enough drugs to drop an elephant."

He wants to cut me. He said that the feelings of guilt and worthlessness, and the heaviness of a heart blackened by sin, will go away. "It is *not* a lobotomy," he said.

I don't like the guy. I don't trust him. I'm not convinced, but I can't go on like this. If I am not having a panic attack I am engulfed in tedious, unrelenting depression. I am overcome with a deadening sense of languor; I can't *do* anything. I wanted to give my buddies a good show! What a goddamn fool. I am a goddamn fool!

It has taken me six months to put my thoughts in order, but I wanted to do it in case I am a vegetable after the operation. I know that my buddy Jorgeson was a real American hero. I wish that he had lived to be something else, if not a painter of pictures then even some kind of fuckup with a factory job and four divorces, bankruptcy petitions, in and out of jail. I wish he had been that. I wish he had been *anything* rather than a real American hero. So, then, if I am to feel somewhat *indifferent* to life after the operation, all the better. If not, not.

If I had a more conventional sense of morality I would shitcan those dress blues, and I'd send that Navy Cross to Jorgeson's brother. Jorgeson was the one who won it, who pulled the John Wayne number up there near Khe Sanh and saved my life, although I lied and took the credit for all of those dead NVA. He had created a stunning body count—nothing like Theogenes, but Jorgeson only had something like twelve minutes total in the theater of war.

The high command almost awarded me the Medal of Honor, but of course there were no witnesses to what I claimed I had done, and I had saved no one's life. When I think back on it, my tale probably did not sound as credible as I thought it had at the time. I was only nineteen years old and not all that practiced a liar. I figure if they *had* given me the Medal of Honor, I would have stood in the ring up at Camp Las Pulgas in Pendleton and let that light-heavyweight from artillery fucking kill me.

Now I'm thinking I might call Hey Baby and ask how he's doing. No shit, a couple of neuropsychs—we probably have a lot in common. I could apologize to him. But I learned from my fits that you don't have to do that. Good and evil are only illusions. Still, I cannot help but wonder sometimes if my vision of the Supreme Reality was any more real than the demons visited upon schizophrenics and madmen. Has it all been just a stupid neurochemical event? Is there no God at all? The human heart rebels against this.

If they fuck up the operation, I hope I get to keep my dogs somehow—maybe stay at my sister's place. If they send me to the nuthouse I lose the dogs for sure.

---

1. Why does the narrator love the statue *The Pugilist at Rest*?
2. Are the narrator's vicious sadism, his loss of the will to power, his failing belief in God, and his depression all due to neurochemical events?

3. Why, between their two stretches together in the Marines, does the narrator think about Jorgeson "a lot"?

4. Why does the narrator find "peace and renewal" in such statements as Schopenhauer's "How hollow and unreal a thing is life, how deceitful are its pleasures, what horrible aspects it possesses"?

T. CORAGHESSAN BOYLE (1948–) was born in Peekskill, New York. He studied music at the State University of New York at Potsdam but discovered his interest in writing short stories and plays after enrolling in a creative writing course. He earned an MFA at the Iowa Writers' Workshop in 1974. His first collection of stories, *The Descent of Man* (1979) and first novel, *Water Music* (1981), announced the arrival of a gifted comic writer, and in the years since, he has averaged a new book every year and a half. Verbally inventive in the manner of James Joyce and Thomas Pynchon, Boyle has taken on as subject matter everything from the foibles of the counterculture to the sex research of Alfred Kinsey. He has been teaching English at the University of Southern California in Los Angeles for more than thirty years.

Greasy Lake

It's about a mile down on the dark side of Route 88.
—Bruce Springsteen

There was a time when courtesy and winning ways went out of style, when it was good to be bad, when you cultivated decadence like a taste. We were all dangerous characters then. We wore torn-up leather jackets, slouched around with toothpicks in our mouths, sniffed glue and ether and what somebody claimed was cocaine. When we wheeled our parents' whining station wagons out into the street we left a patch of rubber half a block long. We drank gin and grape juice, Tango, Thunderbird, and Bali Hai. We were nineteen. We were bad. We read André Gide and struck elaborate poses to show that we didn't give a shit about anything. At night, we went up to Greasy Lake.

Through the center of town, up the strip, past the housing developments and shopping malls, street lights giving way to the thin streaming illumination of the headlights, trees crowding the asphalt in a black unbroken wall: that was the way out to Greasy Lake. The Indians had called it Wakan, a reference to the clarity of its waters. Now it was fetid and murky, the mud banks glittering with broken glass and strewn with beer cans and the charred remains of bonfires. There was a single ravaged island a hundred yards from shore, so stripped of vegetation it looked as if the air force had strafed it. We went up to the lake because everyone went there, because we wanted to snuff the rich scent of possibility on the breeze, watch a girl take off her clothes and plunge into the festering murk, drink beer, smoke pot, howl at the stars, savor the incongruous full-throated roar of rock and roll against the primeval susurrus of frogs and crickets. This was nature.

I was there one night, late, in the company of two dangerous characters. Digby wore a gold star in his right ear and allowed his father to pay his tuition at Cornell; Jeff was thinking of quitting school to become a painter/musician/head-shop proprietor. They were both expert in the social graces, quick with a sneer, able to manage a Ford with lousy shocks over a rutted and gutted blacktop road at eighty-five while rolling a joint as compact as a Tootsie Roll Pop stick. They could lounge against a bank of booming speakers and trade "man"s with the best of them or roll out across the dance floor as if their joints worked on bearings. They were slick and quick and they wore their mirror shades at breakfast and dinner, in the shower, in closets and caves. In short, they were bad.

I drove. Digby pounded the dashboard and shouted along with Toots and the Maytals while Jeff hung his head out the window and streaked the side of my mother's Bel Air with vomit. It was early June, the air soft as a hand on your cheek, the third night of summer vacation. The first two nights we'd been out till dawn, looking for something we never found. On this, the third night, we'd cruised the strip sixty-seven times, been in and out of every bar and club we could think of in a twenty-mile radius, stopped twice for bucket chicken and forty-cent hamburgers, debated going to a party at the house of a girl Jeff's sister knew, and chucked two dozen raw eggs at mailboxes and hitchhikers. It was 2:00 a.m.; the bars were closing. There was nothing to do but take a bottle of lemon-flavored gin up to Greasy Lake.

The taillights of a single car winked at us as we swung into the dirt lot with its tufts of weed and washboard corrugations; '57 Chevy, mint, metallic blue. On the far side of the lot, like the exoskeleton of some gaunt chrome insect, a chopper leaned against its kickstand. And that was it for excitement: some junkie half-wit biker and a car freak pumping his girlfriend. Whatever it was we were looking for, we weren't about to find it at Greasy Lake. Not that night.

But then all of a sudden Digby was fighting for the wheel. "Hey, that's Tony Lovett's car! Hey!" he shouted, while I stabbed at the brake pedal and the Bel Air nosed up to the gleaming bumper of the parked Chevy. Digby leaned on the horn, laughing, and instructed me to put my brights on. I flicked on the brights. This was hilarious. A joke. Tony would experience premature withdrawal and expect to be confronted by grim-looking state troopers with flashlights. We hit the horn, strobed the lights, and then jumped out of the car to press our witty faces to Tony's windows; for all we knew we might even catch a glimpse of some little fox's tit, and then we could slap backs with red-faced Tony, roughhouse a little, and go on to new heights of adventure and daring.

The first mistake, the one that opened the whole floodgate, was losing my grip on the keys. In the excitement, leaping from the car with the gin in one hand and a roach clip in the other, I spilled them in the grass—in the dark, rank, mysterious nighttime grass of Greasy Lake. This was a tactical error, as damaging and irreversible in its way as Westmoreland's decision to dig in at Khe Sanh. I felt it like a jab of intuition, and I stopped there by the open door, peering vaguely into the night that puddled up round my feet.

The second mistake—and this was inextricably bound up with the first—was identifying the car as Tony Lovett's. Even before the very bad character in greasy jeans and engineer boots ripped out of the driver's door, I began to realize that this chrome blue was much lighter than the robin's-egg of Tony's car, and that Tony's car didn't have rear-mounted speakers. Judging from their expressions, Digby and Jeff were privately groping toward the same inevitable and unsettling conclusion as I was.

In any case, there was no reasoning with this bad greasy character—clearly he was a man of action. The first lusty Rockette kick of his steel-toed boot caught me under the chin, chipped my favorite tooth, and left me sprawled in the dirt. Like a fool, I'd gone down on one knee to comb the stiff hacked grass for the keys, my mind making connections in the most dragged-out, testudineous way, knowing that things had gone wrong, that I was in a lot of trouble, and that the lost ignition key was my grail and my salvation. The three or four succeeding blows were mainly absorbed by my right buttock and the tough piece of bone at the base of my spine.

Meanwhile, Digby vaulted the kissing bumpers and delivered a savage kung-fu blow to the greasy character's collarbone. Digby had just finished a course in martial arts for phys-ed credit and had spent the better part of the past two nights telling us apocryphal tales of Bruce Lee types and of the raw power invested in lightning blows shot from coiled wrists, ankles, and elbows. The greasy character was unimpressed. He merely backed off a step, his face like a Toltec mask, and laid Digby out with a single whistling roundhouse blow. . . but by now Jeff had got into the act, and I was beginning to extricate myself from the dirt, a tinny compound of shock, rage, and impotence wadded in my throat.

Jeff was on the guy's back, biting at his ear. Digby was on the ground, cursing. I went for the tire iron I kept under the driver's seat. I kept it there because bad characters always keep tire irons under the driver's seat, for just such an occasion as this. Never mind that I hadn't been involved in a fight since sixth grade, when a kid with a sleepy eye and two streams of mucus depending from his nostrils hit me in the knee with a Louisville slugger; never mind that I'd touched the tire iron exactly twice before, to change tires: it was there. And I went for it.

I was terrified. Blood was beating in my ears, my hands were shaking, my heart turning over like a dirt bike in the wrong gear. My antagonist was shirtless, and a single cord of muscle flashed across his chest as he bent forward to peel Jeff from his back like a wet overcoat. "Motherfucker," he spat, over and over, and I was aware in that instant that all four of us—Digby, Jeff, and myself included—were chanting "motherfucker, motherfucker," as if it were a battle cry. (What happened next? the detective asks the murderer from beneath the turned-down brim of his porkpie hat. I don't know, the murderer says, something came over me. Exactly.)

Digby poked the flat of his hand in the bad character's face and I came at him like a kamikaze, mindless, raging, stung with humiliation—the whole thing, from the initial boot in the chin to this murderous primal instant involving no more than sixty hyperventilating, gland-flooding seconds—I came at him and brought the tire iron down across his ear. The effect was instantaneous, astonishing. He was a stunt man and this was Hollywood, he was a big grimacing toothy balloon and I was a man with a straight pin. He collapsed. Wet his pants. Went loose in his boots.

A single second, big as a zeppelin, floated by. We were standing over him in a circle, gritting our teeth, jerking our necks, our limbs and hands and feet twitching with glandular discharges. No one said anything. We just stared down at the guy, the car freak, the lover, the bad greasy character laid low. Digby looked at me; so did Jeff. I was still holding the tire iron, a tuft of hair clinging to the crook like dandelion fluff, like down. Rattled, I dropped it in the dirt, already envisioning the headlines, the pitted faces of the police inquisitors, the gleam of handcuffs, clank of bars, the big black shadows rising from the back of the cell. . . when suddenly a raw torn shriek cut through me like all the juice in all the electric chairs in the country.

It was the fox. She was short, barefoot, dressed in panties and a man's shirt. "Animals!" she screamed, running at us with her fists clenched and wisps of blow-dried hair in her face There was a silver chain round her ankle, and her toenails flashed in the glare of the headlights. I think it was the toenails that did it. Sure, the gin and the cannabis and even the Kentucky Fried may have had a hand in it, but it was the sight of those flaming toes that set us off—the toad emerging from the loaf in *Virgin Spring*, lipstick smeared on a child: she was already tainted. We were on her like Bergman's deranged brothers—see no evil, hear none, speak none—panting, wheezing, tearing at her clothes, grabbing for flesh. We were bad characters, and we were scared and hot and three steps over the line—anything could have happened.

It didn't.

Before we could pin her to the hood of the car, our eyes masked with lust and greed and the purest primal badness, a pair of headlights swung into the lot. There we were, dirty, bloody, guilty, dissociated from humanity and civilization, the first of the Ur-crimes behind us, the second in progress, shreds of nylon panty and spandex brassiere dangling from our fingers, our flies open, lips licked—there we were, caught in the spotlight. Nailed.

We bolted. First for the car, and then, realizing we had no way of starting it, for the woods. I thought nothing. I thought escape. The headlights came at me like accusing fingers. I was gone.

Ram-bam-bam, across the parking lot, past the chopper and into the feculent undergrowth at the lake's edge, insects flying up in my face, weeds whipping, frogs and snakes and red-eyed turtles splashing off into the night: I was already ankle-deep in muck and tepid water and still going strong. Behind me, the girl's screams rose in intensity, disconsolate, incriminating, the screams of the Sabine women, the Christian martyrs, Anne Frank dragged from the garret. I kept going, pursued by those cries, imagining cops and bloodhounds. The water was up to my knees when I realized what I was doing: I was going to swim for it. Swim the breadth of Greasy Lake and hide myself in the thick clot of woods on the far side. They'd never find me there.

I was breathing in sobs, in gasps. The water lapped at my waist as I looked out over the moon-burnished ripples, the mats of algae that clung to the surface like scabs. Digby and Jeff had vanished. I paused. Listened. The girl was quieter now, screams tapering to sobs, but there were male voices, angry, excited, and the high-pitched ticking of the second car's engine. I waded deeper, stealthy, hunted, the ooze sucking at my sneakers. As I was about to take the plunge—at the very instant I dropped my shoulder for the first slashing stroke—I blundered into something. Something unspeakable, obscene, something soft, wet, moss-grown. A patch of weed? A log? When I reached out to touch it, it gave like a rubber duck, it gave like flesh.

In one of those nasty little epiphanies for which we are prepared by films and TV and childhood visits to the funeral home to ponder the shrunken painted forms of dead grandparents, I understood what it was that bobbed there so inadmissibly in the dark. Understood, and stumbled back in horror and revulsion, my mind yanked in six different directions (I was nineteen, a mere child, an infant, and here in the space of five minutes I'd struck down one greasy character and blundered into the waterlogged carcass of a second), thinking, The keys, the keys, why did I have to go and lose the keys? I stumbled back, but the muck took hold of my feet—a sneaker snagged, balance lost—and suddenly I was pitching face forward into the buoyant black mass, throwing out my hands in desperation while simultaneously conjuring the image of reeking frogs and muskrats revolving in slicks of their own deliquescing juices. AAAAArrrgh! I shot from the water like a torpedo, the dead man rotating to expose a mossy beard and eyes cold as the moon. I must have shouted out, thrashing around in the weeds, because the voices behind me suddenly became animated.

"What was that?"

"It's them, it's them: they tried to, tried to . . . *rape* me!" Sobs.

A man's voice, flat Midwestern accent. "You sons a bitches, we'll kill you!"

Frogs, crickets.

Then another voice, harsh, *r*-less, Lower East Side: "Motherfucker!" I recognized the verbal virtuosity of the bad greasy character in the engineer boots. Tooth chipped, sneakers gone, coated in mud and slime and worse, crouching breathless in the weeds waiting to have my ass thoroughly and definitively kicked and fresh from the hideous stinking embrace of a three-days-dead corpse, I suddenly felt a rush of joy and vindication: the son of a bitch was alive! Just as quickly, my bowels turned to ice. "Come on out of there, you pansy motherfuckers!" the bad greasy character was screaming. He shouted curses till he was out of breath.

The crickets started up again, then the frogs. I held my breath. All at once there was a sound in the reeds, a swishing, a splash: thunk-a-thunk. They were throwing rocks. The frogs fell silent. I cradled my head. Swish, swish, thunk-a-thunk. A wedge of feldspar the size of a cue hall glanced off my knee. I bit my finger.

It was then that they turned to the car. I heard a door slam, a curse, and then the sound of the headlights shattering—almost a good-natured sound, celebratory, like corks popping from the necks of bottles. This was succeeded by the dull booming of the fenders, metal on metal, and then the icy crash of the windshield. I inched forward, elbows and knees, my belly pressed to the muck, thinking of guerrillas and commandos and *The Naked and the Dead*. I parted the weeds and squinted the length of the parking lot.

The second car—it was a Trans-Am—was still running, its high beams washing the scene in a lurid stagy light. Tire iron flailing, the greasy bad character was laying into the side of my mother's Bel Air like an avenging demon, his shadow riding up the trunks of the trees. Whomp. Whomp. Whomp-whomp. The other two guys—blond types, in fraternity jackets—were helping out with tree branches and skull-sized boulders. One of them was gathering up bottles, rocks, muck, candy wrappers, used condoms, pop-tops, and other refuse and pitching it through the window on the driver's side. I could see the fox, a white bulb behind the windshield of the '57 Chevy. "Bobbie," she whined over the thumping, "come *on*." The greasy character paused a moment, took one good swipe at the left taillight, and then heaved the tire iron halfway across the lake. Then he fired up the '57 and was gone.

Blond head nodded at blond head. One said something to the other, too low for me to catch. They were no doubt thinking that in helping to annihilate my mother's car they'd committed a fairly rash act, and thinking too that there were three bad characters connected with that very car watching them from the woods. Perhaps other possibilities occurred to them as well—police, jail cells, justices of the peace, reparations, lawyers, irate parents, fraternal censure. Whatever they were thinking, they suddenly dropped branches, bottles, and rocks and sprang for their car in unison, as if they'd choreographed it. Five seconds. That's all it took. The engine shrieked, the tires squealed, a cloud of dust rose from the rutted lot and then settled back on darkness.

I don't know how long I lay there, the bad breath of decay all around me, my jacket heavy as a bear, the primordial ooze subtly reconstituting itself to accommodate my upper thighs and testicles. My jaws ached, my knee throbbed, my coccyx was on fire. I contemplated suicide, wondered if I'd need bridgework, scraped the recesses of my brain for some sort of excuse to give my parents—a tree had fallen on the car, I was blindsided by a bread truck, hit and run, vandals had got to it while we were playing chess at Digby's. Then I thought of the dead man. He was probably the only person on the planet worse off than I was. I thought about him, fog on the lake, insects chirring eerily, and felt the tug of fear, felt the darkness opening up inside me like a set of jaws. Who was he, I wondered, this victim of time and circumstance bobbing sorrowfully in the lake at my back. The owner of the chopper, no doubt, a bad older character come to this. Shot during a murky drug deal, drowned while drunkenly frolicking in the lake. Another headline. My car was wrecked; he was dead.

When the eastern half of the sky went from black to cobalt and the trees began to separate themselves from the shadows, I pushed myself up from the mud and stepped out into the open. By now the birds had begun to take over for the crickets, and dew lay slick on the leaves. There was a smell in the air, raw and sweet at the same time, the smell of the sun firing buds and opening blossoms. I contemplated the car. It lay there like a wreck along the highway, like a steel sculpture left over from a vanished civilization. Everything was still. This was nature.

I was circling the car, as dazed and bedraggled as the sole survivor of an air blitz, when Digby and Jeff emerged from the trees behind me. Digby's face was crosshatched with smears of dirt; Jeff's jacket was gone and his shirt was torn across the shoulder. They slouched across the lot, looking sheepish, and silently came up beside me to gape at the ravaged automobile. No one said a word. After a while Jeff swung open the driver's door and began to scoop the broken glass and garbage off the seat. I looked at Digby. He shrugged. "At least they didn't slash the tires," he said.

It was true: the tires were intact. There was no windshield, the headlights were staved in, and the body looked as if it had been sledgehammered for a quarter a shot at the county fair, but the tires were inflated to regulation pressure. The car was drivable. In silence, all three of us bent to scrape the mud and shattered glass from the interior. I said nothing about the biker. When we were finished, I reached in my pocket for the keys, experienced a nasty stab of recollection, cursed myself, and turned to search the grass. I spotted them almost immediately, no more than five feet from the open door, glinting like jewels in the first tapering shaft of sunlight. There was no reason to get philosophical about it: I eased into the seat and turned the engine over.

It was at that precise moment that the silver Mustang with the flame decals rumbled into the lot. All three of us froze; then Digby and Jeff slid into the car and slammed the door. We watched as the Mustang rocked and bobbed across the ruts and finally jerked to a halt beside the forlorn chopper at the far end of the lot. "Let's go," Digby said. I hesitated, the Bel Air wheezing beneath me.

Two girls emerged from the Mustang. Tight jeans, stiletto heels, hair like frozen fur. They bent over the motorcycle, paced back and forth aimlessly, glanced once or twice at us, and then ambled over to where the reeds sprang up in a green fence round the perimeter of the lake. One of them cupped her hands to her mouth. "Al," she called. "Hey, Al!"

"Come on," Digby hissed. "Let's get out of here."

But it was too late. The second girl was picking her way across the lot, unsteady on her heels, looking up at us and then away. She was older—twenty-five or -six—and as she came closer we could see there was something wrong with her: she was stoned or drunk, lurching now and waving her arms for balance. I gripped the steering wheel as if it were the ejection lever of a flaming jet, and Digby spat out my name, twice, terse and impatient.

"Hi," the girl said.

We looked at her like zombies, like war veterans, like deaf-and-dumb pencil peddlers.

She smiled, her lips cracked and dry. "Listen," she said, bending from the waist to look in the window, "you guys seen Al?" Her pupils were pinpoints, her eyes glass. She jerked her neck. "That's his bike over there—Al's. You seen him?"

Al. I didn't know what to say. I wanted to get out of the car and retch, I wanted to go home to my parents' house and crawl into bed. Digby poked me in the ribs. "We haven't seen anybody," I said.

The girl seemed to consider this, reaching out a slim veiny arm to brace herself against the car. "No matter," she said, slurring the *t*'s, "he'll turn up." And then, as if she'd just taken stock of the whole scene—the ravaged car and our battered faces, the desolation of the place—she said: "Hey, you guys look like some pretty bad characters—been fightin', huh?" We stared straight ahead, rigid as catatonics. She was fumbling in her pocket and muttering something. Finally she held out a handful of tablets in glassine wrappers: "Hey, you want to party, you want to do some of these with me and Sarah?"

I just looked at her. I thought I was going to cry. Digby broke the silence. "No, thanks," he said, leaning over me. "Some other time."

I put the car in gear and it inched forward with a groan, shaking off pellets of glass like an old dog shedding water after a bath, heaving over the ruts on its worn springs, creeping toward the highway. There was a sheen of sun on the lake. I looked back. The girl was still standing there, watching us, her shoulders slumped, hand outstretched.

---

1. Why does the narrator begin the story by remembering a time "when it was good to be bad"?
2. Why does the narrator twice say of the fetid and murky waters of Greasy Lake and the trashed park: "This was nature"?
3. When the narrator and his friends first arrive at Greasy Lake, why does the narrator decide, "Whatever it was we were looking for, we weren't about to find it at Greasy Lake. Not that night"? What, if anything, do the narrator and his friends "find" as a result of subsequent events?
4. At the end of the story, why does the girl's invitation to do drugs cause the narrator to think he might cry?

MARY GORDON (1949–) has spent much of her writing career investigating her interest in women's identities, particularly the intersection between sexuality and spirituality. She was born in Long Island, New York, into a devout Catholic family and received her education at Barnard College and Syracuse University. Her first novel, *Final Payments* (1978), brought her immediate fame. Gordon's subsequent novels include *The Company of Women* (1981), *Men and Angels* (1985), and *The Other Side* (1989). She has also published essays, memoirs, and three volumes of short fiction, including *The Stories of Mary Gordon* (2006), in which "The Baby" appears. Among the awards she has received are O. Henry awards in 1983, 1997, and 2000 and a Guggenheim Fellowship. Gordon is a professor of English at Barnard College.

The Baby

When people asked Kathleen if she was homesick in America, she said she wasn't, and it was the truth. She'd come over with Kevin from Ennis, County Clare, a week after their wedding; they had a honeymoon at Niagara Falls. People teased her about it afterwards, and she pretended to know why. She laughed along with them, and made a face to show she got it, but she never did.

At first it was like a big holiday. There was the wedding, and the airplane ride, the food on the little trays. There was her trip to Niagara Falls on the train, Kevin telling her she was great not to be feeling the jet lag. And her first night ever in a hotel. Her first night really alone with Kevin. The week after the wedding they'd spent in her parents' house; her brothers had cleared out of their room and were sleeping on the sitting room floor. It made her and Kevin self-conscious, trying to sleep together in her brother James's bed, too narrow for them, only they couldn't give up what seemed like the treat of sleeping in the same bed. The times they'd been together before in the back of someone's car or in a field she'd felt a little bad about it, but she hadn't wanted to say anything for fear of spoiling Kevin's time. Maybe he'd felt bad about it too, it seemed to mean so much him sleeping in her brother's cramped bed, with the pictures of footballers looking down on them. "It's great not to have to sneak around, not to have to skulk home afterwards, to look your mam in the eye, not feeling lonely for you in the bed, thinking of you while my brothers were snoring," he said.

Kevin had no sisters; he'd come from a family of seven, all boys. And in her family, she'd been the only girl. Everyone was thrilled when she and Kevin had the baby and it was a girl. They named it Margaret after Kevin's aunt, who'd died young, but they called her Maggie and not Peg, as the aunt had been called, to break the bad luck. So that was another part of the holiday, having Maggie fifteen months after she'd set foot in the States, decorating the nursery and buying baby clothes. Kevin was doing well so they could afford to splurge, and she'd banked her whole salary while she'd been pregnant.

Her life had been wonderful the last five years, everything was better than it had been at home. She even looked better a bit older. She always knew she'd been good-looking, but there were little things that had tormented her that seemed to have gone away after the baby. Her face used to break out, and that had stopped. And there were secret deformities that possibly no one had noticed but were a torture to Kathleen. Before the baby her palms and fingertips had always been damp, so that she'd dreaded shaking hands with anyone for fear she might disgust them. And her fingernails had had little ridges cut into them, so that she felt she never could wear nail varnish, because it would draw attention. But now her hands were perfectly fine; she didn't think of them at all now.

After the baby, after she got her figure back, she'd looked at herself naked in the full-length mirror. She'd never done that before in her life. She was surprised at how pleased she was at the sight of herself, surprised and a bit ashamed. She understood what Kevin meant now, that her breasts were round and lovely. She liked that she had a waist, some women didn't even if they were thin, and if she wished her thighs were a bit smaller, she knew it wasn't really serious. She'd always known she had nice eyes, green like the sea, Kevin said, and she began wearing a bit of makeup, blue eye shadow and black mascara, and she was pleased with the way it made her eyes look bigger and brought out the color.

She'd got used to feeling good about things; it had seemed strange at first, a different way from the people at home she'd known most of her life. When they walked into church on Sundays or when they went dancing sometimes on Saturday nights, if they could get a sitter for Maggie, she knew that people looked at her and Kevin and admired them and she didn't feel she had to pretend anymore that it wasn't happening. She liked the way Lawrence at the Hair Emporium cut her hair. She knew he was queer, and she wondered what they'd think of that at home, but she liked him and he liked her too. He told her about his boyfriend and that they were saving up for a house. He was very complimentary about her hair. He said very few had the red highlights without being brassy. He said not to worry about it being a little oily. He recommended a special shampoo. The price shocked her, but she went for it, although she kept it from Kevin. That was the good thing about having her own job, she didn't have to be asking her husband for every blessed penny.

She wasn't even afraid anymore that Kevin had quit his job as an air conditioner repairman, the one he'd got his green card on, and was selling mobile phones and home systems. Rockland County was a boom location, he said, and the brogue never hurt. She even liked the name of the town they lived in: New City. She didn't tell anyone that she liked the name because it sounded new. She knew they'd think she was simple for having an idea like that.

She was very proud of their house, she didn't worry that one day they wouldn't be able to make the mortgage; she planted petunias and zinnias and she thought it was great that because the house was sided with aluminum they'd never have to paint it. At first she wasn't sure she liked that shade of yellow, but she'd come to see that it was fine, it always cheered you up, no matter what the weather.

Maggie was three now, and she'd gone back to work two afternoons a week in the cafeteria of the elementary school while Maggie went to preschool. She didn't like the net she had to wear around her hair, and she hated the feel of the plastic gloves, but it was worth it because the hours were perfect. Maggie went to school from eleven to three and she worked from eleven thirty to two thirty. With Kevin making his own hours, he could pick Maggie up sometimes and she had an hour or so on her own.

But the best thing about her job was the girls she worked with. She couldn't believe her luck. The four of them that worked together were like sisters. They called her the baby. They all had some Irish blood, but Joanne was half Italian, and Marty's father was Polish and Italian. Lois had the least Irish in her, only a great-grandmother, but she was the one Kathleen was closest to. She had a bit of a weight problem and Kathleen was sympathetic. She never got impatient with her like the others did, she never teased her about it, even when she went on the popcorn and grapefruit diet. She knew Lois needed encouragement.

Joanne was married to a man who sold TVs and other appliances; he didn't do too well. She liked suggesting that he was good in bed. She'd gone into debt to have what she called "a boob job" but Kathleen didn't like to think about that, having plastic bags put in you so you'd look bigger. Marty's husband drank, but she was loyal. She was very thin, maybe a bit too thin, and this was hard for Lois, the way she always made a point of having to eat more to keep her weight up. But Marty was right, when she lost a pound or two it really showed on her face, it aged her. Marty's and Joanne's children were all grown up, so they loved making a pet of Maggie. On Kevin and Kathleen's fifth anniversary they chipped in to send them to the Marriott in Bear Mountain for a special weekend, and they all stayed at the house to watch Maggie. They put a gift-wrapped package in the back of the car. It was a sexy nightgown. Kevin was thrilled with it, but Kathleen thought it made her look too pale. When they got home, she saw that Maggie didn't seem to miss them at all. She was very attached to Lois. Lois was the one who spoiled her most. It made Kathleen sad, knowing how much she would have loved a baby. She kept asking Kevin wouldn't he try to fix Lois up with one of his friends. Kevin said Lois was great but his friends weren't her type.

Every Friday after work the four of them went to Harrigan's Pub for happy hour. The whole thing was pretending to be an Irish pub, but Kevin and Kathleen laughed because they hadn't a clue. The brothers who ran it, Joe and Jeff Harrigan, loved it when Kathleen came in; they loved to hear Kathleen order for everyone. "That brogue just knocks me out, just knocks me out," Jeff would say. They never let her pay for her drinks. When he put in the karaoke, the four girls began singing together, and they were up there every happy hour. They taught Kathleen to sing songs that were around when they were young, songs she hadn't sung before. They liked one by the Carpenters called "Close to You." Apparently the girl who sang it originally died because she'd taken too many laxatives. "Could you credit that," Kathleen said, and they laughed at her for the expression. She didn't think a thing like that could happen in Ireland, people weren't so appearance-conscious there. But she didn't tell them that because she didn't want them to think she was criticizing America. She thought America was great, she didn't even know if she'd move back home if she had the chance. Kevin said they would when they'd saved enough, but they didn't seem to put very much away.

Jeff Harrigan got Irish songs for the karaoke. He made Kathleen sing them. She told herself she didn't have to, it was her choice, but she didn't like the way they looked at her when she was up there. He asked her to learn "H-A-double-R-I, G-A-N spells Harrigan," and they split their sides laughing because she pronounced it "haitch," beginning with a breath, instead of "aitch." When somebody got drunk, they always asked her to sing "When Irish Eyes Are Smiling." She didn't know how to tell them she'd only just learned it; they never sang it at home.

She and the girls started practicing routines and their big hit was "My Boyfriend's Back." They'd all wag their fingers at the guys in the audience, and everyone cracked up. Their finale was "Lean on Me." She thought the words were really great. "Lean on me, when you're not strong, I'll be your strength, I'll help you carry on." When they sang that, they all leaned into each other, and everyone always clapped. She liked singing with the girls, it was just when they made her sing the Irish songs by herself it made her feel self-conscious. But singing in the group was great gas. When she said "great gas," they fell over themselves laughing.

It must have been at Harrigan's that they came up with the plan of the four of them going to Ireland. She'd gone back every year. If you didn't go in high season (she went during the spring vacation), the fare was dirt-cheap really and once she got home there were no expenses. Her father picked her and Maggie up at Shannon and they were right home in her own bedroom in forty-five minutes. It was great living that near the airport. When people asked her where she came from she'd said, "Ennis, County Clare," and that didn't mean anything to them until she said, "Forty-five minutes from Shannon." They all relaxed; they could place it in their minds. But all the time she was growing up she never thought a thing of being near the airport.

Her mother spoiled her and Maggie when they were there. Her sisters-in-law noticed it. All her brothers had married and settled near the town, and she knew how the wives felt, never getting a holiday for themselves, never being waited on like Kathleen was by her mother. One of her brothers' wives was particularly spiteful about it. Kathleen had known Brid Callahan all her life; they'd been in the same class and Brid had always disliked her. Brid was clever, but the nuns didn't take to her, not like they did Kathleen and some of the other girls who didn't do so well at academics. Kathleen never understood why of all the ones he could have had—and he could have had any girl in town, he was the kind of boy—her brother Jimmy chose Brid. Jimmy was the sweetest boy in the world, the next youngest of them, just before Kathleen. He had Kathleen's eyes, only bigger, and beautiful teeth as white as milk. And his skin was so white the freckles made it look like you could see through it. His skin and his teeth made him seem very light, and he moved lightly, but the lightness also came from something about him that made it seem he never cared if he got his way or not.

Jimmy was the brother Kathleen was closest to and it was a blow for her when he married Brid. She was the brains of the outfit, everyone said, and that was good for Jimmy, he didn't seem too cut out for the rough and tumble of making a living. He was good at carpentry, and what with the building boom they'd done well with Brid managing the accounts. She'd taken the money and invested it in a gas station and convenience store. The year before she'd had Jimmy build on to it and was starting a bed and breakfast. She certainly had go, Kathleen had to say that, accomplishing all this with two-year-old twins. But she'd never like Brid. She made it hard for Kathleen to have a minute to herself with Jimmy and she was always passing remarks about people being waited on hand and foot.

Kathleen always kept hoping that in time things would get easier with her and Brid, and the day at Harrigan's when the idea came up about all of the girls going with her to Ireland she thought it was perfect because they could all stay at Brid's new B & B. Not her, of course, but the other three. She didn't know whether Brid would give them a cut rate, but she thought there was at least a chance of it.

They were all over the moon about the trip and Kevin loved teasing her about them. "The witches coven come to Ennis. I'll be ringing my mates to tell them to look out for their lives." The girls were pretending to hit at him, and teasing back. "They'll be grateful to their dying day. We'll show them what the real thing is." Kathleen understood that they prized Kevin because, among the four of them, she had the only husband who could be recognized as a real man.

"Would you want to leave Maggie and me for a week?" he asked Kathleen. "Just go off by yourself with your girlfriends. Really let your hair down. Then I could join you."

At first the thought made her sick. She'd never been separated from Maggie for more than a night. And then she knew her mother would be terribly disappointed.

"It's just a week, Kath," he said. "Then I'll be there and we'll make it up to her. We'll go home for Christmas too this year."

"Oh, she'll take it out on me anyway," Kathleen said.

"You're your own person, Kath. You've lived in America, you're different. It would do them a bit of good over there to see a woman with some freedom. Your mother has to understand you're not the same girl she put on the plane five years ago."

Kathleen didn't like to hear that. She hoped it wasn't true. But Kevin was right: they'd come to America for freedom and opportunity. And they'd found it.

The girls booked their flight for August 15, the Feast of the Assumption, Marty said and laughed, they all knew they'd been thinking it, all of them had gone to Catholic school.

"What'll the weather be like?" Lois asked.

"Well, I can't promise. It can be unpredictable."

"It won't be like the New York steam bath," Lois said. They all understood that she felt the heat because of her weight.

The drinks were free on the flight, and they each had several. Except for Kathleen. She'd read an article that said that alcohol could be dehydrating, and made the jet lag worse. She'd found she did better just drinking lots of water. The girls seemed loud on the plane, and she wondered why she hadn't noticed it before, if she was just being oversensitive, worrying that the Irish on the plane would think badly of them. It was one of the things the Irish said about Americans: that they were loud.

They'd been hoping to get some sleep on the plane, but none of them could get comfortable. Joanne said she was sure that when she'd flown to California the seats had been wider. "That was American Airlines though," she said, and Kathleen felt chastised.

They were exhausted after the flight, and Kathleen was worried they might be a bit hungover. They weren't looking their best, and she regretted that. Marty and Joanne were sharp dressers; their hair was dyed—Marty was red-haired and Joanne streaky blonde, they all went to Lawrence the same as her and she'd always admired the way they used makeup. But now they looked different. She thought for the first time that they were older than her. That she was young, but perhaps they weren't young. She wished they looked better for her family's first sight of them. She didn't know who'd pick her up, but she hoped it was her father because the look of people wasn't something he noticed.

It was Jimmy who picked them up. That was fine, she was proud of him, she was convinced that just seeing him would perk her friends right up. But they were only just polite to him, they said hello but barely; they seemed to expect him to carry their luggage and she thought they talked to him as they would to a porter. She was afraid she was being oversensitive. She was always afraid people would take advantage of Jimmy. His good nature. Even though he was older, she'd always felt she had to look out for him.

The weather didn't help. "Jesus, it's pissing down with rain," Kathleen said.

"I never heard you use that kind of language in America," Marty said, and Kathleen couldn't tell if she was kidding.

"You should have been here yesterday," Jimmy said, "the sun would have blinded you."

"It's always my luck. I always have bad weather on vacation," Lois said. Kathleen thought she should be careful; people didn't like to hear overweight people complain.

"It might break," Jimmy said, but Kathleen could tell he wasn't hopeful.

The rain had never bothered her. Especially when she came home from America, it seemed comforting and right, she felt cleansed, but gently, rinsed, as if she were undergoing some treatment particularly good for the complexion. The kind of thing very rich women might arrange for when they got what were called facials. The girls had talked about it to her: facials were steam cleaning and all sorts of lotions. But when the rain fell on Kathleen's face at home she felt as if she hadn't realized how all the makeup and grime of America had clogged her pores, dried the skin around her lips. She felt she got her baby skin back after walking in the rain. She thought now of the girls calling her "the baby," and that she was the baby of her family. She knew there was something in her that made people want to protect her. She didn't know what that was.

Her mother had laid out an enormous breakfast for them. Eggs and bacon and sausage, fried tomatoes, mushrooms, fried bread.

"This is going right to my arteries," Joanne said. "Fried bread. Grease and carbohydrates. I've died and gone to heaven."

Kathleen could tell her mother wasn't sure whether or not she was being praised.

Lois asked for fresh fruit. She was on Weight Watchers. Kathleen's mother blushed; she said she'd look around for some. Kathleen said she'd do some shopping after they'd had a rest. Lois said she'd need to go with her; there were things she needed "for her program," or the whole thing would go up in smoke.

"Brid will have the rooms ready for you now," Jimmy said.

"I'll get down on my knees to anyone who will show me to my bed," Marty said. Jimmy laughed, and Kathleen could see that pleased Marty. She relaxed; everything would be all right.

Jimmy drove them to the B & B. "We're staying in a gas station?" Joanne said.

"No," Kathleen said. "It's just attached."

But she could see they were disappointed. They'd probably dreamed of a thatched cottage, of their eyes falling on green fields.

Whereas what they could see outside their window was a twenty-foot-high sign saying Esso.

The way Brid was acting made Kathleen sick. She was acting like a nervous dog, anxious to please, saying how great it was to have them with her. That she felt she must have built the whole B & B with them in mind. They'd be her first guests. It was a blessing, she said. Bull, Kathleen wanted to say, you had the idea for this two years before you knew we were coming. And as for blessing, Brid never darkened the door of a church.

The girls thought Brid was wonderful. She offered them tea in their rooms. "You must be dead, longing for bed," she said.

Kathleen suggested they'd be better off trying to stay awake, trying to get on Irish time.

"I've never heard of that," Brid said. "And it's that damp, you might want to put on your electric blanket. It's under your sheets; the switch is just at the side of the bed."

"Lead me to it," Marty said. "Sandman here I come."

The way Brid laughed at that was really phony, Kathleen thought. As if she knew what they meant. Kathleen couldn't remember whether Irish people had the sandman the way they did in America, but she was pretty sure they didn't, and Brid was faking so they'd think she was something great.

Jimmy brought their bags into their rooms and they settled down to sleep. Kathleen was annoyed that they hadn't taken her advice about trying to get on Irish time, and she was worried. If they didn't get on Irish time, they'd feel wretched for days. And the whole holiday was only meant to last a week.

"Your friends are much older than you, except the stout one," Kathleen's mother said. "Haven't you friends your own age, pet?"

She'd made lots of plans for things that they could see; she'd take them to Blarney Castle, to the ruined Abbey, to the Cliffs of Moher, to the Burren.

She asked her mother if she could borrow the car to get what Lois needed for her diet from the store in Ennis.

"You can, of course," her mother said. "We'll try and make a great time for them."

She tried to think what Lois would want to eat. She bought celery and carrots and yogurt. She bought large bottles of diet Coke. But she'd never had to watch her weight herself, so she was guessing.

"I need nonfat yogurt. Don't they have nonfat?" Lois said.

"This was all they had."

"Four percent fat. Sugar, the works. I might as well forget about it," Lois said and began to cry. Kathleen was mortified in front of her mother, but her mother was running the water loud rinsing the carrots and celery and cutting them up small, as if she were going to put them in a soup. That was the wrong way, Kathleen knew, but she didn't know how to tell her mother.

Her mother had made them ham sandwiches for lunch, with raspberries and vanilla ice cream for dessert. When she offered second helpings Lois took one. Kathleen felt like a fool, making a special trip to buy food for her diet.

It was hard to get them to go on the outings Kathleen had planned with the rain coming down in sheets. They got into the car, trying to be cheerful, but they were all asleep every time Kathleen tried to point something out.

"Is there any way you could remind your friends breakfast's over a 9:30, Kathleen," Brid said. "It's clearly posted in the rooms. After all they're paying guests, like anyone else."

"You have no others, Brid," Kathleen said. "Maybe you'd accommodate them. They're having a rough time with the jet lag."

"I have my schedule, the B & B's not the only thing. I have the petrol pump and the counter at the convenience store, I'm not on holiday like you. No one's waiting on me hand and foot."

Kathleen said she'd mention it to them, but she never did.

She didn't know what else to do with them except take them around in the car and pretend they weren't sleeping. She'd tried to find a nice place for lunch every day, but she forgot that Irish pubs had a certain limited menu, which repeated itself from place to place.

"You'd make a fortune with a good old Greek diner here," Joanne said. "God what I wouldn't give for a bacon cheeseburger. I don't know what they call bacon here but it's nothing I'd call by the name."

"It's more like what we call Canadian bacon," Marty said, and Kathleen knew she was trying to be nice.

"Crisp is a foreign concept to them here," Joanne said.

"Crisps is their name for potato chips," Lois said, and they all laughed.

After the drive and the lunch, they'd all go back to bed. They were better in the evenings, and Kathleen was proud of them as they sat around her mother's table. Her father was silent. He'd never heard women talk like this. Her mother seemed to be having a good time, and when Jimmy drove by he seemed to have a good laugh with them, and that made everyone feel good.

He took them to the pub every night and Kathleen was glad to see how much they enjoyed it. They were generous buying people drinks, and Kathleen wished that the people in the town were equally generous. She tried not to be counting, but she couldn't help noticing that after a while her friends weren't being treated as much as they treated the men. It made her nervous and it made her even more nervous to see Lois deep in conversation with Kieran Donnelly, who was known for nothing good. She felt sick at Lois's excitement when she talked about him.

"I was asking Kieran about how they thatched the roofs and he invited me out to his place so he could show me," she said.

Kathleen knew Kieran's house; it was an old whitewashed house he lived in with his father. But his father was dead now, so he must live alone. The house was in a dark patch of trees a quarter mile from the Gort Road. She was quite sure it hadn't a thatched roof.

But she told herself that she hadn't been there for a long time, maybe she'd misremembered. Still she thought she should give Lois a warning about Kieran. He was a drinker and he was known to bring a not nice type of woman back to his house when he went to Limerick for the day. He was a good plumber but unreliable, everyone was always complaining that you couldn't trust him to show up.

"You just think anyone who's interested in me would have to have something wrong with him," Lois said, bursting into tears. Kathleen didn't remember that in America she'd cried so much.

"No, that's not it, Lois. Only I've known Kieran all my life."

"Well, I'm not planning on settling down with him. Don't worry about that. I'm not that bad off that I'd land myself in a place like this."

Kathleen didn't say anything, but she felt bad for what she wanted to say, "Find out yourself then what he's up to," to Lois, who was her best friend. She wouldn't have said anything like that to Lois before. Everything was topsy-turvy now.

Lois came back from Kieran's looking sullen and disappointed, but she didn't say a word about what had gone on. It was after that she started taking out her Weight Watchers' books and writing things down on the blue and white charts.

"I don't even want to think about the number of points I'm over," Lois said.

Kathleen and all the girls knew Weight Watchers was on a point system: you got a certain number of points for everything you ate, and you were supposed to lose weight if you didn't go over the weekly points.

"But I don't see what I could have done. There's nothing to eat here that I can eat. There isn't any way I could get to a supermarket and buy some of the things I need, is there?"

"You can, of course," said Kathleen, ashamed for her country and its famously poor cuisine. "We'll go to the big market outside of Limerick tomorrow."

The idea of going to a supermarket cheered the girls up; they invited Kathleen to do the Ouija board with them in their room, but Kathleen said she was tired. She was glad she was staying in her mother's house instead of the B & B. She was glad she had somewhere to go.

By the morning, the plan had grown and bloomed: the girls had decided they were going to make a meal for Kathleen's family to show their gratitude. A real Italian meal. Had Kathleen forgotten they all had Italian blood?

They were going to make it a surprise. So they didn't want Kathleen involved in it, not even the shopping. They'd worked it all out with Jimmy in the pub the night before. He'd drive them into Limerick to do their shopping. Kathleen would have the day to herself.

"The day to myself." She was ashamed at the joy that spread over the whole of her skin when she heard the words. It had been a long time since she'd had a day to herself. Years. But how many?

She saw the girls off waving from the parking area between the doorway to the B & B and the petrol pump. There was no car available to her, but she didn't mind the half-mile walk back to her parents' house, even though it was along the main road with nothing to look at but a few new houses, which looked as if they'd stolen the land from the trees and stood there glancing at the road, shamefully naked. As she walked on the side of the road, she was a bit worried at the cars whizzing by. She was sure there hadn't been that much traffic when she still lived here. And it was only five years ago she'd left. What would it be like five years from now? Crossing the road, she had to remind herself to look the opposite way from the way she looked in America. It always took her a few days to get that straight. She wondered which was the better way of doing it, driving on the right side or the left. She reckoned that each side probably thought their side was right, and each of them probably had good arguments.

She borrowed her mother's wellies to walk through the fields to the stream she always liked. She enjoyed the squelch her rubbery feet made in the wet grass and the low bellow of the cattle and the foolish bleating of the sheep. She'd hoped the girls would take this walk with her, but they hadn't the footwear for it, their sneakers would be ruined, it was that wet. She wondered should she have told them to bring some sort of boots, but they would have been heavy in their luggage, and there was nothing like wellies in America. Nothing that would really have served.

She felt that the light rain on her skin was doing her whole body good, her insides, not just her skin. She didn't know why people made such a thing about sunshine. If you just put your head in the right place gray skies and a soft rain and wet grass could be just as beautiful. It was just that sunshine had better PR.

She sat by the stream and threw stones in the water, enjoying the look of them sinking in the clear. Maybe I am young for my age, she thought. She imagined how nice it would be sitting there with Maggie throwing stones and twigs into the water. Then she worried that Maggie wouldn't like the wet weather, and would fuss about having to wear her raincoat all the time. She'd take her to Gort and get her a new raincoat. Your Irish raincoat, they'd call it. It would be something to show her friends back home. Kathleen wondered if she wore a raincoat when she was a child. She couldn't remember, but she couldn't remember having been wet. It would be great when Kevin and Maggie came here next week. In two days, the girls would be gone and she'd have three days with her parents. She looked forward to that.

She could hear the girls giggling when Jimmy stopped the car. The sun was shining, it was beginning to be warm; they'd driven with the windows open. Jimmy looked pleased with himself, and the girls looked more like themselves, laughing and teasing like she was used to.

Kathleen and her mother watched out the kitchen window.

"Mother of God, they've bought enough food to feed an army," Kathleen's mother said. "How many do they think they're feeding and what size do they think my kitchen is? Where am I going to put all the stuff?"

Kathleen felt worried about the size of the refrigerator. It hardly came to her waist; it was less than a quarter as big as her fridge in New York. There was no way the girls would understand that.

But they were in their best moods, and showed Kathleen and her mother out of the kitchen. "The Irish are banished. Italians rule," Marty said, holding two cans of tomatoes over her head. "Kathleen, would you believe, we had to go three places for parsley. Apparently they think it's a gourmet item here."

"Yes, they would so," Kathleen said, realizing she never used "so" at the end of the sentence like that when she was in New York.

She wanted to go for a walk with her mother, but her mother was jittery about strangers in her kitchen.

"They work in a kitchen, mam," Kathleen said. "They're professionals."

"But they don't know our ways. I'm not fond of their saying the Irish are banished."

"It's their sense of humor."

"Funny kind of joke. More like an insult to me."

"They wouldn't have meant it that way, mam. They'd be mortified if they thought they'd insulted you."

"Aren't there any nice Irish girls in New York for you to be friends with?"

"They are Irish, mam. All of them have Irish blood."

"Funny they didn't mention it. You think Maggie's all right without you?"

"She's fine. Kevin's with her. They're having a ball, they'll be here in three days."

"I'd never have left you at three years old."

"Do you think I'd have done it if I thought it was bad for her?"

"Don't you be talking to me like that. D'ye think I'm one of those Americans? Getting tanned and playing tennis at my age? The sky's the limit with that lot."

Kathleen didn't know exactly what her mother was talking about. They walked along in silence. Kathleen asked her mother if she wanted to go to the movies.

"See a fill-um in the middle of the day with the sun cracking the pavestones?"

"Just for a change, mam."

"All right then, for a change." Kathleen knew her mother agreed because she didn't want to fight and couldn't think of anything to say that wouldn't start a fight. They drove into Gort. It was an English movie. People said it was supposed to be funny. She didn't think her mother would like it, but she hoped it would take her mind off what was going on in her kitchen. But she didn't like it, and she said, "I guess you have a different sense of humor if you're from a different place."

She dropped her mother at Brid's and said she'd go home to set the table. She was walking in the grass at the back of the house; she could hear the girls through the kitchen window.

"I've been in trailers that had bigger kitchens than this," Joanne said.

"I knew it was simple, but this is depressing as hell. The poor baby. No wonder she couldn't wait to get out," Marty said. "I mean that shower. I think it was made of Styrofoam, and if that's their idea of hot water."

"They're very nice, though," Lois said.

"I like that Brid. She's got gumption. More than her husband with his big blue eyes," said Marty.

"We ought to get something for them, to thank her. Brid, I mean."

"Do you think there are really stores that we could go to that sell stuff that's tacky enough? That lamp made out of fake shells. And the fabric on the sofa. I thought I was going to die it was so itchy."

"I don't think we have the right to complain. We're staying there for free, so we have to be nice about things."

Kathleen felt terror in the middle of her chest, as if she'd been stung below one of her ribs. They thought Brid was letting them stay for free. Where had they gotten that idea? She was sure she'd never said that. Should she have told them right away what the cost would be? She'd hoped she'd be able to work that out with Brid, that Brid would give them a break. But she'd never dreamed of asking Brid not to charge them.

She'd have to make up the money. She couldn't imagine how she'd do it. She thought of telling them they'd have to pay. But their faces when she told them were a horrifying prospect. Anything would have to be better than that.

She'd have to call Kevin. She tried to make herself walk slowly to Brid's house and say calmly that she'd told Kevin she'd call at this time, but that she'd reverse the charges, like it was normal she was doing it from here instead of her parents'.

"Fine then," Brid said. She was standing behind the counter at the convenience store, being oh so pleasant to an American couple who were buying candy and soft drinks.

"Isn't it great for you the weather broke?" she said, smiling. Kathleen saw she'd spent a fortune at the dentist.

"Oh, we didn't come to Ireland for the weather, or the food. It's the spirit of the people," the woman said. She was wearing a turquoise running suit and her husband had an identical one in teal. They both wore immaculate white sneakers. Trainers, they were called in Ireland, Kathleen remembered.

When she heard Kevin's voice she burst into tears.

"I suppose I could tell them they have to pay for it, but, oh, Kevin, the thought of it kills me."

"No, no, I understand," he said.

"Only, how will I get the money?"

"Not a problem. Put it on the Visa. Tell Brid the girls gave you a certain sum of money and you deposited it in your bank in America."

"Brid would never believe me. She'd know something was up. I'd never hear the end of it. Isn't there anything else? Couldn't we borrow money off the Visa?"

"Go see Martin Cunningham in the Ennis bank. Tell him you need five hundred pounds off the Visa."

"What'll he think I need it for? He'll think I need to go to England for an abortion."

"He'll think no such thing, Kathleen. Besides, what do you care what he thinks?"

"He'd have it all over town."

"Of course he won't, he's a professional. Don't make it a problem, baby."

"Don't you call me baby. Ever ever again."

"Don't you be chewing out my guts because your friends let you down. I'm on your side, remember? I'll be with you in two days. I should have known better than to let you loose in the world on your own."

Her palms felt moist the way they used to all the time before she had the baby. She wondered if they'd feel like that all the time now. She kept walking up and down the sidewalk in front of the bank, then she realized she was looking conspicuous. She walked in and walked up to Martin Cunningham's desk.

"Well, Kathleen, aren't you a sight for sore eyes? How long are you home for?"

"Two weeks," she said, and she was blushing. "Only, you see, Mr. Cunningham, Kevin's coming next week and I'm afraid I've overspent what he gave me to tide me over. I'm just off the phone with him, he said I could get a cash advance on the Visa."

"You can, of course," he said. "Just hand it over, said the dodo."

She had no idea what he meant by that dodo bit. She was worried that the lie came to her so easily.

He took the card and came back with a slip for her to sign. Then he went away again and came back with five hundred pounds.

"Anything else we could be doing for you?"

"No, you're grand," she said. "Thanks."

She ran out the door before she could start worrying that he was looking at her funny.

As she drove home, she wondered how they'd make the money up. They just made it month to month, and they were careful. Maybe it meant they couldn't come over again at Christmas. Or maybe she'd get another job. Kevin was always saying she could make more money somewhere else. With her looks and her way with people. She was getting to be known in town; people knew her from church, and with the singing in Harrigan's.

She'd taken Jimmy's car and she left it in front of the B & B. Slowly, she walked the half mile to her parents' house. The nausea that began when she thought of the Visa bill grew when she smelt the heavy smell of the tomato sauce. She couldn't bear the thought of eating it. She knew what would happen. She'd walk into the kitchen and they'd give her a piece of bread dipped in the sauce. She'd cut it up into small pieces with a knife and fork and eat it slowly, piece by piece. When they asked her how it was, she'd tell them it was fantastic.

---

1. Why doesn't Kathleen like to hear Kevin say, "Your mother has to understand you're not the same girl she put on the plane five years ago"? Why does Kathleen hope "it wasn't true"?
2. Why is Kathleen ashamed of the joy she feels when she realizes that she will have the day to herself?
3. By the end of the story, why will Kathleen not tolerate being called baby?
4. What does Kathleen understand about herself when she decides to tell her friends that the tomato sauce is "fantastic"?

ROHINTON MISTRY (1952–) was born in Bombay (now Mumbai), India, and immigrated to Canada in his early twenties. His first book, *Tales from Firozsha Baag* (1987), was published in the United States under the title *Swimming Lessons and Other Stories from Firozsha Baag*. The interrelated stories of the volume feature the mostly Parsi inhabitants of a deteriorating apartment building in Bombay. Critics heaped generous praise on Mistry's debut work for its rich detail and sharply rendered characters. Mistry's novels include *Such a Long Journey* (1991), which won the Governor General's Award for best fiction; *A Fine Balance: A Novel* (1996); and *Family Matters* (2002). *A Fine Balance* has invited critical comparisons with Leo Tolstoy, Charles Dickens, and Salman Rushdie; it won the Los Angeles Times Book Prize for fiction as well as the Commonwealth Writers' Prize.

The Collectors

1

When Dr. Burjor Mody was transferred from Mysore to assume the principalship of the Bombay Veterinary College, he moved into Firozsha Baag with his wife and son Pesi. They occupied the vacant flat on the third floor of C Block, next to the Bulsara family.

Dr. Mody did not know it then, but he would be seeing a lot of Jehangir, the Bulsara boy; the boy who sat silent and brooding, every evening, watching the others at play, and called *chaarikhao* by them—quite unfairly, since he never tattled or told tales—(Dr. Mody would call him, affectionately, the observer of C Block). And Dr. Mody did not know this, either, at the time of moving, that Jehangir Bulsara's visits at ten a.m. every Sunday would become a source of profound joy for himself. Or that just when he would think he had found someone to share his hobby with, someone to mitigate the perpetual disappointment about his son Pesi, he would lose his precious Spanish dancing lady stamp and renounce Jehangir's friendship, both in quick succession. And then two years later, he himself would—but *that* is never knowable.

Soon after moving in, Dr. Burjor Mody became the pride of the Parsis in C Block. C Block, like the rest of Firozsha Baag, had a surfeit of low-paid bank clerks and bookkeepers, and the arrival of Dr. Mody permitted them to feel a little better about themselves. More importantly, in A Block lived a prominent priest, and B Block boasted a chartered accountant. Now C Block had a voice in Baag matters as important as the others did.

While C Block went about its routine business, confirming and authenticating the sturdiness of the object of their pride, the doctor's big-boned son Pesi established himself as leader of the rowdier elements among the Baag's ten-to-sixteen population. For Pesi, too, it was routine business; he was following a course he had mapped out for himself ever since the family began moving from city to city on the whims and megrims of his father's employer, the government.

To account for Pesi's success was the fact of his brutish strength. But he was also the practitioner of a number of minor talents which appealed to the crowd where he would be leader. The one no doubt complemented the other, the talents serving to dissemble the brutish qualifier of strength, and the brutish strength encouraging the crowd to perceive the appeal of his talents.

Hawking, for instance, was one of them. Pesi could summon up prodigious quantities of phlegm at will, accompanied by sounds such as the boys had seldom heard except in accomplished adults: deep, throaty, rasping, resonating rolls which culminated in a pthoo, with the impressive trophy landing in the dust at their feet, its size leaving them all slightly envious. Pesi could also break wind that sounded like questions, exclamations, fragments of the chromatic scale, and clarion calls, while the others sniffed and discussed the merits of pungency versus tonality. This ability earned him the appellation of Pesi *paad-maroo*, and he wore the sobriquet with pride.

Perhaps his single most important talent was his ability to improvise. The peculiarities of a locale were the raw material for his inventions. In Firozsha Baag, behind the three buildings, or blocks, as they were called, were spacious yards shared by all three blocks. These yards planted in Pesi's fecund mind the seed from which grew a new game: stoning-the-cats.

Till the arrival of the Mody family the yards were home for stray and happy felines, well fed on scraps and leftovers disgorged regularly as clockwork, after mealtimes, by the three blocks. The ground floors were the only ones who refrained. They voiced their protests in a periodic cycle of reasoning, pleading, and screaming of obscenities, because the garbage collected outside their windows where the cats took up permanent residency, miaowing, feasting, and caterwauling day and night. If the cascade of food was more than the cats could devour, the remainder fell to the fortune of the rats. Finally, flies and insects buzzed and hovered over the dregs, little pools of pulses and curries fermenting and frothing, till the *kuchrawalli* came next morning and swept it all away.

The backyards of Firozsha Baag constituted its squalid underbelly. And this would be the scenario for stoning-the-cats, Pesi decided. But there was one hitch: the backyards were off limits to the boys. The only way in was through the *kuchrawalli*'s little shack standing beyond A Block, where her huge ferocious dog, tied to the gate, kept the boys at bay. So Pesi decreed that the boys gather at the rear windows of their homes, preferably at a time of day when the adults were scarce, with the fathers away at work and the mothers not yet finished with their afternoon naps. Each boy brought a pile of small stones and took turns, chucking three stones each. The game could just as easily have been stoning-the-rats; but stoned rats quietly walked away to safety, whereas the yowls of cats provided primal satisfaction and verified direct hits: no yowl, no point.

The game added to Pesi's popularity—he called it a howling success. But the parents (except the ground floor) complained to Dr. Mody about his son instigating their children to torment poor dumb and helpless creatures. For a veterinarian's son to harass animals was shameful, they said.

As might be supposed, Pesi was the despair of his parents. Over the years Dr. Mody had become inured to the initial embarrassment in each new place they moved to. The routine was familiar: first, a spate of complaints from indignant parents claiming their sons *bugree nay dhoor thai gaya*—were corrupted to become useless as dust; next, the protestations giving way to sympathy when the neighbours saw that Pesi was the worm in the Modys' mango.

And so it was in Firozsha Baag. After the furor about stoning-the-cats had died down, the people of the Baag liked Dr. Mody more than ever. He earned their respect for the initiative he took in Baag matters, dealing with the management for things like broken lifts, leaking water tanks, crumbling plaster, and faulty wiring. It was at his urging that the massive iron gate, set in the stone wall which ran all around the buildings, compound, and backyards, was repaired, and a watchman installed to stop beggars and riffraff. (And although Dr. Mody would be dead by the time of the *Shiv Sena* riots, the tenants would remember him for the gate which would keep out the rampaging mobs.) When the Bombay municipality tried to appropriate a section of Baag property for its road-widening scheme, Dr. Mody was in the forefront of the battle, winning a compromise whereby the Baag only lost half the proposed area. But the Baag's esteem did nothing to lighten the despair for Pesi that hung around the doctor.

At the birth of his son, Dr. Mody had deliberated long and hard about the naming. Peshotan, in the Persian epic *Shah-Nameh*, was the brother of the great Asfandyar, and a noble general, lover of art and learning, and man of wise counsel. Dr. Mody had decided his son would play the violin, acquire the best from the cultures of East and West, thrill to the words of Tagore and Shakespeare, appreciate Mozart and Indian ragas; and one day, at the proper moment, he would introduce him to his dearest activity, stamp collecting.

But the years passed in their own way. Fate denied fruition to all of Dr. Mody's plans; and when he talked about stamps, Pesi laughed and mocked his beloved hobby. This was the point at which, hurt and confused, he surrendered his son to whatever destiny was in store. A perpetual grief entered to occupy the void left behind after the aspirations for his son were evicted.

The weight of grief was heaviest around Dr. Mody when he returned from work in the evenings. As the car turned into the compound he usually saw Pesi before Pesi saw him, in scenes which made him despair, scenes in which his son was abusing someone, fighting, or making lewd gestures.

But Dr. Mody was careful not to make a public spectacle of his despair. While the car made its way sluggishly over the uneven flagstones of the compound, the boys would stand back and wave him through. With his droll comments and jovial countenance he was welcome to disrupt their play, unlike two other car owners of Firozsha Baag: the priest in A Block and the chartered accountant in B who habitually berated, from inside their vehicles, the sons of bank clerks and bookkeepers for blocking the driveway with their games. Their well-worn curses had become so predictable and ineffective that sometimes the boys chanted gleefully, in unison with their nemeses: "Worse than *saala* animals!" or "*junglee* dogs-cats have more sense!" or "you *sataans* ever have any lesson *paani* to do or not!"

There was one boy who always stayed apart from his peers—the Bulsara boy, from the family next door to the Modys. Jehangir sat on the stone steps every evening while the gentle land breezes, drying and cooling the sweaty skins of the boys at play, blew out to sea. He sat alone through the long dusk, a source of discomfiture to the others. They resented his melancholy, watching presence.

Dr. Mody noticed Jehangir, too, on the stone steps of C Block, the delicate boy with the build much too slight for his age. Next to a hulk like Pesi he was diminutive, but things other than size underlined his frail looks: he had slender hands, and forearms with fine downy hair. And while facial fuzz was incipient in most boys of his age (and Pesi was positively hirsute), Jehangir's chin and upper lip were smooth as a young woman's. But it pleased Dr. Mody to see him evening after evening. The quiet contemplation of the boy on the steps and the noise and activity of the others at play came together in the kind of balance that Dr. Mody was always looking for and was quick to appreciate.

Jehangir, in his turn, observed the burly Dr. Mody closely as he walked past him each evening. When he approached the steps after parking his car, Jehangir would say "*Sahibji*" in greeting, and smile wanly. He saw that despite Dr. Mody's constant jocularity there was something painfully empty about his eyes. He noticed the peculiar way he scratched the greyish red patches of psoriasis on his elbows, both elbows simultaneously, by folding his arms across his chest. Sometimes Jehangir would arise from the stone steps and the two would go up together to the third floor. Dr. Mody asked him once, "You don't like playing with the other boys? You just sit and watch them?" The boy shook his head and blushed, and Dr. Mody did not bring up the matter after that.

Gradually, a friendship of sorts grew between the two. Jehangir touched a chord inside the doctor which had lain silent for much too long. Now affection for the boy developed and started to linger around the region hitherto occupied by grief bearing Pesi's name.

2

One evening, while Jehangir sat on the stone steps waiting for Dr. Mody's car to arrive, Pesi was organizing a game of *naargolio*. He divided the boys into two teams, then discovered he was one short. He beckoned to Jehangir, who said he did not want to play. Scowling, Pesi handed the ball to one of the others and walked over to him. He grabbed his collar with both hands, jerking him to his feet. *"Arré choosya!"* he yelled, "want a pasting?" and began dragging him by the collar to where the boys had piled up the seven flat stones for *naargolio*.

At that instant, Dr. Mody's car turned into the compound, and he spied his son in one of those scenes which could provoke despair. But today the despair was swept aside by rage when he saw that Pesi's victim was the gentle and quiet Jehangir Bulsara. He left the car in the middle of the compound with the motor running. Anger glinted in his eyes. He kicked over the pile of seven flat stones as he walked blindly towards Pesi who, having seen his father, had released Jehangir. He had been caught by his father often enough to know that it was best to stand and wait. Jehangir, meanwhile, tried to keep back the tears.

Dr. Mody stopped before his son and slapped him hard, once on each cheek, with the front and back of his right hand. He waited, as if debating whether that was enough, then put his arm around Jehangir and led him to the car.

He drove to his parking spot. By now, Jehangir had control of his tears, and they walked to the steps of C Block. The lift was out of order. They climbed the stairs to the third floor and knocked. He waited with Jehangir.

Jehangir's mother came to the door. "*Sahibji*, Dr. Mody," she said, a short, middle-aged woman, very prim, whose hair was always in a bun. Never without a *mathoobanoo*, she could do wonderful things with that square of fine white cloth which was tied and knotted to sit like a cap on her head, snugly packeting the bun. In the evenings, after the household chores were done, she removed the *mathoobanoo* and wore it in a more conventional manner, like a scarf.

"*Sahibji*," she said, then noticed her son's tear-stained face. "*Arré*, Jehangoo, what happened, who made you cry?" Her hand flew automatically to the *mathoobanoo*, tugging and adjusting it as she did whenever she was concerned or agitated.

To save the boy embarrassment, Dr. Mody intervened: "Go, wash your face while I talk to your mother." Jehangir went inside, and Dr. Mody told her briefly about what had happened. "Why does he not play with the other boys?" he asked finally.

"Dr. Mody, what to say. The boy never wants even to go out. *Khoedai salaamat raakhé*, wants to sit at home all the time and read storybooks. Even this little time in the evening he goes because I force him and tell him he will not grow tall without fresh air. Every week he brings new-new storybooks from school. First, school library would allow only one book per week. But he went to Father Gonzalves who is in charge of library and got special permission for two books. God knows why he gave it."

"But reading is good, Mrs. Bulsara."

"I know, I know, but a mania like this, all the time?"

"Some boys are outdoor types, some are indoor types. You shouldn't worry about Jehangir, he is a very good boy. Look at my Pesi, now there is a case for worry," he said, meaning to reassure her.

"No, no. You mustn't say that. Be patient, *Khoedai* is great," said Mrs. Bulsara, consoling him instead. Jehangir returned, his eyes slightly red but dry. While washing his face he had wet a lock of his hair which hung down over his forehead.

"Ah, here comes my indoor champion," smiled Dr. Mody, and patted Jehangir's shoulder, brushing back the lock of hair. Jehangir did not understand, but grinned anyway; the doctor's joviality was infectious. Dr. Mody turned again to the mother. "Send him to my house on Sunday at ten o'clock. We will have a little talk."

After Dr. Mody left, Jehangir's mother told him how lucky he was that someone as important and learned as Burjor Uncle was taking an interest in him. Privately, she hoped he would encourage the boy towards a more all-rounded approach to life and to the things other boys did. And when Sunday came she sent Jehangir off to Dr. Mody's promptly at ten.

Dr. Mody was taking his bath, and Mrs. Mody opened the door. She was a dour-faced woman, spare and lean—the opposite of her husband in appearance and disposition, yet retaining some quality from long ago which suggested that it had not always been so. Jehangir had never crossed her path save when she was exchanging civilities with his mother, while making purchases out by the stairs from the vegetablewalla or fruitwalla.

Not expecting Jehangir's visit, Mrs. Mody stood blocking the doorway and said: "Yes?" Meaning, what nuisance now?

"Burjor Uncle asked me to come at ten o'clock."

"Asked you to come at ten o'clock? What for?"

"He just said to come at ten o'clock."

Grudgingly, Mrs. Mody stepped aside. "Come in then. Sit down there." And she indicated the specific chair she wanted him to occupy, muttering something about a *baap* who had time for strangers' children but not for his own son.

Jehangir sat in what must have been the most uncomfortable chair in the room. This was his first time inside the Modys' flat, and he looked around with curiosity. But his gaze was quickly restricted to the area of the floor directly in front of him when he realized that he was the object of Mrs. Mody's watchfulness.

Minutes ticked by under her vigilant eye. Jehangir was grateful when Dr. Mody emerged from the bedroom. Being Sunday, he had eschewed his usual khaki half pants for loose and comfortable white pyjamas. His *sudra* hung out over it, and he strode vigorously, feet encased in a huge pair of *sapaat*. He smiled at Jehangir, who happily noted the crow's-feet appearing at the corners of his eyes. He was ushered into Dr. Mody's room, and man and boy both seemed glad to escape the surveillance of the woman.

The chairs were more comfortable in Dr. Mody's room. They sat at his desk and Dr. Mody opened a drawer to take out a large book.

"This was the first stamp album I ever had," said Dr. Mody. "It was given to me by my Nusserwanji Uncle when I was your age. All the pages were empty." He began turning them. They were covered with stamps, each a feast of colour and design. He talked as he turned the pages, and Jehangir watched and listened, glancing at the stamps flying past, at Dr. Mody's face, then at the stamps again.

Dr. Mody spoke not in his usual booming, jovial tones but softly, in a low voice charged with inspiration. The stamps whizzed by, and his speech was gently underscored by the rustle of the heavily laden pages that seemed to turn of their own volition in the quiet room. (Jehangir would remember this peculiar rustle when one day, older, he'd stand alone in this very room, silent now forever, and turn the pages of Nusserwanji Uncle's album.) Jehangir watched and listened. It was as though a mask had descended over Dr. Mody, a faraway look upon his face, and a shining in the eyes which heretofore Jehangir had only seen sad with despair or glinting with anger or just plain and empty, belying his constant drollery. Jehangir watched, and listened to the euphonious voice hinting at wondrous things and promises and dreams.

The album on the desk, able to produce such changes in Dr. Mody, now worked its magic through him upon the boy. Jehangir, watching and listening, fascinated, tried to read the names of the countries at the top of the pages as they sped by: Antigua . . . Australia . . . Belgium . . . Bhutan . . . Bulgaria . . . and on through to Malta and Mauritius . . . Romania and Russia . . . Togo and Tonga . . . and a final blur through which he caught Yugoslavia and Zanzibar.

"Can I see it again?" he asked, and Dr. Mody handed the album to him.

"So what do you think? Do you want to be a collector?"

Jehangir nodded eagerly and Dr. Mody laughed. "When Nusserwanji Uncle showed me his collection I felt just like that. I'll tell your mother what to buy for you to get you started. Bring it here next Sunday, same time."

And next Sunday Jehangir was ready at nine. But he waited by his door with a Stamp Album For Beginners and a packet of 100 Assorted Stamps—All Countries. Going too early would mean sitting under the baleful eyes of Mrs. Mody.

Ten o'clock struck and the clock's tenth bong was echoed by the Modys' door chimes. Mrs. Mody was expecting him this time and did not block the doorway. Wordlessly, she beckoned him in. Burjor Uncle was ready, too, and came out almost immediately to rescue him from her arena.

"Let's see what you've got there," he said when they were in his room. They removed the cellophane wrapper, and while they worked Dr. Mody enjoyed himself as much as the boy. His deepest wish appeared to be coming true: he had at last found someone to share his hobby with. He could not have hoped for a finer neophyte than Jehangir. His young recruit was so quick to learn how to identify and sort stamps by countries, learn the different currencies, spot watermarks. Already he was skilfully folding and moistening the little hinges and mounting the stamps as neatly as the teacher.

When it was almost time to leave, Jehangir asked if he could examine again Nusserwanji Uncle's album, the one he had seen last Sunday. But Burjor Uncle led him instead to a cupboard in the corner of the room. "Since you enjoy looking at my stamps, let me show you what I have here." He unlocked its doors.

Each of the cupboard's four shelves was piled with biscuit tins and sweet tins: round, oval, rectangular, square. It puzzled Jehangir: all this bore the unmistakable stamp of the worthless hoardings of senility, and did not seem at all like Burjor Uncle. But Burjor Uncle reached out for a box at random and showed him inside. It was chockfull of stamps! Jehangir's mouth fell open. Then he gaped at the shelves, and Burjor Uncle laughed. "Yes, all these tins are full of stamps. And that big cardboard box at the bottom contains six new albums, all empty."

Jehangir quickly tried to assign a number in his mind to the stamps in the containers of Maghanlal Biscuitwalla and Lokmanji Mithaiwalla, to all of the stamps in the round tins and the oval tins, the square ones and the oblong ones. He failed.

Once again Dr. Mody laughed at the boy's wonderment. "A lot of stamps. And they took me a lot of years to collect. Of course, I am lucky I have many contacts in foreign countries. Because of my job, I meet the experts from abroad who are invited by the Indian government. When I tell them about my hobby they send me stamps from their countries. But no time to sort them, so I pack them in boxes. One day, after I retire, I will spend all my time with my stamps." He paused, and shut the cupboard doors. "So what you have to do now is start making lots of friends, tell them about your hobby. If they also collect, you can exchange duplicates with them. If they don't, you can still ask them for all the envelopes they may be throwing away with stamps on them. You do something for them, they will do something for you. Your collection will grow depending on how smart you are."

He hesitated, and opened the cupboard again. Then he changed his mind and shut it—it wasn't yet time for the Spanish dancing lady stamp.

3

On the pavement outside St. Xavier's Boys School, not far from the ornate iron gates, stood two variety stalls. They were the stalls of *Patla Babu* and *Jhaaria Babu*. Their real names were never known. Nor was known the exact source of the schoolboy inspiration that named them thus, many years ago, after their respective thinness and fatness.

Before the schoolboys arrived in the morning, the two would unpack their cases and set up the displays, beating the beggars to the choice positions. Occasionally, there were disputes if someone's space was violated. The beggars did not harbour great hopes for alms from schoolboys but they stood there, nonetheless, like mute lessons in realism and the harshness of life. Their patience was rewarded when they raided the dustbins after breaks and lunches.

At the end of the school day the pavement community packed up. The beggars shuffled off into the approaching dark, *Patla Babu* went home with his cases, and *Jhaaria Babu* slept near the school gate under a large tree to whose trunk he chained his boxes during the night.

The two sold a variety of nondescript objects and comestibles, uninteresting to any save the eyes and stomachs of schoolboys: *supari*, A-1 chewing gum (which, in a most ungumlike manner, would, after a while, dissolve in one's mouth), *jeeragoli*, marbles, tops, *aampapud* during the mango season, pens, Camel Ink, pencils, rulers, and stamps in little cellophane packets.

Patla Babu and *Jhaaria Babu* lost some of their goods regularly due to theft. This was inevitable when doing business outside a large school like St. Xavier's, with a population as varied as its was. The loss was an operating expense stoically accepted, like the success or failure of the monsoons, and they never complained to the school authorities or held it against the boys. Besides, business was good despite the losses: insignificant items like a packet of *jeeragoli* worth ten paise, or a marble of the kind that sold three for five paise. More often than not, the stealing went on for the excitement of it, out of bravado or on a dare. It was called "flicking" and was done without any malice towards *Patla* and *Jhaaria*.

Foremost among the flickers was a boy in Jehangir's class called Eric D'Souza. A tall, lanky fellow who had been suspended a couple of times, he had had to repeat the year on two occasions, and held out the promise of more repetitions. Eric also had the reputation of doing things inside his half pants under cover of his desk. In a class of fifty boys it was easy to go unobserved by the teacher, and only his immediate neighbours could see the ecstasy on his face and the vigorous back and forth movement of his hand. When he grinned at them they looked away, pretending not to have noticed anything.

Jehangir sat far from Eric and knew of his habits only by hearsay. He was oblivious to Eric's eye which had been on him for quite a while. In fact, Eric found Jehangir's delicate hands and fingers, his smooth legs and thighs very desirable. In class he gazed for hours, longingly, at the girlish face, curly hair, long eyelashes.

Jehangir and Eric finally got acquainted one day when the class filed out for games period. Eric had been made to kneel down by the door for coming late and disturbing the class, and Jehangir found himself next to him as he stood in line. From his kneeling position Eric observed the smooth thighs emerging from the half pants (half pants was the school uniform requirement), winked at him and, unhindered by his underwear, inserted a pencil up the pant leg. He tickled Jehangir's genitals seductively with the eraser end, expertly, then withdrew it. Jehangir feigned a giggle, too shocked to say anything. The line started to move for the playground.

Shortly after this incident, Eric approached Jehangir during breaktime. He had heard that Jehangir was desperate to acquire stamps.

"*Arré* man, I can get you stamps, whatever kind you want," he said.

Jehangir stopped. He had been slightly confused ever since the pass with the pencil; Eric frightened him a little with his curious habits and forbidden knowledge. But it had not been easy to accumulate stamps. Sundays with Burjor Uncle continued to be as fascinating as the first. He wished he had new stamps to show—the stasis of his collection might be misinterpreted as lack of interest. He asked Eric: "Ya? You want to exchange?"

"No *yaar*, I don't collect. But I'll get them for you. As a favour, man."

"Ya? What kind do you have?"

"I don't have, man. Come on with me to *Patla* and *Jhaaria*, just show me which ones you want. I'll flick them for you."

Jehangir hesitated. Eric put his arm around him: "C'mon man, what you scared for, I'll flick. You just show me and go away." Jehangir pictured the stamps on display in cellophane wrappers: how well they would add to his collection. He imagined album pages bare no more but covered with exquisite stamps, each one mounted carefully and correctly, with a hinge, as Burjor Uncle had showed him to.

They went outside, Eric's arm still around him. Crowds of schoolboys were gathered around the two stalls. A multitude of groping, exploring hands handled the merchandise and browsed absorbedly, a multitude that was a prerequisite for flicking to begin. Jehangir showed Eric the individually wrapped stamps he wanted and moved away. In a few minutes Eric joined him triumphantly.

"Got them?"

"Ya ya. But come inside. He could be watching, man."

Jehangir was thrilled. Eric asked, "You want more or what?"

"Sure," said Jehangir.

"But not today. On Friday. If you do me a favour in visual period on Thursday."

Jehangir's pulse speeded slightly—visual period, with its darkened hall and projector, and the intimacy created by the teacher's policing abilities temporarily suspended. He remembered Eric's pencil. The cellophane-wrapped stamp packets rustled and crackled in his hand.

And there was the promise of more. There had been nothing unpleasant about the pencil. In fact it had felt quite, well, exciting. He agreed to Eric's proposal.

On Thursday, the class lined up to go to the Visual Hall. Eric stood behind Jehangir to ensure their seats would be together.

When the room was dark he put his hand on Jehangir's thigh and began caressing it. He took Jehangir's hand and placed it on his crotch. It lay there inert. Impatient, he whispered, "Do it, man, c'mon!" But Jehangir's lacklustre stroking was highly unsatisfactory. Eric arrested the hand, reached inside his pants and said, "OK, hold it tight and rub it like this." He encircled Jehangir's hand with his to show him how. When Jehangir had attained the right pressure and speed he released his own hand to lean back and sigh contentedly. Shortly, Jehangir felt a warm stickiness fill his palm and fingers, and the hardness he held in his hand grew flaccid.

Eric shook off the hand. Jehangir wiped his palm with his hanky. Eric borrowed the hanky to wipe himself. "Want me to do it for you?" he asked. But Jehangir declined. He was thinking of his hanky. The odour was interesting, not unpleasant at all, but he would have to find some way of cleaning it before his mother found it.

The following day, Eric presented him with more stamps. Next Thursday's assignation was also fixed.

And on Sunday Jehangir went to see Dr. Mody at ten o'clock. The wife let him in, muttering something under her breath about being bothered by inconsiderate people on the one day that the family could be together.

Dr. Mody's delight at the new stamps fulfilled Jehangir's every expectation: "Wonderful, wonderful! Where did you get them all? No, no, forget it, don't tell me. You will think I'm trying to learn your tricks. I already have enough stamps to keep me busy in my retirement. Ha! ha!"

After the new stamps had been examined and sorted Dr. Mody said, "Today, as a reward for your enterprise, I'm going to show you a stamp you've never seen before." From the cupboard of biscuit and sweet tins he took a small satin-covered box of the type in which rings or bracelets are kept. He opened it and, without removing the stamp from inside, placed it on the desk.

The stamp said España Correos at the bottom and its denomination was noted in the top left corner: 3 PTAS. The face of the stamp featured a flamenco dancer in the most exquisite detail and colour. But it was something in the woman's countenance, a look, an ineffable sparkle he saw in her eyes, which so captivated Jehangir.

Wordlessly, he studied the stamp. Dr. Mody waited restlessly as the seconds ticked by. He kept fidgeting till the little satin-covered box was shut and back in his hands, then said, "So you like the Spanish dancing lady. Everyone who sees it likes it. Even my wife who is not interested in stamp collecting thought it was beautiful. When I retire I can spend more time with the Spanish dancing lady. And all my other stamps." He relaxed once the stamp was locked again in the cupboard.

Jehangir left, carrying that vision of the Spanish dancer in his head. He tried to imagine the stamp inhabiting the pages of his album, to greet him every time he opened it, with the wonderful sparkle in her eyes. He shut the door behind him and immediately, as though to obliterate his covetous fantasy, loud voices rose inside the flat.

He heard Mrs. Mody's, shrill in argument, and the doctor's, beseeching her not to yell lest the neighbours would hear. Pesi's name was mentioned several times in the quarrel that ensued, and accusations of neglect, and something about the terrible affliction on a son of an unloving father. The voices followed Jehangir as he hurried past the inquiring eyes of his mother, till he reached the bedroom at the other end of the flat and shut the door.

When the school week started, Jehangir found himself looking forward to Thursday. His pulse was racing with excitement when visual period came. To save his hanky this time he kept some paper at hand.

Eric did not have to provide much guidance. Jehangir discovered he could control Eric's reactions with variations in speed, pressure, and grip. When it was over and Eric offered to do it to him, he did not refuse.

The weeks sped by and Jehangir's collection continued to grow, visual period by visual period. Eric's and his masturbatory partnership was whispered about in class, earning the pair the title of *moothya-maroo*. He accompanied Eric on the flicking forays, helping to swell the milling crowd and add to the browsing hands. Then he grew bolder, studied Eric's methods, and flicked a few stamps himself.

But this smooth course of stamp collecting was about to end. *Patla Babu* and *Jhaaria Babu* broke their long tradition of silence and complained to the school. Unlike marbles and *supari*, it was not a question of a few paise a day. When Eric and Jehangir struck, their haul could be totalled in rupees reaching double digits; the loss was serious enough to make the *Babus* worry about their survival.

The school assigned the case to the head prefect to investigate. He was an ambitious boy, always snooping around, and was also a member of the school debating team and the Road Safety Patrol. Shortly after the complaint was made he marched into Jehangir's class one afternoon just after lunch break, before the teacher returned, and made what sounded very much like one of his debating speeches: "Two boys in this class have been stealing stamps from *Patla Babu* and *Jhaaria Babu* for the past several weeks. You may ask: who are those boys? No need for names. They know who they are and I know who they are, and I am asking them to return the stamps to me tomorrow. There will be no punishment if this is done. The *Babus* just want their stamps back. But if the missing stamps are not returned, the names will be reported to the principal and to the police. It is up to the two boys."

Jehangir tried hard to appear normal. He was racked with trepidation, and looked to the unperturbed Eric for guidance. But Eric ignored him. The head prefect left amidst mock applause from the class.

After school, Eric turned surly. Gone was the tender, cajoling manner he reserved for Jehangir, and he said nastily: "You better bring back all those fucking stamps tomorrow." Jehangir, of course, agreed. There was no trouble with the prefect or the school after the stamps were returned.

But Jehangir's collection shrunk pitiably overnight. He slept badly the entire week, worried about explaining to Burjor Uncle the sudden disappearance of the bulk of his collection. His mother assumed the dark rings around his eyes were due to too much reading and not enough fresh air. The thought of stamps or of *Patla Babu* or *Jhaaria Babu* brought an emptiness to his stomach and a bitter taste to his mouth. A general sense of ill-being took possession of him.

He went to see Burjor Uncle on Sunday, leaving behind his stamp album. Mrs. Mody opened the door and turned away silently. She appeared to be in a black rage, which exacerbated Jehangir's own feelings of guilt and shame.

He explained to Burjor Uncle that he had not bothered to bring his album because he had acquired no new stamps since last Sunday, and also, he was not well and would not stay for long.

Dr. Mody was concerned about the boy, so nervous and uneasy; he put it down to his feeling unwell. They looked at some stamps Dr. Mody had received last week from his colleagues abroad. Then Jehangir said he'd better leave.

"But you *must* see the Spanish dancing lady before you go. Maybe she will help you feel better. Ha! ha!" and Dr. Mody rose to go to the cupboard for the stamp. Its viewing at the end of each Sunday's session had acquired the significance of an esoteric ritual.

From the next room Mrs. Mody screeched: "Burjorji! Come here at once!" He made a wry face at Jehangir and hurried out.

In the next room, all the vehemence of Mrs. Mody's black rage of that morning poured out upon Dr. Mody: "It has reached the limit now! No time for your own son and Sunday after Sunday sitting with some stranger! What does he have that your own son does not? Are you a *baap* or what? No wonder Pesi has become this way! How can I blame the boy when his own *baap* takes no interest . . ."

"Shh! The boy is in the next room! What do you want, that all the neighbours hear your screaming?"

"I don't care! Let them hear! You think they don't know already? You think you are . . ."

Mrs. Bulsara next door listened intently. Suddenly, she realized that Jehangir was in there. Listening from one's own house was one thing—hearing a quarrel from inside the quarrellers' house was another. It made feigning ignorance very difficult.

She rang the Modys' doorbell and waited, adjusting her *mathoobanoo*. Dr. Mody came to the door.

"Burjorji, forgive me for disturbing your stamping and collecting work with Jehangir. But I must take him away. Guests have arrived unexpectedly. Jehangir must go to the Irani, we need cold drinks."

"That's okay, he can come next Sunday." Then added, "He *must* come next Sunday," and noted with satisfaction the frustrated turning away of Mrs. Mody who waited out of sight of the doorway. "Jehangir! Your mother is calling."

Jehangir was relieved at being rescued from the turbulent waters of the Mody household. They left without further conversation, his mother tugging in embarrassment at the knots of her *mathoobanoo*.

As a result of this unfortunate outburst, a period of awkwardness between the women was unavoidable. Mrs. Mody, though far from garrulous, had never let her domestic sorrows and disappointments interfere with the civilities of neighbourly relations, which she respected and observed at all times. Now for the first time since the arrival of the Modys in Firozsha Baag these civilities experienced a hiatus.

When the *muchhiwalla* arrived next morning, instead of striking a joint deal with him as they usually did, Mrs. Mody waited till Mrs. Bulsara had finished. She stationed an eye at her peephole as he emphasized the freshness of his catch. "Look *bai*, it is *saféd paani*," he said, holding out the pomfret and squeezing it near the gills till white fluid oozed out. After Mrs. Bulsara had paid and gone, Mrs. Mody emerged, while the former took her turn at the peephole. And so it went for a few days till the awkwardness had run its course and things returned to normal.

But not so for Jehangir; on Sunday, he once again had to leave behind his sadly depleted album. To add to his uneasiness, Mrs. Mody invited him in with a greeting of "Come *bawa* come," and there was something malignant about her smile.

Dr. Mody sat at his desk, shoulders sagging, his hands dangling over the arms of the chair. The desk was bare—not a single stamp anywhere in sight, and the cupboard in the corner locked. The absence of his habitual, comfortable clutter made the room cold and cheerless. He was in low spirits; instead of the crow's-feet at the corners of his eyes were lines of distress and dejection.

"No album again?"

"No. Haven't got any new stamps yet," Jehangir smiled nervously.

Dr. Mody scratched the psoriasis on his elbows. He watched Jehangir carefully as he spoke. "Something very bad has happened to the Spanish dancing lady stamp. Look," and he displayed the satin-covered box minus its treasure. "It is missing." Half fearfully, he looked at Jehangir, afraid he would see what he did not want to. But it was inevitable. His last sentence evoked the head prefect's thundering debating-style speech of a few days ago, and the ugliness of the entire episode revisited Jehangir's features—a final ignominious postscript to Dr. Mody's loss and disillusion.

Dr. Mody shut the box. The boy's reaction, his silence, the absence of his album, confirmed his worst suspicions. More humiliatingly, it seemed his wife was right. With great sadness he rose from his chair. "I have to leave now, something urgent at the college." They parted without a word about next Sunday.

Jehangir never went back. He thought for a few days about the missing stamp and wondered what could have happened to it. Burjor Uncle was too careful to have misplaced it; besides, he never removed it from its special box. And the box was still there. But he did not resent him for concluding he had stolen it. His guilt about *Patla Babu* and *Jhaaria Babu*, about Eric and the stamps was so intense, and the punishment deriving from it so inconsequential, almost nonexistent, that he did not mind this undeserved blame. In fact, it served to equilibrate his scales of justice.

His mother questioned him the first few Sundays he stayed home. Feeble excuses about homework, and Burjor Uncle not having new stamps, and it being boring to look at the same stuff every Sunday did not satisfy her. She finally attributed his abnegation of stamps to sensitivity and a regard for the unfortunate state of the Modys' domestic affairs. It pleased her that her son was capable of such concern. She did not press him after that.

4

Pesi was no longer to be seen in Firozsha Baag. His absence brought relief to most of the parents at first, and then curiosity. Gradually, it became known that he had been sent away to a boarding school in Poona.

The boys of the Baag continued to play their games in the compound. For better or worse, the spark was lacking that lent unpredictability to those languid coastal evenings of Bombay; evenings which could so easily trap the unwary, adult or child, within a circle of lassitude and depression in which time hung heavy and suffocating.

Jehangir no longer sat on the stone steps of C Block in the evenings. He found it difficult to confront Dr. Mody day after day. Besides, the boys he used to watch at play suspected some kind of connection between Pesi's being sent away to boarding school, Jehangir's former friendship with Dr. Mody, and the emerging of Dr. Mody's constant sorrow and despair (which he had tried so hard to keep private all along, and had succeeded, but was now visible for all to see). And the boys resented Jehangir for whatever his part was in it—they bore him open antagonism.

Dr. Mody was no more the jovial figure the boys had grown to love. When his car turned into the compound in the evenings, he still waved, but no crow's-feet appeared at his eyes, no smile, no jokes.

Two years passed since the Mody family's arrival in Firozsha Baag.

In school, Jehangir was as isolated as in the Baag. Most of his effeminateness had, of late, transformed into vigorous signs of impending manhood. Eric D'Souza had been expelled for attempting to sodomize a junior boy. Jehangir had not been involved in this affair, but most of his classmates related it to the furtive activities of their callow days and the stamp flicking. *Patla Babu* and *Jhaaria Babu* had disappeared from the pavement outside St. Xavier's. The Bombay police, in a misinterpretation of the nation's mandate, *garibi hatao*—eradicate poverty, conducted periodic roundups of pavement dwellers, sweeping into their vans beggars and street vendors, cripples and alcoholics, the homeless and the hungry, and dumped them somewhere outside the city limits; when the human detritus made its way back into the city, another cleanup was scheduled. *Patla* and *Jhaaria* were snared in one of these raids, and never found their way back. Eyewitnesses said their stalls were smashed up and *Patla Babu* received a *lathi* across his forehead for trying to salvage some of his inventory. They were not seen again.

Two years passed since Jehangir's visits to Dr. Mody had ceased.

It was getting close to the time for another transfer for Dr. Mody. When the inevitable orders were received, he went to Ahmedabad to make arrangements. Mrs. Mody was to join her husband after a few days. Pesi was still in boarding school, and would stay there.

So when news arrived from Ahmedabad of Dr. Mody's death of heart failure, Mrs. Mody was alone in the flat. She went next door with the telegram and broke down.

The Bulsaras helped with all the arrangements. The body was brought to Bombay by car for a proper Parsi funeral. Pesi came from Poona for the funeral, then went back to boarding school.

The events were talked about for days afterwards, the stories spreading first in C Block, then through A and B. Commiseration for Mrs. Mody was general. The ordeal of the body during the two-day car journey from Ahmedabad was particularly horrifying, and was discussed endlessly. Embalming was not allowed according to Parsi rituals, and the body in the trunk, although packed with ice, had started to smell horribly in the heat of the Deccan Plateau which the car had had to traverse. Some hinted that this torment suffered by Dr. Mody's earthly remains was the Almighty's punishment for neglecting his duties as a father and making Mrs. Mody so unhappy. Poor Dr. Mody, they said, who never went a day without a bath and talcum powder in life, to undergo this in death. Someone even had, on good authority, a count of the number of eau de cologne bottles used by Mrs. Mody and the three occupants of the car over the course of the journey—it was the only way they could draw breath, through cologne-watered handkerchiefs. And it was also said that ever after, these four could never tolerate eau de cologne—opening a bottle was like opening the car trunk with Dr. Mody's decomposing corpse.

A year after the funeral, Mrs. Mody was still living in Firozsha Baag. Time and grief had softened her looks, and she was no longer the harsh and dour-faced woman Jehangir had seen during his first Sunday visit. She had decided to make the flat her permanent home now, and the trustees of the Baag granted her request "in view of the unfortunate circumstances."

There were some protests about this, particularly from those whose sons or daughters had been postponing marriages and families till flats became available. But the majority, out of respect for Dr. Mody's memory, agreed with the trustees' decision. Pesi continued to attend boarding school.

One day, shortly after her application had been approved by the trustees, Mrs. Mody visited Mrs. Bulsara. They sat and talked of old times, when they had first moved in, and about how pleased Dr. Mody had been to live in a Parsi colony like Firozsha Baag after years of travelling, and then the disagreements she had had with her husband over Pesi and Pesi's future; tears came to her eyes, and also to Mrs. Bulsara's, who tugged at a corner of her *mathoobanoo* to reach it to her eyes and dry them. Mrs. Mody confessed how she had hated Jehangir's Sunday visits although he was such a fine boy, because she was worried about the way poor Burjorji was neglecting Pesi: "But he could not help it. That was the way he was. Sometimes he would wish *Khoedai* had given him a daughter instead of a son. Pesi disappointed him in everything, in all his plans, and . . ." and here she burst into uncontrollable sobs.

Finally, after her tears subsided she asked, "Is Jehangir home?" He wasn't. "Would you ask him to come and see me this Sunday? At ten? Tell him I won't keep him long."

Jehangir was a bit apprehensive when his mother gave him the message. He couldn't imagine why Mrs. Mody would want to see him.

On Sunday, as he prepared to go next door, he was reminded of the Sundays with Dr. Mody, the kindly man who had befriended him, opened up a new world for him, and then repudiated him for something he had not done. He remembered the way he would scratch the greyish red patches of psoriasis on his elbows. He could still picture the sorrow on his face as, with the utmost reluctance, he had made his decision to end the friendship. Jehangir had not blamed Dr. Mody then, and he still did not; he knew how overwhelmingly the evidence had been against him, and how much that stamp had meant to Dr. Mody.

Mrs. Mody led him in by his arm: "Will you drink something?"

"No, thank you."

"Not feeling shy, are you? You always were shy." She asked him about his studies and what subjects he was taking in high school. She told him a little about Pesi, who was still in boarding school and had twice repeated the same standard. She sighed. "I asked you to come today because there is something I wanted to give you. Something of Burjor Uncle's. I thought about it for many days. Pesi is not interested, and I don't know anything about it. Will you take his collection?"

"The album in his drawer?" asked Jehangir, a little surprised.

"Everything. The album, all the boxes, everything in the cupboard. I know you will use it well. Burjor would have done the same."

Jehangir was speechless. He had stopped collecting stamps, and they no longer held the fascination they once did. Nonetheless, he was familiar with the size of the collection, and the sheer magnitude of what he was now being offered had its effect. He remembered the awe with which he had looked inside the cupboard the first time its doors had been opened before him. So many sweet tins, cardboard boxes, biscuit tins . . .

"You will take it? As a favour to me, yes?" she asked a second time, and Jehangir nodded. "You have some time today? Whenever you like, just take it." He said he would ask his mother and come back.

There was a huge, old iron trunk which lay under Jehangir's bed. It was dented in several places and the lid would not shut properly. Undisturbed for years, it had rusted peacefully beneath the bed. His mother agreed that the rags it held could be thrown away and the stamps temporarily stored in it till Jehangir organized them into albums. He emptied the trunk, wiped it out, lined it with brown paper and went next door to bring back the stamps.

Several trips later, Dr. Mody's cupboard stood empty. Jehangir looked around the room in which he had once spent so many happy hours. The desk was in exactly the same position, and the two chairs. He turned to go, almost forgetting, and went back to the desk. Yes, there it was in the drawer, Dr. Mody's first album, given him by his Nusserwanji Uncle.

He started to turn the heavily laden pages. They rustled in a peculiar way—what was it about that sound? Then he remembered: that first Sunday, and he could almost hear Dr. Mody again, the soft inspired tones speaking of promises and dreams, quite different from his usual booming, jovial voice, and that faraway look in his eyes which had once glinted with rage when Pesi had tried to bully him . . .

Mrs. Mody came into the room. He shut the album, startled: "This is the last lot." He stopped to thank her but she interrupted: "No, no. What is the thank-you for? You are doing a favour to me by taking it, you are helping me to do what Burjor would like." She took his arm. "I wanted to tell you. From the collection one stamp is missing. With the picture of the dancing lady."

"I know!" said Jehangir. "That's the one Burjor Uncle lost and thought that I . . ."

Mrs. Mody squeezed his arm which she was still holding and he fell silent. She spoke softly, but without guilt: "He did not lose it. I destroyed it." Then her eyes went moist as she watched the disbelief on his face. She wanted to say more, to explain, but could not, and clung to his arm. Finally, her voice quavering pitiably, she managed to say, "Forgive an old lady," and patted his cheek. Jehangir left in silence, suddenly feeling very ashamed.

Over the next few days, he tried to impose some order on that greatly chaotic mass of stamps. He was hoping that sooner or later his interest in philately would be rekindled. But that did not happen; the task remained futile and dry and boring. The meaningless squares of paper refused to come to life as they used to for Dr. Mody in his room every Sunday at ten o'clock. Jehangir shut the trunk and pushed it back under his bed where it had lain untroubled for so many years.

From time to time his mother reminded him about the stamps: "Do something Jehangoo, do something with them." He said he would when he felt like it and had the time; he wasn't interested for now.

Then, after several months, he pulled out the trunk again from under his bed. Mrs. Bulsara watched eagerly from a distance, not daring to interrupt with any kind of advice or encouragement: her Jehangoo was at that difficult age, she knew, when boys automatically did the exact reverse of what their parents said.

But the night before, Jehangir's sleep had been disturbed by a faint and peculiar rustling sound seeming to come from inside the trunk. His reasons for dragging it out into daylight soon became apparent to Mrs. Bulsara.

The lid was thrown back to reveal clusters of cockroaches. They tried to scuttle to safety, and he killed a few with his slipper. His mother ran up now, adding a few blows of her own *chappal*, as the creatures began quickly to disperse. Some ran under the bed into hard-to-reach corners; others sought out the trunk's deeper recesses.

A cursory examination showed that besides cockroaches, the trunk was also infested with white ants. All the albums had been ravaged. Most of the stamps which had not been destroyed outright were damaged in one way or another. They bore haphazard perforations and brown stains of the type associated with insects and household pests.

Jehangir picked up an album at random and opened it. Almost immediately, the pages started to fall to pieces in his hands. He remembered what Dr. Mody used to say: "This is my retirement hobby. I will spend my retirement with my stamps." He allowed the tattered remains of Burjor Uncle's beloved pastime to drop back slowly into the trunk.

He crouched beside the dented, rusted metal, curious that he felt no loss or pain. Why, he wondered. If anything, there was a slight sense of relief. He let his hands stray through the contents, through worthless paper scraps, through shreds of the work of so many Sunday mornings, stopping now and then to regard with detachment the bizarre patterns created by the mandibles of the insects who had feasted night after night under his bed, while he slept.

With an almost imperceptible shrug, he arose and closed the lid. It was doubtful if anything of value remained in the trunk.

---

1. Why does Dr. Mody want to share his love of stamp collecting with Jehangir?

2. Why does Mrs. Mody want Jehangir to have Dr. Mody's stamp collection, then admit to him that she destroyed the stamp of the Spanish dancing lady? Why did Mrs. Mody destroy that stamp?

3. What explains Jehanjir's slight sense of relief rather than loss or pain when he discovers that the stamp collection has been destroyed?

LORRIE MOORE (1957–) was born in Glen Falls, New York, and educated at St. Lawrence University and Cornell University, where she earned her MFA. Her first collection of stories, tellingly titled *Self-Help* (1985), allowed her to mock that all-purpose genre while considering the lives of emotionally needy and ultimately sympathetic characters. Other collections have helped to buttress Moore's reputation as a leading contemporary writer of short fiction. *Like Life* (1990) and *Birds of America* (1998) are populated by smart protagonists, usually women, who quite frequently are comic, verbal showoffs trying to mask their desperation. Winner of numerous literary prizes, including the O. Henry Award and the PEN/Malamud Award, Moore has also written several novels. She is currently a professor of English at the University of Wisconsin–Madison.

You're Ugly, Too

You had to get out of them occasionally, those Illinois towns with the funny names: Paris, Oblong, Normal. Once, when the Dow Jones dipped two hundred points, the Paris paper boasted a banner headline: NORMAL MAN MARRIES OBLONG WOMAN. They knew what was important. They did! But you had to get out once in a while, even if it was just across the border to Terre Haute, for a movie.

Outside of Paris, in the middle of a large field, was a scatter of brick buildings, a small liberal arts college with the improbable name of Hilldale-Versailles. Zoë Hendricks had been teaching American history there for three years. She taught "The Revolution and Beyond" to freshmen and sophomores, and every third semester she had the Senior Seminar for Majors, and although her student evaluations had been slipping in the last year and a half—*Professor Hendricks is often late for class and usually arrives with a cup of hot chocolate, which she offers the class sips of*—generally, the department of nine men was pleased to have her. They felt she added some needed feminine touch to the corridors—that faint trace of Obsession and sweat, the light, fast clicking of heels. Plus they had had a sex-discrimination suit, and the dean had said, well, it was time.

The situation was not easy for her, they knew. Once, at the start of last semester, she had skipped into her lecture hall singing "Getting to Know You"—both verses. At the request of the dean, the chairman had called her into his office, but did not ask her for an explanation, not really. He asked her how she was and then smiled in an avuncular way. She said, "Fine," and he studied the way she said it, her front teeth catching on the inside of her lower lip. She was almost pretty, but her face showed the strain and ambition of always having been close but not quite. There was too much effort with the eyeliner, and her earrings, worn no doubt for the drama her features lacked, were a little frightening, jutting out from the side of her head like antennae.

"I'm going out of my mind," said Zoë to her younger sister, Evan, in Manhattan. *Professor Hendricks seems to know the entire sound track to* The King and I. *Is this history?* Zoë phoned her every Tuesday.

"You always say that," said Evan, "but then you go on your trips and vacations and then you settle back into things and then you're quiet for a while and then you say you're fine, you're busy, and then after a while you say you're going crazy again, and you start all over." Evan was a part-time food designer for photo shoots. She cooked vegetables in green dye. She propped up beef stew with a bed of marbles and shopped for new kinds of silicone sprays and plastic ice cubes. She thought her life was "OK." She was living with her boyfriend of many years, who was independently wealthy and had an amusing little job in book publishing. They were five years out of college, and they lived in a luxury midtown high-rise with a balcony and access to a pool. "It's not the same as having your own pool," Evan was always sighing, as if to let Zoë know that, as with Zoë, there were still things she, Evan, had to do without.

"Illinois. It makes me sarcastic to be here," said Zoë on the phone. She used to insist it was irony, something gently layered and sophisticated, something alien to the Midwest, but her students kept calling it sarcasm, something they felt qualified to recognize, and now she had to agree. It wasn't irony. *What is your perfume?* a student once asked her. *Room freshener*, she said. She smiled, but he looked at her, unnerved.

Her students were by and large good midwesterners, spacey with estrogen from large quantities of meat and cheese. They shared their parents' suburban values; their parents had given them things, things, things. They were complacent. They had been purchased. They were armed with a healthy vagueness about anything historical or geographic. They seemed actually to know very little about anything, but they were extremely good-natured about it. "All those states in the East are so tiny and jagged and bunched up," complained one of her undergraduates the week she was lecturing on "The Turning Point of Independence: The Battle at Saratoga." "Professor Hendricks, you're from Delaware originally, right?" the student asked her.

"Maryland," corrected Zoë.

"Aw," he said, waving his hand dismissively. "New England."

Her articles—chapters toward a book called *Hearing the One About: Uses of Humor in the American Presidency*—were generally well received, though they came slowly for her. She liked her pieces to have something from every time of day in them—she didn't trust things written in the morning only—so she reread and rewrote painstakingly. No part of a day, its moods, its light, was allowed to dominate. She hung on to a piece for over a year sometimes, revising at all hours, until the entirety of a day had registered there.

The job she'd had before the one at Hilldale-Versailles had been at a small college in New Geneva, Minnesota, Land of the Dying Shopping Mall. Everyone was so blond there that brunettes were often presumed to be from foreign countries. *Just because Professor Hendricks is from Spain doesn't give her the right to be so negative about our country.* There was a general emphasis on cheerfulness. In New Geneva you weren't supposed to be critical or complain. You weren't supposed to notice that the town had overextended and that its shopping malls were raggedy and going under. You were never to say you weren't fine thank you and yourself. You were supposed to be Heidi. You were supposed to lug goat milk up the hills and not think twice. Heidi did not complain. Heidi did not do things like stand in front of the new IBM photocopier, saying, "If this fucking Xerox machine breaks on me one more time, I'm going to slit my wrists."

But now, in her second job, in her fourth year of teaching in the Midwest, Zoë was discovering something she never suspected she had: a crusty edge, brittle and pointed. Once she had pampered her students, singing them songs, letting them call her at home, even, and ask personal questions. Now she was losing sympathy. They were beginning to seem different. They were beginning to seem demanding and spoiled.

"You act," said one of her Senior Seminar students at a scheduled conference, "like your opinion is worth more than everybody else's in the class."

Zoë's eyes widened. "I *am* the teacher," she said. "I *do* get paid to act like that." She narrowed her gaze at the student, who was wearing a big leather bow in her hair, like a cowgirl in a TV ranch show. "I mean, otherwise *everybody* in the class would have little offices and office hours." *Sometimes Professor Hendricks will take up the class's time just talking about movies she's seen.* She stared at the student some more, then added, "I bet you'd like that."

"Maybe I sound whiny to you," said the girl, "but I simply want my history major to mean something."

"Well, there's your problem," said Zoë, and with a smile, she showed the student to the door. "I like your bow," she added.

Zoë lived for the mail, for the postman, that handsome blue jay, and when she got a real letter, with a real full-price stamp, from someplace else, she took it to bed with her and read it over and over. She also watched television until all hours and had her set in the bedroom, a bad sign. *Professor Hendricks has said critical things about Fawn Hall, the Catholic religion, and the whole state of Illinois. It is unbelievable.* At Christmastime she gave twenty-dollar tips to the mailman and to Jerry, the only cabbie in town, whom she had gotten to know from all her rides to and from the Terre Haute airport, and who, since he realized such rides were an extravagance, often gave her cut rates.

"I'm flying in to visit you this weekend," announced Zoë.

"I was hoping you would," said Evan. "Charlie and I are having a party for Halloween. It'll be fun."

"I have a costume already. It's a bonehead. It's this thing that looks like a giant bone going through your head."

"Great," said Evan.

"It is, it's great."

"Alls I have is my moon mask from last year and the year before. I'll probably end up getting married in it."

"Are you and Charlie getting *married*?" Foreboding filled her voice.

"Hmmmmmmnnno, not immediately."

"Don't get married."

"Why?"

"Just not yet. You're too young."

"You're only saying that because you're five years older than I am and *you're* not married."

"*I'm* not married? Oh, my God," said Zoë. "I forgot to get married."

Zoë had been out with three men since she'd come to Hilldale-Versailles. One of them was a man in the Paris municipal bureaucracy who had fixed a parking ticket she'd brought in to protest and who then asked her to coffee. At first she thought he was amazing—at last, someone who did not want Heidi! But soon she came to realize that all men, deep down, wanted Heidi. Heidi with cleavage. Heidi with outfits. The parking ticket bureaucrat soon became tired and intermittent. One cool fall day, in his snazzy, impractical convertible, when she asked him what was wrong, he said, "You would not be ill served by new clothes, you know." She wore a lot of gray-green corduroy. She had been under the impression that it brought out her eyes, those shy stars. She flicked an ant from her sleeve.

"Did you have to brush that off in the car?" he said, driving. He glanced down at his own pectorals, giving first the left, then the right, a quick survey. He was wearing a tight shirt.

"Excuse me?"

He slowed down at a yellow light and frowned. "Couldn't you have picked it up and thrown it outside?"

"The ant? It might have bitten me. I mean, what difference does it make?"

"It might have bitten you! Ha! How ridiculous! Now it's going to lay eggs in my car!"

The second guy was sweeter, lunkier, though not insensitive to certain paintings and songs, but too often, too, things he'd do or say would startle her. Once, in a restaurant, he stole the garnishes off her dinner plate and waited for her to notice. When she didn't, he finally thrust his fist across the table and said, "Look," and when he opened it, there was her parsley sprig and her orange slice, crumpled to a wad. Another time he described to her his recent trip to the Louvre. "And there I was in front of Géricault's *Raft of the Medusa*, and everyone else had wandered off, so I had my own private audience with it, all those painted, drowning bodies splayed in every direction, and there's this motion in that painting that starts at the bottom left, swirling and building, and building, and building, and going up to the right-hand corner, where there's this guy waving a flag, and on the horizon in the distance you could see this teeny tiny boat. . . ." He was breathless in the telling. She found this touching and smiled in encouragement. "A painting like that," he said, shaking his head. "It just makes you shit."

"I have to ask you something," said Evan. "I know every woman complains about not meeting men, but really, on my shoots, I meet a lot of men. And they're not all gay, either." She paused. "Not anymore."

"What are you asking?"

The third guy was a political science professor named Murray Peterson, who liked to go out on double dates with colleagues whose wives he was attracted to. Usually the wives would consent to flirt with him. Under the table sometimes there was footsie, and once there was even kneesie. Zoë and the husband would be left to their food, staring into their water glasses, chewing like goats. "Oh, Murray," said one wife, who had never finished her master's in physical therapy and wore great clothes. "You know, I know everything about you: your birthday, your license plate number. I have everything memorized. But then that's the kind of mind I have. Once at a dinner party I amazed the host by getting up and saying good-bye to every single person there, first *and* last names."

"I knew a dog who could do that," said Zoë, with her mouth full. Murray and the wife looked at her with vexed and rebuking expressions, but the husband seemed suddenly twinkling and amused. Zoë swallowed. "It was a Talking Lab, and after about ten minutes of listening to the dinner conversation this dog knew everyone's name. You could say, 'Bring this knife to Murray Peterson,' and it would."

"Really," said the wife, frowning, and Murray Peterson never called again.

"Are you seeing anyone?" said Evan. "I'm asking for a particular reason, I'm not just being like Mom."

"I'm seeing my house. I'm tending to it when it wets, when it cries, when it throws up." Zoë had bought a mint-green ranch house near campus, though now she was thinking that maybe she shouldn't have. It was hard to live in a house. She kept wandering in and out of the rooms, wondering where she had put things. She went downstairs into the basement for no reason at all except that it amused her to own a basement. It also amused her to own a tree. The day she moved in, she had tacked to her tree a small paper sign that said *Zoë's Tree.*

Her parents, in Maryland, had been very pleased that one of their children had at last been able to afford real estate, and when she closed on the house they sent her flowers with a congratulations card. Her mother had even UPS'd a box of old decorating magazines saved over the years, photographs of beautiful rooms her mother used to moon over, since there never had been any money to redecorate. It was like getting her mother's pornography, that box, inheriting her drooled-upon fantasies, the endless wish and tease that had been her life. But to her mother it was a rite of passage that pleased her. "Maybe you will get some ideas from these," she had written. And when Zoë looked at the photographs, at the bold and beautiful living rooms, she was filled with longing. Ideas and ideas of longing.

Right now Zoë's house was rather empty. The previous owner had wallpapered around the furniture, leaving strange gaps and silhouettes on the walls, and Zoë hadn't done much about that yet. She had bought furniture, then taken it back, furnishing and unfurnishing, preparing and shedding, like a womb. She had bought several plain pine chests to use as love seats or boot boxes, but they came to look to her more and more like children's coffins, so she returned them. And she had recently bought an Oriental rug for the living room, with Chinese symbols on it she didn't understand. The salesgirl had kept saying she was sure they meant *Peace* and *Eternal Life*, but when Zoë got the rug home, she worried. What if they didn't mean *Peace* and *Eternal Life*? What if they meant, say, *Bruce Springsteen*. And the more she thought about it, the more she became convinced she had a rug that said *Bruce Springsteen*, and so she returned that, too.

She had also bought a little baroque mirror for the front entryway, which she had been told, by Murray Peterson, would keep away evil spirits. The mirror, however, tended to frighten *her*, startling her with an image of a woman she never recognized. Sometimes she looked puffier and plainer than she remembered. Sometimes shifty and dark. Most times she just looked vague. *You look like someone I know*, she had been told twice in the last year by strangers in restaurants in Terre Haute. In fact, sometimes she seemed not to have a look of her own, or any look whatsoever, and it began to amaze her that her students and colleagues were able to recognize her at all. How did they know? When she walked into a room, how did she look so that they knew it was her? Like this? Did she look like this? And so she returned the mirror.

"The reason I'm asking is that I know a man I think you should meet," said Evan. "He's fun. He's straight. He's single. That's all I'm going to say."

"I think I'm too old for fun," said Zoë. She had a dark bristly hair in her chin, and she could feel it now with her finger. Perhaps when you had been without the opposite sex for too long, you began to resemble them. In an act of desperate invention, you began to grow your own. "I just want to come, wear my bonehead, visit with Charlie's tropical fish, ask you about your food shoots."

She thought about all the papers on "Our Constitution: How It Affects Us" she was going to have to correct. She thought about how she was going in for ultrasound tests on Friday, because, according to her doctor and her doctor's assistant, she had a large, mysterious growth in her abdomen. Gallbladder, they kept saying. Or ovaries or colon. "You guys practice medicine?" asked Zoë, aloud, after they had left the room. Once, as a girl, she brought her dog to a vet, who had told her, "Well, either your dog has worms or cancer or else it was hit by a car."

She was looking forward to New York.

"Well, whatever. We'll just play it cool. I can't wait to see you, hon. Don't forget your bonehead," said Evan.

"A bonehead you don't forget," said Zoë.

"I suppose," said Evan.

The ultrasound Zoë was keeping a secret, even from Evan. "I feel like I'm dying," Zoë had hinted just once on the phone.

"You're not dying," said Evan. "You're just annoyed."

"Ultrasound," Zoë now said jokingly to the technician who put the cold jelly on her bare stomach. "Does that sound like a really great stereo system, or what?" She had not had anyone make this much fuss over her bare stomach since her boyfriend in graduate school, who had hovered over her whenever she felt ill, waved his arms, pressed his hands upon her navel, and drawled evangelically, "Heal! Heal for thy Baby Jesus' sake!" Zoë would laugh and they would make love, both secretly hoping she would get pregnant. Later they would worry together, and he would sink a cheek to her belly and ask whether she was late, was she late, was she sure, she might be late, and when after two years she had not gotten pregnant, they took to quarreling and drifted apart.

"OK," said the technician absently.

The monitor was in place, and Zoë's insides came on the screen in all their gray and ribbony hollowness. They were marbled in the finest gradations of black and white, like stone in an old church or a picture of the moon. "Do you suppose," she babbled at the technician, "that the rise in infertility among so many couples in this country is due to completely different species trying to reproduce?" The technician moved the scanner around and took more pictures. On one view in particular, on Zoë's right side, the technician became suddenly alert, the machine he was operating clicking away.

Zoë stared at the screen. "That must be the growth you found there," suggested Zoë.

"I can't tell you anything," said the technician rigidly. "Your doctor will get the radiologist's report this afternoon and will phone you then."

"I'll be out of town," said Zoë.

"I'm sorry," said the technician.

Driving home, Zoë looked in the rearview mirror and decided she looked—well, how would one describe it? A little wan. She thought of the joke about the guy who visits his doctor and the doctor says, "Well, I'm sorry to say you've got six weeks to live."

"I want a second opinion," says the guy. *You act like your opinion is worth more than everyone else's in the class.*

"You want a second opinion? OK," says the doctor. "You're ugly, too." She liked that joke. She thought it was terribly, terribly funny.

She took a cab to the airport, Jerry the cabbie happy to see her.

"Have fun in New York," he said, getting her bag out of the trunk. He liked her, or at least he always acted as if he did. She called him "Jare."

"Thanks, Jare."

"You know, I'll tell you a secret: I've never been to New York. I'll tell you two secrets: I've never been on a plane." And he waved at her sadly as she pushed her way in through the terminal door. "Or an escalator!" he shouted.

The trick to flying safe, Zoë always said, was never to buy a discount ticket and to tell yourself you had nothing to live for anyway, so that when the plane crashed it was no big deal. Then, when it didn't crash, when you had succeeded in keeping it aloft with your own worthlessness, all you had to do was stagger off, locate your luggage, and, by the time a cab arrived, come up with a persuasive reason to go on living.

"You're here!" shrieked Evan over the doorbell, before she even opened the door. Then she opened it wide. Zoë set her bags on the hall floor and hugged Evan hard. When she was little, Evan had always been affectionate and devoted. Zoë had always taken care of her, advising, reassuring, until recently, when it seemed Evan had started advising and reassuring *her*. It startled Zoë. She suspected it had something to do with Zoë's being alone. It made people uncomfortable. "How *are* you?"

"I threw up on the plane. Besides that, I'm OK."

"Can I get you something? Here, let me take your suitcase. Sick on the plane. Eeeyew."

"It was into one of those sickness bags," said Zoë, just in case Evan thought she'd lost it in the aisle. "I was very quiet."

The apartment was spacious and bright, with a view all the way downtown along the East Side. There was a balcony and sliding glass doors. "I keep forgetting how nice this apartment is. Twentieth floor, doorman . . ." Zoë could work her whole life and never have an apartment like this. So could Evan. It was Charlie's apartment. He and Evan lived in it like two kids in a dorm, beer cans and clothes strewn around. Evan put Zoë's bag away from the mess, over by the fish tank. "I'm so glad you're here," she said. "Now what can I get you?"

Evan made them a snack—soup from a can, and saltines.

"I don't know about Charlie," she said, after they had finished. "I feel like we've gone all sexless and middle-aged already."

"Hmmm," said Zoë. She leaned back into Evan's sofa and stared out the window at the dark tops of the buildings. It seemed a little unnatural to live up in the sky like this, like birds that out of some wrongheaded derring-do had nested too high. She nodded toward the lighted fish tanks and giggled. "I feel like a bird," she said, "with my own personal supply of fish."

Evan sighed. "He comes home and just sacks out on the sofa, watching fuzzy football. He's wearing the psychic cold cream and curlers, if you know what I mean."

Zoë sat up, readjusted the sofa cushions. "What's fuzzy football?"

"We haven't gotten cable yet. Everything comes in fuzzy. Charlie just watches it that way."

"Hmmm, yeah, that's a little depressing," Zoë said. She looked at her hands. "Especially the part about not having cable."

"This is how he gets into bed at night." Evan stood up to demonstrate. "He whips all his clothes off, and when he gets to his underwear, he lets it drop to one ankle. Then he kicks up his leg and flips the underwear in the air and catches it. I, of course, watch from the bed. There's nothing else. There's just that."

"Maybe you should just get it over with and get married."

"Really?"

"Yeah. I mean, you guys probably think living together like this is the best of both worlds, but . . ." Zoë tried to sound like an older sister; an older sister was supposed to be the parent you could never have, the hip, cool mom. ". . . I've always found that as soon as you think you've got the best of both worlds"—she thought now of herself, alone in her house; of the toad-faced cicadas that flew around like little caped men at night, landing on her screens, staring; of the size fourteen shoes she placed at the doorstep, to scare off intruders; of the ridiculous inflatable blow-up doll someone had told her to keep propped up at the breakfast table—"it can suddenly twist and become the worst of both worlds."

"Really?" Evan was beaming. "Oh, Zoë. I have something to tell you. Charlie and I *are* getting married."

"Really." Zoë felt confused.

"I didn't know how to tell you."

"Yes, well, I guess the part about fuzzy football misled me a little."

"I was hoping you'd be my maid of honor," said Evan, waiting. "Aren't you happy for me?"

"Yes," said Zoë, and she began to tell Evan a story about an award-winning violinist at Hilldale-Versailles, how the violinist had come home from a competition in Europe and taken up with a local man, who made her go to all his summer softball games, made her cheer for him from the stands, with the wives, until she later killed herself. But when she got halfway through, to the part about cheering at the softball games, Zoë stopped.

"What?" said Evan. "So what happened?"

"Actually, nothing," said Zoë lightly. "She just really got into softball. I mean, really. You should have seen her."

Zoë decided to go to a late-afternoon movie, leaving Evan to chores she needed to do before the party—*I have to do them alone*, she'd said, a little tense after the violinist story. Zoë thought about going to an art museum, but women alone in art museums had to look good. They always did. Chic and serious, moving languidly, with a great handbag. Instead, she walked over and down through Kips Bay, past an earring boutique called Stick It in Your Ear, past a beauty salon called Dorian Gray's. That was the funny thing about *beauty*, thought Zoë. Look it up in the yellow pages, and you found a hundred entries, hostile with wit, cutesy with warning. But look up *truth*—ha! There was nothing at all.

Zoë thought about Evan getting married. Would Evan turn into Peter Pumpkin Eater's wife? Mrs. Eater? At the wedding would she make Zoë wear some flouncy lavender dress, identical with the other maids'? Zoë hated uniforms, had even, in the first grade, refused to join Elf Girls, because she didn't want to wear the same dress as everyone else. Now she might have to. But maybe she could distinguish it. Hitch it up on one side with a clothespin. Wear surgical gauze at the waist. Clip to her bodice one of those pins that said in loud letters, SHIT HAPPENS.

At the movie—*Death by Number*—she bought strands of red licorice to tug and chew. She took a seat off to one side in the theater. She felt strangely self-conscious sitting alone and hoped for the place to darken fast. When it did, and the coming attractions came on, she reached inside her purse for her glasses. They were in a Baggie. Her Kleenex was also in a Baggie. So were her pen and her aspirin and her mints. Everything was in Baggies. This was what she'd become: *a woman alone at the movies with everything in a Baggie.*

At the Halloween party, there were about two dozen people. There were people with ape heads and large hairy hands. There was someone dressed as a leprechaun. There was someone dressed as a frozen dinner. Some man had brought his two small daughters: a ballerina and a ballerina's sister, also dressed as a ballerina. There was a gaggle of sexy witches—women dressed entirely in black, beautifully made up and jeweled. "I hate those sexy witches. It's not in the spirit of Halloween," said Evan. Evan had abandoned the moon mask and dolled herself up as a hausfrau, in curlers and an apron, a decision she now regretted. Charlie, because he liked fish, because he owned fish, collected fish, had decided to go as a fish. He had fins and eyes on the side of his head. "Zoë! How are you! I'm sorry I wasn't here when you first arrived!" He spent the rest of his time chatting up the sexy witches.

"Isn't there something I can help you with here?" Zoë asked her sister. "You've been running yourself ragged." She rubbed her sister's arm, gently, as if she wished they were alone.

"Oh, God, not at all," said Evan, arranging stuffed mushrooms on a plate. The timer went off, and she pulled another sheetful out of the oven. "Actually, you know what you can do?"

"What?" Zoë put on her bonehead.

"Meet Earl. He's the guy I had in mind for you. When he gets here, just talk to him a little. He's nice. He's fun. He's going through a divorce."

"I'll try." Zoë groaned. "OK? I'll try." She looked at her watch.

When Earl arrived, he was dressed as a naked woman, steel wool glued strategically to a body stocking, and large rubber breasts protruding like hams.

"Zoë, this is Earl," said Evan.

"Good to meet you," said Earl, circling Evan to shake Zoë's hand. He stared at the top of Zoë's head. "Great bone."

Zoë nodded. "Great tits," she said. She looked past him, out the window at the city thrown glitteringly up against the sky; people were saying the usual things: how it looked like jewels, like bracelets and necklaces unstrung. You could see Grand Central station, the clock of the Con Ed building, the red-and-gold-capped Empire State, the Chrysler like a rocket ship dreamed up in a depression. Far west you could glimpse the Astor Plaza, its flying white roof like a nun's habit. "There's beer out on the balcony, Earl—can I get you one?" Zoë asked.

"Sure, uh, I'll come along. Hey, Charlie, how's it going?"

Charlie grinned and whistled. People turned to look. "Hey, Earl," someone called, from across the room. "Va-va-va-voom."

They squeezed their way past the other guests, past the apes and the sexy witches. The suction of the sliding door gave way in a whoosh, and Zoë and Earl stepped out onto the balcony, a bonehead and a naked woman, the night air roaring and smoky cool. Another couple was out here, too, murmuring privately. They were not wearing costumes. They smiled at Zoë and Earl. "Hi," said Zoë. She found the plastic-foam cooler, dug into it, and retrieved two beers.

"Thanks," said Earl. His rubber breasts folded inward, dimpled and dented, as he twisted open the bottle.

"Well," sighed Zoë anxiously. She had to learn not to be afraid of a man, the way, in your childhood, you learned not to be afraid of an earthworm or a bug. Often, when she spoke to men at parties, she rushed things in her mind. As the man politely blathered on, she would fall in love, marry, then find herself in a bitter custody battle with him for the kids and hoping for a reconciliation, so that despite all his betrayals she might no longer despise him, and in the few minutes remaining, learn, perhaps, what his last name was and what he did for a living, though probably there was already too much history between them. She would nod, blush, turn away.

"Evan tells me you're a professor. Where do you teach?"

"Just over the Indiana border into Illinois."

He looked a little shocked. "I guess Evan didn't tell me that part."

"She didn't?"

"No."

"Well, that's Evan for you. When we were kids we both had speech impediments."

"That can be tough," said Earl. One of his breasts was hidden behind his drinking arm, but the other shone low and pink, full as a strawberry moon.

"Yes, well, it wasn't a total loss. We used to go to what we called peach pearapy. For about ten years of my life I had to map out every sentence in my mind, way ahead, before I said it. That was the only way I could get a coherent sentence out."

Earl drank from his beer. "How did you do that? I mean, how did you get through?"

"I told a lot of jokes. Jokes you know the lines to already—you can just say them. I love jokes. Jokes and songs."

Earl smiled. He had on lipstick, a deep shade of red, but it was wearing off from the beer. "What's your favorite joke?"

"Uh, my favorite joke is probably . . . OK, all right. This guy goes into a doctor's office and—"

"I think I know this one," interrupted Earl, eagerly. He wanted to tell it himself. "A guy goes into a doctor's office, and the doctor tells him he's got some good news and some bad news—that one, right?"

"I'm not sure," said Zoë. "This might be a different version."

"So the guy says, 'Give me the bad news first,' and the doctor says, 'OK. You've got three weeks to live.' And the guy cries, 'Three weeks to live! Doctor, what is the good news?' And the doctor says, 'Did you see that secretary out front? I finally fucked her.' "

Zoë frowned.

"That's not the one you were thinking of?"

"No." There was accusation in her voice. "Mine was different."

"Oh," said Earl. He looked away and then back again. "You teach history, right? What kind of history do you teach?"

"I teach American, mostly—eighteenth and nineteenth century." In graduate school, at bars, the pickup line was always: "So what's your century?"

"Occasionally I teach a special theme course," she added, "say, 'Humor and Personality in the White House.' That's what my book's on." She thought of something someone once told her about bowerbirds, how they build elaborate structures before mating.

"Your book's on *humor*?"

"Yeah, and, well, when I teach a theme course like that, I do all the centuries." *So what's your century?*

"All three of them."

"Pardon?" The breeze glistened her eyes. Traffic revved beneath them. She felt high and puny, like someone lifted into heaven by mistake and then spurned.

"Three. There's only three."

"Well, four, really." She was thinking of Jamestown, and of the Pilgrims coming here with buckles and witch hats to say their prayers.

"I'm a photographer," said Earl. His face was starting to gleam, his rouge smearing in a sunset beneath his eyes.

"Do you like that?"

"Well, actually I'm starting to feel it's a little dangerous."

"Really?"

"Spending all your time in a darkroom with that red light and all those chemicals. There's links with Parkinson's, you know."

"No, I didn't."

"I suppose I should wear rubber gloves, but I don't like to. Unless I'm touching it directly, I don't think of it as real."

"Hmmm," said Zoë. Alarm buzzed through her, mildly, like a tea.

"Sometimes, when I have a cut or something, I feel the sting and think, *Shit*. I wash constantly and just hope. I don't like rubber over the skin like that."

"Really."

"I mean, the physical contact. That's what you want, or why bother?"

"I guess," said Zoë. She wished she could think of a joke, something slow and deliberate, with the end in sight. She thought of gorillas, how when they had been kept too long alone in cages, they would smack each other in the head instead of mating.

"Are you . . . in a relationship?" Earl suddenly blurted.

"Now? As we speak?"

"Well, I mean, I'm sure you have a relationship to your *work*." A smile, a weird one, nestled in his mouth like an egg. She thought of zoos in parks, how when cities were under siege, during world wars, people ate the animals. "But I mean, with a *man*."

"No, I'm not in a relationship with a *man*." She rubbed her chin with her hand and could feel the one bristly hair there. "But my last relationship was with a very sweet man," she said. She made something up. "From Switzerland. He was a botanist—a weed expert. His name was Jerry. I called him 'Jare.' He was so funny. You'd go to the movies with him and all he would notice were the plants. He would never pay attention to the plot. Once, in a jungle movie, he started rattling off all these Latin names, out loud. It was very exciting for him." She paused, caught her breath. "Eventually he went back to Europe to, uh, study the edelweiss." She looked at Earl. "Are you involved in a relationship? With a *woman*?"

Earl shifted his weight, and the creases in his body stocking changed, splintering outward like something broken. His pubic hair slid over to one hip, like a corsage on a saloon girl. "No," he said, clearing his throat. The steel wool in his underarms was inching toward his biceps. "I've just gotten out of a marriage that was full of bad dialogue, like 'You want more *space*? I'll give you more space!' *Clonk*. Your basic Three Stooges."

Zoë looked at him sympathetically. "I suppose it's hard for love to recover after that."

His eyes lit up. He wanted to talk about love. "But *I* keep thinking love should be like a tree. You look at trees and they've got bumps and scars from tumors, infestations, what have you, but they're still growing. Despite the bumps and bruises, they're . . . straight."

"Yeah, well," said Zoë, "where I'm from, they're all married or gay. Did you see that movie *Death by Number*?"

Earl looked at her, a little lost. She was getting away from him. "No," he said.

One of his breasts had slipped under his arm, tucked there like a baguette. She kept thinking of trees, of gorillas and parks, of people in wartime eating the zebras. She felt a stabbing pain in her abdomen.

"Want some hors d'oeuvres?" Evan came pushing through the sliding door. She was smiling, though her curlers were coming out, hanging bedraggled at the ends of her hair like Christmas decorations, like food put out for the birds. She thrust forward a plate of stuffed mushrooms.

"Are you asking for donations or giving them away," said Earl, wittily. He liked Evan, and he put his arm around her.

"You know, I'll be right back," said Zoë.

"Oh," said Evan, looking concerned.

"Right back. I promise."

Zoë hurried inside, across the living room, into the bedroom, to the adjoining bath. It was empty; most of the guests were using the half bath near the kitchen. She flicked on the light and closed the door. The pain had stopped and she didn't really have to go to the bathroom, but she stayed there anyway, resting. In the mirror above the sink she looked haggard beneath her bonehead, violet grays showing under the skin like a plucked and pocky bird. She leaned closer, raising her chin a little to find the bristly hair. It was there, at the end of the jaw, sharp and dark as a wire. She opened the medicine cabinet, pawed through it until she found some tweezers. She lifted her head again and poked at her face with the metal tips, grasping and pinching and missing. Outside the door she could hear two people talking low. They had come into the bedroom and were discussing something. They were sitting on the bed. One of them giggled in a false way. She stabbed again at her chin, and it started to bleed a little. She pulled the skin tight along the jawbone, gripped the tweezers hard around what she hoped was the hair, and tugged. A tiny square of skin came away with it, but the hair remained, blood bright at the root of it. Zoë clenched her teeth. "Come on," she whispered. The couple outside in the bedroom were now telling stories, softly, and laughing. There was a bounce and squeak of mattress, and the sound of a chair being moved out of the way. Zoë aimed the tweezers carefully, pinched, then pulled gently away, and this time the hair came, too, with a slight twinge of pain and then a great flood of relief. "Yeah!" breathed Zoë. She grabbed some toilet paper and dabbed at her chin. It came away spotted with blood, and so she tore off some more and pressed hard until it stopped. Then she turned off the light and opened the door, to return to the party.

"Excuse me," she said to the couple in the bedroom. They were the couple from the balcony, and they looked at her, a bit surprised. They had their arms around each other, and they were eating candy bars.

Earl was still out on the balcony, alone, and Zoë rejoined him there.

"Hi," she said. He turned around and smiled. He had straightened his costume out a bit, though all the secondary sex characteristics seemed slightly doomed, destined to shift and flip and zip around again any moment.

"Are you OK?" he asked. He had opened another beer and was chugging.

"Oh, yeah. I just had to go to the bathroom." She paused. "Actually I have been going to a lot of doctors recently."

"What's wrong?" asked Earl.

"Oh, probably nothing. But they're putting me through tests." She sighed. "I've had sonograms. I've had mammograms. Next week I'm going in for a candygram." He looked at her worriedly. "I've had too many gram words," she said.

"Here, I saved you these." He held out a napkin with two stuffed mushroom caps. They were cold and leaving oil marks on the napkin.

"Thanks," said Zoë, and pushed them both in her mouth. "Watch," she said, with her mouth full. "With my luck, it'll be a gallbladder operation."

Earl made a face. "So your sister's getting married," he said, changing the subject. "Tell me, really, what you think about love."

"*Love?*" Hadn't they done this already? "I don't know." She chewed thoughtfully and swallowed. "All right. I'll tell you what I think about love. Here is a love story. This friend of mine—"

"You've got something on your chin," said Earl, and he reached over to touch it.

"*What?*" said Zoë, stepping back. She turned her face away and grabbed at her chin. A piece of toilet paper peeled off it, like tape. "It's nothing," she said. "It's just—it's nothing."

Earl stared at her.

"At any rate," she continued, "this friend of mine was this award-winning violinist. She traveled all over Europe and won competitions; she made records, she gave concerts, she got famous. But she had no social life. So one day she threw herself at the feet of this conductor she had a terrible crush on. He picked her up, scolded her gently, and sent her back to her hotel room. After that she came home from Europe. She went back to her old hometown, stopped playing the violin, and took up with a local boy. This was in Illinois. He took her to some Big Ten bar every night to drink with his buddies from the team. He used to say things like "Katrina here likes to play the violin," and then he'd pinch her cheek. When she once suggested that they go home, he said, 'What, you think you're too famous for a place like this? Well, let me tell you something. You may think you're famous, but you're not *famous* famous.' Two famouses. 'No one here's ever heard of you.' Then he went up and bought a round of drinks for everyone but her. She got her coat, went home, and shot a gun through her head."

Earl was silent.

"That's the end of my love story," said Zoë.

"You're not at all like your sister," said Earl.

"Ho, really," said Zoë. The air had gotten colder, the wind singing minor and thick as a dirge.

"No." He didn't want to talk about love anymore. "You know, you should wear a lot of blue—blue and white—around your face. It would bring out your coloring." He reached an arm out to show her how the blue bracelet he was wearing might look against her skin, but she swatted it away.

"Tell me, Earl. Does the word *fag* mean anything to you?"

He stepped back, away from her. He shook his head in disbelief. "You know, I just shouldn't try to go out with career women. You're all stricken. A guy can really tell what life has done to you. I do better with women who have part-time jobs."

"Oh, yes?" said Zoë. She had once read an article entitled "Professional Women and the Demographics of Grief." Or no, it was a poem: *If there were a lake, the moonlight would dance across it in conniptions*. She remembered that line. But perhaps the title was "The Empty House: Aesthetics of Barrenness." Or maybe "Space Gypsies: Girls in Academe." She had forgotten.

Earl turned and leaned on the railing of the balcony. It was getting late. Inside, the party guests were beginning to leave. The sexy witches were already gone. "Live and learn," Earl murmured.

"Live and get dumb," replied Zoë. Beneath them on Lexington there were no cars, just the gold rush of an occasional cab. He leaned hard on his elbows, brooding.

"Look at those few people down there," he said. "They look like bugs. You know how bugs are kept under control? They're sprayed with bug hormones, female bug hormones. The male bugs get so crazy in the presence of this hormone, they're screwing everything in sight: trees, rocks—everything but female bugs. Population control. That's what's happening in this country," he said drunkenly. "Hormones sprayed around, and now men are screwing rocks. Rocks!"

In the back the Magic Marker line of his buttocks spread wide, a sketchy black on pink like a funnies page. Zoë came up, slow, from behind and gave him a shove. His arms slipped forward, off the railing, out over the street. Beer spilled out of his bottle, raining twenty stories down to the street.

"Hey, what are you doing?!" he said, whipping around. He stood straight and readied and moved away from the railing, sidestepping Zoë. "What the *hell* are you doing?"

"Just kidding," she said. "I was just kidding." But he gazed at her, appalled and frightened, his Magic Marker buttocks turned away now toward all of downtown, a naked pseudo-woman with a blue bracelet at the wrist, trapped out on a balcony with—with *what*? *"Really, I was just kidding!"* Zoë shouted. The wind lifted the hair up off her head, skyward in spines behind the bone. If there were a lake, the moonlight would dance across it in conniptions. She smiled at him, and wondered how she looked.

---

1. What inspires Zoë to tell Evan the "love story" about the violinist?
2. Why is Zoë so concerned about the bristly hair on her chin?
3. Why does Zoë give Earl a shove from behind out on the balcony?

SUDDEN FICTION

WILLIAM MAXWELL (1908–2000) was born in Lincoln, Illinois, and educated at the University of Illinois and Harvard University. He became a fiction editor at the *New Yorker*, where he remained for forty years, editing the work of some of the greatest twentieth-century writers, including John Cheever, Eudora Welty, and J. D. Salinger. Although Maxwell lived most of his life in the midst of New York City's cosmopolitan literary scene, many of his short stories and novels, including *They Came Like Swallows* (1937) and *The Folded Leaf* (1945), depict life in the rural Midwest in spare, elegant prose. Maxwell also wrote many brief stories that he referred to as "half fable, half fairy tale."

The Country Where Nobody Ever Grew Old and Died

There used to be, until roughly a hundred and fifty years ago, a country where nobody ever grew old and died. The gravestone with its weathered inscription, the wreath on the door, the black arm band, and the friendly reassuring smile of the undertaker were unknown there. This is not as strange as it at first seems. You do not have to look very far to find a woman who does not show her age or a man who intends to live forever. In this country, people did live forever, and nobody thought anything about it, but at some time or other somebody had thought about it, because there were certain restrictions on the freedom of the inhabitants. The country was not large, and there would soon not have been enough land to go around. So, instead of choosing an agreeable site and building a house on it, married couples chose an agreeable house and bought the right to add a story onto it. In this way, gradually, the houses, which were of stone, and square, and without superfluous ornamentation, became towers. The prevailing style of architecture was very much like that of the Italian hill towns. Arriving at the place where you lived, you rang the concierge's bell and sat down in a wicker swing, with your parcels on your lap, and were lifted to your own floor by ropes and pulleys.

A country where there were no children would be sadness incarnate. People didn't stop having them, but they were placed in such a way that the smallest number of children could be enjoyed by the greatest number of adults. If you wanted to raise a family, you applied for a permit and waited your turn. Very often by the time the permit came, the woman was too old to have a child and received instead a permit to help bring up somebody else's child.

Young women who were a pleasure to look at were enjoyed the way flowers are enjoyed, but leaving one's youth behind was not considered to be a catastrophe, and the attitudes and opinions of the young were not anxiously subscribed to. There is, in fact, some question whether the young of that country really were young, as we understand the word. Most people appeared to be on the borderline between maturity and early middle age, as in England in the late eighteenth century, when the bald pate and the head of thick brown hair were both concealed by a powdered wig, and physical deterioration was minimized by the fashions in dress and by what constituted good manners.

All the arts flourished except history. If you wanted to know what things were like in the period of Erasmus or Joan of Arc or Ethelred the Unready, you asked somebody who was alive at the time. People tended to wear the clothes of the period in which they came of age, and so walking down the street was like thumbing through a book on the history of costume. The soldiers, in every conceivable kind of armor and uniform, were a little boy's dream.

As one would expect, that indefatigable traveler Lady Mary Wortley Montagu spent a considerable time in this interesting country before she settled down in Venice, and so did William Beckford. Lady Mary's letters about it were destroyed by her daughter after her death, because they happened to contain assertions of a shocking nature, for which proof was lacking, about a contemporary figure who would have relished a prosecution for libel. For Beckford's experiences, see his *Dreams, Waking Thoughts, and Incidents* (Leipzig, 1832).

One might have supposed that in a country where death was out of the question, morbidity would be unknown. This was true for I have no idea how many centuries and then something very strange happened. The young, until this moment entirely docile and unimaginative, began having scandalous parties at which they pretended that they were holding a funeral. They even went so far as to put together a makeshift pine coffin, and took turns lying in it, with their eyes closed and their hands crossed, and a lighted candle at the head and foot. This occurred during Beckford's stay, and it is just possible that he had something to do with it. Though he could be very amusing, he was a natural mischief-maker and an extremely morbid man.

The mock funerals were the first thing that happened. The second was the trial, *in absentia*, of a gypsy woman who was accused of taking money with intent to defraud. This was not an instance of a poor foolish widow's being persuaded to bring her husband's savings to a fortuneteller in order to have the money doubled. In the first place, there were no widows, and the victim was a young man.

The plaintiff—just turned twenty-one, Beckford says, and exceedingly handsome—stated under oath that he had consulted the gypsy woman in the hope of learning from her the secret of how to commit suicide. For it seems that in this country as everywhere else gypsies were a race apart and a law unto themselves. They did not choose to live forever, so they didn't. When one of them decided that life had no further interest for him, he did something. What, nobody knew. It was assumed that the gypsy bent on terminating his existence sat down under a tree or by a riverbank, some nice quiet place where he wouldn't be disturbed, and in a little while the other gypsies came and disposed of the body.

The plaintiff testified that the gypsy woman studied his hand, and then she looked in her crystal ball, and then she excused herself in order to get something on the other side of a curtain. That was the last anybody had seen of her or of the satchel full of money which the plaintiff had brought with him.

The idea that a personable young man, on the very threshold of life, had actually wanted to die caused a tremendous stir. The public was barred from the trial, but Beckford was on excellent terms with the wife of the Lord Chief Justice and managed to attend the hearing in the guise of a court stenographer. The story is to be found in the Leipzig edition of his book and no other, which suggests that he perhaps did have something to do with the events he describes, and that from feelings of remorse, or shame, wrote about them and then afterward wished to suppress what he had written. At all events we have his very interesting account. The jury found for the plaintiff and against the gypsy woman. After the verdict was read aloud in the court, the attorney for the defense made an impassioned and—in the light of what happened afterward—heartbreaking speech. If only it had been taken seriously! He asked that the verdict stand, but that no effort be made to find his client, and that no other gypsy be questioned or molested in any way by the police. The court saw the matter in a different light, and during the next few days the police set about rounding up every single gypsy in the country. The particular gypsy woman who had victimized the young man with a bent for self-destruction was never found. The others were subjected to the most detailed questioning. When that produced no information, the rack and the thumbscrew were applied, to no purpose. You might as well try to squeeze kindness out of a stone as torture a secret out of a gypsy. But there was living with the gypsies at that time a middle-aged man who had been stolen by them as a child and who had spent his life among them. When he was brought into the courtroom between two bailiffs the attorney for the defense lowered his head and covered his eyes with his hand. The man was put on the witness stand and, pale and drawn after a night of torture, gave his testimony. Shortly after this, the gravestone, the wreath, the arm band, and the smiling undertaker, so familiar everywhere else in the world, made their appearance here also, and the country was no longer unique.

---

1. Why does the narrator think it is not as strange as it may seem that the people of this country never grew old or died?

2. Why does the narrator note that in this country there were "certain restrictions on the freedom of the inhabitants"?

3. Why does death come to this country as a result of the trial of a gypsy woman?

GRACE PALEY (1922–2007) was born to Russian Jewish immigrants and grew up in the Bronx. She briefly attended Hunter College, and then studied poetry with W. H. Auden at the New School for Social Research in Manhattan. After starting out as a poet, in 1959 Paley published *The Little Disturbances of Man*, a collection of stories that focused on the everyday lives of women. Other important collections include *Enormous Changes at the Last Minute* (1974) and *Later the Same Day* (1985). *The Collected Stories* (1994) earned the National Book Award.

Wants

I saw my ex-husband in the street. I was sitting on the steps of the new library.

Hello, my life, I said. We had once been married for twenty-seven years, so I felt justified.

He said, What? What life? No life of mine.

I said, OK. I don't argue when there's real disagreement. I got up and went into the library to see how much I owed them.

The librarian said $32 even and you've owed it for eighteen years. I didn't deny anything. Because I don't understand how time passes. I have had those books. I have often thought of them. The library is only two blocks away.

My ex-husband followed me to the Books Returned desk. He interrupted the librarian, who had more to tell. In many ways, he said, as I look back, I attribute the dissolution of our marriage to the fact that you never invited the Bertrams to dinner.

That's possible, I said. But really, if you remember: First, my father was sick that Friday, then the children were born, then I had those Tuesday night meetings, then the war began. Then we didn't seem to know them anymore. But you're right. I should have had them to dinner.

I gave the librarian a check for $32. Immediately she trusted me, put my past behind her, wiped the record clean, which is just what most other municipal and/or state bureaucracies will not do.

I checked out the two Edith Wharton books I had just returned because I'd read them so long ago and they are more apropos now than ever. They were *The House of Mirth* and *The Children*, which is about how life in the United States in New York changed in twenty-seven years fifty years ago.

A nice thing I do remember is breakfast, my husband said. I was surprised. All we ever had was coffee. Then I remembered there was a hole in the back of the kitchen closet which opened into the apartment next door. There, they always ate sugar-cured smoked bacon. It gave us a very grand feeling about breakfast, but we never got stuffed and sluggish.

That was when we were poor, I said.

When were we ever rich? he asked.

Oh, as time went on, as our responsibilities increased, we didn't go in need. You took adequate financial care, I reminded him. The children went to camp four weeks a year and in decent ponchos with sleeping bags and boots, just like everyone else. They looked very nice. Our place was warm in winter, and we had nice red pillows and things.

I wanted a sailboat, he said. But you didn't want anything.

Don't be bitter, I said. It's never too late.

No, he said with a great deal of bitterness. I may get a sailboat. As a matter of fact I have money down on an eighteen-foot two-rigger. I'm doing well this year and can look forward to better. But as for you, it's too late. You'll always want nothing.

He had a habit throughout the twenty-seven years of making a narrow remark which, like a plumber's snake, could work its way through the ear down the throat, halfway to my heart. He would then disappear, leaving me choking with equipment. What I mean is, I sat down on the library steps and he went away.

I looked through *The House of Mirth*, but lost interest. I felt extremely accused. Now, it's true, I'm short of requests and absolute requirements. But I do want *something*.

I want, for instance, to be a different person. I want to be the woman who brings these two books back in two weeks. I want to be the effective citizen who changes the school system and addresses the Board of Estimate on the troubles of this dear urban center.

I *had* promised my children to end the war before they grew up.

I wanted to have been married forever to one person, my ex-husband or my present one. Either has enough character for a whole life, which as it turns out is really not such a long time. You couldn't exhaust either man's qualities or get under the rock of his reasons in one short life.

Just this morning I looked out the window to watch the street for a while and saw that the little sycamores the city had dreamily planted a couple of years before the kids were born had come that day to the prime of their lives.

Well! I decided to bring those two books back to the library. Which proves that when a person or an event comes along to jolt or appraise me I *can* take some appropriate action, although I am better known for my hospitable remarks.

---

1. Why does the narrator address her ex-husband as "my life"? Does her justification for that phrase make sense?

2. Why does her ex-husband follow her to the Books Returned desk to say, "I attribute the dissolution of our marriage to the fact that you never invited the Bertrams to dinner"?

3. What does the ex-husband mean when he says to the narrator: "You'll always want nothing"? What is the narrator's complaint about her ex-husband's way of communicating?

4. Why has the narrator waited eighteen years to return the library books?

DONALD BARTHELME (1931–1989) served in the U.S. Army in Korea and Japan, worked as a reporter for the *Houston Post*, and, in the early sixties, was managing editor of *Location* magazine, a short-lived art and literary review in New York City. He moved to Denmark in 1965, received a Guggenheim Fellowship, and published his first novel, *Snow White*, in 1967. Barthelme has been variously described as a postmodernist, a surrealist, and a metafictionist; his work is characterized by seemingly random events and strange juxtapositions of people, places, and things. His collection *Sixty Stories* (1981) won the PEN/Faulkner Award for Fiction and the Los Angeles Times Book Prize.

A City of Churches

"Yes," Mr. Phillips said, "ours is a city of churches all right."

Cecelia nodded, following his pointing hand. Both sides of the street were solidly lined with churches, standing shoulder to shoulder in a variety of architectural styles. The Bethel Baptist stood next to the Holy Messiah Free Baptist, St Paul's Episcopal next to Grace Evangelical Covenant. Then came the First Christian Science, the Church of God, All Souls, Our Lady of Victory, the Society of Friends, the Assembly of God, and the Church of the Holy Apostles. The spires and steeples of the traditional buildings were jammed in next to the broad imaginative flights of the "contemporary" designs.

"Everyone here takes a great interest in church matters," Mr. Phillips said.

Will I fit in? Cecelia wondered. She had come to Prester to open a branch office of a car-rental concern.

"I'm not especially religious," she said to Mr. Phillips, who was in the real-estate business.

"Not *now*," he answered. "Not *yet*. But we have many fine young people here. You'll get integrated into the community soon enough.

The immediate problem is, where are you to live? Most people," he said, "live in the church of their choice. All of our churches have many extra rooms. I have a few belfry apartments that I can show you. What price range were you thinking of?"

They turned a corner and were confronted with more churches. They passed St. Luke's, the Church of the Epiphany, All Saints Ukrainian Orthodox, St. Clement's, Fountain Baptist, Union Congregational, St. Anargyri's, Temple Emanuel, the First Church of Christ Reformed. The mouths of all the churches were gaping open. Inside, lights could be seen dimly.

"I can go up to a hundred and ten," Cecelia said. "Do you have any buildings here that are *not* churches?"

"None," said Mr. Phillips. "Of course many of our fine church structures also do double duty as something else." He indicated a handsome Georgian façade. "That one," he said, "houses the United Methodist and the Board of Education. The one next to it, which is Antioch Pentecostal, has the barbershop."

It was true. A red and white striped barber pole was attached inconspicuously to the front of the Antioch Pentecostal.

"Do many people rent cars here?" Cecelia asked. "Or would they, if there was a handy place to rent them?"

"Oh, I don't know," said Mr. Phillips. "Renting a car implies that you want to go somewhere. Most people are pretty content right here. We have a lot of activities. I don't think I'd pick the car-rental business if I was just starting out in Prester. But you'll do fine." He showed her a small, extremely modern building with a severe brick, steel, and glass front. "That's St. Barnabas. Nice bunch of people over there. Wonderful spaghetti suppers."

Cecelia could see a number of heads looking out of the windows. But when they saw that she was staring at them, the heads disappeared.

"Do you think it's healthy for so many churches to be gathered together in one place?" she asked her guide. "It doesn't seem . . . *balanced*, if you know what I mean."

"We are famous for our churches," Mr. Phillips replied. "They are harmless. Here we are now."

. . .

He opened a door and they began climbing many flights of dusty stairs. At the end of the climb they entered a good-sized room, square, with windows on all four sides. There was a bed, a table, and two chairs, lamps, a rug. Four very large bronze bells hung in the exact center of the room.

"What a view!" Mr. Phillips exclaimed. "Come here and look."

"Do they actually ring these bells?" Cecelia asked.

"Three times a day," Mr. Phillips said, smiling. "Morning, noon, and night. Of course when they're rung you have to be pretty quick at getting out of the way. You get hit in the head by one of these babies and that's all she wrote."

"God Almighty," said Cecelia involuntarily. Then she said, "Nobody lives in the belfry apartments. That's why they're empty."

"You think so?" Mr. Phillips said.

"You can only rent them to new people in town," she said accusingly.

"I wouldn't do that," Mr. Phillips said. "It would go against the spirit of Christian fellowship."

"This town is a little creepy, you know that?"

"That may be, but it's not for you to say, is it? I mean, you're new here. You should walk cautiously, for a while. If you don't want an upper apartment I have a basement over at Central Presbyterian. You'd have to share it. There are two women in there now."

"I don't want to share," Cecelia said. "I want a place of my own."

"Why?" the real-estate man asked curiously. "For what purpose?"

"Purpose?" asked Cecelia. "There is no particular purpose. I just want—"

"That's not usual here. Most people live with other people. Husbands and wives. Sons with their mothers. People have roommates. That's the usual pattern."

"Still, I prefer a place of my own."

"It's very unusual."

"Do you have any such places? Besides bell towers, I mean?"

"I guess there are a few," Mr. Phillips said, with clear reluctance. "I can show you one or two, I suppose."

He paused for a moment.

"It's just that we have different values, maybe, from some of the surrounding communities," he explained. "We've been written up a lot. We had four minutes on the *CBS Evening News* one time. Three or four years ago. 'A City of Churches,' it was called."

"Yes, a place of my own is essential," Cecelia said, "if I am to survive here."

'That's kind of a funny attitude to take," Mr. Phillips said. "What denomination are you?"

Cecelia was silent. The truth was, she wasn't anything.

"I said, what denomination are you?" Mr. Phillips repeated.

"I can will my dreams," Cecelia said. "I can dream whatever I want. If I want to dream that I'm having a good time, in Paris or some other city, all I have to do is go to sleep and I will dream that dream. I can dream whatever I want."

"What do you dream, then, mostly?" Mr. Phillips said, looking at her closely.

"Mostly sexual things," she said. She was not afraid of him.

"Prester is not that kind of a town," Mr. Phillips said, looking away.

They went back down the stairs.

The doors of the churches were opening, on both sides of the street. Small groups of people came out and stood there, in front of the churches, gazing at Cecelia and Mr. Phillips.

A young man stepped forward and shouted, *"Everyone in this town already has a car! There is no one in this town who doesn't have a car!"*

"Is that true?" Cecelia asked Mr. Phillips.

"Yes," he said. "It's true. No one would rent a car here. Not in a hundred years."

"Then I won't stay," she said. "I'll go somewhere else."

"You must stay," he said. "There is already a car-rental office for you. In Mount Moriah Baptist, on the lobby floor. There is a counter and a telephone and a rack of car keys. And a calendar."

"I won't stay," she said. "Not if there's not any sound business reason for staying."

"We want you," said Mr. Phillips. "We want you standing behind the counter of the car-rental agency, during regular business hours. It will make the town complete."

"I won't," she said. "Not me."

"You must. It's essential."

"I'll dream," she said. "Things you won't like."

"We are discontented," said Mr. Phillips. "Terribly, terribly discontented. Something is wrong."

"I'll dream the Secret," she said. "You'll be sorry."

"We are like other towns, except that we are perfect," he said. "Our discontent can only be held in check by perfection. We need a car-rental girl. Someone must stand behind that counter."

"I'll dream the life you are most afraid of," Cecelia threatened.

"You are ours," he said, gripping her arm. "Our car-rental girl. Be nice. There is nothing you can do."

"Wait and see," Cecelia said.

---

1. What does it mean that many of the city's churches "do double duty as something else"? Why does Mr. Phillips tell Cecelia that the city's churches are "harmless"?

2. Why does Cecelia threaten Mr. Phillips by saying she will dream the life he is afraid of? What is "the Secret" Cecelia threatens to dream?

3. What does Mr. Phillips mean when he tells Cecelia: "You are ours . . . Our car-rental girl. Be nice. There is nothing you can do"?

DON SHEA (1940–) was born in New York City and earned his BA and MA from New York University. He joined IBM as a programmer in 1965, when the profession was almost unknown, and became a technology management consultant with Booz Allen Hamilton. In 1988 he quit business and began to write stories, which have been published in magazines including the *North American Review*, the *Gettysburg Review, Crosscurrents*, and *Kansas Quarterly*; his work has appeared in the anthologies *Flash Fiction* (1992) and *Flash Fiction Forward* (2006). Shea's work has been nominated twice for the Pushcart Prize.

True Love

They met at a national entomology conference. To his eye, she was a woman of extraordinary physical grace and beauty, the last thing he expected to find at a professional conference.

He was struck by her slender, hairless forearms, the delicate curve of her neck, the proud way she carried her rather small head.

His tall thin frame and slightly bulging eyes reminded her of the subjects of her first highly successful entomological research project. It was a strong and fond memory. The project had established her reputation for creative insectology.

He approached her during the cocktail hour after the first day's papers.

"Hello," he said, "I'm Lloyd Gaynor."

"Gaynor? Oh, yes. Termites."

He was pleased.

Her name was Phyllis Turner and he knew and admired her work on fire ants. Fortuitously, he was seated next to her at the dinner. Their mutual attraction was very strong, so strong that their exchanges took on a quality of escalation, advancing their intimacy in a series of minute but rapid steps, a breathless spiral like a ritual dance.

BRING ON

An attraction strong enough to evoke real fear.

A revelation occurred over the mocha bombe and espresso that excited her more than she cared to show. She realized that as part of the research he was describing in termite neurobiology he had developed a computer model that could save her six months in her statistical analysis of fire ant brain function. She expressed her interest in a low key, oblique way. He was encouraging but noncommittal.

BIOLOGY OF THE NERVOUS SYSTEM.

Shortly after the dinner, by unspoken agreement, they ascended in the hotel elevator to her floor and entered her room. They undressed without speaking, he in the bathroom, she in the bedroom.

He entered the bedroom and paused, standing beside the bed. She stood naked across the bed from him. They examined each other's pale, slender, almost hairless bodies. HAIRLESS...?

He spoke first.

"The female praying mantis is nearsighted and dangerous. When the male is impelled to mate, he approaches her slowly and with great caution, sometimes waiting motionless for up to twenty minutes before the next short advance. When he finally summons the courage to dash forward and mount her from the rear, she typically responds by twisting her upper body around and biting off his head. This act quite literally removes his innate fear of her, since it removes the neurons and ganglia in which that fear resides. He then copulates to a successful conclusion and dies, presumably as happily as any creature can without its head. After he dies, she eats the rest of him."

He paused and looked at her expectantly. His long thin penis extended out and upward with mute pink urgency.

When she spoke, she used the same light didactic tone as he.

"The female empid fly also has a nasty habit of eating the male when he approaches her during mating season. To divert her from this purpose, the male typically finds a morsel of food and wraps it elaborately in a silk balloon formed by his glandular secretions. The time it takes the female to unwrap his gift is often long enough for him to copulate successfully and escape unscathed. But in one empid species, whether through cleverness, laziness, or just bad faith, the male fails to put any food inside the balloon. The female is hoodwinked into copulation with an empty promise."

These things they said to each other were well known to both, as indeed they were to any first-year graduate student of entomology.

There was a pause after she spoke. They continued to stare at each other. It could have gone either way.

Then they fell upon each other.

---

1. What explains the immediate and mutual attraction that develops between Phyllis and Lloyd?

2. Why does Lloyd describe the mating of the praying mantis? Why does Phyllis speak of the empid fly?

3. Does Phyllis and Lloyd's relationship constitute "true love"?

KIM CHURCH (1956–) was born and raised in Lexington, North Carolina. She holds a degree in English from the University of North Carolina at Greensboro and a law degree from the University of North Carolina at Chapel Hill. She practiced law for a number of years as a civil trial attorney before beginning to write fiction. Her stories have appeared in *Flash Fiction Forward* (2006) as well as magazines such as *Painted Bride Quarterly*, *Mississippi Review*, and *Shenandoah*. She has been nominated for a Pushcart Prize.

Bullet

I know what a bullet can do. Everybody has an idea, everybody's seen close-ups—gaudy wounds, geysers of blood, arms and legs flopping, life kathumping to a close. TV bullet drama. But there are other, not-so-spectacular ways a bullet can work.

My husband wore a bullet on a chain around his neck. He had blond chest hair, red skin from the sun and drinking, and that bright silver necklace. Hobart. When he held me, his bullet would grind into the bone at the base of my throat. I still have a dark place there. I call it a birthmark but it's a bruise that never went away. "Am I your sweet meat?" he used to ask me. "Say it. Say, Hobart, you're my sweet meat."

Here's what I learned from marriage: I am not brave. I never will be. But I am patient, and I can outlast anyone.

A man came in the store last night. He didn't shop around, just marched straight up to the counter, shoved his hand in his pocket and said, "This bullet's for you," so I gave him all the money from my drawer, stuffed it in a sack like he said, and he—quick!—slapped the counter and left. Slapped down his bullet like he was paying cash, is what I told the police.

It was brass, not silver. Smaller than Hobart's and without the shine. Greasy, like some people's pocket change.

The robbery was all over this morning's news. They showed a picture of the store while the newswoman announced that the man who held it up hadn't used a gun. He didn't even say gun. The newswoman made a big point of this. She almost broke into a smile when she told how he'd disappeared before the police could find him. "Successful," she called him, making him sound heroic.

I wonder what I would say if she interviewed me.

"How did you feel when you realized what had happened?"

"I don't know. Sick. Mad. But mostly I was just glad he left without hurting me. Mostly I felt grateful."

"You were grateful?" Like it's the wrong answer. Like grateful isn't enough to satisfy a TV audience.

"Gratefulness can fool you," I would tell her. "It's a stronger feeling than you think. In fact, I'd put gratefulness up there with the big ones. It can feel like love, or grief, that strong."

I know this to be true. Or maybe how it works is, gratefulness makes you able to feel the big feelings you wouldn't be able to otherwise.

"Where's the bullet now?"

"The police took it. I've asked to have it back when they're through."

"Why? What'll you do with it?"

Keep it with the other one, I'm thinking. "Put it in my jewelry box, where I can look at it from time to time."

Because (not that I would say this on the news) I know what will happen. One day my robber will die. Maybe some gung-ho store clerk will shoot him when he reaches in his pocket. Maybe he'll come down with a fluke disease. Only forty-six years old, people will say. What a shame, what a waste.

Yes, I will say. I'll be tender, because I can afford to be. Yes, it is.

---

1. What explains the fact that the bruise on the narrator's neck "never went away"?
2. Why does the narrator claim that she "can outlast anyone"?
3. Why does the narrator want the bullet from the robbery back?

ANN HOOD (1956–) went to work for TWA as a flight attendant shortly after finishing her BA at the University of Rhode Island in 1978. During the next several years, finding time on layovers, while commuting to and from airports, and during long-distance flights, she began to write the stories that would later become her first published novel, *Somewhere Off the Coast of Maine* (1987). After she was laid off by TWA in 1981, Hood focused on her writing, obtaining an MA from New York University and attending the Bread Loaf Writers' conference, where she completed the novel. Subsequent novels include *Waiting to Vanish* (1988), *Three-Legged Horse* (1989), and *Ruby* (1998). Her collection of short stories, *An Ornithologist's Guide to Life*, appeared in 2004. She has won two Pushcart Prizes and the Paul Bowles Prize for Short Fiction.

The Doctor

The doctor who killed my father wants to take me for coffee. *Starbucks*, he says. *The Coffee Café. Java Man.* He gives me options. He tells me he wants to talk about my father's treatment, his cancer, how hard he tried to save his life. *I didn't kill him*, he always says. *I just couldn't save him*. The distinction is lost on me. After all, I'm the one who had to walk into my father's room every day, grinning, lighthearted. I'm the one who had to explain about metastasizing, lymph nodes, Taxol; my father was a welder, a man who read *Reader's Digest* on the toilet and sometimes the Sunday paper. He did not really know what was out there.

The doctor who killed my father is as handsome as an Italian movie star: dark curly hair and a droopy handlebar mustache. He is from Chicago. He is divorced. He sees his kids every other weekend and alternating holidays. I learned all this during the long weeks of my father's illness. *Won't see you this weekend*, he'd say. *Got my kids.*

While I tried to get my father to drink his Ensure, I would imagine the doctor at their soccer games or buying them Happy Meals.

Even though I was falling in love with the doctor, I hated him, too. My father wasn't an every-other-weekend-and-alternating-holidays father. He drove me to school each morning, stopping at Dunkin' Donuts for Bavarian creams. He nursed me through measles, chicken pox, my tonsillectomy. He moved me from apartment to apartment, from broken heart to broken heart. He was a guy who was always around. Sometimes I would watch the doctor from my father's hospital room window as he walked across the parking lot to his red station wagon. *Il Dottore*, I would think. The doctor. The doctor who can't help.

The next time he calls, it's a Saturday evening that fall, five months after my father died. I am standing at my kitchen sink, staring at the neighbor's elaborate jack-o'-lanterns. A witch on a broomstick and a frightened cat that seems to leap out of the pumpkin, poised in midair. My other neighbor has lined her back porch with luminarias: paper bags with lit votives inside. In fact, my entire neighborhood is glowing. Except for my house.

"How about an espresso with sambuca?" the doctor asks me. "We could go to Lucinda's? Do you know it?"

His house, like mine, is quiet.

"I know it," I say.

When I was not with someone, my father was my Saturday-night date. We used to go for barbecue ribs, or lobster dinners. We used to share a bottle of wine, a pitcher of beer.

"I didn't kill him," the doctor is saying in a voice so low I can barely hear him.

"I know," I say again.

That morning of the day my father died, the doctor grabbed my arm hard. *I have tried everything*, he told me. *And still your father is going to die*. And I said, *Try something else. Do you hear me?* He shook his head. *We've run out of options.*

The doctor sighs. He laughs awkwardly, relieved. "You do see it then. It's an insidious disease. Horrible."

Darkness has fallen in that quick way it does this time of year. I am alone.

"Please," the doctor says, and he sounds eager, needy. "I would like to see you again. Under different circumstances. Better ones."

He was right about everything. The chances for survival, the progress of the disease, my father's inescapable death. But I do not want him to have everything. He can't lose my father and win the girl, too.

"No. I'm really not interested. Please don't keep calling."

When I hang up, I reach for the can that is sitting on the counter. It opens with a sigh. I set up the coffeemaker for one cup. As it brews, I watch the glow of the tiny red light, waiting to hear the almost imperceptible click that tells me it is time.

---

1. Does the narrator fail to distinguish between the doctor killing her father and not being able to save him?

2. How can the narrator refer to the doctor as "the doctor who killed my father" and yet later acknowledge, "He was right about everything"?

3. Why does the narrator not want the doctor "to have everything"?

MELANIE RAE THON (1957–) writes stories that focus on marginal people living in very small towns like White Falls, Idaho, the setting of her most acclaimed novel *Iona Moon* (1993). This may be because Thon grew up in just such a town: Kalispell, Montana. Her short story collections *Girls in the Grass* (1991) and *First, Body* (1996) explore issues related to youthful sexuality and social ills such as racial discrimination and incest. Although it is sometimes criticized for its persistently grim subject matter, Thon's highly stylized prose is praised for its ability to convey truths about the cruelty of society. In addition to writing, Thon has taught at various institutions, including Emerson College, the University of Massachusetts, and Syracuse University.

Blind Fish

My father says nobody whose word can be trusted has pulled a sturgeon from this lake since 1927, but divers searching for drowned children and drowned mothers swear they've seen fish bigger than themselves hiding in the lake's deepest trenches.

A freshwater sturgeon can grow twelve feet long. One old fish with barbels that look like whiskers might live a hundred years if no hungry human hooks or spears her.

They resist change.

Their Jurassic ancestors would find them sweetly familiar, still recognizable, though there are a hundred fifty million years between them.

They resemble sharks, or mermaids, or monsters.

Their snouts are flat, their skulls bony. Swim bladders in their guts allow them to breathe air for several hours. Long enough to roll in the shallows and spawn over rocks. Long enough to flop on the beach while they wait for the fisherman with a club to kill them. In courtship, they tumble and leap near the bottom. Or so we are told. What human has ever seen this?

They are loved for their delicate flesh and even more loved for their delicate caviar. You can kill the female and eat all of her, or you can catch her to strip the eggs, and this is said to be more merciful.

They are bottom feeders but not scavengers. This distinction is important. With their barbels they search the sediment for living prey: insect larvae, snails, worms, crayfish.

They are not vicious.

Big as they are, they won't attack you.

Hours after it is caught, a half-frozen, fifteen-inch pike can bite hard enough to draw blood as you try to gut it. But a sturgeon will look at you with its sad eyes as if to say, *I'm older than your grandmother. What are you doing?*

They are not blind after all; they see you. When they surface to feed in the shoals, their vision miraculously returns to them. Amazed, they understand that loss of sense is a choice of environment, a fact in the lake's treacherous canyons, but not, in the end, irreversible. Seeing you, they are not grateful for sight. They think, *We did not miss much.*

Don't be deceived by the scales. A sturgeon is soft inside, and delicious.

Some claim there are monsters in this lake. They have pictures to prove it. But the pictures are always grainy, out of focus, so the monster might be a log tossed by a wave, a trick of light, a sturgeon breaching.

The monster might be your own memory, wild horses, your mother who can breathe air but who doesn't want to, who goes down instead, who seeks the deepest trench, the one unmeasured, carved by the glacier that dug this lake, then melted to fill it.

If you fall in the water, you're safe where it's white. That's the foam, near the surface. Where it's green, you have hope. Swim toward the light. Keep your faith. Imagine all the people on shore who still love you. If it's black and you're blind, you can lose your direction, make mistakes or grow weary. That far down, the weight of water is oppressive, which is why, I suppose, the sturgeon's scales are hard as enamel, why its body is flat and has five bony ridges, why it rises out of the lake to swim miles upstream where it spawns in the dangerous river.

---

1. Why is the story titled “Blind Fish” when the sturgeons “are not blind after all”?
2. What is the significance of the story’s references to drowned mothers and to a mother who can breathe air but doesn’t want to?
3. What effects are achieved by attributing human thoughts and characteristics to the sturgeons? What effects are achieved by identifying humans as analogous to sturgeons?
4. Why does the narrator urge someone who falls in the water to “swim toward the light. Keep your faith. Imagine all the people on shore who still love you”?

DAVID GALEF (1959–) was born in New York City and educated at Princeton and Columbia universities. He has published widely in various genres, including novels, poems, short stories, children's books, and literary criticism; he has also translated works from Japanese, publishing two volumes of Japanese proverbs. Galef's fiction includes the novels *Flesh* (1995), *Turning Japanese* (1998), and *How to Cope with Suburban Stress* (2006), which has been translated into Russian, and a collection of short stories, *Laugh Track* (2002). He has taught literature and creative writing at the University of Mississippi and at Montclair State University in New Jersey.

My Date with Neanderthal Woman

I didn't know whether to bring flowers, which don't say much to someone from a basic subsistence culture. But a raw beefsteak might come across as too suggestive, and I'd read somewhere that Neanderthals were supposed to be vegetarians. I opted for the middle road, a box of chocolates.

I arrived just as the sun was sinking below the tree line. Glena lived in a cave by the edge of the forest and had, I'd heard, a more natural sense of time than those of us dominated by Rolexes and cell phones. Still, she wasn't there when I hurt my hand knocking on the cave entrance.

I tried twice, the second time with my foot. Then I called out, emphasizing the glottal *G* I'd heard when her name was pronounced by the TransWorld Dating Agency. She appeared as if suddenly planted in front of me, barrel-chested and bandy-legged, not much taller than a high-cut tree stump. Her furry brown hair was matted with sweat, but she smiled in a flat-faced way as I held out the chocolate.

Grabbing the box, she ripped it open and crowed in delight. She stuffed several candies with their wrappers into her mouth and chewed vigorously. The agency had told me not to waste time with complicated verbal behavior, so I just pointed at her and myself and said, "Glena, Robert."

She nodded, then pointed to the chocolate and rubbed her belly. Such a primal response! Frankly, I'd grown tired of modern women and their endless language games. She offered me one of the remaining chocolates from the box, and I was touched: pure reciprocity, though she looked disappointed that I didn't eat the wrappers. I mimed eating and pointed away from the forest. I would take her out to dinner.

Neanderthals, I recalled, were often on the cusp of starvation. She seemed to understand and followed me obediently as I led her to Chez Asperge, a small French-fusion-vegan restaurant not far from the woods.

Chez Asperge is elegant but casual, and we were greeted heartily by Claude the maitre d'. I didn't know the place had a dress code. In fact, the little loincloth Glena wore made me feel overdressed. Anyway, the situation was fixed with a borrowed jacket, which Glena wore in a charmingly asymmetric fashion.

God, I hate all the introductory explanations of a first date—which is why I was so happy none of that mattered to Glena. With a familiarity as if she'd known me for years, she spread her arms on the table and scooped up the mashed lentil dip. It's true, a woman who enjoys her food is sexy. Of course, she offered me some, and I showed her how to spread it on pita. But knives seemed to frighten her, and I'm sorry about that scar on the table. Still, we had a lovely meal—she particularly enjoyed the raw vegetable plate.

After dinner, I walked her home along the forest path. Movies and clubs could come later. I didn't want to overstimulate her. Even electric lights made her twitch. But along the path the moon was out, illuminating Glena's short but powerful body in a way that was weirdly beautiful. When I reached for her hand, she jerked back—different cultures have different intimacy rites, the agency guy said—so I took pains to explain that my intentions were honorable. Maybe she couldn't understand the words, yet I think she got the gist. Anyway, there's a limit to what I can achieve by gestures.

Eventually, her hand crept into mine and nearly crushed it. My miming of pain, hopping on one foot and flailing, made her laugh. A sense of humor is important in a relationship.

We paused at the entrance to her cave. She smiled, the gaps in her teeth drawing me in. Her earthy aroma was a definite aphrodisiac. What came next was sort of a kiss, followed by a rib-cracking embrace that the osteopath says is healing nicely. Still, whenever I think about it, I feel twinges. What a woman! I'd like to invite her out this weekend, but I can't e-mail her. Maybe I'll just drop by her cave accidentally on purpose with a bouquet of broccoli.

Yes, I know all the objections. Some couples are separated by decades, but we're separated by millennia. I like rock music and she likes the music of rocks. I'm modern Homo sapiens and she's Neanderthal, but I think we can work out our differences if we try.

---

1. What is being satirized in this story?
2. What fantasy or fantasies does Glena embody for the narrator?
3. What does this story illuminate about the narrator's relationship to women?

RACHEL CUSK (1967–) was born in Canada and grew up in Los Angeles; she finished her education in England, where she now lives. A mother of two, Cusk chronicles the emotional struggles faced by women of her generation, and she has been lauded for her dark, subtle comedy and elegant prose. In addition to her novels, she has written a highly praised work of nonfiction, *A Life's Work: On Becoming a Mother* (2002). Named among the best of young British novelists by *Granta* magazine, Cusk won the Whitbread First Novel Award for *Saving Agnes* (1992) and the Somerset Maugham Award for *The Country Life* (1997). "After Caravaggio's Sacrifice of Isaac" was originally written for a BBC series inspired by paintings.

After Caravaggio's Sacrifice of Isaac

One of the things about having children is the feeling they give you that they know all about you. It's like they've come from inside you and had a good look round while they were there. My son Ian gives me this feeling. I often catch him staring at me when my back is turned, like he's reading something private. Then I think, *he knows*, or *he's found out*, even though when it comes down to it I've got nothing to hide. I say to him, have I got egg on my face then?—something like that, and when he laughs I see that he's still just a boy and that I'm a man, even though a minute before it wasn't clear at all. It sounds a funny thing to say, but it's easy to forget how much children depend on you. It's important for them that you don't lose your authority. My wife said to me, during our bad time, one day he'll thank you Alan, and in those strange moments that seem to come so close to the truth and then don't I believe she might be right. When Ian was a baby we had him circumcised. My wife thought it was more hygienic. I didn't like it, but Sally said to me, he won't remember, they don't remember things. That's the way she is: she won't let it bother her.

I dream about Ian, not the same dream, different dreams, but they're all sort of similar. Like, we're getting on a train, me and him, and I put him on with all our bags and then I get off because I want to buy a newspaper or something and next thing I know the train's pulling away with me still on the platform and Ian looking at me through the window. Or, I'll have a whole dream about something else entirely, and then at the end I'll realize that all the time I was dreaming I was supposed to be looking after Ian and I don't know where he is. My mother left me on a bus once, when I was just a tot. There were so many of us she was always forgetting one. I went all round London on the number 73 crying my eyes out. You'd think I'd *meant* to leave you, she says. Didn't do you any harm, did it? she says. Just like Sally really. I've always tried to be different with Ian, but I sometimes wonder whether it was that trying that made things go wrong in the first place, whether if I'd been like Sally or my mum none of it would ever have happened. What I mean is that loving Ian made me expect more from life. It made me think there were better things out there.

It was right after he was born that I started looking at paintings. After what she'd been through with the birth Sally couldn't bear him near her. His crying made her mad; even if he was at the other end of the house she'd hear him crying and go mad. I didn't know what to think: it was totally unlike her. In the end I had to take unpaid leave off work. I used to take him out and just walk about with him round London, and that's how I first went to an art gallery. I was walking past and I saw a big poster for an exhibition and the picture on it caught my eye. It was a picture of a woman holding a baby. I didn't have a clue what it was then, but just looking at it made me feel things, with Sally at home being the way she was, and so I went in. What amazed me was how many people were in there, at ten o'clock on a Tuesday morning, just looking at paintings when they should have been at work. At least, that's what I *expected* myself to think: you know, lazy sods, arty-farty scroungers. But I didn't think that. I started to, and then I just didn't. It was something to do with Ian. He was asleep in his pram, but his being there was like some kind of passport, some bridge to another place. It felt right being there with him. It was an exhibition of Renaissance art, but as I say I didn't have a clue, I just went round and looked at things and kept getting this feeling of another side of life. You could say it was a call. Looking back to that day I can see now that I might have been a bit confused. I was seeing the writing on the wall with Sally: in my mind I think I was consciously separating myself and Ian from her. When I thought "we," it was me and Ian I was thinking about. And I worried about that thought, and when I looked at the pictures they told me not to worry, they told me everything was all right. They were sympathetic, if that doesn't sound too silly.

That was the beginning, anyway. I met Gerte a bit later, when I signed up for the evening class she was teaching on the History of Art. Ian was three by then. I was a bit stuck. I'd had all these ideas about art, but they hadn't seemed to come to anything. I was still in my job, even though when I went back after Sally had got better I'd decided to leave. From the first minute back I knew I couldn't stand it anymore, I knew I'd changed, and every day I spent there felt like a day wearing shoes that are too small, that cramp and pinch and torture your feet until all you can think about is getting them off. But I stayed all the same. I didn't have the courage to leave. I didn't have the confidence in myself. I just had the dissatisfaction. It took meeting Gerte to give me the confidence to go with it. Once I'd been chosen by her, I thought I could do anything. I looked back at the life I'd lived and thought, how could you have done this and that, how could you have been so ordinary? I was ashamed, ashamed of Sally, ashamed of our house and the things in it, ashamed of our friends and the things we talked about. The only thing I wasn't ashamed of was Ian. Like I say, he was my passport. He was what made me worth something. When Gerte chose me, inside myself I knew that somehow he was the reason; not because she loved him—she didn't—but because I did.

Gerte was from Germany. She taught art history at a university there and she came to England for a year on an exchange programme. She was the opposite of Sally, she was very well educated and delicate and beautiful. Her face belonged in one of those paintings she talked about, a Giotto, a Bellini. Whenever I looked at it I got that feeling, the feeling that everything would be all right. I was obsessed with her from the start. What's funny is that I never felt I was being unfaithful to Sally, even when I actually was. Gerte was better than Sally; it was as simple as that. I was learning about taste and beauty and value, and learning about these things justified what I felt about Gerte. It was a fact; but there are other facts, which don't have anything to do with taste and beauty and value. That's what I didn't see—I never saw it, even when I was standing at the front door with my bags packed.

Gerte spoke to me at the end of the third class. You look at me so much, she said, you'll wear my face away. She said that and then she walked away very lightly, like a ghost, leaving the door swinging on its hinges behind her. The significance of that moment, of her words and her look and the swinging door, seemed to reach right down to the root of my life. I felt that my whole existence was the frame for that moment, in the way that a pond exists for the pebble thrown into it and pulses with its rings long after the pebble has disappeared. I shuddered in just such a way; I felt a force pass through me. I thought it signified something, but now I realize it was a careless, idle gesture, a throw-away remark that I failed somehow to consign to the dustbin. Gerte hadn't yet seen anything in me that she wanted. I hadn't yet roused in her the desire to win, to possess. When I asked to buy her a drink, the next week, she seemed surprised. I was like some mad compass, febrile, sensitive, vibrating to everything she did and said, while she seemed solid and fixed and decided. At the pub she asked me a lot of questions, in the way people do who are bored. I told her things; eventually I told her about Ian. I remember her face, as if something had suddenly caught her eye, something beautiful and rare, something valuable. You love him, she said. Yes, I said. More than your wife? she said. Yes, I said. More than anything. I thought it would be all right, saying that to her, but a feeling of pressure rose in my chest, like I used to get as a child when I'd done something I knew was wrong.

I got so used to that feeling over the next few weeks that I stopped noticing it, it became the atmosphere of my time with Gerte, became indistinguishable from love. Why can't you stay, she would say across the dark, when I rose from her bed to get dressed. You know why, I would say. And she would sigh out my son's name and my heart would pound. Sometimes she spoke about Germany and the life I could lead there with her, and this made me very happy, I made a sort of story of it in my head so that for a while I lived two lives, one actual and one possible. That these possibilities adhered to me filled me with amazement and fear. I felt that without them I would die. How much do you love me, she would say, and because I had the certainty of Ian but not of her I felt that I could encompass him in myself, could speak on his behalf as well as my own. More than anything, I would say.

It's him or me, that's how she put it in the end. If you loved me, you would give him up. Then I would believe that you loved me. She was going back to Germany. Can't I bring him too, I said. If you did I would never know, she said, who you loved more. That's what love is like, when there are no facts. Sally knows about facts. She booked my cab for the airport. When I left Ian cried and ran out of the house after me and held on to my leg. I had to pick him up and carry him back to the house with him screaming. Go to your mum, I said, but he wouldn't, I had to force him off me and shut the door on him. When he looks at me now in that strange way, deep down I always think that it's because he's remembered that night. He couldn't, of course: the way things worked out he wouldn't know any different. I remember Gerte's face at the airport, lit with pleasure at the sight of me, so that I couldn't understand what she said, she had to repeat it over and over. I know now, she said. You can go home to your son. Go on, go home. So I did. Sally was still in the hall. That's when she said that one day Ian would thank me. You're a good man, Alan, she said.

---

1. Why does the narrator consider Ian to be his "passport"?
2. Why do the pictures he sees in the art gallery tell Adam that "everything was all right"? Why does looking at Gerte's face make Adam feel that "everything would be all right"?
3. What does Adam mean when he says, "That's what love is like, when there are no facts"?
4. How does Cusk's story reflect the biblical story of Abraham and Isaac (Genesis 22:1–19)? In what ways does Cusk's story follow Caravaggio's interpretation of the biblical story?

NOVELLAS

HERMAN MELVILLE (1819–1891) was a successful author by the age of thirty, having written several popular accounts of his experiences as a ship's crew member and adventurer in the South Seas, most notably *Typee* (1846), *Omoo* (1847), and *White-Jacket* (1850). Under the influence of Nathaniel Hawthorne, however, Melville began to explore deeper and darker literary territory. The resulting novels and stories are those for which he is highly regarded today even though they were initially critical and commercial failures. Among these are *Moby-Dick* (1851), "Bartleby the Scrivener" (1853), *The Confidence-Man* (1857), and *Billy Budd* (1888–1891). In his last decades, Melville lived in financially secure obscurity as a New York City customs inspector.

Benito Cereno

In the year 1799, Captain Amasa Delano, of Duxbury, in Massachusetts, commanding a large sealer and general trader, lay at anchor, with a valuable cargo, in the harbour of St. Maria—a small, desert, uninhabited island toward the southern extremity of the long coast of Chili. There he had touched for water.

On the second day, not long after dawn, while lying in his berth, his mate came below, informing him that a strange sail was coming into the bay. Ships were then not so plenty in those waters as now. He rose, dressed, and went on deck.

The morning was one peculiar to that coast. Everything was mute and calm; everything grey. The sea, though undulated into long roods of swells, seemed fixed, and was sleeked at the surface like waved lead that has cooled and set in the smelter's mould. The sky seemed a grey mantle. Flights of troubled grey fowl, kith and kin with flights of troubled grey vapours among which they were mixed, skimmed low and fitfully over the waters, as swallows over meadows before storms. Shadows present, foreshadowing deeper shadows to come.

To Captain Delano's surprise, the stranger, viewed through the glass, showed no colours; though to do so upon entering a haven, however uninhabited in its shores, where but a single other ship might be lying, was the custom among peaceful seamen of all nations. Considering the lawlessness and loneliness of the spot, and the sort of stories, at that day associated with those seas, Captain Delano's surprise might have deepened into some uneasiness had he not been a person of a singularly undistrustful good nature, not liable, except on extraordinary and repeated excitement, and hardly then, to indulge in personal alarms, any way involving the imputation of malign evil in man. Whether, in view of what humanity is capable, such a trait implies, along with a benevolent heart, more than ordinary quickness and accuracy of intellectual perception, may be left to the wise to determine.

But whatever misgivings might have obtruded on first seeing the stranger, would almost, in any seaman's mind, have been dissipated by observing that the ship, in navigating into the harbour, was drawing too near the land, for her own safety's sake, owing to a sunken reef making out off her bow. This seemed to prove her a stranger, indeed, not only to the sealer, but the island; consequently, she could be no wonted freebooter on that ocean. With no small interest, Captain Delano continued to watch her—a proceeding not much facilitated by the vapours partly mantling the hull, through which the far matin light from her cabin streamed equivocally enough; much like the sun—by this time crescented on the rim of the horizon, and apparently, in company with the strange ship, entering the harbour—which, wimpled by the same low, creeping clouds, showed not unlike a Lima intriguante's one sinister eye peering across the plaza from the Indian loophole of her dusk *saya-y-manta*.

It might have been but a deception of the vapours, but, the longer the stranger was watched, the more singular appeared her manoeuvres. Ere long it seemed hard to decide whether she meant to come in or no—what she wanted, or what she was about. The wind, which had breezed up a little during the night, was now extremely light and baffling, which the more increased the apparent uncertainty of her movements.

Surmising, at last, that it might be a ship in distress, Captain Delano ordered his whaleboat to be dropped, and, much to the wary opposition of his mate, prepared to board her, and, at the least, pilot her in. On the night previous, a fishing party of the seamen had gone a long distance to some detached rocks out of sight from the sealer, and, an hour or two before daybreak, had returned, having met with no small success. Presuming that the stranger might have been long off soundings, the good captain put several baskets of the fish, for presents, into his boat, and so pulled away. From her continuing too near the sunken reef, deeming her in danger, calling to his men, he made all haste to apprise those on board of their situation. But, sometime ere the boat came up, the wind, light though it was, having shifted, had headed the vessel off, as well as partly broken the vapours from about her.

Upon gaining a less remote view, the ship, when made signally visible on the verge of the leaden-hued swells, with the shreds of fog here and there raggedly furring her, appeared like a whitewashed monastery after a thunderstorm, seen perched upon some dun cliff among the Pyrenees. But it was no purely fanciful resemblance which now, for a moment, almost led Captain Delano to think that nothing less than a shipload of monks was before him. Peering over the bulwarks were what really seemed, in the hazy distance, throngs of dark cowls; while, fitfully revealed through the open portholes, other dark moving figures were dimly descried, as of Black Friars pacing the cloisters.

Upon a still nigher approach, this appearance was modified, and the true character of the vessel was plain—a Spanish merchantman of the first class; carrying Negro slaves, amongst other valuable freight, from one colonial port to another. A very large, and, in its time, a very fine vessel, such as in those days were at intervals encountered along that main; sometimes superseded Acapulco treasure ships, or retired frigates of the Spanish king's navy, which, like superannuated Italian palaces, still, under a decline of masters, preserved signs of former state.

As the whaleboat drew more and more nigh, the cause of the peculiar pipe-clayed aspect of the stranger was seen in the slovenly neglect pervading her. The spars, ropes, and great part of the bulwarks looked woolly, from long unacquaintance with the scraper, tar, and the brush. Her keel seemed laid, her ribs put together, and she launched, from Ezekiel's Valley of Dry Bones.

In the present business in which she was engaged, the ship's general model and rig appeared to have undergone no material change from their original warlike and Froissart pattern. However, no guns were seen.

The tops were large, and were railed about with what had once been octagonal network, all now in sad disrepair. These tops hung overhead like three ruinous aviaries, in one of which was seen perched, on a ratlin, a white noddy, a strange fowl, so called from its lethargic somnambulistic character, being frequently caught by hand at sea. Battered and mouldy, the castellated forecastle seemed some ancient turret, long ago taken by assault, and then left to decay. Towards the stern, two high-raised quarter galleries—the balustrades here and there covered with dry, tindery sea moss—opening out from the unoccupied state cabin, whose dead lights, for all the mild weather, were hermetically closed and caulked—these tenantless balconies hung over the sea as if it were the grand Venetian canal. But the principal relic of faded grandeur was the ample oval of the shieldlike stern piece, intricately carved with the arms of Castile and Leon, medallioned about by groups of mythological or symbolical devices; uppermost and central of which was a dark satyr in a mask, holding his foot on the prostrate neck of a writhing figure, likewise masked.

Whether the ship had a figurehead, or only a plain beak, was not quite certain, owing to canvas wrapped about that part, either to protect it while undergoing a refurbishing, or else decently to hide its decay. Rudely painted or chalked, as in a sailor freak, along the forward side of a sort of pedestal below the canvas, was the sentence, "*Seguid vuestro jefe*," (follow your leader); while upon the tarnished headboards, nearby, appeared, in stately capitals, once gilt, the ship's name, "SAN DOMINICK," each letter streakingly corroded with tricklings of copper-spike rust; while, like mourning weeds, dark festoons of sea grass slimily swept to and fro over the name, with every hearselike roll of the hull.

As at last the boat was hooked from the bow along toward the gangway amidship, its keel, while yet some inches separated from the hull, harshly grated as on a sunken coral reef. It proved a huge bunch of conglobated barnacles adhering below the water to the side like a wen; a token of baffling airs and long calms passed somewhere in those seas.

Climbing the side, the visitor was at once surrounded by a clamorous throng of whites and blacks, but the latter outnumbering the former more than could have been expected, Negro transportation ship as the stranger in port was. But, in one language, and as with one voice, all poured out a common tale of suffering; in which the Negresses, of whom there were not a few, exceeded the others in their dolorous vehemence. The scurvy, together with a fever, had swept off a great part of their number, more especially the Spaniards. Off Cape Horn, they had narrowly escaped shipwreck; then, for days together, they had lain tranced without wind; their provisions were low; their water next to none; their lips that moment were baked.

While Captain Delano was thus made the mark of all eager tongues, his one eager glance took in all the faces, with every other object about him.

Always upon first boarding a large and populous ship at sea, especially a foreign one, with a nondescript crew such as lascars or Manila men, the impression varies in a peculiar way from that produced by first entering a strange house with strange inmates in a strange land. Both house and ship, the one by its walls and blinds, the other by its high bulwarks like ramparts, hoard from view their interiors till the last moment; but in the case of the ship there is this addition: that the living spectacle it contains, upon its sudden and complete disclosure, has, in contrast with the blank ocean which zones it, something of the effect of enchantment. The ship seems unreal; these strange costumes, gestures, and faces, but a shadowy tableau just emerged from the deep, which directly must receive back what it gave.

Perhaps it was some such influence as above is attempted to be described which, in Captain Delano's mind, heightened whatever, upon a staid scrutiny, might have seemed unusual; especially the conspicuous figures of four elderly grizzled Negroes, their heads like black, doddered willow tops, who, in venerable contrast to the tumult below them, were couched sphynx-like, one on the starboard cathead, another on the larboard, and the remaining pair face-to-face on the opposite bulwarks above the main chains. They each had bits of unstranded old junk in their hands, and, with a sort of stoical self-content, were picking the junk into oakum, a small heap of which lay by their sides. They accompanied the task with a continuous, low, monotonous chant; droning and drooling away like so many grey-headed bagpipers playing a funeral march.

The quarterdeck rose into an ample elevated poop, upon the forward verge of which, lifted, like the oakum pickers, some eight feet above the general throng, sat along in a row, separated by regular spaces, the cross-legged figures of six other blacks; each with a rusty hatchet in his hand, which, with a bit of brick and a rag, he was engaged like a scullion in scouring; while between each two was a small stack of hatchets, their rusted edges turned forward awaiting a like operation. Though occasionally the four oakum pickers would briefly address some person or persons in the crowd below, yet the six hatchet polishers neither spoke to others, nor breathed a whisper among themselves, but sat intent upon their task, except at intervals, when, with the peculiar love in Negroes of uniting industry with pastime, two-and-two they sideways clashed their hatchets together, like cymbals, with a barbarous din. All six, unlike the generality, had the raw aspect of unsophisticated Africans.

But that first comprehensive glance which took in those ten figures, with scores less conspicuous, rested but an instant upon them, as, impatient of the hubbub of voices, the visitor turned in quest of whomsoever it might be that commanded the ship.

But as if not unwilling to let nature make known her own case among his suffering charge, or else in despair of restraining it for the time, the Spanish captain, a gentlemanly, reserved-looking, and rather young man to a stranger's eye, dressed with singular richness, but bearing plain traces of recent sleepless cares and disquietudes, stood passively by, leaning against the main mast, at one moment casting a dreary, spiritless look upon his excited people, at the next an unhappy glance toward his visitor. By his side stood a black of small stature, in whose rude face, as occasionally, like a shepherd's dog, he mutely turned it up into the Spaniard's, sorrow and affection were equally blended.

Struggling through the throng, the American advanced to the Spaniard, assuring him of his sympathies, and offering to render whatever assistance might be in his power. To which the Spaniard returned, for the present, but grave and ceremonious acknowledgments, his national formality dusked by the saturnine mood of ill health.

But losing no time in mere compliments, Captain Delano, returning to the gangway, had his baskets of fish brought up; and as the wind still continued light, so that some hours at least must elapse ere the ship could be brought to the anchorage, he bade his men return to the sealer, and fetch back as much water as the whaleboat could carry, with whatever soft bread the steward might have, all the remaining pumpkins on board, with a box of sugar, and a dozen of his private bottles of cider.

Not many minutes after the boat's pushing off, to the vexation of all, the wind entirely died away, and the tide turning, began drifting back the ship helplessly seaward. But trusting this would not long last, Captain Delano sought with good hopes to cheer up the strangers, feeling no small satisfaction that, with persons in their condition he could—thanks to his frequent voyages along the Spanish Main—converse with some freedom in their native tongue.

While left alone with them, he was not long in observing some things tending to heighten his first impressions; but surprise was lost in pity, both for the Spaniards and blacks, alike evidently reduced from scarcity of water and provisions, while long-continued suffering seemed to have brought out the less good-natured qualities of the Negroes, besides, at the same time, impairing the Spaniard's authority over them. But, under the circumstances, precisely this condition of things was to have been anticipated. In armies, navies, cities, or families—in nature herself—nothing more relaxes good order than misery. Still, Captain Delano was not without the idea, that had Benito Cereno been a man of greater energy, misrule would hardly have come to the present pass. But the debility, constitutional or induced by the hardships, bodily and mental, of the Spanish captain, was too obvious to be overlooked. A prey to settled dejection, as if long mocked with hope he would not now indulge it, even when it had ceased to be a mock, the prospect of that day or evening at furthest, lying at anchor, with plenty of water for his people, and a brother captain to counsel and befriend, seemed in no perceptible degree to encourage him. His mind appeared unstrung, if not still more seriously affected. Shut up in these oaken walls, chained to one dull round of command, whose unconditionality cloyed him, like some hypochondriac abbot he moved slowly about, at times suddenly pausing, starting, or staring, biting his lip, biting his fingernail, flushing, paling, twitching his beard, with other symptoms of an absent or moody mind. This distempered spirit was lodged, as before hinted, in as distempered a frame. He was rather tall, but seemed never to have been robust, and now with nervous suffering was almost worn to a skeleton. A tendency to some pulmonary complaint appeared to have been lately confirmed. His voice was like that of one with lungs half gone, hoarsely suppressed, a husky whisper. No wonder that, as in this state he tottered about, his private servant apprehensively followed him. Sometimes the Negro gave his master his arm, or took his handkerchief out of his pocket for him; performing these and similar offices with that affectionate zeal which transmutes into something filial or fraternal acts in themselves but menial; and which has gained for the Negro the repute of making the most pleasing body servant in the world; one, too, whom a master need be on no stiffly superior terms with, but may treat with familiar trust; less a servant than a devoted companion.

Marking the noisy indocility of the blacks in general, as well as what seemed the sullen inefficiency of the whites, it was not without humane satisfaction that Captain Delano witnessed the steady good conduct of Babo.

But the good conduct of Babo, hardly more than the ill behaviour of others, seemed to withdraw the half-lunatic Don Benito from his cloudy languor. Not that such precisely was the impression made by the Spaniard on the mind of his visitor. The Spaniard's individual unrest was, for the present, but noted as a conspicuous feature in the ship's general affliction. Still, Captain Delano was not a little concerned at what he could not help taking for the time to be Don Benito's unfriendly indifference toward himself. The Spaniard's manner, too, conveyed a sort of sour and gloomy disdain, which he seemed at no pains to disguise. But this the American in charity ascribed to the harassing effects of sickness, since, in former instances, he had noted that there are peculiar natures on whom prolonged physical suffering seems to cancel every social instinct of kindness; as if forced to black bread themselves, they deemed it but equity that each person coming nigh them should, indirectly, by some slight or affront, be made to partake of their fare.

But ere long Captain Delano bethought him that, indulgent as he was at the first, in judging the Spaniard, he might not, after all, have exercised charity enough. At bottom it was Don Benito's reserve which displeased him; but the same reserve was shown toward all but his personal attendant. Even the formal reports which, according to sea usage, were at stated times made to him by some petty underling (either a white, mulatto, or black), he hardly had patience enough to listen to, without betraying contemptuous aversion. His manner upon such occasions was, in its degree, not unlike that which might be supposed to have been his imperial countryman's, Charles V, just previous to the anchoritish retirement of that monarch from the throne.

This splenetic disrelish of his place was evinced in almost every function pertaining to it. Proud as he was moody, he condescended to no personal mandate. Whatever special orders were necessary, their delivery was delegated to his body servant, who in turn transferred them to their ultimate destination, through runners, alert Spanish boys or slave boys, like pages or pilot fish within easy call continually hovering round Don Benito. So that to have beheld this undemonstrative invalid gliding about, apathetic and mute, no landsman could have dreamed that in him was lodged a dictatorship beyond which, while at sea, there was no earthly appeal.

Thus, the Spaniard, regarded in his reserve, seemed as the involuntary victim of mental disorder. But, in fact, his reserve might, in some degree, have proceeded from design. If so, then in Don Benito was evinced the unhealthy climax of that icy though conscientious policy, more or less adopted by all commanders of large ships, which, except in signal emergencies, obliterates alike the manifestation of sway with every trace of sociality; transforming the man into a block, or rather into a loaded cannon, which, until there is call for thunder, has nothing to say.

Viewing him in this light, it seemed but a natural token of the perverse habit induced by a long course of such hard self-restraint, that, notwithstanding the present condition of his ship, the Spaniard should still persist in a demeanour, which, however harmless—or it may be, appropriate—in a well-appointed vessel, such as the *San Dominick* might have been at the outset of the voyage, was anything but judicious now. But the Spaniard perhaps thought that it was with captains as with gods: reserve, under all events, must still be their cue. But more probably this appearance of slumbering dominion might have been but an attempted disguise to conscious imbecility—not deep policy, but shallow device. But be all this as it might, whether

Don Benito's manner was designed or not, the more Captain Delano noted its pervading reserve, the less he felt uneasiness at any particular manifestation of that reserve toward himself.

Neither were his thoughts taken up by the captain alone. Wonted to the quiet orderliness of the sealer's comfortable family of a crew, the noisy confusion of the *San Dominick*'s suffering host repeatedly challenged his eye. Some prominent breaches not only of discipline but of decency were observed. These Captain Delano could not but ascribe, in the main, to the absence of those subordinate deck officers to whom, along with higher duties, is entrusted what may be styled the police department of a populous ship. True, the old oakum pickers appeared at times to act the part of monitorial constables to their countrymen, the blacks; but though occasionally succeeding in allaying trifling outbreaks now and then between man and man, they could do little or nothing toward establishing general quiet. The *San Dominick* was in the condition of a transatlantic emigrant ship, among whose multitude of living freight are some individuals, doubtless, as little troublesome as crates and bales; but the friendly remonstrances of such with their ruder companions are of not so much avail as the unfriendly arm of the mate. What the *San Dominick* wanted was what the emigrant ship has, stern superior officers. But on these decks not so much as a fourth mate was to be seen.

The visitor's curiosity was roused to learn the particulars of those mishaps which had brought about such absenteeism, with its consequences; because, though deriving some inkling of the voyage from the wails which at the first moment had greeted him, yet of the details no clear understanding had been had. The best account would, doubtless, be given by the captain. Yet at first the visitor was loth to ask it, unwilling to provoke some distant rebuff. But plucking up courage, he at last accosted Don Benito, renewing the expression of his benevolent interest, adding, that did he (Captain Delano) but know the particulars of the ship's misfortunes, he would, perhaps, be better able in the end to relieve them. Would Don Benito favour him with the whole story?

Don Benito faltered; then, like some somnambulist suddenly interfered with, vacantly stared at his visitor, and ended by looking down on the deck. He maintained this posture so long, that Captain Delano, almost equally disconcerted, and involuntarily almost as rude, turned suddenly from him, walking forward to accost one of the Spanish seamen for the desired information. But he had hardly gone five paces, when with a sort of eagerness Don Benito invited him back, regretting his momentary absence of mind, and professing readiness to gratify him.

While most part of the story was being given, the two captains stood on the afterpart of the main deck, a privileged spot, no one being near but the servant.

"It is now a hundred and ninety days," began the Spaniard, in his husky whisper, "that this ship, well officered and well manned, with several cabin passengers—some fifty Spaniards in all—sailed from Buenos Ayres bound to Lima, with a general cargo, Paraguay tea and the like—and," pointing forward, "that parcel of Negroes, now not more than a hundred and fifty, as you see, but then numbering over three hundred souls. Off Cape Horn we had heavy gales. In one moment, by night, three of my best officers, with fifteen sailors, were lost, with the main yard; the spar snapping under them in the slings, as they sought, with heavers, to beat down the icy sail. To lighten the hull, the heavier sacks of mata were thrown into the sea, with most of the water pipes lashed on deck at the time. And this last necessity it was, combined with the prolonged detentions afterwards experienced, which eventually brought about our chief causes of suffering. When—"

Here there was a sudden fainting attack of his cough, brought on, no doubt, by his mental distress. His servant sustained him, and drawing a cordial from his pocket placed it to his lips. He a little revived. But unwilling to leave him unsupported while yet imperfectly restored, the black with one arm still encircled his master, at the same time keeping his eye fixed on his face, as if to watch for the first sign of complete restoration, or relapse, as the event might prove.

The Spaniard proceeded, but brokenly and obscurely, as one in a dream.

—"Oh, my God! rather than pass through what I have, with joy I would have hailed the most terrible gales; but—"

His cough returned and with increased violence; this subsiding, with reddened lips and closed eyes he fell heavily against his supporter.

"His mind wanders. He was thinking of the plague that followed the gales," plaintively sighed the servant; "my poor, poor master!" wringing one hand, and with the other wiping the mouth. "But be patient, *señor*," again turning to Captain Delano, "these fits do not last long; master will soon be himself."

Don Benito reviving, went on; but as this portion of the story was very brokenly delivered, the substance only will here be set down.

It appeared that after the ship had been many days tossed in storms off the Cape, the scurvy broke out, carrying off numbers of the whites and blacks. When at last they had worked round into the Pacific, their spars and sails were so damaged, and so inadequately handled by the surviving mariners, most of whom were become invalids, that, unable to lay her northerly course by the wind, which was powerful, the unmanageable ship for successive days and nights was blown northwestward, where the breeze suddenly deserted her, in unknown waters, to sultry calms. The absence of the water pipes now proved as fatal to life as before their presence had menaced it. Induced, or at least aggravated, by the more than scanty allowance of water, a malignant fever followed the scurvy; with the excessive heat of the lengthened calm, making such short work of it as to sweep away, as by billows, whole families of the Africans, and a yet larger number, proportionably, of the Spaniards, including, by a luckless fatality, every officer on board. Consequently, in the smart west winds eventually following the calm, the already rent sails having to be simply dropped, not furled, at need, had been gradually reduced to the beggar's rags they were now. To procure substitutes for his lost sailors, as well as supplies of water and sails, the captain at the earliest opportunity had made for Baldivia, the southernmost civilized port of Chili and South America; but upon nearing the coast the thick weather had prevented him from so much as sighting that harbour. Since which period, almost without a crew, and almost without canvas and almost without water, and at intervals giving its added dead to the sea, the *San Dominick* had been battledored about by contrary winds, inveigled by currents, or grown weedy in calms. Like a man lost in woods, more than once she had doubled upon her own track.

"But throughout these calamities," huskily continued Don Benito, painfully turning in the half embrace of his servant, "I have to thank those Negroes you see, who, though to your inexperienced eyes appearing unruly, have, indeed, conducted themselves with less of restlessness than even their owner could have thought possible under such circumstances."

Here he again fell faintly back. Again his mind wandered: but he rallied, and less obscurely proceeded.

"Yes, their owner was quite right in assuring me that no fetters would be needed with his blacks; so that while, as is wont in this transportation, those Negroes have always remained upon deck—not thrust below, as in the Guineamen—they have, also, from the beginning, been freely permitted to range within given bounds at their pleasure."

Once more the faintness returned—his mind roved—but, recovering, he resumed:

"But it is Babo here to whom, under God, I owe not only my own preservation, but likewise to him, chiefly, the merit is due, of pacifying his more ignorant brethren, when at intervals tempted to murmurings."

"Ah, master," sighed the black, bowing his face, "don't speak of me; Babo is nothing; what Babo has done was but duty."

"Faithful fellow!" cried Captain Delano. "Don Benito, I envy you such a friend; slave I cannot call him."

As master and man stood before him, the black upholding the white, Captain Delano could not but bethink him of the beauty of that relationship which could present such a spectacle of fidelity on the one hand and confidence on the other. The scene was heightened by the contrast in dress, denoting their relative positions. The Spaniard wore a loose Chili jacket of dark velvet; white small clothes and stockings, with silver buckles at the knee and instep; a high-crowned sombrero, of fine grass; a slender sword, silver mounted, hung from a knot in his sash; the last being an almost invariable adjunct, more for utility than ornament, of a South American gentleman's dress to this hour. Excepting when his occasional nervous contortions brought about disarray, there was a certain precision in his attire, curiously at variance with the unsightly disorder around; especially in the belittered ghetto, forward of the main mast, wholly occupied by the blacks.

The servant wore nothing but wide trousers, apparently, from their coarseness and patches, made out of some old topsail; they were clean, and confined at the waist by a bit of unstranded rope, which, with his composed, deprecatory air at times, made him look something like a begging friar of St. Francis.

However unsuitable for the time and place, at least in the blunt-thinking American's eyes, and however strangely surviving in the midst of all his afflictions, the toilette of Don Benito might not, in fashion at least, have gone beyond the style of the day among South Americans of his class. Though on the present voyage sailing from Buenos Ayres, he had avowed himself a native and resident of Chili, whose inhabitants had not so generally adopted the plain coat and once plebeian pantaloons; but, with a becoming modification, adhered to their provincial costume, picturesque as any in the world. Still, relatively to the pale history of the voyage, and his own pale face, there seemed something so incongruous in the Spaniard's apparel, as almost to suggest the image of an invalid courtier tottering about London streets in the time of the plague.

The portion of the narrative which, perhaps, most excited interest, as well as some surprise, considering the latitudes in question, was the long calms spoken of, and more particularly the ship's so long drifting about. Without communicating the opinion, of course, the American could not but impute at least part of the detentions both to clumsy seamanship and faulty navigation. Eyeing Don Benito's small, yellow hands, he easily inferred that the young captain had not got into command at the hawsehole but the cabin window, and if so, why wonder at incompetence, in youth, sickness, and aristocracy united? Such was his democratic conclusion.

But drowning criticism in compassion, after a fresh repetition of his sympathies, Captain Delano having heard out his story, not only engaged, as in the first place, to see Don Benito and his people supplied in their immediate bodily needs, but, also, now further promised to assist him in procuring a large permanent supply of water, as well as some sails and rigging; and, though it would involve no small embarrassment to himself, yet he would spare three of his best seamen for temporary deck officers; so that without delay the ship might proceed to Concepción, there fully to refit for Lima, her destined port.

Such generosity was not without its effect, even upon the invalid. His face lighted up; eager and hectic, he met the honest glance of his visitor. With gratitude he seemed overcome.

"This excitement is bad for master," whispered the servant, taking his arm, and with soothing words gently drawing him aside.

When Don Benito returned, the American was pained to observe that his hopefulness, like the sudden kindling in his cheek, was but febrile and transient.

Ere long, with a joyless mien, looking up toward the poop, the host invited his guest to accompany him there, for the benefit of what little breath of wind might be stirring.

As during the telling of the story, Captain Delano had once or twice started at the occasional cymballing of the hatchet polishers, wondering why such an interruption should be allowed, especially in that part of the ship, and in the ears of an invalid; and, moreover, as the hatchets had anything but an attractive look, and the handlers of them still less so, it was, therefore, to tell the truth, not without some lurking reluctance, or even shrinking, it may be, that Captain Delano, with apparent complaisance, acquiesced in his host's invitation. The more so, since with an untimely caprice of punctilio, rendered distressing by his cadaverous aspect, Don Benito, with Castilian bows, solemnly insisted upon his guest's preceding him up the ladder leading to the elevation; where, one on each side of the last step, sat four armorial supporters and sentries, two of the ominous file. Gingerly enough stepped good Captain Delano between them, and in the instant of leaving them behind, like one running the gauntlet, he felt an apprehensive twitch in the calves of his legs.

But when, facing about, he saw the whole file, like so many organ grinders, still stupidly intent on their work, unmindful of everything beside, he could not but smile at his late fidgeting panic.

Presently, while standing with Don Benito, looking forward upon the decks below, he was struck by one of those instances of insubordination previously alluded to. Three black boys, with two Spanish boys, were sitting together on the hatchets, scraping a rude wooden platter, in which some scanty mess had recently been cooked. Suddenly, one of the black boys, enraged at a word dropped by one of his white companions, seized a knife, and though called to forbear by one of the oakum pickers, struck the lad over the head, inflicting a gash from which blood flowed.

In amazement, Captain Delano inquired what this meant. To which the pale Benito dully muttered, that it was merely the sport of the lad.

"Pretty serious sport, truly," rejoined Captain Delano. "Had such a thing happened on board the *Bachelor's Delight*, instant punishment would have followed."

At these words the Spaniard turned upon the American one of his sudden, staring, half-lunatic looks; then, relapsing into his torpor, answered, "Doubtless, doubtless, *señor.*"

Is it, thought Captain Delano, that this helpless man is one of those paper captains I've known, who by policy wink at what by power they cannot put down? I know no sadder sight than a commander who has little of command but the name.

"I should think, Don Benito," he now said, glancing toward the oakum picker who had sought to interfere with the boys, "that you would find it advantageous to keep all your blacks employed, especially the younger ones, no matter at what useless task, and no matter what happens to the ship. Why, even with my little band, I find such a course indispensable. I once kept a crew on my quarterdeck thrumming mats for my cabin, when, for three days, I had given up my ship—mats, men, and all—for a speedy loss, owing to the violence of a gale in which we could do nothing but helplessly drive before it."

"Doubtless, doubtless," muttered Don Benito.

"But," continued Captain Delano, again glancing upon the oakum pickers and then at the hatchet polishers, nearby, "I see you keep some at least of your host employed."

"Yes," was again the vacant response.

"Those old men there, shaking their pows from their pulpits," continued Captain Delano, pointing to the oakum pickers, "seem to act the part of old dominies to the rest, little heeded as their admonitions are at times. Is this voluntary on their part, Don Benito, or have you appointed them shepherds to your flock of black sheep?"

"What posts they fill, I appointed them," rejoined the Spaniard in an acrid tone, as if resenting some supposed satiric reflection.

"And these others, these Ashantee conjurors here," continued Captain Delano, rather uneasily eyeing the brandished steel of the hatchet polishers, where in spots it had been brought to a shine, "this seems a curious business they are at, Don Benito?"

"In the gales we met," answered the Spaniard, "what of our general cargo was not thrown overboard was much damaged by the brine. Since coming into calm weather, I have had several cases of knives and hatchets daily brought up for overhauling and cleaning."

"A prudent idea, Don Benito. You are part owner of ship and cargo, I presume; but not of the slaves, perhaps?"

"I am owner of all you see," impatiently returned Don Benito, "except the main company of blacks, who belonged to my late friend, Alexandro Aranda."

As he mentioned this name, his air was heartbroken, his knees shook; his servant supported him.

Thinking he divined the cause of such unusual emotion, to confirm his surmise, Captain Delano, after a pause, said, "And may I ask, Don Benito, whether—since awhile ago you spoke of some cabin passengers—the friend, whose loss so afflicts you, at the outset of the voyage accompanied his blacks?"

"Yes."

"But died of the fever?"

"Died of the fever. Oh, could I but—"

Again quivering, the Spaniard paused.

"Pardon me," said Captain Delano slowly, "but I think that, by a sympathetic experience, I conjecture, Don Benito, what it is that gives the keener edge to your grief. It was once my hard fortune to lose at sea a dear friend, my own brother, then supercargo. Assured of the welfare of his spirit, its departure I could have borne like a man; but that honest eye, that honest hand—both of which had so often met mine—and that warm heart; all, all—like scraps to the dogs—to throw all to the sharks! It was then I vowed never to have for fellow voyager a man I loved, unless, unbeknown to him, I had provided every requisite, in case of a fatality, for embalming his mortal part for interment on shore. Were your friend's remains now on board this ship, Don Benito, not thus strangely would the mention of his name affect you."

"On board this ship?" echoed the Spaniard. Then, with horrified gestures, as directed against some spectre, he unconsciously fell into the ready arms of his attendant, who, with a silent appeal toward Captain Delano, seemed beseeching him not again to broach a theme so unspeakably distressing to his master.

This poor fellow now, thought the pained American, is the victim of that sad superstition which associates goblins with the deserted body of man, as ghosts with an abandoned house. How unlike are we made! What to me, in like case, would have been a solemn satisfaction, the bare suggestion, even, terrifies the Spaniard into this trance. Poor Alexandro Aranda! what would you say could you here see your friend—who, on former voyages, when you for months were left behind, has, I dare say, often longed, and longed, for one peep at you—now transported with terror at the least thought of having you anyway nigh him.

At this moment, with a dreary graveyard toll, betokening a flaw, the ship's forecastle bell, smote by one of the grizzled oakum pickers, proclaimed ten o'clock through the leaden calm; when Captain Delano's attention was caught by the moving figure of a gigantic black, emerging from the general crowd below, and slowly advancing toward the elevated poop. An iron collar was about his neck, from which depended a chain, thrice wound round his body; the terminating links padlocked together at a broad band of iron, his girdle.

"How like a mute Atufal moves," murmured the servant.

The black mounted the steps of the poop, and, like a brave prisoner, brought up to receive sentence, stood in unquailing muteness before Don Benito, now recovered from his attack.

At the first glimpse of his approach, Don Benito had started, a resentful shadow swept over his face; and, as with the sudden memory of bootless rage, his white lips glued together.

This is some mulish mutineer, thought Captain Delano, surveying, not without a mixture of admiration, the colossal form of the Negro.

"See, he waits your question, master," said the servant.

Thus reminded, Don Benito, nervously averting his glance, as if shunning, by anticipation, some rebellious response, in a disconcerted voice, thus spoke:

"Atufal, will you ask my pardon now?"

The black was silent.

"Again, master," murmured the servant, with bitter upbraiding eyeing his countryman; "Again, master; he will bend to master yet."

"Answer," said Don Benito, still averting his glance, "say but the one word *pardon*, and your chains shall be off."

Upon this, the black, slowly raising both arms, let them lifelessly fall, his links clanking, his head bowed; as much as to say, "No, I am content."

"Go," said Don Benito, with inkept and unknown emotion.

Deliberately as he had come, the black obeyed.

"Excuse me, Don Benito," said Captain Delano, "but this scene surprises me; what means it, pray?"

"It means that that Negro alone, of all the band, has given me peculiar cause of offence. I have put him in chains; I—"

Here he paused; his hand to his head, as if there were a swimming there, or a sudden bewilderment of memory had come over him; but meeting his servant's kindly glance seemed reassured, and proceeded:

"I could not scourge such a form. But I told him he must ask my pardon. As yet he has not. At my command, every two hours he stands before me."

"And how long has this been?"

"Some sixty days."

"And obedient in all else? And respectful?"

"Yes."

"Upon my conscience, then," exclaimed Captain Delano, impulsively, "he has a royal spirit in him, this fellow."

"He may have some right to it," bitterly returned Don Benito; "he says he was king in his own land."

"Yes," said the servant, entering a word, "those slits in Atufal's ears once held wedges of gold; but poor Babo here, in his own land, was only a poor slave; a black man's slave was Babo, who now is the white's."

Somewhat annoyed by these conversational familiarities, Captain Delano turned curiously upon the attendant, then glanced inquiringly at his master; but, as if long wonted to these little informalities, neither master nor man seemed to understand him.

"What, pray, was Atufal's offence, Don Benito?" asked Captain Delano; "if it was not something very serious, take a fool's advice, and, in view of his general docility, as well as in some natural respect for his spirit, remit his penalty."

"No, no, master never will do that," here murmured the servant to himself, "proud Atufal must first ask master's pardon. The slave there carries the padlock, but master here carries the key."

His attention thus directed, Captain Delano now noticed for the first time that, suspended by a slender silken cord, from Don Benito's neck hung a key. At once, from the servant's muttered syllables divining the key's purpose, he smiled and said: "So, Don Benito—padlock and key—significant symbols, truly."

Biting his lip, Don Benito faltered.

Though the remark of Captain Delano, a man of such native simplicity as to be incapable of satire or irony, had been dropped in playful allusion to the Spaniard's singularly evidenced lordship over the black; yet the hypochondriac seemed in some way to have taken it as a malicious reflection upon his confessed inability thus far to break down, at least, on a verbal summons, the entrenched will of the slave. Deploring this supposed misconception, yet despairing of correcting it, Captain Delano shifted the subject; but finding his companion more than ever withdrawn, as if still slowly digesting the lees of the presumed affront above-mentioned, by and by Captain Delano likewise became less talkative, oppressed, against his own will, by what seemed the secret vindictiveness of the morbidly sensitive Spaniard. But the good sailor himself, of a quite contrary disposition, refrained, on his part, alike from the appearance as from the feeling of resentment, and if silent, was only so from contagion.

Presently the Spaniard, assisted by his servant, somewhat discourteously crossed over from Captain Delano; a procedure which, sensibly enough, might have been allowed to pass for idle caprice of ill humour, had not master and man, lingering round the corner of the elevated skylight, begun whispering together in low voices. This was unpleasing. And more: the moody air of the Spaniard, which at times had not been without a sort of valetudinarian stateliness, now seemed anything but dignified; while the menial familiarity of the servant lost its original charm of simple-hearted attachment.

In his embarrassment, the visitor turned his face to the other side of the ship. By so doing, his glance accidentally fell on a young Spanish sailor, a coil of rope in his hand, just stepped from the deck to the first round of the mizzen rigging. Perhaps the man would not have been particularly noticed, were it not that, during his ascent to one of the yards, he, with a sort of covert intentness, kept his eye fixed on Captain Delano, from whom, presently, it passed, as if by a natural sequence, to the two whisperers.

His own attention thus redirected to that quarter, Captain Delano gave a slight start. From something in Don Benito's manner just then, it seemed as if the visitor had, at least partly, been the subject of the withdrawn consultation going on—a conjecture as little agreeable to the guest as it was little flattering to the host.

The singular alternations of courtesy and ill breeding in the Spanish captain were unaccountable, except on one of two suppositions—innocent lunacy, or wicked imposture.

But the first idea, though it might naturally have occurred to an indifferent observer, and, in some respects, had not hitherto been wholly a stranger to Captain Delano's mind, yet, now that, in an incipient way, he began to regard the stranger's conduct something in the light of an intentional affront, of course the idea of lunacy was virtually vacated. But if not a lunatic, what then? Under the circumstances, would a gentleman, nay, any honest boor, act the part now acted by his host? The man was an impostor. Some low-born adventurer, masquerading as an oceanic grandee; yet so ignorant of the first requisites of mere gentlemanhood as to be betrayed into the present remarkable indecorum. That strange ceremoniousness, too, at other times evinced, seemed not uncharacteristic of one playing a part above his real level. Benito Cereno—Don Benito Cereno—a sounding name. One, too, at that period, not unknown, in the surname, to supercargoes and sea captains trading along the Spanish Main, as belonging to one of the most enterprising and extensive mercantile families in all those provinces; several members of it having titles; a sort of Castilian Rothschild, with a noble brother, or cousin, in every great trading town of South America. The alleged Don Benito was in early manhood, about twenty-nine or thirty. To assume a sort of roving cadetship in the maritime affairs of such a house, what more likely scheme for a young knave of talent and spirit? But the Spaniard was a pale invalid. Never mind. For even to the degree of simulating mortal disease, the craft of some tricksters had been known to attain. To think that, under the aspect of infantile weakness, the most savage energies might be couched—those velvets of the Spaniard but the velvet paw to his fangs.

From no train of thought did these fancies come; not from within, but from without; suddenly, too, and in one throng, like hoarfrost; yet as soon to vanish as the mild sun of Captain Delano's good nature regained its meridian.

Glancing over once again toward Don Benito—whose side face, revealed above the skylight, was now turned toward him—Captain Delano was struck by the profile, whose clearness of cut was refined by the thinness incident to ill health, as well as ennobled about the chin by the beard. Away with suspicion. He was a true offshoot of a true hidalgo Cereno.

Relieved by these and other better thoughts, the visitor, lightly humming a tune, now began indifferently pacing the poop, so as not to betray to Don Benito that he had at all mistrusted incivility, much less duplicity; for such mistrust would yet be proved illusory, and by the event; though, for the present, the circumstance which had provoked that distrust remained unexplained. But when that little mystery should have been cleared up, Captain Delano thought he might extremely regret it, did he allow Don Benito to become aware that he had indulged in ungenerous surmises. In short, to the Spaniard's black-letter text, it was best, for a while, to leave open margin.

Presently, his pale face twitching and overcast, the Spaniard, still supported by his attendant, moved over toward his guest, when, with even more than his usual embarrassment, and a strange sort of intriguing intonation in his husky whisper, the following conversation began:

"*Señor*, may I ask how long you have lain at this isle?"

"Oh, but a day or two, Don Benito."

"And from what port are you last?"

"Canton."

"And there, *señor*, you exchanged your seal skins for teas and silks, I think you said?"

"Yes. Silks, mostly."

"And the balance you took in specie, perhaps?"

Captain Delano, fidgeting a little, answered—

"Yes; some silver; not a very great deal, though."

"Ah—well. May I ask how many men have you on board, *señor*?"

Captain Delano slightly started, but answered:

"About five-and-twenty, all told."

"And at present, *señor*, all on board, I suppose?"

"All on board, Don Benito," replied the captain now with satisfaction.

"And will be tonight, *señor*?"

At this last question, following so many pertinacious ones, for the soul of him Captain Delano could not but look very earnestly at the questioner, who, instead of meeting the glance, with every token of craven discomposure dropped his eyes to the deck; presenting an unworthy contrast to his servant, who, just then, was kneeling at his feet adjusting a loose shoe buckle; his disengaged face meantime, with humble curiosity, turned openly up into his master's downcast one.

The Spaniard, still with a guilty shuffle, repeated his question:

"And—and will be tonight, *señor*?"

"Yes, for aught I know," returned Captain Delano—"but nay," rallying himself into fearless truth, "some of them talked of going off on another fishing party about midnight."

"Your ships generally go—go more or less armed, I believe, *señor*?"

"Oh, a six-pounder or two, in case of emergency," was the intrepidly indifferent reply, "with a small stock of muskets, sealing spears, and cutlasses, you know."

As he thus responded, Captain Delano again glanced at Don Benito, but the latter's eyes were averted; while abruptly and awkwardly shifting the subject, he made some peevish allusion to the calm, and then, without apology, once more, with his attendant, withdrew to the opposite bulwarks, where the whispering was resumed.

At this moment, and ere Captain Delano could cast a cool thought upon what had just passed, the young Spanish sailor before mentioned was seen descending from the rigging. In act of stooping over to spring inboard to the deck, his voluminous, unconfined frock, or shirt, of coarse woollen, much spotted with tar, opened out far down the chest, revealing a soiled undergarment of what seemed the finest linen, edged, about the neck, with a narrow blue ribbon, sadly faded and worn. At this moment the young sailor's eye was again fixed on the whisperers, and Captain Delano thought he observed a lurking significance in it, as if silent signs of some Freemason sort had that instant been interchanged.

This once more impelled his own glance in the direction of Don Benito, and, as before, he could not but infer that himself formed the subject of the conference. He paused. The sound of the hatchet polishing fell on his ears. He cast another swift side look at the two. They had the air of conspirators. In connection with the late questionings, and the incident of the young sailor, these things now begat such return of involuntary suspicion that the singular guilelessness of the American could not endure it. Plucking up a gay and humorous expression, he crossed over to the two rapidly, saying: "Ha, Don Benito, your black here seems high in your trust; a sort of privy counsellor, in fact."

Upon this, the servant looked up with a good-natured grin, but the master started as from a venomous bite. It was a moment or two before the Spaniard sufficiently recovered himself to reply; which he did, at last, with cold constraint: "Yes, *señor*, I have trust in Babo."

Here Babo, changing his previous grin of mere animal humour into an intelligent smile, not ungratefully eyed his master.

Finding that the Spaniard now stood silent and reserved, as if involuntarily, or purposely giving hint that his guest's proximity was inconvenient just then, Captain Delano, unwilling to appear uncivil even to incivility itself, made some trivial remark and moved off; again and again turning over in his mind the mysterious demeanour of Don Benito Cereno.

He had descended from the poop, and, wrapped in thought, was passing near a dark hatchway, leading down into the steerage, when, perceiving motion there, he looked to see what moved. The same instant there was a sparkle in the shadowy hatchway, and he saw one of the Spanish sailors, prowling there, hurriedly placing his hand in the bosom of his frock, as if hiding something. Before the man could have been certain who it was that was passing, he slunk below out of sight. But enough was seen of him to make it sure that he was the same young sailor before noticed in the rigging.

What was that which so sparkled? thought Captain Delano. It was no lamp—no match—no live coal. Could it have been a jewel? But how come sailors with jewels?—or with silk-trimmed undershirts either? Has he been robbing the trunks of the dead cabin passengers? But if so, he would hardly wear one of the stolen articles on board ship here. Ah, ah—if now that was, indeed, a secret sign I saw passing between this suspicious fellow and his captain awhile since; if I could only be certain that in my uneasiness my senses did not deceive me, then—

Here, passing from one suspicious thing to another, his mind revolved the point of the strange questions put to him concerning his ship.

By a curious coincidence, as each point was recalled, the black wizards of Ashantee would strike up with their hatchets, as in ominous comment on the white stranger's thoughts. Pressed by such enigmas and portents, it would have been almost against nature, had not, even into the least distrustful heart, some ugly misgivings obtruded.

Observing the ship now helplessly fallen into a current, with enchanted sails, drifting with increased rapidity seaward; and noting that, from a lately intercepted projection of the land, the sealer was hidden, the stout mariner began to quake at thoughts which he barely durst confess to himself. Above all, he began to feel a ghostly dread of Don Benito. And yet when he roused himself, dilated his chest, felt himself strong on his legs, and coolly considered it—what did all these phantoms amount to?

Had the Spaniard any sinister scheme, it must have reference not so much to him (Captain Delano) as to his ship (the *Bachelor's Delight*). Hence the present drifting away of the one ship from the other, instead of favouring any such possible scheme, was, for the time at least, opposed to it. Clearly any suspicion, combining such contradictions, must need be delusive. Beside, was it not absurd to think of a vessel in distress—a vessel by sickness almost dismanned of her crew—a vessel whose inmates were parched for water—was it not a thousand times absurd that such a craft should, at present, be of a piratical character; or her commander, either for himself or those under him, cherish any desire but for speedy relief and refreshment? But then, might not general distress, and thirst in particular, be affected? And might not that same undiminished Spanish crew, alleged to have perished off to a remnant, be at that very moment lurking in the hold? On heartbroken pretence of entreating a cup of cold water, fiends in human form had got into lonely dwellings, nor retired until a dark deed had been done. And among the Malay pirates, it was no unusual thing to lure ships after them into their treacherous harbours, or entice boarders from a declared enemy at sea, by the spectacle of thinly manned or vacant decks, beneath which prowled a hundred spears with yellow arms ready to upthrust them through the mats. Not that Captain Delano had entirely credited such things. He had heard of them—and now, as stories, they recurred. The present destination of the ship was the anchorage. There she would be near his own vessel. Upon gaining that vicinity, might not the *San Dominick*, like a slumbering volcano, suddenly let loose energies now hid?

He recalled the Spaniard's manner while telling his story. There was a gloomy hesitancy and subterfuge about it. It was just the manner of one making up his tale for evil purposes, as he goes. But if that story was not true, what was the truth? That the ship had unlawfully come into the Spaniard's possession? But in many of its details, especially in reference to the more calamitous parts, such as the fatalities among the seamen, the consequent prolonged beating about, the past sufferings from obstinate calms, and still continued suffering from thirst; in all these points, as well as others, Don Benito's story had corroborated not only the wailing ejaculations of the indiscriminate multitude, white and black, but likewise—what seemed impossible to be counterfeit—by the very expression and play of every human feature, which Captain Delano saw. If Don Benito's story was throughout an invention, then every soul on board, down to the youngest Negress, was his carefully drilled recruit in the plot: an incredible inference. And yet, if there was ground for mistrusting the Spanish captain's veracity, that inference was a legitimate one.

In short, scarce an uneasiness entered the honest sailor's mind but, by a subsequent spontaneous act of good sense, it was ejected. At last he began to laugh at these forebodings; and laugh at the strange ship for, in its aspect, someway siding with them, as it were; and laugh, too, at the odd-looking blacks, particularly those old scissors grinders, the Ashantees; and those bedridden old knitting women, the oakum pickers; and, in a human way, he almost began to laugh at the dark Spaniard himself, the central hobgoblin of all.

For the rest, whatever in a serious way seemed enigmatical, was now good-naturedly explained away by the thought that, for the most part, the poor invalid scarcely knew what he was about; either sulking in black vapours, or putting random questions without sense or object. Evidently, for the present, the man was not fit to be entrusted with the ship. On some benevolent plea withdrawing the command from him, Captain Delano would yet have to send her to Concepción in charge of his second mate, a worthy person and good navigator—a plan which would prove no wiser for the *San Dominick* than for Don Benito; for—relieved from all anxiety, keeping wholly to his cabin—the sick man, under the good nursing of his servant, would probably, by the end of the passage, be in a measure restored to health and with that he should also be restored to authority.

Such were the American's thoughts. They were tranquillizing. There was a difference between the idea of Don Benito's darky preordaining Captain Delano's fate, and Captain Delano's lightly arranging Don Benito's. Nevertheless, it was not without something of relief that the good seaman presently perceived his whaleboat in the distance. Its absence had been prolonged by unexpected detention at the sealer's side, as well as its returning trip lengthened by the continual recession of the goal.

The advancing speck was observed by the blacks. Their shouts attracted the attention of Don Benito, who, with a return of courtesy, approaching Captain Delano, expressed satisfaction at the coming of some supplies, slight and temporary as they must necessarily prove.

Captain Delano responded; but while doing so, his attention was drawn to something passing on the deck below: among the crowd climbing the landward bulwarks, anxiously watching the coming boat, two blacks, to all appearances accidentally incommoded by one of the sailors, flew out against him with horrible curses, which the sailor someway resenting, the two blacks dashed him to the deck and jumped upon him, despite the earnest cries of the oakum pickers.

"Don Benito," said Captain Delano quickly, "do you see what is going on there? Look!"

But, seized by his cough, the Spaniard staggered, with both hands to his face, on the point of falling. Captain Delano would have supported him, but the servant was more alert, who, with one hand sustaining his master, with the other applied the cordial. Don Benito, restored, the black withdrew his support, slipping aside a little, but dutifully remaining within call of a whisper. Such discretion was here evinced as quite wiped away, in the visitor's eyes, any blemish of impropriety which might have attached to the attendant, from the indecorous conferences before mentioned; showing, too, that if the servant were to blame, it might be more the master's fault than his own, since when left to himself he could conduct thus well.

His glance thus called away from the spectacle of disorder to the more pleasing one before him, Captain Delano could not avoid again congratulating Don Benito upon possessing such a servant, who, though perhaps a little too forward now and then, must upon the whole be invaluable to one in the invalid's situation.

"Tell me, Don Benito," he added, with a smile—"I should like to have your man here myself—what will you take for him? Would fifty doubloons be any object?"

"Master wouldn't part with Babo for a thousand doubloons," murmured the black, overhearing the offer, and taking it in earnest, and, with the strange vanity of a faithful slave appreciated by his master, scorning to hear so paltry a valuation put upon him by a stranger. But Don Benito, apparently hardly yet completely restored, and again interrupted by his cough, made but some broken reply.

Soon his physical distress became so great, affecting his mind, too, apparently, that, as if to screen the sad spectacle, the servant gently conducted his master below.

Left to himself, the American, to while away the time till his boat should arrive, would have pleasantly accosted some one of the few Spanish seamen he saw; but recalling something that Don Benito had said touching their ill conduct, he refrained, as a shipmaster indisposed to countenance cowardice or unfaithfulness in seamen.

While, with these thoughts, standing with eye directed forward toward that handful of sailors—suddenly he thought that some of them returned the glance and with a sort of meaning. He rubbed his eyes, and looked again; but again seemed to see the same thing. Under a new form, but more obscure than any previous one, the old suspicions recurred, but, in the absence of Don Benito, with less of panic than before. Despite the bad account given of the sailors, Captain Delano resolved forthwith to accost one of them. Descending the poop, he made his way through the blacks, his movement drawing a queer cry from the oakum pickers, prompted by whom the Negroes, twitching each other aside, divided before him; but, as if curious to see what was the object of this deliberate visit to their ghetto, closing in behind, in tolerable order, followed the white stranger up. His progress thus proclaimed as by mounted kings-at-arms, and escorted as by a Caffre guard of honour, Captain Delano, assuming a good-humoured, offhand air, continued to advance; now and then saying a blithe word to the Negroes, and his eye curiously surveying the white faces, here and there sparsely mixed in with the blacks, like stray white pawns venturously involved in the ranks of the chessmen opposed.

While thinking which of them to select for his purpose, he chanced to observe a sailor seated on the deck engaged in tarring the strap of a large block, with a circle of blacks squatted round him inquisitively eyeing the process.

The mean employment of the man was in contrast with something superior in his figure. His hand, black with continually thrusting it into the tar pot held for him by a Negro, seemed not naturally allied to his face, a face which would have been a very fine one but for its haggardness. Whether this haggardness had aught to do with criminality could not be determined; since, as intense heat and cold, though unlike, produce like sensations, so innocence and guilt, when, through casual association with mental pain, stamping any visible impress, use one seal—a hacked one.

Not again that this reflection occurred to Captain Delano at the time, charitable man as he was. Rather another idea. Because observing so singular a haggardness to be combined with a dark eye, averted as in trouble and shame, and then, however illogically, uniting in his mind his own private suspicions of the crew with the confessed ill opinion on the part of their captain, he was insensibly operated upon by certain general notions, which, while disconnecting pain and abashment from virtue, as invariably link them with vice.

If, indeed, there be any wickedness on board this ship, thought Captain Delano, be sure that man there has fouled his hand in it, even as now he fouls it in the pitch. I don't like to accost him. I will speak to this other, this old Jack here on the windlass.

He advanced to an old Barcelona tar, in ragged red breeches and dirty nightcap, cheeks trenched and bronzed, whiskers dense as thorn hedges. Seated between two sleepy-looking Africans, this mariner, like his younger shipmate, was employed upon some rigging—splicing a cable—the sleepy-looking blacks performing the inferior function of holding the outer parts of the ropes for him.

Upon Captain Delano's approach, the man at once hung his head below its previous level; the one necessary for business. It appeared as if he desired to be thought absorbed, with more than common fidelity, in his task. Being addressed, he glanced up, but with what seemed a furtive, diffident air, which sat strangely enough on his weather-beaten visage, much as if a grizzly bear, instead of growling and biting, should simper and cast sheep's eyes. He was asked several questions concerning the voyage—questions purposely referring to several particulars in Don Benito's narrative—not previously corroborated by those impulsive cries greeting the visitor on first coming on board. The questions were briefly answered, confirming all that remained to be confirmed of the story. The Negroes about the windlass joined in with the old sailor, but, as they became talkative, he by degrees became mute, and at length quite glum, seemed morosely unwilling to answer more questions, and yet, all the while, this ursine air was somehow mixed with his sheepish one.

Despairing of getting into unembarrassed talk with such a centaur, Captain Delano, after glancing round for a more promising countenance, but seeing none, spoke pleasantly to the blacks to make way for him; and so, amid various grins and grimaces, returned to the poop, feeling a little strange at first, he could hardly tell why, but upon the whole with regained confidence in Benito Cereno.

How plainly, thought he, did that old whiskerando yonder betray a consciousness of ill desert. No doubt, when he saw me coming, he dreaded lest I, apprised by his captain of the crew's general misbehaviour, came with sharp words for him, and so down with his head. And yet—and yet, now that I think of it, that very old fellow, if I err not, was one of those who seemed so earnestly eyeing me here awhile since. Ah, these currents spin one's head round almost as much as they do the ship. Ha, there now's a pleasant sort of sunny sight; quite sociable, too.

His attention had been drawn to a slumbering Negress, partly disclosed through the lacework of some rigging, lying, with youthful limbs carelessly disposed, under the lee of the bulwarks, like a doe in the shade of a woodland rock. Sprawling at her lapped breasts was her wide-awake fawn, stark naked, its black little body half lifted from the deck, crosswise with its dam's; its hands, like two paws, clambering upon her; its mouth and nose ineffectually rooting to get at the mark; and meantime giving a vexatious half-grunt, blending with the composed snore of the Negress.

The uncommon vigour of the child at length roused the mother. She started up, at distance facing Captain Delano. But, as if not at all concerned at the attitude in which she had been caught, delightedly she caught the child up, with maternal transports, covering it with kisses.

There's naked nature, now; pure tenderness and love, thought Captain Delano, well pleased.

This incident prompted him to remark the other Negresses more particularly than before. He was gratified with their manners; like most uncivilized women, they seemed at once tender of heart and tough of constitution; equally ready to die for their infants or fight for them. Unsophisticated as leopardesses; loving as doves. Ah! thought Captain Delano, these perhaps are some of the very women whom Mungo Park saw in Africa, and gave such a noble account of.

These natural sights somehow insensibly deepened his confidence and ease. At last he looked to see how his boat was getting on; but it was still pretty remote. He turned to see if Don Benito had returned; but he had not.

To change the scene, as well as to please himself with a leisurely observation of the coming boat, stepping over into the mizzen chains he clambered his way into the starboard quarter gallery; one of those abandoned Venetian-looking water balconies previously mentioned; retreats cut off from the deck. As his foot pressed the half-damp, half-dry seamosses matting the place, and a chance phantom cat's-paw—an islet of breeze, unheralded, unfollowed—as this ghostly cat's-paw came fanning his cheek, as his glance fell upon the row of small, round deadlights, all closed like coppered eyes of the coffined, and the state cabin door, once connecting with the gallery, even as the deadlights had once looked out upon it, but now caulked fast like a sarcophagus lid, to a purple-black, tarred-over panel, threshold, and post; and he bethought him of the time, when that state cabin and this state balcony had heard the voices of the Spanish king's officers, and the forms of the Lima viceroy's daughters had perhaps leaned where he stood—as these and other images flitted through his mind, as the cat's-paw through the calm, gradually he felt rising a dreamy inquietude, like that of one who alone on the prairie feels unrest from the repose of the noon.

He leaned against the carved balustrade, again looking off toward his boat; but found his eye falling upon the ribboned grass, trailing along the ship's waterline, straight as a border of green box; and parterres of seaweed, broad ovals and crescents, floating nigh and far, with what seemed long formal alleys between, crossing the terraces of swells, and sweeping round as if leading to the grottoes below. And overhanging all was the balustrade by his arm, which, partly stained with pitch and partly embossed with moss, seemed the charred ruin of some summerhouse in a grand garden long running to waste.

Trying to break one charm, he was but becharmed anew. Though upon the wide sea, he seemed in some far inland country; prisoner in some deserted château, left to stare at empty grounds, and peer out at vague roads, where never wagon or wayfarer passed.

But these enchantments were a little disenchanted as his eye fell on the corroded main chains. Of an ancient style, massy and rusty in link, shackle, and bolt, they seemed even more fit for the ship's present business than the one for which probably she had been built.

Presently he thought something moved nigh the chains. He rubbed his eyes, and looked hard. Groves of rigging were about the chains; and there, peering from behind a great stay, like an Indian from behind a hemlock, a Spanish sailor, a marlingspike in his hand, was seen, who made what seemed an imperfect gesture toward the balcony—but immediately, as if alarmed by some advancing step along the deck within, vanished into the recesses of the hempen forest, like a poacher.

What meant this? Something the man had sought to communicate, unbeknown to anyone, even to his captain. Did the secret involve aught unfavourable to his captain? Were those previous misgivings of Captain Delano's about to be verified? Or, in his haunted mood at the moment, had some random, unintentional motion of the man, while busy with the stay, as if repairing it, been mistaken for a significant beckoning?

Not unbewildered, again he gazed off for his boat. But it was temporarily hidden by a rocky spur of the isle. As with some eagerness he bent forward, watching for the first shooting view of its beak, the balustrade gave way before him like charcoal. Had he not clutched an outreaching rope he would have fallen into the sea. The crash, though feeble, and the fall, though hollow, of the rotten fragments, must have been overheard. He glanced up. With sober curiosity peering down upon him was one of the old oakum pickers, slipped from his perch to an outside boom; while below the old Negro—and, invisible to him, reconnoitring from a porthole like a fox from the mouth of its den—crouched the Spanish sailor again. From something suddenly suggested by the man's air, the mad idea now darted into Captain Delano's mind; that Don Benito's plea of indisposition, in withdrawing below, was but a pretence: that he was engaged there maturing some plot, of which the sailor, by some means gaining an inkling, had a mind to warn the stranger against; incited, it may be, by gratitude for a kind word on first boarding the ship. Was it from foreseeing some possible interference like this, that Don Benito had, beforehand, given such a bad character of his sailors, while praising the Negroes; though, indeed, the former seemed as docile as the latter the contrary? The whites, too, by nature, were the shrewder race. A man with some evil design, would not he be likely to speak well of that stupidity which was blind to his depravity, and malign that intelligence from which it might not be hidden? Not unlikely, perhaps. But if the whites had dark secrets concerning Don Benito, could then Don Benito be any way in complicity with the blacks? But they were too stupid. Besides, who ever heard of a white so far a renegade as to apostatize from his very species almost, by leaguing in against it with Negroes? These difficulties recalled former ones. Lost in their mazes, Captain Delano, who had now regained the deck, was uneasily advancing along it, when he observed a new face: an aged sailor seated cross-legged near the main hatchway. His skin was shrunk up with wrinkles like a pelican's empty pouch; his hair frosted; his countenance grave and composed. His hands were full of ropes, which he was working into a large knot. Some blacks were about him obligingly dipping the strands for him, here and there, as the exigencies of the operation demanded.

Captain Delano crossed over to him, and stood in silence surveying the knot; his mind, by a not uncongenial transition, passing from its own entanglements to those of the hemp. For intricacy such a knot he had never seen in an American ship, or indeed any other. The old man looked like an Egyptian priest, making Gordian knots for the temple of Ammon. The knot seemed a combination of double-bowline knot, treble-crown knot, backhanded well knot, knot-in-and-out knot, and jamming knot.

At last, puzzled to comprehend the meaning of such a knot, Captain Delano, addressed the knotter:

"What are you knotting there, my man?"

"The knot," was the brief reply, without looking up.

"So it seems; but what is it for?"

"For someone else to undo," muttered back the old man, plying his fingers harder than ever, the knot being now nearly completed.

While Captain Delano stood watching him, suddenly the old man threw the knot toward him, and said in broken English—the first heard in the ship—something to this effect—"Undo it, cut it, quick." It was said lowly, but with such condensation of rapidity, that the long, slow words in Spanish, which had preceded and followed, almost operated as covers to the brief English between.

For a moment, knot in hand, and knot in head, Captain Delano stood mute; while, without further heeding him, the old man was now intent upon other ropes. Presently there was a slight stir behind Captain Delano. Turning, he saw the chained Negro, Atufal, standing quietly there. The next moment the old sailor rose, muttering, and, followed by his subordinate Negroes, removed to the forward part of the ship, where in the crowd he disappeared.

An elderly Negro, in a clout like an infant's, and with a pepper-and-salt head, and a kind of attorney air, now approached Captain Delano. In tolerable Spanish, and with a good-natured, knowing wink, he informed him that the old knotter was simple witted, but harmless; often playing his old tricks. The Negro concluded by begging the knot, for of course the stranger would not care to be troubled with it. Unconsciously, it was handed to him. With a sort of congé, the

Negro received it, and turning his back ferreted into it like a detective customhouse officer after smuggled laces. Soon, with some African word, equivalent to pshaw, he tossed the knot overboard.

All this is very queer now, thought Captain Delano, with a qualmish sort of emotion; but as one feeling incipient seasickness, he strove, by ignoring the symptoms, to get rid of the malady. Once more he looked off for his boat. To his delight, it was now again in view, leaving the rocky spur astern.

The sensation here experienced, after at first relieving his uneasiness, with unforeseen efficiency, soon began to remove it. The less distant sight of that well-known boat—showing it, not as before, half blended with the haze, but with outline defined, so that its individuality, like a man's, was manifest; that boat, *Rover* by name, which, though now in strange seas, had often pressed the beach of Captain Delano's home, and, brought to its threshold for repairs, had familiarly lain there, as a Newfoundland dog; the sight of that household boat evoked a thousand trustful associations, which, contrasted with previous suspicions, filled him not only with lightsome confidence, but somehow with half-humorous self-reproaches at his former lack of it.

"What, I, Amasa Delano—Jack of the Beach, as they called me when a lad—I, Amasa; the same that, duck satchel in hand, used to paddle along the waterside to the schoolhouse made from the old hulk—I, little Jack of the Beach, that used to go berrying with cousin Nat and the rest; I to be murdered here at the ends of the earth, on board a haunted pirate ship by a horrible Spaniard? Too nonsensical to think of! Who would murder Amasa Delano? His conscience is clean. There is someone above. Fie, fie, Jack of the Beach! you are a child indeed; a child of the second childhood, old boy; you are beginning to dote and drool, I'm afraid."

Light of heart and foot, he stepped aft, and there was met by Don Benito's servant, who, with a pleasing expression, responsive to his own present feelings, informed him that his master had recovered from the effects of his coughing fit, and had just ordered him to go present his compliments to his good guest, Don Amasa, and say that he (Don Benito) would soon have the happiness to rejoin him.

There now, do you mark that? again thought Captain Delano, walking the poop. What a donkey I was. This kind gentleman who here sends me his kind compliments, he, but ten minutes ago, dark lantern in hand, was dodging round some old grindstone in the hold, sharpening a hatchet for me, I thought. Well, well; these long calms have a morbid effect on the mind, I've often heard, though I never believed it before. Ha! glancing toward the boat, there's *Rover*, a good dog, a white bone in her mouth. A pretty big bone though, seems to me.—What? Yes, she has fallen afoul of the bubbling tide rip there. It sets her the other way, too, for the time. Patience.

It was now about noon, though, from the greyness of everything, it seemed to be getting toward dusk.

The calm was confirmed. In the far distance, away from the influence of land, the leaden ocean seemed laid out and leaded up, its course finished, soul gone, defunct. But the current from landward, where the ship was, increased; silently sweeping her further and further toward the tranced waters beyond.

Still, from his knowledge of those latitudes, cherishing hopes of a breeze, and a fair and fresh one, at any moment, Captain Delano, despite present prospects, buoyantly counted upon bringing the *San Dominick* safely to anchor ere night. The distance swept over was nothing; since, with a good wind, ten minutes' sailing would retrace more than sixty minutes' drifting. Meantime, one moment turning to mark *Rover* fighting the tide rip, and the next to see Don Benito approaching, he continued walking the poop.

Gradually he felt a vexation arising from the delay of his boat; this soon merged into uneasiness; and at last, his eye falling continually, as from a stage box into the pit, upon the strange crowd before and below him, and by and by recognizing there the face—now composed to indifference—of the Spanish sailor who had seemed to beckon from the main chains, something of his old trepidations returned.

Ah, thought he—gravely enough—this is like the ague: because it went off, it follows not that it won't come back.

Though ashamed of the relapse, he could not altogether subdue it; and so, exerting his good nature to the utmost, insensibly he came to a compromise.

Yes, this is a strange craft; a strange history, too, and strange folks on board. But—nothing more.

By way of keeping his mind out of mischief till the boat should arrive, he tried to occupy it with turning over and over, in a purely speculative sort of way, some lesser peculiarities of the captain and crew. Among others, four curious points recurred.

First, the affair of the Spanish lad assailed with a knife by the slave boy; an act winked at by Don Benito. Second, the tyranny in Don Benito's treatment of Atufal, the black; as if a child should lead a bull of the Nile by the ring in his nose. Third, the trampling of the sailor by the two Negroes; a piece of insolence passed over without so much as a reprimand. Fourth, the cringing submission to their master of all the ship's underlings, mostly blacks; as if by the least inadvertence they feared to draw down his despotic displeasure.

Coupling these points, they seemed somewhat contradictory. But what then, thought Captain Delano, glancing toward his now nearing boat—what then? Why, this Don Benito is a very capricious commander. But he is not the first of the sort I have seen; though it's true he rather exceeds any other. But as a nation—continued he in his reveries—these Spaniards are all an odd set; the very word *Spaniard* has a curious, conspirator, Guy Fawkish twang to it. And yet, I dare say, Spaniards in the main are as good folks as any in Duxbury, Massachusetts. Ah, good! At last *Rover* has come.

As, with its welcome freight, the boat touched the side, the oakum pickers, with venerable gestures, sought to restrain the blacks, who, at the sight of three gurried water casks in its bottom, and a pile of wilted pumpkins in its bow, hung over the bulwarks in disorderly raptures.

Don Benito with his servant now appeared; his coming, perhaps, hastened by hearing the noise. Of him Captain Delano sought permission to serve out the water, so that all might share alike, and none injure themselves by unfair excess. But sensible, and, on Don Benito's account, kind as this offer was, it was received with what seemed impatience; as if aware that he lacked energy as a commander, Don Benito, with the true jealousy of weakness, resented as an affront any interference. So, at least, Captain Delano inferred.

In another moment the casks were being hoisted in, when some of the eager Negroes accidentally jostled Captain Delano, where he stood by the gangway; so that, unmindful of Don Benito, yielding to the impulse of the moment, with good-natured authority he bade the blacks stand back; to enforce his words making use of a half-mirthful, half-menacing gesture. Instantly the blacks paused, just where they were, each Negro and Negress suspended in his or her posture, exactly as the word had found them—for a few seconds continuing so—while, as between the responsive posts of a telegraph, an unknown syllable ran from man to man among the perched oakum pickers. While Captain Delano's attention was fixed by this scene, suddenly the hatchet polishers half rose, and a rapid cry came from Don Benito.

Thinking that at the signal of the Spaniard he was about to be massacred, Captain Delano would have sprung for his boat, but paused, as the oakum pickers, dropping down into the crowd with earnest exclamations, forced every white and every Negro back, at the same moment, with gestures friendly and familiar, almost jocose, bidding him, in substance, not be a fool. Simultaneously the hatchet polishers resumed their seats, quietly as so many tailors, and at once, as if nothing had happened, the work of hoisting in the casks was resumed, whites and blacks singing at the tackle.

Captain Delano glanced toward Don Benito. As he saw his meagre form in the act of recovering itself from reclining in the servant's arms, into which the agitated invalid had fallen, he could not but marvel at the panic by which himself had been surprised on the darting supposition that such a commander, who upon a legitimate occasion, so trivial, too, as it now appeared, could lose all self-command, was, with energetic iniquity, going to bring about his murder.

The casks being on deck, Captain Delano was handed a number of jars and cups by one of the steward's aides, who, in the name of Don Benito, entreated him to do as he had proposed: dole out the water. He complied, with republican impartiality as to this republican element, which always seeks one level, serving the oldest white no better than the youngest black; excepting, indeed, poor Don Benito, whose condition, if not rank, demanded an extra allowance. To him, in the first place, Captain Delano presented a fair pitcher of the fluid; but, thirsting as he was for fresh water, Don Benito quaffed not a drop until after several grave bows and salutes: a reciprocation of courtesies which the sight-loving Africans hailed with clapping of hands.

Two of the less-wilted pumpkins being reserved for the cabin table, the residue were minced up on the spot for the general regalement. But the soft bread, sugar, and bottled cider, Captain Delano would have given the Spaniards alone, and in chief Don Benito; but the latter objected; which disinterestedness, on his part, not a little pleased the American; and so mouthfuls all around were given alike to whites and blacks; excepting one bottle of cider, which Babo insisted upon setting aside for his master.

Here it may be observed that as, on the first visit of the boat, the American had not permitted his men to board the ship, neither did he now; being unwilling to add to the confusion of the decks.

Not uninfluenced by the peculiar good humour at present prevailing, and for the time oblivious of any but benevolent thoughts, Captain Delano, who from recent indications counted upon a breeze within an hour or two at furthest, despatched the boat back to the sealer with orders for all the hands that could be spared immediately to set about rafting casks to the watering place and filling them. Likewise he bade word be carried to his chief officer, that if against present expectation the ship was not brought to anchor by sunset, he need be under no concern, for as there was to be a full moon that night, he (Captain Delano) would remain on board ready to play the pilot, should the wind come soon or late.

As the two captains stood together, observing the departing boat—the servant as it happened having just spied a spot on his master's velvet sleeve, and silently engaged rubbing it out—the American expressed his regrets that the *San Dominick* had no boats; none, at least, but the unseaworthy old hulk of the longboat, which, warped as a camel's skeleton in the desert, and almost as bleached, lay pot-wise inverted amidships, one side a little tipped, furnishing a subterraneous sort of den for family groups of the blacks, mostly women and small children; who, squatting on old mats below, or perched above in the dark dome, on the elevated seats, were descried, some distance within, like a social circle of bats, sheltering in some friendly cave; at intervals, ebon flights of naked boys and girls, three or four years old, darting in and out of the den's mouth.

"Had you three or four boats now, Don Benito," said Captain Delano, "I think that, by tugging at the oars, your Negroes here might help along matters some. Did you sail from port without boats, Don Benito?"

"They were stove in the gales, *señor.*"

"That was bad. Many men, too, you lost then. Boats and men. Those must have been hard gales, Don Benito."

"Past all speech," cringed the Spaniard.

"Tell me, Don Benito," continued his companion with increased interest, "tell me, were these gales immediately off the pitch of Cape Horn?"

"Cape Horn?—who spoke of Cape Horn?"

"Yourself did, when giving me an account of your voyage," answered Captain Delano with almost equal astonishment at this eating of his own words, even as he ever seemed eating his own heart, on the part of the Spaniard. "You yourself, Don Benito, spoke of Cape Horn," he emphatically repeated.

The Spaniard turned, in a sort of stooping posture, pausing an instant, as one about to make a plunging exchange of elements, as from air to water.

At this moment a messenger boy, a white, hurried by, in the regular performance of his function carrying the last expired half-hour forward to the forecastle, from the cabin timepiece, to have it struck at the ship's large bell.

"Master," said the servant, discontinuing his work on the coat sleeve, and addressing the rapt Spaniard with a sort of timid apprehensiveness, as one charged with a duty, the discharge of which, it was foreseen, would prove irksome to the very person who had imposed it, and for whose benefit it was intended, "master told me never mind where he was, or how engaged, always to remind him, to a minute, when shaving time comes. Miguel has gone to strike the half-hour afternoon. It is *now*, master. Will master go into the cuddy?"

"Ah—yes," answered the Spaniard, starting, somewhat as from dreams into realities; then turning upon Captain Delano, he said that ere long he would resume the conversation.

"Then if master means to talk more to Don Amasa," said the servant, "why not let Don Amasa sit by master in the cuddy, and master can talk, and Don Amasa can listen, while Babo here lathers and strops."

"Yes," said Captain Delano, not unpleased with this sociable plan, "yes, Don Benito, unless you had rather not, I will go with you."

"Be it so, *señor.*"

As the three passed aft, the American could not but think it another strange instance of his host's capriciousness, this being shaved with such uncommon punctuality in the middle of the day. But he deemed it more than likely that the servant's anxious fidelity had something to do with the matter; inasmuch as the timely interruption served to rally his master from the mood which had evidently been coming upon him.

The place called the cuddy was a light deck cabin formed by the poop, a sort of attic to the large cabin below. Part of it had formerly been the quarters of the officers; but since their death all the partitionings had been thrown down, and the whole interior converted into one spacious and airy marine hall; for absence of fine furniture and picturesque disarray, of odd appurtenances, somewhat answering to the wide, cluttered hall of some eccentric bachelor-squire in the country, who hangs his shooting jacket and tobacco pouch on deer antlers, and keeps his fishing rod, tongs, and walking stick in the same corner.

The similitude was heightened, if not originally suggested, by glimpses of the surrounding sea; since, in one aspect, the country and the ocean seem cousins-german.

The floor of the cuddy was matted. Overhead, four or five old muskets were stuck into horizontal holes along the beams. On one side was a claw-footed old table lashed to the deck; a thumbed missal on it, and over it a small, meagre crucifix attached to the bulkhead. Under the table lay a dented cutlass or two, with a hacked harpoon, among some melancholy old rigging, like a heap of poor friar's girdles. There were also two long, sharp-ribbed settees of malacca cane, black with age, and uncomfortable to look at as inquisitors' racks, with a large, misshapen armchair, which, furnished with a rude barber's crutch at the back, working with a screw, seemed some grotesque Middle Age engine of torment. A flag locker was in one corner, exposing various coloured bunting, some rolled up, others half unrolled, still others tumbled. Opposite was a cumbrous washstand, of black mahogany, all of one block, with a pedestal, like a font, and over it a railed shelf, containing combs, brushes, and other implements of the toilet. A torn hammock of stained grass swung near; the sheets tossed, and the pillow wrinkled up like a brow, as if whoever slept here slept but illy, with alternate visitations of sad thoughts and bad dreams.

The further extremity of the cuddy, overhanging the ship's stern, was pierced with three openings, windows or portholes, according as men or cannon might peer, socially or unsocially, out of them. At present neither men nor cannon were seen, though huge ringbolts and other rusty iron fixtures of the woodwork hinted of twenty-four-pounders.

Glancing toward the hammock as he entered, Captain Delano said, "You sleep here, Don Benito?"

"Yes, *señor*, since we got into mild weather."

"This seems a sort of dormitory, sitting room, sail loft, chapel, armoury, and private closet together, Don Benito," added Captain Delano, looking round.

"Yes, *señor*; events have not been favourable to much order in my arrangements."

Here the servant, napkin on arm, made a motion as if waiting his master's good pleasure. Don Benito signified his readiness, when, seating him in the malacca armchair, and for the guest's convenience drawing opposite it one of the settees, the servant commenced operations by throwing back his master's collar and loosening his cravat.

There is something in the Negro which, in a peculiar way, fits him for avocations about one's person. Most Negroes are natural valets and hairdressers; taking to the comb and brush congenially as to the castanets, and flourishing them apparently with almost equal satisfaction. There is, too, a smooth tact about them in this employment, with a marvellous, noiseless, gliding briskness, not ungraceful in its way, singularly pleasing to behold, and still more so to be the manipulated subject of. And above all is the great gift of good humour. Not the mere grin or laugh is here meant. Those were unsuitable. But a certain easy cheerfulness, harmonious in every glance and gesture; as though God had set the whole Negro to some pleasant tune.

When to all this is added the docility arising from the unaspiring contentment of a limited mind, and that susceptibility of blind attachment sometimes inhering in indisputable inferiors, one readily perceives why those hypochondriacs, Johnson and Byron—it may be something like the hypochondriac, Benito Cereno—took to their hearts, almost to the exclusion of the entire white race, their serving men, the Negroes, Barber and Fletcher. But if there be that in the Negro which exempts him from the inflicted sourness of the morbid or cynical mind, how, in his most prepossessing aspects, must he appear to a benevolent one? When at ease with respect to exterior things, Captain Delano's nature was not only benign, but familiarly and humorously so. At home, he had often taken rare satisfaction in sitting in his door, watching some free man of colour at his work or play. If on a voyage he chanced to have a black sailor, invariably he was on chatty, and half-gamesome terms with him. In fact, like most men of a good, blithe heart, Captain Delano took to Negroes, not philanthropically, but genially, just as other men to Newfoundland dogs.

Hitherto the circumstances in which he found the *San Dominick* had repressed the tendency. But in the cuddy, relieved from his former uneasiness, and, for various reasons, more sociably inclined than at any previous period of the day, and seeing the coloured servant, napkin on arm, so debonair about his master, in a business so familiar as that of shaving, too, all his old weakness for Negroes returned.

Among other things, he was amused with an odd instance of the African love of bright colours and fine shows, in the black's informally taking from the flag locker a great piece of bunting of all hues, and lavishly tucking it under his master's chin for an apron.

The mode of shaving among the Spaniards is a little different from what it is with other nations. They have a basin, specially called a barber's basin, which on one side is scooped out, so as accurately to receive the chin, against which it is closely held in lathering; which is done, not with a brush, but with soap dipped in the water of the basin and rubbed on the face.

In the present instance saltwater was used for lack of better; and the parts lathered were only the upper lip, and low down under the throat, all the rest being cultivated beard.

These preliminaries being somewhat novel to Captain Delano he sat curiously eyeing them, so that no conversation took place, nor for the present did Don Benito appear disposed to renew any.

Setting down his basin, the Negro searched among the razors, as for the sharpest, and having found it, gave it an additional edge by expertly stropping it on the firm, smooth, oily skin of his open palm; he then made a gesture as if to begin, but midway stood suspended for an instant, one hand elevating the razor, the other professionally dabbling among the bubbling suds on the Spaniard's lank neck. Not unaffected by the close sight of the gleaming steel, Don Benito nervously shuddered, his usual ghastliness was heightened by the lather, which lather, again, was intensified in its hue by the contrasting sootiness of the Negro's body. Altogether the scene was somewhat peculiar, at least to Captain Delano, nor, as he saw the two thus postured, could he resist the vagary, that in the black he saw a headsman, and in the white, a man at the block. But this was one of those antic conceits, appearing and vanishing in a breath, from which, perhaps, the best regulated mind is not free.

Meantime the agitation of the Spaniard had a little loosened the bunting from around him, so that one broad fold swept curtainlike over the chair arm to the floor, revealing, amid a profusion of armorial bars and ground colours—black, blue, and yellow—a closed castle in a blood-red field diagonal with a lion rampant in a white.

"The castle and the lion," exclaimed Captain Delano—"why, Don Benito, this is the flag of Spain you use here. It's well it's only I, and not the king, that sees this," he added with a smile, "but"—turning toward the black—"it's all one, I suppose, so the colours be gay," which playful remark did not fail somewhat to tickle the Negro.

"Now, master," he said, readjusting the flag, and pressing the head gently further back into the crotch of the chair; "now master," and the steel glanced nigh the throat.

Again Don Benito faintly shuddered.

"You must not shake so, master. See, Don Amasa, master always shakes when I shave him. And yet master knows I never yet have drawn blood, though it's true, if master will shake so, I may some of these times. Now, master," he continued. "And now, Don Amasa, please go on with your talk about the gale, and all that, master can hear, and between times master can answer."

"Ah yes, these gales," said Captain Delano; "but the more I think of your voyage, Don Benito, the more I wonder, not at the gales, terrible as they must have been, but at the disastrous interval following them. For here, by your account, have you been these two months and more getting from Cape Horn to St. Maria, a distance which I myself, with a good wind, have sailed in a few days. True, you had calms, and long ones, but to be becalmed for two months, that is, at least, unusual. Why, Don Benito, had almost any other gentleman told me such a story, I should have been half disposed to a little incredulity."

Here an involuntary expression came over the Spaniard, similar to that just before on the deck, and whether it was the start he gave, or a sudden gawky roll of the hull in the calm, or a momentary unsteadiness of the servant's hand; however it was, just then the razor drew blood, spots of which stained the creamy lather under the throat; immediately the black barber drew back his steel, and remaining in his professional attitude, back to Captain Delano, and face to Don Benito, held up the trickling razor, saying, with a sort of half-humorous sorrow, "See, master—you shook so—here's Babo's first blood."

No sword drawn before James the First of England, no assassination in that timid king's presence, could have produced a more terrified aspect than was now presented by Don Benito.

Poor fellow, thought Captain Delano, so nervous he can't even bear the sight of barber's blood; and this unstrung, sick man, is it credible that I should have imagined he meant to spill all my blood, who can't endure the sight of one little drop of his own? Surely, Amasa Delano, you have been beside yourself this day. Tell it not when you get home, sappy Amasa. Well, well, he looks like a murderer, doesn't he? More like as if himself were to be done for. Well, well, this day's experience shall be a good lesson.

Meantime, while these things were running through the honest seaman's mind, the servant had taken the napkin from his arm, and to Don Benito had said: "But answer Don Amasa, please, master, while I wipe this ugly stuff off the razor, and strop it again."

As he said the words, his face was turned half round, so as to be alike visible to the Spaniard and the American, and seemed by its expression to hint that he was desirous, by getting his master to go on with the conversation, considerately to withdraw his attention from the recent annoying accident. As if glad to snatch the offered relief, Don Benito resumed, rehearsing to Captain Delano, that not only were the calms of unusual duration, but the ship had fallen in with obstinate currents and other things he added, some of which were but repetitions of former statements, to explain how it came to pass that the passage from Cape Horn to St. Maria had been so exceedingly long, now and then mingling with his words incidental praises, less qualified than before, to the blacks, for their general good conduct.

These particulars were not given consecutively, the servant now and then using his razor, and so, between the intervals of shaving, the story and panegyric went on with more than usual huskiness.

To Captain Delano's imagination, now again not wholly at rest, there was something so hollow in the Spaniard's manner, with apparently some reciprocal hollowness in the servant's dusky comment of silence, that the idea flashed across him, that possibly master and man, for some unknown purpose, were acting out, both in word and deed, nay, to the very tremor of Don Benito's limbs, some juggling play before him. Neither did the suspicion of collusion lack apparent support, from the fact of those whispered conferences before mentioned. But then, what could be the object of enacting this play of the barber before him? At last, regarding the notion as a whimsy, insensibly suggested, perhaps, by the theatrical aspect of Don Benito in his harlequin ensign, Captain Delano speedily banished it.

The shaving over, the servant bestirred himself with a small bottle of scented waters, pouring a few drops on the head, and then diligently rubbing; the vehemence of the exercise causing the muscles of his face to twitch rather strangely.

His next operation was with comb, scissors, and brush; going round and round, smoothing a curl here, clipping an unruly whisker hair there, giving a graceful sweep to the temple lock, with other impromptu touches evincing the hand of a master; while, like any resigned gentleman in barber's hands, Don Benito bore all, much less uneasily, at least, than he had done the razoring; indeed, he sat so pale and rigid now, that the Negro seemed a Nubian sculptor finishing off a white statue head.

All being over at last, the standard of Spain removed, tumbled up, and tossed back into the flag locker, the Negro's warm breath blowing away any stray hair which might have lodged down his master's neck; collar and cravat readjusted; a speck of lint whisked off the velvet lapel; all this being done, backing off a little space, and pausing with an expression of subdued self-complacency, the servant for a moment surveyed his master, as, in toilet at least, the creature of his own tasteful hands.

Captain Delano playfully complimented him upon his achievement; at the same time congratulating Don Benito.

But neither sweet waters, nor shampooing, nor fidelity, nor sociality, delighted the Spaniard. Seeing him relapsing into forbidding gloom, and still remaining seated, Captain Delano, thinking that his presence was undesired just then, withdrew, on pretence of seeing whether, as he had prophesied, any signs of a breeze were visible.

Walking forward to the main mast, he stood awhile thinking over the scene, and not without some undefined misgivings, when he heard a noise near the cuddy, and turning, saw the Negro, his hand to his cheek. Advancing, Captain Delano perceived that the cheek was bleeding. He was about to ask the cause, when the Negro's wailing soliloquy enlightened him.

"Ah, when will master get better from his sickness; only the sour heart that sour sickness breeds made him serve Babo so; cutting Babo with the razor, because, only by accident, Babo had given master one little scratch; and for the first time in so many a day, too. Ah, ah, ah," holding his hand to his face.

Is it possible, thought Captain Delano; was it to wreak in private his Spanish spite against this poor friend of his, that Don Benito, by his sullen manner, impelled me to withdraw? Ah, this slavery breeds ugly passions in man! Poor fellow!

He was about to speak in sympathy to the Negro, but with a timid reluctance he now reentered the cuddy.

Presently master and man came forth; Don Benito leaning on his servant as if nothing had happened.

But a sort of love quarrel, after all, thought Captain Delano.

He accosted Don Benito, and they slowly walked together. They had gone but a few paces, when the steward—a tall, rajah-looking mulatto, orientally set off with a pagoda turban formed by three or four madras handkerchiefs wound about his head, tier on tier—approaching with a salaam, announced lunch in the cabin.

On their way thither, the two captains were preceded by the mulatto, who, turning round as he advanced, with continual smiles and bows, ushered them in, a display of elegance which quite completed the insignificance of the small bareheaded Babo, who, as if not unconscious of inferiority, eyed askance the graceful steward. But in part, Captain

Delano imputed his jealous watchfulness to that peculiar feeling which the full-blooded African entertains for the adulterated one. As for the steward, his manner, if not bespeaking much dignity of self-respect, yet evidenced his extreme desire to please; which is doubly meritorious, as at once Christian and Chesterfieldian.

Captain Delano observed with interest that while the complexion of the mulatto was hybrid, his physiognomy was European; classically so.

"Don Benito," whispered he, "I am glad to see this usher-of-the-golden-rod of yours; the sight refutes an ugly remark once made to me by a Barbados planter that when a mulatto has a regular European face, look out for him; he is a devil. But see, your steward here has features more regular than King George's of England; and yet there he nods, and bows, and smiles; a king, indeed—the king of kind hearts and polite fellows. What a pleasant voice he has, too?"

"He has, *señor.*"

"But, tell me, has he not, so far as you have known him, always proved a good, worthy fellow?" said Captain Delano, pausing, while with a final genuflexion the steward disappeared into the cabin; "come, for the reason just mentioned, I am curious to know."

"Francesco is a good man," rather sluggishly responded Don Benito, like a phlegmatic appreciator, who would neither find fault nor flatter.

"Ah, I thought so. For it were strange indeed, and not very creditable to us white skins, if a little of our blood mixed with the African's, should, far from improving the latter's quality, have the sad effect of pouring vitriolic acid into black broth; improving the hue, perhaps, but not the wholesomeness."

"Doubtless, doubtless, *señor*, but"—glancing at Babo—"not to speak of Negroes, your planter's remark I have heard applied to the Spanish and Indian intermixtures in our provinces. But I know nothing about the matter," he listlessly added.

And here they entered the cabin.

The lunch was a frugal one. Some of Captain Delano's fresh fish and pumpkins, biscuit and salt beef, the reserved bottle of cider, and the *San Dominick*'s last bottle of Canary.

As they entered, Francesco, with two or three coloured aids, was hovering over the table giving the last adjustments. Upon perceiving their master they withdrew, Francesco making a smiling congé, and the Spaniard, without condescending to notice it, fastidiously remarking to his companion that he relished not superfluous attendance.

Without companions, host and guest sat down, like a childless married couple, at opposite ends of the table, Don Benito waving Captain Delano to his place, and, weak as he was, insisting upon that gentleman being seated before himself.

The Negro placed a rug under Don Benito's feet, and a cushion behind his back, and then stood behind, not his master's chair, but Captain Delano's. At first, this a little surprised the latter. But it was soon evident that, in taking his position, the black was still true to his master; since by facing him he could the more readily anticipate his slightest want.

"This is an uncommonly intelligent fellow of yours, Don Benito," whispered Captain Delano across the table.

"You say true, *señor.*"

During the repast, the guest again reverted to parts of Don Benito's story, begging further particulars here and there. He inquired how it was that the scurvy and fever should have committed such wholesale havoc upon the whites, while destroying less than half of the blacks. As if this question reproduced the whole scene of plague before the Spaniard's eyes, miserably reminding him of his solitude in a cabin where before he had had so many friends and officers round him, his hand shook, his face became hueless, broken words escaped; but directly the sane memory of the past seemed replaced by insane terrors of the present. With starting eyes he stared before him at vacancy. For nothing was to be seen but the hand of his servant pushing the Canary over toward him. At length a few sips served partially to restore him. He made random reference to the different constitutions of races, enabling one to offer more resistance to certain maladies than another. The thought was new to his companion.

Presently Captain Delano, intending to say something to his host concerning the pecuniary part of the business he had undertaken for him, especially—since he was strictly accountable to his owners—with reference to the new suit of sails, and other things of that sort; and naturally preferring to conduct such affairs in private, was desirous that the servant should withdraw; imagining that Don Benito for a few minutes could dispense with his attendance. He, however, waited awhile; thinking that, as the conversation proceeded, Don Benito, without being prompted, would perceive the propriety of the step.

But it was otherwise. At last catching his host's eye, Captain Delano, with a slight backward gesture of his thumb, whispered, "Don Benito, pardon me, but there is an interference with the full expression of what I have to say to you."

Upon this the Spaniard changed countenance; which was imputed to his resenting the hint, as in some way a reflection upon his servant. After a moment's pause, he assured his guest that the black's remaining with them could be of no disservice; because since losing his officers he had made Babo (whose original office, it now appeared, had been captain of the slaves) not only his constant attendant and companion, but in all things his confidant.

After this, nothing more could be said; though, indeed, Captain Delano could hardly avoid some little tinge of irritation upon being left ungratified in so inconsiderable a wish, by one, too, for whom he intended such solid services. But it is only his querulousness, thought he; and so filling his glass he proceeded to business.

The price of the sails and other matters was fixed upon. But while this was being done, the American observed that, though his original offer of assistance had been hailed with hectic animation, yet now when it was reduced to a business transaction, indifference and apathy were betrayed. Don Benito, in fact, appeared to submit to hearing the details more out of regard to common propriety, than from any impression that weighty benefit to himself and his voyage was involved.

Soon, this manner became still more reserved. The effort was vain to seek to draw him into social talk. Gnawed by his splenetic mood, he sat twitching his beard, while to little purpose the hand of his servant, mute as that on the wall, slowly pushed over the Canary.

Lunch being over, they sat down on the cushioned transom, the servant placing a pillow behind his master. The long continuance of the calm had now affected the atmosphere. Don Benito sighed heavily, as if for breath.

"Why not adjourn to the cuddy," said Captain Delano; "there is more air there." But the host sat silent and motionless.

Meantime his servant knelt before him, with a large fan of feathers. And Francesco, coming in on tiptoes, handed the Negro a little cup of aromatic waters, with which at intervals he chafed his master's brow, smoothing the hair along the temples as a nurse does a child's. He spoke no word. He only rested his eye on his master's, as if, amid all Don Benito's distress, a little to refresh his spirit by the silent sight of fidelity.

Presently the ship's bell sounded two o'clock; and through the cabin windows a slight rippling of the sea was discerned; and from the desired direction.

"There," exclaimed Captain Delano, "I told you so, Don Benito, look!"

He had risen to his feet, speaking in a very animated tone, with a view the more to rouse his companion. But though the crimson curtain of the stern window near him that moment fluttered against his pale cheek, Don Benito seemed to have even less welcome for the breeze than the calm.

Poor fellow, thought Captain Delano, bitter experience has taught him that one ripple does not make a wind, any more than one swallow a summer. But he is mistaken for once. I will get his ship in for him, and prove it.

Briefly alluding to his weak condition, he urged his host to remain quietly where he was, since he (Captain Delano) would with pleasure take upon himself the responsibility of making the best use of the wind.

Upon gaining the deck, Captain Delano started at the unexpected figure of Atufal, monumentally fixed at the threshold, like one of those sculptured porters of black marble guarding the porches of Egyptian tombs.

But this time the start was, perhaps, purely physical. Atufal's presence, singularly attesting docility even in sullenness, was contrasted with that of the hatchet polishers, who in patience evinced their industry; while both spectacles showed, that lax as Don Benito's general authority might be, still, whenever he chose to exert it, no man so savage or colossal but must, more or less, bow.

Snatching a trumpet which hung from the bulwarks, with a free step Captain Delano advanced to the forward edge of the poop, issuing his orders in his best Spanish. The few sailors and many Negroes, all equally pleased, obediently set about heading the ship toward the harbour.

While giving some directions about setting a lower stu'n'sail, suddenly Captain Delano heard a voice faithfully repeating his orders. Turning, he saw Babo, now for the time acting, under the pilot, his original part of captain of the slaves. This assistance proved valuable. Tattered sails and warped yards were soon brought into some trim. And no brace or halyard was pulled but to the blithe songs of the inspirited Negroes.

Good fellows, thought Captain Delano, a little training would make fine sailors of them. Why see, the very women pull and sing, too. These must be some of those Ashantee Negresses that make such capital soldiers, I've heard. But who's at the helm? I must have a good hand there.

He went to see.

The *San Dominick* steered with a cumbrous tiller, with large horizontal pullies attached. At each pulley end stood a subordinate black, and between them, at the tiller head, the responsible post, a Spanish seaman, whose countenance evinced his due share in the general hopefulness and confidence at the coming of the breeze.

He proved the same man who had behaved with so shamefaced an air on the windlass.

"Ah—it is you, my man," exclaimed Captain Delano—"well, no more sheep's eyes now—look straightforward and keep the ship so. Good hand, I trust? And want to get into the harbour, don't you?"

"Si *señor,*" assented the man with an inward chuckle, grasping the tiller head firmly. Upon this, unperceived by the American, the two blacks eyed the sailor askance.

Finding all right at the helm, the pilot went forward to the forecastle, to see how matters stood there.

The ship now had way enough to breast the current. With the approach of evening, the breeze would be sure to freshen.

Having done all that was needed for the present, Captain Delano, giving his last orders to the sailors, turned aft to report affairs to Don

Benito in the cabin; perhaps additionally incited to rejoin him by the hope of snatching a moment's private chat while his servant was engaged upon deck.

From opposite sides, there were, beneath the poop, two approaches to the cabin; one further forward than the other, and consequently communicating with a longer passage. Marking the servant still above, Captain Delano, taking the nighest entrance—the one last named, and at whose porch Atufal still stood—hurried on his way, till, arrived at the cabin threshold, he paused an instant, a little to recover from his eagerness. Then, with the words of his intended business upon his lips, he entered. As he advanced toward the Spaniard, on the transom, he heard another footstep, keeping time with his. From the opposite door, a salver in hand, the servant was likewise advancing.

"Confound the faithful fellow," thought Captain Delano; "what a vexatious coincidence."

Possibly, the vexation might have been something different, were it not for the buoyant confidence inspired by the breeze. But even as it was, he felt a slight twinge, from a sudden involuntary association in his mind of Babo with Atufal.

"Don Benito," said he, "I give you joy; the breeze will hold, and will increase. By the way, your tall man and timepiece, Atufal, stands without. By your order, of course?"

Don Benito recoiled, as if at some bland satirical touch, delivered with such adroit garnish of apparent good breeding as to present no handle for retort.

He is like one flayed alive, thought Captain Delano; where may one touch him without causing a shrink?

The servant moved before his master, adjusting a cushion; recalled to civility, the Spaniard stiffly replied: "You are right. The slave appears where you saw him, according to my command; which is, that if at the given hour I am below, he must take his stand and abide my coming."

"Ah now, pardon me, but that is treating the poor fellow like an ex-king denied. Ah, Don Benito," smiling, "for all the license you permit in some things, I fear lest, at bottom, you are a bitter hard master."

Again Don Benito shrank; and this time, as the good sailor thought, from a genuine twinge of his conscience.

Conversation now became constrained. In vain Captain Delano called attention to the now perceptible motion of the keel gently cleaving the sea; with lacklustre eye, Don Benito returned words few and reserved.

By and by, the wind having steadily risen, and still blowing right into the harbour, bore the *San Dominick* swiftly on. Rounding a point of land, the sealer at distance came into open view.

Meantime Captain Delano had again repaired to the deck, remaining there some time. Having at last altered the ship's course, so as to give the reef a wide berth, he returned for a few moments below.

I will cheer up my poor friend, this time, thought he.

"Better and better, Don Benito," he cried as he blithely reentered; "there will soon be an end to your cares, at least for awhile. For when, after a long, sad voyage, you know, the anchor drops into the haven, all its vast weight seems lifted from the captain's heart. We are getting on famously, Don Benito. My ship is in sight. Look through this sidelight here; there she is; all a-taunt-o! The *Bachelor's Delight*, my good friend. Ah, how this wind braces one up. Come, you must take a cup of coffee with me this evening. My old steward will give you as fine a cup as ever any sultan tasted. What say you, Don Benito, will you?"

At first, the Spaniard glanced feverishly up, casting a longing look toward the sealer, while with mute concern his servant gazed into his face. Suddenly the old ague of coldness returned, and dropping back to his cushions he was silent.

"You do not answer. Come, all day you have been my host; would you have hospitality all on one side?"

"I cannot go," was the response.

"What? It will not fatigue you. The ships will lie together as near as they can, without swinging foul. It will be little more than stepping from deck to deck; which is but as from room to room. Come, come, you must not refuse me."

"I cannot go," decisively and repulsively repeated Don Benito.

Renouncing all but the last appearance of courtesy, with a sort of cadaverous sullenness, and biting his thin nails to the quick, he glanced, almost glared, at his guest; as if impatient that a stranger's presence should interfere with the full indulgence of his morbid hour. Meantime the sound of the parted waters came more and more gurglingly and merrily in at the windows; as reproaching him for his dark spleen; as telling him that, sulk as he might, and go mad with it, nature cared not a jot; since, whose fault was it, pray?

But the foul mood was now at its depth as the fair wind at its height.

There was something in the man so far beyond any mere unsociality or sourness previously evinced, that even the forbearing good nature of his guest could no longer endure it. Wholly at a loss to account for such demeanour, and deeming sickness with eccentricity, however extreme, no adequate excuse, well satisfied, too, that nothing in his own conduct could justify it, Captain Delano's pride began to be roused. Himself became reserved. But all seemed one to the Spaniard. Quitting him, therefore, Captain Delano once more went to the deck.

The ship was now within less than two miles of the sealer. The whaleboat was seen darting over the interval.

To be brief, the two vessels, thanks to the pilot's skill, ere long in neighbourly style lay anchored together.

Before returning to his own vessel, Captain Delano had intended communicating to Don Benito the practical details of the proposed services to be rendered. But, as it was, unwilling anew to subject himself to rebuffs, he resolved, now that he had seen the *San Dominick* safely moored, immediately to quit her, without further allusion to hospitality or business. Indefinitely postponing his ulterior plans, he would regulate his future actions according to future circumstances. His boat was ready to receive him; but his host still tarried below. Well, thought Captain Delano, if he has little breeding, the more need to show mine. He descended to the cabin to bid a ceremonious, and, it may be, tacitly rebukeful adieu. But to his great satisfaction, Don Benito, as if he began to feel the weight of that treatment with which his slighted guest had, not indecorously, retaliated upon him, now supported by his servant, rose to his feet, and grasping Captain Delano's hand, stood tremulous, too much agitated to speak. But the good augury hence drawn was suddenly dashed, by his resuming all his previous reserve, with augmented gloom, as, with half-averted eyes, he silently reseated himself on his cushions. With a corresponding return of his own chilled feelings, Captain Delano bowed and withdrew.

He was hardly midway in the narrow corridor, dim as a tunnel, leading from the cabin to the stairs, when a sound, as of the tolling for execution in some jail yard, fell on his ears. It was the echo of the ship's flawed bell, striking the hour, drearily reverberated in this subterranean vault. Instantly, by a fatality not to be withstood, his mind, responsive to the portent, swarmed with superstitious suspicions. He paused. In images far swifter than these sentences, the minutest details of all his former distrusts swept through him.

Hitherto, credulous good nature had been too ready to furnish excuses for reasonable fears. Why was the Spaniard, so superfluously punctilious at times, now heedless of common propriety in not accompanying to the side his departing guest? Did indisposition forbid? Indisposition had not forbidden more irksome exertion that day. His last equivocal demeanour recurred. He had risen to his feet, grasped his guest's hand, motioned toward his hat; then, in an instant, all was eclipsed in sinister muteness and gloom. Did this imply one brief, repentant relenting at the final moment, from some iniquitous plot, followed by remorseless return to it? His last glance seemed to express a calamitous, yet acquiescent farewell to Captain Delano forever. Why decline the invitation to visit the sealer that evening? Or was the Spaniard less hardened than the Jew, who refrained not from supping at the board of him whom the same night he meant to betray? What imported all those daylong enigmas and contradictions, except they were intended to mystify, preliminary to some stealthy blow? Atufal, the pretended rebel, but punctual shadow, that moment lurked by the threshold without. He seemed a sentry, and more. Who, by his own confession, had stationed him there? Was the Negro now lying in wait?

The Spaniard behind—his creature before: to rush from darkness to light was the involuntary choice.

The next moment, with clenched jaw and hand, he passed Atufal, and stood unarmed in the light. As he saw his trim ship lying peacefully at her anchor, and almost within ordinary call; as he saw his household boat, with familiar faces in it, patiently rising and falling on the short waves by the *San Dominick*'s side; and then, glancing about the decks where he stood, saw the oakum pickers still gravely plying their fingers; and heard the low, buzzing whistle and industrious hum of the hatchet polishers, still bestirring themselves over their endless occupation; and more than all, as he saw the benign aspect of nature, taking her innocent repose in the evening; the screened sun in the quiet camp of the west shining out like the mild light from Abraham's tent; as his charmed eye and ear took in all these, with the chained figure of the black, the clenched jaw and hand relaxed. Once again he smiled at the phantoms which had mocked him, and felt something like a tinge of remorse, that, by indulging them even for a moment, he should, by implication, have betrayed an almost atheist doubt of the ever-watchful Providence above.

There was a few minutes' delay, while, in obedience to his orders, the boat was being hooked along to the gangway. During this interval, a sort of saddened satisfaction stole over Captain Delano, at thinking of the kindly offices he had that day discharged for a stranger. Ah, thought he, after good actions one's conscience is never ungrateful, however much so the benefited party may be.

Presently, his foot, in the first act of descent into the boat, pressed the first round of the side ladder, his face presented inward upon the deck. In the same moment, he heard his name courteously sounded; and, to his pleased surprise, saw Don Benito advancing—an unwonted energy in his air, as if, at the last moment, intent upon making amends for his recent discourtesy. With instinctive good feeling, Captain Delano, revoking his foot, turned and reciprocally advanced. As he did so, the Spaniard's nervous eagerness increased, but his vital energy failed; so that, the better to support him, the servant, placing his master's hand on his naked shoulder, and gently holding it there, formed himself into a sort of crutch.

When the two captains met, the Spaniard again fervently took the hand of the American, at the same time casting an earnest glance into his eyes, but, as before, too much overcome to speak.

I have done him wrong, self-reproachfully thought Captain Delano; his apparent coldness has deceived me; in no instance has he meant to offend.

Meantime, as if fearful that the continuance of the scene might too much unstring his master, the servant seemed anxious to terminate it. And so, still presenting himself as a crutch, and walking between the two captains, he advanced with them toward the gangway; while still, as if full of kindly contrition, Don Benito would not let go the hand of Captain Delano, but retained it in his, across the black's body.

Soon they were standing by the side, looking over into the boat, whose crew turned up their curious eyes. Waiting a moment for the Spaniard to relinquish his hold, the now embarrassed Captain Delano lifted his foot, to overstep the threshold of the open gangway; but still Don Benito would not let go his hand. And yet, with an agitated tone, he said, "I can go no further; here I must bid you adieu. Adieu, my dear, dear Don Amasa. Go—go!" suddenly tearing his hand loose, "go, and God guard you better than me, my best friend."

Not unaffected, Captain Delano would now have lingered; but catching the meekly admonitory eye of the servant, with a hasty farewell he descended into his boat, followed by the continual adieus of Don Benito, standing rooted in the gangway.

Seating himself in the stern, Captain Delano, making a last salute, ordered the boat shoved off. The crew had their oars on end. The bowsman pushed the boat a sufficient distance for the oars to be lengthwise dropped. The instant that was done, Don Benito sprang over the bulwarks, falling at the feet of Captain Delano; at the same time, calling toward his ship, but in tones so frenzied, that none in the boat could understand him. But, as if not equally obtuse, three Spanish sailors, from three different and distant parts of the ship, splashed into the sea, swimming after their captain, as if intent upon his rescue.

The dismayed officer of the boat eagerly asked what this meant. To which, Captain Delano, turning a disdainful smile upon the unaccountable Benito Cereno, answered that, for his part, he neither knew nor cared; but it seemed as if the Spaniard had taken it into his head to produce the impression among his people that the boat wanted to kidnap him. "Or else—give way for your lives," he wildly added, starting at a clattering hubbub in the ship, above which rang the tocsin of the hatchet polishers; and seizing Don Benito by the throat he added, "this plotting pirate means murder!" Here, in apparent verification of the words, the servant, a dagger in his hand, was seen on the rail overhead, poised, in the act of leaping, as if with desperate fidelity to befriend his master to the last; while, seemingly to aid the black, the three Spanish sailors were trying to clamber into the hampered bow. Meantime, the whole host of Negroes, as if inflamed at the sight of their jeopardized captain, impended in one sooty avalanche over the bulwarks.

All this, with what preceded, and what followed, occurred with such involutions of rapidity, that past, present, and, future seemed one.

Seeing the Negro coming, Captain Delano had flung the Spaniard aside, almost in the very act of clutching him, and, by the unconscious recoil, shifting his place, with arms thrown up, so promptly grappled the servant in his descent, that with dagger presented at Captain Delano's heart, the black seemed of purpose to have leaped there as to his mark. But the weapon was wrenched away, and the assailant dashed down into the bottom of the boat, which now, with disentangled oars, began to speed through the sea.

At this juncture, the left hand of Captain Delano, on one side, again clutched the half-reclined Don Benito, heedless that he was in a speechless faint, while his right foot, on the other side, ground the prostrate Negro; and his right arm pressed for added speed on the after oar, his eye bent forward, encouraging his men to their utmost.

But here, the officer of the boat, who had at last succeeded in beating off the towing Spanish sailors, and was now, with face turned aft, assisting the bowsman at his oar, suddenly called to Captain Delano, to see what the black was about; while a Portuguese oarsman shouted to him to give heed to what the Spaniard was saying.

Glancing down at his feet, Captain Delano saw the freed hand of the servant aiming with a second dagger—a small one, before concealed in his wool—with this he was snakishly writhing up from the boat's bottom, at the heart of his master, his countenance lividly vindictive, expressing the centred purpose of his soul; while the Spaniard, half choked, was vainly shrinking away, with husky words, incoherent to all but the Portuguese.

That moment, across the long benighted mind of Captain Delano, a flash of revelation swept, illuminating in unanticipated clearness Benito Cereno's whole mysterious demeanour, with every enigmatic event of the day, as well as the entire past voyage of the *San Dominick*. He smote Babo's hand down, but his own heart smote him harder. With infinite pity he withdrew his hold from Don Benito. Not Captain Delano, but Don Benito, the black, in leaping into the boat, had intended to stab.

Both the black's hands were held, as, glancing up toward the *San Dominick*, Captain Delano, now with the scales dropped from his eyes, saw the Negroes, not in misrule, not in tumult, not as if frantically concerned for Don Benito, but with mask torn away, flourishing hatchets and knives, in ferocious piratical revolt. Like delirious black dervishes, the six Ashantees danced on the poop. Prevented by their foes from springing into the water, the Spanish boys were hurrying up to the topmost spars, while such of the few Spanish sailors, not already in the sea, less alert, were descried, helplessly mixed in, on deck, with the blacks.

Meantime Captain Delano hailed his own vessel, ordering the ports up, and the guns run out. But by this time the cable of the *San Dominick* had been cut; and the fag end, in lashing out, whipped away the canvas shroud about the beak, suddenly revealing, as the bleached hull swung round toward the open ocean, death for the figurehead, in a human skeleton; chalky comment on the chalked words below, "*Follow your leader.*"

At the sight, Don Benito, covering his face, wailed out: " 'Tis he, Aranda! my murdered, unburied friend!"

Upon reaching the sealer, calling for ropes, Captain Delano bound the Negro, who made no resistance, and had him hoisted to the deck. He would then have assisted the now almost helpless Don Benito up the side; but Don Benito, wan as he was, refused to move, or be moved, until the Negro should have been first put below out of view. When, presently assured that it was done, he no more shrank from the ascent.

The boat was immediately despatched back to pick up the three swimming sailors. Meantime, the guns were in readiness, though, owing to the *San Dominick* having glided somewhat astern of the sealer, only the aftermost one could be brought to bear. With this, they fired six times; thinking to cripple the fugitive ship by bringing down her spars. But only a few inconsiderable ropes were shot away. Soon the ship was beyond the guns' range, steering broad out of the bay; the blacks thickly clustering round the bowsprit, one moment with taunting cries toward the whites, the next with upthrown gestures hailing the now dusky expanse of ocean—cawing crows escaped from the hand of the fowler.

The first impulse was to slip the cables and give chase. But, upon second thought, to pursue with whale boat and yawl seemed more promising.

Upon inquiring of Don Benito what firearms they had on board the *San Dominick*, Captain Delano was answered that they had none that could be used; because, in the earlier stages of the mutiny, a cabin passenger, since dead, had secretly put out of order the locks of what few muskets there were. But with all his remaining strength, Don Benito entreated the American not to give chase, either with ship or boat; for the Negroes had already proved themselves such desperadoes, that, in case of a present assault, nothing but a total massacre of the whites could be looked for. But, regarding this warning as coming from one whose spirit had been crushed by misery, the American did not give up his design.

The boats were got ready and armed. Captain Delano ordered twenty-five men into them. He was going himself when Don Benito grasped his arm.

"What! Have you saved my life, *señor*, and are you now going to throw away your own?"

The officers also, for reasons connected with their interests and those of the voyage, and a duty owing to the owners, strongly objected against their commander's going. Weighing their remonstrances a moment, Captain Delano felt bound to remain; appointing his chief mate—an athletic and resolute man, who had been a privateer's man, and, as his enemies whispered, a pirate—to head the party. The more to encourage the sailors, they were told that the Spanish captain considered his ship as good as lost; that she and her cargo, including some gold and silver, were worth upwards of ten thousand doubloons. Take her, and no small part should be theirs. The sailors replied with a shout.

The fugitives had now almost gained an offing. It was nearly night; but the moon was rising. After hard, prolonged pulling, the boats came up on the ship's quarters, at a suitable distance laying upon their oars to discharge their muskets. Having no bullets to return, the Negroes sent their yells. But, upon the second volley, Indian-like, they hurtled their hatchets. One took off a sailor's fingers. Another struck the whaleboat's bow, cutting off the rope there, and remaining stuck in the gunwale, like a woodman's axe. Snatching it, quivering from its lodgment, the mate hurled it back. The returned gauntlet now stuck in the ship's broken quarter gallery, and so remained.

The Negroes giving too hot a reception, the whites kept a more respectful distance. Hovering now just out of reach of the hurtling hatchets, they, with a view to the close encounter which must soon come, sought to decoy the blacks into entirely disarming themselves of their most murderous weapons in a hand-to-hand fight, by foolishly flinging them, as missiles, short of the mark, into the sea. But ere long perceiving the stratagem, the Negroes desisted, though not before many of them had to replace their lost hatchets with handspikes; an exchange which, as counted upon, proved in the end favourable to the assailants.

Meantime, with a strong wind, the ship still clove the water; the boats alternately falling behind, and pulling up, to discharge fresh volleys.

The fire was mostly directed toward the stern, since there, chiefly, the Negroes, at present, were clustering. But to kill or maim the Negroes was not the object. To take them, with the ship, was the object. To do it, the ship must be boarded; which could not be done by boats while she was sailing so fast.

A thought now struck the mate. Observing the Spanish boys still aloft, high as they could get, he called to them to descend to the yards, and cut adrift the sails. It was done. About this time, owing to causes hereafter to be shown, two Spaniards, in the dress of sailors and conspicuously showing themselves, were killed; not by volleys, but by deliberate marksman's shots; while, as it afterwards appeared, during one of the general discharges, Atufal, the black, and the Spaniard at the helm likewise were killed. What now, with the loss of the sails, and loss of leaders, the ship became unmanageable to the Negroes.

With creaking masts she came heavily round to the wind; the prow slowly swinging into view of the boats, its skeleton gleaming in the horizontal moonlight, and casting a gigantic ribbed shadow upon the water. One extended arm of the ghost seemed beckoning the whites to avenge it.

"Follow your leader!" cried the mate; and, one on each bow, the boats boarded. Scaling spears and cutlasses crossed hatchets and handspikes. Huddled upon the longboat amidships, the Negresses raised a wailing chant, whose chorus was the clash of the steel.

For a time, the attack wavered; the Negroes wedging themselves to beat it back; the half-repelled sailors, as yet unable to gain a footing, fighting as troopers in the saddle, one leg sideways flung over the bulwarks, and one without, plying their cutlasses like carters' whips. But in vain. They were almost overborne, when, rallying themselves into a squad as one man, with a huzza, they sprang inboard; where, entangled, they involuntarily separated again. For a few breaths' space there was a vague, muffled, inner sound as of submerged swordfish rushing hither and thither through shoals of blackfish. Soon, in a reunited band, and joined by the Spanish seamen, the whites came to the surface, irresistibly driving the Negroes toward the stern. But a barricade of casks and sacks, from side to side, had been thrown up by the main mast. Here the Negroes faced about, and though scorning peace or truce, yet fain would have had a respite. But, without pause, overleaping the barrier, the unflagging sailors again closed. Exhausted, the blacks now fought in despair. Their red tongues lolled, wolflike, from their black mouths. But the pale sailors' teeth were set; not a word was spoken; and, in five minutes more, the ship was won.

Nearly a score of the Negroes were killed. Exclusive of those by the balls, many were mangled; their wounds—mostly inflicted by the long-edged scaling spears—resembling those shaven ones of the English at Prestonpans, made by the poled scythes of the Highlanders. On the other side, none were killed, though several were wounded; some severely, including the mate. The surviving Negroes were temporarily secured, and the ship, towed back into the harbour at midnight, once more lay anchored.

Omitting the incidents and arrangements ensuing, suffice it that, after two days spent in refitting, the two ships sailed in company for Concepción in Chili, and thence for Lima in Peru; where, before the viceregal courts, the whole affair, from the beginning, underwent investigation.

Though, midway on the passage, the ill-fated Spaniard, relaxed from constraint, showed some signs of regaining health with free will; yet, agreeably to his own foreboding, shortly before arriving at Lima, he relapsed, finally becoming so reduced as to be carried ashore in arms. Hearing of his story and plight, one of the many religious institutions of the City of Kings opened an hospitable refuge to him, where both physician and priest were his nurses, and a member of the order volunteered to be his one special guardian and consoler, by night and by day.

The following extracts, translated from one of the official Spanish documents, will, it is hoped, shed light on the preceding narrative, as well as, in the first place, reveal the true port of departure and true history of the *San Dominick*'s voyage, down to the time of her touching at the island of Santa Maria.

But, ere the extracts come, it may be well to preface them with a remark.

The document selected, from among many others, for partial translation, contains the deposition of Benito Cereno; the first taken in the case. Some disclosures therein were, at the time, held dubious for both learned and natural reasons. The tribunal inclined to the opinion that the deponent, not undisturbed in his mind by recent events, raved of some things which could never have happened. But subsequent depositions of the surviving sailors, bearing out the revelations of their captain in several of the strangest particulars, gave credence to the rest. So that the tribunal, in its final decision, rested its capital sentences upon statements which, had they lacked confirmation, it would have deemed it but duty to reject.

. . .

I, Don José de Abos and Padilla, His Majesty's Notary for the Royal Revenue, and Register of this Province, and Notary Public of the Holy Crusade of this Bishopric, etc.

Do certify and declare, as much as is requisite in law, that, in the criminal cause commenced the twenty-fourth of the month of September, in the year seventeen hundred and ninety-nine, against the Senegal Negroes of the ship *San Dominick*, the following declaration before me was made.

Declaration of the first witness, Don Benito Cereno.

The same day, and month, and year, His Honour, Doctor Juan Martinez de Dozas, Councillor of the Royal Audience of this Kingdom, and learned in the law of this Intendancy, ordered the captain of the ship *San Dominick*, Don Benito Cereno, to appear; which he did in his litter, attended by the monk Infelez; of whom he received, before Don José de Abos and Padilla, Notary Public of the Holy Crusade, the oath, which he took by God, our Lord, and a sign of the Cross; under which he promised to tell the truth of whatever he should know and should be asked; and being interrogated agreeably to the tenor of the act commencing the process, he said, that on the twentieth of May last, he set sail with his ship from the port of Valparaiso, bound to that of Callao; loaded with the produce of the country and one hundred and sixty blacks, of both sexes, mostly belonging to Don Alexandro Aranda, gentleman, of the city of Mendoza; that the crew of the ship consisted of thirty-six men, beside the persons who went as passengers; that the Negroes were in part as follows:

[*Here, in the original, follows a list of some fifty names, descriptions, and ages, compiled from certain recovered documents of Aranda's, and also from recollections of the deponent, from which portions only are extracted.*]

—One, from about eighteen to nineteen years, named José, and this was the man that waited upon his master, Don Alexandro, and who speaks well the Spanish, having served him four or five years; . . . a mulatto, named Francesco, the cabin steward, of a good person and voice, having sung in the Valparaiso churches, native of the province of Buenos Ayres, aged about thirty-five years. . . . A smart Negro, named Dago, who had been for many years a gravedigger among the Spaniards, aged forty-six years. . . . Four old Negroes, born in Africa, from sixty to seventy, but sound, caulkers by trade, whose names are as follows: the first was named Muri, and he was killed (as was also his son named Diamelo); the second, Nacta; the third, Yola, likewise killed; the fourth, Ghofan; and six full-grown Negroes, aged from thirty to forty-five, all raw, and born among the Ashantees—Martinqui, Yan, Lecbe, Mapenda, Yambaio, Akim; four of whom were killed; . . . a powerful Negro named Atufal, who, being supposed to have been a chief in Africa, his owners set great store by him. . . . And a small Negro of Senegal, but some years among the Spaniards, aged about thirty, which Negro's name was Babo; . . . that he does not remember the names of the others, but that still expecting the residue of Don Alexandro's papers will be found, will then take due account of them all, and remit to the court; . . . and thirty-nine women and children of all ages.

[*After the catalogue, the deposition goes on as follows*:]

. . . That all the Negroes slept upon deck, as is customary in this navigation, and none wore fetters, because the owner, his friend Aranda, told him that they were all tractable; . . . that on the seventh day after leaving port, at three o'clock in the morning, all the Spaniards being asleep except the two officers on the watch, who were the boatswain, Juan Robles, and the carpenter, Juan Bautista Gayete, and the helmsman and his boy, the Negroes revolted suddenly, wounded dangerously the boatswain and the carpenter, and successively killed eighteen men of those who were sleeping upon deck, some with handspikes and hatchets, and others by throwing them alive overboard, after tying them; that of the Spaniards upon deck, they left about seven, as he thinks, alive and tied, to manoeuvre the ship and three or four more who hid themselves, remained also alive. Although in the act of revolt the Negroes made themselves masters of the hatchway, six or seven wounded went through it to the cockpit, without any hindrance on their part; that in the act of revolt, the mate and another person, whose name he does not recollect, attempted to come up through the hatchway, but having been wounded at the onset, they were obliged to return to the cabin; that the deponent resolved at break of day to come up the companionway, where the Negro Babo was, being the ringleader, and Atufal, who assisted him, and having spoken to them, exhorted them to cease committing such atrocities, asking them, at the same time, what they wanted and intended to do, offering, himself, to obey their commands; that, notwithstanding this, they threw, in his presence, three men, alive and tied, overboard; that they told the deponent to come up, and that they would not kill him; which having done, the Negro Babo asked him whether there were in those seas any Negro countries where they might be carried, and he answered them, No; that the Negro Babo afterwards told him to carry them to Senegal, or to the neighbouring islands of St. Nicholas; and he answered, that this was impossible, on account of the great distance, the necessity involved of rounding Cape Horn, the bad condition of the vessel, the want of provisions, sails, and water; but that the Negro Babo replied to him he must carry them in anyway; that they would do and conform themselves to everything the deponent should require as to eating and drinking; that after a long conference, being absolutely compelled to please them, for they threatened him to kill all the whites if they were not, at all events, carried to Senegal, he told them that what was most wanting for the voyage was water; that they would go near the coast to take it, and hence they would proceed on their course; that the Negro Babo agreed to it; and the deponent steered toward the intermediate ports, hoping to meet some Spanish or foreign vessel that would save them; that within ten or eleven days they saw the land, and continued their course by it in the vicinity of Nasca; that the deponent observed that the Negroes were now restless and mutinous, because he did not effect the taking in of water, the Negro Babo having required, with threats, that it should be done, without fail, the following day; he told him he saw plainly that the coast was steep, and the rivers designated in the maps were not to be found, with other reasons suitable to the circumstances; that the best way would be to go to the island of Santa Maria, where they might water and victual easily, it being a desert island, as the foreigners did; that the deponent did not go to Pisco, that was near, nor make any other port of the coast, because the Negro Babo had intimated to him several times, that he would kill all the whites the very moment he should perceive any city, town, or settlement of any kind on the shores to which they should be carried: that having determined to go to the island of Santa Maria, as the deponent had planned, for the purpose of trying whether, in the passage or in the island itself, they could find any vessel that should favour them, or whether he could escape from it in a boat to the neighbouring coast of Arruco; to adopt the necessary means he immediately changed his course, steering for the island; that the Negroes Babo and Atufal held daily conferences, in which they discussed what was necessary for their design of returning to Senegal, whether they were to kill all the Spaniards, and particularly the deponent; that eight days after parting from the coast of Nasca, the deponent being on the watch a little after daybreak, and soon after the Negroes had their meeting, the Negro Babo came to the place where the deponent was, and told him that he had determined to kill his master, Don Alexandro Aranda, both because he and his companions could not otherwise be sure of their liberty, and that, to keep the seamen in subjection, he wanted to prepare a warning of what road they should be made to take did they or any of them oppose him; and that, by means of the death of Don Alexandro, that warning would best be given; but, that what this last meant, the deponent did not at the time comprehend, nor could not, further than that the death of Don Alexandro was intended; and moreover, the Negro Babo proposed to the deponent to call the mate Raneds, who was sleeping in the cabin, before the thing was done, for fear, as the deponent understood it, that the mate, who was a good navigator, should be killed with Don Alexandro and the rest; that the deponent, who was the friend from youth of Don Alexandro, prayed and conjured, but all was useless; for the Negro Babo answered him that the thing could not be prevented, and that all the Spaniards risked their death if they should attempt to frustrate his will in this matter, or any other; that, in this conflict, the deponent called the mate, Raneds, who was forced to go apart, and immediately the Negro Babo commanded the Ashantee Martinqui and the Ashantee Lecbe to go and commit the murder; that those two went down with hatchets to the berth of Don Alexandro; that, yet half alive and mangled, they dragged him on deck; that they were going to throw him overboard in that state, but the Negro Babo stopped them, bidding the murder be completed on the deck before him, which was done, when, by his orders, the body was carried below, forward; that nothing more was seen of it by the deponent for three days; . . . that Don Alonzo Sidonia, an old man, long resident at Valparaiso, and lately appointed to a civil office in Peru, whither he had taken passage, was at the time sleeping in the berth opposite Don Alexandro's; that, awakening at his cries, surprised by them, and at the sight of the Negroes with their bloody hatchets in their hands, he threw himself into the sea through a window which was near him, and was drowned, without it being in the power of the deponent to assist or take him up; . . . that, a short time after killing Aranda, they brought upon deck his german-cousin, of middle age, Don Francisco Masa, of Mendoza, and the young Don Joaquin,

Marques de Aramboalaza, then lately from Spain, with his Spanish servant Ponce, and the three young clerks of Aranda, José Mozairi, Lorenzo Bargas, and Hermenegildo Gandix, all of Cádiz; that Don Joaquin and Hermenegildo Gandix, the Negro Babo for purposes hereafter to appear, preserved alive; but Don Francisco Masa, José Mozairi, and Lorenzo Bargas, with Ponce, the servant, beside the boatswain, Juan Robles, the boatswain's mates, Manuel Viscaya and Roderigo Hurta, and four of the sailors, the Negro Babo ordered to be thrown alive into the sea, although they made no resistance, nor begged for anything else but mercy; that the boatswain, Juan Robles, who knew how to swim, kept the longest above water, making acts of contrition, and, in the last words he uttered, charged this deponent to cause mass to be said for his soul to our Lady of Succour: . . . that, during the three days which followed, the deponent, uncertain what fate had befallen the remains of Don Alexandro, frequently asked the Negro Babo where they were, and, if still on board, whether they were to be preserved for interment ashore, entreating him so to order it; that the Negro Babo answered nothing till the fourth day, when at sunrise, the deponent coming on deck, the Negro Babo showed him a skeleton, which had been substituted for the ship's proper figurehead, the image of Christopher Colón, the discoverer of the New World; that the Negro Babo asked him whose skeleton that was, and whether, from its whiteness, he should not think it a white's; that, upon his covering his face, the Negro Babo, coming close, said words to this effect: "Keep faith with the blacks from here to Senegal, or you shall in spirit, as now in body, follow your leader," pointing to the prow; . . . that the same morning the Negro Babo took by succession each Spaniard forward, and asked him whose skeleton that was, and whether, from its whiteness, he should not think it a white's; that each Spaniard covered his face; that then to each the Negro Babo repeated the words in the first place said to the deponent; . . . that they (the Spaniards), being then assembled aft, the Negro Babo harangued them, saying that he had now done all; that the deponent (as navigator for the Negroes) might pursue his course, warning him and all of them that they should, soul and body, go the way of Don Alexandro if he saw them (the Spaniards) speak or plot anything against them (the Negroes)—a threat which was repeated every day; that, before the events last mentioned, they had tied the cook to throw him overboard, for it is not known what thing they heard him speak, but finally the Negro Babo spared his life, at the request of the deponent; that a few days after, the deponent, endeavouring not to omit any means to preserve the lives of the remaining whites, spoke to the Negroes peace and tranquillity, and agreed to draw up a paper, signed by the deponent and the sailors who could write, as also by the Negro Babo, for himself and all the blacks, in which the deponent obliged himself to carry them to Senegal, and they not to kill any more, and he formally to make over to them the ship, with the cargo, with which they were for that time satisfied and quieted. . . . But the next day, the more surely to guard against the sailors' escape, the Negro Babo commanded all the boats to be destroyed but the longboat, which was unseaworthy, and another, a cutter in good condition, which, knowing it would yet be wanted for lowering the water casks, he had it lowered down into the hold.

[*Various particulars of the prolonged and perplexed navigation ensuing here follow, with incidents of a calamitous calm, from which portion one passage is extracted, to wit*:]

—That on the fifth day of the calm, all on board suffering much from the heat, and want of water, and five having died in fits, and mad, the Negroes became irritable, and for a chance gesture, which they deemed suspicious—though it was harmless—made by the mate, Raneds, to the deponent, in the act of handing a quadrant, they killed him; but that for this they afterwards were sorry, the mate being the only remaining navigator on board, except the deponent.

. . .

—That omitting other events, which daily happened, and which can only serve uselessly to recall past misfortunes and conflicts, after seventy-three days' navigation, reckoned from the time they sailed from Nasca, during which they navigated under a scanty allowance of water, and were afflicted with the calms before mentioned, they at last arrived at the island of Santa Maria, on the seventeenth of the month of August, at about six o'clock in the afternoon, at which hour they cast anchor very near the American ship, *Bachelor's Delight*, which lay in the same bay, commanded by the generous Captain Amasa Delano; but at six o'clock in the morning, they had already descried the port, and the Negroes became uneasy, as soon as at distance they saw the ship, not having expected to see one there; that the Negro Babo pacified them, assuring them that no fear need be had; that straightway he ordered the figure on the bow to be covered with canvas, as for repairs, and had the decks a little set in order; that for a time the Negro Babo and the Negro Atufal conferred; that the Negro Atufal was for sailing away, but the Negro Babo would not, and, by himself, cast about what to do; that at last he came to the deponent, proposing to him to say and do all that the deponent declares to have said and done to the American captain; . . . that the Negro Babo warned him that if he varied in the least, or uttered any word, or gave any look that should give the least intimation of the past events or present state, he would instantly kill him, with all his companions, showing a dagger, which he carried hid, saying something which, as he understood it, meant that that dagger would be alert as his eye; that the Negro Babo then announced the plan to all his companions, which pleased them; that he then, the better to disguise the truth, devised many expedients, in some of them uniting deceit and defence; that of this sort was the device of the six Ashantees before named, who were his bravos; that them he stationed on the break of the poop, as if to clean certain hatchets (in cases, which were part of the cargo), but in reality to use them, and distribute them at need, and at a given word he told them that, among other devices, was the device of presenting Atufal, his right-hand man, as chained, though in a moment the chains could be dropped; that in every particular he informed the deponent what part he was expected to enact in every device, and what story he was to tell on every occasion, always threatening him with instant death if he varied in the least: that, conscious that many of the Negroes would be turbulent, the Negro Babo appointed the four aged Negroes, who were caulkers, to keep what domestic order they could on the decks; that again and again he harangued the Spaniards and his companions, informing them of his intent, and of his devices, and of the invented story that this deponent was to tell, charging them lest any of them varied from that story; that these arrangements were made and matured during the interval of two or three hours, between their first sighting the ship and the arrival on board of Captain Amasa Delano; that this happened at about half-past seven in the morning, Captain Amasa Delano coming in his boat, and all gladly receiving him; that the deponent, as well as he could force himself, acting then the part of principal owner, and a free captain of the ship, told Captain Amasa Delano, when called upon, that he came from Buenos Ayres, bound to Lima, with three hundred Negroes; that off Cape Horn, and in a subsequent fever, many Negroes had died; that also, by similar casualties, all the sea officers and the greatest part of the crew had died.

[*And so the deposition goes on, circumstantially recounting the fictitious story dictated to the deponent by Babo, and through the deponent imposed upon Captain Delano; and also recounting the friendly offers of Captain Delano, with other things, but all of which is here omitted. After the fictitious, strange story, etc., the deposition proceeds*:]

—That the generous Captain Amasa Delano remained on board all the day, till he left the ship anchored at six o'clock in the evening, deponent speaking to him always of his pretended misfortunes, under the forementioned principles, without having had it in his power to tell a single word, or give him the least hint, that he might know the truth and state of things; because the Negro Babo, performing the office of an officious servant with all the appearance of submission of the humble slave, did not leave the deponent one moment; that this was in order to observe the deponent's actions and words, for the Negro Babo understands well the Spanish; and besides, there were thereabout some others who were constantly on the watch, and likewise understood the Spanish; . . . that upon one occasion, while deponent was standing on the deck conversing with Amasa Delano, by a secret sign the Negro Babo drew him (the deponent) aside, the act appearing as if originating with the deponent; that then, he being drawn aside, the Negro Babo proposed to him to gain from Amasa Delano full particulars about his ship, and crew, and arms; that the deponent asked "For what?"; that the Negro Babo answered he might conceive; that, grieved at the prospect of what might overtake the generous Captain Amasa Delano, the deponent at first refused to ask the desired questions, and used every argument to induce the Negro Babo to give up this new design;

that the Negro Babo showed the point of his dagger; that, after the information had been obtained, the Negro Babo again drew him aside, telling him that that very night he (the deponent) would be captain of two ships instead of one, for that, great part of the American's ship's crew being to be absent fishing, the six Ashantees, without anyone else, would easily take it; that at this time he said other things to the same purpose; that no entreaties availed; that before Amasa Delano's coming on board, no hint had been given touching the capture of the American ship; that to prevent this project the deponent was powerless; . . .—that in some things his memory is confused, he cannot distinctly recall every event; . . .—that as soon as they had cast anchor at six of the clock in the evening, as has before been stated, the American captain took leave to return to his vessel; that upon a sudden impulse, which the deponent believes to have come from God and his angels, he, after the farewell had been said, followed the generous Captain Amasa Delano as far as the gunwale, where he stayed, under the pretence of taking leave, until Amasa Delano should have been seated in his boat; that on shoving off, the deponent sprang from the gunwale, into the boat, and fell into it, he knows not how, God guarding him; that—

[*Here, in the original, follows the account of what further happened at the escape, and how the* San Dominick *was retaken, and of the passage to the coast; including in the recital many expressions of "eternal gratitude" to the "generous Captain Amasa Delano." The deposition then proceeds with recapitulatory remarks, and a partial renumeration of the Negroes, making record of their individual part in the past events, with a view to furnishing, according to command of the court, the data whereon to found the criminal sentences to be pronounced. From this portion is the following*:]

—That he believes that all the Negroes, though not in the first place knowing to the design of revolt, when it was accomplished, approved it. . . . That the Negro, José, eighteen years old, and in the personal service of Don Alexandro, was the one who communicated the information to the Negro Babo, about the state of things in the cabin, before the revolt; that this is known, because, in the preceding midnight, he used to come from his berth, which was under his master's, in the cabin, to the deck where the ringleader and his associates were, and had secret conversations with the Negro Babo, in which he was several times seen by the mate; that, one night, the mate drove him away twice; . . . that this same Negro José was the one who, without being commanded to do so by the Negro Babo, as Lecbe and Martinqui were, stabbed his master, Don Alexandro, after he had been dragged half-lifeless to the deck; . . . that the mulatto steward, Francesco, was of the first band of revolters, that he was, in all things, the creature and tool of the Negro Babo; that, to make his court, he, just before a repast in the cabin, proposed, to the Negro Babo, poisoning a dish for the generous Captain Amasa Delano; this is known and believed, because the Negroes have said it; but that the Negro Babo, having another design, forbade Francesco; . . . that the Ashantee Lecbe was one of the worst of them; for that, on the day the ship was retaken, he assisted in the defence of her, with a hatchet in each hand, with one of which he wounded, in the breast, the chief mate of Amasa Delano, in the first act of boarding; this all knew; that, in sight of the deponent, Lecbe struck, with a hatchet, Don Francisco Masa when, by the Negro Babo's orders, he was carrying him to throw him overboard, alive; beside participating in the murder, before mentioned, of Don Alexandro Aranda, and others of the cabin passengers; that, owing to the fury with which the Ashantees fought in the engagement with the boats, but this Lecbe and Yan survived; that Yan was bad as Lecbe; that Yan was the man who, by Babo's command, willingly prepared the skeleton of Don Alexandro, in a way the Negroes afterwards told the deponent, but which he, so long as reason is left him, can never divulge; that Yan and Lecbe were the two who, in a calm by night, riveted the skeleton to the bow; this also the Negroes told him; that the Negro Babo was he who traced the inscription below it; that the Negro Babo was the plotter from first to last; he ordered every murder, and was the helm and keel of the revolt; that Atufal was his lieutenant in all; but Atufal, with his own hand, committed no murder; nor did the Negro Babo; . . . that Atufal was shot, being killed in the fight with the boats, ere boarding; . . . that the Negresses, of age, were knowing to the revolt, and testified themselves satisfied at the death of their master, Don Alexandro; that, had the Negroes not restrained them, they would have tortured to death, instead of simply killing, the Spaniards slain by command of the Negro Babo; that the Negresses used their utmost influence to have the deponent made away with; that, in the various acts of murder, they sang songs and danced—not gaily, but solemnly; and before the engagement with the boats, as well as during the action, they sang melancholy songs to the Negroes, and that this melancholy tone was more inflaming than a different one would have been, and was so intended; that all this is believed, because the Negroes have said it.

—That of the thirty-six men of the crew—exclusive of the passengers (all of whom are now dead), which the deponent had knowledge of—six only remained alive, with four cabin boys and ship boys, not included with the crew; . . .—that the Negroes broke an arm of one of the cabin boys and gave him strokes with hatchets.

[*Then follow various random disclosures referring to various periods of time. The following are extracted*:]

—That during the presence of Captain Amasa Delano on board, some attempts were made by the sailors, and one by Hermenegildo Gandix, to convey hints to him of the true state of affairs; but that these attempts were ineffectual, owing to fear of incurring death, and furthermore owing to the devices which offered contradictions to the true state of affairs; as well as owing to the generosity and piety of Amasa Delano, incapable of sounding such wickedness; . . . that Luys Galgo, a sailor about sixty years of age, and formerly of the king's navy, was one of those who sought to convey tokens to Captain Amasa Delano; but his intent, though undiscovered, being suspected, he was, on a pretence, made to retire out of sight, and at last into the hold, and there was made away with. This the Negroes have since said; . . . that one of the ship boys feeling, from Captain Amasa Delano's presence, some hopes of release, and not having enough prudence, dropped some chance word respecting his expectations, which being overheard and understood by a slave boy with whom he was eating at the time, the latter struck him on the head with a knife, inflicting a bad wound, but of which the boy is now healing; that likewise, not long before the ship was brought to anchor, one of the seamen, steering at the time, endangered himself by letting the blacks remark a certain unconscious hopeful expression in his countenance, arising from some cause similar to the above; but this sailor, by his heedful after conduct, escaped; . . . that these statements are made to show the court that from the beginning to the end of the revolt, it was impossible for the deponent and his men to act otherwise than they did; . . .—that the third clerk, Hermenegildo Gandix, who before had been forced to live among the seamen, wearing a seaman's habit, and in all respects appearing to be one for the time; he, Gandix, was killed by a musket ball fired through a mistake from the American boats before boarding; having in his fright ran up the mizzen rigging, calling to the boats—"don't board," lest upon their boarding the Negroes should kill him; that this inducing the Americans to believe he some way favoured the cause of the Negroes, they fired two balls at him, so that he fell wounded from the rigging, and was drowned in the sea; . . .—that the young Don Joaquin, Marques de Aramboalaza, like Hermenegildo Gandix, the third clerk, was degraded to the office and appearance of a common seaman; that upon one occasion, when Don Joaquin shrank, the Negro Babo commanded the Ashantee Lecbe to take tar and heat it, and pour it upon Don Joaquin's hands; . . .—that Don Joaquin was killed owing to another mistake of the Americans, but one impossible to be avoided, as upon the approach of the boats, Don Joaquin, with a hatchet tied edge out and upright to his hand, was made by the Negroes to appear on the bulwarks; whereupon, seen with arms in his hands and in a questionable attitude, he was shot for a renegade seaman; . . .—that on the person of Don Joaquin was found secreted a jewel, which, by papers that were discovered, proved to have been meant for the shrine of our Lady of Mercy in Lima; a votive offering, beforehand prepared and guarded, to attest his gratitude, when he should have landed in Peru, his last destination, for the safe conclusion of his entire voyage from Spain; . . .—that the jewel, with the other effects of the late Don Joaquin, is in the custody of the brethren of the Hospital de Sacerdotes, awaiting the decision of the honourable court; . . .—that, owing to the condition of the deponent, as well as the haste in which the boats departed for the attack, the Americans were not forewarned that there were, among the apparent crew, a passenger and one of the clerks disguised by the Negro Babo; . . .—that, beside the Negroes killed in the action, some were killed after the capture and re-anchoring at night, when shackled to the ringbolts on deck; that these deaths were committed by the sailors, ere they could be prevented. That so soon as informed of it, Captain Amasa Delano used all his authority, and, in particular with his own hand, struck down Martinez Gola, who, having found a razor in the pocket of an old jacket of his, which one of the shackled Negroes had on, was aiming it at the Negro's throat; that the noble Captain Amasa Delano also wrenched from the hand of Bartholomew Barlo, a dagger secreted at the time of the massacre of the whites, with which he was in the act of stabbing a shackled Negro, who, the same day, with another Negro, had thrown him down and jumped upon him; . . .—that, for all the events, befalling through so long a time, during which the ship was in the hands of the Negro Babo, he cannot here give account; but that, what he has said is the most substantial of what occurs to him at present, and is the truth under the oath which he has taken; which declaration he affirmed and ratified, after hearing it read to him.

He said that he is twenty-nine years of age, and broken in body and mind; that when finally dismissed by the court, he shall not return home to Chili, but betake himself to the monastery on Mount Agonia without; and signed with his honour, and crossed himself, and, for the time, departed as he came, in his litter, with the monk Infelez, to the Hospital de Sacerdotes.

BENITO CERENO.

DOCTOR ROZAS.

If the deposition of Benito Cereno has served as the key to fit into the lock of the complications which preceded it, then, as a vault whose door has been flung back, the *San Dominick*'s hull lies open today.

Hitherto the nature of this narrative, besides rendering the intricacies in the beginning unavoidable, has more or less required that many things, instead of being set down in the order of occurrence, should be retrospectively, or irregularly given; this last is the case with the following passages, which will conclude the account:

During the long, mild voyage to Lima, there was, as before hinted, a period during which Don Benito a little recovered his health, or, at least in some degree, his tranquillity. Ere the decided relapse which came, the two captains had many cordial conversations—their fraternal unreserve in singular contrast with former withdrawments.

Again and again, it was repeated, how hard it had been to enact the part forced on the Spaniard by Babo.

"Ah, my dear Don Amasa," Don Benito once said, "at those very times when you thought me so morose and ungrateful—nay when, as you now admit, you half thought me plotting your murder—at those very times my heart was frozen; I could not look at you, thinking of what, both on board this ship and your own, hung, from other hands, over my kind benefactor. And as God lives, Don Amasa, I know not whether desire for my own safety alone could have nerved me to that leap into your boat, had it not been for the thought that, did you, unenlightened, return to your ship, you, my best friend, with all who might be with you, stolen upon, that night, in your hammocks, would never in this world have wakened again. Do but think how you walked this deck, how you sat in this cabin, every inch of ground mined into honeycombs under you. Had I dropped the least hint, made the least advance toward an understanding between us, death, explosive death—yours as mine—would have ended the scene."

"True, true," cried Captain Delano, starting, "you saved my life, Don Benito, more than I yours; saved it, too, against my knowledge and will."

"Nay, my friend," rejoined the Spaniard, courteous even to the point of religion, "God charmed your life, but you saved mine. To think of some things you did—those smilings and chattings, rash pointings and gesturings. For less than these, they slew my mate, Raneds; but you had the Prince of Heaven's safe conduct through all ambuscades."

"Yes, all is owing to Providence, I know; but the temper of my mind that morning was more than commonly pleasant, while the sight of so much suffering—more apparent than real—added to my good nature, compassion, and charity, happily interweaving the three. Had it been otherwise, doubtless, as you hint, some of my interferences with the blacks might have ended unhappily enough. Besides that, those feelings I spoke of enabled me to get the better of momentary distrust, at times when acuteness might have cost me my life, without saving another's. Only at the end did my suspicions get the better of me, and you know how wide of the mark they then proved."

"Wide, indeed," said Don Benito, sadly; "you were with me all day; stood with me, sat with me, talked with me, looked at me, ate with me, drank with me; and yet, your last act was to clutch for a villain, not only an innocent man, but the most pitiable of all men. To such degree may malign machinations and deceptions impose. So far may even the best men err, in judging the conduct of one with the recesses of whose condition he is not acquainted. But you were forced to it; and you were in time undeceived. Would that, in both respects, it was so ever, and with all men."

"I think I understand you; you generalize, Don Benito; and mournfully enough. But the past is passed; why moralize upon it? Forget it. See, yon bright sun has forgotten it all, and the blue sea, and the blue sky; these have turned over new leaves."

"Because they have no memory," he dejectedly replied; "because they are not human."

"But these mild trades that now fan your cheek, Don Benito, do they not come with a humanlike healing to you? Warm friends, steadfast friends are the trades."

"With their steadfastness they but waft me to my tomb, *señor*," was the foreboding response.

"You are saved, Don Benito," cried Captain Delano, more and more astonished and pained; "you are saved; what has cast such a shadow upon you?"

"The Negro."

There was silence, while the moody man sat, slowly and unconsciously gathering his mantle about him, as if it were a pall.

There was no more conversation that day.

But if the Spaniard's melancholy sometimes ended in muteness upon topics like the above, there were others upon which he never spoke at all; on which, indeed, all his old reserves were piled. Pass over the worst and, only to elucidate, let an item or two of these be cited. The dress so precise and costly, worn by him on the day whose events have been narrated, had not willingly been put on. And that silver-mounted sword, apparent symbol of despotic command, was not, indeed, a sword, but the ghost of one. The scabbard, artificially stiffened, was empty.

As for the black—whose brain, not body, had schemed and led the revolt, with the plot—his slight frame, inadequate to that which it held, had at once yielded to the superior muscular strength of his captor, in the boat. Seeing all was over, he uttered no sound, and could not be forced to. His aspect seemed to say: since I cannot do deeds, I will not speak words. Put in irons in the hold, with the rest, he was carried to Lima. During the passage Don Benito did not visit him. Nor then, nor at any time after, would he look at him. Before the tribunal he refused. When pressed by the judges he fainted. On the testimony of the sailors alone rested the legal identity of Babo. And yet the Spaniard would, upon occasion, verbally refer to the Negro, as has been shown; but look on him he would not, or could not.

Some months after, dragged to the gibbet at the tail of a mule, the black met his voiceless end. The body was burned to ashes; but for many days, the head, that hive of subtlety, fixed on a pole in the plaza, met, unabashed, the gaze of the whites; and across the plaza looked toward St. Bartholomew's church, in whose vaults slept then, as now, the recovered bones of Aranda; and across the Rimae bridge looked toward the monastery, on Mount Agonia without; where, three months after being dismissed by the court, Benito Cereno, borne on the bier, did, indeed, follow his leader.

---

1. What is accomplished in this story by initially depicting the situation onboard the *San Dominick* through the eyes of Captain Delano? How do the excerpts from the deposition alter our interpretation of events, apart from clarifying more fully what transpired on the *San Dominick*?
2. What does Melville mean when he states, "In armies, navies, cities, or families—in nature herself—nothing more relaxes good order than misery"?
3. What is the significance of Don Alexandro's skeleton being substituted for the ship's proper figurehead, the image of Christopher Colón?
4. How do Don Benito's final revelations change Captain Delano's perception of social reality?

WILLA CATHER (1873–1947) was born in Virginia and raised in the town of Red Cloud, Nebraska. After the success of her first short story collection, *The Troll Garden* (1905), and a journalism career as managing editor of the New York magazine *McClure's*, she devoted herself to writing fiction, producing a series of well-received novels. These include *My Ántonia* (1918), *One of Ours* (1922), for which she won the Pulitzer Prize, *A Lost Lady* (1923), and *Death Comes for the Archbishop* (1927). Many of Cather's works, marked by a simple, lyrical style, portray stalwart individuals coming to terms with the challenges, victories, and defeats of living on the American frontier. "Tom Outland's Story" is the middle section of her novel *The Professor's House* (1925) and is frequently treated as a distinct narrative in its own right.

Tom Outland's Story

1

The thing that sidetracked me and made me so late coming to college was a somewhat unusual accident, or string of accidents. It began with a poker game, when I was a call boy in Pardee, New Mexico.

One cold, clear night in the fall I started out to hunt up a freight crew that was to go out soon after midnight. It was just after payday, and one of the fellows had tipped me off that there would be a poker game going on in the card room behind the Ruby Light saloon. I knew most of my crew would be there, except Conductor Willis, who had a sick baby at home. The front windows were dark, of course. I went up the back alley, through a tumbledown ice house and a court, into a 'dobe room that didn't open into the saloon proper at all. It was crowded, and hot and stuffy enough. There were six or seven in the game, and a crowd of fellows were standing about the walls, rubbing the whitewash off on to their coat shoulders. There was a birdcage hanging in one window, covered with an old flannel shirt, but the canary had wakened up and was singing away for dear life. He was a beautiful singer—an old Mexican had trained him—and he was one of the attractions of the place.

I happened along when a jackpot was running. Two of the fellows I'd come for were in it, and they naturally wanted to finish the hand. I stood by the door with my watch, keeping time for them. Among the players I saw two sheep men who always liked a lively game, and one of the bystanders told me you had to buy a hundred dollars' worth of chips to get in that night. The crowd was fussing about one fellow, Rodney Blake, who had come in from his engine without cleaning up. That wasn't customary; the minute a man got in from his run, he took a bath, put on citizen's clothes, and went to a barber. This Blake was a new fireman on our division. He'd come up town in his greasy overalls and sweaty blue shirt, with his face streaked up with smoke. He'd been drinking; he smelled of it, and his eyes were out of focus. All the other men were clean and freshly shaved, and they were sore at Blake—said his hands were so greasy they marked the cards. Some of them wanted to put him out of the game, but he was a big, heavy-built fellow, and nobody wanted to be the man to do it. It didn't please them any better when he took the jackpot.

I got my two men and hurried them out, and two others from the row along the wall took their places. One of the chaps who left with me asked me to go up to his house and get his grip with his work clothes. He'd lost every cent of his pay cheque and didn't want to face his wife. I asked him who was winning.

"Blake. The dirty boomer's been taking everything. But the fellows will clean him out before morning."

About two o'clock, when my work for that night was over and I was going home to sleep, I just dropped in at the card room to see how things had come out. The game was breaking up. Since I left them at midnight, they had changed to stud poker, and Blake, the fireman, had cleaned everybody out. He was cashing in his chips when I came in. The bank was a little short, but Blake made no fuss about it. He had something over sixteen hundred dollars lying on the table before him in bank notes and gold. Some of the crowd were insulting him, trying to get him into a fight and loot him. He paid no attention and began to put the money away, not looking at anybody. The bills he folded and put inside the band of his hat. He filled his overalls pockets with the gold, and swept the rest of it into his big red neckerchief.

I'd been interested in this fellow ever since he came on our division; he was close-mouthed and unfriendly. He was one of those fellows with a settled, mature body and a young face, such as you often see among working men. There was something calm, and sarcastic, and mocking about his expression—that, too, you often see among working men. When he had put all his money away, he got up and walked toward the door without a word, without saying good night to anybody.

"Manners of a hog, and a dirty hog!" little Barney Shea yelled after him. Blake's back was just in the doorway; he hitched up one shoulder, but didn't turn or make a sound.

I slipped out after him and followed him down the street. His walk was unsteady, and the gold in his baggy overalls pockets clinked with every step he took. I ran a little way and caught up with him. "What are you going to do with all that money, Blake?" I asked him.

"Lose it, tomorrow night. I'm no hog for money. Damned barber-pole dudes!"

I thought I'd better follow him home. I knew he lodged with an old Mexican woman, in the yellow quarter, behind the roundhouse. His room opened on to the street, by a sky blue door. He went in, didn't strike a light or make a stab at undressing, but threw himself just as he was on the bed and went to sleep. His hat stuck between the iron rods of the bedhead, the gold ran out of his pockets and rolled over the bare floor in the dark.

I struck a match and lit a candle. The bed took up half the room; on the dresser was a grip with his clean clothes in it, just as he'd brought it in from his run. I took out the clothes and began picking up the money; got the bills out of his hat, emptied his pockets, and collected the coins that lay in the hollow of the bed about his hips, and put it all into the grip. Then I blew out the light and sat down to listen. I trusted all the boys who were at the Ruby Light that night, except Barney Shea. He might try to pull something off on a stranger, down in Mexican town. We had a quiet night, however, and a cold one. I found Blake's winter overcoat hanging on the wall and wrapped up in it. I wasn't a bit sorry when the roosters began to crow and the dogs began barking all over Mexican town. At last the sun came up and turned the desert and the 'dobe town red in a minute. I began to shake the man on the bed. Waking men who didn't want to get up was part of my job, and I didn't let up on him until I had him on his feet.

"Hello, kid, come to call me?"

I told him I'd come to call him to a Harvey House breakfast. "You owe me a good one. I brought you home last night."

"Sure, I'm glad to have company. Wait till I wash up a bit." He took his soap and towel and comb and went out into the patio, a neat little sanded square with flowers and vines all around, and washed at the trough under the pump. Then he called me to come and pump water on his head. After he'd stood the gush of cold water for a few seconds, he straightened up with his teeth chattering.

"That ought to get the whisky out of a fellow's head, oughtn't it? Felt good, Tom." Presently he began feeling his side pockets. "Was I dreaming something, or did I take a string of jackpots last night?"

"The money's in your grip," I told him. "You don't deserve it, for you were too drunk to take care of it. I had to come after you and pick it up out of the mud."

"All right. I'll go halvers. Easy come, easy go."

I told him I didn't want anything off him but breakfast, and I wanted that pretty soon.

"Go easy, son. I've got to change my shirt. This one's wet."

"It's worse than wet. You oughtn't to go up town without changing. You're a stranger here, and it makes a bad impression."

He shrugged his shoulders and looked superior. He had a square-built, honest face and steady eyes that didn't carry a cynical expression very well. I knew he was a decent chap, though he'd been drinking and acting ugly ever since he'd been on our division.

After breakfast we went out and sat in the sun at a place where the wooden sidewalk ran over a sand gully and made a sort of bridge. I had a long talk with him. I was carrying the grip with his winnings in it, and I finally persuaded him to go with me to the bank. We put every cent of it into a savings account that he couldn't touch for a year.

From that night Blake and I were fast friends. He was the sort of fellow who can do anything for somebody else, and nothing for himself. There are lots like that among working men. They aren't trained by success to a sort of systematic selfishness. Rodney had been unlucky in personal relations. He'd run away from home when he was a kid because his mother married again—a man who had been paying attention to her while his father was still alive. He got engaged to a girl down on the Southern Pacific, and she double-crossed him, as he said. He went to Old Mexico and let his friends put all his savings into an oil well, and they skinned him. What he needed was a pal, a straight fellow to give an account to. I was ten years younger, and that was an advantage. He liked to be an older brother. I suppose the fact that I was a kind of stray and had no family, made it easier for him to unbend to me. He surely got to think a lot of me, and I did of him. It was that winter I had pneumonia. Mrs. O'Brien couldn't do much for me; she was overworked, poor woman, with a houseful of children. Blake took me down to his room, and he and the old Mexican woman nursed me. He ought to have had boys of his own to look after. Nature's full of such substitutions, but they always seem to me sad, even in botany.

I wasn't able to be about until spring, and then the doctor and Father Duchene said I must give up night work and live in the open all summer. Before I knew anything about it, Blake had thrown up his job on the Santa Fe, and got a berth for him and me with the Sitwell Cattle Company. Jonas Sitwell was one of the biggest cattle men in our part of New Mexico. Roddy and I were to ride the range with a bunch of grass cattle all summer, then take them down to a winter camp on the Cruzados river and keep them on pasture until spring.

We went out about the first of May, and joined our cattle twenty miles south of Pardee, down toward the Blue Mesa. The Blue Mesa was one of the landmarks we always saw from Pardee—landmarks mean so much in a flat country. To the northwest, over toward Utah, we had the Mormon Buttes, three sharp blue peaks that always sat there. The Blue Mesa was south of us, and was much stronger in colour, almost purple. People said the rock itself had a deep purplish cast. It looked, from our town, like a naked blue rock set down alone in the plain, almost square, except that the top was higher at one end. The old settlers said nobody had ever climbed it, because the sides were so steep and the Cruzados river wound round it at one end and undercut it.

Blake and I knew that the Sitwell winter camp was down on the Cruzados river, directly under the mesa, and all summer long, while we drifted about with our cattle from one water hole to another, we planned how we were going to climb the mesa and be the first men up there. After supper, when we lit our pipes and watched the sunset, climbing the mesa was our staple topic of conversation. Our job was a cinch; the actual work wouldn't have kept one man busy. The Sitwell people were good to their hands. John Rapp, the foreman, came along once a month in his spring wagon, to see how the cattle were doing and to bring us supplies and bundles of old newspapers.

Blake was a conscientious reader of newspapers. He always wanted to know what was going on in the world, though most of it displeased him. He brooded on the great injustices of his time; the hanging of the anarchists in Chicago, which he could just remember, and the Dreyfus case. We had long arguments about what we read in the papers, but we never quarrelled. The only trouble I had with Blake was in getting to do my share of the work. He made my health a pretext for taking all the heavy chores, long after I was as well as he was. I'd brought my Caesar along, and had promised Father Duchene to read a hundred lines a day. Blake saw that I did it—made me translate the dull stuff aloud to him. He said if I once knew Latin, I wouldn't have to work with my back all my life like a burro. He had great respect for education, but he believed it was some kind of hocus-pocus that enabled a man to live without work. We had *Robinson Crusoe* with us, and Roddy's favourite book, *Gulliver's Travels*, which he never tired of.

Late in October, Rapp, the foreman, came along to accompany us down to the winter camp. Blake stayed with the cattle about fifteen miles to the east, where the grass was still good, and Rapp and I went down to air out the cabin and stow away our winter supplies.

2

The cabin stood in a little grove of piñons, about thirty yards back from the Cruzados river, facing south and sheltered on the north by a low hill. The grama grass grew right up to the doorstep, and the rabbits were running about and the grasshoppers hitting the door when we pulled up and looked at the place. There was no litter around, it was as clean as a prairie dog's house. No outbuildings, except a shed for our horses. The hillside behind was sandy and covered with tall clumps of deer-horn cactus, but there was nothing but grass to the south, with streaks of bright yellow rabbit brush. Along the river the cottonwoods and quaking asps had already turned gold. Just across from us, overhanging us, indeed, stood the mesa, a pile of purple rock, all broken out with red sumach and yellow aspens up in the high crevices of the cliffs. From the cabin, night and day, you could hear the river, where it made a bend round the foot of the mesa and churned over the rocks. It was the sort of place a man would like to stay in forever.

I helped Rapp open the wooden shutters and sweep out the cabin. We put clean blankets on the bunks, and stowed away bacon and coffee and canned stuff on the shelves behind the cookstove. I confess I looked forward to cooking on an iron stove with four holes. Rapp explained to me that Blake and I wouldn't be able to enjoy all this luxury together for a time. He wanted the herd kept some distance to the north as long as the grass held out up there, and Roddy and I could take turn about, one camping near the cattle and one sleeping in a bed.

"There's not pasture enough down here to take them through a long winter," he said, "and it's safest to keep them grazing up north while you can. Besides, if you bring them down here while the weather's so warm, they get skittish, and that mesa over there makes trouble. They swim the river and bolt into the mesa, and that's the last you ever see of them. We've lost a lot of critters that way. The mesa has been populated by runaways from our herd, till now there's a fine bunch of wild cattle up there. When the wind's right, our cows over here get the scent of them and make a break for the river. You'll have to watch 'em close when you bring 'em down."

I asked him whether nobody had ever gone over to get the lost cattle out.

Rapp glared at me. "Out of that mesa? Nobody has ever got into it yet. The cliffs are like the base of a monument, all the way round. The only way into it is through that deep canyon that opens on the water level, just where the river makes the bend. You can't get in by that, because the river's too deep to ford and too swift to swim. Oh, I suppose a horse could swim it, if cattle can, but I don't want to be the man to try."

I remarked that I had had my eye on the mesa all summer and meant to climb it.

"Not while you're working for the Sitwell Company, you don't! If you boys try any nonsense of that sort, I'll fire you quick. You'd break your bones and lose the herd for us. You have to watch them close to keep them from going over, I tell you. If it wasn't for that mesa, this would be the best winter range in all New Mexico."

After the foreman left us, we settled down to easy living and fine weather; blue and gold days, and clear, frosty nights. We kept the cattle off to the north and east and alternated in taking charge of them. One man was with the herd while the other got his sleep and did the cooking at the cabin. The mesa was our only neighbour, and the closer we got to it, the more tantalizing it was. It was no longer a blue, featureless lump, as it had been from a distance. Its skyline was like the profile of a big beast lying down; the head to the north, higher than the flanks around which the river curved. The north end we could easily believe impassable—sheer cliffs that fell from the summit to the plain, more than a thousand feet. But the south flank, just across the river from us, looked accessible by way of the deep canyon that split the bulk in two, from the top rim to the river, then wound back into the solid cube so that it was invisible at a distance, like a mouse track winding into a big cheese. This canyon didn't break the solid outline of the mesa, and you had to be close to see that it was there at all. We faced the mesa on its shortest side; it was only about three miles long from north to south, but east and west it measured nearly twice that distance. Whether the top was wooded we couldn't see—it was too high above us; but the cliffs and canyon on the river side were fringed with beautiful growth, groves of quaking asps and piñons and a few dark cedars, perched up in the air like the hanging gardens of Babylon. At certain hours of the day, those cedars, growing so far up on the rocks, took on the bluish tint of the cliffs themselves.

It was light up there long before it was with us. When I got up at daybreak and went down to the river to get water, our camp would be cold and grey, but the mesa top would be red with sunrise, and all the slim cedars along the rocks would be gold—metallic, like tarnished gold foil. Some mornings it would loom up above the dark river like a blazing volcanic mountain. It shortened our days, too, considerably. The sun got behind it early in the afternoon, and then our camp would lie in its shadow. After a while the sunset colour would begin to stream up from behind it. Then the mesa was like one great ink-black rock against a sky on fire.

No wonder the thing bothered us and tempted us; it was always before us, and was always changing. Black thunderstorms used to roll up from behind it and pounce on us like a panther without warning. The lightning would play round it and jab into it so that we were always expecting it would fire the brush. I've never heard thunder so loud as it was there. The cliffs threw it back at us, and we thought the mesa itself, though it seemed so solid, must be full of deep canyons and caverns, to account for the prolonged growl and rumble that followed every crash of thunder. After the burst in the sky was over, the mesa went on sounding like a drum, and seemed itself to be muttering and making noises.

One afternoon I was out hunting turkeys. Just as the sun was getting low, I came through a sea of rabbit brush, still yellow, and the horizontal rays of light, playing into it, brought out the contour of the ground with great distinctness. I noticed a number of straight mounds, like plough furrows, running from the river inland. It was too late to examine them. I cut a scrub willow and stuck a stake into one of the ridges, to mark it. The next day I took a spade down to the plantation of rabbit brush and dug around in the sandy soil. I came upon an old irrigation main, unmistakable, lined with hard smooth cobbles and 'dobe cement, with sluices where the water had been let out into trenches. Along these ditches I turned up some pieces of pottery, all of it broken, and arrowheads, and a very neat, well-finished stone pickax.

That night I didn't go back to the cabin, but took my specimens out to Blake, who was still north with the cattle. Of course, we both knew there had been Indians all over this country, but we felt sure that Indians hadn't used stone tools for a long while back. There must have been a colony of pueblo Indians here in ancient times: fixed residents, like the Taos Indians and the Hopis, not wanderers like the Navajos.

To people off alone, as we were, there is something stirring about finding evidences of human labour and care in the soil of an empty country. It comes to you as a sort of message, makes you feel differently about the ground you walk over every day. I liked the winter range better than any place I'd ever been in. I never came out of the cabin door in the morning to go after water that I didn't feel fresh delight in our snug quarters and the river and the old mesa up there, with its top burning like a bonfire. I wanted to see what it was like on the other side, and very soon I took a day off and forded the river where it was wide and shallow, north of our camp. I rode clear around the mesa, until I met the river again where it flowed under the south flank.

On that ride I got a better idea of its actual structure. All the way round were the same precipitous cliffs of hard blue rock, but in places it was mixed with a much softer stone. In these soft streaks there were deep dry watercourses which could certainly be climbed as far as they went, but nowhere did they reach to the top of the mesa. The top seemed to be one great slab of very hard rock, lying on the mixed mass of the base like the top of an old-fashioned marble table. The channels worn out by water ran for hundreds of feet up the cliffs, but always stopped under this great rimrock, which projected out over the erosions like a granite shelf. Evidently, it was because of this unbroken top layer that the butte was inaccessible. I rode back to camp that night, convinced that if we ever climbed it, we must take the route the cattle took, through the river and up the one canyon that broke down to water level.

3

We brought the bunch of cattle down to the winter range in the latter part of November. Early in December the foreman came along with generous provisions for Christmas. This time he brought with him a supercargo, a pitiful wreck of an old man he had picked up at Tarpin, the railroad town thirty miles northeast of us, where the Sitwells bought their supplies. This old man was a castaway Englishman, Henry Atkins by name. He had been a valet, and a hospital orderly, and a cook, and for many years was a table steward on the Anchor Line. Lately he had been cooking for a sheep outfit that were grazing in the cattle country, where they weren't wanted. They had done something shady and had to get out in a hurry. They dropped old Henry at Tarpin, where he soon drank up all his wages. When Rapp picked him up there, he was living on handouts.

"I've told him we can't pay him anything," Rapp explained. "But if he wants to stay here and cook for you boys till I make my next trip, he'll have plenty to eat and a roof over him. He was sleeping in the livery stable in Tarpin. He says he's a good cook, and I thought he might liven things up for you at Christmastime. He won't bother you, he's not got any of the mean ways of a bum—I know a bum when I see one. Next time I come down I'll bring him some old clothes from the ranch, and you can fire him if you want to. All his baggage is that newspaper bundle, and there's nothing in it but shoes—a pair of patent leathers and a pair of sneakers. The important thing is, never, on any account, go off skylarking, you two, and leave him with the cattle. Not for an hour, mind you. He ain't strong enough, and he's got no head."

Life was a holiday for Blake and me after we got old Henry. He was a wonderful cook and a good housekeeper. He kept that cabin shining like a playhouse; used to dress it all out with piñon boughs, and trimmed the kitchen shelves with newspapers cut in fancy patterns. He had learned to make up cots when he was a hospital orderly, and he made our bunks feel like a Harvey House bed. To this day that's the best I can say for any bed. And he was such a polite, mannerly old boy; simple and kind as a child. I used to wonder how anybody so innocent and defenceless had managed to get along at all, to keep alive for nearly seventy years in as hard a world as this. Anybody could take advantage of him. He held no grudge against any of the people who had misused him. He loved to tell about the celebrated people he'd been steward to, and the liberal tips they had given him. There with us, where he couldn't get at whisky, he was a model of good behaviour. "Drink is me weakness, you might say," he occasionally remarked apologetically. He shaved every morning and was as clean as a pin. We got to be downright fond of him, and the three of us made a happy family.

Ever since we'd brought our herd down to the winter camp, the wild cattle on the mesa were more in evidence. They came down to the river to drink oftener, and loitered about, grazing in that low canyon so much that we began to call it Cow Canyon. They were fine-looking beasts, too. One could see they had good pasture up there. Henry had a theory that we ought to be able to entice them over to our side with salt. He wanted to kill one for beefsteaks. Soon after he joined us we lost two cows. Without warning they bolted into the mesa, as the foreman had said. After that we watched the herd closer; but a few days before Christmas, when Blake was off hunting and I was on duty, four fine young steers sneaked down to the water's edge through the brush, and before I knew it they were swimming the river—seemed to do it with no trouble at all. They frisked out on the other side, ambled up the canyon, and disappeared. I was furious to have them steal a march on me, and I swore to myself I'd follow them over and drive them back.

The next morning we took the herd a few miles east, to keep them out of mischief. I made some excuse to Blake, cut back to the cabin, and asked Henry to put me up a lunch. I told him my plan, but warned him not to bear tales. If I wasn't home when Blake came in at night, then he could tell him where I'd gone.

Henry went down to the river with me to watch me across. It had grown colder since morning, and looked like snow. The old man was afraid of a storm; said I might get snowed in. But I'd got my nerve up, and I didn't want to put off making a try at it. I strapped my blanket and my lunch on my shoulders, hung my boots around my neck to keep them dry, stuffed my socks inside my hat, and we waded in. My horse took the water without any fuss, though he shivered a good deal. He stepped out very carefully, and when it got too deep for him, he swam without panic. We were carried downstream a little by the current, but I didn't have to slide off his back. He found bottom after a while, and we easily made a landing. I waved goodbye to Henry on the other side and started up the canyon, running beside my horse to get warm.

The canyon was wide at the water's edge, and though it corkscrewed back into the mesa by abrupt turns, it preserved this open, roomy character. It was, indeed, a very deep valley with gently sloping sides, rugged and rocky, but well grassed. There was a clear trail. Horses have no sense about making a trail, but you can trust cattle to find the easiest possible path and to take the lowest grades. The bluish rock and the suntanned grass, under the unusual purple-grey of the sky, gave the whole valley a very soft colour, lavender and pale gold, so that the occasional cedars growing beside the boulders looked black that morning. It may have been the hint of snow in the air, but it seemed to me that I had never breathed in anything that tasted so pure as the air in that valley. It made my mouth and nostrils smart like charged water, seemed to go to my head a little and produce a kind of exaltation. I kept telling myself that it was very different from the air on the other side of the river, though that was pure and uncontaminated enough.

When I had gone up this canyon for a mile or so, I came upon another, opening out to the north—a box canyon, very different in character. No gentle slope there. The walls were perpendicular, where they weren't actually overhanging, and they were anywhere from eight hundred to a thousand feet high, as we afterward found by measurement. The floor of it was a mass of huge boulders, great pieces of rock that had fallen from above ages back, and had been worn round and smooth as pebbles by the long action of water. Many of them were as big as haystacks, yet they lay piled on one another like a load of gravel. There was no footing for my horse among those smooth stones, so I hobbled him and went on alone a little way, just to see what it was like. My eyes were steadily on the ground—a slip of the foot there might cripple one.

It was such rough scrambling that I was soon in a warm sweat under my damp clothes. In stopping to take breath, I happened to glance up at the canyon wall. I wish I could tell you what I saw there, just *as* I saw it, on that first morning, through a veil of lightly falling snow. Far up above me, a thousand feet or so, set in a great cavern in the face of the cliff, I saw a little city of stone, asleep. It was as still as sculpture—and something like that. It all hung together, seemed to have a kind of composition: pale little houses of stone nestling close to one another, perched on top of each other, with flat roofs, narrow windows, straight walls, and in the middle of the group, a round tower.

It was beautifully proportioned, that tower, swelling out to a larger girth a little above the base, then growing slender again. There was something symmetrical and powerful about the swell of the masonry. The tower was the fine thing that held all the jumble of houses together and made them mean something. It was red in colour, even on that grey day. In sunlight it was the colour of winter oak leaves. A fringe of cedars grew along the edge of the cavern, like a garden. They were the only living things. Such silence and stillness and repose—immortal repose. That village sat looking down into the canyon with the calmness of eternity. The falling snowflakes, sprinkling the piñons, gave it a special kind of solemnity. I can't describe it. It was more like sculpture than anything else. I knew at once that I had come upon the city of some extinct civilization, hidden away in this inaccessible mesa for centuries, preserved in the dry air and almost perpetual sunlight like a fly in amber, guarded by the cliffs and the river and the desert.

As I stood looking up at it, I wondered whether I ought to tell even Blake about it; whether I ought not to go back across the river and keep that secret as the mesa had kept it. When I at last turned away, I saw still another canyon branching out of this one, and in its wall still another arch, with another group of buildings. The notion struck me like a rifle ball that this mesa had once been like a beehive; it was full of little cliff-hung villages, it had been the home of a powerful tribe, a particular civilization.

That night when I got home Blake was on the riverbank waiting for me. I told him I'd rather not talk about my trip until after supper—that I was beat out. I think he'd meant to upbraid me for sneaking off, but he didn't. He seemed to realize from the first that this was a serious matter to me, and he accepted it in that way.

After supper, when we had lit our pipes, I told Blake and Henry as clearly as I could what it was like over there, and we talked it over. The town in the cliffs explained the irrigation ditches. Like all pueblo Indians, these people had had their farms away from their dwellings. For a stronghold they needed rock, and for farming, soft earth and a water main.

"And this proves," said Roddy, "that there must have been a trail into the mesa at the north end, and that they carried their harvest over by the ford. If this Cow Canyon was the only entrance, they could never have farmed down here." We agreed that he should go over on the first warm day, and try to find a trail up to the Cliff City, as we already called it.

We talked and speculated until after midnight. It was Christmas Eve, and Henry said it was but right we should do something out of the ordinary. But after we went to bed, tired as I was, I was unable to sleep. I got up and dressed and put on my overcoat and slipped outside to get sight of the mesa. The wind had come up and was blowing the squall clouds across the sky. The moon was almost full, hanging directly over the mesa, which had never looked so solemn and silent to me before. I wondered how many Christmases had come and gone since that round tower was built. I had been to Acoma and the Hopi villages, but I'd never seen a tower like that one. It seemed to me to mark a difference. I felt that only a strong and aspiring people would have built it, and a people with a feeling for design. That cluster of buildings, in its arch, with the dizzy drop into empty air from its doorways and the wall of cliff above, was as clear in my mind as a picture. By closing my eyes I could see it against the dark, like a magic-lantern slide.

Blake got over the river before New Year's day, but he didn't find any way of getting from the bottom of the box canyon up into the Cliff City. He felt sure that the inhabitants of that sky village had reached it by a trail from the top of the mesa down, not from the bottom of the canyon up. He explored the branch canyons a little, and found four other villages, smaller than the first, placed in similar arches.

These arches we had often seen in other canyons. You can find them in the Grand Canyon, and all along the Rio Grande. Whenever the surface rock is much harder than the rock beneath it, the softer stone begins to crack and crumble with weather just at the line where it meets the hard rimrock. It goes on crumbling and falling away, and in time this washout grows to be a spacious cavern. The Cliff City sat in an unusually large cavern. We afterward found that it was three hundred and sixty feet long, and seventy feet high in the centre. The red tower was fifty feet in height.

Blake and I began to make plans. Our engagement with the Sitwell Company terminated in May. When we turned our cattle over to the foreman, we would go into the mesa with what food and tools we could carry, and try to find a trail down the north end, where we were sure there must once have been one. If we could find an easier way to get in and out of the mesa, we would devote the summer, and our winter's wages, to exploring it. From Tarpin, the nearest railroad, we could get supplies and tools, and help if we needed it. We thought we could manage to do the work ourselves if old Henry would stay with us. We didn't want to make our discovery any more public than necessary. We were reluctant to expose those silent and beautiful places to vulgar curiosity. Finally we outlined our plan to Henry, telling him we couldn't promise him regular wages.

"We won't mention it," he said, waving his hand. "I'd ask nothing better than to share your fortunes. In me youth it was me ambition to go to Egypt and see the tombs of the Pharaohs."

"You may get a bad cold going over the river, Henry," Blake warned him. "It's bad crossing—makes you dizzy when you take to swimming. You have to keep your head."

"I was never seasick in me life," he declared, "and at that, I've helped in the cook's galley on the Anchor Line when she was fair standing on her head. You'll find me strong and active when I'm once broke into the work. I come of an enduring family, though, to be sure, I've abused me constitution somewhat."

Henry liked to talk about his family, and the work they'd done, and the great age to which they lived, and the brandy puddings his mother made. "Eighteen we was in all, when we sat down at table," he would often say with his thin, apologetic smile. "Mother and father, and ten living, and four dead, and two stillborn." Roddy and I used to strain our imagination trying to visualize such a family dinner party.

Everything worked out well for us. The foreman showed so much interest in our plans that we told him everything. He insisted that we should stay on at the winter camp as long as we needed a home base, and use up whatever supplies were left. When he paid us off, he sold us our two horses at a very reasonable figure.

4

Blake and I got over to the mesa together for the first time early in May. We carried with us all the food we could, and an ax and spade. It took us several days to find a trail leading from the bottom of the box canyon up to the Cliff City. There were gaps in it; it was broken by ledges too steep for a man to climb. Lying beside one of these, we found an old dried cedar trunk, with toe notches cut in it. That was a plain suggestion. We felled some trees and threw them up over the gaps in the path. Toward the end of the week, when our provisions were getting low, we made the last lap in our climb, and stepped upon the ledge that was the floor of the Cliff City.

In front of the cluster of buildings, there was an open space, like a courtyard. Along the outer edge of this yard ran a low stone wall. In some places the wall had fallen away from the weather, but the buildings themselves sat so far back under the rimrock that the rain had never beat on them. In thunderstorms I've seen the water come down in sheets over the face of that cavern without a drop touching the village.

The courtyard was not choked by vegetation, for there was no soil. It was bare rock, with a few old, flat-topped cedars growing out of the cracks, and a little pale grass. But everything seemed open and clean, and the stones, I remember, were warm to the touch, smooth and pleasant to feel.

The outer walls of the houses were intact, except where sometimes an outjutting corner had crumbled. They were made of dressed stones, plastered inside and out with 'dobe, and were tinted in light colours, pink and pale yellow and tan. Here and there a cedar log in the ceiling had given way and let the second-story chamber down into the first; except for that, there was little rubbish or disorder. As Blake remarked, wind and sun are good housekeepers.

This village had never been sacked by an enemy, certainly. Inside the little rooms water jars and bowls stood about unbroken, and yucca-fibre mats were on the floors.

We could give only a hurried look over the place, as our food was exhausted, and we had to get back over the river before dark. We went about softly, tried not to disturb anything—even the silence. Besides the tower, there seemed to be about thirty little separate dwellings. Behind the cluster of houses was a kind of back courtyard, running from end to end of the cavern; a long, low, twilit space that got gradually lower toward the back until the rimrock met the floor of the cavern, exactly like the sloping roof of an attic. There was perpetual twilight back there, cool, shadowy, very grateful after the blazing sun in the front courtyard. When we entered it we heard a soft trickling sound, and we came upon a spring that welled out of the rock into a stone basin and then ran off through a cobble-lined gutter and dripped down the cliffs. I've never anywhere tasted water like it; as cold as ice, and so pure. Long afterward Father Duchene came out to spend a week with us on the mesa; he always carried a small drinking glass with him, and he used to fill it at the spring and take it out into the sunlight. The water looked like liquid crystal, absolutely colourless, without the slight brownish or greenish tint that water nearly always has. It threw off the sunlight like a diamond.

Beside this spring stood some of the most beautifully shaped water jars we ever found—I gave Mrs. St. Peter one of them—standing there just as if they'd been left yesterday. In the back court we found a great many things besides jars and bowls: a row of grinding stones, and several clay ovens, very much like those the Mexicans use today. There were charred bones and charcoal, and the roof was thick with soot all the way along. It was evidently a kind of common kitchen, where they roasted and baked and probably gossiped. There were corncobs everywhere, and ears of corn with the kernels still on them—little, like popcorn. We found dried beans, too, and strings of pumpkin seeds, and plum seeds, and a cupboard full of little implements made of turkey bones.

Late that afternoon Roddy and I crossed the river and got back to our cabin to rest for a few days.

The second time we went over, we found a long winding trail leading from the Cliff City up to the top of the mesa—a narrow path worn deep into the stone ledges that overhung the village, then running back into the wood of stunted piñons on the summit. Following this to the north end of the mesa, we found what was left of an old road down to the plain. But making this road passable was a matter of weeks, and we had to get workmen and tools from Tarpin. It was a narrow foot-path, barely wide enough for a sure-footed mule, and it wound down through Black Canyon, dropping in loops along the face of terrifying cliffs. About a hundred feet above the river, it ended—broke right off into the air. A wall of rock had fallen away there, probably from a landslide. That last piece of road cost us three weeks' hard work, and most of our winter's wages. We kept the workmen on long enough to build us a tight log cabin on the mesa top, a little way back from the ledge that hung over the Cliff City.

While we were engaged in road building, we made a short cut from our cabin down to the Cliff City and Cow Canyon. Just over the Cliff City, there was a crack in the ledge, a sort of manhole, and in this we hung a ladder of pine trunks spliced together with light chains, leaving the branch forks for footholds. By climbing down this ladder we saved about two miles of winding trail, and dropped almost directly into Cow Canyon, where we meant always to leave one of the horses grazing. Taking this route, we could at any time make a quick exit from the mesa—we were used to swimming the river now, and in summer our wet clothes dried very quickly.

Bill Hook, the liveryman at Tarpin, who'd sheltered old Henry when he was down and out, proved a good friend to us. He got our workmen back and forth for us, brought our supplies up onto the mesa on his pack mules, and when one of us had to stay in town overnight he let us sleep in his hay barn to save a hotel bill. He knew our expenses were heavy, and did everything for us at a bottom price.

By the first of July our money was nearly gone, but we had our road made, and our cabin built on top of the mesa. We brought old Henry up by the new horse trail and began housekeeping. We were now ready for what we called excavating. We built wide shelves all around our sleeping room, and there we put the smaller articles we found in the Cliff City. We numbered each specimen, and in my daybook I wrote down just where and in what condition we had found it, and what we thought it had been used for. I'd got a merchant's ledger in Tarpin, and every night after supper, while Roddy read the newspapers, I sat down at the kitchen table and wrote up an account of the day's work.

Henry, besides doing the housekeeping, was very eager to help us in the "rew-ins," as he called them. He was more patient than we, and would dig with his fingers half a day to get a pot out of a rubbish pile without breaking it. After all, the old man had a wider knowledge of the world than either of us, and it often came in handy. When we were working in a pale pink house, with two stories, and a sort of balcony before the upper windows, we came on a closet in the wall of the upstairs room; in this were a number of curious things, among them a deerskin bag full of little tools. Henry said at once they were surgical instruments; a stone lancet, a bunch of fine bone needles, wooden forceps, and a catheter.

One thing we knew about these people; they hadn't built their town in a hurry. Everything proved their patience and deliberation. The cedar joists had been felled with stone axes and rubbed smooth with sand. The little poles that lay across them and held up the clay floor of the chamber above, were smoothly polished. The door lintels were carefully fitted (the doors were stone slabs held in place by wooden bars fitted into hasps). The clay dressing that covered the stone walls was tinted, and some of the chambers were frescoed in geometrical patterns, one colour laid on another. In one room was a painted border, little tents, like Indian tepees, in brilliant red.

But the really splendid thing about our city, the thing that made it delightful to work there, and must have made it delightful to live there, was the setting. The town hung like a bird's nest in the cliff, looking off into the box canyon below, and beyond into the wide valley we called Cow Canyon, facing an ocean of clear air. A people who had the hardihood to build there, and who lived day after day looking down upon such grandeur, who came and went by those hazardous trails, must have been, as we often told each other, a fine people. But what had become of them? What catastrophe had overwhelmed them?

They hadn't moved away, for they had taken none of their belongings, not even their clothes. Oh, yes, we found clothes; yucca moccasins, and what seemed like cotton cloth, woven in black and white. Never any wool, but sheepskins tanned with the fleece on them. They may have been mountain sheep; the mesa was full of them. We talked of shooting one for meat, but we never did. When a mountain sheep comes out on a ledge hundreds of feet above you, with his trumpet horns, there's something noble about him—he looks like a priest. We didn't want to shoot at them and make them shy. We liked to see them. We shot a wild cow when we wanted fresh meat.

At last we came upon one of the original inhabitants—not a skeleton, but a dried human body, a woman. She was not in the Cliff City; we found her in a little group of houses stuck up in a high arch we called the Eagle's Nest. She was lying on a yucca mat, partly covered with rags, and she had dried into a mummy in that water-drinking air. We thought she had been murdered; there was a great wound in her side, the ribs stuck out through the dried flesh. Her mouth was open as if she were screaming, and her face, through all those years, had kept a look of terrible agony. Part of the nose was gone, but she had plenty of teeth, not one missing, and a great deal of coarse black hair. Her teeth were even and white, and so little worn that we thought she must have been a young woman. Henry named her Mother Eve, and we called her that. We put her in a blanket and let her down with great care, and kept her in a chamber in the Cliff City.

Yes, we found three other bodies, but afterward. One day, working in the Cliff City, we came upon a stone slab at one end of the cavern, that seemed to lead straight into the rock. It was set in cement, and when we loosened it we found it opened into a small, dark chamber. In this there had been a platform, of fine cedar poles laid side by side, but it had crumbled. In the wreckage were three bodies, one man and two women, wrapped in yucca fibre, all in the same posture and apparently prepared for burial. They were the bodies of old people. We believed they were among the aged who were left behind when the tribe went down to live on their farms in the summer season; that they had died in the absence of the villagers, and were put into this mortuary chamber to await the return of the tribe, when they would have their funeral rites. Probably these people burned their dead. Of course an archaeologist could have told a great deal about that civilization from those bodies. But they never got to an archaeologist—at least, not on this side of the world.

5

The first of August came, and everything was going well with us. We hadn't met with any bad luck, and though we had very little money left, there was Blake's untouched savings account in the bank at Pardee, and we had plenty of credit in Tarpin. The merchants there took an interest and were friendly. But the little new moon, that looked so innocent, brought us trouble. We lost old Henry, and in a terrible way. From the first we'd been a little bothered by rattlesnakes—you generally find them about old stone quarries and old masonry. We had got them pretty well cleared out of the Cliff City, hadn't seen one there for weeks. But one Sunday we took Henry and went on an exploring expedition at the north end of the mesa, along Black Canyon. We caught sight of a little bunch of ruins we'd never noticed before, and made a foolhardy scramble to get up to them. We almost made it, and then there was a stretch of rock wall so smooth we couldn't climb it without a ladder. I was the tallest of the three, and Henry was the lightest; he thought he could get up there if he stood on my shoulders. He was standing on my back, his head just above the floor of the cavern, groping for something to hoist himself by, when a snake struck him from the ledge—struck him square in the forehead. It happened in a flash. He came down and brought the snake with him. By the time we picked him up and turned him over, his face had begun to swell. In ten minutes it was purple, and he was so crazy it took the two of us to hold him and keep him from jumping down the chasm. He was struck so near the brain that there was nothing to do. It lasted nearly two hours. Then we carried him home. Roddy dropped down the ladder into Cow Canyon, caught his horse, and rode into Tarpin for the coroner. Father Duchene was preaching there at the mission church that Sunday, and came back with him.

We buried Henry on the mesa. Father Duchene stayed on with us a week to keep us company. We were so cut up that we were almost ready to quit. But he had been planning to come out to see our find for a long while, and he got our minds off our trouble. He worked hard every day. He went over everything we'd done, and examined everything minutely: the pottery, cloth, stone implements, and the remains of food. He measured the heads of the mummies and declared they had good skulls. He cut down one of the old cedars that grew exactly in the middle of the deep trail worn in the stone, and counted the rings under his pocket microscope. You couldn't count them with the unassisted eye, for growing out of a tiny crevice in the rock as that tree did, the increase of each year was so scant that the rings were invisible except with a glass. The tree he cut down registered three hundred and thirty-six years' growth, and it could have begun to grow in that well-worn path only after human feet had ceased to come and go there.

Why had they ceased? That question puzzled him, too. Smallpox, any epidemic, would have left unburied bodies. Father Duchene suggested what Dr. Ripley, in Washington, afterward surmised: that the tribe had been exterminated, not here in their stronghold, but in their summer camp, down among the farms across the river. Father Duchene had been among the Indians nearly twenty years then, he had seventeen Indian pueblos in his parish, and he spoke several Indian dialects. He was able to explain the use of many of the implements we found, especially those used in religious ceremonies. The night before he left us, he summed up the results of his week's study, something like this:

"The two square towers on the mesa top, to which you have given little attention, were unquestionably granaries. Under the stones and earth fallen from the walls, there is a quantity of dried corn on the ear. Not a great harvest, for life must have come to an end here in the summer, when the new crop was not yet garnered and the last year's grain was getting low. The semicircular ridge on the mesa top, which you can see distinctly among the piñons when the sun is low and brings it into high relief, is the buried wall of an amphitheatre, where probably religious exercises and games took place. I advise you not to dig into it. It is probably the most important thing here, and should be left for scholars to excavate.

"The tower you so much admire in the cliff village may have been a watch tower, as you think, but from the curious placing of those narrow slits, like windows, I believe it was used for astronomical observations. I am inclined to think that your tribe were a superior people. Perhaps they were not so when they first came upon this mesa, but in an orderly and secure life they developed considerably the arts of peace. There is evidence on every hand that they lived for something more than food and shelter. They had an appreciation of comfort, and went even further than that. Their life, compared to that of our roving Navajos, must have been quite complex. There is unquestionably a distinct feeling for design in what you call the Cliff City. Buildings are not grouped like that by pure accident, though convenience probably had much to do with it. Convenience often dictates very sound design.

"The workmanship on both the wood and stone of the dwellings is good. The shapes and decoration of the water jars and food bowls is better than in any of the existing pueblos I know, better even than the pottery made at Acoma. I have seen a collection of early pottery from the island of Crete. Many of the geometrical decorations on these jars are not only similar, but, if my memory is trustworthy, identical.

"I see your tribe as a provident, rather thoughtful people, who made their livelihood secure by raising crops and fowl—the great number of turkey bones and feathers are evidence that they had domesticated the wild turkey. With grain in their storerooms, and mountain sheep and deer for their quarry, they rose gradually from the condition of savagery. With the proper variation of meat and vegetable diet, they developed physically and improved in the primitive arts. They had looms and mills, and experimented with dyes. At the same time, they possibly declined in the arts of war, in brute strength and ferocity.

"I see them here, isolated, cut off from other tribes, working out their destiny, making their mesa more and more worthy to be a home for man, purifying life by religious ceremonies and observances, caring respectfully for their dead, protecting the children, doubtless entertaining some feelings of affection and sentiment for this stronghold where they were at once so safe and so comfortable, where they had practically overcome the worst hardships that primitive man had to fear. They were, perhaps, too far advanced for their time and environment.

"They were probably wiped out, utterly exterminated, by some roving Indian tribe without culture or domestic virtues, some horde that fell upon them in their summer camp and destroyed them for their hides and clothing and weapons, or from mere love of slaughter. I feel sure that these brutal invaders never even learned of the existence of this mesa, honeycombed with habitations. If they had come here, they would have destroyed. They killed and went their way.

"What I cannot understand is why you have not found more human remains. The three bodies you found in the mortuary chamber were prepared for burial by the old people who were left behind. But what of the last survivors? It is possible that when autumn wore on, and no one returned from the farms, the aged banded together, went in search of their people, and perished in the plain.

"Like you, I feel a reverence for this place. Wherever humanity has made that hardest of all starts and lifted itself out of mere brutality, is a sacred spot. Your people were cut off here without the influence of example or emulation, with no incentive but some natural yearning for order and security. They built themselves into this mesa and humanized it."

Father Duchene warmly agreed with Blake that I ought to go to Washington and make some report to the government, so that the proper specialists would be sent out to study the remains we had found.

"You must go to the director of the Smithsonian Institution," he said. "He will send us an archaeologist who will interpret all that is obscure to us. He will revive this civilization in a scholarly work. It may be that you will have thrown light on some important points in the history of your country."

After he left us, Blake and I began to make definite plans for my trip to Washington. Blake was to work on the railroad that winter and save as much money as possible. The expense of my journey would be paid out of what we called the jackpot account, in the bank at Pardee. All our further expenses on the mesa would be paid by the government. Roddy often hinted that we would get a substantial reward of some kind. When we broke or lost anything at our work, he used to smile and say: "Never mind. I guess our Uncle Sam will make that good to us."

We had a beautiful autumn that year, soft, sunny, like a dream. Even up there in the air we had so little wind that the gold hung on the poplars and quaking aspens late in November. We stayed out on the mesa until after Christmas. We wanted our archaeologist, when he came, to find everything in good order. We cleared up any litter we'd made in digging things out, stored all the specimens, even the mummies, in our cabin, and padlocked the doors and windows before we left it. I had written up my daybook carefully to the very end, had even written out some of Father Duchene's deductions. This book I left in concealment on the mesa. I climbed up to the Eagle's Nest in which we had found the mummy of the murdered woman we called Mother Eve, where I had noticed a particularly neat little cupboard in the wall. I put my book in this niche and sealed it up with cement. Mother Eve had greatly interested Father Duchene, by the way. He laughed and said she was well named. He didn't believe her death could throw any light on the destruction of her people. "I seem to smell," he said slyly, "a personal tragedy. Perhaps when the tribe went down to the summer camp, our lady was sick and would not go. Perhaps her husband thought it worthwhile to return unannounced from the farms some night, and found her in improper company. The young man may have escaped. In primitive society the husband is allowed to punish an unfaithful wife with death."

When the first snow began to fly, we said goodbye to our mesa and rode into Tarpin. It took several days to outfit me for my journey to Washington. We bought a trunk (I'd never owned one in my life), and a supply of white shirts, an overcoat that was as heavy as lead and just about as cold, and two suits of clothes. That conscienceless trader worked off on me a clawhammer coat he must have had in stock for twenty years. He easily persuaded Roddy that it was the proper thing for dress occasions. I think Roddy expected that I would be received by ambassadors—perhaps I did.

Roddy drew six hundred dollars out of the bank to stake me, and bought my ticket and Pullman through to Washington. He went to the station with me the morning I left, and a hard handshake was goodbye.

For a long while after my train pulled out, I could see our mesa bulking up blue on the skyline. I hated to leave it, but I reflected that it had taken care of itself without me for a good many hundred years. When I saw it again, I told myself, I would have done my duty by it; I would bring back with me men who would understand it, who would appreciate it and dig out all its secrets.

6

I got off the train, just behind the Capitol building, one cold bright January morning. I stood for a long while watching the white dome against a flashing blue sky, with a very religious feeling. After I had walked about a little and seen the parks, so green though it was winter, and the Treasury building, and the War and Navy, I decided to put off my business for a little and give myself a week to enjoy the city. That was the most sensible thing I did while I was there. For that week I was wonderfully happy.

My sightseeing over, I got to work. First I went to see the representative from our district, to ask for letters of introduction. He was cordial enough, but he gave me bad advice. He was very positive that I ought to report to the Indian Commission, and gave me a letter to the commissioner. The commissioner was out of town, and I wasted three days waiting about his office, being questioned by clerks and secretaries. They were not very busy, and seemed to find me entertaining. I thought they were interested in my mission, and interest was what I wanted to arouse. I didn't know how influential these people might be—they talked as if they had great authority. I had brought along in my telescope bag some good pieces of pottery—not the best, I was afraid of accident, but some that were representative—and all the photographs Blake and I had taken. We had only a small Kodak, and these pictures didn't make much show—looked, indeed, like grubby little 'dobe ruins such as one can find almost anywhere. They gave no idea of the beauty and vastness of the setting. The clerks at the Indian Commission seemed very curious about everything and made me talk a lot. I was green and didn't know any better. But when one of the fellows there tried to get me to give him my best bowl for his cigarette ashes, I began to suspect the nature of their interest.

At last the commissioner returned, but he had pressing engagements, and I hung around several days more before he would see me. After questioning me for about half an hour, he told me that his business was with living Indians, not dead ones, and that his office should have informed me of that in the beginning. He advised me to go back to our congressman and get a letter to the Smithsonian Institution. I packed up my pottery and got out of the place, feeling pretty sore. The head clerk followed me down the corridor and asked me what I'd take for that little bowl he'd taken a fancy to. He said it had no market value, I'd find Washington full of such things; there were cases of them in the cellar at the Smithsonian that they'd never taken the trouble to unpack, hadn't any place to put them.

I went back to my congressman. This time he wasn't so friendly as before, but he gave me a letter to the Smithsonian. There I went through the same experience. The director couldn't be seen except by appointment, and his secretary had to be convinced that your business was important before he would give you an appointment with his chief. After the first morning I found it difficult to see even the secretary. He was always engaged. I was told to take a seat and wait, but when he was disengaged he was hurrying off to luncheon. I would sit there all morning with a group of unfortunate people: girls who wanted to get typewriting to do, nice polite old men who wanted to be taken out on surveys and expeditions next summer. The secretary would at last come out with his overcoat on, and would hurry through the waiting room reading a letter or a report, without looking up.

The office assistants cheered me along, and I kept this up for some days, sitting all morning in that room, studying the patterns of the rugs, and the shoes of the patient waiters who came as regularly as I. One day after the secretary had gone out, his stenographer, a nice little Virginia girl, came and sat down in an empty chair next to mine and began talking to me. She wasn't pretty, but her kind eyes and soft Southern voice took hold of me at once. She wanted to know what I had in my telescope, and why I was there, and where I came from, and all about it. Nearly everyone else had gone out to lunch—that seemed to be the one thing they did regularly in Washington—and we had the waiting room to ourselves. I talked to her a good deal. Her name was Virginia Ward. She was a tiny little thing, but she had lovely eyes and such gentle ways. She seemed indignant that I had been put off so long after having come so far.

"Now you just let me fix it up for you," she said at last. "Mr. Wagner is bothered by a great many foolish people who waste his time, and he is suspicious. The best way will be for you to invite him to lunch with you. I'll arrange it. I keep a list of his appointments, and I know he is not engaged for luncheon tomorrow. I'll tell him that he is to lunch with a nice boy who has come all the way from New Mexico to inform the department about an important discovery. I'll tell him to meet you at the Shoreham, at one. That's expensive, but it would do no good to invite him to a cheap place. And, remember, you must ask him to order the luncheon. It will maybe cost you ten dollars, but it will get you somewhere."

I felt grateful to the nice little thing—she wasn't older than I. I begged her wouldn't she please come to lunch with me herself today, and talk to me.

"Oh, no!" she said, blushing red as a poppy. "Why, I'm afraid you think——"

I told her I didn't think anything but how nice she was to me, and how lonesome I was. She went with me, but she wouldn't go to any swell place. She told me a great many useful things.

"If you want to get attention from anybody in Washin'ton," she said, "ask them to lunch. People here will do almost anything for a good lunch."

"But the director of the Smithsonian, for instance," I said, "surely you don't mean that the high-up ones like that——? Why would he want to bother with a cowpuncher from New Mexico, when he can lunch with scientists and ambassadors?"

She had a pretty little fluttery Southern laugh. "You just name a hotel like the Shoreham to the director, and try it! There has to be somebody to pay for a lunch, and the scientists and ambassadors don't do that when they can avoid it. He'd accept your invitation, and the next time he went to dine with the secretary of state he'd make a nice little story of it, and paint you up so pretty you'd hardly know yourself."

When I asked her whether I'd better take my pottery—it was there under the table between us—to the Shoreham to show Mr. Wagner, she tittered again. "I wouldn't bother. If you show him enough of the Shoreham pottery, that will be more effective."

The next morning, when the secretary arrived at his office, he stopped by my chair and said he had an engagement with me for one o'clock. That was a good idea, he added: his mind was freer when he was away from office routine.

I had been in Washington twenty-two days when I took the secretary out to lunch. It was an excellent lunch. We had a bottle of Château d'Yquem. I'd never heard of such a wine before, but I remember it because it cost five dollars. I drank only one glass, and that pleased him too, for he drank the rest. Though he was friendly and talked a great deal, my heart sank lower, for he wouldn't let me explain my mission to him at all. He kept telling me that he knew all about the Southwest. He had been sent by the Smithsonian to conduct parties of European archaeologists through all the show places, Frijoles and Canyon de Chelly, and Taos and the Hopi pueblos. When some Austrian archduke had gone to hunt in the Pecos range, he had been sent by his chief and the German ambassador to manage the tour, and he had done it with such success that both he and the director were given decorations from the Austrian Crown, in recognition of his services. Then I had to listen to a long story about how well he was treated by the archduke when he went to Vienna with his chief the following summer. I had to hear about balls and receptions, and the names and titles of all the people he had met at the duke's country estate. I was amazed and ashamed that a man of fifty, a man of the world, a scholar with ever so many degrees, should find it worth his while to show off before a boy, and a boy of such humble pretensions, who didn't know how to eat the *hors d'oevres* any more than if an assortment of coconuts had been set before him with no hammer.

Imagine my astonishment when, as he was drinking his liqueur, he said carelessly: "By the way, I was successful in arranging an interview with the director for you. He will see you at four o'clock on Monday."

That was Thursday. I spent the time between then and Monday trying to find out something more about the kind of people I had come among. I persuaded Virginia Ward to go to the theatre with me, and she told me that it always took a long while to get anything through with the director, that I mustn't lose heart, and she would always be glad to cheer me up. She lived with her mother, a widow lady, and they had me come to dinner and were very nice to me.

All this time I was living with a young married couple who interested me very much, for they were unlike any people I had ever known. The husband was "in office," as they say there, he had some position in the War Department. How it did use to depress me to see all the hundreds of clerks come pouring out of that big building at sunset! Their lives seemed to me so petty, so slavish. The couple I lived with gave me a prejudice against that kind of life. I couldn't help knowing a good deal about their affairs. They had only a small flat, and rented me one room of it, so I was very much in their confidence and couldn't help overhearing. They asked me not to mention the fact that I paid rent, as they had told their friends I was making them a visit. It was like that in everything; they spent their lives trying to keep up appearances, and to make his salary do more than it could. When they weren't discussing where she should go in the summer, they talked about the promotions in his department; how much the other clerks got and how they spent it, how many new dresses their wives had. And there was always a struggle going on for an invitation to a dinner or a reception, or even a tea party. When once they got the invitation they had been scheming for, then came the terrible question of what Mrs. Bixby should wear.

The secretary of war gave a reception; there was to be dancing and a great showing of foreign uniforms. The Bixbys were in painful suspense until they got a card. Then for a week they talked about nothing but what Mrs. Bixby was going to wear. They decided that for such an occasion she must have a new dress. Bixby borrowed twenty-five dollars from me, and took his lunch hour to go shopping with his wife and choose the satin. That seemed to me very strange. In New Mexico the Indian boys sometimes went to a trader's with their wives and bought shawls or calico, and we thought it rather contemptible. On the night of the reception the Bixbys set off gaily in a cab; the dress they considered a great success. But they had bad luck. Somebody spilt claret-cup on Mrs. Bixby's skirt before the evening was half over, and when they got home that night I heard her weeping and reproaching him for having been so upset about it, and looking at nothing but her ruined dress all evening. She said he cried out when it happened. I don't doubt it.

Every cab, every party, was more than they could afford. If he lost an umbrella, it was a real misfortune. He wasn't lazy, he wasn't a fool and he meant to be honest; but he was intimidated by that miserable sort of departmental life. He didn't know anything else. He thought working in a store or a bank not respectable. Living with the Bixbys gave me a kind of low-spiritedness I had never known before. During my days of waiting for appointments, I used to walk for hours around the fence that shuts in the White House grounds, and watch the Washington monument colour with those beautiful sunsets, until the time when all the clerks streamed out of the Treasury building and the War and Navy. Thousands of them, all more or less like the couple I lived with. They seemed to me like people in slavery, who ought to be free. I remember the city chiefly by those beautiful, hazy, sad sunsets, white columns and green shrubbery, and the monument shaft still pink while the stars were coming out.

I got my interview with the director of the Smithsonian at last. He gave me his attention, he was interested. He told me to come again in three days and meet Dr. Ripley, who was the authority on prehistoric Indian remains and had excavated a lot of them. Then came an exciting and rather encouraging time for me. Dr. Ripley asked the right sort of questions, and evidently knew his business. He said he'd like to take the first train down to my mesa. But it required money to excavate, and he had none. There was a bill up before Congress for an appropriation. We'd have to wait. I must use my influence with my representative. He took my pottery to study it. (I never got it back, by the way.) There was a Dr. Fox, connected with the Smithsonian, who was also interested. They told me a good many things I wanted to know, and kept me dangling about the office. Of course they were very kind to take so much trouble with a green boy. But I soon found that the director and all his staff had one interest which dwarfed every other. There was to be an international exposition of some sort in Europe the following summer, and they were all pulling strings to get appointed on juries or sent to international congresses—appointments that would pay their expenses abroad; and give them a salary in addition. There was, indeed, a bill before Congress for appropriations for the Smithsonian; but there was also a bill for exposition appropriations, and that was the one they were really pushing. They kept me hanging on through March and April, but in the end it came to nothing. Dr. Ripley told me he was sorry, but the sum Congress had allowed the Smithsonian wouldn't cover an expedition to the South-west.

Virginia Ward, who had been so kind to me, went out to lunch with me that day, and admitted I had been let down. She was almost as much disappointed as I. She said the only thing Dr. Ripley really cared about was getting a free trip to Europe and acting on a jury, and maybe getting a decoration. "And that's what the director wants, too," she said. "They don't care much about dead and gone Indians. What they do care about is going to Paris, and getting another ribbon on their coats."

The only other person besides Virginia who was genuinely concerned about my affair was a young Frenchman, a lieutenant attached to the French embassy, who came to the Smithsonian often on business connected with this same international exposition. He was nice and polite to Virginia, and she introduced him to me. We used to walk down along the Potomac together. He studied my photographs and asked me such intelligent questions about everything that it was a pleasure to talk to him. He had a fine attitude about it all; he was thoughtful, critical, and respectful. I feel sure he'd have gone back to New Mexico with me if he'd had the money. He was even poorer than I.

I was utterly ashamed to go home to Roddy, dead broke after all the money I'd spent, and without a thing to show for it. I hung on in Washington through May, trying to get a job of some sort, to at least earn my fare home. My letters to Blake had been pretty blue for some time back. If I'd been sensible, I'd have kept my troubles to myself. He was easily discouraged, and I knew that. At last I had to write him for money to go home. It was slow in coming, and I began to telegraph. I left Washington at last, wiser than I came. I had no plans, I wanted nothing but to get back to the mesa and live a free life and breathe free air, and never, never again to see hundreds of little black-coated men pouring out of white buildings. Queer, how much more depressing they are than workmen coming out of a factory.

I was terribly disappointed when I got off the train at Tarpin and Roddy wasn't at the station to meet me. It was late in the afternoon, almost dark, and I went straight to the livery stable to ask Bill Hook for news of Blake. Hook, you remember, had done all our hauling for us, and had been a good friend. He gave me a glad hand and said Blake was out on the mesa.

"I expect maybe he's had his feelings hurt here. He's been shy of this town lately. You see, Tom, folks weren't bothered none about that mesa so long as you fellows were playing Robinson Crusoe out there, digging up curios. But when it leaked out that Blake had got a lot of money for your stuff, then they begun to feel jealous—said them ruins didn't belong to Blake any more than to anybody else. It'll blow over in time; people are always like that when money changes hands. But right now there's a good deal of bad feeling."

I told him I didn't know what he was talking about.

"You mean you ain't heard about the German, Fechtig? Well, Rodney's got some surprise waiting for you! Why, he's had the damnedest luck! He's cleaned up a neat little pile on your stuff."

I begged him to tell me what stuff he meant.

"Why, your curios. This German, Fechtig, come along; he'd been buying up a lot of Indian things out here, and he bought your whole outfit and paid four thousand dollars down for it. The transaction made quite a stir here in Tarpin. I'm not kicking. I made a good thing out of it. My mules were busy three weeks packing the stuff out of there on their backs, and I held the Dutchman up for a fancy price. He had packing cases made at the wagon shop and took 'em up to the mesa full of straw and sawdust, and packed the curios out there. I lost one of my mules, too. You remember Jenny? Well, they were leading her down with a big box on her, and right there where the trail runs so narrow around a bump in the cliff above Black Canyon, she lost her balance and fell clean to the bottom, her load on her. Pretty near a thousand feet, I guess. We never went down to hold a postmortem, but Fechtig paid for her like a gentleman."

I remember I sat down on the sofa in Hook's office because I couldn't stand up any longer, and the smell of the horse blankets began to make me deathly sick. In a minute I went over, like a girl in a novel. Hook pulled me out on the sidewalk and gave me some whisky out of his pocket flask.

When I felt better I asked him how long this German had been gone, and what he had done with the things.

"Oh, he cleared out three weeks ago. He didn't waste no time. He treated everybody well, though; nobody's sore at him. It's your partner they're turned against. Fechtig took the stuff right along with him, chartered a freight car, and travelled in the car with it. I reckon it's on the water by now. He took it straight through into Old Mexico, and was to load it on a French boat. Seems he was afraid of having trouble getting curiosities out of the United States ports. You know you can take anything out of the City of Mexico."

I had heard all I wanted to hear. I went to the hotel, got a room, and lay down without undressing to wait for daylight. Hook was to drive me and my trunk out to the mesa early the next morning. All I'd been through in Washington was nothing to what I went through that night. I thought Blake must have lost his mind. I didn't for a minute believe he'd meant to sell me out, but I cursed his stupidity and presumption. I had never told him just how I felt about those things we'd dug out together, it was the kind of thing one doesn't talk about directly. But he must have known; he couldn't have lived with me all summer and fall without knowing. And yet, until that night, I had never known myself that I cared more about them than about anything else in the world.

At the first blink of daylight I jumped up from my damnable bed and went round to the stable to rout Hook out of his bunk. We had breakfast and got out of town with his best team. On the way to the mesa we had a breakdown, one of the old dry wheels smashed to splinters. Hook had to unhitch and ride back to Tarpin and get another. Everything took an unreasonably long time, and the afternoon was half gone when he put me and my trunk down at the foot of the Black Canyon trail. Every inch of that trail was dear to me, every delicate curve about the old piñon roots, every chancy track along the face of the cliffs, and the deep windings back into shrubbery and safety. The wild-currant bushes were in bloom, and where the path climbed the side of a narrow ravine, the scent of them in the sun was so heavy that it made me soft, made me want to lie down and sleep. I wanted to see and touch everything, like homesick children when they come home.

When I pulled out on top of the mesa, the rays of sunlight fell slantingly through the little twisted piñons—the light was all in between them, as red as a daylight fire, they fairly swam in it. Once again I had that glorious feeling that I've never had anywhere else, the feeling of being *on the mesa*, in a world above the world. And the air, my God, what air!—Soft, tingling, gold, hot with an edge of chill on it, full of the smell of piñon—it was like breathing the sun, breathing the colour of the sky. Down there behind me was the plain, already streaked with shadow, violet and purple and burnt orange until it met the horizon. Before me was the flat mesa top, thinly sprinkled with old cedars that were not much taller than I, though their twisted trunks were almost as thick as my body. I struck off across it, my long black shadow going ahead.

I made straight for the cabin, it was about three miles from the spot where the trail emerged at the top. I saw smoke rising before I could see the hut itself. Blake was in the doorway when I got there. I didn't look at his face, but I could feel that he looked at mine.

"Don't say anything, Tom. Don't rip me up until you hear all about it," he said as I came toward him.

"I've heard enough to about do for me," I blurted out. "What made you do it, Blake? What made you do it?"

"It was a chance in a million, boy. There wasn't any time to consult you. There's only one man in thousands that wants to buy relics and pay real money for them. I could see how your Washington campaign was coming out. I know you'd thought about big figures, so had I. But that was all a pipe dream. Four thousand's not so bad, you don't pick it up every day. And he bore all the expenses. Why, it was a terrible expensive job, getting all that frail stuff out of here. Who else would have bought it, I want to know? We'd have had to pack it around at Harvey Houses, selling it at a dollar a bowl, like the poor Indians do. I took the best chance going, for both of us, Tom."

I didn't say anything, because there was too much to say. I stood outside the cabin until the gold light went blue and a few stars came out, hardly brighter than the bright sky they twinkled in, and the swallows came flying over us, on their way to their nests in the cliffs. It was the time of day when everything goes home. From habit and from weariness I went in through the door. The kitchen table was spread for supper, I could smell a rabbit stew cooking on the stove. Blake lit the lantern and begged me to eat my supper. I didn't go into the bunk-room, for I knew the shelves in there were empty. I heard Blake talking to me as you hear people talking when you are asleep.

"Who else would have bought them?" he kept saying. "Folks make a lot of fuss over such things, but they don't want to pay good money for them."

When I at last told him that such a thing as selling them had never entered my head, I'm sure he thought I was lying. He reminded me about how we used to talk of getting big money from the government.

I admitted I'd hoped we'd be paid for our work, and maybe get a bonus of some kind, for our discovery. "But I never thought of selling them, because they weren't mine to sell—nor yours! They belonged to this country, to the state, and to all the people. They belonged to boys like you and me, that have no other ancestors to inherit from. You've gone and sold them to a country that's got plenty of relics of its own. You've gone and sold your country's secrets, like Dreyfus."

"That man was innocent. It was a frame-up," Blake murmured. It was a point he would never pass up.

"Whether he's guilty or not, you are! If there was only anybody in Washington I could telegraph to, and have that German held up at the port!"

"That's just it. If there was anybody in Washington that cared a damn, I wouldn't have sold 'em. But you pretty well found out there ain't."

"We could have kept them, then," I told him. "I've got a strong back. I'm not so poor that I have to sell the pots and pans that belonged to my poor grandmothers a thousand years ago. I made all my plans on the train, coming back." (It was a lie, I hadn't.) "I meant to get a job on the railroad and keep our find right here, and come back to it when I had a layoff. I think a lot more of it now than before I went to Washington. And after a while, when that exposition is over and the Smithsonian people get home, they would come out here all right. I've learned enough from them so that I could go on with it myself."

Blake reminded me that I had my way to make in the world, and that I wanted to go to school. "That money's in the bank this minute, in your name, and you're going to college on it. You're not going to be a day labourer like me. After you've got your sheepskin, then you can divide with me."

"You think I'd touch that money?" I looked squarely at him for the first time. "No more than if you'd stolen it. You made the sale. Get what you can out of it. I want to ask you one question: did you ever think I was digging those things up for what I could sell them for?"

Rodney explained that he knew I cared about the things, and was proud of them, but he'd always supposed I meant to "realize" on them, just as he did, and that it would come to money in the end. "Everything does," he added.

"If that nice young Frenchman I met had come down here with me, and offered me four million instead of four thousand, I'd have refused him. There never was any question of money with me, where this mesa and its people were concerned. They were something that had been preserved through the ages by a miracle, and handed on to you and me, two poor cowpunchers, rough and ignorant, but I thought we were men enough to keep a trust. I'd as soon have sold my own grandmother as Mother Eve—I'd have sold any living woman first."

"Save your tears," said Roddy grimly. "She refused to leave us. She went to the bottom of Black Canyon and carried Hook's best mule along with her. They had to make her box extra wide, and she crowded Jenny out an inch or so too far from the canyon wall."

This painful interview went on for hours. I walked up and down the kitchen trying to make Blake understand the kind of value those objects had had for me. Unfortunately, I succeeded. He sat slumping on the bench, his elbows on the table, shading his eyes from the lantern with his hands.

"There's no need to keep this up," he said at last. "You're away out of my depth, but I think I get you. You might have given me some of this Fourth of July talk a little earlier in the game. I didn't know you valued that stuff any different than anything else a fellow might run on to: a gold mine or a pocket of turquoise."

"I suppose you gave him my diary along with the rest?"

"No," said Blake, his voice growing gloomier and darker, "that's in the Eagle's Nest, where you hid it. That's your private property. I supposed I had some share in the relics we dug up—you always spoke of it that way. But I see now I was working for you like a hired man, and while you were away I sold your property."

I said again it wasn't mine or his. He took something out of the pocket of his flannel shirt and laid it on the table. I saw it was a bank passbook, with my name on the yellow cover.

"You may as well keep it," I said. "I'll never touch it. You had no right to deposit it in my name. The townspeople are sore about the money, and they'll hold it against me."

"No they won't. Can't you trust me to fix that?"

"I don't know what I can trust you with, Blake. I don't know where I'm at with you," I said.

He got up and began putting on his coat. "Motives don't count, eh?" he said, his face turned away, as he put his arm into the sleeve.

"They would in anything of our own, between you and me," I told him. "If it was my money you'd lost gambling, or my girl you'd made free with, we could fight it out, and maybe be friends again. But this is different."

"I see. You make it clear." He was quietly stirring around as he spoke. He got his old knapsack off its nail on the wall, opened his trunk and took out some underwear and socks and a couple of shirts. After he had put these into the bag, he slung it over one shoulder, and his canvas water bag over the other. I let these preparations go on without a word. He went to the cupboard over the stove and put some sticks of chocolate into his pocket, then his pipe and a bag of tobacco. Presently I said he'd break his neck if he tried riding down the trail in the dark.

"I'm not riding the trail," he replied curtly. "I'm going down the quick way. My horse is grazing in Cow Canyon."

"I noticed the river's high. It's dangerous crossing," I remarked.

"I got over that way a few days ago. I'm surprised at you, using such common expressions!" he said sarcastically. "*Dangerous crossing*; it's painted on signboards all over the world!" He walked out of the cabin without looking back. I followed him to the V-shaped break in the rimrock, hardly larger than a man's body, where the spliced tree trunks made a swinging ladder down the face of the cliff. I wanted to protest, but only succeeded in finding fault.

"You'll catch your knapsack on those forks and come to grief."

"That's my lookout."

By this time my eyes had grown accustomed to the darkness, and I could see Blake quite clearly—the stubborn, crouching set of his shoulders that I used to notice when he first came to Pardee and was drinking all the time. There was an ache in my arms to reach out and detain him, but there was something else that made me absolutely powerless to do so. He stepped down and settled his foot into the first fork. Then he stopped a moment and straightened his pack, buttoned his coat up to the chin, and pulled his hat on tighter. There was always a night draught in the canyon. He gripped the trunk with his hands. "Well," he said with grim cheerfulness, "here's luck! And I'm glad it's you that's doing this to me, Tom; not me that's doing it to you."

His head disappeared below the rim. I could hear the trees creak under his heavy body, and the chains rattle a little at the splicings. I lay down on the ledge and listened. I could hear him for a long way down, and the sounds were comforting to me, though I didn't realize it. Then the silence closed in. I went to sleep that night hoping I would never waken.

7

The next morning the whinnying of my saddle horse in the shed roused me. I took him down to the foot of the trail where I'd left my trunk, and packed my things up to the cabin on his back. I sat up late that night, waiting for Blake, though I knew he wouldn't come. A few days later I rode into Tarpin for news of him. Bill Hook showed me Roddy's horse. He had sold him to the barn for sixty dollars. The stationmaster told me Blake had bought a ticket to Winslow, Arizona. I wired the station master and the dispatcher at Winslow, but they could give me no information. Father Duchene came along, on his rounds, and I told him the whole story.

He thought Blake would come back sometime, that I'd only miss him if I went out to look for him. He advised me to stay on the mesa that summer and get ahead with my studies, work up my Spanish grammar and my Latin. He had friends all along the Santa Fe, and he was sure we could catch Blake by advertising in the local papers along the road; Albuquerque, Winslow, Flagstaff, Williams, Los Angeles. After few days with him, I went back to the mesa to wait.

I'll never forget the night I got back. I crossed the river an hour before sunset and hobbled my horse in the wide bottom of Cow Canyon. The moon was up, though the sun hadn't set, and it had that glittering silveriness the early stars have in high altitudes. The heavenly bodies look so much more remote from the bottom of a deep canyon than they do from the level. The climb of the walls helps out the eye, somehow. I lay down on a solitary rock that was like an island in the bottom of the valley, and looked up. The grey sagebrush and the blue-grey rock around me were already in shadow, but high above me the canyon walls were dyed flame colour with the sunset, and the Cliff City lay in a gold haze against its dark cavern. In a few minutes it, too, was grey, and only the rimrock at the top held the red light. When that was gone, I could still see the copper glow in the piñons along the edge of the top ledges. The arc of sky over the canyon was silvery blue, with its pale yellow moon, and presently stars shivered into it, like crystals dropped into perfectly clear water.

I remember these things, because, in a sense, that was the first night I was ever really on the mesa at all—the first night that all of me was there. This was the first time I ever saw it as a whole. It all came together in my understanding, as a series of experiments do when you begin to see where they are leading. Something had happened in me that made it possible for me to coordinate and simplify, and that process, going on in my mind, brought with it great happiness. It was possession. The excitement of my first discovery was a very pale feeling compared to this one. For me the mesa was no longer an adventure, but a religious emotion. I had read of filial piety in the Latin poets, and I knew that was what I felt for this place. It had formerly been mixed up with other motives; but now that they were gone, I had my happiness unalloyed.

What that night began lasted all summer. I stayed on the mesa until November. It was the first time I'd ever studied methodically, or intelligently. I got the better of the Spanish grammar and read the twelve books of the *Aeneid*. I studied in the morning, and in the afternoon I worked at clearing away the mess the German had made in packing—tidying up the ruins to wait another hundred years, maybe, for the right explorer. I can scarcely hope that life will give me another summer like that one. It was my high tide. Every morning, when the sun's rays first hit the mesa top, while the rest of the world was in shadow, I wakened with the feeling that I had found everything, instead of having lost everything. Nothing tired me. Up there alone, a close neighbour to the sun, I seemed to get the solar energy in some direct way. And at night, when I watched it drop down behind the edge of the plain below me, I used to feel that I couldn't have borne another hour of that consuming light, that I was full to the brim, and needed dark and sleep.

All that summer, I never went up to the Eagle's Nest to get my diary—indeed, it's probably there yet. I didn't feel the need of that record. It would have been going backward. I didn't want to go back and unravel things step by step. Perhaps I was afraid that I would lose the whole in the parts. At any rate, I didn't go for my record.

During those months I didn't worry much about poor Roddy. I told myself the advertisements would surely get him—I knew his habit of reading newspapers. There are times when one's vitality is too high to be clouded, too elastic to stay down. Hurrying from my cabin in the morning to the spot in the Cliff City where I studied under a cedar, I used to be frightened at my own heartlessness. But the feel of the narrow moccasin-worn trail in the flat rock made my feet glad, like a good taste in the mouth, and I'd forget all about Blake without knowing it. I found I was reading too fast; so I began to commit long passages of Virgil to memory—if it hadn't been for that, I might have forgotten how to use my voice, or gone to talking to myself. When I look into the *Aeneid* now, I can always see two pictures: the one on the page, and another behind that: blue and purple rocks and yellow-green piñons with flat tops, little clustered houses clinging together for protection, a rude tower rising in their midst, rising strong, with calmness and courage—behind it a dark grotto, in its depths a crystal spring.

Happiness is something one can't explain. You must take my word for it. Troubles enough came afterward, but there was that summer, high and blue, a life in itself.

Next winter I went back to Pardee and stayed with the O'Briens again, working on the section and studying with Father Duchene and trying to get some word of Blake. Now that I was back on the railroad, I thought I couldn't fail to find him. I went out to Winslow and to Williams, and I questioned the railroad men. We advertised for him in every possible way, had all the Santa Fe operatives and the police and the Catholic missionaries on the watch for him, offered a thousand dollars reward for whoever found him. But it came to nothing. Father Duchene and our friends down there are still looking. But the older I grow, the more I understand what it was I did that night on the mesa. Anyone who requites faith and friendship as I did, will have to pay for it. I'm not very sanguine about good fortune for myself. I'll be called to account when I least expect it.

In the spring, just a year after I quarrelled with Roddy, I landed here and walked into your garden, and the rest you know.

---

1. Why does Tom believe that it is important for the government to study the Cliff City and "revive this civilization in a scholarly work"?

2. As Roddy is getting ready to leave the mesa, why does he say, "I'm glad it's you that's doing this to me, Tom; not me that's doing it to you"?

3. Why does Tom experience "happiness unalloyed" after the pottery has been sold and Roddy has left?

GRAPHIC STORIES

JAIME HERNANDEZ (1959–) grew up in Oxnard, California. His father was a Mexican immigrant; his mother, from Texas, had deep Mexican roots as well, besides a passionate interest in comic books which she shared with her children. During the late 1970s, Hernandez and his brother Gilbert began drawing cartoons influenced by the Southern California punk rock scene. At the urging of their older brother Mario, they published their first issue of *Love & Rockets* in 1982. The new comics publisher Fantagraphics acquired the rights to the series and the Hernandez brothers immediately became famous among devotees of alternative comics. The brothers have gone on to publish many more issues in the series, and they have each launched comic book series of their own. Jaime Hernandez's include *Penny Century* and *Whoa, Nellie!*

Flies on the Ceiling

ABORTION IS MURDER
PLANNED PARENTHOOD
KILLING OUR
REAGAN
HOGAR DULCE HOGAR

flies on the ceiling
THE STORY OF ISABEL IN MEXICO
XAIME 88-89
2

HEY YOU!

NO, DON'T GO! I'M WONDERING IF YOU CAN HELP ME!

I'VE GOT A LITTLE BOY IN THERE THAT WON'T EAT. IF YOU CAN GET HIM TO, I'LL GLADLY PAY YOU.

I DON'T KNOW HOW YOU DID IT, BUT I SURE DO THANK YOU.
I USED TO HAVE TO CONVINCE MY BROTHERS TO EAT MY COOKING.

I CAN TELL YOU'RE NOT FROM AROUND HERE. DO YOU HAVE A PLACE TO STAY?
NO.

WELL, I NEED SOMEONE WHO CAN COOK AND LOOK AFTER BETO. I CAN'T PAY MUCH, BUT YOU WOULD HAVE A ROOM...
3

YOU DON'T HAVE TO EAT IN YOUR ROOM. EAT WITH US, ISABEL.
EAT WITH US!
SEE? ISN'T THIS MORE LIKE IT? NOW WE'RE MORE LIKE A FAMILY, EH?
YEAH!
4

FLIES ON THE CEILING

JAIME HERNANDEZ

7

FORGIVE ME, DARLING, BUT HE'S FOUND ME AND I CAN'T RISK GETTING YOU AND BETO INVOLVED...
OH, GOD. WHY ME?
I'M NOT THE FIRST PERSON THAT EVER GOT A DIVORCE...
OR AN ABORTION...
OR ATTEMPTED SUICIDE...
NO...
IT'S NOT YOUR SINS BUT YOUR GUILT THAT ALLOWS ME TO COME TO YOU.
I'M ALSO NOT THE FIRST PERSON TO HAVE GUILT.
YOU ARE ALSO AFRAID. I LOVE FOR YOU TO BE AFRAID.
8

FLIES ON THE CEILING

I-I CHANGED MY MIND. I DON'T WANT TO SEE YOU AFTER ALL.
HA HA HAAK!!
10

LUCHA
BRE
!!!
TSK! BABY. IT'LL BE OVER IN MINUTES.
11

WIDOWS
WIDOWS
HOPPERS
13
12

JAIME HERNANDEZ

YOU'RE NOT AFRAID ANY MORE.
ISABEL...?
HE SAID I CAN GO HOME NOW. MY FATHER IS DEAD.
HE ALSO REFUSES TO GIVE ME UP. SAYS HE'LL BE WAITING FOR ME IN THE STATES.
"I MAY TURN UP AS FLIES ON YOUR CEILING," HE SAID...
HEH. FLIES...
The end

---

1. When Isabel first decides to leave Beto and his father, why does she tell the father, "I can't risk getting you and Beto involved"?

2. Why does the voice behind the wall tell Isabel that it is "not your sins but your guilt that allows me to come to you"? Who or what is speaking to her?

3. What is the symbolic meaning of the lizard in the rooster's beak?

4. At the end of the story, why does Isabel decide to leave Beto and his father and return home?

JOE SACCO (1960–) was born in Malta, lived in Australia until he was twelve, then immigrated to the United States. He studied journalism at the University of Oregon, and worked on newspapers in Los Angeles and Portland. Combining traditional journalistic skills of interviewing and reporting with his gift for cartoon artistry, Sacco has published a number of comic books including *Yahoo* (1994), *War Junkie* (1995), and *Palestine* (1996), a series in which Sacco recounts his experiences in the occupied territories. It won the American Book Award. After his stint in the Middle East, Sacco traveled to Bosnia and wrote *Safe Area Gorazde: The War in Eastern Bosnia, 1992–1995. Publishers Weekly* declared the book "an extraordinary work of both journalism and comics nonfiction."

Palestine

Chapter One

Traffic?
I'm swallowing exhaust and my snot's gone black!
And noise?
Car horns are what Egyptians have instead of home entertainment centers!
Whatta town!
CRAZEEE!
15 million heads with their chickens cut off!
And between pyramids and boy pharaohs, I'm zonked!
I'm spinning!
TAXI!
Get me outta here!
CAIRO
I pull up a chair
I take a load off my feet
I'm hanging with the hotel receptionists
It's quieter, and the talk's turned philosophic
THERE ARE MUSLIMS AND THERE ARE MUSLIMS.
And Shreef is a Muslim in love!
Violins, please!
A woman from Prague!
A two-day sigh-fest!
Candlelight and Nile cruises!
Up the Cairo Tower for God knows what amount!
In two days he blew 500 Egyptian pounds!
Best of all, they didn't even do the nasty!
Taha is beside himself with arithmetic!
600% OF YOUR MONTHLY WAGE! HALF A YEAR'S PAY IN TWO DAYS!
I LOVE HER
YOU ARE DRINKING TO FORGET!
SHE SAID SHE WILL LEAVE HER HUSBAND FOR ME! HER CHILDREN!
SHE SAYS SHE LOVES HIM NOW! 500 POUNDS!
1

JOE SACCO

PALESTINE (CHAPTER ONE)

SADAT WAS A VERY INTELLIGENT MAN! HE KNEW ISRAEL WAS STRONG THEN, BUT IN 50 YEARS...?
SADAT HAD A PLAN!
Taha unwinds Sadat's plan
It's a little convoluted
I don't quite follow the tank tactics
Meanwhile, Shreef has compiled a list of his favorite rock:
BARCLAY JAMES HARVEST... PINK FLOYD ... GEORGE MICHAEL ... DEEP PURPLE...
SEE THAT?!
HE'S CHANGED THE CONVERSATION!
THAT'S WHAT HE KNOWS HOW TO TALK ABOUT!
HOW MUCH DO YOU SPEND ON BOOKS?
I AM A POOR MAN AND I SPEND 30 POUNDS A MONTH ON BOOKS!
AND YOU SPEND 500 POUNDS ON HER IN TWO DAYS!
SHE LOVES ME.
LOVE? HA! SHE WOULD LEAVE HER CHILDREN?!
A couple of days later I get my visa and I leave Cairo
Across the Suez and into the Sinai
We pass tanks twisted and burned out since when?
'56?
'67?
'73?
The bus stops a lot, the bus drivers jumping out to have words with each other and the escort
It's a long way to Palestine and slow going
But I've been speeding, man
I've been speeding
I'm already there
3

JOE SACCO

BLIND DATES
Three weeks later and I'm good at this, watch his reaction, 'cause here I am in the Old City of Nablus and we both know I don't belong, now watch this...
SALAAM ALEEKUM!
'Peace be with you.'
He's got to respond:
ALEEKUM ES-SALAAM!
'And peace be with you.'
Now I've got him!
See, he calls me over, he wants to practice his English, he wants to know what I'm doing here, what I think of his country...
his country?
And will I drink tea?
Tea!
Seriously sugared!
Hospitality measured by the lump!
But I'm gracious...
LOVE TEA.
...a perfect guest of Palestine.
4

BUT WHAT DO YOU THINK OF MY COUNTRY?
Back to that again, are we?
Okay okay...
THE HILLS!
It's not what he's fishing for...
THE OLIVE TREES!
...but I'm a charmer...
THE TERRACED FIELDS!
...a real innocent...
...and, by the way, not with Israeli intelligence.
J. SACCO '92
5
But in case he hasn't heard...
THIS OCCUPATION THING LOOKS PRETTY HARSH.
Whamo!!
I've committed myself now!
I'm no longer beating about the bush!
I've hit his nail on the head, too!
YES...
BUT WHAT CAN WE DO?
Indeed!
My point precisely!
You've got my sympathies and—

JOE SACCO

Okay okay, maybe that ain't saying much, sympathy can be lots of hot air; I'll give you my own for instance from years ago when I was in Berlin talking with Claudia about Klinghoffer, and by then I'd come far, I'd figured the Palestinians ought to have a state of their own, you know, to fuck up for themselves just like everybody else, and does his name ring a bell?
Klinghoffer
American Jew
On a pleasure cruise with his wife and their friends...
Genoa, Naples, Alexandria...
After Port Said he was shot in the head by the Palestine Liberation Front...
...dumped with his wheelchair into the Mediterranean.
And by the way I was in love with Claudia, I'd been swooning for months, biding my time, too, I was bursting with the expectation of overripe Euroromance.
YOU GOTTA UNDERSTAND THE AMERICAN MEDIA. THEY WANT HUMAN INTEREST, KLINGHOFFER GETS KILLED AND WE GET THE FULL PROFILE, THE BEREAVING WIDOW, WHERE HE LIVED AND WHAT HE PUT ON HIS CORN FLAKES TILL HE SOUNDS LIKE THE GUY NEXT DOOR WHO BORROWS YOUR LADDER. YOU SEE THE POWER OF THAT?
J. SACCO 8·92
6

It was far into the a.m., we'd been drinking, Claudia, who was half Iraqi, who'd studied Arabic in Damascus where she'd left her Palestinian Romeo whose brother in the PLO was on first names with Yasser – Claudia may or may not have said something of interest at that point...
You better believe I did:
AMERICANS WON'T CARE ABOUT THE PROBLEMS OF PALESTINIANS WHEN AMERICANS GET KILLED IN THESE TERRORIST ATTACKS. ONE AMERICAN DIES LIKE THAT, IT ECLIPSES ANYTHING PALESTINIANS HAVE TO SAY!
WELL...
I DON'T KNOW SO MUCH ABOUT THESE THINGS...
I knew she did, but...
Conversation over!
A peck on the cheek and–
I went home alone
PALESTINIAN BOYFRIEND! HA! BITCH! TERRORIST GROUPIE!
Unfair? You bet, but I couldn't get the taste out of my mouth, terrorism is the bread Palestinians get buttered on, I'd swallowed that ever since the airliners went sky high in the desert, do you remember that, do you remember Munich and the blown up athletes, the bus and airport massacres?
J. SACCO 8-92
7

I do, my mind gurgles over with televised pools of blood.... I mean sure I had sympathy for a homeland lost, but what were the problems of Palestinians to me next to Klinghoffer, who ate Brand X corn flakes and probably borrowed my ladder...
He went over the side of the Achille Lauro and into my consciousness.
And if Palestinians have been sinking for decades, expelled, bombed and kicked black and blue, even when it's made the evening news I never caught a name or recall a face, to say nothing about their corn flakes.
But now my buddy on the West Bank wants to make some introductions, to set me up, he wants me to shake hands with his people's pain...
THIS WOMAN, SHE HAS EIGHT CHILDREN. HER HUSBAND VERY OLD, VERY SICK. THE GOVERNMENT GIVES HER NOTHING!
J. SACCO 8-92
8

THIS ONE: HIS FATHER IS IN PRISON. HOW LONG IN PRISON? FOUR YEARS!
THIS ONE: HIS SON IS KILLED BY SOLDIERS!
HE WON'T STOP?
DON'T MIND.
THIS ONE: HIS SON IS IN PRISON!
THIS ONE: TWO SONS IN PRISON!
J. SACCO 8·92

9

Palestinian victims all right!
The real-life adaptation of all those affidavits I've been reading!
The flesh and blood stuff!
Up close and almost personal!
But it's time for me to go!..
Now he's thanking my ass!
He's touched!
I've come all this way!
YOU WRITE SOME-THING ABOUT US?
I SHOWED YOU, YOU SAW!
YOU TELL ABOUT US?
Of course of course!
I'm off to fill my notebook!
I will alert the world to your suffering!
Watch your local comic-book store...
10
I walk back to where the taxis are waiting.
Mission accomplished!
Told you I was good at this!

In Jerusalem I made pals with an American Jew named Dave; he was taking time out from his kibbutz experience to sightsee the Holy City.

REALLY COOL AT NIGHT, DON'TCHA THINK?

YEAH.

AMAZING.

KINDA FUNNY BEING HERE AT THE WESTERN WALL GETTING INTO MY HERITAGE.

ON FRIDAY I HAD SHABBAT DINNER WITH THIS ORTHODOX RABBI ORIGINALLY FROM NEW YORK.

YEAH? HOW'D IT GO?

INTERESTING.

RETURN

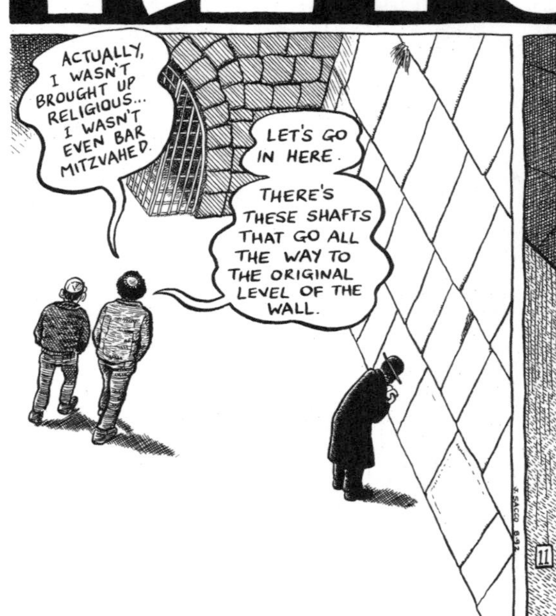

ACTUALLY, I WASN'T BROUGHT UP RELIGIOUS... I WASN'T EVEN BAR MITZVAHED.
LET'S GO IN HERE.
THERE'S THESE SHAFTS THAT GO ALL THE WAY TO THE ORIGINAL LEVEL OF THE WALL.

DEEP, HUH?
It goes down, down
Like the feelings you can get for this city, it's hard to see the bottom

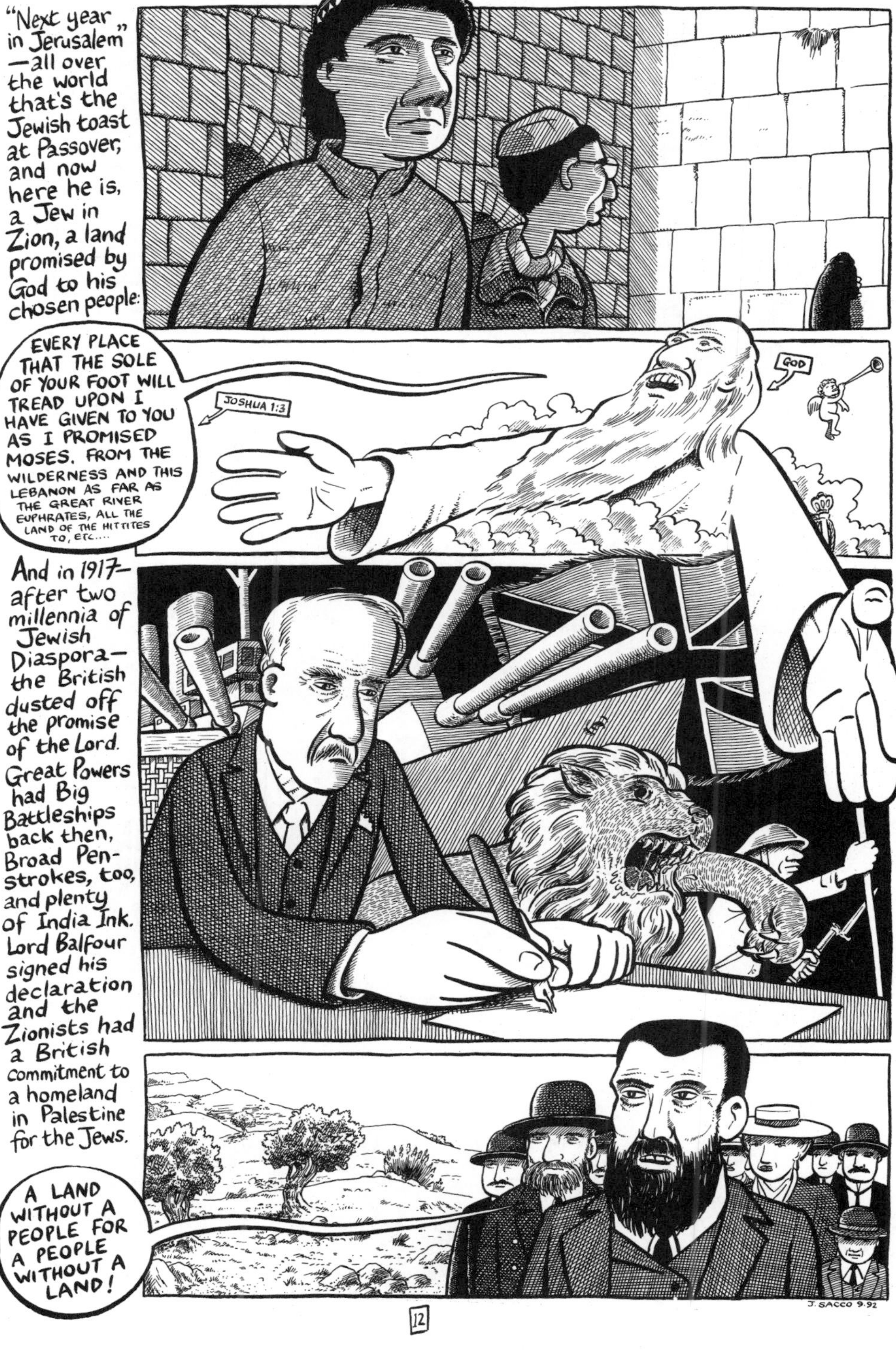

"Next year in Jerusalem"—all over the world that's the Jewish toast at Passover, and now here he is, a Jew in Zion, a land promised by God to his chosen people:

EVERY PLACE THAT THE SOLE OF YOUR FOOT WILL TREAD UPON I HAVE GIVEN TO YOU AS I PROMISED MOSES. FROM THE WILDERNESS AND THIS LEBANON AS FAR AS THE GREAT RIVER EUPHRATES, ALL THE LAND OF THE HITTITES TO, ETC....

JOSHUA 1:3

GOD

And in 1917—after two millennia of Jewish Diaspora—the British dusted off the promise of the Lord. Great Powers had Big Battleships back then, Broad Pen-strokes, too, and plenty of India Ink. Lord Balfour signed his declaration and the Zionists had a British commitment to a homeland in Palestine for the Jews.

A LAND WITHOUT A PEOPLE FOR A PEOPLE WITHOUT A LAND!

J. SACCO 9.92

12

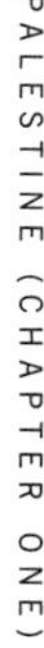

But things weren't as cut and dry as *that* Zionist slogan. Plenty of Arabs lived in Palestine; in 1917 Arabs outnumbered Jewish inhabitants ten-to-one. But you know mathematics, it doesn't always fit into the equation:

LORD BALFOUR AGAIN

ZIONISM, BE IT RIGHT OR WRONG, GOOD OR BAD, IS ROOTED IN AGE-LONG TRADITION, IN PRESENT NEEDS, IN FUTURE HOPES, OF FAR PROFOUNDER IMPORT THAN THE DESIRE AND PREJUDICES OF 700,000 ARABS WHO NOW INHABIT THAT ANCIENT LAND.

And, incidentally:

WE DO NOT PROPOSE EVEN TO GO THROUGH THE FORM OF CONSULTING THE WISHES OF THE PRESENT INHABITANTS OF THE COUNTRY.

Decision made! History follows on such heels and refugees after that... But if it's been downhill for Palestinians ever since, Israelis have soared to greater heights, who can deny it?

J. SACCO 9-92

Come over, see for yourself! Like these kids: the International Student Set! The hostel's crawling with 'em! Dutch, Australian, South African ...they're on their way to kibbutzim, they're gonna get communal, they're gonna pick oranges in Galilee or the Negev...
...some who've already done their stint sit around trading vomit stories, especially the English, who won't call it a holiday unless they've puked every night, they say there's nothing to do on them farms after sundown except plow vodka...
But Mary Ann the Argentine hasn't been boozin, she's just come off a three-week Volunteers for Israel program...
...YOU MEAN WITH THE ISRAELI ARMY? SCRUBBING TANKS?
IT'S NOT JUST THAT. IT HELPED ME UNDERSTAND THE CULTURE.
ISRAEL NEEDS A STRONG ARMY. IT'S SURROUNDED BY ENEMIES.
I THINK IT'S SO WONDERFUL HOW YOUNG ISRAELIS HAVE SUCH A SENSE OF THEIR COUNTRY, OF THEIR IDENTITY... I THINK IT'S A BEAUTIFUL THING.
AND WHERE ARE YOU FROM?
Dave's got to think about it...
A weekend in the Holy City and now he's not sure...
ISRAEL AND AMERICA.
WELL, ACTUALLY I'M AN AMERICAN.
BUT THIS FEELS LIKE HOME TO ME.
I AM HOME! I AM HOME! I AM HOME!
And so he is, he's got full Israeli citizenship if he wants, that's the Law of Return, any Jew from anywhere can "return" here ...from Moldavia, from Ethiopia, from Christchurch, New Zealand...
J. SACCO 9.92
14

Weeks later, in Jabalia refugee camp, I met an old Palestinian who told me about the home he fled in 1948 after Israel declared independence and the Arab armies invaded...

THE JEWS CAME AND OCCUPIED THE VILLAGE AND ARRESTED EVERYONE LEFT BEHIND, INCLUDING MY FATHER, WHO WAS AN OLD MAN AND COULDN'T MOVE...

I WALKED WITH MY WIFE, WHO WAS PREGNANT, FOR FOUR DAYS...

THE EGYPTIAN ARMY REFUSED TO TAKE US IN TRUCKS...

THE JEWS BOMBED US...

EVEN THE ANTS RAN AFTER US...

IT WAS A BLACK DAY WHEN I LEFT MY LAND.

He returned, as it were, a few years ago.

He got a permit from the Israeli authorities.

For a few hours he could leave the Gaza Strip...

He could cross into what is now Israel to visit his home village...

I TOOK MY FAMILY TO SEE MY LAND...

WHERE MY HOUSE WAS AND MY SCHOOL...

SOME PEOPLE ARE PARALYZED AFTER THEY HAVE A CHANCE TO GO BACK AND SEE.

THEY DESTROYED EVERYTHING.

THERE IS NO SIGN THAT WE EVER LIVED THERE.

J. SACCO 9-92

15

PALESTINE (CHAPTER ONE)

HEY!
YOU AMERICAN?
YEAH, YOU!
YOU WANT PART OF A SANDWICH?
UM... WHERE YOU GUYS FROM?
Ohmy Gawd!!
Is she nervous?
Or plain stoopid?
Either way, our soldier takes it in stride...
WE'RE FROM ISRAEL.
Got that straight?
Now come on!
Let's salvage this flirtation...
Sheesh!
Looks like mom's a little smitten herself!
Betcha she's never had beefcake like this on her Fuji Color!
HIYA, FELLAHS!
Big Sur
Too late!
Mom and pop's arrival extinguishes all hope...
17
HOW OLD ARE YOU BOYS? YOU SHOULDN'T BE SMOKING.
HOLD IT!
IT'S DANGEROUS FOR YOUR HEALTH. YOU CAN GET CANCER.
HOLD IT!

HEY, THERE'S A LOT OF PEOPLE DOWN THERE...
IS SOMETHING GOING ON?
I want to interject...
I read all about it this morning, didn't I:
It's Silwan, an all-Arab village. A week ago Jewish settlers booted out several Palestinian households, moved in, rolled out the barbed wire, sent up the Star of David... and with Uzis and the Attorney General's green light, who's gonna argue?
AWW, SOMETHING'S ALWAYS GOIN' ON.
And that's why I'm here...
...to see what's going on...
...so I walk down through Dung Gate...
...I walk straight into...
Democracy!
A demonstration!
A counterdemonstration!
A sweet sight for a right-to-assembly nut like me...
Also, I'm a free speech junkie...
And this is Israel!
(Okay, annexed land, but let's skip it)
It's 'the Middle East's only democracy'!
And here's both sides of the settler issue for consideration!
PEACE NOW TRAITORS NOW
PEACE NOW TRAITORS NOW
PEACE NOW TRAITORS NOW
PEACE NOW
STOP THE
STOP ALL THE

By far the more numerous end of this afternoon's political spectrum is the Peace Now crowd, they've bussed in from all over Israel to express solidarity with the Palestinians of Silwan. I fall in with one of them...
MAYBE THESE SETTLERS DID IT LEGALLY, I DON'T KNOW, BUT THAT'S NOT THE POINT.
IT'S A PROVOCATION, THAT'S OBVIOUS...
...AND RIGHT WHEN PEACE TALKS ARE STARTING UP...
STOP ALL THE SETTLEMENTS NEGOTIATE NOW
Sure, he says, Israel should get out of the Occupied Territories, and there ought to be a Palestinian state...
...AND IF IT DOESN'T HAPPEN IN THE NEXT 10 YEARS, IT'LL BE IN 20 OR 30...
Meanwhile, like most able-bodied Israeli men up till late middle age, he's required to do several weeks a year in the reserves, including duty in the West Bank...
The Democracy continues around us...
It's a pretty day for a peaceful Peace Now demonstration...
HOW DO YOU RECONCILE YOUR POLITICAL VIEWS WITH BEING A MEMBER OF AN OCCUPYING ARMY?
And, by the way, let's make one thing clear:
I KNOW PEOPLE WHO REFUSED TO SERVE THERE AND WENT TO JAIL, BUT IT'S GOOD THERE ARE GUYS LIKE ME IN.
ARABS IN THE TERRITORIES DON'T GET JUSTICE, BUT IF I REPORT SOME HOTHEAD SOLDIER WHO DOES SOMETHING ILLEGAL, THAT SETS THE WHEELS IN MOTION...
HE COULD GET IN TROUBLE, EXPELLED FROM THE ARMY... HEAVY PUNISHMENT FOR A GUY THAT MAKES THE ARMY HIS LIFE.
LOOK, I'M A ZIONIST AND I BELIEVE IN A STRONG ISRAEL.
IT'S BECAUSE WE'RE STRONG THE ARABS HAVE GIVEN UP ON THROWING US INTO THE SEA...
THEY'RE READY TO NEGOTIATE NOW.
19
J. SACCO 9.92

A little later the Democracy's all but over...
People are heading back home to watch themselves on T.V.
Palestinian kids go through the crowd sweet-talking Peace Now protesters out of their signs.
I'm halfway up the hill when I hear shouting...
A mini-demonstration!
maybe 50 people
STOP SETTLEMENTS NEGOTIATE NOW
Some kids, some women
They march a few dozen yards...
...chanting their heads off...
...raising more decibels in two minutes than I've heard all afternoon...
I mean, they're screaming like their lives depended on it!

VALLEY of KIDRON
HALLO!
HELLO!
JEWISH? JEWISH?
ME? NO, NOT JEWISH.
YOU COME? YOU COME?
DOWN THERE? YOU GOTTA BE KIDDING!
YES! COME! COME!
YOU SPEAK JEWISH?
NO!
NICE? NICE?
YOU SPEAK JEWISH?
NO!
OKAY, I KNOW SOME WORDS: SHALOM, KIBBUTZ, KNESSET.

JOE SACCO

PALESTINE (CHAPTER ONE)

Then...
Birds up a tree!
The boys turn to scoop stones!
They want to bust a bird's brains in!
The birds make their getaway, and the boys don't notice!
But there's no stopping 'em!
They scoop!
Fire!
Scoop!
Fire!
Scoop!
Fire!
Scoop!
Fire!
Nice kids, you know, but they're beginning to bore me. I say my goodbyes and...
MONEY!
MONEY?
TEN!
TEN SHEKELS?! BUT I THOUGHT WE WERE FRIENDS!
WE SHOW YOU! WE SHOW YOU!
BUT YOU DIDN'T SAY FOR MONEY!
LOOKIT, HERE'S THREE AND A HALF!
NO! NO!
They won't take it! They close my fist over the coins...
HERE! HERE!
TEN! FIVE ME! FIVE HIM!
BUT THIS ISN'T FAIR...
23
J. SACCO 8.92

JOE SACCO

I cough up a few more coins...
They let me go...
WE ARE BAD? WE ARE BAD?
You think I tell them they're bad?
You think I tell them off?
Those little terrorists?
After that artillery display?
FUCKING KIDS! THE FAT BASTARD ESPECIALLY! PROBABLY WASN'T FROM SILWAN! PROBABLY RIPPED ME ON THAT, TOO! GODDAMN PIPSQUEEK
ASSHOLES... GODDAMN
Back in Jerusalem's Old City I walk by Palestinian shopkeepers...
They get me sick...
Their big, sad eyes...
Their empty pockets...
I want to kick them...
SHAKE HANDS! SHAKE HANDS!
Fat chance, buddy! I know that bullshit from Cairo...
SEE! HE DOESN'T WANT PEACE!
24

---

1. Why does Shreef say, “There are Muslims and there are Muslims”?
2. Why does the narrator refer to the episodes involving Klinghoffer, the airliner hijackings, and the massacre of Israeli athletes in Munich?
3. What does the narrator mean when he says, “The Democracy continues around us,” while observing the demonstrations in Silwan?
4. Why do the Palestinian boys shake the narrator down for ten shekels? How does this shape his view of the Israeli-Palestinian conflict?

ALISON BECHDEL (1960–) was born in Lock Haven, Pennsylvania. Her father was a high school English teacher, funeral director, and antiques dealer, and her mother a high school English teacher and actress. Bechdel received her BA from Oberlin College in 1981. Two years later she launched her syndicated cartoon *Dykes to Watch Out For*. From 1986 to 1990 she worked as production manager for the gay and lesbian newspaper *Equal Time* in Minneapolis. She has published numerous collections of cartoons based on her syndicated series, including *Hot, Throbbing Dykes to Watch Out For* (1997) and *Invasion of Dykes to Watch Out For* (2005). Her graphic novel *Fun Home: A Family Tragicomic,* published in 2006, headed *Time* magazine's list of the year's ten best books. "A Happy Death" is the second chapter of *Fun Home.*

A Happy Death

CHAPTER 2

A HAPPY DEATH

THERE'S NO PROOF, ACTUALLY, THAT MY FATHER KILLED HIMSELF.

HIS DEATH WAS QUITE POSSIBLY HIS CONSUMMATE ARTIFICE, HIS MASTERSTROKE.

THERE'S NO PROOF, BUT THERE ARE SOME SUGGESTIVE CIRCUMSTANCES. THE FACT THAT MY MOTHER HAD ASKED HIM FOR A DIVORCE TWO WEEKS BEFORE.

THE COPY OF CAMUS' *A HAPPY DEATH* THAT HE'D BEEN READING AND LEAVING AROUND THE HOUSE IN WHAT MIGHT BE CONSTRUED AS A DELIBERATE MANNER.

CAMUS' FIRST NOVEL, IT'S ABOUT A CONSUMPTIVE HERO WHO DOES NOT DIE A PARTICULARLY HAPPY DEATH. MY FATHER HAD HIGHLIGHTED ONE LINE.

spared him a great deal of loneliness. He had been unfair: while his imagination and vanity had given her too much importance, his pride had given her too little. He discovered the cruel paradox by which we always deceive ourselves twice about the people we love – first to their advantage, then to their disadvantage. Today he understood that Marthe had been genuine with him – that she had been what she was, and that he owed her a good deal. It was beginning to ra[...] of the street; t[...] saw Marthe's sudd[...] by a burst of gratitude he could not express – in the old

A FITTING EPITAPH FOR MY PARENTS' MARRIAGE.

BUT DAD WAS ALWAYS READING SOMETHING. SHOULD WE HAVE BEEN SUSPICIOUS WHEN HE STARTED PLOWING THROUGH PROUST THE YEAR BEFORE?

WAS THAT A SIGN OF DESPERATION? IT'S SAID, AFTER ALL, THAT PEOPLE REACH MIDDLE AGE THE DAY THEY REALIZE THEY'RE NEVER GOING TO READ *REMEMBRANCE OF THINGS PAST*. DAD ALSO LEFT A MARGINAL NOTATION IN ANOTHER BOOK.

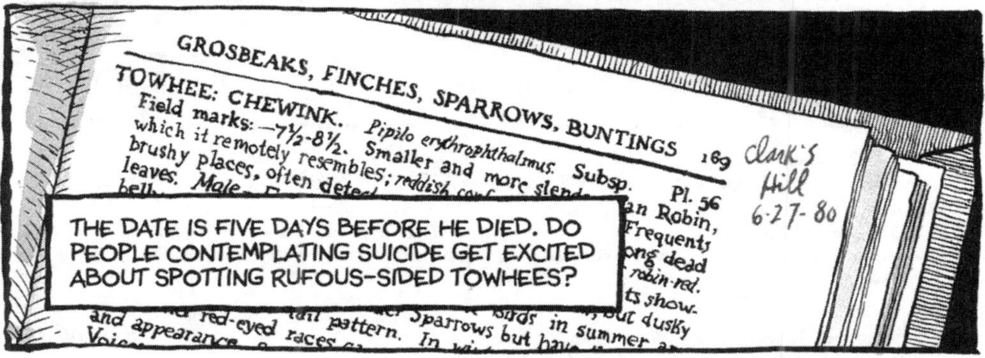

GROSBEAKS, FINCHES, SPARROWS, BUNTINGS 169
TOWHEE: CHEWINK. Pipilo erythrophthalmus. Subsp. Pl. 56
Field marks: —7½-8½. Smaller and more slend[...]
which it remotely resembles; reddish conf[...]
brushy places, often detec[...]
Clark's Hill 6-27-80
THE DATE IS FIVE DAYS BEFORE HE DIED. DO PEOPLE CONTEMPLATING SUICIDE GET EXCITED ABOUT SPOTTING RUFOUS-SIDED TOWHEES?

MAYBE HE DIDN'T NOTICE THE TRUCK COMING BECAUSE HE WAS PREOCCUPIED WITH THE DIVORCE. PEOPLE OFTEN HAVE ACCIDENTS WHEN THEY'RE DISTRAUGHT.

BUT THESE ARE JUST QUIBBLES. I DON'T BELIEVE IT WAS AN ACCIDENT.

IMPORTANT MESSAGE

FOR Allison Bechdel

DATE 7-2-80 TIME 12:27 AM PM

WHILE YOU WERE AWAY

M Your Mother

OF

PHONE NO.

TELEPHONED	✓	PLEASE CALL	
[...]ED [...]EE YOU		WILL CALL AGAIN	
[...]S [...]EE YOU		RUSH	
[...]URNED [...]UR CALL			

MESSAGE Call home as soon as possible – it's an emergency

AFTER I HAD MADE THE FIVE-HOUR DRIVE HOME FROM COLLEGE AND EVERYONE ELSE HAD GONE TO BED, MOM AND I DISCUSSED IT.

IT'S POSSIBLE THAT WE CHOSE TO BELIEVE THIS BECAUSE IT WAS LESS PAINFUL.
IF HE'D INTENDED TO DIE, THERE WAS A CERTAIN CONSOLATION IN THE FACT THAT HE SUCCEEDED WITH SUCH APLOMB.
I THINK IT WAS SOMETHING HE ALWAYS MEANT TO DO.

HIS HEADSTONE IS AN OBELISK, A STRIKING ANACHRONISM AMONG THE UNGAINLY GRANITE SLABS IN THE NEW END OF THE CEMETERY.

HAUGH
IT'S ALSO A SHAPE THAT IN LIFE HE WAS UNABASHEDLY FIXATED ON.

HE HAD AN OBELISK COLLECTION, IN FACT, AND HIS PRIZE SPECIMEN WAS ONE IN KNEE-HIGH JADE THAT PROPPED OPEN THE DOOR TO HIS LIBRARY.

HIS ULTIMATE OBELISK IS NOT CARVED FROM FLESHY, TRANSLUCENT MARBLE LIKE THE TOMBSTONES IN THE OLD PART OF THE CEMETERY.

ANNA FEARON
Daughter
Wm & BEULAH TEMPLE
Born Jan. 20, 1782
Died
Nov. 4, 1870
Aged
88 y. 9 mos.

MOM COULDN'T CONVINCE THE MONUMENT MAKER TO DO IT.

IT WON'T LAST. IN TEN, TWENTY YEARS YOU'LL HAVE LICHEN, EROSION. TRUST ME, YOU WANT GRANITE.
STRECK Monuments

THE GRANITE IS HANDSOME, CRISP... AND, WELL, LIFELESS.

BRUCE ALLEN
BECHDEL
1936 — 1980

ON A MAP OF MY HOMETOWN, A CIRCLE A MILE AND A HALF IN DIAMETER CIRCUMSCRIBES:

(A) DAD'S GRAVE,

(B) THE SPOT ON ROUTE 150 WHERE HE DIED, NEAR AN OLD FARMHOUSE HE WAS RESTORING,

(C) THE HOUSE WHERE HE AND MY MOTHER RAISED OUR FAMILY, AND

(D) THE FARM WHERE HE WAS BORN.

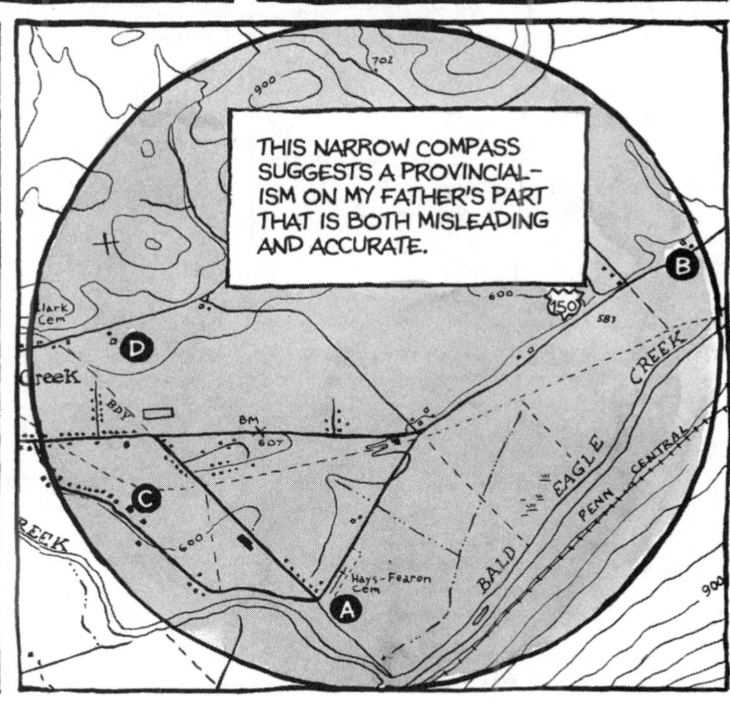
THIS NARROW COMPASS SUGGESTS A PROVINCIALISM ON MY FATHER'S PART THAT IS BOTH MISLEADING AND ACCURATE.
Clark Cem
Creek
Hays-Fearon Cem
BALD EAGLE CREEK
PENN CENTRAL
150
A
B
C
D

Beech
HIS MOTHER'S BROTHER
MANY OF HIS RELATIVES DISPLAYED A SIMILAR RELUCTANCE TO STRAY.
HIS MOTHER'S SISTER
HIS MOTHER
OUR HOUSE
HIS SISTER SUE
HIS SISTER RUTH
(WHEN AUNT SUE'S SON AND DAUGHTER GREW UP, THEY EACH BUILT A HOUSE IN THE FIELD BETWEEN OUR HOUSE AND HERS.)
HIS BROTHER ED

BUT IT'S PUZZLING WHY MY URBANE FATHER, WITH HIS UNWHOLESOME INTEREST IN THE DECORATIVE ARTS, REMAINED IN THIS PROVINCIAL HAMLET.

COME OUT TO CAMP! YOU DON'T HAFTA SHOOT NOTHIN'. WE'LL JUST SIT AROUND THE STOVE AND GET BOMBED.
OLD SCHOOL CHUM
Sunbeam Ranch

AND WHY MY CULTURED MOTHER, WHO HAD STUDIED ACTING IN NEW YORK CITY, WOULD LIVE THERE CHEEK BY JOWL WITH HIS FAMILY IS MORE PUZZLING STILL.

HELEN? DON'T STOP. I'M JUST SHOWING OFF YOUR HOUSE TO SOME FRIENDS.
AUNT SUE

IT WAS MADE CLEAR THAT MY BROTHERS AND I WOULD NOT REPEAT THEIR MISTAKE.

DON'T YOU KIDS GET ANY IDEAS ABOUT DRAGGING A TRAILER INTO THE BACKYARD. AFTER YOU GRADUATE FROM HIGH SCHOOL, I DON'T WANT TO SEE YOU AGAIN.
(MY COUSIN'S HOUSE BEING DELIVERED.)

MY PARENTS HAD IN FACT GOTTEN AS FAR AS EUROPE, WHERE MY FATHER WAS STATIONED IN THE ARMY. MOM FLEW THERE TO MARRY HIM.

THEY LIVED IN WEST GERMANY FOR ALMOST A YEAR DURING DAD'S SERVICE, IN SOME DEGREE OF EXPATRIATE SPLENDOR.

BUT THEN, THE STORY GOES, MY GRANDFATHER HAD A HEART ATTACK AND DAD HAD TO GO HOME AND RUN THE FAMILY BUSINESS.

PREGNANT WITH ME
BECHDEL? YOU JUST GOT A MESSAGE FROM YOUR SISTER. CALL HOME ASAP.

THIS WAS A FUNERAL PARLOR BEGUN BY MY GREAT-GRANDFATHER, EDGAR T. BECHDEL.

THE CHANGE IN PLANS WAS A CRUEL BLOW. I WAS BORN SOON AFTER THEY GOT BACK.

FOR A SHORT TIME WE ALL LIVED WITH MY GRANDMOTHER AND AILING GRANDFATHER AT THE FUNERAL HOME.

LESS THAN A YEAR LATER, WE MOVED TO A RENTED FEDERAL-STYLE FARMHOUSE AND MY BROTHER CHRISTIAN WAS BORN.

DAD STARTED TEACHING HIGH SCHOOL ENGLISH. FUNERAL DIRECTING PROVIDED ONLY A PART-TIME INCOME IN OUR THINLY POPULATED REGION.

ALISON BECHDEL

BY THE TIME WE MOVED TO THE GOTHIC REVIVAL HOUSE AND JOHN WAS BORN, EUROPE HAD DISAPPEARED FROM MY PARENTS' HORIZON.

IT WAS SOMEWHERE DURING THOSE EARLY YEARS THAT I BEGAN CONFUSING US WITH THE ADDAMS FAMILY.

LONG BEFORE I COULD READ, I WOULD PUZZLE OVER A BOOK OF ADDAMS CARTOONS.

THE CAPTIONS ELUDED ME, AS DID THE IRONIC REVERSAL OF SUBURBAN CONFORMITY. HERE WERE THE FAMILIAR DARK, LOFTY CEILINGS, PEELING WALLPAPER, AND MENACING HORSEHAIR FURNISHINGS OF MY OWN HOME.

WORLD
IN ONE OCCULT AND WORDLESS CARTOON...

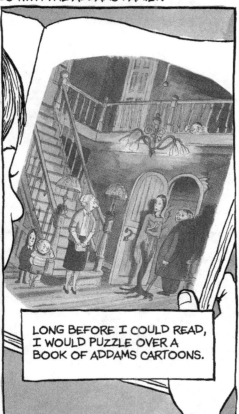

...A WORRIED GIRL HAD A STRING RUNNING FROM HER MOUTH TO A TRAP DOOR.

THE LAMP NEXT TO HER LOOKED JUST LIKE MY LAMP. IN FACT, THE GIRL LOOKED JUST LIKE ME.

THE RESEMBLANCE IN MY FIRST-GRADE SCHOOL PHOTO IS EERIE.

WEARING A BLACK VELVET DRESS MY FATHER HAD WRESTLED ME INTO, I APPEAR TO BE IN MOURNING.

MY MOTHER, WITH HER LUXURIANT BLACK HAIR AND PALE SKIN, BORE A MORE THAN PASSING LIKENESS TO MORTICIA.

MOM, HOW COME YOU NEVER GO OUTSIDE?
I TOLD YOU, I'M A VAMPIRE.
NOCTURNE

AND ON WARM SUMMER NIGHTS, IT WAS NOT UNUSUAL FOR A BAT TO SWOOP THROUGH OUR LIVING ROOM.

BUT WHAT GAVE THE COMPARISON REAL WEIGHT WAS THE FAMILY BUSINESS...

...AND THE CAVALIER ATTITUDE WHICH, INEVITABLY, WE CAME TO TAKE TOWARD IT.

CAN I GET IN?
RUPERT

THE "FUN HOME," AS WE CALLED IT, WAS UP ON MAIN STREET.

MY GRANDMOTHER LIVED IN THE FRONT. THE BUSINESS WAS IN THE BACK.

I REMEMBER SEEING MY GRANDFATHER LAID OUT THERE WHEN I WAS THREE. PEOPLE WERE AMUSED BY WHAT SEEMED TO ME A REASONABLE ENOUGH REQUEST.

MY FATHER HAD BEEN GIVEN A FREE HAND WITH THE INTERIOR DECORATION OF THE VIEWING AREA, AND THE ROOMS WERE HUNG WITH DARK VELVET DRAPERY. THIS ENSURED A SOMBER MOOD ON THE SUNNIEST OF DAYS.

THERE WAS A MINIMUM OF FURNITURE, AND A VAST EXPANSE OF TEXTURED OLIVE WALL-TO-WALL CARPETING.

MY BROTHERS AND I HAD LOTS OF CHORES AT THE FUN HOME, BUT ALSO MANY INTERESTING OPPORTUNITIES FOR PLAY.

WE WERE STRICTLY FORBIDDEN TO CLIMB INTO THE CASKETS.

AND THE CRUSHABLE CAPSULES FILLED WITH SMELLING SALTS.

THESE WERE FOR REVIVING PEOPLE WHEN THEY FAINTED FROM SHOCK OR GRIEF, WHICH, DISAPPOINTINGLY, NEVER SEEMED TO HAPPEN.

WHEN A NEW SHIPMENT OF CASKETS CAME IN, WE'D LIFT THEM WITH A WINCH TO THE SHOWROOM ON THE SECOND FLOOR OF THE GARAGE.

THOUGH THERE WERE NEVER ANY DEAD PEOPLE IN THE SHOWROOM, IT HAD THE OTHERWORLDLY AMBIENCE OF A MAUSOLEUM.

IT WAS USUALLY AFTER SCHOOL, IN A MELANCHOLY, FADING LIGHT, THAT WE FOUND OURSELVES UP THERE UNWRAPPING CASKETS.
A RICH SCENT OF CEDAR HUNG IN THE AIR.

MORE VELVET DRAPES MUFFLED ANY SOUNDS FROM OUTSIDE AND HEIGHTENED THE SENSATION THAT TIME WAS AT A STANDSTILL.
Burial Wear

LIKE A MEDIUM CHANNELING LOST SOULS, THE FILAMENT OF A SPACE HEATER VIBRATED TUNELESSLY TO OUR FOOTFALLS.

IT WASN'T THE SORT OF PLACE YOU WANTED TO BE ALONE IN.

ON THE OTHER HAND, IT WAS NOT PARTICULARLY SCARY TO SPEND THE NIGHT IN THE FUNERAL HOME PROPER, EVEN WHEN WE HAD A DEAD PERSON.

MY BROTHERS AND I OFTEN SLEPT THERE WITH MY GRANDMOTHER.

PERMANENT GREASE STAIN FROM MY DEAD GRANDFATHER'S VITALIS

TO QUIET US DOWN, GRAMMY WOULD LET US SWEEP THE CEILING WITH THE BEAM OF HER FLASHLIGHT IN SEARCH OF BUGS.

WHEN WE SPOTTED ONE, SHE WOULD DECLARE IT TO BE EITHER A "PISS-ANT" OR AN "ANTIE-MIRE"-- A TAXONOMIC DIFFERENTIATION I WAS NEVER CLEAR ON--AND SQUASH IT WITH A RAG ON THE END OF A BROOM.

AFTER THIS, WE WOULD BEG HER TO TELL US A STORY.

THE STORY, I SHOULD SAY, BECAUSE THERE WAS ONE TALE THAT HELD US IN SUCH THRALL THAT THE REST OF MY GRANDMOTHER'S REPERTOIRE--HER STILLBORN TWINS, THE TIME MY AUNT HAD WORMS--PALED BEFORE IT.

TELL US THE STORY OF WHEN DAD GOT STUCK IN THE MUD!
ALL RIGHT. SETTLE DOWN, NOW.

WUNST UPON A TIME, WHEN YOUR DADDY WAS A LITTLE BOY, HE WANDERED OFF.

"HE WAS LITTLER THAN YOU, JOHN, NO MORE THAN THREE. IT WAS SPRINGTIME."

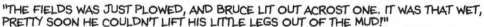

"THE FIELDS WAS JUST PLOWED, AND BRUCE LIT OUT ACROST ONE. IT WAS THAT WET, PRETTY SOON HE COULDN'T LIFT HIS LITTLE LEGS OUT OF THE MUD!"

"BUT JUST THEN, ALONG COMES MORT DEHAAS WITH THE MAIL, AND HE SEES BRUCE A WAY OUT THERE, JUST A TINY SPECK."

WHAT IF THE MAILMAN DIDN'T SEE HIM?
WOULD HE OF DIED?
WELL, I DON'T KNOW, DEARS. BUT MORT COMMENCED TO WALK OUT ACROST THE MUDDY FIELD TO WHERE BRUCE WAS.

"HE GAVE HIM A YANK, AND HE WAS THAT STUCK, HIS OVERSHOES COME OFF!"

(I KNOW MORT WAS A MAILMAN, BUT I ALWAYS PICTURED HIM AS A MILKMAN, ALL IN WHITE-- A REVERSE GRIM REAPER.)

"HE BRUNG YOUR DADDY INTO THE KITCHEN IN HIS STOCKING FEET, AND I UNDRESSED HIM RIGHT THERE."

LOSE SOMETHIN', DOROTHY?
OH, MY LANDS!

UNDRESSED HIM?!
WHY?
WHY, HE WAS ALL OVER MUD, DEARS.
THEN WHAT?!

AND HERE THE STORY REACHED ITS BIZARRE, GRIMMSIAN CLIMAX.

THEN I WRAPPED HIM IN A QUILT AND PUT HIM IN THE OVEN.

SHE WAS REFERRING, OF COURSE, TO A COOK-STOVE.

BUT ALL WE COULD ENVISION WAS THE MODERN OVEN SHE HAD NOW, WITH ITS RED-HOT ELEMENTS.

THE TALE WAS ENDLESSLY COMPELLING.

AGAIN!
WUNST MORE, THEN WE'LL GO TO SLEEP.

BY DAY, IT WAS DIFFICULT TO IMAGINE DAD EVER HELPLESS, NAKED, OR TRUSSED UP IN THE OVEN.

WHEN YOU'RE DONE, DO THE VACUUMING.
THAT'S CHRISTIAN'S JOB.

THOUGH THE WAY GRAMMY HELPED HIM TIE HIS SURGICAL GOWN IN BACK WAS EVOCATIVE.

DO IT, OR I'LL GIVE YOU SOMETHING TO WHINE ABOUT.

DAD WORKED BACK IN THE INNER SANCTUM, THE EMBALMING ROOM.

THIS SMELLED OF BACTERICIDAL SOAP AND EMBALMING FLUID. IT WAS DOMINATED BY A PORCELAIN ENAMEL PREP TABLE AND A CURIOUS WALL CHART.

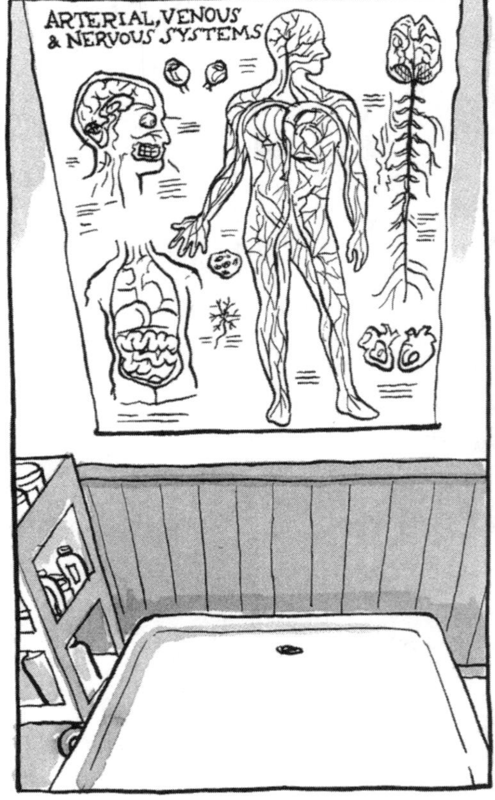

I DIDN'T NORMALLY SEE THE BODIES BEFORE THEY WERE DRESSED AND IN A CASKET.
ALISON!
BUT ONE DAY DAD CALLED ME BACK THERE.

THE MAN ON THE PREP TABLE WAS BEARDED AND FLESHY, JARRINGLY UNLIKE DAD'S USUAL TRAFFIC OF DESICCATED OLD PEOPLE.

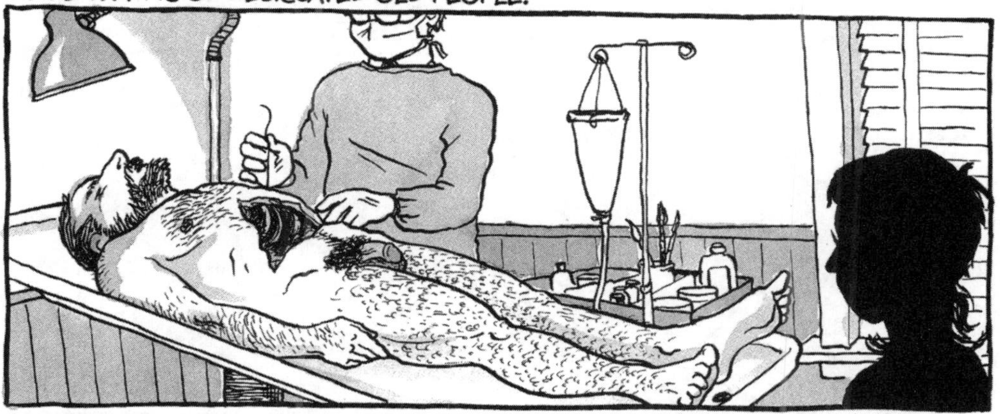

THE STRANGE PILE OF HIS GENITALS WAS SHOCKING, BUT WHAT REALLY GOT MY ATTENTION WAS HIS CHEST, SPLIT OPEN TO A DARK RED CAVE.

THERE WAS SOME PRACTICAL EXCHANGE WITH MY FATHER DURING WHICH I STUDIOUSLY BETRAYED NO EMOTION.

HAND ME THOSE SCISSORS OVER BY THE SINK.

IT FELT LIKE A TEST. MAYBE THIS WAS THE SAME OFFHANDED WAY HIS OWN NOTORIOUSLY COLD FATHER HAD SHOWN HIM **HIS** FIRST CADAVER.

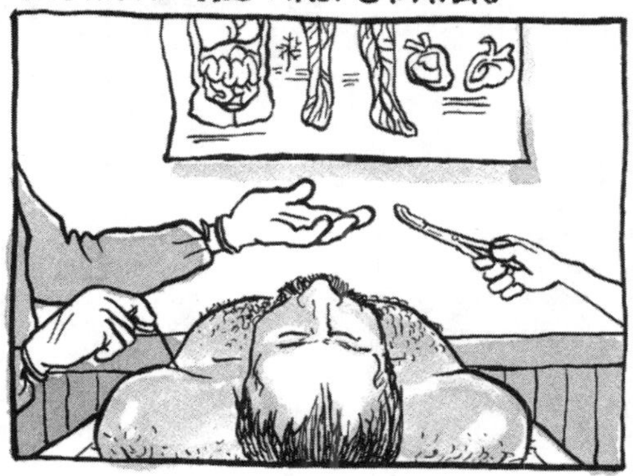

OR MAYBE HE FELT THAT HE'D BECOME TOO INURED TO DEATH, AND WAS HOPING TO ELICIT FROM ME AN EXPRESSION OF THE NATURAL HORROR HE WAS NO LONGER CAPABLE OF.

OR MAYBE HE JUST NEEDED THE SCISSORS.

IS THAT ALL?
MM-HMM.

I HAVE MADE USE OF THE FORMER TECHNIQUE MYSELF, HOWEVER, THIS ATTEMPT TO ACCESS EMOTION VICARIOUSLY.

FOR YEARS AFTER MY FATHER'S DEATH, WHEN THE SUBJECT OF PARENTS CAME UP IN CONVERSATION I WOULD RELATE THE INFORMATION IN A FLAT, MATTER-OF-FACT TONE...

MY DAD'S DEAD. HE JUMPED IN FRONT OF A TRUCK.
...EAGER TO DETECT IN MY LISTENER THE FLINCH OF GRIEF THAT ELUDED ME.

THE EMOTION I HAD SUPPRESSED FOR THE GAPING CADAVER SEEMED TO STAY SUPPRESSED.

GOD, I'M SORRY.

EVEN WHEN IT WAS DAD HIMSELF ON THE PREP TABLE.

THERE'S BEEN AN ACCIDENT.

I WAS AWAY AT SCHOOL THAT SUMMER, GENERATING BAR CODES FOR ALL THE BOOKS IN THE COLLEGE LIBRARY.

I HAVE TO GO HOME. MY FATHER GOT HIT BY A TRUCK.
PRIMITIVE MODEM

OH MY GOD. IS HE OKAY?
UMM...

I BICYCLED BACK TO MY APARTMENT, MARVELING AT THE DISSONANCE BETWEEN THIS APPARENTLY CAREFREE ACTIVITY AND MY NEWLY TRAGIC CIRCUMSTANCES.

AS I TOLD MY GIRLFRIEND WHAT HAD HAPPENED, I CRIED QUITE GENUINELY FOR ABOUT TWO MINUTES.

JOAN DROVE HOME WITH ME AND WE ARRIVED THAT EVENING. MY LITTLE BROTHER JOHN AND I GREETED EACH OTHER WITH GHASTLY, UNCONTROLLABLE GRINS.

IT COULD BE ARGUED THAT DEATH IS INHERENTLY ABSURD, AND THAT GRINNING IS NOT NECESSARILY AN INAPPROPRIATE RESPONSE. I MEAN ABSURD IN THE SENSE OF RIDICULOUS, UNREASONABLE. ONE SECOND A PERSON IS THERE, THE NEXT THEY'RE NOT.

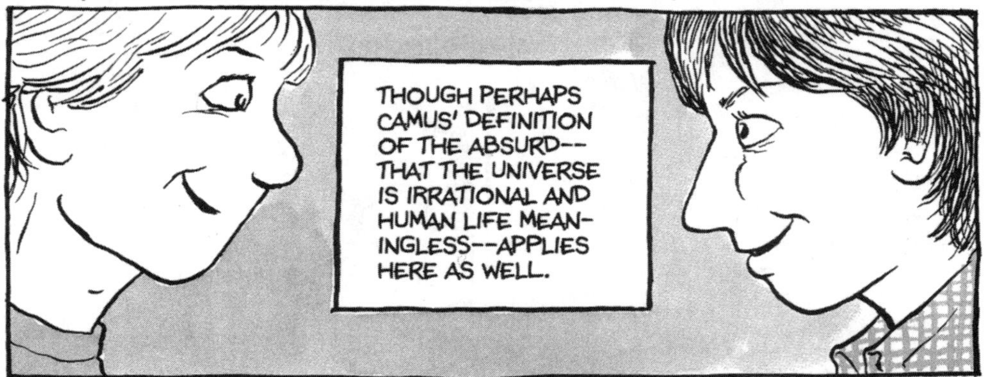
THOUGH PERHAPS CAMUS' DEFINITION OF THE ABSURD--THAT THE UNIVERSE IS IRRATIONAL AND HUMAN LIFE MEANINGLESS--APPLIES HERE AS WELL.

IN COLLEGE, I NEEDED *THE MYTH OF SISYPHUS* FOR A CLASS. DAD OFFERED TO SEND ME HIS OLD COPY, BUT I RESISTED HIS INTERFERENCE.

S.222
INTRO. TO WESTERN PHILOSOPHY
THE MYTH OF SISYPHUS
CAMUS · The Myth of

I WISH I COULD SAY I'D ACCEPTED HIS BOOK, THAT I STILL HAD IT, THAT HE'D UNDERLINED ONE PARTICULAR PASSAGE.

longing for death.
The subject of this essay is precisely this relationship between the absurd and suicide, the exact degree to which suicide is a solution to the absurd. The principle can be established that for a man who does not cheat, what he believes to be true must determine his action. Belief in the absurdity of existence must then dictate his conduct. It is legitimate to wonder, clearly and without false pathos, whether a conclusion of this importance requires forsaking as rapidly as possible an incomprehensible condition. I am

IT'S NOT THAT I THINK HE KILLED HIMSELF OUT OF EXISTENTIALIST CONVICTION. FOR ONE THING, IF HE'D READ CAREFULLY, HE WOULD HAVE GOTTEN TO CAMUS' CONCLUSION THAT SUICIDE IS ILLOGICAL.

BUT I SUSPECT MY FATHER OF BEING A HAPHAZARD SCHOLAR.

BECHDEL! PUT THAT GODDAMN BOOK DOWN. WE'RE GOING OUT.
ΦΚΨ
The Myth of Sisyphus

A SNAPSHOT OF HIM IN A FRAT BROTHER'S SPORTS CAR REMINDS ME OF CARTIER-BRESSON'S PHOTOS OF CAMUS.

MAYBE IT'S JUST THE CIGARETTE. IN EVERY PHOTO I'VE SEEN OF CAMUS, THERE'S A BUTT DANGLING FROM HIS GALLIC LIP.

Death
a novel
TO BE FAIR, EVERYONE SMOKED THEN.

BUT CAMUS' LUNGS WERE FULL OF HOLES FROM TUBERCULOSIS. WHO WAS HE TO CAST LOGICAL ASPERSIONS AT SUICIDE?

HE COULDN'T HAVE LASTED MUCH LONGER EVEN IF HE HADN'T DIED IN A CAR CRASH AT FORTY-SIX.

CAMUS WAS KNOWN TO HAVE SAID TO HIS FRIENDS ON VARIOUS OCCASIONS THAT DYING IN A CAR ACCIDENT WOULD BE *UNE MORT IMBÉCILE.*

IN JANUARY OF 1960, THE SPORTS CAR HE WAS RIDING IN CAROMED OFF ONE PLANE TREE AND WRAPPED AROUND ANOTHER.
PARIS
Herald Tribune
THE WRITER ALBERT CAMUS KILLED IN AUTOMOBILE ACCIDENT
NIXON MAY HURT
MY PARENTS WERE STILL IN EUROPE.

CAMUS ALSO SAID, IN *THE MYTH OF SISYPHUS,* THAT WE ALL LIVE AS IF WE DON'T KNOW WE'RE GOING TO DIE.

Yet one will never be sufficiently surprised that everyone lives as if no one "knew." This is because in reality there is no experience of death. Properly speaking, nothing has been experienced but what has been lived and made conscious. Here, it is barely possible to speak of the experience of others' deaths. It is a substitute, and illusion, and it never quite convinces us. That melancholy convention cannot be persuasive. The horror comes in reality from the mathematical aspect of the event. If time

BUT THEN, HE WASN'T A MORTICIAN.

I SUSPECT THAT FOR MY FATHER, DEATH WAS ALL TOO CONVINCING.

IN THE LETTERS HE SENT ME AT COLLEGE, SOMETIMES HE SEEMED THE PERFECT ABSURD HERO, SISYPHUS SHOULDERING HIS BOULDER WITH DETACHED JOY.

The weekend was of little consequense entertainmentwise. I was called at 3:30 AM for Fay Murray's death. That shot that Friday Saturday. Some highlights of my work her yellow lace bikini rose-embroidered panties. Her died red hair after three months of hospitalizati Her hairdersser and her hairpieces. Her bitter green velvet jumpsuit with gold sequined trim and plunging neckline. Well I did my best with red lips, green eyeshadow, lots of rouge and eyebrow pencil and low and behold there lay Fay. She had lovely flawlessly smoothskin. Everyone was pleased and you would never have guessed she was <u>seventy.</u>

OTHER TIMES, HE WAS DESPAIRING.

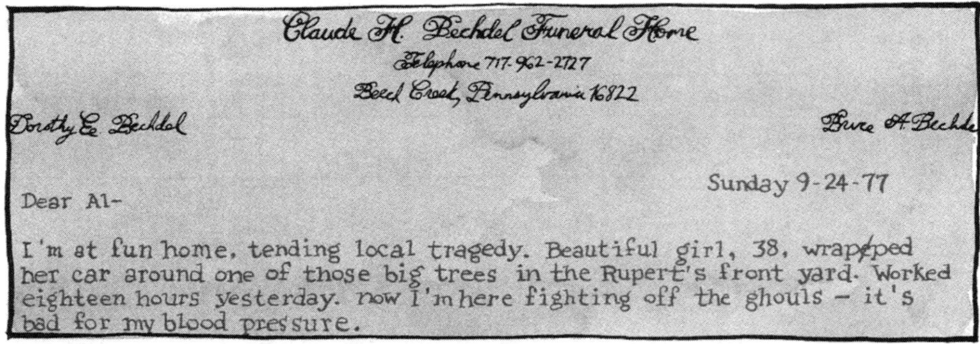

Claude H. Bechdel Funeral Home
Telephone 717-962-2727
Beech Creek, Pennsylvania 16822

Dorothy E. Bechdel Bruce A. Bechde

Sunday 9-24-77

Dear Al-

I'm at fun home, tending local tragedy. Beautiful girl, 38, wrapped her car around one of those big trees in the Rupert's front yard. Worked eighteen hours yesterday. now I'm here fighting off the ghouls - it's bad for my blood pressure.

I DON'T HAVE ANY LETTERS ABOUT THE SUICIDES HE DEALT WITH, LIKE THE LOCAL DOCTOR WHO SHOT HIMSELF A FEW MONTHS BEFORE DAD'S OWN DEATH.

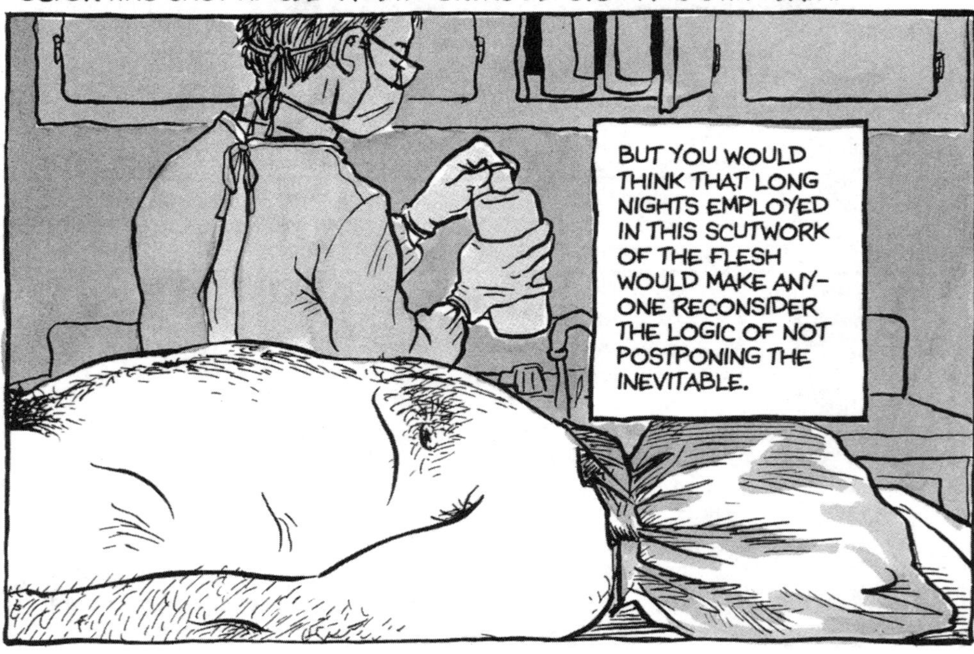

BUT YOU WOULD THINK THAT LONG NIGHTS EMPLOYED IN THIS SCUTWORK OF THE FLESH WOULD MAKE ANYONE RECONSIDER THE LOGIC OF NOT POSTPONING THE INEVITABLE.

YOU WOULD ALSO THINK THAT A CHILDHOOD SPENT IN SUCH CLOSE PROXIMITY TO THE WORKADAY INCIDENTALS OF DEATH WOULD BE GOOD PREPARATION.

THAT WHEN SOMEONE YOU KNEW ACTUALLY DIED, MAYBE YOU'D GET TO SKIP A PHASE OR TWO OF THE GRIEVING PROCESS--"DENIAL" AND "ANGER," FOR EXAMPLE--

BUT IN FACT, ALL THE YEARS SPENT VISITING GRAVEDIGGERS, JOKING WITH BURIAL-VAULT SALESMEN, AND TEASING MY BROTHERS WITH CRUSHED VIALS OF SMELLING SALTS ONLY MADE MY OWN FATHER'S DEATH MORE INCOMPREHENSIBLE.

WHO EMBALMS THE UNDERTAKER WHEN HE DIES?

IT WAS LIKE RUSSELL'S PARADOX...

...THE FAMOUS CONUNDRUM OF THE CLEAN-SHAVEN BARBER WHOSE SIGN READS, "I SHAVE ALL THOSE MEN, AND ONLY THOSE MEN, WHO DO NOT SHAVE THEMSELVES."

THE BARBER, EQUALLY UNABLE TO SHAVE HIMSELF, AND TO NOT SHAVE HIMSELF, IS IMPOSSIBLE.

YET SOMEHOW, THERE HE IS.
MY FATHER COULD HAVE USED A BARBER. HIS FACE WAS ROUGH AND DRY, SCRAPED CLEAN WITH NO HELP FROM THE EXPENSIVE LOTIONS AND AFTERSHAVES ON THE SILVER TRAY IN HIS BATHROOM AT HOME.

HIS WIRY HAIR, WHICH HE HAD DAILY TAKEN GREAT PAINS TO STYLE, WAS BRUSHED STRAIGHT UP ON END AND REVEALED A SURPRISINGLY RECEDED HAIRLINE.

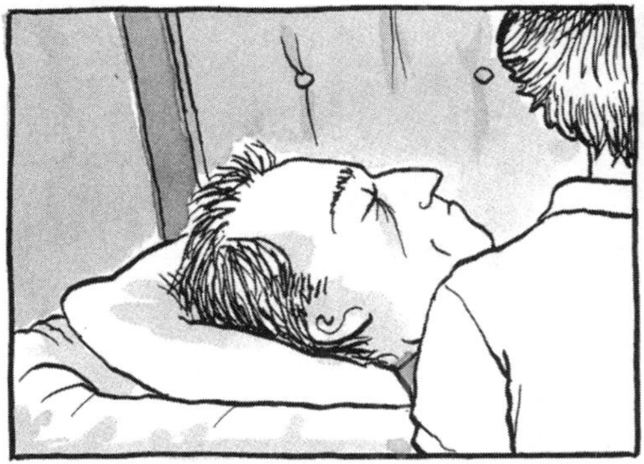

I WASN'T EVEN SURE IT WAS HIM UNTIL I FOUND THE TINY BLUE TATTOO ON HIS KNUCKLE WHERE HE'D ONCE BEEN ACCIDENTALLY STABBED WITH A PENCIL.

DRY-EYED AND SHEEPISH, MY BROTHERS AND I LOOKED FOR AS LONG AS WE SENSED IT WAS APPROPRIATE.

IF ONLY THEY MADE SMELLING SALTS TO INDUCE GRIEF-STRICKEN SWOONS, RATHER THAN SNAP YOU OUT OF THEM.

THE SOLE EMOTION I COULD MUSTER WAS IRRITATION, WHEN THE PINCH-FUNERAL DIRECTOR LAID HIS HAND ON MY ARM CONSOLINGLY.

I SHOOK IT OFF WITH A VIOLENCE THAT WAS, IN FACT, RATHER CONSOLING.

THIS SAME IRRITATION WOULD OVERTAKE ME FOR YEARS AFTERWARD WHEN I VISITED DAD'S GRAVE.

ON ONE OCCASION I FOUND IT DESECRATED WITH A CHEESY FLAG, PLACED THERE BY SOME WELL-MEANING ARMED SERVICES ORGANIZATION.

I JAVELINED THIS, UGLY BRASS HOLDER AND ALL, INTO THE CORNFIELD THAT IMMEDIATELY ADJOINS HIS PLOT AT THE EDGE OF THE CEMETERY.

AGAIN, THERE WAS SOME FLEETING CONSOLATION IN THE SHEER VIOLENCE OF MY GESTURE.

STUCK IN THE MUD FOR GOOD THIS TIME.

---

1. Why is the story of the father stuck in the mud the children's favorite story about him?
2. What is the significance of the map of the father's relatives?
3. How does the reading of Camus help the narrator understand her father's death?
4. Does the narrator believe her father's death was "a happy death"?

About Shared Inquiry

Shared Inquiry™ is the effort to achieve a more thorough understanding of a text by discussing questions, responses, and insights with fellow readers. Careful listening is essential. The leader guides the discussion by asking questions about specific ideas, problems of meaning, and passages in the text, but does not seek to impose a personal interpretation on the group.

During discussion, participants consider a number of possible ideas and weigh the evidence for each. Ideas that are entertained and then refined or abandoned are not thought of as mistakes, but rather as valuable parts of the interpretive process. Participants gain experience in communicating complex ideas and in supporting, testing, and expanding their thoughts. Everyone in the group contributes to the discussion. While participants may disagree with one another, they treat one another's ideas respectfully.

This process helps develop an understanding of important texts and ideas, rather than merely cataloging knowledge about them. These guidelines keep conversation focused on the text and assure that all participants have a voice.

1. **Read the story carefully before participating in the discussion.** This ensures that all participants are equally prepared to talk about the work.

2. **Support your ideas with evidence from the text.** This keeps the discussion focused on understanding the story and enables the group to weigh textual support for different interpretive possibilities.

3. **Discuss the themes and formal elements of the story and try to understand them fully before exploring issues that go beyond the story itself.** Adequate reflection about the story and about the textual evidence for various interpretations will make the exploration of related issues more productive.

4. **Listen to other participants and respond to them directly.** Shared Inquiry is about the give-and-take of ideas, the willingness to listen to others and talk with them respectfully. Directing your comments and questions to other participants in the discussion, not always to the leader, will make the discussion livelier and more dynamic.

5. **Expect the leader to only ask questions.** Effective leaders help participants develop their own ideas, with everyone gaining a new understanding in the process. When participants hang back and wait for the leader to suggest answers, the discussion tends to falter.

Acknowledgments

All possible care has been taken to trace ownership and secure permission for each selection in this anthology. The Great Books Foundation wishes to thank the following authors, publishers, and representatives for permission to reprint copyrighted material:

The Lady with a Dog, from THE OXFORD CHEKHOV: VOLUME IX, by Anton Chekhov, translated and edited by Ronald Hingley. Copyright © 1975 by Ronald Hingley. Reprinted by permission of Oxford University Press.

Indian Camp, from THE SHORT STORIES OF ERNEST HEMINGWAY, by Ernest Hemingway. Copyright © 1925 by Charles Scribner's Sons. Copyright renewed 1953 by Ernest Hemingway. Reprinted by permission of Scribner, an imprint of Simon & Schuster Adult Publishing Group.

The Yellow Wallpaper, from THE YELLOW WALLPAPER AND OTHER STORIES, by Charlotte Perkins Gilman. Copyright © 1997 by Dover Publications. Reprinted by permission of Dover Publications, Inc.

The Diver, from COMPLETE COLLECTED STORIES, by V. S. Pritchett. Copyright © 1990 by V. S. Pritchett. Reprinted by permission of Random House, Inc.

Gimpel the Fool, from A TREASURY OF YIDDISH STORIES, by Isaac Bashevis Singer, translated by Saul Bellow, edited by Irving Howe and Eliezer Greenberg. Copyright © 1953, 1954 by Viking Press Inc.; renewed 1981, 1982 by Viking Penguin Inc. Reprinted by permission of Viking Penguin, a division of Penguin Group (USA) Inc.

The Wall, from THE WALL AND OTHER STORIES, by Jean-Paul Sartre, translated by Lloyd Alexander. Copyright © 1948 by New Directions Publishing Corp. Copyright © 1975 by Lloyd Alexander. Reprinted by permission of New Directions Publishing Corp.

The Country Husband, from THE STORIES OF JOHN CHEEVER, by John Cheever. Copyright © 1955, renewed 1978 by John Cheever. Reprinted by permission of Alfred A. Knopf, a division of Random House, Inc.

Looking for Mr. Green, from MOSBY'S MEMOIRS AND OTHER STORIES, by Saul Bellow. Copyright © 1951, renewed 1979 by Saul Bellow. Reprinted by permission of Viking Penguin, a division of Penguin Group (USA) Inc.

The Ledge, by Lawrence Sargent Hall. Copyright © 1957, 1987 by Bowdoin College. Used by permission of Bowdoin College.

Sonny's Blues, from GOING TO MEET THE MAN, by James Baldwin, published by Vintage Books. Copyright © 1957 by James Baldwin. First appeared in the *Partisan Review*, Summer 1957. Reprinted by permission of the James Baldwin Estate.

Argument and Persuasion, from WILLOW TEMPLE, by Donald Hall. Copyright © 2003 by Donald Hall. Reprinted by permission of Houghton Mifflin Company.

Lost in the Funhouse, from LOST IN THE FUNHOUSE, by John Barth. Copyright © 1967 by the Atlantic Monthly Company. Reprinted by permission of Doubleday, a division of Random House, Inc.

The Professor's Houses, from UNLOCKING THE AIR AND OTHER STORIES, by Ursula K. Le Guin. Copyright © 1982 by Ursula K. Le Guin. First appeared in the *New Yorker.* Reprinted by permission of the author and the author's agents, the Viginia Kidd Agency, Inc.

Tomorrow and Tomorrow and So Forth, from THE EARLY STORIES: 1953–1975, by John Updike. Copyright © 2003 by John Updike. Reprinted by permission of Alfred A. Knopf, a division of Random House, Inc.

Cathedral, from CATHEDRAL, by Raymond Carver. Copyright © 1981, 1982, 1983 by Raymond Carver. Reprinted by permission of Alfred A. Knopf, Inc., a division of Random House, Inc.

The Man from Mars, from DANCING GIRLS AND OTHER STORIES, by Margaret Atwood. Copyright © 1977, 1982 by O. W. Toad, Ltd. Reprinted by permission of Simon & Schuster Adult Publishing Group.

The Pugilist at Rest, from THE PUGILIST AT REST, by Thom Jones. Copyright © 1993 by Thom Jones. Reprinted by permission of Little, Brown & Company.

Greasy Lake, from GREASY LAKE & OTHER STORIES, by T. Coraghessan Boyle. Copyright © 1979, 1981, 1982, 1983, 1984, 1985 by T. Coraghessan Boyle. Reprinted by permission of Viking Penguin, a division of Penguin Group (USA) Inc.

The Baby, from THE STORIES OF MARY GORDON, by Mary Gordon. Copyright © 2006 by Mary Gordon. Reprinted by permission of Pantheon Books, a division of Random House, Inc.

The Collectors, from SWIMMING LESSONS AND OTHER STORIES FROM FIROZSHA BAAG, by Rohinton Mistry. Copyright © 1987 by Rohinton Mistry. Reprinted by permission of the author.

You're Ugly, Too, from LIKE LIFE: STORIES, by Lorrie Moore. Copyright © 1990 by Lorrie Moore. Reprinted by permision of Alfred A. Knopf, a division of Random House, Inc.

The Country Where Nobody Ever Grew Old and Died, from ALL THE DAYS AND NIGHTS, by William Maxwell. Copyright © 1994 by William Maxwell. Reprinted by permission of Alfred A. Knopf, a division of Random House, Inc.

Wants, from THE COLLECTED STORIES, by Grace Paley. Copyright © 1994 by Grace Paley. Reprinted by permission of Farrar, Straus & Giroux, LLC.

A City of Churches, from SADNESS, by Donald Barthelme. Copyright © 1972 by Donald Barthelme. Reprinted by permission of the Wylie Agency, Inc.

True Love, by Don Shea. Copyright © 1990 by Don Shea. First appeared in *Kansas Quarterly*, Vol. 22, No. 2. Reprinted by permission of the author.

Bullet, by Kim Church. Copyright © 2005 by Kim Church. First appeared in *Painted Bride Quarterly*, Issue 69. Reprinted by permission of the author.

The Doctor, by Ann Hood. Copyright © 1997 by Ann Hood. First appeared in *Story* magazine (Spring 1998). Reprinted by permission of Brandt & Hochman Literary Agency, Inc.

Blind Fish, from SWEET HEARTS, by Melanie Rae Thon. Copyright © 2000 by Melanie Rae Thon. Reprinted by permission of Houghton Mifflin Harcourt Publishing Company.

My Date With Neanderthal Woman, by David Galef. Copyright © 2003 by David Galef. Reprinted by permission of the author.

After Caravaggio's Sacrifice of Isaac, by Rachel Cusk. Copyright © 2003 by Rachel Cusk. First appeared in *Granta* 81 (Spring 2003). Reprinted by permission of the Wylie Agency, Inc.

Flies on the Ceiling, by Jaime Hernandez, from LOVE AND ROCKETS, BOOK 9: FLIES ON THE CEILING. Copyright © 1988 by Jaime Hernandez. Reprinted by permission of Fantagraphics Books.

Palestine (Chapter One), from PALESTINE, by Joe Sacco. Copyright © 1993, 2001 by Joe Sacco. Reprinted by permission of Fantagraphics Books.

A Happy Death, from FUN HOME: A FAMILY TRAGICOMIC, by Alison Bechdel. Copyright © 2006 by Alison Bechdel. Reprinted by permission of Houghton Mifflin Company.